Avon Books by Jack Hoffenberg

LAURELTON, GEORGIA
THE SCENE OF <u>SOW NOT IN ANGER</u> HAS MORE FASCINATING PEOPLE FOR YOU TO MEET!

Drew Warren—They said she and her brother had been "too close," that his death had ruined her for any other man.

Corey Armour—He wants Drew Warren to escape the ghosts that plague her mind, and to come to him as a woman free and whole.

Theo and Chase Warren—The two brothers were locked in a titanic struggle for control of an empire.

Elizabeth Shackleford—She believed that a northern education and a respected position would allow a black woman to love a white man in Laurelton.

Lyle Emerson—Wounded in Vietnam, his love for Liz Shackleford healed the hurts of war and plunged him into even more deadly combat.

Dr. Rhama—Black and angry, articulate, and terrifying, his cool authority was the trigger that could set off apocalyptic violence.

Unforgettable people caught in the blazing turmoil of today's south. For them, love became a heroic act, and traditional power turned to ashes overnight.

The monumental saga of the Warren tobacco dynasty in Georgia continues: Grandpa Anderson Warren, who predicted the rosy future of ready-made cigarettes at the turn of the century; his ineffectual son Theodore, who thinks about selling out to a conglomerate; his 27-year-old daughter Drew, who is battling the bottle and a lesbian streak. In addition, Mr. Hoffenberg keeps about a dozen subplots rolling along merrily, using enough characters to exhaust Central Casting, dealing with everything from domestic spats and business chicanery to race riots and the Vietnam war. The writing is slick and the reader is kept busy every minute.

Publishers' Weekly

Jack Hoffenberg

Reap in Tears

AVON BOOKS
A division of
The Hearst Corporation
959 Eighth Avenue
New York, New York 10019

Copyright © 1965 by Jack Hoffenberg
Published by arrangement with the author.

All rights reserved, which includes the right to reproduce this book or portions thereof in any form whatsoever. For information address Avon Books.

First Avon Printing, October, 1968
Eleventh Printing

AVON TRADEMARK REG. U.S. PAT. OFFICE AND IN OTHER COUNTRIES, MARCA REGISTRADA, HECHO EN U.S.A.

AVON
PUBLISHERS OF BARD, CAMELOT, DISCUS, EQUINOX AND FLARE BOOKS

AVON BOOKS
A division of
The Hearst Corporation
959 Eighth Avenue
New York, New York 10019

First Avon Printing, October, 1969
Eleventh Printing

AVON TRADEMARK REG. U.S. PAT. OFF. AND
FOREIGN COUNTRIES, REGISTERED TRADEMARK—
MARCA REGISTRADA, HECHO EN CHICAGO, U.S.A.

Printed in the U.S.A.

This Book,
with deep affection,
is dedicated to
JOE *and* **SELMA GROSS**

Sow not your Seed in Anger,
Nor with Hatred, nor with Fears;
For Ye who Sow in Anger
Shall for certain reap in tears.

BOOK I

CHAPTER I

1

The room reflected the personality of the man who stood beside the heavy column of gold-shot drapery looking out over the complex of buildings and bustling activities that were part of the Warren Tobacco Company of South Laurelton. There was a certain opulence, even ostentatiousness, about the office, with its hand-rubbed paneled walls, polished random-width pegged boards of the floor peeping out from the edges of a rug that had been hand-loomed in Belgium long ago when monarchs reigned in Europe, now considered an art treasure. Other trappings, the glove-leather sofas and chairs arranged in separate conversation groups, a tasteful selection of rare oils and modern watercolors recessed into the walls, the bar hidden behind a section of paneling, were in character with the overall decor of the room.

Beyond the floor-to-ceiling double doors was the office of his private secretary, Miss Mitchell, and beyond that, the twelfth floor of the Warren Building was given over to large, handsome offices, dining room, kitchen, exercise room, steam baths, handball and squash courts for the exclusive use of Warren executives and their guests. The remaining eleven floors housed the many departments required to maintain the endless flow of communications and contact with the widespread organization at home and abroad; acres of calculators, typewriters, telephones, teletype machines and computers, pouring out reports on sales, advertising, production, transportation, engineering, warehousing, purchasing, real estate acquisitions, rentals and leases, finance, accounting and personnel, all geared to the world's cigarette habit.

But the man himself, Theodore Warren, remained oblivious to all movement going on around and below him. He was a tall, austere man of inordinately good looks and strong features, with the possible exception of some weakness about the mouth. His eyes were a cool blue, his brown hair showing wisps of gray at the temples. His clothes, tailored by an exclusive house in London, were made of cloth selected by him on occasional business and pleasure trips abroad, at other times from swatches airmailed to him.

His boots and shirts were custom-made, his ties mere accents of color worn like a light touch of delicate seasoning added to a salad, all blending perfectly to achieve a façade that bespoke his stature in the world of business. His voice was soft with the musical cadence of a cultured Georgian, but could turn granite-hard when, as it had sometimes happened, gentleness had been mistaken for underlying softness. It had never disturbed him that from his earliest childhood he had never been called "Ted" or "Theo" by anyone; always it was Theodore, later, Mr. Warren. But then, he had never heard his father called by any name other than Anderson; never Andy, not even by his most intimate friend or his late wife.

The presidency was an office Theodore had neither sought nor expected to attain, satisfied with his former obscure position as vice-president without specific duties until age and failing health forced Anderson Warren to step into the less arduous position of Chairman of the Board and named Theodore to succeed him. Theodore would gladly have stepped aside for Kenneth Armour, who was Anderson's executive vice-president and chief legal counsel, but for Anderson's vanity, or need, to keep a Warren at the head of the company which he had founded in 1911.

And there was Chase, Theodore's older brother, whose ambitions had led him to break with Anderson, move to New York and create an empire of his own. Chase—

One of the four telephones on the long, low cabinet behind his desk buzzed softly and a red button glowed in its base. Theodore let it buzz twice more before he went to the cabinet and lifted the receiver.

"Yes, Mrs. Mitchell."

14

"Mr. Armour for his ten-thirty appointment, Mr. Warren," Mrs. Mitchell said.

"Give me ten minutes before you send him in," Theodore Warren replied.

"Yes, sir."

He replaced the receiver in its cradle and went back to the window and continued to stare out into the bright, hot sunlit day. There was no real reason for the ten-minute delay. He knew what Kenneth Armour wanted, but he had no answer for him, nor would he have one for the Company's executive vice-president and chief legal counsel if he delayed the interview an hour, a day, a week; yet he took some perverse, childish pleasure in keeping Armour waiting.

From the window, he looked beyond the immediate structures toward the bridge that crossed the Cottonwood River into Laurelton proper, a city that would have remained a normal, sleepy agricultural community had it not been for the phenomenal drive of Jonas Taylor, most prominent and best-remembered of a line of Taylors, who had brought industry alive here. It was Jonas who had engineered the first major step when he persuaded the Carolina-Georgia to run its tracks through Laurelton instead of Fairview at the turn of the century, thus creating an industrial complex that now served many needs of the nation with products of Laurelton's soil and manufacture: cotton and processed textiles, cottonseed oil, lumber and its many by-products, aviation and electronics components, paper products, truck transportation, banking and finance.

And, Theodore mused, Tobacco; for it was Jonas Taylor, always in search of new profitable markets and increased payrolls who had encouraged Anderson Warren, his cousin from Loudon, North Carolina, to remain in Laurelton to develop and grow tobacco leaf that was far superior to any grown in Georgia at that time, early in the century.

Those, Theodore reflected now, were the days of the giants; men of towering strength like Jonas Taylor and Anderson Warren who had built industries for men of today who, with their boards of directors, kept their eyes on the stock market and nervous fingers on the pulses of their stockholders; mere housekeepers of that which had been left behind by their creators. They were the true pioneers who had combined vision and stamina with audacious courage to carve and mold a nation into greatness that had been felt around the world. Meanwhile they amassed fortunes unhindered by massive taxes, untroubled by labor unions and government interference, and used their wealth to create more, newer, and greater industries to attract more workers

15

and their families; people who needed houses, food, clothing, schools, colleges, churches, transportation, streets, highways, parks; they provided sewers, lighting, water and power facilities; expanded city, county and state government services; erected courthouses and other necessary civic buildings.

Jonas Taylor and his banker son, Ames, were dead now. And soon, Anderson Warren would join them.

Theodore turned away from the window with a sigh and examined the original Hendley portrait of his father which occupied the place of honor over the fireplace, then its reproduction which had appeared on the cover of *Time*, laminated between two sheets of clear glass; this man who had come to Laurelton with his wife, Cleo, and son, Chase, in a canvas-covered wagon drawn by two mules, their entire wealth and possessions with them, and Theodore as yet unborn; seeking a new home and land where Anderson could plant his precious store of tobacco seed, to form roots that would become the empire known as the Warren Tobacco Company.

Theodore wondered idly what Jonas Taylor and Anderson Warren had looked like in those early days. Anderson had been 25, Taylor in his mid-30s. The Hendley portrait, *Tobacco Tycoon*, painted only 15 years ago from sketches made in this room, stared back, mocking him. The artist had seen beneath the old man's formidable exterior and had managed, despite stern, shaggy white eyebrows and tightly drawn lips beneath a hawklike nose, to capture a rare glint of humor in his bright, sparkling eyes; as though he were quietly laughing at a world he had taken on, beaten, and would soon leave behind, scarcely missing it.

Theodore checked the time on his wafer-thin platinum Patek, then went to his desk and touched a concealed button which would tell Mrs. Mitchell he was ready for Kenneth Armour.

At once, the beige phone buzzed softly. "Yes?"

"Mr. Chase Warren, calling from London, Mr. Warren," Mrs. Mitchell said.

The mention of his brother's name startled him. "Chase?" he asked as though in doubt.

"Yes, sir."

He hesitated, the fingers holding the receiver flexing, tightening; then he heard Mrs. Mitchell ask, "Mr. Warren?"

"Put him through and ask Mr. Armour to wait, please."

"Yes, sir."

Chase Warren's voice was so clear, he might easily have

16

been in the same room, a voice Theodore hadn't heard in many years, yet familiar at once at his first spoken word.

"Theodore?"

"Yes."

"Chase here. I've just finished talking with my New York office. They tell me there was an item in the *Times* about Father."

In the thirty-some years that had passed, it was still there, that irritating inflection in Chase's tone, the big-brother-to-little-brother attitude. Chase was 67, Theodore 58. "What's it all about?" Chase's voice boomed across the wire.

Again the uncertainty and hesitation, then, "Carl Ballard took Father up to Johns Hopkins on Sunday for some tests. Carl called from Baltimore the day before yesterday—"

"What was the verdict?"

"I didn't talk with Carl personally. I was in Atlanta. It—it doesn't look very good. They'll be home tomorrow morning."

"Did they operate?"

"Carl said there was no point in doing an exploratory. They did a liver biopsy. The pathology report shows cancer, probably originating elsewhere."

There was a slight pause and a shrug in Chase's voice. "Well, we can't be too surprised. He must be close to ninety. He can't expect to live forever."

Stiffly, Theodore's reply edged with resentment, "I hadn't expected he would."

"Well— I've got to be over here for a little while. I'm tied up in some shipping negotiations, then a conference in Athens. If you should need to reach me, my office in New York will know where I am."

Theodore did not reply at once. "You still on, Theodore?"

"Ah—yes. Chase, wait a moment. There's something about the Company that Ken Armour—"

Chase's tight tone indicated total disinterest. "The Company? I'm sure you don't want my opinions or advice—"

"Father's death—"

"The Company is your problem, Mr. President. I'm sure you and Ken can handle its affairs without me." Boastfully now, "I've got twenty companies to look after without having to add another one to my burdens. Good-bye now." Chase hung up abruptly and Theodore stared vacantly into the mouth of the dead phone.

The arrogant sonofabitch, Theodore thought. Father is dying and all he cares about is a shipping contract and whatever the hell else he's mixed up with.

17

One of the huge double doors opened then and Mrs. Mitchell, a small, graying woman, stood to one side as Kenneth Armour strode past her and crossed the large expanse of carpet to Theodore's desk. "Good morning, Theodore."

"Good morning, Ken."

Armour sank into the deep, leather visitor's chair and crossed his legs. He was equally as tall as Theodore but slender, his manner alert, far more the picture of a president than Theodore Warren. "Anything new from Dr. Ballard?" he asked.

"No. They're due in with the 7:08 tomorrow morning."

Armour nodded. He waited until Mrs. Mitchell closed the door. "Theodore," he said, "I don't like to push the Intercon matter at a time like this, but Tom Shelby phoned from Richmond late yesterday. Kirk Dillingham has been pressing for an answer to his proposal."

"I've read your latest summary and recommendation, Ken, but I haven't made up my mind about it. There's Chase to consider, too. He is a son, and—"

"I talked with Chase in New York when the offer was first made. He didn't seem to care one way or the other."

"I didn't know that. Just what did he say about it?"

"That he didn't believe Anderson would mention him in his will beyond a token amount of stock, not enough to matter."

"And I suppose it makes no difference to him that the Company will pass out of Warren hands if we accept Intercon's offer."

We're back to *that*, Armour thought. "Theodore," he said aloud, displaying the kind of patience a parent would take with a reluctant child, "we've got to face up to one important fact. A company name, even his own, has little sentimental value to Chase, only the profits the company produces. When I first broached the subject of Intercon's offer to him months ago, Chase was all for it."

"I expect that he would be."

"Can you really blame him?"

Not entirely, Theodore told himself, wondering whether he was fighting the idea of merging Warren with Intercon or, for purely personal reasons, fighting Chase Warren.

It had begun many months ago when it became obvious that Anderson Warren's health was deteriorating dangerously. Until then, no one would have dared mention the words "merger" or "sell-out," but as rumor spread through the industry, there had been tentative offers, dismissed abruptly by Anderson. When the Surgeon General's unfavorable report on the relationship between smoking and lung cancer had been made public, Kenneth Armour had proposed a novel program to diversify—acquire unrelated subsidiaries in the event the 1964 report would be taken seriously by the public.

On his own, Armour had brought a list of recommendations to Anderson's attention, scattered plants for which he sought permission to open quiet negotiations, none related to the tobacco industry. A toy plant in Massachusetts, a candy factory in Ohio in need of money to expand, a plastics plant in Illinois, two producers of food products. Other possibilities he had explored were in the realm of razor blades, ballpoint pens—

"Goddamn it, no!" Anderson had thundered. "I'm a tobacco man! I've been a tobacco man all my life, and I'll damn well die a tobacco man! The Surgeon General's reports don't prove anything. People in our laboratories, in the industry's laboratories, ain't come up with anything definite or conclusive, no more than they can lay the blame on where smog comes from. I don't think those people in Washington can change lifelong habits with a piece of paper. People are going to keep on smoking, you mark my words, and until Washington or somebody else comes up with something as good, or better, to take its place, Warren will keep on making cigarettes, what it knows best and does best!

"Plastics, toys, candy, they're for people like Chase and his father-in-law to monkey around with; syndicates, buying into companies to milk their assets dry, sell 'em off and pick up a hotel or a newspaper or some other goddamned toy to play with. The answer is, No! Now let's get back to work."

To bear Anderson's theories out, despite a sharp drop in cigarette consumption down to 511 billion that year, the loss was soon wiped out the following year by the rapid change-over to filter tips; in fact, cigarette sales and consumption now reached the new height of 542 billion, with still more brand names and menthols being introduced and sales increasing each succeeding year. Yet, other manufacturers were not as stubbornly resistant to diversification as Anderson Warren.

Later, when the rumors of Anderson's ill health became more widespread, Intercon, seeking to add to its widespread trucking lines, paper mills, hotel-motel chain, motion picture interests, publishing, and other holdings, submitted a tentative offer through Kenneth Armour; a sound offer with substantial cash and stock in Intercon. Armour had brought the offer to Theodore.

There were obstacles, Theodore pointed out. "What about

19

the Taylors?" he asked Armour. "Taylor money helped create the Warren Tobacco Company. Taylor Industries has been supplying us with paper, foil, cellophane, cardboard and fiberboard. They have pioneered our electronic equipment in competition with some of Intercon's subsidiaries—"

"But on a noncompetitive basis, Theodore. And for profit, not sentiment or charity."

"—and let me remind you, Ken, Taylor Industries is a substantial stockholder in Warren—"

"Which has paid them handsome dividends over the years and given them the inside track as a principal supplier."

Theodore looked up with a wry grin. "And what about loyalty, Ken? I remember there were periods of war shortages, when Taylor supplied Warren first."

Armour shrugged. "Loyalty is a wonderful attribute among friends, Theodore, but in business it becomes a luxury few can afford."

"I thought you might feel that way about it, but the Taylors are not merely involved in doing business with us. They're kin."

Another shrug. "I can't argue that point, but one day, the inevitable must happen. For your sake, I hope Chase and you see matters the same way."

"I don't need to be reminded that when my father dies, Chase could become a factor I'll have to face," Theodore said dryly.

"All I'm asking is that you keep an open mind toward this offer and consider the possibilities. What Intercon is asking for is reassurance—"

Theodore began showing signs of wearying of the conversation. "All right, Ken," he said, "I'll keep an open mind. Is there anything else now? If not—"

Now, Armour was saying, "There's still the offer to retain you as president at your present salary, with all fringe benefits, the usual stock options—"

"As long as I go along with Kirk Dillingham's policy changes?"

"Naturally."

"Ken, I've told you before. If—and I repeat, *if*—I decide to seriously consider the Intercon offer, I will not become a part of the new organization. I haven't changed my mind about that."

"Then—"

"Not yet, Ken. I won't make a final decision while my father is still alive."

"I understand, Theodore. I'll phone Dillingham's man,

20

Shelby, and bring him up to date on the situation as it stands at this moment."

"And remember to give him no assurances of my acceptance of the offer."

"Yes, of course."

"Then shall we let it stand as it is for the moment?" Theodore stood up to signal an end to the discussion. Armour rose and said, "I'll phone Shelby this afternoon." As he turned to leave, Theodore said, "What do you hear from Corey?"

"He's doing well, thank you."

"Isn't he due home soon?"

"His last letter wasn't very explicit, but it should be soon, I hope."

"Yes, well—thank you, Ken."

When Armour left, Theodore wondered why he continued to show this firm resistance to the Intercon offer, why his thinking was so confused, unable to separate the personal elements from the pure business aspect. Certainly, the Company meant little enough to him; he had never felt himself an integral part of it except for that period— *That period* was the key; 1943, when Louise got her Reno divorce and went to Europe, never to return. And remembering Louise and that period of happiness in his life, he could not omit the part his brother Chase had played in its disintegration. Nearly twenty-five years ago, he thought, and it's still there, as fresh as if it had happened only last year.

He shook the thought off, returning to Ken Armour. How much would Ken get out of the merger or buy-out? Surely he would be rewarded with a generous block of Intercon stock for acting as intermediary, his "finder's fee"; even be retained as chief counsel, perhaps move up to the presidency of the newer, expanded, king-sized, mentholated, filtered company which would be built up around the ultra-respectable Warren name.

Certainly, money was the least consideration. The Company was healthy and hearty. Even if, after Anderson Warren's death, Theodore sold out completely, there would be more than he and his daughter, Drew, could spend in their lifetimes; or when Drew married, her children's. When she reached 21, Drew had already received the million-dollar trust fund which Anderson had established on her birth, and another million from her Grandmother Cleo's estate. Also, the trust fund of her brother, Bruce, when he died in a tragic automobile accident; all a mere token of what was yet to come. When Anderson died, Drew would inherit twenty times that, with more to come later; sooner, if Theodore accepted Intercon's offer.

Ah, he thought, if Louise— If Bruce hadn't died— If Chase—

It all came back to Chase; the childhood rivalry, the resentment, the enmity that had come later. And his curious feeling toward Ken Armour who had been closer to Anderson than either son.

Chase, who had bedded Louise before Theodore married her; Ken Armour, who had, on Anderson's orders, handled the divorce settlement while Theodore remained hidden in New York, unable or unwilling to cope with the magnitude of the whole sordid business.

Almost twenty-five years since Louise had left Laurelton, never to return, a condition stipulated in the settlement agreement; remarried to an obscure Italian title, living in Rome, with a palazzo in Venice and a home on the Riviera. Never again to see Bruce, dead now, with no word from her despite the wide publicity the accident had received; and carefully avoiding Drew, a few years ago when Drew tried to seek her out; cutting herself free from everything Warren except the money and her own memories.

Well, Theodore thought now, we'll see. We'll see.

2

The old man lay on his bed beside the window, its curtain drawn back, watching the night shadows; trees, farms, a stretch of glistening water, an occasional sleeping village, all blending into a long panoramic mural of blacks and grays, unrolling like a vast canvas as the train glided swiftly southward. There were no lights in his private bedroom at this hour—two, perhaps three o'clock in the morning; it no longer mattered—and the darkness seemed to give him a certain peace and comfort he could not achieve in daylight.

In one corner of the compartment, which took up the entire width of the car except for a narrow corridor, a nurse dozed fitfully in a deep armchair, legs propped up on a matching leather ottoman, the white of her uniform a vague, indistinct blur; one more shadow among other shadows when outside lights intruded.

In other compartments between this and the lounge, dining and kitchen areas, Dr. Carl Ballard and the members of his personal staff, valet and cook, slept. Somewhere up ahead, the train's electric horn shattered the quiet night with a warning blast and the black steel monster streaked past a small town with haughty contempt for its two red signal lights that wigwagged at a lonely crossing where no one waited. In a twinkling, the few town lights had been left behind and the landscape returned to a patchwork of abstract grays and blacks of varying depths. In her chair, the nurse stirred, turned from one side to the other and dozed on.

"*How long, Lord?*" the old man asked silently. "*How much longer? I am far past my allotted span, used up, drained, tired of a world that has no need for old men. I've got the mark of death on me and I'm willing to go. I don't want to be a burden, Lord. Take me out of it——*"

A wave of pain struck him then and his thin body shuddered and bucked with its violent blow. He tried to brace himself against the assault, but the old man, who until recently had never known deep physical pain, and only rare and small illnesses, no longer had the strength to repress the agonizing sound that escaped through his thin, compressed lips. "Ah-h-h-h—— Oh, S-Sweet Jesu-us——"

The light beside the nurse's chair came on quickly and she moved swiftly across the carpeted floor in white-stockinged feet. The beam from her flashlight struck his pain-gaunt, wrinkled face, grimaced with agony, eyes closed, hands balled into bony fists that pressed into his mid-section, body twisted and knees drawn up in an effort to fight off the torment of his sickness. She turned on the bed lamp and reached for the stand on which numerous instruments, bottles, tubes and boxes of medicines were laid out within convenient grasp; deciding between Demerol and morphine. The morphine would bring quicker relief. Sterile syringe, cellophane-wrapped needle, morphine vial. She slipped a rubber tourniquet over the old man's thin arm and drew it tight, then plunged the needle through the rubber cap of the vial, sucked the pain-killing liquid into its barrel, shot a few drops to clear the air out, then turned back and injected the remainder of the fluid into his arm.

He lay back, gasping, waiting for the drug to take hold. The nurse gave him a Thorazine tablet to swallow with water, then held her fingers over his wrist, perhaps to let him know he wasn't alone. And, finally, the tenseness went out of his body as the morphine rolled the pain back, easing, subsiding. His mouth relaxed into aged slackness and the night sounds grew fainter in his ears as his breathing became more regular. Soon he was asleep.

The nurse rearranged his pillow, straightened the covers over him. She made an entry on the chart and replaced it in its slot on the side of the medical cabinet, turned the bed lamp off and returned to her chair. She sat watching the

23

body beneath the covers, swaying with the motion of the train, then snapped the flashlight off and closed her eyes, hearing the soft noises of the train and the light, sleeping moans of the old man whose great wealth could buy him almost anything in the world. Except Time.

3

In the early morning darkness, a hound bayed mournfully and from somewhere in the distance came a furious barking in reply. Drew Warren stirred in her bed, trying to hold on to the fringe of a dream that had begun to unfold, but the sad howl in the black night and the barking continued. She gave up finally and turned on her reading lamp. It was just past three and she last remembered the time at 1:30 when she closed her book and fell into a light, restless sleep. She reached for a cigarette and her lighter, then turned the lamp off, concentrating on the red tip glowing in the dark. Outside, the furious burst of barking subsided and all was quiet once again.

The night air was heavy and still and yet the old house creaked and moaned, reminding Drew of a time long ago when she would lie in bed and listen to these very same sounds, trying to form them into words because her brother Bruce had told her they were the voices of ghosts. She had been frightened for a long time after that and when she heard the ghost voices would run to her grandfather's room and crawl into bed beside her grandmother. After Grandmother Cleo's death, she no longer feared the voices because she knew that Cleo's voice was among them to protect her, whispering that all was well.

And reassured, Drew was able to add other voices of her own choice; the phantom voice of the mother she couldn't remember, of the sad, lonely man who was her father, of story book characters she had adopted as her friends, of Bruce, who had started the whole business; and finally, the voice of Corey Armour, not dead, not fictitious, but far away in Viet Nam.

She finished the cigarette and crushed it out in the ashtray, then lay back, telling herself to relax. But it wouldn't work and sleep eluded her; nor could she recapture the thread of the dream that had begun to unreel, although she knew it had, for a change, been pleasant. Her pillow was moist with perspiration, her thick hair damp at the back of her neck. During the night, she had kicked the top sheet to

24

one side and her nightgown clung uncomfortably to her body.

She considered taking another sleeping pill, but only for a moment, remembering the difficulty she had experienced in breaking the four-and-a-half to six-grain habit she had acquired during the year when she had wandered aimlessly through Europe after Bruce's death. She turned the light on, got out of bed and found the brandy bottle on her writing desk, but it was empty. In mild despair, she crossed the room and went through the open French doors where the curtains hung motionless and dispiritedly, out on the veranda, and stood at the waist-high railing, leaning against one of the eight huge, round columns, looking over the distant lights of Laurelton, the bridge that crossed the Cottonwood River and the few, dim pinpricks of yellow, red and green in West Laurelton, known more familiarly as Angeltown.

Even here, there was no movement of air this night. The house, which she described privately as Ugly Victorian, had been built in 1920, a huge, rambling monstrosity that defied improvement. Its plumbing never seemed to work properly, the electrical system would fail at inopportune moments and the elaborate air-conditioning system could not be made to function when needed most. The house was an expensive perverse anachronism that refused to be made over to conform with the present. Even its color; originally, its exterior had been painted a golden tobacco leaf brown with green shutters. Now, despite many coatings of white paint, the brown still seemed to come through stubbornly in ugly splotches of discoloration.

She stood at the rail for a while, feeling the damp nightgown against her body, then lay down on the towel-textured chaise, hoping sleep would come, the dream return—

It was another summer. She was 16 and marvelous biological changes had begun to take place. As a child, Drew Warren had developed a strong tendency toward shyness. When she was three, her mother and father had separated and were later divorced. Bruce, who was three years older, had been removed from school in order to protect him from local gossip, and the two were almost totally isolated on Brookhill, with only their Grandfather Anderson and Grandmother Cleo, housekeeper and butler Leona and Shad Waters, their four-year-old son, Cord, other servants, gardeners, grooms and estate workers. During that period, Bruce and Cord were her constant refuge from loneliness.

Months later, when local interest in the scandal of Theodore and Louise diminished, Bruce returned to school. Drew was adrift, with only Cord for a playmate, always remote and in conscious awe of her. Grandmother Cleo tried to entertain her with stories and games of her own childhood, but it wasn't the same without Bruce and his friends Sam Driscoll, Perry Willard, Hughie Brock, Les Delevan, Lin Dorsey and Corey Armour.

When her own school years began three years later, there were other complications. There appeared in the *Herald* a photo study of Laurelton children on that momentous day of their lives. Drew Warren's picture, captioned "Tobacco Heiress Begins School," had been featured most prominently and was picked up by national newspaper syndicates and news weeklies. From that day, she realized that there was something different and special that set her apart from other children. The principal and teachers treated her with deference and further complicated matters by their marked attention during recess periods. Nor did it lessen her burden to arrive at school with Bruce in a limousine driven by Shad Waters, and be picked up by him at the end of the school day.

Occasionally, children were brought to Brookhill to play or attend parties, but these were spiritless affairs with the small guests on their very best and most unnatural behavior. What she liked most was when Bruce's coterie of schoolmates and friends came out to ride and swim and play their boy games, with Drew watching enviously from a distance.

At 12, the situation had not bettered itself. She was too tall, too gangling, too flat and too plain, resembling a boy more than a girl. Despite stuffing herself with rich foods, double desserts, malts with eggs and pure cream, she gained nowhere except in height. At 13, she topped off at five feet six inches, an awkward height among her contemporaries.

Other girls of 13 and 14 were beginning to fill out where it counted most—and were becoming noticeable—boasting bras, comparing measurements, wearing sweaters and tight jeans that left little more to be discovered; and that little more becoming even less of a mystery when the weather warmed and skimpy bathing suits took over. Growing bolder as they discovered the strangely new, awesome powers of unexplored sex, testing those powers on as yet uninitiated, albeit interested boys.

And then, suddenly, she was 16 and the miracle occurred. Her body began to fill out in proportion to her height and she never grew tired of examining the remarkable changes that seemed to be taking place from day to day; the curves, rounded thighs, maturing breasts, and rear

26

projection with, as Bruce put it admiringly, "all the dips and bulges in the right places." Drew sent off subscriptions to New York for the latest foreign fashion magazines, ordered imports through local shops, scrounged among those in Atlanta and went through endless experiments with makeup and strange, even weird, hairdos, and finally eliminated the exotic for simple elegance that allowed her face and figure to become what they were—her predominant and most attractive physical assets.

By the time she was 17, she had both friends and admirers but the quality of shyness in her remained despite the many new social opportunities that were offered. Theodore Warren returned from one of his unexplained, mysterious absences, this time from a lengthy stay abroad and coincident with Drew's 17th birthday. Others had passed unnoticed but now he put in a call to an Atlanta dealer and had an ultra-smart Ferrari delivered during the evening of her party, a match for the one Bruce was driving.

Life was becoming beautiful and exciting to live and between Bruce and Drew, Brookhill began to take on an atmosphere rivaling the Laurelton Country Club. There were parties, music, drinking and so much to learn and absorb that had been unimportant before.

Anderson Warren disapproved much of what he called "this damn nonsense of giving children too much too soon" but realized that this was a permissive age and could not deny his grandchildren their right to grow up in their own time and generation. Theodore was spending much of his time in Atlanta where, Bruce told Drew, there was an attractive widow who was occupying their father's time. Drew was curious, but not shocked. Long ago she had become somewhat indifferent toward Theodore and was more interested in Bruce's frequent and temporary attachments to various local girls which included two of Drew's own classmates.

Interest and curiosity led Drew into a brief and strange relationship with Sandra Caldwell, who was 19, and with whom Bruce had had an affair which was known to many, including Drew, who had come upon them late one afternoon in the bathhouse at Brookhill. The discovery caused Bruce to break off the affair, but soon after led to an uninhibited discussion between Sandra and Drew at the country club which was followed by an experience between them which created a disturbing excitement, then disgust in Drew. She learned that Sandra had told Bruce about it, apparently to revenge herself on Bruce, who warned Drew of the dangers of unnatural attachments between members of the same sex.

Once awakened, however, the effort to restrain her surging desires produced a debilitating effect on Drew. She became overly conscious of hidden meanings in what had once been bright, casual conversation among her group. The sight of well-formed bodies cavorting in and about the swimming pool brought on erotic thoughts. The throbbing motion of a horse under her excited her into prolonged riding exercises. Soon, she began to look forward to the end of the school term when she and Bruce, as usual, would go off to the Warren cottage at Loon Lake for the summer and a change from familiar associations.

When the term ended, many of their friends left Laurelton for summer vacations. The Driscolls were off to their place at Sea Island, Lin Dorsey to a camp in Maine, Hugh Brock to visit relatives in La Jolla. Perry Willard and Les Delevan were taking summer jobs in town. Polk Holderby, who was Corey Armour's close friend and classmate, was going abroad with his parents, as were others. Kenneth and Catherine Armour were remaining in town and Corey had been planning a summer driving trip through California, Oregon and Washington immediately following the Fourth of July tennis tournament at the Laurelton Country Club, in which Bruce Warren was also entered.

In that event, Corey picked up the junior singles championship in the morning and during the afternoon teamed with Casper Hartung to easily beat Bruce and Harvey Kohlman in the doubles, bringing home another plaque and a cup to add to his growing trophy collection.

Early on the following morning at the Armour home, the front door bell rang. Corey, still in pajamas and robe, was at breakfast, Tish in the kitchen, Kenneth and Catherine still upstairs. When he answered the bell, Corey found Bruce there, tall, fair, smiling and handsome. Bruce would be beginning his sophomore year at the University of Georgia where Corey would be entering as a freshman that fall.

"Hi, Corey," Bruce greeted. "Hope I didn't get you out of bed."

Surprised by the early visit, "Not at all, Bruce. Come in."

"Just for a few minutes."

"Sure. I'm finishing breakfast. Have some coffee with me."

"I'll have a cup, thanks. Congratulations again, Corey. You were in damn good form yesterday. Never better."

"You had an off day," Corey replied modestly.

"Don't put me on. I was at my best and you had me all

28

the way. Hell, I felt like I had a shovel in my hand instead of a racket."

"Well—" Corey grinned and added, "Maybe you ought to play less and practice more. Your serve was what beat you, you know."

"That's what the pro told me, but there isn't time to work with him. Drew and I are leaving for Loon Lake on Saturday morning. I know you've been planning a driving trip—"

"Yes. I was thinking about leaving on Monday."

Bruce smiled engagingly. "Any chance of changing your mind for you? Drew suggested that if you come along to Loon Lake with us, we could both sharpen up. We've got some beautiful courts up there, riding trails, sailing and swimming at our front door. There's some night life in the village at Blue Lake nearby and we could have a ball. How about it, Corey?"

"Well, I—"

"Driving several thousand miles alone is a kind of square thing, isn't it? We'd have lots of company at the lake. Our Warren cousins come down from Maryland and Virginia for an annual get-together, but there's plenty of room and a bunch of live swingers in the colony. Drew and I would like you to come with us."

The idea was suddenly appealing, yet Corey's plans were virtually complete. "Gee, Bruce, it sounds great, but I don't know—"

"We could leave together on Saturday. If you come along, we'll take both cars. I'll carry the luggage in mine and you can drive Drew's Ferrari."

"I'd have to think about it—"

Then Kenneth Armour, dressed for work, came into the breakfast room and became involved in the discussion, seeing both willingness and hesitation in Corey, and urged him to accept the invitation. "Frankly, I'd feel a lot better about your being up at Loon Lake than worrying about you driving through strange country alone, Corey. Why don't you take today to think it over and let Bruce know tonight?"

"Will you, Corey?" Bruce asked, elated.

"I'll phone you tonight," Corey said.

When Bruce left, Catherine Armour came down for breakfast and was surprised to find Kenneth still at home, discussing Loon Lake with Corey.

"Loon Lake?" Catherine said, showing mild astonishment. "I thought it was all settled, the driving trip, I mean. I think it would be a lot more educational and broadening

29

than wasting the entire summer fooling around with the Warren children."

"I think it can be just as broadening and educational to strengthen social contacts that may become valuable later on," Kenneth said pointedly. "Why don't you run along, Corey, and think about it. You'll need other clothes if you decide to go."

Corey went upstairs to dress and Kenneth turned sharply on Catherine. "You might have been a little more cooperative."

"Why?" Catherine asked.

"Don't put on your naïve act for me, Catherine. You know what a close association with the Warrens can mean to Corey's future."

"What it has meant to yours?"

"It hasn't hurt me, has it?"

"Only that your ambitions have bound you hand and foot to Anderson Warren since you indentured yourself to him."

"Let's not start another argument about my ambitions and yours, please. We're talking about a simple matter: whether or not Corey should spend an enjoyable vacation with friends at Loon Lake. It doesn't deserve a high-level quarrel, does it?"

"And I suppose you aren't thinking in terms of Corey and that girl, are you?"

"The name of *that girl* is Drew Warren, and if Corey and she become interested in each other, where is the harm?"

"Only that I don't like the thought of my son—"

"*Our* son."

"—being used by you to weld yourself tighter to the Warrens. Besides, when that old man dies—"

"Goddam it, Catherine," Kenneth exploded angrily, "can't you learn to refer to people by name instead of *that girl* or *that old man?* Anderson Warren happens to be Drew's grandfather, and a legend in this community and state—"

"I'm not interested in a history lecture and don't raise your voice to me in that way."

"I might remind you that we live very well on what I earn as Warren's chief legal counsel and executive vice-president. *That* doesn't seem to disturb your sense of balance, does it?"

Catherine's voice turned icy cold. "And I might remind you that I was not penniless when we were married, nor am I without means of my own."

"Admitted. Your father saw to it—"

30

"Only because he saw through you much better than I could."

"All right, we've plowed through that bit of ground again and again. Let's give it the final touch—"

Catherine laughed without humor. "Are you going to suggest divorce again, Kenneth?"

"It would solve a lot of problems for both of us, wouldn't it?"

"Your problems. You'd love that, wouldn't you? A quiet divorce while Corey is away. Then you could live openly with your precious young tart instead of having to sneak off to meet her in dirty little motels or hotels in Macon, Augusta, Atlanta, and where else, Kenneth?"

"All right, Catherine. You don't want a divorce and you know I can't force one on you, so let's drop it for now. The question is, a peaceful, enjoyable vacation for Corey—"

Catherine stood up abruptly, coffee cup and saucer in hand, her face lined with anger. "Corey is old enough to make up his own mind, so I needn't discuss it with you any further." She turned and went out of the room.

Corey telephoned his acceptance to Bruce that night then spent the rest of the day rearranging his plans, storing his car, repacking clothing, adding other items he would need.

The drive into North Carolina's Blue Ridge Mountains was delightful and pleasant, Drew more enticingly attractive than ever before and showing signs of having lost some of her shyness. They started at four in the morning, drove straight through and reached Loon Lake shortly after midnight.

The Maryland and Virginia Warrens had arrived on the Wednesday and Friday before, each with a Negro couple to look after their needs. A couple of servants had been sent ahead by the Warrens a week before to open the large cottage. From Maryland there were Lucas, who was 19, Brad, 17, and Charlotte, 15. The Virginia Warrens were Clyde, 20, Laurellen, 17, and Christian, 14. With Bruce, Drew and Corey, they made a total of nine, plus the servants who occupied a small house at the rear of the estate.

The first day together was spent getting settled and in general reunion. This was the first year they would be without supervision of the Maryland or Virginia parents who had previously spent alternate summers at the lake as chaperons. Unhindered by elders, there was an unspoken atmosphere of new freedom among them.

It was evident that the northern Warrens had been care-

31

fully briefed and were on guard not to inquire after Theodore, the skeleton in the Georgia Warren closet. His was the only divorce on record in the family line, his life erratic and mysterious, known to have been in several sanitariums as a suspected alcoholic or for psychiatric treatment. None of this generation had ever seen him in person.

Luke, at 19, was a burly first string fullback at the University of Maryland whose ambitions lay toward a career in professional football. Brad was a bright, innocuous youth interested in space aviation, looking ahead to taking up his scholarship at Lehigh University. Charlotte was a wan, colorless, unexciting girl who dreamed of a career on the stage. Of the Virginia contingent, Clyde was a sober, serious prelaw student whose car trunk disgorged what appeared to be a near-complete law library to study while keeping an eye on Laurellen and Chris. Laurellen was a sullen, voluptuous nymph who looked and acted far older than the rest and was apparently the despair of her parents and two brothers.

Within a week, social patterns were set among the Warrens and the Loon Lake summer colony, the cottage established as headquarters for the younger set. Bruce and Corey dominated the tennis courts every morning, but by noon the house and lake swarmed with visitors. Nights were for driving, boating, dancing and the outdoor movie at Blue Lake, which was only eight miles away, these among other diversions available for the influx of summer residents and visitors. Hotels, motels, rooming houses and nearby camping grounds were packed to capacity as the season got under way.

To Drew's disappointment, Bruce had reignited an earlier romance with Anna Marie McPherson and managed to pair Corey with her twin sister, Angie. Luke rampaged about like a stallion turned loose among a field of mares and Laurellen made an immediate conquest of a local boy, Charley Evans, who was 24 and the son of the filling station owner in Blue Lake. Drew had her choice of any number of boys who were competing openly for her company, which she casually divided among them.

The roads to the Warren cottage became cluttered with speeding vehicles of every curious make and their boat dock was seldom empty of sail or motor craft. And as usual, the elderly neighbors complained of excessive noise, suspected drinking and outlandish carryings-on. Harassed sheriff's deputies would know little peace until after Labor Day, when Loon Lake would regain its normal fall and winter sanity.

way, there was the game and I sat with Dad and some of his friends. They won by a lopsided score, forty-two to six, and Luke made four of the six touchdowns and everybody went crazy wild. I remembered back to the time I was only five years old, when they celebrated V-J Day and we were in Washington, Mama, Daddy, Clyde and me. Chris was only two, so he was left at home. I didn't know what all the fuss and noise was about, but it was great fun. People, strangers, kissing each other, dancing in the streets and all. Well, it was the same thing all over again after that game. Everybody was drinking, snake-dancing and whooping and hollering, tearing down the goal posts, carrying on like crazy.

"Dad went back to Washington after the game and when the team was dressed, the real excitement began. Alumni, students, everybody had gone wild over that silly old football game. And Luke was the big hero of the day. We could hardly get anything to eat for all the drinking going on. I got woozy and—I don't know what happened until I woke up in this room in a motel somewhere between College Park and Washington. With Luke. And I didn't have a stitch of clothes on and I hurt all over. I started to get out of bed and Luke woke up, still drunk. I began to cry, but he put a hand over my mouth and—and—he held me down and did it to me again—"

"Laurellen—" Drew's eyes were wide open with shock now—"Luke? You—?"

Laurellen nodded. "Like an animal. I fainted." She paused, breathing hard, reliving it over again. "In the morning, he said he was sorry. Just like that. 'I'm sorry, kid,' he said, like he'd stepped on my foot. I couldn't say anything, I was so sick of him and ashamed of myself. He drove me into Washington and left me in the lobby of Dad's hotel. I took a long hot bath and when Dad woke up we drove home. That's why your cousin, Lucas Warren, is ashamed to be around me. I guess I embarrass him."

"Why did he come to Loon Lake at all?" Drew asked.

"He had to come here or else stay home and not go anywhere. I wish he hadn't. I didn't want to come, but I couldn't think of a good reason for not coming. The day we got here, he took me aside and—he wanted to know if—we could get together again. I spit in his face."

Laurellen was crying openly now and Drew put her arms around her, seething with fury, wanting to find Luke and expose him before the world. Then Laurellen pulled away and said, "Nothing happened. I was lucky. It almost killed me, those next weeks, waiting for my period to come on. But it did. If it hadn't, I was thinking about killing myself."

"What about this Charley Evans?"

Laurellen's face brightened with a smile. "Charley? He's fun."

"Does he know—"

"Not about Luke. You're the only one I've told about that."

"I mean—"

"Oh, sure. We're doing it." She laughed and added, "What have I got to lose after Luke? Once it's gone, that's it and you don't have to worry about it any more, except to be careful."

"Laurellen—"

Laurellen stood up. "I just wanted to warn you. Watch out for him." She turned and walked out of the room.

Drew decided there was nothing she could tell Bruce, nor would anything she said to Laurellen make any difference in her outings with Charley Evans; but after that night, Drew couldn't look at Lucas Warren without feeling that a good, old-fashioned lynching might not be out of order.

Toward the end of July, Perry Willard and Les Delevan came up for a week and the activity livened up with picnics, hiking, riding, swimming and tennis by day, parties, movies and dancing by night. Perry and Drew paired off, Les choosing Laurellen. When Perry and Les left for Laurelton, Loon Lake became considerably duller.

On a warm night in mid-August, Drew walked down to the lake and sat on the edge of the dock, her feet dangling in the cool water. She heard a car drive up, Corey's and Bruce's voices, back from Blue Lake. They went inside and all grew quiet again. A few minutes later, another car pulled in, braked to a noisy stop on the gravel. Luke, she thought, remembering Laurellen, burdened with her agonizing secret.

Then she felt the dock swaying with motion and the scuffing of soft footsteps on the boards behind her, hoping it was Corey. But it was Luke, still dressed in tight khaki pants, white T-shirt, rope-soled sneakers and the ever-present white sweater with its bright orange, block-lettered "M" on its left side. She felt a tenseness come over her as he crouched down and sat beside her, the fumes of whiskey still on him.

"Hiya, beautiful," he said with a wide, toothy grin. Drew did not look up or answer. "You know, Cousin, you been avoidin' me and that ain't the kind of hospitality I been expectin'."

38

"I don't know what you expect and I'm not interested," Drew replied.

"Well, leastways, we're cousins, ain't we? Kissin' cousins? So how about a kiss, Cousin?" He put a heavy arm around her shoulder and drew her toward him. Drew pulled back angrily. "Luke—" she began.

"What, honey?"

"Get your arm away from me."

"Now you ain't all that unfriendly, are you, Cousin? Why I'll just bet if that pretty Armour boy ever put his arm around you, you'd roll over and open wide for him."

"Luke, you're a dirty-mouthed, filthy-minded—"

"Heah, heah, now. That ain't no way to talk. Ain't the least bit ladylike to alienate a well-meanin' cousin—"

She pulled out of his grasp and almost fell off the dock, but he caught her tightly and brushed his lips over her cheek. "Let go, Luke, or I'll call out for help," Drew said angrily.

Luke laughed and held on. "Now that would whip up a storm, wouldn't it? Drag your brother and Cousin Clyde and your tennis player right out of their beds—"

"And Laurellen," Drew added.

"So that's it. Laurellen been shootin' her mouth off? Well, lemme tell you, Cousin, she didn't put up nearly as much of a fight as you are right now. What's more, she's lousy in bed—"

Suddenly angered, she tried to pull out of his grasp. "You filthy animal, *let go of me!*"

Behind his bulk, she saw a light go on at Bruce's window, then at Corey's, heard Bruce call out, "Drew! Is that you?"

Before Lucas could clamp a hand over her mouth, she screamed, "Core—!" The hand covered her mouth then and Lucas pushed her down against the decking, covering her body with his own. "Shut up, you little bitch, or I'll strangle you!"

Drew twisted under his crushing weight. One of his hands was pressed over her mouth, the other holding her down, feeling her breasts, his hips grinding into her groin. She was terrified, straining to free herself, her halter askew, partially exposing her nakedness, trying to get her teeth into the flesh of his hand. And then, suddenly, the weight lifted and she rolled out from under him. Turning, facing upward, she saw Corey's face behind Luke's, one arm locked around his throat, dragging him backwards. She stood up and adjusted her halter as Bruce arrived, Clyde behind him, Laurellen just reaching the dock. Lucas had torn free from Corey's grip and they were facing each other.

39

"Now don't you guys be gettin' any wrong ideas," Lucas said with uncertainty.

Bruce had gone to Drew, who was crying, trembling with anger and oncoming hysteria. Corey said, "Take her up to the house, Bruce."

"I'll take care of him, Corey," Bruce replied angrily.

"You take care of Drew. I can handle him."

"Now listen, pretty boy—" Lucas began, when Corey took a step toward him and hit him, a jarring right to the mouth. Lucas fell back, recovered and came toward Corey slowly. "All right, kid," he said scornfully, "you been askin' for it. Now you got it."

Brad and Charlotte had joined the watchers. Christian was probably asleep, and if the servants in their own quarters had heard the disturbance, they evidently had no intention of getting involved in white people's ruckusing. The dock was narrow, barely sufficient for Corey and Lucas to circle around each other, and Lucas, fists balled up, moved in heavily, taunting Corey. "Come on, tennis player, make your play."

"You slimy filth," Corey said. "Your own cousin."

"My cousin, kid, not yours. You gonna make somethin' of it or you tryin' to talk yourself out of a beating?"

Clyde said, "Will somebody tell me what the devil this is all about?"

"Go back to your books, brain boy," Lucas said with contempt, his eyes still glued on Corey. "All of you, go on back to bed. Nothin' happened and nothin's gonna happen. Beat it."

Laurellen touched it off. "What happened, Clyde, is that your Cousin Luke probably tried to rape your Cousin Drew. He's a specialist at it."

"You lyin' bitch!" Lucas snarled.

"Don't tell me I'm lying, Luke. I saw it from my window. I was watching!" Laurellen retorted.

Corey leaped in then and hit Lucas twice, bringing blood to his nose. Lucas rushed, hit Corey's shoulder and missed with a left to his face. Corey caught Lucas with a hard right to the middle and thought he had broken his hand. Lucas backed off, gasping for breath.

"Luke!" It was Clyde.

"Shut up and stay out of this, Clyde!" Luke said.

"Luke, I swear I'll call the sheriff's office—"

"You do just that, brain boy." To Corey, "Okay, Armour, get set."

They exchanged blows, circling, snapping fists, flailing arms. Lucas got inside Corey's guard and knocked him to the decking. Corey got up and Lucas hit him with a left that floored him again, the advantage of perhaps thirty pounds in his favor. But speed and footwork were on Corey's side. He danced in and out, zeroed in on Lucas' jaw with a right, followed up with a hard left. Lucas remained upright, taking Corey's blows, then threw a right to Corey's midriff, dropping him to one knee. Corey could hear Laurellen encouraging him. He saw Lucas coming toward him, ready to deliver the moment he stood up. Lucas, Corey realized, was too heavy, too strong for him, that sooner or later, he must be worn down. He took a deep breath and measured his target and the distance, Lucas' middle, then rose into a low crouch and rushed him. His head struck Lucas' belly and Lucas was thrown backward, too late to save himself from going off the dock into deep water. Corey went in after him and the advantage once more became his.

When Lucas came up gasping, Corey was treading water behind him. He threw an armlock around Lucas' neck, turned, twisted and drew him under. Lucas was helpless against Corey's superior swimming power. Corey brought him up for a moment, stung him with a hard blow to his jaw, then dragged him under again. Twice more he allowed Lucas to come up, gasping for breath, dragging him under again, holding him down until he felt Lucas go totally limp. It was all over.

He brought Lucas up, towed him to the dock by his long hair, where Clyde and Bruce, who had returned to the dock, hauled him out. Corey climbed up, rolled Lucas over face down and applied artificial respiration. When Lucas came to, the fight had gone out of him. He lay on the dock breathing hard, mouth open, eyes closed. The others looked down on him for a few minutes, then went up to the house. Bruce remained behind to tell Lucas to pack up and be gone by early morning or risk arrest by the sheriff.

In the morning, before anyone else was astir, Luke was gone.

From that night until they said their farewells and goodbyes on the morning after Labor Day, Corey was seldom far away from Drew. He dropped Angie MacPherson and his other girls and spent most of his days and nights with Drew, and when Bruce kidded him about this, Corey replied, "Hell, I'm just tapering off. This kind of a summer is too long for me."

But there was something in Bruce's manner that seemed to leave Corey's reply hanging in midair. "What is it, Bruce?" he asked.

"Well— Drew isn't Angie MacPherson, you know."

41

"That's a pretty rotten thing to suggest, isn't it?"

"Look, Corey, she— All right, I'll ask you right out. You aren't fooling around with Drew, are you?"

Corey was stunned into silence.

"Well?" Bruce asked.

"I don't think I'll answer that, Bruce. If you haven't any more respect for me, I think you'd have some for Drew."

"Don't get so high and mighty. Remember, I've seen you with Angie—"

Corey angered beyond speech, turned away in silent fury. "Corey, listen—" Corey kept walking, Bruce behind him now. "—I apologize. I'm sorry."

"I think you should apologize to Drew," Corey said.

"Okay, let's forget it. It's just that she's at that age, ripe—"

"And you're an evil-minded bastard, so okay. Let's skip it."

They returned to Laurelton as they had left it, Bruce with his and Drew's smaller possessions, Drew with Corey in her car.

It was September and Polk was back from Europe, the others from their vacation rounds; all preparing to leave for the University the following week, Drew to remain behind at Laurelton High as a junior. But it had been the most wonderful and exciting summer of her life, that summer when she was 17 and knew she was in love with Corey Armour.

Shortly after dawn, the sun crept up over Drew's body and soon reached her face. Leona came softly into her room, found her on the chaise on the veranda and shook her awake gently, reminding her that she must meet the 7:08 that was bringing her grandfather home from Baltimore.

Drew yawned sleepily, then went to her bathroom for a cold shower.

4

On that hot Friday morning the mirror-polished Rolls drew up at the C&G depot in Laurelton and turned left, away from the general parking area, toward the special reserved section behind a chain link fence. On the public platform, several waiting passengers idling on the near end watched with curiosity the gleaming black car, the only Rolls in Laurelton and Cairn County since Jonas Taylor's had been retired after his death, this one a mobile monument to old Anderson Warren. A few brief comments were passed between the onlookers, then their attention turned back to normal conversations and their newspapers, checking their watches against the station clock in anticipation of the 7:08 express which would take them to their various businesses, luncheon, shopping and weekend appointments in Atlanta.

Even at this early hour, the air was oppressively humid and the first layers of industrial smoke from across the Cottonwood River in West and South Laurelton had begun to drift toward East Laurelton proper with the promise of increased eye irritation to come. Already, crisp seersucker, silk and linen suits and dresses were wilted by body perspiration, collars dampened, and thirteen minutes to go before the citybound wayfarers would be able to step into the blessed relief of the air-conditioned train.

The Rolls came to a stop at the fence and its chauffeur, Shadrach Waters, lightly tapped the horn twice. On the back seat, Drew Warren tugged the edge of a white glove down and looked at her wrist watch. The time was 6:55. A uniformed special officer emerged from the station master's office and crossed a graveled path to unlock and open the gate, then approached the car with two fingers raised to the visor of his cap in salute. The rear window rolled down and Drew Warren leaned forward to respond to his greeting. The officer nodded, then returned to the gate and swung it open to permit the Rolls to enter. The car window rolled up again to keep the morning heat from invading its air-cooled interior as Shad pulled up at one end of the platform that fronted the one-storied brick building.

At 7:00, Shad Waters, wearing his black uniform with precise military correctness, got out of the car and went to the private platform and greeted the granite-bodied stationmaster with a formal, "Good morning, Mist' Davidson," and Davidson looked at the large open-faced watch he pulled out of his vest pocket and said solemnly, "She's on time. You need any help gettin' him off?" Shad replied, "No, sir. I don't think we'll be needin' no help, thank you."

Then the 7:08 rounded the bend less than half a mile away, its raucous horn announcing its imminent arrival. Moments later it slipped smoothly, arrogantly, past rows of box cars and work engines, into the yards. It came to a halt before it reached the public platform, then chuffed backward easily to the private platform, where two trainmen uncoupled the long, sleek private car that bore the single gilt-lettered name: WARREN, spaced out along the center one-third of its body. Shad returned to the Rolls, shut off

43

its motor and held the rear door open for his passenger. The rest of the train moved forward into the station to discharge and embark its normal cargo of mail and passengers.

On the private platform, Mr. Davidson, who wore a vest and dark blue suit the year around, said politely, "Good mornin', Miss Warren. Hope the heat isn't botherin' you too much."

"Good morning, Mr. Davidson. I don't mind it at all."

Davidson nodded in his usual brusque manner. "Hope the old gentleman is feelin' better. You-all need any help, just call me."

"Thank you. Between Shad and the nurse, I don't think we'll need to call on you."

Davidson nodded again and disappeared into the building. Shad had gone ahead to assist Drew aboard and at that moment, Dr. Carl Ballard appeared on the observation platform to take her gloved hand. "Good morning, Drew," he greeted soberly.

"Good morning, Dr. Carl. Is Gran awake?"

"He's awake and meaner than a cottonmouth. Giving the nurse fits. Won't let her or his valet get him dressed. Come in. There's fresh coffee and it's a lot cooler inside than out here in this furnace."

"Thank you." To Shad, "Go along and see if you can help Grandfather get dressed. Don't bother with the luggage now. We'll send someone back for it later."

Shad went forward to the bedroom compartment while Dr. Ballard poured coffee for them in the luxurious lounge section. Drew settled down in the large swivel chair at the window. She was dressed in a blue silk-linen suit dress with touches of white at the V-throat and pockets and whose very simplicity and exquisite lines spoke for its exclusiveness. She wore a small, matching beret-type hat with the scantiest reference to an eyebrow-length veil, wrist-long white gloves, her long legs sheathed in flesh-toned nylon. Her blue pumps were related closely to her bag.

She was 27 years old and one glance at her flawless skin, temporarily darkened by the summer sun, suggested that neither time nor the elements would ever destroy its incredibly lovely texture. From beneath the blue beret, a waterfall of silky black bangs cascaded in practiced carelessness over her forehead, ending where the veil left off, exposing large, dark eyes. Her nose was patrician and thin, her lips full and generous with only a hint of artificial coloring added, her chin firm and held high. A single strand of magnificent pearls, which were duplicated in her earrings, hung from

44

her neck in a rope that flowed over the fullness of her curving breasts.

Dr. Ballard placed the coffee on the table before Drew and dropped into the facing chair. She took a cigarette from the carved ivory box and Ballard lighted it for her, frowning.

"I thought I'd convinced you about cigarettes, Drew," he said.

Her lips curved upward into an impish smile. "It's quite silly, don't you think, Dr. Carl? The Warrens have been existing on cigarettes all their lives, created an empire with them." She exhaled a stream of smoke. "Gran will be eighty-nine on the nineteenth of next month and he once told Bruce and me he couldn't remember when, once he began to manufacture them, he hadn't been a three-pack-a-day smoker. And, at the moment, I'm not your patient. He is." A pause, then, "How is he, Dr. Carl?"

"Once he stopped fighting the trip, he was fine. A very interesting and enjoyable traveling companion. Full of stories I'd never heard before, and I thought I'd heard them all. You know, he told me things—"

"You're being evasive, Dr. Carl."

Ballard sipped at his coffee, then said, "All right, Drew. I told you when I telephoned from Baltimore not to expect too much—"

"Dr. Carl—"

"All right. I suppose you want it without the usual professional embellishments."

"Yes, please."

"Very well. In short, the Johns Hopkins people seem to have confirmed my earlier diagnosis. They did a needle biopsy. Cancer of the liver is a certainty, but possibly more widespread—"

"Possibly?"

"They suggested a laparotomy, an exploratory operation, to get the complete story. I talked with your granddaddy about it and he decided not to go through with it. So we packed up and left."

"Terminal?"

"Without question, terminal."

The door opened inward from the observation platform and Theodore Warren entered. "Sorry I'm a little late," he apologized, then to Drew, "Just as I was leaving, I received a phone call from Ken Armour." Carl Ballard stood up to pour another cup of coffee, but Theodore waved it aside.

"I was just repeating to Drew what I'd told her on the phone," Ballard said.

"Where is he?"

"In his bedroom compartment with Shad, getting dressed."

Drew said, "What about the pain, Dr. Carl?"

"We're controlling that as best we can with drugs. He's already worked up an immunity to codeine. We're giving him Demerol by mouth, morphine by injection when it's indicated. Also a tranquillizer, Thorazine, and Nembutal to induce sleep. I'll want a nurse around the clock for him. He'll be able to get up and around for a while, but I'd rather keep him in bed, resting as much as possible. He won't allow himself to be taken to a hospital—"

Both Theodore and Drew nodded, accepting this last as characteristic of the man who had contributed an entire wing, which bore Cleo Warren's name, to the Laurelton Memorial Hospital. Ballard replaced his empty cup on its saucer, ready for the inevitable question he had answered many times during his career. Theodore asked it. "How long, Dr. Carl?"

Ballard turned his palms upward and outward. "That's not within my province, Theodore. It belongs to an authority higher and wiser than mine. In over thirty years of practice, I've had to speculate too much with life to guess at death. Medically, we are agreed that the condition is fairly widespread, but we saw no advantage or benefit, at his advanced age, in subjecting him to major exploratory surgery. It could have ended there on the operating table."

"It may have been more humane," Drew said.

"Drew—" Theodore said in mild remonstrance.

"That," Ballard said, "isn't for anyone, doctor, patient, relative or bystander to decide, Drew. In a man of advanced age, cancer cells have been known to metastasize less rapidly than in a younger, more active person."

"Could you approximate—?"

"Guess is the word. It would be only that."

"Please—"

"I'd say two months, a week or ten days, more or less, either way. I can't pinpoint it to the day."

Theodore stood up and went toward the bedroom compartment. "I'll look in on him and then go along to the office. I'm sure he'll be in better hands with Drew and Shad and you, Carl."

When he went out, Ballard said, "What about our other problem, Drew?"

Her face flushed with a hint of crimson. "It's under control, Dr. Carl," she said.

"Sure?"

46

"I haven't had very much to drink since you've been gone."

"Good. Don't let this thing with your grandfather touch it off, eh?"

"I won't. At least, I don't think I will." She changed the subject quickly. "Two months," she said, as though pronouncing a death sentence. "Poor Gran."

She put her cup down and stubbed the cigarette out. Ballard sighed. "Drew, you're not a child. Be realistic. Cancer or not, Anderson Warren is less than a month away from his eighty-ninth birthday. It's a blessing to grow old without the usual infirmities or the slightest sign of mental deterioration that befall so many others much earlier in life. Even the Hopkins people were amazed over his alertness and clarity of mind, his awareness and acceptance of his condition. Your grandfather has lived a long and useful life and accomplished more good in passing through this crazy world than most men do."

Ballard saw the tears beginning to well up in her eyes and leaned across the table to take one of her hands into his own. "Drew, I'll let you in on a secret. He is content to go. When I told him what I've just told you, he said, 'Carl, it isn't given to many what the good Lord has seen fit to give me. I think I can honestly say I've tried my best to be a decent man, a good husband, father and grandfather. But no matter how hard we try, none of us is perfect. At a time like this, a man's got time to look back and count up his failures. Somehow, they become more important than his successes, which don't seem to matter any more. I guess if I had it to do all over again, I'd probably make the same mistakes. Anyway, I can't complain. If it makes you feel any better, I'm not afraid to die.' "

Ballard paused and looked directly at Drew but she had turned away, using a wisp of handkerchief to dry her eyes.

"He doesn't want you to cry or mourn for him, only to remember him as a man who did his best. It will help and comfort him a lot if you keep from showing pity he doesn't want. You're probably closer to him than any living person, Drew, so he'll most likely want to lean on you a little." Ballard broke off suddenly as the nurse, Erna Keller, appeared in the doorway. Ballard looked past Drew, eyebrows raised in question. "He's not ready yet, Doctor," the nurse said. "Good morning, Miss Warren," as Drew turned toward her. "I don't know what's come over him all of a sudden. He told me to get out while his man helps him get dressed. As though I hadn't dressed him and undressed him before." She was almost in tears.

"It's all right, Erna," Ballard said. "Sit down and let's give Shad a chance—"

"I didn't even go near him. I was putting things in my bag, clearing the drugs away while Shad was getting him up. He snapped at me—"

"He's been through a lot this past week, Erna," Ballard said placatingly. "Sit down and have a cup of coffee. You can get the rest of it packed when he's dressed. I'll want you to go along to Brookhill until I can get a relief nurse. I've got to stop off at the hospital first, then my office."

In his bedroom compartment, Anderson Warren, trousers drawn up and belted, stood beside his bed and held on to a post while Shad Waters unfolded a fresh white shirt and opened it. Theodore Warren moved over to help him, but Anderson waved him aside. "You don't need to come home with us, Theodore," he said gruffly. "Drew and Shad here are enough to take care of me, and there's that nurse—"

"I just wanted to see you," Theodore began.

"Well, I'm still in one piece, just as cantankerous as ever, and I'm sure you got a lot more important things on your mind than me."

"All right, Father, I'll run along and see you at home later in the day."

"You do that. I won't be going nowhere."

Theodore left by the rear door, avoiding the longer trip through the forward lounge compartment. The old man thrust one thin arm into a shirt sleeve, then held the bed post with his left hand while Shad pulled the right sleeve up over his arm and shoulder. When the shirt was buttoned, Warren sat down on the side of the bed while Shad removed his bedroom slippers and placed soft, gaiter-type shoes on his feet.

"You want to wear a necktie, Mist' Anderson?" Shad asked. "Won't nobody see you on the way home."

"Of course I want to wear a necktie."

"Yessir." Warren sat patiently while Shad looped the tie under his collar and knotted it. "There we are. Miss Drew said to leave everything else and we'll send somebody back for it."

Anderson Warren crossed the room and went to the medical stand, searching through the miscellany of medical paraphernalia, digging into the partially packed medical bag. "You lookin' for somethin', Mist' Anderson?" Shad asked.

"Just my fountain pen. I was making some notes with it last night. That nurse keeps moving things around— Get my coat, Shad."

"I don't see no pen here, Mist' Anderson."

"Just get my coat and stop talking," Warren said petulantly.

"Yessir."

Shad opened the wardrobe and removed the thin silk jacket from its hanger, came to the old man and held it for him. "That train valet, he didn't even press this— Here's your pen, Mist' Anderson, right here in the inside pocket 'longside your pencil."

The old man turned from the medical stand. "Eh? Oh, so it is. She must have put it back there." He held out his thin arms, fists clenched, as Shad slipped the coat over his shoulders. "I'm ready, Shad," he said more brightly. "Let's get out of this traveling coffin, hey?"

"Yessir, Mist' Anderson."

On the observation platform, Anderson Warren shook off any attempt by Shad or the nurse to help him down the steps, but permitted Drew to link her arm into his as curious eyes from the stationmaster's office looked on from behind window panes. Once on the back seat of the Rolls beside Drew, Shad and the nurse on the front seat, Dr. Ballard gave Miss Keller some final instructions, then spoke to Anderson briefly. The car pulled away as Ballard went toward the cab station.

During the drive to Brookhill, Anderson's head turned from side to side to drink in the scenery, perhaps consciously aware that he might never see it again and must remember it. When they reached the house, he insisted on walking alone up the wide steps to where Shad's wife, Leona, stood before the open door, hands folded under her long, white apron.

"Hello, Leona," Anderson said.

"Good mornin', Mist' Anderson," Leona replied with a rehearsed smile. "My, you look real fine. Them people treat you good up there?"

"Did wonders for me. I feel like I'm twenty-one again."

"Your room is all ready for you, Mist' Anderson. You going to be nice an' comf'table."

"I don't think I'll go up for a while. Want to look around a little."

Erna Keller flashed a quick look at Drew. "I think the doctor wants you to—"

"I know what the doctor wants, Erna. Also, I know what I want and I want to not go to my room right now, so you run along and I'll be there in a little while. Drew?"

"Yes, Gran."

Erna Keller hadn't moved. "I said for you to go along,

49

Erna, and don't worry," he said sharply. "Miss Drew will be with me. Somethin' I got to do."

Drew nodded her own approval toward the nurse and said, "I'll have him back shortly, Erna, and I won't let him tire himself." To Shad and Leona, "Help Miss Keller with anything she needs."

"Ain't nothin' more to do—" Leona began, but Anderson had moved off toward the rear of the house, Drew at his side. Emerging on the back porch, he took Drew's arm to negotiate the steps, one hand gripping the side rail. They walked slowly down the bricked path and through the opening in the white picket fence. Beyond the fence, about 60 yards away, stood Anderson Warren's goal—the Warren mausoleum.

The sprawling mansion stood almost in the center of the estate and had been built in 1920 when Anderson Warren discovered that 1) cigarette consumption had reached an unprecedented peak in America, 2) WARRENS were among the leading favorites with smokers, 3) the trend away from hand-rolled cigarettes and cigars toward machine-rolled cigarettes was very likely to continue, and 4) that he had become a millionaire. It was then that he decided to give Cleo the first really important gift of her life—a house that would be second to none in the community, not even, by God, Jonas Taylor's mansion, Laurel.

Anderson had given Cleo her way as far as the design of the house and its furnishings were concerned, but he reserved the choice of its location for himself. He found what he wanted in the eastern end of Laurelton, just beyond the Riverton-Fairview road, a 640-acre farm that had been allowed to run down by lack of wartime manpower and other shortages. What attracted him to it was its respectable elevation, a hill in its very center, surrounded by a grove of oaks, pines, and dogwood trees, and providing a view that overlooked Laurelton as far as the Cottonwood River.

The house, in its time, became a modern showpiece; a huge, rambling three-storied affair with wide verandas and pillars surrounded by lacy railings, intricate scrollwork, bay windows and an observation platform extending out from the third floor and facing the town.

Then, there had been stables, barns and a smokehouse, a small herd of dairy cows, flower and vegetable gardens, chickens, pigs and a dog kennel. The estate took its name, Brookhill, from the small stream that ran through it and in later years was tapped to build the large swimming pool. The exterior of the house had later been modified and repainted from its original tobacco color to white with green shutters and trim, its interior modernized and fitted out with every present-day electrical and electronic and plumbing improvement. It was a roomy, comfortable house even though it retained much of its original flavor and ugliness and had never achieved the grace and dignity of the Taylors' Georgian mansion, Laurel.

So, the house was Cleo's; but when it was finished and they had moved into it, Anderson decided on a building project of his own—a family mausoleum; a place where present and future Warrens would lie in death as they had not always lived—together.

He called in his architect and sent for a consultant from Atlanta to discuss the project, from which came months of conferences over sketches that became drawings which, in turn, were translated into paintings, complete in detail and specifications. The ground was carefully chosen to allow a circle of oak trees to remain as natural guardians of the mausoleum. By the time the first shovel, in Anderson's own hands, turned the first of the red earth, slabs of marble, painstakingly selected by the architect's European agents, began arriving from Italy along with numerous pieces of statuary and a door of bronze panels by Ghiberti that depicted the phases of birth, life and death.

Slowly, the central structure rose under Anderson's watchful eye, who often created minor havoc by making last-minute changes during construction. The cold interior north and south walls, he insisted, must be warmed with bronze bas-reliefs. In the center of the crypt area, between two huge urns, he ordered a wide marble bench installed to face the east and west walls, which had been pierced to hold twelve crypts, with room for more when and if necessity demanded.

Outside the marble structure, encircled by an open fence of wrought-iron leaves and vines, broad lawns stretched in every direction to the encircling oak trees, the ground was studded with bronze faun and deer implanted to add an illusion of life to the marble house of death; among these the headstones of faithful servants whose presence seemed to imply service in death as well as in life.

The mausoleum became, as it had been designed to become, a haven of peace and rest in time of stress. Here, over the years, Anderson had come, often with Cleo, to seek solace from worrisome, nagging problems, to walk across its lawns or sit inside the marble building in contemplation, seeking relief from a temporarily troubled world.

Its first occupant had been Clyde, the son who had come after Chase and before Theodore, dead in infancy almost

51

before he had begun to take form, two weeks after his birth in 1904 on the very night Anderson, Cleo and Chase had come to Laurelton from their native Loudon, North Carolina. Clyde's small coffin had been removed from the public cemetery years later to become the mausoleum's first tenant.

It had been Anderson's belief and certainty that he would become its second tenant, but the Lord had seen fit to deny him and had taken Cleo from him eighteen years before when she died peacefully in her sleep; then his grandson, Bruce, killed in a tragic accident at the age of 25. Now, as he and Drew entered the crypt room, there was little doubt in either of their minds who would be next. Anderson sat on the bench directly in front of the bronze plaque that marked Cleo's resting place. There were freshly cut flowers in each of the small urns beside it. The collection of bronze and marble figures, the bas-reliefs, gave the room the appearance of a small, private museum.

When Drew moved to sit beside him, Anderson said, "Drew, honey, I wonder if you'd mind leaving me alone with your grandmother for a few minutes."

"I—you'll be all right, Gran?"

"Of course. Five minutes is all I want. You come back for me then."

Drew went out and Anderson stared intently at the bronze plaque. "Cleo, honey," he said, "it won't be long. Maybe a few days, a week or two at the most. Whatever there is on your side of this world, a garden of peace, or darkness, I'll know soon. Which one it is, at least we'll sleep side by side again, and forever. I won't try to tell you what's on my mind now, like I've done so many times before. When we're together, there'll be time enough. And if there's only darkness that follows death, no use me talking in vain."

He looked from side to side, then stood up and made his way to the large urn on the near side of the marble bench. From his jacket pocket, he removed the plastic container of pills he had taken from the medication table in his bedroom compartment on the train and buried it in the soft earth, covered it carefully and returned to his place on the bench, "I ain't going to ask you to forgive me for what I'm going to do, Cleo," he said. "If you're where I think you are, I know you understand I don't mean to sin."

When Drew returned, she found him sitting where she had left him. "Gran?" she said softly.

He looked up and smiled at her. "I'm ready now, Drew," he said.

In his own bed, Anderson Warren lay back against two

52

pillows, luxuriating in familiar comfort. The week-long trip to Baltimore, the examinations by probing doctors and fussing nurses, the attacks of pain and the long return trip had tired him beyond endurance. He hadn't wanted to make the trip, but Carl Ballard's and Drew's persuasions had overcome his objections. All right, he thought, that part of it is over; now I can be let alone.

In near-sitting position, he looked out of the floor-to-ceiling window-doors. From the veranda, he would be able to look down on bustling, growing Laurelton. Once he was able to see as far as the tall center spires of the bridge that crossed the Cottonwood, the river itself, the haze of smoke over the Warren Tobacco complex he had begun in 1911 with the help of his cousin, Jonas Taylor, and later, Jonas' son, Ames, both dead now; but his vision had been dimmed by the lengthening years and it was only his earlier memory of that invigorating sight that drew the picture so clearly across his mind.

"There now, Mr. Warren, how's that?" Erna Keller asked.

"Lovely, Erna, lovely. I'm sorry I lost my temper on the train this morning."

"Don't even mention it, Mr. Warren."

"Thank you. Will you send my granddaughter in now, please?"

"Only for a short visit, Mr. Warren. Dr. Ballard wants you to have your medication now so you can sleep—"

"Not just yet, Erna. You send Miss Drew in and I'll take the medicine after she leaves. I'll have more than enough time for sleep soon."

Erna turned toward the table on which she had laid out the various bottles and trays and instruments and began searching among them. Warren turned his head in her direction and said, "Now, Erna. I want to see Drew now."

"I—yes, sir." She went out swiftly and returned in a few moments with Drew behind her. "Wait outside, Erna," Anderson Warren ordered.

"No more than fifteen minutes, Miss Drew," the nurse admonished and went out again.

"Gran," Drew lied as she stood over him at bedside, "you look rested already. But you do need to get more sleep."

"Sleep. I God, honey, I slept all the way down from Baltimore. Every time I woke up, that danged nurse or Carl Ballard were there popping pills in my mouth or sticking a needle in my arm or behind. I feel like one of your grandma's pincushions. Anything been happening around here?"

"Not much. There was a demonstration in town, but it didn't amount to anything."

"Where?"

"At one of the movie houses. Some youngsters from across the bridge trying to get it integrated. It only lasted an hour."

"Don't guess they like the one Wayne Taylor and I put up the money for two years ago over in Angeltown——"

"They like it, Gran, but that's not the point any more. They want all theaters desegregated, the way the schools and the buses and some of the stores and restaurants have——"

"Well, it'll come, it'll come. We've gone a long way, fur-ther'n anybody else in the whole state, the whole South, but it can't all happen overnight. This damfool black power thing's done more to hurt their own people than anything else. Black power, an axe handle-slinging governor, that danged fool next door spouting poison wherever he goes——"

"Gran, please. You're getting yourself worked up in a lather. I'm going to call Miss Keller——"

"No, not yet, not yet, Drew——"

"Then let's change the subject, shall we?"

"All right. I don't suppose I could talk you into giving me one of your cigarettes, could I?"

"To prove I'm not an entirely unreasonable female," Drew said with a smile, "be my guest." She took a pack from her jacket pocket, extracted and lighted one, put it be-tween his lips. He drew on it hungrily, then lay back and relaxed, thinking, *This close to the end, even Ballard's be-ginning to give in to the will of the Lord.* He looked up into Drew's face and said, "You know, don't you, Drew? Dr. Carl tell you——?"

Through her smile, she said sadly, "Yes," and took his right hand into her own.

"Then I want you to know this. I don't feel badly about it and I don't want you to."

"Gran, please let's not talk about it now."

"Things I got to say to you, Drew. I owe you so much."

"That's nonsense. You've given me so much of every-thing. You don't owe anyone a single, solitary thing."

Anderson Warren sighed. "I wonder if your father would agree with you——"

"Hush, Gran, or I'll have to leave. You're talking too much."

"I God, Drew, give in to me just a little," he pleaded.

"Only if you stop talking about things that upset you.

54

And me." She looked at the clock on the nightstand. "Eight minutes more, then I've got to go."

He clutched at her hand with his own bony claw. "Eight minutes. Agreed." Then, "What about you, Drew?"

"What about me?"

"Well, getting married and settled down, for one thing."

"Oh, that again." She laughed lightly. "You're not going to start nagging me about that, are you?"

"Why the hell not? You're as ripe for it as any woman ever was—"

"Practically an old maid, aren't I?"

"You're almost 27—"

"Way past middle age. Does it show so much, my gray hair and wrinkled face?"

"You had a whole year gallivanting around Europe to make your mind up. Is it still that Armour boy, Corey?"

"You know, for a nice old man, you're pretty nosy."

"You hear anything from him?" Anderson persisted.

"I've had a few letters from him, answers to those I wrote him. The last real news I had was from Lyle Emerson when he got home from the Army hospital up north. You know—"

"The teacher fellow who lost his leg when Cord got killed, wasn't he?"

"Yes. He saw Corey in Saigon only a day before they flew him back. That was almost a year ago."

"Should be comin' home soon, shouldn't he?"

"Some time this fall, I think. That's what his father told me the last time I saw him."

"Well, you goin'a marry him?"

"Stop fishing, Gran. We were good friends, that's all."

"That wasn't all and you know it. You two were thicker'n ticks on a dog's back before he went off to college and you run off to Europe. You love him?"

"Maybe. I don't know. It's been a long time. Things change. People change."

"That's what I'm asking. Did you change?"

"You're still fishing in blind waters. I don't know. Period."

"I like that boy. Better'n any of the others."

"Why, Gran? You never said anything one way or the other about him before. Why Corey over anyone else?"

"I guess I saw something in him. Character, you could call it. Gutty. The way he stood up to his father. Same way me and my brothers stood up to our father, long, long ago."

"There's something I've always been curious about. Corey's father. Your ambivalence toward—"

"My what?"

"Ambivalence. A ten-center meaning love and hate, or like and dislike, of a person at the same time."

"A real ten-center, that one." Anderson chuckled throatily. "Well, you put your finger on it. I like Ken Armour for certain things and I dislike him for others. I like the way he gets things done for the Company, but there were times I didn't like the way he went about getting 'em done. Also, some personal things— But it's you we're talking about, not Ken Armour, Drew. You. Getting married."

"Like day follows night, Gran, I suppose it will happen. Who, how, when, I can't say now, but I can promise I won't become an old spinster."

"That much," Anderson said, "I'll agree on. The *who* interests me most of all." He paused to take several deep breaths. "No, don't leave, you're not tiring me. Drew, when I go, you're going to be a rich young woman, maybe one of the richest in the state. You'll be getting something like ten-twelve million dollars right off, with a lot more to come later. That's one hell of a lot of money for a girl to have lyin' around. Still, I can't bring myself to tie it all up in damfool complicated trusts so you can't put your hands on it 'til it's too late to use and enjoy, havin' you hate me for it. Nor do I want you flinging it around like it all grew on trees for the pickin'.

"Money can be terrible burdensome, you know. You'll be pretty much on your own. You can't count much on your father. If your Uncle Chase were here—"

It was an old story that Drew knew must be faced soon. Theodore Warren, living within the fence he had built around himself, content to let the Company run along with other hands at the helm. Uncle Chase, who had forsaken the Company years ago for New York, living in his own world of high finance, dealing in stocks, banks, an insurance company, oil, hotels, and only he knew what else.

"Your Uncle Chase," Anderson continued musingly, "if he wanted, he could've made Warren the number-one tobacco company in the country. The world. Onliest thing was, he could never touch anything unless he had absolute control of it. Your father, he don't care a green fig about the Company, except for what it provides.

"I built the Company from the ground up. Red earth and some of the best tobacco seed in the country. Your Grandma Cleo, rest her sweet soul, and I watched it grow into the biggest thing of its kind in the state. When Chase got married and took to high finance, I thought your daddy

56

—" He broke off suddenly, then, "All I ever wanted was to have a Warren at the head of the Company—"

"There's still Father, Gran—"

"Yes, there is, Drew, but he's content to let somebody else do the work while he reaps the benefits. He's got no deep feeling for the roots we've got planted here, no more'n Chase has. I God, I wish—" Again he was silent, and Drew knew he couldn't bring himself, even now, to mention her brother, Bruce; and that unspoken wish—that she might have been born a boy to carry the name Warren into the Company.

"Gran," she said, "I've overstayed my leave. I've got to go now."

The old man said, "That Corey, Drew. He comes of good family, even though his daddy's got a fever to become a rich man. Lewis and Marcus Armour were fine lawyers and honest judges—"

"Gran, I think I know how Corey feels about coming into a ready-made job in the Company. Besides, Corey doesn't need or want Warren money. If anything, the over-abundance of Warren money may well be more of a hindrance than a help—"

"Maybe I ought to disinherit you outright," Anderson said with a light chuckle.

"So Corey would marry me out of sympathy? Wouldn't that be a reverse form of bribery, you old fox?"

"Old fox. I wonder. Lord, I wonder—"

He was overly wearied and his pale blue eyes closed. He lay back for a few moments, his hand still holding Drew's. And then, through the touch of his hand, she felt a violent shudder as the pain struck him, heard his agonizing, "Ah—h-h-" unable to repress it. She went hurriedly to the door, just as it opened to admit Dr. Ballard and Erna Keller.

Swiftly, Ballard turned to the medication table and selected a sterile syringe and needle, pushed it through the rubber collar of a vial of morphine while Erna applied alcohol to Anderson Warren's arm with a square of absorbent cotton. The morphine administered, he checked Warren's pulse, then listened to his heart through the stethoscope while Miss Keller wrapped the sleeve of the blood pressure machine around his arm.

"Dr. Carl—?" Drew began.

Ballard looked up and said sternly, "He's asleep, Drew, worn out. He should have gone right to bed when he got home."

"I'm sorry, Dr. Carl. He wanted to take a look at the grounds. It would have been cruel not to allow him—"

57

"It might be more cruel to indulge him, Drew."

Without a word in response to his mild rebuke, Drew went out. Ballard walked to the medical table, looked over the array of drugs on its top, then searched through its drawers. "Are you sure, Erna?" he asked.

Erna Keller shook her head from side to side. "I declare they were there on the train this morning, Doctor," she said emphatically. "I gave him two before we came into the depot, just as you told me. Later, when I was gathering up, I'm positive I put them in my bag with the other drugs. When we got here and I laid everything out, they were gone. I thought maybe you put them in your bag by accident—"

She saw the unspoken "Damn!" form on his lips. "You were with him all the time, weren't you?" he said.

"Except when he sent me out so his Nigra man could help him get dressed, remember, when you and Miss Drew were—"

"How many were in the container?"

"It was a fresh one I got from the hospital the day before we left. Here's the chart—two, four, six. There were thirty-six fifty-milligram tablets to start with and there's twelve on the chart, so there were twenty-four left."

For a moment, Ballard studied Anderson Warren's relaxed, sleeping face, then he said with a sigh, "All right, Erna. I'll phone in a prescription and have Ada Elgin bring them when she comes out to relieve you. I don't suppose it will do much good, but—"

"It may have fallen on the floor of the train," Erna suggested with an air of helplessness.

"I doubt it. For what it may be worth, let's search this room. Inside the pillow cases, under the mattress, anything that looks like a possible hiding place. I'll go through his things in the closet—"

CHAPTER II

1. West Laurelton, December, 1957

Lutie Shackleford shuffled across the narrow hallway into the small, dark, airless room and bent over the sleeping form of her son, Duke, who would be 16 years old on Christmas Day. He lay on the iron cot between the thin slab of mattress and an old, worn Army blanket, knees drawn up in fetal position, shoulders hunched forward to keep out the penetrating cold. When she touched his smooth cheek with her worn hand, he moaned in his sleep, turned from the wall toward her.

"Duke," she called softly.

Duke mumbled a few sleepy, unintelligible words.

"Duke," she called again, her hand moving to his shoulder, rubbing it gently.

"Huh? Oh. A'right, Ma."

"It quarter to five, son."

"Okay. Okay, Ma. I'm up."

"You sure you don' want me to fix you somethin' to eat 'fore you go?"

"No, Ma. You go on back to sleep. Il'l be home by 7:30."

"I'll have you a good breakfus' ready."

She shuffled back to her room across the hallway, shivering in the thin cotton slip that barely contained her bulk, crawled back into her bed beside Sam, feeling the warmth of his flesh. Her bare leg touched the cast that ran from mid-thigh down under his foot, stirrup-like. Six weeks out of work now. The good Lord only knew how many more before the cast would be removed so he could get back to his job in the box factory. A fall when he stepped into a hole caused by a missing brick in the pavement. If it had to happen, Lord, why couldn't it of been on the job so's he could be drawin' full pay 'stead of half pay? And just when things were moving along on a barely even keel. Shackleford luck. Christmas and Duke's birthday just a little over three weeks away.

And Duke, she thought. Lord bless that Duke. Working his paper route from 5:00 until 7:30 every morning, then at his job at Clark's from 8:45 to 5:30. Then doing odd jobs at that poolroom until late at night. No wonder he's so tired, losing his appetite, getting thin. But never a complaint from him. Bringing in ten, sometimes fifteen, dollars every week. Thank the Lord he had that old bicycle they'd bought him two years ago come Christmas at Dan Crystal's second-hand shop. What a difference between Duke and Ivy, that shiftless daughter of Sam's brother, Matt. Eighteen, working at the Riverside Burial Society and Insurance Office and putting every cent she earned on her back. Lord, just don't let my Elizabeth take on none of her habits. That girl is a bad case. Wasn't for Matt dying in Parkton Prison, I'd throw her out—

In the pitch-blackness across the hall, Duke Shackleford got off the cot and grabbed for his shirt and pants as the bone-chilling cold air enveloped his near-naked body. He shivered as he dressed in the dark, taking long, deep breaths to bring himself fully awake. With less than five hours of sleep, he could count on two-and-a-half hours of pedaling his bike over his paper route, breakfast, then off to Clark's for eight hours of opening boxes and cases, stacking merchandise, delivering orders in the nine-year-old pickup truck, sweeping up, eating a sandwich while driving. Home for supper with Ma and Pa and Elizabeth, then out on his own to try to hustle a dollar here or there; from Benny Tupper, if he could snag a piece of merchandise from Clark's, sometimes helping out as rack boy, cleaning up behind the lunch counter, washing dishes, sweeping up, running errands.

Duke had been raised in Baptist tradition, but once out of school and on his own, he could see no reason for believing in a God who permitted the brutality, filth, disease and human miseries he encountered every day. Religion, he thought, was a refuge for the weak, the beaten.

He had been through the 8th grade in the Booker T. Washington Elementary School in Angeltown. He had worked in the stripping sheds for the Warren Tobacco Company. He had spent nights at Miss Katie Willard's Recreational and Vocational Center where Sam Shackleford had sent him to learn a trade, but all he learned there, and enjoyed more than anything else, was to box. Man, that was it. To put them gloves just where you wanted, fight without fear of punishment. And that white cop, Lee Durkin, who ran the Police Athletic League, standing there urging him on. Hell, if he'd stayed with it he could have been champ of his division. Everybody said so. Ah-h, what chance did a nigger have of being champ of anything in the South?

He reached into his pants pocket and pulled out the crushproof pack of Warrens, lit a match and searched through the eight remaining cigarettes for the four reefers he knew were there. He found one, put it into his mouth and touched the flame to it, sucking deeply and greedily as he sat on the edge of the cot and laced his sneakers on. He took three more deep drags before he felt any reaction, then lay back on the cot until he had finished, getting the extra jolt out of the last half inch of the cigarette.

Ah. Better now. The chill was gone. In the dark, he began to visualize color, could almost hear melodic, rhythmic sound. He sat up suddenly, then stood as he pulled on the old, oversized sweater that had been his father's, picked up the thin windbreaker from the chair beside his bed and went out to the kitchen. He took a slab of cold cornbread from the battered tin breadbox, munching it as he went out back where his bike stood leaning against the outhouse.

Duke liked the paper route in the spring, summer and early fall, but hated it during the cold winter months. He had had it since he was twelve and, aside from the money, there was something unbelievably free and clean unleashed in him as he rode through the near-empty streets, a bodyless spirit floating through air. There were no white folks around then, hardly any colored. It was as though he were the only living thing in a world he owned. No small room, no hard cot, no dirt or filth, no evil or hatred, no poor. Goddam. Goddam. Best part of the day or night, he thought. Best time to be alive. Everything else stinks.

At the rear of the *Herald* office, he and fifteen other boys —three colored, twelve white—picked up their folded papers, put them into shoulder bags and wire bike baskets. Sleepily, wordlessly. White boys on one side of the rail, Duke and the other three colored boys on the other, the white boys taken care of first at the counter. Fanning out in all directions to cover Laurelton, some of the older white boys with cars of their own to cover the outlying areas, Duke heading back toward Velie Street in Angeltown where his route began. As he wheeled along, throwing papers with long-practiced accuracy into darkened doorways and hallways and on porches, he ticked off the names of each occupant.

"Mornin', Mist' Archer."

"Mornin', Miz Campbell."

"Mornin', Apex Pharmacy."

And after each greeting, at this time of the year, "Don't you fo'get youah paper boy come Chris'mus."

At 7:15 he was through, weary enough to crawl back

into his cot and sleep the rest of the day through. The reefer effect had worn off long ago and the tiredness and cold came sweeping back over and through him, spirit lowered as he reached home. He wheeled his bike up the broken path to the house, a four-room pineboard affair whose walls were multi-layered with newspapers to keep the cold from whistling through the cracks. Goddam it, he thought, some day I'm goin'a make it big an' we goin'a move outa this shithouse into a real place. Ma, Pa, Elizabeth an' me. Not that goddam Ivy. I'll have a say who moves in an' lives with us.

He snapped the lock through the wheel spokes and went into the house through the kitchen, heard the sound and smelled the odor of sizzling bacon in the hot skillet, bringing the juices of hunger running into his mouth.

"Duke?" Lutie called softly.

"It me, Ma. Breakfus' ready?"

"Soon's you sit down to table."

She forked bacon onto a thick plate alongside the broad slab of fried mush, spooned a gleaming mound of white grits to one side and carried it to him. While she poured his coffee, he doused the mush with thick black molasses. Lutie poured another cup of coffee for herself and sat down opposite him, watching him bolt the food down.

"Don' gobble so, Duke," she said.

"I'n gobblin', Ma. I'm eatin'. How's Pa?"

She shook her head from side to side. "He had a bad night. He hate it, doin' nothin' all day long, thinkin' about you havin' to work day an' night to keep us all."

"Us an' that Ivy—"

"Duke—" It was a plea for peace. "We can't help it about Ivy. Her daddy died up in Parkton Prison, she got no place else to go."

"Least she could do is pay somethin' foah her keep."

"You don't understan', Duke. She's 18. She needs a lot of things to get her 'round to meet people, some nice fella she c'n marry."

And Duke thought, Oh, Mama, you sure got a lot to learn about Miss Ivy Shackleford.

"Duke," Lutie said as he forked some bacon into his mouth, "you got to stop comin' home so late nights. You jus' wore thin keepin' up your paper route, then puttin' in a full day at Clark's. Boy your age needs more sleep'n you gettin'."

He swallowed the mouthful of food and sucked at his coffee cup. "How about *her?* She work all day an' stay out later'n I do. Don' come home 'til two, sometimes three."

"Ivy? What she got to do with you? It you I care about. You an' Lizbeth an' Pa. You need more rest."

He grinned up at her. "Chris'mus comin', Ma. I pick up a few extra dollars a week workin' at Banjo Nichols' place. With Pa on half pay, we c'n use what we get. Lizabeth needs things, too."

"I don' like the people hangs 'roun' that poolroom."

Duke laughed. "Nothin' wrong wif 'em people, Ma. You ain' seen the kin' I see along the paper route sometimes. Drunks sleepin' in doorways, in alleys. Women on Velie Street still entertainin' their customers—"

"Lord, I wish you could jus' work at Clark's."

"That ain' no blessing, Ma. That goddam stingy ol' skin-flint."

"Don' use that kind of talk in this house, Duke. He a good man."

"Iffen you don' have to work for him."

"Leastways, he given you a job an' most boys your age they doin' nothin' cept hangin' roun' gettin' into trouble."

"He getten his money's worth outa my hide."

Lutie sighed deeply. "It sure hard to be alive."

"Ain't so hard 'cept if you're a—"

"Don' say it, Duke," Lutie broke in quickly.

"—nigger. I ain' afraid to say it. Hell, that's what we born, and that's how we live, that's how we die. Born black, born losers. Jus' niggers."

"Oh, Lord, don' le's start on that again, Duke."

"Shit, why not?" Over her protest at the word he had used, he went on, angry now. "It's true, ain' it? All that pink an' rosy prayin' about goin' to heaven, that's nothin' but preacher talk. Don' mean a thing. We get there, what we goin'a find? We goin'a find it's a white man's Lord and a white man's heaven, ain' we, jus' like it's a white man's world?"

"Duke, honey, you too young to start hatin' so soon. Ain' nothin' we try to teach you stickin' in your head? You pickin' up a lot of dirty talk in that poolroom."

"It's the truth, ain' it? Well, ain' it? Look at us, Ma. You, Pa, and me. Workin' like dogs so's you, Pa, Elizabeth an' me can sleep in our stinkin' house in stinkin' little rooms. Pa's a good man, never did nothin' to hurt nobody, did he? Uncle Matt, somebody come after him with a knife an' he bust his head open with an axe handle. Self-defense if a white man protects hisself, murder if a nigger does the same thing. The time I got locked up, you remember? White judge, he say I was stealin' lumber. Jus' because I was pickin' up some old boards off'n a trash pile. 'Cept it was a

63

white man's trash pile, so that make it stealin'. Sendin' me up to Mayfield for three months."

He saw her head bend over the coffee cup again, avoiding his hot, staring eyes. Duke looked away from her hurt, drank the rest of his coffee. "I'm goin' out back a minute. I be right back."

He went to the outhouse, sat there smoking his second reefer down to the very end to get the maximum jolt. Back in the house, he pulled the light windbreaker on over his sweater.

Elizabeth came in to have her hair combed and plaited before eating her breakfast and going down to the corner to meet her friends with whom she walked the mile to school. She was thin and the clothes she wore had been made over from some of Lutie's warmer things.

"Hi, Duke," she called out.

"Hush, Lizabeth. You wake yoah daddy," Lutie cautioned.

"Hi, punkin," Duke greeted. "You learnin' anything in 'at ol' school?"

"Teacher thinks so. She says I'm the smartest."

"Tha's good, punkin. Some day you'll be the smartest of the smartest. You behave an' maybe I bring you a present. I got to go now."

Lutie said, "You goin' ask Mist' Clark to see about that warm coat come Sat'dy?"

"I don' need it, Ma. It'll be warmin' up soon."

During the day he swept the floor, straightened merchandise, helped unload two delivery trucks, unpacked nine cases, delivered fourteen orders in the pickup, wrapped and packed take-with and mail orders, went to the post office, refolded merchandise that had been picked over by customers, ran to the drugstore to bring coffee for Mr. Clark and the three sales clerks, swept the small office upstairs, hauled trash outside, swept the floor again, covered the tables of exposed merchandise. At 5:40 he bicycled home, stopping to deliver two orders on the way.

At 6:30 o'clock he sat down to his supper, alone with Lutie. Sam Shackleford had eaten earlier and gone back to his bed to keep his leg warm under the cover. The cold sent incredible thrusts of pain shooting through his entire leg. Elizabeth had eaten with Sam and gone to the room she shared with her cousin, Ivy, studying her lessons by kerosene lamp. After supper, Duke went to his room to lie down and smoke his last reefer.

His room was a catchall, Duke its only occupant; a storage place for odds and ends of furniture, two old battered trunks, and a cardboard wardrobe where Ivy kept her clothes, since there was no room for it in Elizabeth's room.

Duke hated the idea of Ivy moving about his room, among his things, barging in on him to get this or that while he was in the room. Ivy was a complete mystery to him. She was two years his senior, eighteen, six years older than Elizabeth, and it worried him that his young sister might be taking on some of Ivy's habits. Ivy wasn't very tall and looked to be no older than he, but she was as light-skinned as Elizabeth, fully developed, bosomy, and with more than enough good looks to attract the male eye. Her clothes were cheap, flashily styled and hugged her tightly across the buttocks so that her passage along the street evoked quick whistles of admiration and sighs of desire from the boys and men who generally hung around in front of the stores, taverns, movies and poolrooms along Velie Street where she worked.

There were times when she looked at Duke with something akin to sisterly affection, yet she could smile at him in a certain irritating way that told him he was too young, too immature, too *nothing* to merit her attention. It annoyed him that on those occasions when he came into his room and found her in the act of dressing, half-naked, all-revealing, she paid no more attention to him than if he were a three-year-old. Or his sister Elizabeth.

He saw Ivy around. She was running with the older, faster crowd, the hipsters with the know-how, the angles, the money. Henry Billis, who was head of the insurance office where she worked, frequently brought her home in the early hours of morning. Duke had watched them kissing and fondling each other in Henry's car, and Henry, a married man with four children, one as old as Duke, caressing her intimately before he released her to go into the house. He had seen her in Benny Tupper's car; with Big Jake Runnels, Mace Bodie, Toby Lake, eating at the Blue Cat, drinking in Danny Joiner's tavern. He knew she was on pot, probably got them from the same source he did—Benny Tupper, who made his money pushing reefers—but for a different price.

He thought Ivy had already left the house as he lay on his cot with the door closed, drawing on the last inch of his reefer. He'd pick up more at Banjo's. Benny owed him at least four packs. While he was out on his delivery run that afternoon, he had delivered a package to Banjo's Place for Benny. Two sweaters, two shirts and a pair of tan gloves. Taken at various times, stashed away in the back room, and surreptitiously placed on the truck with the delivery orders

65

after he had been checked out by Mr. Clark. Good for at least six dollars in cash and four packs of reefers.

The door opened. He looked up toward it from his cot. It was Ivy. She looked down and gave him that little-boy look. "I forgot my scarf," she said.

Duke didn't answer, moved his head downward and curled his hand over the remaining inch of reefer. Ivy walked with that seductive movement across the room to her wardrobe, took out the scarf, put it around her neck, then came over and stood beside the cot, looking down. That smile.

"How you feelin'?" she asked.

"On top."

"You strung out on pot?"

"Whyn't you jus' mind your own business, Ivy?"

"Yoah ma wouldn' like it if she knew."

"My pa wouldn' like it if he knew about you."

She tossed her head lightly, still smiling, showing white teeth. "I'm old enough to do anything I please."

"Far's you concerned, so'm I."

"You ain' been aroun' long enough, boy. You got a long ways to go."

"I been there an' I'm doin' a'right."

"Well, glad to hear you growin' up." Her smile indicated disbelief in her own words. And Duke knew it and it angered him.

"Listen, girl. Just 'cause you layin' up with Henry Billis an' Benny an' Mace an' a few other hustlers, don't think nobody else don' know nothin'."

The smile was gone now. "You goddam fresh little nigger," she snapped with sudden viciousness. "You start any of that kinda talk aroun' here an' you goin'a come out on the wrong side."

"You jus' take care o' your business an' leave me to mine. Pa ever fin' out where you spendin' your time, an' with who, you ain't goin'a be able to sit down for a month o' Sundays. He th'ow yoah cute little ass outa here mighty quick."

Her lips compressed and the retort died on her lips. She turned away from him and went out of the room. His reefer had died and he lit it again, took the last two puffs and dropped the butt on the floor. His foot ground it out, then he picked up the torn paper, scattered the few remaining grains into the floor cracks with his foot. Time to go. He pulled on the windbreaker and his cap, went past his father's room and saw that Sam was still asleep. In the

66

kitchen, he called out, "So long, Ma, Elizabeth," then went outside and unlocked his bike.

There was little action at the poolroom. Jake Runnels and Jody Wells were shooting a game of straight pool while Toby Lake, never too far from Big Jake's side, sat on the bench against the wall watching, encouraging Jake with soft calls of appreciation for the more difficult shots. Duke saw Banjo Nichols behind the lunch counter and moved over to talk to him. "Where's Hobie tonight, Mist' Banjo?"

"I don' know. Sonofabitch didn't show up, didn't call up."

"Anything I c'n do for you?"

"You run this counter tonight?"

"Sure. Nothin' to it."

"Okay. Hobie shows up, I pay you for the night anyhow."

Duke went behind the counter and began making the sandwiches to be put into waxed paper bags and displayed on plates. Ham, roast beef, pork, some sliced chicken. "An' jus' remember, kid," Banjo warned, "you ain't got no friends when you work behind this counter. Everybody pays."

"Sure, I know."

Three of the five tables hadn't been uncovered, and Banjo turned his attention to these, turning on the overhead lights. This close to Christmas, business generally fell off at Banjo's. The hustlers who usually waited for the suckers were busy with part-time jobs for cash. Duke picked up a few dirty dishes and put them in the sink, empty bottles in their compartmented boxes. When he had finished with the sandwiches, he washed the dishes, then came out and brushed the three uncovered tables that were still not in use. At nine o'clock, Hobie Morris, eyes bloodshot, clothes rumpled, showed up. Banjo turned his eyes toward him, showing anger. "Well, where the hell you been?"

"Wasn't my fault, Banjo," Hobie said hoarsely. "I was on my way here when two cops pick me up, I don' even know what foah. They straddle me over the trunk of their prowl car, search me, then give me a hard time about holdin' up the Late Night Fillin' Station las' night. I got mad, so they taken me in to the station house an' try to sweat me some more, but they got nothin' on me and lemme go just half hour ago."

"Bastards," Banjo ground out. "A'right. Duke here, he done mosta your work a'ready. Get back o'the counter. I'll pay him foah what he done."

Banjo motioned Duke nearer, counted out three one-dollar bills. "Okay, kid?"

"Sure, Banjo. Okay." It was more than Duke had expected. He folded the bills and tucked them into his pocket, turned and saw Benny Tupper come through the door, smiling toothily, nodding to Banjo, then to Duke.

Benny was the hip slick. Always neat and pressed, shoes shined, smiling, big Buick sitting outside. And always with a roll of bills in his pocket. Benny had it made. Benny didn't have to take nothing off the white bastards who ran everything in town. He didn't even have to go near them, except to make a payoff to two or three of them so he could operate. And Benny was an operator.

"Hi, Banjo, Jake, Toby, you-all." Then to Duke, "Hiya, kid. Come on have a san'wich an' a coke, keep me company. I'm hungry." They went to the counter together. "Hi, Hobie. What's new, cat?"

Hobie at once went into his recitation of the police roust on him while Benny and Duke ate their sandwiches and drank their coke and coffee. Hobie's back was turned toward them, still telling his story, but Benny wasn't paying attention. "You get the package I left for you, Benny?" Duke asked.

"Sure." He put one hand in his trouser pocket and took out a thick wad of bills. "Here, kid. Eight bucks okay? I got some smokes f'you, too. B'fore I leave, I'll put 'em in the backroom john, on top the water tank."

Duke nodded happily as he took the money and slipped it into his pocket. "Thanks, Benny."

"Nothin', kid." For a few moments he chewed on his sandwich, then washed it down with more coffee. "Lissen. You think you could pick me up one of them brown suede jackets? I c'd use one. You get two of 'em, I got a customer for the other one."

"They hard to get, Benny. They in the cases up front. They go for a'most thirty bucks apiece."

"Give you seven-fifty apiece an' five packs o'smokes, you get youah hands on 'em."

"Okay, I'll try. May take a little bit o'doin'. Got to find time when everybody's busy with somethin' else."

"Okay." Benny leaned closer to Duke, grinning broadly. "Somethin' else, kid. Any fancy ladies' stuff you c'n pick up, I c'n use it."

"Sure. That ain't so hard to get to. All over the store."

"Tha's fine." He looked around as though insuring that his next words wouldn't be overheard. "Lissen, Duke."

"What?"

"Ivy."

Duke stiffened. "What about Ivy?"

"She tellin' me you gettin' a little hard-nosed to live with, talkin' about tellin' your Pa some things about her. Now, you don' want to do nothin' like that, do you? It kinda bust things up foah her. Foah me, too." Benny winked elaborately, conspiratorially. "I got me a notion you got Ivy wrong, Duke. She a nice gal, 'jus' out foah a little fun. You don't want to do nothin' to hurt her, do you?"

"No-o, Benny. It just, she always puttin' me down like I'm a little snot-nose kid, laughin' at me behin' my back, sometimes to my face."

"Well, I was sayin' somethin' like 'at to her myself. I tellin' her if she treat you like a man, you treat her like a lady." Benny looked around again. "You workin' tonight?"

"No. Not since Hobie show up."

"Tell you what. I'm goin' out soon's I finish this. You wait about ten minutes, then go back to the john an' pick up yoah smokes. Long about ten o'clock, you be on the corner Mercer an' Pratt, in front of the barbershop. I'll come by an' pick you up. Okay?"

"Sure, okay."

At ten minutes past ten, Duke saw the Buick pull up. He opened the door and started to get in, then saw Ivy in the front seat and drew back.

"Get in the back, Duke," Benny said. Afraid to disobey, and not fully trusting Ivy, Duke shut the front door and opened the one in the back, got in. And found himself sitting beside another girl, a stranger to him. Older than himself. About Ivy's age, smiling invitingly, welcoming him. Good to look at and smelling like something out of heaven. Benny tossed a pack of reefers back to them. "Come on, light up, cats. We goin' for a little ride."

The car headed down Mercer and back on Velie, south through the poorest part of Angeltown, picking up the back road to the river. At the dead end, Benny turned left and drove along the bank for a while, the light of the cold winter moon making a path from the near bank across to the east side of the Cottonwood.

"Your name Duke?" the girl with him asked as their reefers glowed in the darkness. "That's a nice name. I'm Delia."

"H—h'lo, Delia."

"What you doin' so far away? Come on over closer."

Duke inched his way across the seat toward her. From the front seat, Ivy turned, an enigmatic smile on her face, and said, "Now don't you go flappin' your mouth about

69

this, Duke. Ain't no need for your ma or pa to know nothin' about it." She turned back as Benny's arm curled around her shoulders and drew her closer to him.

"You want another one?" Delia asked.

She was already lighting a second cigarette for herself and offered the pack to Duke. He had never smoked two so close together, but he took one now, lighting it from hers, their faces no more than inches apart. He lay back against the soft cushion in the warmth of the car, one arm around Delia. Feeling her right hand running down the inside of his left thigh. Soft and gentle. And that wonderful lightness about everything. That feeling of being on top. The very top. Jesus, Lord, nothing else mattered. Not Ivy, his mother, father, Mr. Clark, white people who looked at him like he was dirt under their feet. Nothing. Nobody. Delia leaned over and kissed him. His arm tightened around her, feeling a yielding, soft breast, the warmth of her lips on his own. He kissed her hard and held on, clinging to Paradise. When their cigarettes were finished and thrown through the lowered window, he put both arms around her, began to feel the softness of her through her dress, his own maleness surging with hot excitement to assert itself.

"Take it easy," Delia whispered soothingly into his ear. "You got the whole night ahead of you."

They turned off on a little side road and moved along slowly for about two hundred yards, then another sharp turn and Benny applied the brakes and shut off the lights. The car stopped in front of a small shack, one of the many used by fishermen during the summer. Benny walked up to it, unlocked the padlock and threw the door open. Delia, Ivy and Duke followed him inside. Benny found an oil lamp and lit it, made sure the heavy curtains were in place over the two windows, even to stepping outside to check that no light was showing through the curtains or at their edges.

That was all there was to the shack. One room. Four chairs, a table, two narrow beds. Benny, Ivy and Delia were doing most of the talking, loose, almost hilarious talk, suggestive and good-natured. Duke felt his youth and awkwardness, left out of it all, unable, yet wanting to take part in it. Then Benny pulled Ivy down on one of the beds with him and Delia moved over toward the other, taking Duke's hand, leading him to it.

"Blow out the lamp, Deel, will you?" Benny called. Delia did. In the darkness and over their murmurings, Duke could hear the rustling of clothes coming from the bed where Benny and Ivy lay. Delia came back and began taking off her dress. Duke couldn't see her, but heard the swish of her garments. He stood frozen, but then Delia came to him and began to help him. Somehow, he was no longer cold. Perhaps the reefers. The touch of Delia's flesh. She was urging him into the bed and he heard the small moans and squeals coming from Benny and Ivy.

"I want another smoke," Duke said.

"Wait. I got 'em here," Delia said. She found them, lit two and handed him one, then got into the bed beside him. They lay close together, pulling on their cigarettes. The tension in Duke began to ease.

Delia knew her way around. She found him, fondled him, kissed and embraced him. He was floating as if in some heavenly dream. And then the sudden thought occurred to him: *Goddam! It ain't a white man's world or heaven or God after all!* Then Delia pulled him toward her and he was really on top of his new world. She guided him, crooned to him, whispered into his ear, paced him as he stroked her warmth and felt her violent response; her tongue in his mouth, then her lips on his face and neck, talking, giving, holding nothing back, cautioning him, "Don't go yet. Not yet. Hold on. Hold on." And when he was at his peak, poised over her in aroused tumult, "Now. Now, Duke! Goddam it, *now!*" And he let go. Then the sensation of falling, falling, but not alone; Delia was falling with him, locked in his arms, he in hers, tearing at each other, fighting to hang on to the last ecstatic moment. A moment somewhere between life and death. And then they had landed in some soft meadow where everything was peaceful and warm and serene.

Delia slept in his arms as he lay content with the weight of her on his arm, his hand touching her at will where and as he pleased, marveling, panting—

"Duke. Duke!" It was Benny, standing beside the bed, whispering his name.

"Yeah, Benny."

"Delia asleep?"

"Yeah."

"So's Ivy. Le's go outside a coupla minutes. I got to talk to you."

"Sure, Benny." He got up and put his clothes on. Delia hadn't moved.

Outside, they sat in the car. "How you like it, Duke?" Benny asked.

"Man—that—that's it, the livin' it!" Duke said with honest fervor.

"Well, there's more of it if you want it."

71

Duke waited. "You want it?" Benny asked.

"Sure. Sure I want it."

"Well, it ain't for free. Tonight, you my guest. But if you want more, you got to have the stuff to pay your way."

"Well, thanks, Benny. I guess that's all for me. I ain't got nothing to go along with the rest of this."

"Sure you have, boy. Like I said before, all you got to have is a little guts. That's how I get it. You can, too."

"How you mean, Benny?"

"Lissen. You know what pot does for you? Pick you up an' put you in another world? Feels great. Big man an' all. Is great, man."

"Sure."

"Well, how'd you like to work for me? Deliver the stuff an' pick up the money? You be my runner. I got too much to handle all by myself an' I need somebody I c'n trust. You keep your job at Clark's, work for me nights. Reefers. White stuff."

"What white stuff you talkin' about, Benny?"

"Man—horse, that's what I'm talkin' about."

Heroin. Now he knew the main source of Benny's money. "I—I—don't know, Benny."

"Well, wait'll you try it. You get a shot of that inside you, you not only think you great, man, you are great. All the guts you need to get anything you want. Money, cars, women. That reefer shit, that's for kids. Shit for the birds. You wanna be a man, you got to *be* a man."

"That H, Benny. It's dynamite, ain't it?"

"Come on inside. I show you."

They went inside again and Benny lit the oil lamp. Ivy's voluptuous body lay half uncovered on one bed, Delia curled up under the blanket on the other. Duke watched as Benny took four cellophane wrappers out of a secret inner pants pocket, got out a small alcohol burner from a drawer in the table, a bent spoon. He poured the powder from one wrapper into the spoon, added a few drops of water, held a burning match under it, watched the white powder dissolve. Another match. The third match did it. From a small imitation leather case, Benny withdrew a syringe, sucked up the fluid into its barrel.

"Here, you do this for me." Benny handed Duke a round roll of rubber, shaped like a thin hose. "Slip it up on my arm an' pull it tight." A vein, like a long, brown worm, popped up and Benny quickly jabbed the needle into the vein, forced the plunger down slowly, withdrew the needle and sat in the chair, eyes closed, smiling, waiting. Then, "Ah, man. *Man!* That's it. Nothin' like it. Ah! Ah—"

Duke watched with fascination. The expression of complete joy was not only in Benny's utterances, but written across his relaxed, placid face. Sexual. Almost Godlike. He stood over Benny for a few moments, totally absorbed, then Benny opened his eyes and grinned broadly. "You still with me, cat? Come on. I'll give you a shot before I give it to the girls."

Duke didn't know how to say no. This was too—*much* —not to experience. He watched the process again. The rubber garter on his arm, the dark worm that rose along his arm, the prick of the needle, watching the plunger force the happiness fluid into his vein. He sat in the chair, eyes closed, the world reeling around him. Like he was drunk, by God. Yet, there was no nausea. In fact, nothing; an absence of feeling. And then the warmth of it struck him, the peace, the greatness in him beginning to express itself, like nothing he had ever known.

When he opened his eyes again, Ivy had just had her shot, standing naked beside the bed as Benny was withdrawing the needle. Delia, with only a towel around her hips, was standing close to Ivy, one arm around her, their bodies touching. Then Delia giggled. "How about some o' that for mama?"

"You next, baby. You goin' get yours," Benny said.

Ivy was lying on the bed while Delia took her shot. Duke came over and stood looking down on Ivy, lying there in her own bliss, her nude body squirming in seductive rhythm. He saw her with a new glow; with colors, music. Beautiful. They were all beautiful and he was beautiful, too. Ivy's eyes opened and stared up at him and he looked away toward Delia, shivering with some marvelous feeling of delight. Duke moved toward Delia and she came at him, embracing him, locking her arms around his waist, kissing him. He started to lead her back to their bed when Benny took him by the arm. "You get in th' sack with Ivy. My turn with Delia."

There was no fear in him of Ivy now. Nor awe. He went to the bed where she lay and got in beside her. He drew the blanket over them and turned her body toward him, pulled her closer. She smiled at him as if in a dream. "Hello, li'l fella," she said softly.

"Little fella, hell. I'm all the man you need."

"You ain't never proved it to me," she taunted.

"I'm goin' prove it right now."

"Be my gues'," she invited.

He kissed her hard on the mouth he had often dreamed

73

about, on the tight, hard breasts that had for so long tormented him, felt the Venus figure he had watched so many times moving across his room, ran his hands up and down the velvety flesh of her legs and thighs which had provoked him time and time again. And heard her soft breath become a moan of want, of hunger, of need for him. He raised himself over her and then submerged himself into her as though he were attacking an enemy, taking pleasure in her counter-attack, knowing that he was pleasing her by the furious raking and clawing of her nails across his back, in his hair, her lips crushed against his, biting his chin and neck.

2

There was money now, but he could not afford to flash or show it around the house, unable to explain its source. Christmas was drawing near and he wanted more than anything else to walk in on that morning, his birthday, and shower a sheaf of green on his mother and father and sister as though money was raining down from the skies; but he would have to be careful. Sam Shackleford wasn't a stupid man.

By comparison, his job at Clark's had become nothing, a drag, but he needed the job as a front and remained at work, hating it, stealing what he could, delivering it to Hobie at Banjo's, to be held until Benny came by to pick it up. At night, he rode his bike around to Benny's apartment, picked up the cellophane wrappers and boxes of reefers, went over the list with Benny, the amounts to be collected, then out to make his deliveries and pick up the money.

There was one disappointment. He couldn't have a car to work with. Not only was he too young, but Benny thought he would be noticed less if he continued to ride his bicycle. No one would suspect he was carrying heroin and marijuana cigarettes inside his shirt, or that a youngster on a bicycle would be carrying large amounts of money.

A week went by. Another. One more until Christmas. He had seen Delia twice in Benny's apartment, had taken Ivy twice. Manlike. Like the man he had become. No doubt about that now. Delia said so. Ivy had said so. And Ivy could hardly keep her eyes off him now whenever they were in the same room, pursing her lips lightly at him in the motion of a secret kiss when Ma and Pa were in the room, from behind their backs.

During the third week, only three days away from Christmas, he felt a pain go through him and knew it was the

74

need for a shot. His nose began to itch and run, his mouth was dry, his throat raspy. He could hardly wait until dark to get over to Benny's, stifling his agony for over an hour until Benny arrived and gave him his shot. The pain lifted, the clouds faded. He was home again in his new, better world. A world in which he was King. Himself. Benny. Delia. Ivy. No pain, no aches, no human misery. It was as if living his true life was now the dream part, that the dream had become his real life; one from which he could awaken and forget the pain of living.

They made up the list together and Benny left him to make his own rounds. He was getting ready to leave when someone knocked on the door. He went to it, called out, then slipped the latch and chain, just as Benny had showed him. It was Ivy. More beautiful than ever. A queen. She came to him on the sofa.

"You didn' come home after work. Your ma was worried."

He passed it off lightly. "She got nothin' to worry about me. I'm okay. Just fine. Where's Delia?"

"I don't know. I thought she'd be here. You goin' home?"

"No. I got some rounds to make."

"Right away?"

"Well, Benny don' like me to be late. The customers neither. Honey, you sure somethin','," he added admiringly.

"You like this dress on me?" she asked. "Bran' new."

"I like it better offen you."

"Well, now you seen it, ain' no use keepin' it on, is it? I got to meet Henry Billis ten o'clock."

"The hell with Henry Billis."

"Look, I got to meet him. I got a job to keep."

She undressed and lay down beside him. "Duke, you some kinda all right. You young, but you a big man where it counts the most."

Half an hour later she dressed and Duke left to make his rounds, locking the door behind them. "Lissen, what kin' of a man is Henry Billis? He any good?"

Ivy laughed. "I tol' you, I got a job to keep. Why you think I come aroun' to see you first, he so good?"

He laughed with her and they parted on the pavement. He unlocked his bike and started down Velie Street. He was late and he had an even dozen stops to make. A boarding house, the janitor at the Cross of Peace office building, Elite Eats, a woman in a private house on Mercer, Mac's filling station, the Domino Club—

It was 11:15 when he got back to Benny's apartment. Half a block away from the house he saw the knot of people standing outside the entrance and around the police squad car. And then he saw them coming out of the building with Benny, wrists shackled behind him, being pushed toward the car by one cop, Delia next, another cop pushing her in the same direction. Duke slid off the seat of his bike, standing there, holding it by the handles, steadying himself to keep from falling.

He was sweating as the car drove off, watched the people drift slowly away, a hard knot at the pit of his stomach, the pain of fear in him, hands wet and trembling, grateful to Ivy for having delayed him; also, that she hadn't been picked up with Benny and Delia. Shaking so badly he couldn't ride the bike. He leaned it against the wall and sat on the wooden steps in front of a house, his world collapsed. In his shirt was the money he had collected: $264. But no H. No reefers.

In a daze, he locked the bike and walked up the street to Banjo's Place. When he entered, the men looked at him with curiosity, but no one spoke to him. He knew it was written on his face, the disaster. And then Banjo motioned him into the back room. "We just heard they picked Benny up, kid," Banjo said.

Duke nodded. "Yeah. If I'da been on time, they'd of got me, too."

"You made it just in time to miss it. What you figger to do now?"

"I don' know, Banjo. I'm scared—"

"You jus' better be. They ofay cops, they ain't as dumb as Benny thought they was. They knowed about him for a long time, jus' waitin' to catch him with somethin' on him. You better believe they know you been runnin' for him, too."

"How they know—?"

"How? Hell, kid, ever'body know it 'roun' here. How you think I know? Same way they do. They got people, maybe even some of our own people, keepin' an eye on things in Angeltown, stoolin' for 'em. Ain't too much they don' know, boy."

"What can I do, Banjo?"

"Bes' thing you c'n do is get outa town, that's what you bes' do. Don' even go home. Chances are they got somebody watchin' yo' house. An' don' try leavin' from the bus depot here. You get a hitch somewhere, maybe down to Tenboro or Fairview, even Atlanna, if you can, then get you a bus ticket somewheres north."

"North? Hell, I'n never been more'n ten miles outside

Laurelton my whole life. I don' know nobody anyplace else, Banjo."

"Well, lemme think. You got any money?"

"Somethin' over two hundred I collected tonight. Benny's money."

"Not where he is, it ain't. It's your money now. How about New York? You think you c'd get that far?"

"Any place so's I don' get locked up again, Banjo."

"Well, it'll cost you. I got a friend up there in Harlem. I give you a note to him. He owes me a favor, got a piece of somethin' goin' for hisself. Maybe he'll do somethin' for you. Okay?"

"Okay, Banjo."

"Wait here." Banjo wrote a note and the name and address of his friend. "Lissen. You take this an' you better sleep in the back room here tonight. Before light, I'll get Hobie to drive you down to Tenboro so's you c'n catch the early bus out. That'll cost you a hunderd an' fifty. Keep the rest of your money hid away an' don' show no more'n a dollar or two at a time, else you wind up with nothin'."

"Sure. Thanks, Banjo. I come back one day, I pay you back the favor." He counted out one hundred and fifty dollars of Benny's money and handed it over to Banjo.

"The favor you c'n do me is forget I he'p you. You curl up on that chair an' go to sleep. Hobie'll wake you up later."

On the following morning, Duke Shackleford left Laurelton behind him. In Tenboro, he bought a bus ticket to Charlotte, making the rest of the journey to New York in separate, easy stages.

Easy except for his need for a fix he could not get, sick with his need for it. Benny had never disclosed his source. Duke would have to kick his habit cold.

CHAPTER III

1. Saigon, August, 1967

At the check-in counter, Corey Armour handed a copy of his orders to the sergeant, was assigned a seat on the stateside-bound transport, watched his flight bag being tagged and heaved onto a tower of baggage on a waiting cart. "Your flight will be announced pretty soon, Lieutenant," the sergeant in sweat-streaked coveralls said without looking up. He turned his attention to the next man in line with a surly, "Okay, Corporal, let's go."

Other homebound passengers who had checked in earlier were ganged up in small groups, showing moods that ranged from hilarity to solemnity, voices high-pitched with anticipation, some in low key, two men discussing odds for and against an air tragedy befalling their plane before reaching its destination. A few kept apart from the groups, preferring their solitary company and thoughts, perhaps feeling a sense of immeasurable relief to be out of the "mean little war" that had become a damned large, nasty war. Just as there were some who felt an unaccountable measure of guilt at leaving friends behind to carry on.

It is an oversimplification to say that one is born and dies and that the period in between is his span of life; that he lives but once. Corey Armour knew this was not so. In a war, he lives many times before he dies, reliving it, remembering over and over again the events and people who have touched his life and those his own has touched, trying to fight off the boredom that comes between moments of combat with the enemy; the long waiting period between life and possible death.

"Hi, Corey!" It was Captain Joe Lanham, a security officer in the Saigon area.

"Hello, Joe. You on this flight?"

"Wish I were. No, I'm catching a chopper down to Vinh Binh to check on a new security operation. Finally made the big one, hey?"

"Yep. Should be home in about ten days."

"Why so long?"

"I'm carrying some special Ordnance reports back to Ab-

78

erdeen Proving Grounds in Maryland, then to Fort Meade for separation processing. After that, home."

"Well, happy flight and good luck. There's my ride warming up. Got to shove."

"Happy landings, Joe."

"Thanks. Same to you."

War, Corey thought again, is for remembering. A name, a vagrant face, a dream in the still of night, waking, wondering where you are. A name like Vinh Binh to associate with Tra Vinh and Aplong Hoi a year ago. Lyle Emerson. And Cord Waters.

He had come in from patrol and reported no enemy contact to the debriefing officer in Intelligence. The Cong had been active in the area recently and Staff wanted some Cong prisoners to determine tactical combat details in order to mount a quick reaction strike. Another patrol had picked up a young Cong boy, badly wounded, who had died before an interrogator could question him. Corey went to a table and got a cup of coffee and a sandwich when the door opened and a Cong prisoner, blindfolded, barefooted, stripped to the waist, hands tied behind his back, was pushed inside the debriefing shack. He heard the soft, rolling voice before he turned "—picked him up around Binh Chanh about 1900, Captain. They asked me to bring him on in for questioning."

When he turned, he saw the man who had brought the prisoner in. Lyle Emerson, who had taught History at Laurelton High, but here in Saigon, Lyle looked like anything but a high school teacher in sweat-dampened flight suit, unshaven and in need of a haircut. Corey waited until Lyle finished his report and the Cong turned over to eager Vietnamese interrogators.

"Lyle?"

Emerson wheeled around and stared. Corey grinned and removed his helmet, revealing his face to the yellow light. Lyle walked toward Corey in disbelief, recognition coming slowly, his grin widening as his pace quickened. "Corey Armour! Well, I'll be go to hell!" Their hands clasped firmly and swung from side to side like a hammock, each with his free hand on the other's upper arm, eyes examining faces to establish old landmarks. Then questions were released in simultaneous bursts.

"Sonofagun! How long you been—?"

"When did you—?"

"Where are you—?"

"What do you hear from—?"

79

"You run into anybody else from home?"

And the senior Intelligence officer's crisp, "Will you for Chrissakes hold your goddam reunion someplace else? We've got work to do here—"

They walked over to Corey's quarters and drew their answers. Corey had been in Viet Nam a little over eight months, a second lieutenant in Infantry. Emerson had been over longer than a year, a helicopter pilot. They spent the next two hours catching up until Corey's roommate, Benny Berrigan, on call for an early patrol, threw them both out.

Two months went by before they saw each other again. This time at the Base Hospital, where Corey had been operated on for removal of a bullet that had entered his chest and nicked his right lung. Lyle had heard the news from Berrigan and went to see him.

"Your father know about it yet, Corey?" Lyle asked.

"He was notified officially, but he may not know about it yet. He's in Europe on business. I had a cable from his secretary, Shana Pierce."

Lyle nodded and said, "I talked to Doc Willoughby. He tells me you're doing fine. No complications. No ticket home, either."

"The way the mop flops. And no more tennis or swimming for a long while."

"Don't worry, champ. By the time you get home, a little practice and you'll be as good as ever. I guess you know you've been scratched from combat duty for the time being."

"Major Ryerson came by to see me yesterday. He gave me the word."

"What next?"

"I don't know yet. The name of the game is wait and see what they come up with."

When his convalescent period was over, Corey, because he was a graduate law student, had been requested by the JAG's office, but Corey paid a visit to Captain Joel Middleton in Army Press and Information and, based on his meager experience on the University newspaper, wormed himself into an opening in that section, giving him more freedom to move around. Over a drink at the officers' club with Lyle one night, Lyle said suddenly, "Hey, I just remembered. We've got a transferee from somewhere up north the other day. A crew chief replacement. Boy by the name of Cord Waters, from Laurelton, a serg—"

"Cord? Cord out here?"

"Just occurred to me you might know him, you were so buddy-buddy with the Warrens up at Brookhill—"

"Hell, yes. We played together at Brookhill when we were kids. Cord, Bruce, Drew. Cord's father, Shad, taught us all to fish and hunt—"

"I'll tell him where to find you. Good record. I tried to wangle him into my crew, but Billy Aaronson was short an experienced crew chief and got to him first."

"How about right now?"

"Sure. Drink up and let's go."

But Cord Waters was out flying a support mission with Aaronson and it was over a week before Cord came looking for him. Corey took Cord into Saigon for dinner and they talked of home and recalled childhoods until the eleven o'clock curfew. Of Shad and Leona, of Kenneth Armour, who came to call on Anderson Warren at Brookhill at least once a week since the old man had begun failing in health, of Theodore Warren, of Bruce Warren, who was dead—and Drew. Most anxiously of Drew, with Corey trying not to show it.

She had been to Europe, Cord told him, and returned with the news that her efforts to see her mother were a failure. The Taylors had built a new high-rise office building and were completing a twelve-story apartment house over on Lee Drive, near the newest Ta-Ran Shopping Center. "Mist' Curran, he puttin' up shoppin' centers right an' left. Got seven goin' now," Cord said.

Ta-Ran was the trade name for Taylor-Curran, the names merged when John Curran married Susan Taylor, who had backed their first successful shopping center.

"You do any hunting up around Shadow Hills before you came over, Cord?" Corey asked.

"Not much. Not much fun huntin' by yourself. We get back, we'll do some, won't we, Mist' Corey?"

"Sure thing. You just count on it, Cord."

2

Corey heard his flight announced and joined the bustle toward the center gate, nodding to a grinning Ed Sheppard, the fighter bomber squadron commander who had received word only the day before that he had, at 38, become a grandfather. Smoking one of the cigars Ed had been passing around at the club the night before, a group of his squadron mates were on hand to see him off. Most of the other faces were unfamiliar to Corey, although he was greeted by several that were as vague as they were beaming and happy. Once aboard the huge bird, he found his seat beside a sergeant who was already buckled in and asleep, or pretending to be, amid the confusion of getting settled, the double checkoff of passengers against lists.

Takeoff. Airborne.

A new, unfamiliar direction. Eastward over the teeming city, cargo ships lining the docks, others swinging from umbilical cords offshore, patrol vessels, freighters limping in, others riding high and heading for home. Fuel tankers. A heavy cruiser mothering its destroyer flock. A hospital ship, dressed like a nurse in immaculate white, displaying its Red Cross insignia. Mine sweepers. Small, fast gunboats. Sampans. Junks. Then the open sea.

Voices died down to small, whispered conversations. The passengers became resigned to the monotony of the flight and dozed, trying to recapture sleep lost in farewell celebrations, conditioning themselves to a tomorrow without the devastation left behind with its filth, disease and dangers. Gone the whores, pimps, thieves, corrupt officials who operated with smiling confidence and impunity; innocent civilians trapped between two enemies, their homes destroyed by both sides, their possessions lost, themselves killed and maimed; children who had never known a life other than under war conditions and perhaps were better able to cope with the problems of survival than their elders, if only there were enough food. Collaborators, infiltrators, spies, women guerrillas, black market operators, generals' wives who owned many of the price-gouging bars and come-on girls. Homeless young, homeless aged. Buddhists and Catholics conducting their own war within a war, as relentless as the war that surrounded them.

And beyond the restless, surging sea below, home.

Home to the greatest and most powerful of all nations on earth; now infected with antiwar and civil rights demonstrations and riots, burning and looting in protest of American indifference. Millions actually hungry in a country whose surpluses and financial aid were dealt out generously to other countries where, as in South Viet Nam, much of the food, supplies and money never reached those for whom it was intended.

Home, where small groups of overprivileged students demanded the right of assembly, right to dissent, right to free speech, right to free love, right to deny the majority of students their right to go to their classrooms to learn and study; this while university authorities temporized and debated the wisdom of permitting police on campus to put an end to childish vandalism.

Corey, like many among those he was leaving behind,

could understand the perplexity of the millions in America who did not accept the confused reasons why the United States had moved from its initial position of giving sympathetic aid to taking over a fully escalated war as its very own. Now that he was out of it, he saw no more justification for American participation in a civil war in Asia than the entrance of a powerful Russian or Chinese war machine into a civil war in Central or South America.

External wars, internal wars. Both involving America, but not backed or supported by all Americans.

And so, remembering.

Lyle Emerson and Cord Waters.

Almost fourteen months ago. He had seen Cord Waters twice after that first time, once in a Saigon bar, once walking along a downtown street, happy occasions both. Then on a Sunday and he had gotten permission from the doctor to take a workout on the courts, provided he didn't overdo it. At the club, he took on a cocky, bandy-legged major by the name of Dunlop and beat him 6-1, 6-1 and 6-0 without extending himself. Dunlop was the Base singles champion, holder of the William Tilden Title Cup (a beat-up canteen cup someone in Maintenance had found in a trash pile and welded it onto an old piece of discarded engine brass to weight it down). After showering, Corey dressed and went to the bar where he ran into Lyle Emerson.

"Hey, Champ! Saw you knock off Dunlop. You looked like Old Home Week." This last was a reference to Corey's title as singles champion at Laurelton High, later taking the same title at the University. "How about a celebration drink?"

"Thanks. For a while, I didn't think I'd last it out," Corey replied with modesty.

"Hell, he was never close. You're not rushing things, are you?"

"I had the doctor's permission. I was a little winded during the first set but when I stopped thinking about it, I was fine."

"How about some chow. I'm on early call in the morning."

"Great."

They finished their drinks and drove back to Emerson's quarters at the Base, then had early dinner. Back in Lyle's room his roommate and copilot, Joe Dolan, was dressing for an evening in town. "Joe," Lyle said, "shake hands with Corey Armour, a *landsmann* from my home town. Corey, my Shotgun, Joe Dolan."

Joe and Corey shook hands. "You-all sho nuff from Lawlton, Jojah?" Joe asked, mimicking Lyle's accent heavily.

"Sho nuff. Where are you from, Joe?"

"Baltimore." It came out as "Bawl-more." "That li'l ol' town behind the big pile of crab and oyster shells."

Emerson said, "Joe loved it so much he enlisted long before the press gangs got within breathing distance."

"Well, you did, too, didn't you? And you were well over the draft age," Corey said.

"Yep. Old man Emerson, the Fearless." He laughed pleasantly. "I was just six when World War II broke out, only fifteen when Korea erupted, so this was my last big chance. Good background material for a history teacher. Also, I might have a couple of kids of my own to answer to some day."

Dolan adjusted his cap at a rakish angle, picked up a fifth of Lang's and put it into a brown paper sack. At the door, he threw a mock salute. "A rivederci, gentlemen. Enjoy your solitary fun while I gather in some Saigon culture."

"Just make sure it's not the medical type of culture you pick up, Shotgun. And let's try to make it in before curfew. Briefing's at oh-four-hundred and I'd like you to have your eyes open this time."

"Pappy, I'll make it with time to spare. These thirsty days, a fifth don't seem to last as long as it used to."

Alone, Lyle broke out the remains of a bottle of brandy, poured two drinks and lay down on his cot. Corey took the native rocker in preference to the straight-backed chair. "Something important on for tomorrow, Lyle?"

"Just routine. Flying a support mission. They're taking a Viet battalion in by helicopter to flush out some Charlies who've been overactive in the Vinh Binh province. If it's the same kind of intelligence we've been getting lately, it'll be a milk run. How's the press information job going?"

"So-so. No matter how much we pick up or hand out, it seems the TV and press association guys are always ahead of us. They get to go in with the troops while we typewriter jockeys wait around to get the word after it's all over."

"At least it's nice, clean white-collar work."

"After three months of it, I think I'd prefer a little more of a blue-collar job."

"Hell, don't knock it, Corey. Didn't you get enough of it before? Don't ask for it. They might surprise you and give it to you."

"And I might just surprise them and take it."

Emerson laughed. "Christ, nobody seems to know when

84

he's well off." He sat up, rustled through some odds and ends on the shelf and found a pipe and can of tobacco, went through the pipe-smoker's ritual, tamped some aromatic grains into its bowl and lighted it. He looked older than his years, his forehead showing deep ridges, suntanned face lined deeply; but beneath his exterior hardness, he was still a pleasant, shy man of medium stocky build who had once been noted for his ability to keep his students interested and amused. When he suddenly asked for and was granted a leave of absence "to study modern history in the making," there was shocked disbelief in the school community that this mild-mannered man would willingly volunteer for military service; and in the ensuing years, Lyle had won a Bronze Star, Air Medal, and Distinguished Flying Cross for bravery under enemy fire. In Laurelton, he was considered an authentic hero, second only to Lee Durkin who had won his laurels during World War II.

"You're getting to be a short-timer, aren't you, Lyle?" Corey asked over a second drink.

Emerson grinned. "Just about another month. We've gotten some replacements in recently, so I guess I'll put away the war games and pick up where I left off. That is, if my job is still open when I get home."

"You almost sound as though you're going to miss this."

"A part of it, yes. The friends, the camaraderie among all men caught in mutual disaster. To be honest about it, I'm sick of the whole thing, the stupidity of all wars, the goddamned corruption war creates. But I had to see it, feel it, know it by sight, smell and taste. Something you can't experience by reading a newspaper or seeing it in pictures. Hell, I may even try to do a book about it." He looked up suddenly and said, "How much longer for you, Corey?"

Corey grinned. "I thought I'd won a ticket home when I got hit, but I wasn't lucky enough. Less than a year to go."

"Then law practice?"

"At the moment, I don't really know, Lyle. I haven't made up my mind definitely."

Lyle's face registered surprise. "Breaking a long tradition, isn't it? You took law at the University, I know. Your father, grandfather, greatgrandfather—"

"Lawyers and judges all. In fact, I can't recall when an Armour hasn't followed in his father's footsteps since the beginning of time. I grew up with it all around me. It damned near suffocated me."

"You did pass the bar, didn't you, with some record as the youngest—"

"Not quite. I came out seventh on the list and there was

85

a boy from Savannah who was six months younger. I couldn't decide a lot of things then, so I volunteered in order to get my service over with. Basic, Infantry, OCS, eight months of combat, and now a typewriter jockey."

And Emerson thought, That's the way it happens out here; a man who has it takes on a certain confidence in himself, command and fatalism entering into his decisions for the future. But once he gets home to old, familiar surroundings, family and friends, I wonder how it stands up?

Corey was staring at the framed, familiar face of Jill Tinsley on the shelf beside the tobacco can; blonde, smiling, provocatively tempting. Back home there had been considerable talk of an "understanding" between Lyle and Jill; also the problem of parental objections over Lyle's social station and financial position—or the lack of both.

The Tinsleys were, by Laurelton standards, considered wealthy, numbering their friends among the Armours, Taylors, Warrens, Willards and other "first" or "early" families. The Emersons had come to Laurelton from Portsmouth, Virginia, back in the mid–30s when Irma Emerson was offered a teaching job through the influence of her uncle, August Shelton, the Cairn County political leader. Lyle's father, Bart, also a teacher, had taken a minor clerical job in the County Tax Assessor's office until 1941 when several younger teachers enlisted in World War II, or were drafted, leaving a vacancy for Bart.

Corey said, "Hear anything from home recently?"

"Had a letter and a box of cookie crumbs from Jill just last week. You knew my father died last year, didn't you, less than a year after Mother passed on?" When Corey nodded sympathetically, "Nothing newer than what we've been reading in the papers. Some demonstrations in town, civil rights, but none of the rioting and burning we've been hearing about. Some antiwar stuff off and on campus, draft-age students mostly with some parents joining in."

"I wonder," Corey ventured, "what my own attitude would be if I hadn't been here."

"Distance lends disenchantment, you could say, but this business of cheering the enemy on, burning draft cards, sending blood, drugs and other comforts to North Viet Nam, Jesus, it makes me wonder what the hell ever became of American patriotism."

"Maybe they believe this isn't our war at all."

"Don't you believe it, buddy. Any war we're in is our war. Without us, this thing could sweep through Asia like leaf-rot in a tobacco field, like boll weevils in a cotton patch. Hell, I—you—we've seen enough of it to be more antiwar than anybody else, but I felt it was necessary then and I feel it all the more today." He laughed without mirth. "Jill accused me of acting like a romantic kid, running off at the sound of a band and the wave of a flag. Romantic patriotism, she called it."

"Well—I don't know how I feel about it, Lyle, but I'm glad you and I are on the same side of this one."

Emerson grinned. "Sure. I'm like the minister who gives his congregation unshirted hell about church absenteeism, forgetting that those he's giving the shellacking to are there and aren't the ones who need it. Well, when I get back to teaching—" he winked—"I may do a little preaching myself." He poured more brandy for himself and added some to Corey's glass. "What do *you* hear from home?"

"I had one from Dad a couple of weeks ago. Sometimes I don't know who is writing me, Dad or his secretary. The letters sound like a fiscal report to the board of directors, but I can't complain about the four cartons of Warren Imperials I get automatically every two or three weeks."

"How are the Warrens?"

"Fine, I guess. Drew got back from Europe recently. I haven't heard from her in months." Corey stood up and finished his drink. "I'd better get out if you want to sack out for your early briefing. I'll drift by the office to see if I can dig up some background material on—where did you say that strike will be tomorrow morning?"

"Vinh Binh Province. About nine miles south, the capital of Tra Vinh. Aplong Hoi, in the Mekong." Emerson stood up. "How about getting together soon, maybe when this one is over?"

"Sure thing. Is Cord in on this one?"

"Yes. He's on Billy Aaronson's No. 8."

"How is he getting along?"

"Fine. Hell of a boy. Aaronson says he's the best crewman he's ever had. Takes to an M–60 like Gary Cooper took to his Springfield rifle in *Sergeant York*. I'll tell Cord I saw you."

"I wish you would. Tell him I'll look him up when he gets back from this one."

"I'll do that. Take it easy."

3

The battle at Aplong Hoi raged all the next day, a Friday. Two of the helicopters carrying the Vietnamese battalion in were shot down after the T-28 fighter-bombers had swept the area. The soldier-bearing helicopters came in only to run into heavy ground fire from the 50s hidden in the brush and among the protective covering of trees below. The V-C came out of hiding momentarily, taking return fire from the chopper gunners, but managed to shoot down the two craft while they were trying to get out. The other thirteen got away with scattered hits in their sides and bellies.

Then the AH-1s, the support helicopters, came in trying to flush the V-C out of their thickets, but the South Viets had been split and were fighting back as best they could from whatever cover they could find. Within minutes, it was almost impossible to distinguish them from the V-C. Communications broke down and later reports claimed 80-plus V-C guerrillas dead and possibly 110 South Viets killed, all unconfirmed.

By late afternoon, there was only confusion as reports filtered back to Base HQ. After dinner, Corey drifted over to the Intelligence briefing shack, but there was no word of Lyle Emerson. Or Cord Waters. Later, some of the support helicopters on the strike came in, carrying wounded troops, all South Viets. Emerson's No. 13 ("My lucky number," Lyle had said) hadn't returned. Nor had Billy Aaronson's No. 8. He watched as No. 3, 5, 2 and 6 came in, unloaded, fueled up and took off again. He had a cup of coffee at the canteen truck and then heard someone say, "No. 8 coming in. Billy Aaronson's—"

Corey put the cup down and went out to meet it. No. 8 had a row of hits along its port side, two that had pierced the wire screening in one of its battery vents. Aaronson leaped to the ground and began shouting to the litter-bearers from the ambulance that was rolling up. They took off one casualty in a litter. Aaronson helped another man off, his arm in a crude sling, a bandage over his left eye and forehead. The copilot was next, bandaged about the knee and calf on his left leg, blood oozing from the wounds, soaking Aaronson's flight suit as he lifted him down.

When the wounded were aboard the ambulance and hospital-bound, Aaronson leaned against the shot-up side of the helicopter, his face gaunt, his expression grim, seemingly unable to walk to the Jeep that waited to take him to Briefing. Corey lighted a cigarette, went to him and stuck it between his lips. Aaronson pulled at it deeply, coughed and turned away, his eyes brimming with tears of anger and futility. The man behind the wheel of the Jeep tapped his horn gently. Corey took Aaronson's arm, but the helicopter pilot pulled away, pushed himself upright and walked slowly toward the Jeep. Corey got into the back seat.

"Lieutenant Aaronson."

"What?"

"What about Cord Waters?" Aaronson didn't answer.

"You see anything of No. 13, Emerson's chopper?" Corey asked.

Without turning, Aaronson said heavily, "I saw it. You goddamned well better believe I saw it."

"What about Emerson?"

"Friend," Aaronson replied, "the litter case that came off No. 8 was Lyle Emerson. Or what's left of him. I hope to Christ he makes it."

"Lyle? That was Lyle you brought in?"

"Lieutenant, we brought him in. Cost me my crew chief, dead, my copilot and gunner wounded. But we brought him in. Me? They didn't lay a finger on me."

"Sergeant Waters—"

"Dead. Didn't I tell you? Dead. He's still out there. Christ almighty. They were all over the goddam place, under trees, behind bushes, blades of grass. We took a couple dozen hits on No. 8. The goddam .50s were sprinkling us like somebody watering a lawn."

"What happened to Lyle, to Cord Waters?"

Aaronson's head fell forward, chin on chest. "I don't know it clearly. I'll have to sort it out when I unshake myself. All I know is, I'm putting Waters in for a Silver Star. I wish to Christ I could make it the Medal of Honor."

It came out in the debriefing shack.

Of the six support helicopters, Emerson's No. 13 was shot down first, less than a hundred yards east of No. 8. Waters and Pastoris, crew chief and gunner on No. 8, saw it go down and called it to Aaronson. Major Carlson, in No.1, saw it at the same time, crashing into a small, open clearing rimmed by a heavily wooded area. He picked up Aaronson's call, "One-Three is down. One-Three is down. I'm going in to cover—"

And Carlson's reply, "Watch it. Watch it. Those goddam woods—"

Aaronson: "I'm going in. One-Three is taking heavy fire from the tree line—"

Carlson: "Do you see any signs of life?"

Aaronson: "Negative. We're returning fire. Nothing from One-Three."

No. 8 was hovering over No. 13, Waters and Pastoris

firing their M-60s into brush and tree line. Artie Church, the copilot, was firing his sub-machine gun from the opening on his right while Aaronson swung and whipped No. 8 from side to side to give them the clearest possible field of fire. Then the ground firing stopped suddenly. Aaronson moved over the thick brush and got as close to the tree line as he could maneuver, but could make out no sign of activity below. He turned and came back over the clearing, hovering, circling over No. 13, seeing no evidence of movement or life.

Carlson called in again. "No. 8. Check in."

Aaronson: "No. 8 hovering. No sign of life in One-Three or in the surrounding woods."

Carlson: "Can you get in?"

Aaronson: "Negative. Clearing is not large enough."

Carlson: "Then pull out and rejoin. We've got our hands full over here."

Aaronson: "I'm going to lower a man on our recovery sling to check it out. There may be wounded—"

For a moment there was nothing, then Carlson came in again. "All right, but for Christ's sake, hurry it up."

Cord Waters shot the sliding window back and said to Aaronson, "I'll ride it down, Lieutenant."

Aaronson was busy at the controls and replied, "What about Pastoris? He's a lot lighter—"

"Yeah, Lieutenant, but I'm stronger. Besides, Lieutenant Emerson's from my home town—"

"Get going. Take Artie's sub-machine gun with you."

Artie Church slapped a fresh clip into the weapon and handed it back to Waters. "Good luck, Cord."

"That's what I got. Never been shot out of the air yet."

"For all our sakes, let's hope your luck holds out."

Waters rode the sling down, his feet in the canvas hammock, one hand gripping the cable, the other clutched around the automatic weapon. Aaronson dropped him beside One-Three and pulled up, then continued to hover. Waters opened the bullet-riddled door on the copilot's side and saw at once that Joe Dolan was dead. The waist door was open and both the crew chief and gunner were dead. He ran around to the pilot's side. Lyle Emerson was slumped forward over the controls. Waters put one hand out and touched his arm, called, "Lieutenant! Lieutenant! It's me, Cord Waters! Lieutenant—"

Then Lyle Emerson groaned. Cord Waters dropped the weapon, leaped up on the boarding step and began unbuck-

90

ling the safety belts. "Hang on, Lieutenant," he breathed. "Jus'
you hang on. I'll get you out in two shakes. Yessir. We got
old No. 8 waitin' upstairs right now. Hol' on. Here we come
—easy—easy—"

He pulled Emerson partially out of the door, leaped to
the ground and dragged him down the rest of the way. One
of Emerson's legs was torn up badly, a mass of bloodied
flesh, resembling no leg Waters had ever seen, ripped by
machine-gun fire that had burst through the bottom of the
helicopter. Waters laid him down on the grass gently, tore
off his own belt and tied it tightly just above the ghastly
opening, his lips moving in silent prayer. Emerson's dead
weight gave him no problem. Aaronson was maneuvering
No. 8 overhead so that the sling was dangling within easy
reach and as soon as the tourniquet was in place, Waters
got the sling under Emerson, strapped him in tightly, then
stood up and gave the "Take it away" signal. Before the
sling could take up the slack, Emerson opened his eyes and
squinted up at Waters.

Cord said, "You okay now, Mist' Emerson. Don't you
worry none. You on your way up and out—"

Emerson said, "Watch—out—Cord. Tricky bastards—always leave—some—somebody behind—pick us off—"

The sling began moving upward slowly, steadily. Just as
the first pair of hands reached out to haul Emerson in, all
hell broke loose from the brush. Rifle and machine-gun fire
coming in from behind the lines of trees. Bullets thudded
into the downed No. 13 while others slammed into No. 8
above. Waters dropped to the ground, searching frantically
for the sub-machine gun he had thrown aside in order to
get Emerson out of the pilot's seat. He crawled and slith-
ered in a circle, then found it in the high grass.

The fire was being directed mostly at No. 8 and Waters
threw up one hand to wave it away to safety, but Aaronson
held it there. No. 8 was returning the fire, Pastoris on one
M-60, Artie Church on the other. Waters dropped down as
close to the earth as he could, crawling toward One-Three's
belly for cover, thinking, "He'll die if they don't get him
back. Goddam it, get out. Go, man, go. I ll be okay. Get
the Lieutenant out—"

He began returning fire in short bursts, holding the sub-
machine gun with loving hands, the way he would caress a
woman, firmly, yet gently, speaking to it. "Give, baby, give
—there—over there—put it to 'em, baby—"

There was a lull in the firing. Waters looked out from
under No. 13's belly and saw No. 8 still maneuvering over-

head hopefully. "Chrissakes, get out!" he mouthed. "You can't do nothin' for me. Get the Lieutenant back——" He braced himself, got to his knees cautiously, then stood up, again waving No. 8 off. A burst came toward him from the woods and he threw himself down. Too late. The first burst of fire caught him, ripped through his upper body, throwing him backward, killing him instantly.

In No. 8, they were taking the heavier calibered stuff again. Artie Church got it first, then Pastoris. Aaronson craned his neck out of the side window and saw Waters at the very moment he was hit, saw his body buckle and crumple to earth. Sickened, he pulled up and away quickly. "I'll come back for you, Cord," he said to himself. "I'll come back. You won't be left out there alone, boy, I swear it."

On the return trip to Aplong Hoi the following morning, there was little to see, little to do. The Cong were gone. But Billy Aaronson kept his word. He found the clearing and sent his new crew chief and gunner down to recover the dead, douse what was left of the stripped, crippled No. 13 with gasoline and set it afire.

4

Corey Armour tried to see Lyle Emerson at the Base Hospital later that night, but found he was still in the operating room. On the fourth day, he learned from the doctor that Lyle's right leg had been amputated about nine inches above the knee. Lyle was under heavy sedation. Corey returned the next day and the one after that and found Lyle awake, dulled by drugs, barely able to keep his eyes open. He came back again the following day, bringing Lyle's tooth-bitten-stemmed pipe and can of tobacco. He filled it, tamped it, placed it between Lyle's lips and held a match to it, but Lyle made little effort to draw on it. Corey put the pipe back on the table beside the bed.

"Lyle, how are you?" he asked.

"Where's Cord?" Emerson replied.

"He's fine, Lyle," Corey lied. "Down in Ward 27. I saw him just a few minutes ago."

"How is he?"

"He's coming along. Shot up some, but they'll be wheeling him in to see you one day soon. He——uh——asked for you."

"Listen, Corey——"

"What?"

92

"For Christ's sake, you don't have to play games with me like the others. I know he's dead. I could see it in Billy Aaronson's face a little while ago. It's a thing you know." He paused as though out of breath, then said, "He's dead, isn't he?"

Corey could no longer play the game. "Yes, Lyle. Cord is dead. Billy went back the next morning and brought him out. Your boys along with him."

"Oh, Jesus," Lyle breathed. "Jesus Christ almighty. Because of me. He died for me, trying to save me."

"Lyle, it happened the way it was fated to happen. You can't undo what's been done."

"He went down to get me, under fire. He got killed saving my life. He—"

"He would have done it no matter who was down there, Lyle. You've got to accept it."

"Accept another man's life? Like I have to accept a one-legged existence, limping through life, being pitied—"

"Nobody's going to pity you. They'll honor you—"

"Sure. I'll be met at home by an honor parade of anti-Vietniks, students and mothers, burning flags and carrying placards reading, *Sucker! Welcome home, Sucker! Rah! Rah! Rah!*"

His voice had risen to a high pitch and a nurse came hurrying in, a doctor behind her, motioning Corey out of the room.

When he saw Lyle again, some ten days later, the atmosphere was less tense. Emerson was steeped in his own depression, the melancholy of a man resigned to a sentence no higher court could reverse. His face reflected the bitter anguish in his heart, and Corey knew what was eating into him.

Jill Tinsley.

Corey knew more about the Emerson-Tinsley affair than Lyle suspected. Jill had been a close friend of Paula Corbin and Paula had been a member of Corey's clique of friends at college. Lyle and Jill, fighting parental objections to their engagement and marriage, had engaged in a quiet affair, which had resolved nothing except their physical need for each other. Jill was in love with Lyle, but was hardly ready for an irrevocable break with her parents; life in Laurelton under those circumstances would be too much to bear. Nor could Lyle accept the responsibility for forcing the break until Jill was ready to make it, realizing that if they eloped under his persuasion, sooner or later it must come up between them and disrupt their lives.

To Lyle, the affair had begun as a beautiful thing between a man and woman in love, then turned into a cheap sidelight of what love and marriage were intended to mean, what it had meant to his own mother and father. Sneaking about, skulking in the dark, an occasional furtive weekend in some distant town; he could see the strain on Jill, perhaps a transference from himself to her. There were arguments, but no solutions. For a while, Jill refused to see him and Lyle was desolate without her, as desolate as Jill, according to Paula, had been without Lyle. His work suffered and became noticeable to other faculty members. And finally, seeking a way out, one he knew would never come as long as they remained together in the same town, he enlisted in the Army, took the aptitude tests and found himself in flight training. When the need for helicopter pilots became critical, he transferred to that branch.

Meanwhile, he had written to Jill and she had relented, assuming some of the guilt for his action, and came down to the training camp to be with him. But then, Ben Tinsley showed up and there was a scene that left Jill in tears. Ben Tinsley threatened to go to the commanding general and Jill, afraid that the greater harm would fall upon Lyle, gave in and returned to Laurelton. A month later, Lyle was on his way overseas.

Now Lyle needed to talk about it. Jill's letters to him, professing her deep love for him. When he returned, she had written recently, they would leave Laurelton together. Wherever he chose, New York, Los Angeles, Boston, Denver, she would be happy with him. Only come back safely.

Lyle showed Corey a letter that had come with the box of "cookie crumbs," forced him to read it.

It is my life and yours, Lyle. Dad and Mother have lived theirs and I intend that you and I shall live ours. Nothing can change that, now or ever. Anywhere you choose, it will be you and me, together and forever. Please take care and come home as soon as you can. I love you.

JILL

While Corey read that last paragraph, Lyle reached for his pipe and fondled it like a favorite toy, eyes averted from the lower right side of the hospital bed where the emptiness was a constant reminder of his terrible loss. Corey refolded the letter and slipped it back into the blue, scented envelope. "She's a sweet girl, Lyle," he said, "you're still a very lucky guy."

"Oh, I am, I am," Lyle said, but the deep cynicism in his voice was harsh and undeniable. "Believe me, I know I am."

"In your place, I'm sure I'd be proud—"

"Oh, for Christ's sweet sake, Corey, come off it. Nobody can crawl into my place. Not you, not Jill, no one." He paused for a moment, then said, "Now take a look and see how lucky I really am. Look at this."

He reached under his pillow and withdrew another letter. The same blue, the same scent. He held it out toward Corey, who now began to suspect what it might contain, and held back. Lyle tossed it to him and it fell on the bed, only a few inches from Corey's hand. "I got this three days ago. Go ahead, read it," Lyle insisted. "Why should *you* be afraid? It didn't kill me."

Corey picked the letter up reluctantly and began to read.

Dearest Lyle:

The news came through last night and I can't tell you how desperately sorry I am. I'm still in a daze about it, knowing only that I'm glad you're alive. It was a terrible, ghastly thing, but the broadcast and newspapers say you'll come through the operation. I pray you will.

You might like to know that the school board has voted unanimously to hold your teaching job open as long as you want it. You are quite a celebrity at home.

Later.

Darling, I don't quite know how to say this. I know what must be going through your mind and how difficult things are for you, but I must tell you. I have thought this out and I am leaving Laurelton next week to take a job in New York. My cousin Alfred found one for me with a book publishing firm. I feel that I've got to get away from everyone and everything. I can't stand living at home. The change may give me what I need right now, otherwise I shall go out of my mind.

Don't hate me. I know I'm being cowardly. I won't blame you for believing that, but it may be best for both of us.

JILL

The message was brief and clear. Lyle Emerson had been Dear-Johned. Coldly, brutally, effectively. Corey could find no words to say to him, no way to comfort him. For himself, he cursed Jill to hell and back again for what these few words were doing to Lyle. He put the letter down and looked away, unwilling to witness the deep misery of his friend.

"I've got my orders," Emerson said finally.

"When?"

"The end of the week. Walter Reed Medical Center in Washington. Convalescence and rehabilitation. The idea is to put me in with the other amputees they've collected who've already been given their artificial arms and legs. That way, I'm supposed to get the idea quicker."

"Lyle, give them a chance. All they want is the best that can be done for you."

"Sure."

"It takes time. Other men have lived through it—"

"I've already had the buildup and statistics thrown at me. It's part of the course. I expect that all the doctors, nurses and attendants in the Gimp Section at Walter Reed will have one or more members missing in order to show me what can and has been done. One-legged golfers, one-armed mechanics—" His voice trailed off, then, "Thanks for coming by, Corey. I don't mean to take any of this out on you." He squirmed around, seeking a more comfortable position. "I'll have to go back to Laurelton for a while, at least. I've got to see Cord's father and mother."

When Corey didn't reply, "If I get there before you, I'll call your father. Anyone else? Paula? Drew Warren?"

"No. I think not, Lyle," Corey replied. "I've been in touch with most of them."

"Then—"

"I'll see you before you take off."

"No. Please don't, Corey. I appreciate the thought, but never could stand good-byes." He looked up then and extended his hand. "I'll see how things work out in Washington before I try to go home. I don't know how long it will take up there. Take care of yourself, Corey. Don't overdo it with that lung and stay on your white-collar job."

"Sure, Lyle." He took the extended hand and gripped it tightly. "Good-bye," he said. "I'll see you back home."

"Sure," Lyle replied, but his voice was shakily uncertain. Blue veins stood out sharply along the sides of his forehead, his jaws clamped so tightly together that hard knots of muscle were visible there and in his neck.

It was, Corey reflected on his way out, a hell of a way to win a ticket home.

CHAPTER IV

1. *Laurelton, Ga., September, 1967*

When he came awake, the illuminated hands of the clock formed a V at five minutes to one. Anderson Warren remembered then that when the new nurse had come on at midnight, she had given him his pain medication. He had fallen back into a deep sleep immediately. Now it came to him that the dream had wakened him and he wondered how he could have relived so much of his life in so little time, a mere 55 minutes; and so penetratingly, lastingly clear. Usually, he would forget a dream immediately on waking, but this—

The room was in almost total darkness. From the doorway leading into the dressing room, where the nurse slept on Cleo's old chaise, came the faint yellow of her night lamp. He lay back wondering whether he could light one of the cigarettes Drew had left in the drawer of his night table without rousing the nurse and becoming embroiled in an argument; and with a to-hell-with-it attitude, he fumbled in the drawer, found the cigarettes and lighter, lighted one and relaxed, defying the nurse to come rushing in to force him to swallow one of the yellow capsules that brought on a sleep as hard as death itself.

He lay back on his pillow and stared at the red tip of the cigarette in the darkness and let the dream come back to him. Now it was no longer a dream, but had become reality, remembering his brothers Benjamin and Alistair; their wives, Laurie and Martha; his own wife, Cleo, who was sister to Martha; his father, Christian; his mother, Nancy-Ann, who had died when he was fifteen.

And Grandfather Clyde and Grandmother Laura-Ellen, who had been kin to Jonas Taylor—

2. *Loudon, North Carolina, September, 1903*

Saturday, September 19th, 1903, was the day in the life of Anderson Warren he had looked forward to ever since the death of his Grandmother Laura-Ellen; a day so deeply etched into his mind that he would never forget it as long as he lived. It was his long-awaited 25th birthday and Inheritance Day, when his father, Christian Warren, must turn over to him the $6,000 left him by his grandmother.

Seven years before, Anderson's eldest brother, Benjamin, had fought Christian physically, and brutally, then threatened to put the law on him before Christian reluctantly went with him into Loudon and withdrew $6,000 held in trust for Ben's 25th birthday. And on that same evening, Ben and his wife, Laurie, packed hurriedly and caught the night train north to Halifax County, Virginia, where Ben bought 250 acres of land and put as much of it as was fit for cultivation, 160 acres, into tobacco.

Three years later, only two months after Anderson married Cleo Trimble, Christian's middle son, Alistair, who was married to Cleo's older sister, Martha, had gone through the same agonizing experience with his father. Not until after Alistair had beaten Christian into insensibility did he receive his $6,000 inheritance on his 25th birthday. And, duplicating Ben's final action, he and Martha had taken the night train north to the township of Waldorf, in southern Maryland, where Martha's Uncle Rafe had located a 310-acre farm suitable for growing tobacco.

Now it was Anderson, youngest of Christian Warren's children, whose turn had come. He had broached the subject to his father a full month before and recognized the same churlish, ill-tempered mood he had seen in his father on two previous occasions. Christian snarled, "You can't wait 'til the auctions are over? You in so big a hurry to collect your portion an' run north like your brothers, leavin' your ol' daddy alone with twenty-two tenants an' croppers to steal the teeth outen his mouth?"

Anderson replied stonily, "Papa, all's I want to know is, do I get my $6,000 without havin' to fight you for it like Ben an' Alistair had to do."

"You got no more respect for your daddy than to talk like that to me?"

"Papa, I'm nigh on twenty-five years old. Don't talk to me like I was fourteen. You get all the respect you earn an' no more."

Anderson's relationship to his father was as crystal clear as were the physical contrasts between them. Years of hard drinking and no work had reduced Christian's work-hardened muscle to soft, slouching flabbiness. At 25, Anderson was rock-hard, lean and strong. Long days overseeing the Warren tobacco acreage, supervising the Warren tenants and sharecroppers, had turned his skin the color of the dark golden leaf they raised in their North Carolina soil. He was a tall man, generally conceded to be the handsomest of the three Warren boys, despite his angular face and high cheekbones. He had quick, dark, inquisitive eyes, a firm mouth which, together with a strong chin and slightly hawklike nose, gave an instant impression of intelligence, character and strength.

As the youngest, Anderson had had the advantage of a long training period under the close and expert tutelage of his Grandfather Clyde Warren, known throughout Clinton County as a "real tobacco man," as much a part of the brown earth as that which it produced, and the highest praise one planter could bestow upon another in a world of tobacco planters. It indicated a man of superior knowledge whose opinions and judgments were accepted unchallenged. His advice, rarely given unless asked for, was taken as though it were being handed down from on high.

Clyde Warren had traveled widely to other tobacco country in an endless search to sample, compare and experiment with alien seed, improve methods of fertilization, irrigation and curing, forever determined to find a disease-resistant, high-quality seed. On his veranda over minted bourbon, many Sunday afternoons were spent in seminars with neighbors and distant visitors, imparting that which he had learned in Maryland, Virginia, Ohio, Kentucky, Tennessee and Georgia, striving to produce greater yield per acre without forsaking quality.

Clyde's son, Christian, had neither his father's wit, wisdom, foresight, nor dedication to the land. The Warrens were considered wealthy by most local standards. Laura-Ellen, Clyde's wife, a Taylor from Laurelton, Georgia, had brought with her a handsome cash dowry provided by her father, Johnathon Taylor, which Clyde had used to increase his already substantial acreage and bring in more Negro tenants to work on shares. Despite occasional bad years of heavy summer rains and unseasonal winter frost and blight, which often threw many of his neighbors deeply in debt, even into bankruptcy, the Warrens had always been sufficiently secure financially to weather such temporary disaster and loan their tenants the necessary cash to ride out these bad periods.

In time, Clyde Warren came to understand that his son, Christian, would never become a "real tobacco man." Christian's taste for town life was too strong, his love for gambling, socializing, and rutting among Loudon's few fallen women too absorbing. And so Clyde accepted his inevitable defeat philosophically and devoted his attention to Benjamin, who was then 14. As soon as Ben was able to take a supervisory position on the land, Christian gave up all pretense as a planter. Later, Alistair and Anderson happily followed Ben into the fields.

When Anderson was 15, their mother died. It was three days before Christian, who had been spending most of his time in Loudon, could be found and sobered up for his wife's funeral. Then Grandfather Clyde died later that same year.

Grandmother Laura-Ellen became a lost soul, her mind wandering, reliving her youth on Laurel, the Taylor plantation in Georgia. Anderson, her favorite, spent many evenings at her side, listening to the stories of her Taylor ancestors who had been among the first white settlers in Georgia. From the flyleaf of the Bible her father had given her on her wedding day, her grandsons learned of their English forebears; the first Jonas Taylor who had reached America in 1767, his son Johnathon (Laura-Ellen's father), her brother, Gregory. Recorded also were those she had never seen, but had known only through correspondence: Gregory's son, Jonas; Jonas' wife, Charlotte; their son, Ames. And her nephew, the present Jonas, she added with pride, was Laurelton's leading citizen, as his father, and hers, had been before him. In that Bible, copied from the one carried to America by the first Jonas, Laura-Ellen had taught them the verse Johnathon had inscribed:

> *Sow not your Seed in Anger,*
> *Nor with Hatred, nor with Fears;*
> *For Ye who Sow in Anger*
> *Shall for certain Reap in Tears.*

Somehow, without emphasizing the fact, Benjamin, Alistair and Anderson knew that Christian Warren had fallen victim to that prediction.

3

When Clyde Warren died, he left the plantation free and clear of mortgage or other debt and a highly respectable cash balance on deposit in the Clinton County Bank in Loudon. When Laura-Ellen died not too long after, the land was still debt-free, but the cash balance had been reduced to $36,000. Laura-Ellen, by tradition, willed the plantation to her son Christian, along with $18,000. The remaining

$18,000 she ordered held in trust, in equal amounts of $6,000 for each grandson, to be paid on his 25th birthday, which became known among them as Inheritance Day.

When Benjamin reached his Inheritance Day, the cash was gone and Christian was forced to take a mortgage on the land in order to satisfy Ben's inheritance. Similarly, Alistair's inheritance threw the plantation further into debt. And now, Anderson's Inheritance Day was rapidly approaching.

On the thirteenth day of September in 1903, which fell on a Sunday, most of the tobacco buyers had begun to arrive in Loudon to choose the best rooms at the Clinton House, the Loudon Hotel and at most of the more respectable boarding houses. With them had come the usual campfollowers, gamblers, fancy women and pimps, seeking to pick up what money they could during Auction Days, when cash was more abundant than at any other time of the year. The whiskey had begun flowing early, the laughter was loud, the news of leaf prices in Greensboro and Durham reported and repeated over and over again for new ears. The buyers brought the latest word of high-yield crops and crop failures from other areas. There was considerable guessing at increased manufacturing tonnages in cut plug and twist for chewing, fine cut for pipe, leaf for cigars, snuff, and the more recent dude fad, cigarettes. Excitement ran high among young and old, as usual, during these carnival-like days.

Early on Monday morning, the 14th, Christian had his blue roan saddled up and rode into Loudon wearing his best black broadcloth suit, town boots, ruffled shirt, white cravat and gray topper; the gentleman planter who no longer planted. His face was gaunt and lined, but his gray eyes sparkled with expectancy.

The clatter of the roan's hooves wakened Cleo, who had spent a restless night, uncomfortable in the third month of her second pregnancy. She rose and went to her three-year-old son, Chase, who lay asleep in the next room, drew the light coverlet over him, then padded back to her own room and sat on the edge of the bed. Anderson woke up at once. "You all right, Cleo, honey?"

"Just restless. I didn't sleep well last night."

"Uh— Wish I could do somethin' for you."

Cleo laughed wearily. "You could share with me."

Not fully awake, frowning, "Share? How?"

"Well, I'd be glad to carry him all day long if you'd just carry him at night."

101

Anderson moved across the bed to where she sat, put one arm around her waist, the other hand on her abdomen, and pressed his cheek into her side gently. "I only wish I could, Cleo. You worried?"

"Not about the baby. Your daddy just rode off into town." Her meaning was entirely clear to Anderson.

"Uh."

"You think you ought to go into town?"

"It'd only mean a ruckus in advance, honey. I won't be twenty-five 'til Saturday and he ain't about to turn over one thin dime to me before then."

"If there's anything left by Saturday. Auctions will be over by Friday. He'll have the crop money by no later than Thursday night or Friday morning."

"Well—"

"You know well enough what will happen, Anderson. Like last year, the year before that, and before that. Like what happened with Benjamin and Alistair."

"Uh— I know."

"He collected the money and paid off the tenants, but only because they dogged his footsteps every minute of every day. Then the drinking and gambling—"

Sadly, "I know. I know, Cleo."

A brief silence, then, "You going into town?"

"I hate to leave you for four-five days."

"Don't take on so about me, Anderson. I'm only in my third month—"

"But you ain't been feelin' right this time."

"—and there's Becky and Rose to look out for me, you know that."

"I still worry about you."

"That's plain silly. There's nothing to worry about. Except *him*." The emphasis was unmistakable. Cleo sighed deeply. "If anything happens to your inheritance money, we'll never be able to leave here—"

Anderson moved away, sat up, then got out of bed. "I'll ride in tomorrow morning, right after breakfast, before the sales start. You sure you'll be all right?"

"Of course. I didn't have a bit of trouble while I carried Chase, did I?"

"No, but you slept better and weren't throwin' up as much as you been this time." He squinted his eyes, studying her. "You think it could be old age creepin' up on you?"

Cleo swung a small fist toward him. "If I were a man, I'd—"

Anderson laughed loudly. "If you was a man, you wouldn't be in my bed or in your delicate condition." He

102

reached over, caught her fist with one hand, kissed it, then leaned down closer and kissed her mouth tenderly. "Pretty Mama," he whispered.

She returned his kiss and pushed him away playfully. "I'm not your mama."

"No, but I made you one. Twice now." He sat down beside her, kissed her again, arms enveloping her.

"Anderson," Cleo said, "whatever you're up to, this isn't any time to—"

"But it's the place—"

"Now you stop this tomfoolery and get dressed."

Reluctantly, "Yes, ma'am." He stood up and made a courtly bow. "Your servant, ma'am."

Cleo giggled. "Now aren't you a sight in that silly old nightshirt, acting as though you were at a cotillion."

In Loudon on Tuesday, the midday meal was over and the buyers, auctioneers, warehousemen, planters and curious townspeople streamed toward the warehouses where the first sales were about to begin. The Indian-summery day was overly warm, the air pungent with the spicy aroma of cured tobacco. In the carnival atmosphere, children ran among the adults, hooting, screaming happily, calling out to each other. Mule-drawn farm wagons and all manner of carriages and light buggies lined both sides of Medairy and Lanier, Loudon's principal thoroughfares, and choked the narrow side streets. Small bands of boys stood by, minding horses for an expected reward of a nickel, a dime if tobacco prices were running higher than the year before. There was gambling even among the boys; matching pennies, pitching pennies closest to a wall, dice games; for money, marbles, pocket knives or any other swap goods of equal or near-equal value.

Along curbs and fences, on the edge of wooden store platforms and sidewalks, Negro field hands sat and waited, whiling away the time, whittling branches with sharply honed pocket knives, talking quietly together, wondering how much actual cash they would receive after the planters were paid and had computed the "figgerin'," earnings against money and goods which had been advanced and borrowed during the growing season.

Anderson tied his mare to the hitching post in front of Dockweiler's Hardware Store. He gave Timmy Brownell a nickel to look after his mare and said, "You look after her good, Timmy, an' I'll maybe find another nickel somewhere for you, eh?"

103

"Sure, Mr. Warren. I'll rub 'er down, too. How's Miz Warren?"

"Fine. Just fine, Timmy. Your ma?"

"She's fine, too. Complainin', but fine."

Anderson caught up with the crowd as it moved into the first warehouse where the golden crop lay in separate piles of wrapper leaf; cutters, fillers, and smokers, waiting for the auctioneer's sing-song introduction to each lot. Over the heads of the milling crowd, he saw his father-in-law, Paul Trimble, tall, thin, with a permanently creased brow, who was assistant head cashier at Loudon's only bank. Trimble raised one hand aloft to attract Anderson's attention, then moved toward him, pushing through the crowd of town-dressed and overalled bodies, apologizing softly, smiling at those who greeted him as he made his way toward his son-in-law. Anderson was genuinely happy to see Cleo's father, the man who had given two daughters to Warren boys. As they met and shook hands warmly, Anderson said, "Hello, Dad. Don't go throwing your hand up like that. You liable to bid yourself a lot of leaf thataway."

"Hello, Anderson. Good to see you, son. How's—"

"She's fine, Dad. Very fine. Sends you and Mrs. Trimble her love. We figured to drive in with Chase last Sunday for supper—"

"We were expecting you. I thought maybe Cleo—"

"No, nothin' like that. Chase's fault. He was runnin' around barefooted in Cleo's berry patch Friday an' durned if he didn't run a rusty brad into his foot. Swole up so bad, I had to cut into it right deep. He'll be all right by next Sunday. Listen, you hear anything from Martha an' Alistair? We'n heard a word in over three months."

"We had a letter just last Friday. They're all right. Kind of busy, though. Betsey had her fifth birthday and—"

"I know. Cleo made two dresses an' sent 'em to her about three weeks ago."

"You and Cleo can read the letter when you come in on Sunday. You going home tonight?"

"Uh—no. I figger I might stay in 'til the auctions are over."

Trimble nodded knowingly. "I saw him at the Clinton House just before noontime, having dinner with some—uh —friends."

"Uh—" Anderson looked up and waved to Jare Hanley and responded to a greeting from Abner Hill. He kept his head turned away from Trimble as he asked, "He been drinkin'?"

Hesitantly, "I'd guess so." Anderson's brow furrowed up

104

with concern. "Maybe I better go look him up." He made a move to leave.

"Will you be staying with us, Anderson? We've got plenty of room, you know, and Lucy will enjoy seeing you."

"Uh—maybe, Dad. I'll see how things work out."

The crowd had moved down the line, the auctioneer singing out offered bids in his peculiar, ritualistic chant, interpreting winks, nods, smirks, raised fingers and other mystic signs as a rise over the last accepted bid, closing out one lot after another, dropping a ticket with the final price on each lot. The action became spirited with varying independent judgments and comments from planters and the curious. Those whose graded crops lay in piles in other warehouses, and not yet reached, looked on with increasing interest, gauging prices, sampling the mood of the various buyers, the quality of competing lots.

In the main, the crowd was good-humored and jocular as the newest high offered, 7.03 cents per pound, topped last year's high of 6.56 cents. The 1903 crop had been a good one, unharmed by too much rain, frost or blight; and the best of the crop hadn't been reached yet.

The air was pungent with the odors of earth, tobacco, sweating bodies, horses and manure, the floor stained liberally with splotches of recently expelled tobacco juice. There was a fragrance of cigar smoke that floated lazily in layers among and above them as the audience grunted with general approval, gesticulated and slapped backs and dug elbows into each other enthusiastically as prices began to climb, however little.

One quick turn around told Anderson that none of the Warren crop was in this warehouse, otherwise, he assumed, Christian would be here with it; not out of idle curiosity, but to tally the prices it was bringing. He left the warehouse and walked over to the Clinton House at Medairy and Lanier, the business, if not geographical, center of town.

Remembering Benjamin's and Alistair's bitter experiences with, and total alienation from, Christian, Anderson privately expected no less from his profligate father. Long before, he and Cleo had come to their firm decision to leave Loudon, Christian, the plantation, and Cleo's family behind as soon as his Inheritance Day arrived.

"Where to, Anderson?" Cleo had asked with excitement at the prospect of leaving North Carolina for the very first time in her life. "Virginia, Maryland, Kentucky—?"

Anderson shook his head negatively. "I don't think so, Cleo. I been thinkin' on it real hard. I remember Grandpa Clyde tellin' us about Georgia."

105

"Georgia? Is that tobacco country?"

"Some. Could be a lot better, 'cordin' to Grandpa. Plenty of good sandy clay soil and the weather is more kindly to crops than here or up north. You got a milder, longer growin' season, less chance of freeze or sleet. What tobacco they grow down there ain't much for quality or yield, he kept tellin' us. Trouble is, they farm it like most other crops. Tobacco is a special crop, I don't have to tell you. He always said that if a planter, a real tobacco man, took it on hisself to go there and put in a crop with good seed and knowed what he was about, he could make a fine crop. Well, we got plenty of seed of our own and the stuff Ben an' Alistair been sendin' me to try. I God, Cleo, I think we could do durned well."

This could have been Clyde Warren talking to his neighbors on the Warren veranda, looking ahead into the future in the only world he was aware of—tobacco—visualizing a crop even before the seedlings were ready for transplanting in the prepared earth, infecting his audience with his quiet, positive enthusiasm.

"We could, Anderson," Cleo said encouragingly. "We could. You're the best tobacco man in these parts. We could get a small piece of land at first, then—"

So, it had been decided, talked about in whispers that no other ears could hear. *If*—

If he could get his inheritance money when it fell due and forever after be rid of Christian, they would leave at once, before Cleo became too heavy and burdened to make the long trip. Find a good piece of land and get a crop into the earth by springtime, when their new son—neither spoke of it as other than a son—would be born.

4

Christian was not at the Clinton House nor at any of the other public houses in town. Probably off in a shack with a woman somewhere, Anderson thought with anger. He returned to the warehouse area where the buying had concluded for the day. Top price at the closing hour had reached 7.84 cents and the news was reflected in the cheerful faces and good humor of the people. He had his supper with a group of neighbors at the Clinton House, but saw no sign of his father anywhere.

At three o'clock the next afternoon, Christian Warren came into Bailey's Warehouse No. 3, where the auction was in full progress. His eyes were red-rimmed and watery, his

breath laden with alcohol fumes. His clothes were disar-
rayed and rumpled, collar dirty and wilted, cravat askew.
And he was visibly annoyed at the sight of Anderson, who
stepped up behind him and said, "Good afternoon, Papa."

Christian turned around unsteadily and stared into his
son's reproachful look. "Wha—what're you doin' in town
'stead of tendin' to business at home?" he asked angrily.

"Looks like if I wasn't here, they'd be nobody to tend to
our business."

"An' what about the place, who's lookin' after things
there, the crop, the—"

"You talkin' foolish, Papa. There're people to tend the
stock and do what needs be done. The crop's right here in
these warehouses waitin' to be bought—"

"An' you're here with it to keep your eye on me, hey,
boy?"

"Papa, don't let's wrangle. Our people got to be paid—"

"An' who says they won't be?" Christian asked with
heated belligerence.

"—an' my Inheritance Day comes on Saturday," Anderson reminded him with added emphasis.

"So it does an' well I know it." The old man grinned evilly, showing two rows of yellowing teeth, jabbing his right
index finger into Anderson's chest to accent his next words.
"You expectin' to tail me aroun' like a houn' dog 'til Saturday, boy?"

"If I have to, I reckon so. I best remind you one thing—"

"I don't need no remindin' from you or anybody else.
An' you just better be mindin' your manners to your father,
else I'll—"

"You'll what, Papa?" There was no immediate reply to
the challenge as Christian stared vacantly into Anderson's
face. "All's I'm reminding you of," Anderson continued
coldly, "is Ben an' Alistair. You ain't no younger'n you
were then, Papa, and I'm considerable older an' heftier. I
don't want to go through what they did to get the money
Grandma Laura-Ellen left them."

Christian snorted with contempt. "You threatenin' me,
boy?"

"Yes, sir, I'm doin' just that," Anderson stated firmly.

"All right, that tells us both where we stand. But you just
keep it in mind, you ain't twenty-five 'til Saturday. Keep out
of my way 'til then, you hear?"

Christian stalked away to join the circle around the auctioneer. Anderson watched his back and the tilted gray top
hat thoughtfully. How different it would be if this were
Grandpa Clyde, he mused to himself. A knot of men would

107

have formed around him quickly, acknowledging his presence, hanging on to his every word, watching his facial expressions as the new bids came across, even predicting the final high price on the last day of the sales. Hell, even the auctioneers and buyers would have paused to greet him. But Christian stood alone, unnoticed.

It wasn't going to be easy, Anderson knew.

The auctions came to an end at dusk on Thursday. At least a third of the buyers had caught the 6:40 northbound train, but others were staying the night. The average price had topped that of 1902 prices, reaching a very satisfactory high of 9.07 cents per pound, and numerous exuberant, and some quiet, celebrations were in progress. And during this night of general revelry in both the white section and the Negro quarter, there was still no trace of the wily, evasive Christian Warren, sought for by Anderson with mounting apprehension.

The next day, the town of Loudon began clearing out and cleaning up behind the four days of selling and buying. The last of the buyers had split up, some catching the morning 9:02 north, the rest on the southbound 4:50 to pick up what tobacco there might be in Georgia. During the last two nights, Anderson had used part of his time to talk with certain buyers about Georgia land and tobacco. Most of what he learned merely confirmed his Grandfather Clyde's earlier opinions; that Georgia tobacco was generally of inferior quality, planted, harvested and carelessly cured by men with little understanding of the techniques practiced where tobacco was the principal money crop instead of cotton. But the possibilities were there, this in the opinion expressed firmly by Henry Shaffer, dean of the buyers and an old friend of Clyde Warren.

"A real tobacco man like your granddaddy could make as fine a money crop as any here," Mr. Shaffer told Anderson, "long's he's sure of his land, puts in good seed and a season of hard work. What's more, there's a need for it—"

These words, pronounced by "a real tobacco man" like Henry Shaffer, were enough for Anderson. All he needed now was to find his father before he could gamble, drink and roister the crop money away.

Early on Saturday morning, Loudon filled up again. From farms and plantations, white and Negro families, momentarily flush with tobacco money, flooded every road into town. On this one Saturday of the year's fifty-two, the Clinton County Bank and every store remained open until every depositor, borrower and purchaser could be accommodated;

108

paying off notes, cashing planters' drafts, laying in supplies for the oncoming fall and winter. Streets and the few sidewalks were jammed with people moving from store to store, piling purchased goods into wagons and carriages. Stocks of merchandise, brought in for this one huge seasonal buying splurge, were being depleted rapidly as the hours flew by.

Anderson had risen earlier than usual, eaten his breakfast and begun his final and desperate search for Christian. As suppertime approached, he had sought out every possibility without success, even scouring the Negro quarter, asking people if they had seen him. He knew two things: the Warren crop had, as usual, brought in the top price; also, that none of the Warren Negroes had yet been paid their shares, depending on Anderson to bring their money home to them as he had promised he would. According to his calculations, based on the auctioneers' tickets dropped on each pile of Warren tobacco, and with the knowledge of the amount due each tenant, there should be well over $9,000 remaining after the local merchants, the bank and the Warren tenants and croppers had been paid. And $6,000 of that belonged to him.

Back at the Clinton House, where an overflow crowd was pressing to get into the dining room for supper, Anderson saw Paul Trimble pushing his way through the crowd, facial muscles tightened with strain. When he reached Anderson, Trimble said, "You saw him, didn't you?"

"No, sir. No sign of him," Anderson replied. "Why?"

"Oh, my God!"

"What's wrong? You seen him?"

"Yes. He came into the bank about an hour ago. I—Anderson, I'm afraid he—he—"

Anderson took the lapels of Trimble's coat into his fists. "Listen. Tell me. Tell me!"

"I— Well, as I said, he came in about an hour ago. I was busy with a line of people in front of my cage. I saw him at the end of the line, then got busy cashing a large draft. Next time I saw him, maybe fifteen-twenty minutes later, he'd left the line and was sitting at the president's desk. Mr. Freeman was counting out some money for him. I saw him put it in his coat pocket and leave. I couldn't call out 'Stop thief!' or leave my cage. A few minutes ago, when I was relieved for supper, I checked the Warren ledger sheet. There was no balance left."

"No balance? No balance? There ought to've been about $3,000 on deposit even before the auction started."

Trimble shook his head from side to side. "He paid off his outstanding bank loan, drew out every last cent and

109

closed the account, Anderson. *Closed out the account.* I swear to God, it's the truth."

Anderson let go of Trimble's coat lapels, his hands trembling with fury. "Where are you going, Anderson?" Trimble asked as his son-in-law turned and pushed his way out of the lobby.

"I'm goin'a find him if I have to turn Loudon upside down an' inside out. An' when I find him, I'm goin'a kill him."

Trimble's normally white face grew ashen with fear. "Anderson—" he called out, but Anderson strode on, deaf to any plea or effort to stop him. He turned down Lanier, walking in the street where there was a little more room, squeezing between loaded wagons, carriages and saddle horses. The Town Hall clock showed 6:37 and, as though a sudden, entirely new thought struck him, he began to run, leaving Paul Trimble far behind him. *Closed out the account. Closed out the account.* That could mean only one thing.

At the corner of Lanier and Railroad Avenue, the traffic had thinned out and he stepped up his pace. In the distance, he saw with horror that the northbound 6:40 Carolina-Georgia was beginning to pull out of the station, heard its mournful warning whistle. By the time he reached the platform, panting and sweating profusely, the caboose disappeared from sight around the bend. Stationmaster Albert Jessup looked up from behind the bars where he had begun checking cash against the daily ticket stubs spindled on the tall spike in front of him.

"Hidy, Anderson. You wasn't tryin' to catch the 6:40, was you?"

"No, Mr. Jessup. I just wanted to know if—"

Before he could complete the question, Jessup answered it for him. "You just missed your daddy by no more'n two minutes. He forgot somethin'?"

Anderson leaned against the counter, breathing heavily. Slowly, dully, he replied, "Yes. I guess you could put it that way, Mr. Jessup. He forgot somethin'." A pause, then, "Where'd he buy his ticket to, you remember?"

"Sure. Nothin' wrong, is there, Anderson?"

"Where?"

"Richmond. You c'd telegraph ahead to him, any one of a dozen stops before he gets there. You write it out, I can get it to him before he reaches Greensboro."

"No." Anderson turned away, wearied with defeat, the blood drained out of his face. "No, thank you kindly," he said slowly, "it can wait." He went outside and stood wait-

110

ing there until Paul Trimble came puffing up on the platform, breathless, not needing Anderson to tell him what had happened, reading it in his dispirited eyes and grim mouth. Albert Jessup came out on the platform, eyeing the two men. "Just happened to remember something, Anderson," he said.

"What?"

"It's only a suspicion, now that I come to think of it." Cautiously, "You won't get riled, will you?"

"No. Please tell me."

"Well, he and this woman, they got here together only two-three minutes before the 6:40 pulled out. They were together outside, but they come in separate-like. Your daddy, he bought him that ticket to Richmond, and then this woman, she steps up an' buys her a ticket to Richmond, too. Onliest two tickets I sold to Richmond all day, an' both right spang on top of each other—"

"You know who she was?"

"I only seen her once before. Come in with most of the buyers last Sunday. Pretty-like. Fancy clothes. Like the rest of 'em come in for Auction Days. Now I ain't sayin' for certain sure they was travelin' together, but—"

A floater, Anderson thought dully. A painted whore who followed the buyers and gamblers from town to town, taking advantage of tobacco money that flowed freely during the short auction period. Anderson heard Paul Trimble ask, "Did he have any baggage with him, Albert?"

"No, Mr. Trimble. I never saw none. She did—"

Anderson said heavily, "With all that cash on him, I'd guess he didn't much need any extra clothes."

That night, Anderson sat stolidly in the Trimble home discussing with deep and futile embarrassment this new calamity that Christian Warren had visited upon him. And Cleo. Paul Trimble sighed and said, "Of course, we were never too happy over your plan to move to Georgia, what with Martha up there in Maryland with Alistair, but if that's what you and Cleo want, maybe the bank can help you."

"How?" Anderson asked.

"Put the place up for auction. It's prime land, a good house, fine outbuildings, the best curing barns, tenants already on the land in good houses. Under the circumstances, the County Judge'll see things your way, give you ownership in lieu of your inheritance claim. With the other debts and the tenants paid off, you may not get out with the full $6,000, but it ought to come mighty close to it."

"Can you handle it for us, Dad?" Anderson asked.

111

"I'll do my best. On Monday, I'll get our lawyer, Will Herbert, on it. He'll go see Judge Crocker and try to keep the whole thing quiet. Then we'll get Norton Ellerbe in our real estate department to pass the word around and look for a buyer. It's good land—"

"The best!"

"Shouldn't be too much trouble. Take a little time—"

"Not too much, I hope. I'd best ride home tonight. I got to tell Cleo—"

"Bring her and Chase tomorrow for supper and stay over Monday. We'll start moving on it by then."

Shortly after Thanksgiving, Anderson received word from Paul Trimble to come into Loudon. There, after two days of talk and considerable haggling, he signed over the Warren land to Angus Hughes and received his money. He returned home, paid off the tenants first, told them of his plans to leave and asked them to stay on with the new owner. He then returned to town and paid off the rest of his debts to the local merchants.

The balance of the cash, $5,372, he carried home with him in a paper bag. The sale of furniture, tools, livestock, excess clothing and other personal possessions brought another $1,300. And after a few days with the Trimbles, he, Cleo and Chase began their trip south, heading first for Laurelton, his grandmother's ancestral home. Anderson had taken the largest wagon, drawn by his two best mules, his and Cleo's riding horses tied on behind.

Inside the canvas-covered wagon, they placed the bed the three would sleep in. Around the bed, Anderson had piled trunks and boxes filled with clothing, tools and certain household pieces of sentimental value. Around his waist and beneath his work shirt, secure in a canvas belt, Anderson carried his money. Under his pillow was his Grandmother Laura-Ellen's Bible, and in a strongly made box were four sacks of prized tobacco seed.

5

Anderson Warren's first glimpse of Laurelton, for all his Grandmother Laura-Ellen's nostalgic memories, was a soggy, inauspicious and harrowing experience he—nor Cleo —would ever forget. As recorded in his journal of the long trip from Loudon, it was Sunday, January 24th, 1904, their 66th day on the road. There had been time-comsuming layovers in Greensboro, Charlotte, Augusta and, since the Wednesday before, Riverton, one full day short of their destination. The longer stops had been necessary because Cleo had been frequently unwell.

They had left Riverton very early that morning, the skies overhead sullen with heavy, dark clouds, growing more threatening with each slow mile they traveled. The dirt road was narrow and deeply rutted, made no less difficult by the rain which began to fall steadily shortly past the noon hour. Inside the wagon, Cleo lay on the bed retching, gritting her teeth to keep from groaning aloud as recurring pains sent her into paroxysms of agony, although she was only in her seventh month.

By the time they reached the outer limits of Laurelton, the rain was falling in solid sheets. The main thoroughfare ran soupily with red mud and its buildings sagged dejectedly. A strong wind drove the rain in slashing gusts at the dispirited mules, through the front opening into the wagon itself, settling its dampness and wet spray over the bed and clothing that hung inside, on Cleo and Chase, who lay huddled together beneath the covers.

Anderson, seated on the high seat, exposed to the cold rain, calculated the time as between five and six, but it was dark enough to be midnight. The trees along the main street were soaked with rain, branches hanging low as he pulled his weary, rain-hammered team to a halt in front of Willard's Hardware Store. Anderson looped and tied the reins through a ring bolt, turned to untie the canvas flap and peered into the pitch-blackness of the wagon's interior. "You all right, Cleo, honey?" he called out.

He had to strain to hear her low, tremulous reply. "I—I —guess so, Anderson. Wh—where are we?"

"Laurelton, thank God. Chase?"

"Yes, sir."

"You stay here with your mama while I find a place to put us up."

"Yes, sir." Anderson detected the heavy uncertainty in his son's voice.

"You ain't afraid, are you?"

"No, sir."

"Anderson?" It was Cleo, weak and apprehensive.

"What, honey?"

"Hurry, *please!*"

"Cleo, you think—"

"Never mind. Just hurry. *Please!*"

"Uh—right away. I'll be back soon."

Rain gushed down the corrugated iron roof that extended outward from the hardware store and over the wooden walk in front of the building but, open on three sides, it offered only a little more protection than being out in the open. The water gushed like a waterfall as he leaped down from the wagon seat, glistening on his black slicker, filling the dented crown of his wide-brimmed planter's hat. As he landed in a deep puddle, water splashed in every direction, and as he straightened up and stepped under the overhang, he became aware for the first time that he was not alone. From the long bench that ran along the back wall came a soft, "Shuh!"

He stared into the darkness and made out three shapeless forms, almost indistinguishable from the heavy shadows that enveloped them except for the whites of their eyes, their bodies huddling together against the chill.

"Hey! Somebody there?" he called out.

A hesitant voice replied. "Us heah, Mister."

Negroes. "Any place close by where I can bed my family down an' stable my mules and horses?"

Silence, then, "Miz Claypool's. Maybe."

"Where's her place?"

"Down the street a piece. This side. You know it by the sign outside."

"I need a doctor, too. There one nearby?"

"Don' know nothin' 'bout white doctors, Mister. Miz Claypool, she tellen you."

He turned back to the wagon, then heard a soft, muffled pealing through the heavy downpour. He turned back to the Negroes and asked, "That a church?"

"Yassir."

"A white church?"

"Yassir. On'iest black church 'cross th' bridge in Angeltown."

Even at this critical moment, the obvious connotation of "church" and "Angeltown" almost caused him to chuckle through his desperation. "I God," he said, "that's sure the fittenest place for it to be."

He stepped on the wheel hub, up on its rim, and sat on the soaked blanket that served as his seat pad. He freed the reins and flapped them over the backs of the unwilling mules. "Gee, *haw!* Git on, you Abe, you Mose! *Git on!*"

The heavily laden wagon creaked and groaned as the mules strained against the harness and moved slowly down the rutted street through rivers of mud. "Move, goddam you, move!"

Through squinted eyes, Anderson peered through the unbroken curtain of rain, searching for a light in a window. About two hundred yards along the street, where the private residences began, he saw the outlines of the church, its

114

pointed steeple resembling the figure of a ghostly, hooded Klansman. He was tempted to stop and seek aid, but just beyond the church he saw the sign that identified *Mrs. Claypool's Boarding House: Home-Cooked Meals*. He paused only to poke his head inside the cave of the wagon. "You all right, Cleo?" he asked for perhaps the fiftieth time since early that morning.

"I'm—not—sure," she replied weakly.

"We're here, Cleo honey. A place to stay. You hold on an' I'll only be a few minutes."

He leaped down and ran to the door and pounded on it. Moments passed before he pounded again, more vigorously. And then the door opened and he saw a tall, broad-bosomed woman who held an oil lamp in her left hand. "My gracious, Mister, you don't have to break down my door, do you?"

"You Miz Claypool?"

"I am." She held the lamp higher. "Who're you?"

"Ma'am, I need a place for my wife and boy. And a doctor, quick. I think she's birthin' ahead of her time."

"Well, land's sake, man, what're you standin' there gabbin' for? Let's get her inside." She turned her heavy figure toward the interior of the house and called out, "You Annabelle! You Maudie! Get Aaron and Bubber here right away, you hear me! And bring some blankets!"

Late that night, Dr. Cornelius Ballard delivered a small, prematurely born son to Cleo Warren. He spanked and breathed life into the infant, then gave him over to Annabelle, the huge Negro woman who had assisted him, then went downstairs to inform Anderson Warren that it was, for the moment, over. He found the exhausted man in the kitchen, sleeping at the table, head resting on his folded arms. On a small cot that had been brought into the large kitchen, Annabelle's comely daughter, Maudie, had put Chase to bed and was covering him with a blanket. Mrs. Claypool sat across from the sleeping Anderson, sipping tea. When she looked up at the doctor, he merely shook his head from side to side without speaking, an expression of doubt, motioning a thumb toward Warren.

"Poor man," Mrs. Claypool said with tears of sympathy gathering in her eyes. "The baby?"

Ballard went to Warren and shook him awake. Anderson looked up, startled, eyes filmed with sleep. "Doc—Doctor, how is she?" he asked.

"For the moment," Ballard said, "your son is still alive. He is undersized and underweight. You understand that a

115

prematurely born infant—" He shrugged, then added, "I have done everything I can. I don't want to minimize his chances, but I must ask you to be prepared for bad news."

"You don't mean Cl—Cleo?" Anderson stood up to face Ballard. "Doc, you save Cleo, you hear me! Let the boy go if you have to, but you got to save Cleo!"

"Your wife's condition is satisfactory. More than satisfactory. Good stock there, Mr. Warren. But she will need rest, care, and building up. The long ride at this stage of her pregnancy, you understand—"

"Yes, sir. We come a long way, slowsome, from Loudon. That's in North Carolina, maybe 350 or 400 miles north and east of here."

"So I understand. Where are you heading?"

"For the time being, here. Laurelton. I got some kin here."

"In Laurelton?"

"Yes, sir. Name of Taylor. You know any Taylors hereabouts, Doctor?"

The doctor could hardly repress a faint smile as Mrs. Claypool's interest picked up. "I think so," Ballard replied. "That is, if they are the same Taylors I have in mind."

"Well, the last livin' one I heard talked of by my grandmother was named Gregory, her brother. Their father was Johnathon. In her Bible, it says Gregory had him a son, name of Jonas."

"Ah, yes. It would be the same family, but Gregory Taylor passed on back in 1890, if I remember the year correctly. His son, Jonas, is now head of the family. They live beyond Laurelton, about eight miles north of here on his place, Laurel."

"Yes, sir. I heard tell of Laurel. My grandmother, Laura-Ellen, was born there."

"We can send word to him come morning, if you'd like."

"No need for that, Doctor. He wouldn't know me by name. I'll go by an' make myself acquainted with him soon's I feel I can leave Cleo and the baby."

"Well then—" Ballard's face was clouded with doubt. "About the baby, Mr. Warren, I'm sorry I can't be more optimistic, but with the Lord's help— The child is in His hands and I am only His servant."

"I'n arguin' with the Lord's will, Doctor. If it's a choice between Cleo and the baby—"

"I don't think it is a matter of choice, but if it is, it will be dictated by the Lord, Mr. Warren. I say again, with proper care, your wife will be fine."

Mrs. Claypool had poured a cup of tea for the doctor,

116

who sat down and began to sip from the steaming cup. To distract Warren from the subject of wife and child, he said, "I could drop some word off to Jonas Taylor on my way home. It wouldn't be too far out of my way."

Anderson took another cup of tea from Mrs. Claypool. "To hear my Grandmother Laura-Ellen tell it, this Jonas, he got himself a right sizable farm out there on Laurel." It was as much a question as it was a statement. Ballard said with a grin, "Well, if you can call a twenty-five-thousand-acre plantation a 'right sizable farm,' Mr. Warren, I'd say yes."

Anderson's mouth dropped open. "Twenty-five *thousand* acres?"

"About that, I'd guess. A good bit more, if you add the Betterton place to it which he took over."

Anderson whistled silently through pursed lips. Ballard said, "You don't really know much about the Taylor branch of your family, do you, Mr. Warren? Well, your cousin Jonas is the wealthiest man in Laurelton and Cairn County. I'd guess he'll be one of the richest men in the state, if he isn't already."

Anderson looked down at his damp, wrinkled clothing speculatively. "I God," was all he could whisper. And again, "I God!"

Mrs. Claypool said, "In the morning I'll have Annabelle clean your clothes. A little sewing and pressing and you'll—"

Anderson bristled. "I thank you kindly, Miz Claypool," he said stiffly. "I didn't come to Laurelton lookin' for no charity. I got other clothes and in my waist belt I got over six thousand dollars in cash. I'n no poor kin to nobody—"

"I'm sorry if we seemed to imply that, Mr. Warren," Ballard said, "but—"

"Can I see Cleo now?"

"She's had a hard time of it, Mr. Warren. I'll look in on her and if she is sleeping, we'll let her sleep. She needs all the rest she can get. The infant is in Annabelle's very capable hands. I'll look in on him and then leave. I'd suggest you get bedded down with your other son. I'll drop by first thing in the morning."

6

Anderson slept in a chair beside Cleo's bed that night. When morning came, she awoke long enough to ask for the infant and Chase. Reassured that they were being cared for by Mrs. Claypool, Annabelle, and Maudie, Cleo said, "An-

117

derson, you look terrible. Please get some rest, shave, and put on some decent clothes. You look like you just came out of the fields."

"Sure, honey, sure. You feelin' better now?"

"I think so. At least, much better than you look."

"Doctor'll be here soon, Cleo. You go back to sleep."

"We've got to name the baby, Anderson."

"No hurry about it."

"I want to name him for your grandfather. Clyde."

"So be it. Clyde Warren. Now you go back to sleep."

He sat in the chair until Dr. Ballard arrived and sent him out of the room. The rain had stopped just before dawn and the sun was peeping through scattered, pink-tinted clouds, promising a fair day. When Ballard informed him that both Cleo and Clyde were progressing satisfactorily, Anderson took Chase to the stables behind the house and saw that his mules and horses had been properly cared for. With the help of Aaron and Bubber, he got a large trunk and a box of clothing into the house and into the room Mrs. Claypool had assigned to him, next to Cleo's. When he was finished, Cleo was still asleep, Maudie in full charge of the infant Clyde. He bathed in a wooden tub in the stable, dressed in his Sunday black broadcloth suit that Annabelle had pressed and taking Chase's hand into his own, walked to Mc-Ilhenney's Barber Shop to be shaved and have his over-growth of hair trimmed.

"You the new people come in last night?" Tom Mc-Ilhenney asked.

"Uh—" Anderson admitted briefly.

"How's the new citizen?"

"Uh—"

"Hear you come a long way."

"Uh—"

"Well, you couldn't come to a more thrivin' town, Mister. Hope you an' the Missus stay an' prosper with us."

"Uh—"

Both chairs were occupied and there were several men waiting on the bench, some customers, some idlers who dropped in merely to sit, listen and exchange gossip. Anderson heard many names mentioned, among them Jonas Taylor's, and was impressed with the respect shown for his kin. He heard the name of Jonas' son, Ames, mentioned once. One disgruntled man, having been turned down for a loan by the manager of the bank, was only killing time until he could catch up with Jonas in person, hoping for a reprieve, this the most likely place to encounter him. The vote in the barbershop was five-to-three in the petitioner's favor.

Anderson took his place in McIlhenney's chair as the talk turned back to the damage caused by the unusual ferocity of the storm and the rising of the Cottonwood River, which had caused considerable flooding. The shave nearly completed, a carriage had pulled up in front and everyone in the shop grew quiet. One man rose from the bench and held the door open as a large man strode in and called out, " 'Morning, gentlemen." Almost to a man, they replied, " 'Mornin', Mr. Taylor."

Jonas Taylor went to a clothes rack where he hung his hat and coat, then removed his stiff collar and tie, hanging them from a hook imbedded in the wall.

McIlhenney hurried through the powdering process, whipped the covering from Anderson Warren and levered the chair into an upright position. "You're next, Mr. Taylor," he said. As Anderson stood in front of the mirror to adjust his collar and tie, Taylor sat in the chair while McIlhenney reached for the special shaving mug on the shelf, elaborately decorated with gold leaf designs and the name JONAS TAYLOR inscribed on it in old English letters, its own brush sticking up out of it.

" 'Mornin', Mr. Taylor," Tom McIlhenney greeted for a second time. He poured some hot water into the mug and began making lather. "How's the Missus and the boy?"

"Fine, Tom," Taylor replied.

Warren, standing at the mirror, examined the newcomer. He was tall and broad-shouldered, with a strong, hawklike face that was not unattractive. Sort of like Ben, he thought. The hands that gripped the arms of the chair, he noted, were also strong. More than anything else, Jonas Taylor's face showed the supreme confidence, perhaps even arrogance, that bespoke a man who would be totally in charge of any situation in which he was involved. Anderson judged him to be in his 30s, not yet at the middle mark. His opinion was generally reflected in the faces and attitudes of the men who were gathered here, waiting for Laurelton's first citizen to speak; a king on his throne who must not be addressed by his subjects until spoken to.

"And you, Tom?" Taylor asked.

"Tolerable, Mr. Taylor. Tolerable." He adjusted the chair and cloth, then reached for the mug and brush. "Hear you're backin' Mort Fayles for judge—"

Jonas Taylor cut him off short. "Let's get on with it, Tom. I'm in a hurry this morning. Dr. Ballard sent me a message telling me I've got a cousin of some kind come into town last night, just barely in time for his wife to birth a child."

Customers and idlers picked up their ears. McIlhenney threw a quick side glance at Anderson Warren struggling to adjust his tie. and saw the newcomer's neck beginning to turn a deeper red.

"Shuh." Tom replied. "Heard about it first thing this mornin'. Stayin' at Miz Claypool's. Kin to you, you say?

"*I* didn't say," Taylor replied. "*He* says."

"Well " Tom said slowly, "you don't have to go as fur as Miz Claypool's to see him, less'n you want to."

"And why not?"

"Because he's standin' less'n six feet away from where you're sittin' this minute."

As Jonas Taylor sat up in his chair. McIlhenney swiveled it around toward Anderson Warren, who turned his head to stare into the lathered face. Taylor said, "You Anderson Warren?"

"That I am," Anderson replied.

"Where you from, Mr. Warren?"

"Loudon, Clinton County, North Carolina."

Jonas Taylor's head bobbed up and down. A moment passed. "Then you'd be my Aunt Laura-Ellen's boy."

"One of her three grandsons. Her son, Christian, is my father."

McIlhenney's assistant had stopped shaving his customer. Idlers and customers remained silent during the exchange. Then Jonas Taylor's face cracked into a smile. "Welcome to Laurelton, Cousin." He extended a huge hand which matched the one Warren put into it. Chase was standing at his father's side now, one small hand clutching the edge of his coat. "Your boy?" Taylor asked.

"Uh—" Anderson's head nodded. "Name's Chase."

"Howdy, Chase. How old are you?" Jonas Taylor asked.

Chase spoke up loudly showing no sign of shyness. "I'm just four-goin'-on-five."

Taylor laughed. "I've got a boy of my own, nine-goin'-on-ten." The others laughed with him. To Anderson, he said, "I hear congratulations are in order, Cousin."

Anderson grinned self-consciously. "Uh—thank you. A boy. Name of Clyde."

"And Mrs. Warren?"

"Dr. Ballard says she'll be fine."

"I'm happy to hear it. He told me she'd had a difficult time. Since we've already met, suppose I postpone my call until later today when I won't be pressed for time. Say, three o'clock?"

"I'll be waiting. Good day to you now."

Anderson pulled out his snap purse to pay McIlhenney,

120

but Jonas Taylor said, "Rule of the house, Cousin. First visit at McIlhenney's is always free."

"For an honest fact, Mr. Warren," Tom added with a sly grin.

Anderson's face reddened to the circle of grins in the room, knowing that this was not an honest fact. He replaced the purse in his pocket and said formally, "Thank you for your hospitality, Mr. McIlhenney. Good day, gentlemen." Chase's hand disappeared inside Anderson's as they went through the door which one of the idlers held open for them.

Jonas Taylor lay back in the chair and said, "Put it on my bill, Tom."

7

Jonas Taylor, Anderson Warren soon learned, was a most unusually perceptive and complicated man. His eyes were as penetrating as those of a hawk, his brain swift to react to what might seem to anyone else to be a most innocuous remark. As Anderson related his plans, Jonas flicked little probing questions at him that required long and detailed answers. Within a short time, Jonas, whose interests were in banking, cotton, land holdings, a sawmill, freight line, construction and building materials, was able to understand and speak with surprising intelligence on the subject of tobacco.

Later, the people Jonas relied upon for information in other cities sent him pertinent data he needed until he understood tobacco not only in the planting phase but in the buying, freighting, manufacturing, financing and selling ends. At the conclusion of certain investigations he had made, Taylor confirmed a belief which Anderson had not yet voiced, that some small effort was being made to raise tobacco in certain parts of Georgia, but not in sufficient quantities, or in quality, to make a measurable market. "So I've heard," Anderson agreed.

"Then why Georgia, instead of North Carolina, where tobacco production is the highest?" Jonas asked.

"Well—" Anderson confessed in detail the problems created for himself and his brothers by Christian's excesses, that had eventually resulted in the loss of what was left of the Warren land. "So I figgered that long's I had to make a fresh start, I'd make it in a fresh place, maybe where the weather is warmer and kinder to tobacco. Onliest thing I know is tobacco. I've got ideas for greater yield per acre. I've got good, healthy seed from Maryland, Virginia and

North Carolina. I aim to produce a sweeter leaf and improve the curing process—"

"We don't produce that much."

"I know. But I've been watchin' the soil all the way down here. I know that tobacco will grow and do well. Also, I know the market is up there, but just the same, the need keeps growin' every year. I figger if I can produce a good crop, others'll take it up, an' you couldn't want a better, sounder cash crop. If the people around here ain't interested—"

"Hold on, Cousin," Jonas said quickly. "A sound cash crop couldn't be more welcome in Cairn County. Go on. Let's hear more."

"First the land, sandy-clay soil—"

"We've got plenty of that."

"—then labor—"

"Got it to spare."

"—and leave the rest to me."

"We'll start looking as soon as you say the word."

Anderson nodded with relief. "Then suppose you take the money I brought with me and put it in that bank of yours 'til I need it. Place I'm lookin' for should have a house for my family—"

"No need for that, Anderson. I got more room on Laurel than I can ever use up."

"Thank you, no, Jonas. When I find my land, my house is goin'a be on it and my family in it. Then my curing barns, stripping and drying and grading sheds. Me and my family'll live where we grow our tobacco. Maybe later, when everything is goin' the way I want it, I'll build us a house in town here, but not yet. I'm goin'a grow the best tobacco in the South, learn others to do the same, then build up a cooperative and establish a market buyers will come to—"

"And if they don't?"

"Cousin, you don't know tobacco buyers. Or manufacturers. To get their hands on prime quality leaf, they'll outbid each other to the bare bone. From time to time, they gang up to keep prices down, but on the quiet, they come snoopin' around to snatch up quality leaf whenever and wherever they can find it. With a cooperative, *we* can control prices. With cigarette production leapin' ahead all the time, quality is what they need, and what I aim to produce."

"Cigarettes? Those dandified paper-wrapped things?"

"Don't look down on 'em, Jonas. They're big an' gettin' bigger every day of every year. Listen. In '80, there were only 400 million produced. In '90, the total was over three billion of 'em sold. Three *billion!* I don't rightly know what the figure is now, but it's a growin' habit, cleaner than chewin' or snuff, not as expensive as cigars. That's where the big money an' profits goin'a be some day."

8

Within two weeks of his birth, the infant Clyde was dead. A chill, followed by pneumonia, had taken him, and Cleo, still exhausted from the labor of his birth, was inconsolable. For weeks she kept Chase close to her side in desperate fear that he might contract a similar illness, refusing to allow Mrs. Claypool, Annabelle or Maudie to bathe, feed or dress him. She permitted visitors, including Charlotte Taylor and her son, Ames, a minimum of her time. Anderson understood her desire to be alone with Chase and threw himself into a determined search for land that was suitable for his purposes.

The February weather had turned mild and warm and the occasional rains were gentle to the soil. The Cottonwood River had overflowed its banks in many areas south of Laurelton that winter, depositing fertile topsoil brought down from the north. The more Anderson rode about in his search, the more he liked what he saw, particularly south of Angeltown, which lay across the bridge where most of the Negro and white labor force lived, and beyond and below where Jonas Taylor had pointed out large parcels of land. Much of it was flat and rolled gently toward the river, perfect for drainage.

Anderson rode across the land on horseback, tramped over it on foot, stopped frequently to dig his hands into the soil, to lift handfuls of it, to feel and smell and sift it through his fingers, his mind orienting itself to what it lacked or needed, what it already had; visualizing his seedling beds, the planted rows, the hoeing, suckering, harvesting, curing, drying and grading of the broad, velvet-soft orange-and-lemon-colored leaf. In an empty field, he saw not its emptiness, but men and women working between the rows, saw the rewards of their labors, the faces of singing auctioneers and eager buyers.

He found 1,500 acres of cotton-stubbled land, ringed by thick stands of pine and oak, far too much for his present needs. He went to the bank to see Jonas Taylor about the parcel. The bank, he knew, owned the land.

"How much an acre, Jonas?" he asked.

"Well, reasonable, I'd say. Been lying fallow ever since

123

Hardy Johnson walked off it after his cotton crop failed him two years in a row. We took it in for the balance of the mortgage and taxes. You interested in the whole fifteen hundred acres?"

"No, not yet. All's I need for a first crop is maybe a hundred and fifty acres, the part with the house an' two barns on it and enough timber to cut for the curin'. Figger I'll use forty acres to plant, keep maybe four people busy the first year, more later. Say I buy a hundred and fifty acres outright an' take an option on the rest."

"No problems, Anderson. I'll let it go for what it cost me. You don't make your crop, I get my land back. You make it, others'll come swarming in and make the bank a nice profit on everything around it. Also, you'll be giving us a valuable new market."

With Cleo and Chase remaining at Mrs. Claypool's for the time being, Anderson moved into the seven-room house, hired two Negro families, moved them onto the land and began at once to clear timber, cut and stack it. He prepared his seed bed in a newly cleared patch of woodland not much larger than the floor of his small barn. This, he spaded up himself, then covered it evenly with cut timber and brush which he fired. The fire killed any insect eggs that might attack and damage the tender plants to come, as it destroyed weeds, weed seeds and other parasites, while the ashes helped fertilize the earth. When the fire burned out, he raked the bed carefully until it was clean and table-top smooth.

From his hoard of seeds, so tiny that six or seven table-spoonsful were enough to plant the full 40 acres he would eventually sow, he mixed a small quantity with a panful of earth and sowed the carefully prepared bed evenly. Next he stretched large pieces of cheesecloth over the entire bed, pegging the covering down tightly to keep the wind from blowing it away. This would protect the soil from any danger of possible frost and keep out the night chill.

He prepared and sowed another bed, slightly larger than the first and in the same manner, about ten days later, his insurance in case something happened to the first bed. Meanwhile, the two Negro families—two men, their wives, and four field-sized children—were preparing the 40 acres he intended to plant; and while they labored over the staked-out area, Anderson watched his seed beds with the anxiety of a mother cat nursing a litter of kittens. What he dreaded most at this critical stage was blue mold, a fungus that was fatal to tender young tobacco seedlings. So he

124

watched and tended while the 40 acres were plowed and harrowed until every clod was broken up, the fertilizer he had brought in fed into the soil to enrich it.

By the time the danger of frost was past, the warm Georgia sun had turned each tiny seed into a six-inch plant, ready to be transferred into the waiting fields. Gently, Anderson removed each plant, placed it in a basket and carried each basketful to where it would grow to maturity. Here, he taught the Negroes how to place and set each plant along widely spaced rows, measured the distance between them carefully with a stick cut exactly four feet in length, then used a tapered chute to punch holes into the soft earth at proper depth. He worked quickly, expertly, allowing no time for the sensitive plants to die.

Released from their cramped quarters in the seed bed, the plants took on new life, their long roots reaching thirstily deep down into the soil to draw up a plentiful supply of moisture. Soon, the leaves flourished, grew broader and formed evenly around their stalks as they expanded in size and height.

The word spread quickly among farmers and cotton planters and they came alone or in groups to watch, ask questions, discuss tobacco prices. Some became deeply interested in Anderson's answers. Others sniffed and departed, resisting change, unwilling to learn. But the interested returned, more curious than ever as they watched the crop cover the 40 acres with broad, velvety leaves.

There was work for all hands now, from dawn to dark. However scanty and mild, each rain created a carpet of grass and weeds that needed to be hoed out to prevent a depletion of life-giving moisture. The Negroes, used to long hot days hoeing cotton, were expert at this tedious occupation.

Anderson brought in a separate crew to build six log-cabin-type curing barns, adding improvements to the old structures on the Warren plantation back in Loudon. While his adult field hands were busy pulling "suckers" from the base of the leaves, their children searched for and removed the caterpillar-like green moth larvae, called tobacco worms, aided by a large flock of turkeys Anderson brought in, and which spent most of their time happily finding and eating the worms.

The weeks flew by swiftly. Between supervising the building of his curing barns and other sheds, Anderson moved anxiously through his fields in search of other destructive diseases which flourish among tobacco: wilt, mosaic, root rot and wildfire; but here, Anderson's care in selecting his seed proved valuable. Most plants were hardy and disease-resistant.

By August, the tobacco began to ripen into lush, head-high stalks, the entire 40 acres magnificently green and beautiful to look upon. Anderson was ecstatic when he touched each leaf and felt its rich quality between sensitive fingers, equal or superior to any he had ever grown in Loudon—or perhaps it was because this very special crop, from seed to full-grown plant, was all his own, the product of his own labor in his own fields.

My first crop, he told himself over and over again as he walked up and down its rows. I've made my own first crop. Thank you, Grandma Laura-Ellen, thank you for my Inheritance Day.

There was still much work ahead.

9

Long before harvest time, Anderson Warren penned a careful letter to his father-in-law, in which he enclosed another to be delivered to Henry Shaffer. In it, he described the crop to the best of his ability, likened it to the finest he and Grandfather Clyde had ever produced in Loudon, estimated his first crop yield as comparing with the highest in any major tobacco-growing center. He asked Shaffer to come to Laurelton on his way south from Loudon and save Anderson the trouble, possible damage and cost of shipping into the northern auction market.

During the curing period, increasingly curious neighboring farmers came to watch the new, strange process that was taking place, necessary because the leaves must be cured as soon as they were pulled from their stalks in order to retain a greater sugar content. The leaves, picked and placed upon mule-drawn sleds, were then loaded onto a larger wagon and taken to a curing barn for the first test-curing. As each load of green tobacco arrived, the leaves were quickly and tightly tied to tobacco sticks, like bananas on the stalk, then hung from rafters and stacked in piles. When the barn was fully packed, Anderson examined the batch to see that the sticks were so placed that the heat would reach each leaf. Nothing must be allowed to touch or fall upon the heat pipes that circulated through the inside lest the entire barn go up in flames.

Outside the properly ventilated barn was a brick fireplace which would be fed with wood that had been cut during the initial land-clearing. From it, metal pipes ran inside the barn to spread the heat evenly, dry the tobacco quickly. The ventilator windows were shut, the door closed, the stage set. Only enough wood to produce a low heat was used at first. As the pipes inside began to warm up, Anderson checked the temperature, striving for only 25 degrees above that of the outside air. Under this moderate heat, the leaves began to change color from green to yellow. It would take almost 48 hours to turn its color to the desired bright orange-yellow.

More wood, drier than before, was added to increase the temperature, the draft improved. The temperature moved steadily upward to 125, 135, then 150 degrees. The ventilator windows were opened now to allow the damp, sap-laden air to escape and the temperature was again increased. For more than sixteen hours, the heat was kept above 160 degrees.

Day and night, the firewatch had to be kept. Every hand took turns sleeping, eating, and watching around the clock. Anderson was everywhere, his eyes rimmed with red, the color of his face and hands burned by the hot sun until he could hardly be distinguished from his helpers. Friendly neighbors came, bringing food and drink, joining in the vigil, establishing a tradition that would become an annual harvest event.

And when the leaves were completely dry, the fibrous stems still contained moisture that must be removed. This required more heat. The temperature was sent soaring for still another 18 hours and the watch became intensified. Food was eaten in the open, sleepers curled up on the ground. And then, finally, it was over. The first barnful. Only one of 40 such loads that must be similarly cured. 900 pounds of prime leaf to the barnful; 36,000 pounds for his 40 acres, if the rest turned out as well.

Neighbor farmers began to show deeper interest at this point. They talked price, now that they had seen the yield. Computed roughly at a modest six cents per pound, they were seeing a cash crop that would run over $2,000.

The total yield, when the full crop was finally brought in, cured, weighed and graded, came to 32,000 pounds; and when Henry Shaffer came down after the Loudon auctions, he bought the entire crop in at an average 8.13 cents per pound, writing his draft for $2,601.60 in full view of a host of envious farmers and cotton planters.

And a chuckling Jonas Taylor.

Anderson Warren next directed his attention to the house. He turned his field hands loose to thoroughly renovate, repair, reroof and paint it. With the aid of newly made friends and their wives, he bought furniture, selected curtain and drapery materials, wallpaper and rugs to furnish the seven-room house, then brought Cleo and Chase into their first real home in Georgia.

Cleo was still weak and ill of mind over their loss of little Clyde, but Chase was a godsend to her. A teacher before she married Anderson, she occupied herself with Chase's education and Anderson was astounded with the five-year-old boy's amazing ability to read, write and calculate complex arithmetical problems.

Still deeply concerned, Anderson persuaded Mrs. Claypool to allow Annabelle's daughter, Maudie, to go with them. Maude's husband, Reed, objected on the grounds that he was a "house Nigra" and not a field hand, which objection was met by Cleo's promise that he would work indoors and only on the immediate grounds and take no part in the field work. Maudie had already been won over by Chase and Cleo.

As Anderson exercised his option on more of the land, additional Negro families moved down from Angeltown. Jonas sent him a young and capable foreman, Shadrach Waters, who was to become Warren's overseer, bringing his new young wife, Leona, with him. A good year followed the first, enough to break down local resistance to the new and progressive methods introduced by Anderson; and now neighbors were sufficiently interested to put in their own seed beds and experiment with a few acres, using the Warren curing barns that year.

Anderson sent his first-year crew to help them, families that had been patiently schooled, trained, drilled and supervised until they could be safely loaned out. Others caught the "cash crop fever" and borrowed from Jonas Taylor's bank to add land and necessary improvements, to buy seed, fertilizer and equipment. On Jonas' considered advice, "It can't hurt you. All you'll be doing is turn unused land to good purpose and put good hard cash in your pockets," dozens jumped in.

Land prices rose, as did the price of tobacco during those next few years. On Henry's Shaffer's word, more buyers came and bought, taking advantage of the absence of a trained auctioneer to undercut the North Carolina market price. In 1906, this situation was remedied when Anderson Warren formed his Georgia Tobacco Cooperative and brought Jim Hagendorn down from Loudon to act as auctioneer. The 1906 price went to 9.11 cents. In 1907 it rose

128

to a record 11.42. And in the panic that followed in 1908, prices plummeted downward.

Cleo's health fully restored, she became pregnant that fall and in 1909, during the worst year tobacco planters had ever known, gave birth to a strong, healthy son, born after 36 hours of desperate labor and fear. Again, Cleo wanted him to be named after Anderson's father, but perhaps superstitiously, Anderson rejected the name Clyde and suggested Cleo's grandfather's name, Theodore, to which Cleo finally agreed. It was shortly after the christening that Anderson and Cleo learned from Dr. Ballard that she would never again bear a child.

The panic year of 1908 was the forerunner of several that threatened to put an end to tobacco planting in Laurelton. It had begun earlier in other markets where a gigantic northern tobacco trust had been formed to depress and control prices. The 11.42-cent price had, by collusive buying practices, been driven down to a destructive 5.01-cent level which threatened planters with bankruptcy and near-starvation. Those who were able joined with others to withhold their crops in a "no-sell" agreement, and stored their cured leaves in warehouses, sheds and barns.

A bitter war of violence erupted throughout the tobacco-growing areas when the trust sent hired thugs and vandals to put the torch to tobacco-laden buildings. Many were burned to the ground and there were violent deaths on both sides. Vigilante groups were formed to counter the barn-burnings and curb sales by desperate planters, driven by hunger and need to feed their families, to sell at the unprecedented low trust price. More barns were burned, more lives were lost and many smaller planters were driven to turn to other farm products in order to survive, caught between the trust and adamant, militant vigilante forces. Generally, the situation was what some brave editorialists called chaotic anarchy.

In Washington, antitrust suits begun by President Theodore Roosevelt were now being pressed by President William Howard Taft. The tension eased somewhat, but the situation was generally a horror to the planters while they awaited government action and decision. Only the increasing need for tobacco kept those planters alive, but barely.

Anderson Warren's dream had received a shattering blow. He went north to study the situation at first hand, then to Washington to talk with a senator and four congressmen to whom Jonas Taylor had sent him. On his return to Laurelton, his attitude was one of depressing gloom.

"Them goddam trust leeches, they're ruinin' us, Jonas," Anderson said bitterly, "and the trust's got more men working in Washington than we got senators or congressmen."

But Jonas Taylor's lines of communication were evidently more securely laid in high places than were Anderson Warren's. "It won't take much longer, Anderson," he counseled. "The trust is going to be busted wide open. Taft won't allow a handful of greedy men to control the whole tobacco market and keep buying up their competitors so they can fix prices at starvation levels."

"But in the meantime—"

"In the meantime, we've got a bank to help us."

"How, for God's sake?"

"We keep topping current prices offered by the trust and we hold the tobacco off the market, store it like we've been doing right along."

"I'm worried, Jonas. They're goin'a come in and burn us out."

"Like hell they will. We're going to throw armed guards around our warehouses and kill any trust sonofabitch comes within two hundred yards of any one of 'em. When the trust is busted, we'll be ready for all the new companies that'll be operating independently. One thing they'll need more than anything else is the basic ingredient—tobacco. Without it, they can't operate."

Anderson shook his head. "I don't know if I can keep my people together that long, Jonas."

Jonas smiled. "You said *my* people. I guess you've finally become a real son of Georgia."

"It's nothin' to smile over, Jonas."

"Nor for you to fret over, Cousin. It's my money and I'm willing to put it up. That makes it my gamble as much as yours. I'm no tobacco man, but I know markets and I've seen enough to know that tobacco has become as prime a market as cotton, rice, flour, corn or oil. All we've got to do is wait it out."

10

Late in 1910, Jonas returned from a trip to Washington and Atlanta. He sent for Anderson at once. "Get ready, Cousin. The dam is about to bust wide open."

"How do you mean?"

"I had a long talk with Senator Beaumont. He's as close to Taft's ear and the Attorney General as I am to you right now. By this time next year the big trust is going to be

130

stood up against the wall and executed. How's our tobacco holding out?"

"We got it comin' out of our ears."

"Then get set for buyers. The word'll be out before long and they'll be coming through here like a plague of locusts. They're going to miss the tobacco they've burned and there's going to be more manufacturers competing for what's left. And we're going to hold out for top dollar. You're liable to see fifteen- and twenty-cent tobacco yet."

Anderson returned home deep in thought. He sat through his supper without a word, scarcely touching his food. "You're not sick, are you, Anderson?" Cleo asked.

"Sick? Me? No, Cleo. Not sick. Just thinkin' on something come up in a talk I had with Jonas Taylor this afternoon."

At three the next morning he was still wide awake, poring over papers he had littered with figures, still thinking, but with his heart pumping faster, his mind turning over like a train wheel rolling over the Carolina-Georgia tracks.

When Jonas Taylor arrived at his office that day, an excited Anderson was waiting for him, but Jonas was in an evil mood. It was the morning his wife, Charlotte, had told him she was sending their son, Ames, off to Duke University at Durham, North Carolina.

Over the past few years, Anderson had come to understand that there were differences between Jonas and Charlotte. He had heard the rumors of a premarital affair between Jonas and a neighbor, Beth-Anne Betterton; that he had jilted her to marry Charlotte, who had been an Ames of Atlanta. The affair, it was alleged, had driven Beth-Anne to suicide, and her father, Wilfred, had thereupon taken his own life in grief. Later, through a proxy, Jonas had bought the 10,000-acre Betterton plantation that lay beside Laurel. Charlotte had known neither of the two victims, but the sad business had developed a coolness beween Jonas and his wife, that not even the birth of their son, Ames, could heal. And now Ames was being sent away from home, an act Jonas took as a personal affront to his position as master of Laurel, impotent in his effort to win his son's affections from Charlotte.

When his ire had finally dissipated itself, at least for the moment, Jonas asked, "What is it that's disturbing you, Anderson?"

"It's not disturbing, Jonas. Exciting is a more proper word. You got some time to listen?"

"Always got time for an exciting idea, Anderson. Go ahead and tell me what's on your mind."

131

Anderson took a deep breath and let it out slowly. He broke it to his cousin in one word. "Manufacturing," he said simply.

Jonas sat up straight in his chair, a new, brighter light in his eyes, his mouth open with surprise. For several moments the two men sat staring at each other across the desk, then Jonas' lips closed in an appreciative grin that matched the one that had begun to spread across Anderson's face. "By sure God, Anderson," Jonas declared, "that's a powerful interesting idea."

For a moment, they sat and grinned at each other. Then Jonas said, "Why not? Why the hell not? The field will be wide open. If you're there and ready when it cracks open, with more tobacco stock than anybody else——"

"Just what I been thinkin' on all night long," Anderson said. "You want in on it?"

"No. I've enough to keep me busy here. But as an investment, to sell more land, bring more families in to work, my bank will back you. How much you think you'll need and how long you think it will take you to get ready?"

"With money behind me, nine months, a year at the most. I'll need equipment, only the best and newest, and a place in New York to manufacture in and set up a sales and distribution office."

Jonas frowned. "I want the manufacturing here in South Laurelton, the jobs, the payroll, the supplies, the freight, the new housing——"

"Not until I get it rolling, Jonas. Once I get it set up in New York, I'll move the whole thing back here, lock, stock and barrel. Listen——"

11

In 1911, as Jonas had correctly predicted, the government won its antitrust suit and Warren Tobacco Company was ready to move into action among the many newly created independent manufacturers. Its more than ample tobacco supply was fed into its new machinery to produce a single product—cigarettes. The cut plug, twist, cigar, and snuff markets were already flooded with name brands too well known and publicly accepted to be cracked by a newcomer, but the cigarette market had not reached that point of saturation and Anderson Warren used this opening wedge to make WARREN'S BLEND cigarettes a strong contender in this more recent and youngest branch of the tobacco business. It had taken long hours of study and a great deal of courage to single out the cigarette as the future star of the industry, a long gamble at best, but it was Warren's and Taylor's gamble—and slowly, surely, it took hold and began to pay off.

This, Anderson would recall later, was the longest, hardest year of his life. No day was shorter than 16 hours long and often ran the full 24. It was the year he learned to cope with realistic labor problems, the operation of strange, mysterious equipment, the hiring of specialists in every phase from factory to front office, the complexities of debt and finance. The latter was fearsome for a man who had known loss through debt—Christian's—and looked upon it with a mixture of hatred and shame.

In New York, he lived in a two-dollar-a-week room and worked in a filthy loft without heat. He ate poorly, often missing meals. He hungered for Cleo and Chase and could hardly remember Theodore. He longed for the people he had trained in his fields, his neighbors, the comforting talks with Jonas Taylor, the optimism his cousin always managed, somehow, to generate.

He took time to get away from the closeness of his work, but only to talk to tobacconists in their aromatic shops, hold conversations with cigarette smokers, leaving samples of his product; and dreamed his big dreams while he walked among the canyons created by huge buildings that overwhelmed him. His love for the relative quiet of Laurelton never left him. "I'm a country boy and I'll die a country boy," he said often. "I need New York, but I'll hire me a man to live and work here for me. Chase. I God, I'll save this for Chase. Some day—"

In May of that year, Benjamin came up from Virginia to pay him a surprise visit in New York and, on his second day there, they received word from Alistair that their father had died in Baltimore, in a waterfront dive at the foot of Broadway, where Christian had become a homeless, drunken spectacle in a seaman's saloon, mopping floors, washing glasses and dishes and running errands, all for the privilege of sleeping in a filthy, verminous, rat-infested cellar, cadging free drinks when and where he could.

Brought to the emergency room of Johns Hopkins Hospital with multiple stab wounds from the knife of a Norwegian sailor he had tried to rob, Christian was able, in his last moments, to recall Alistair's name and address. And so, for a short time, the three brothers were united in sadness, but without grief, as they laid their father to his ultimate rest in the Greenmount Cemetery.

Before they parted, Ben and Alistair promised to invest in

Anderson's venture through the purchase of stock at the issue price of one dollar per share. Their confidence gave Anderson a sense of pride and determination to double his efforts. His greatest challenge was the $5,000,000 the Laurelton National Bank (Jonas Taylor's) had loaned Warren Tobacco Company, holding mortgages on its land and every lick and stick and wheel and building and the tobacco that was stored in sheds and still in the ground. The wheels were rolling and Anderson Warren was riding the treadmill to success—or doomsday.

134

CHAPTER V

1. New York, September, 1967

Buddy Duke was soaring. Miraculously, he had broken through the Earth's gravity barrier, leaving behind him its cares, problems and pressures, its hatreds, intolerances, evils and violence. Its ugliness. He was in that marvelous state of having left and not having arrived at his destination. Limbo. Here, all was beauty and serenity. He was aglow with well-being; neither hot nor cold. There was no pain, no hunger, no Black or White; nothing to tug at his emotions, compel his attention. Only elation, more thrilling even than the ultimate act of love between man and woman. He was Supreme. God.

The physical Duke Shackleford was light years behind him, gone, dead. Long live Buddy Duke.

He floated easily and there was an absence of Time or Distance. In the Unknown, he could breathe effortlessly and his vision was crystal clear. He could sing, and he did; not with one voice but with many that were blended into perfect tonal quality; accompanied by a chorus of thousands of strings, woodwinds, trumpets and crashing cymbals; and he, alone, was creating this marvelous, heavenly symphony. He, an Audience of One, not only heard it with utmost clarity but could actually *feel* it, *see* it.

And then, as it always happened, there came the Force whose power he had not yet learned to conquer, to defy; the one which, at his moment of superb glory, began to rumble, then roar into his ears, creating a discordant cacophony to drown out the glorious music, shaking him as an earthquake rocks the land, as a hurricane sweeps over the sea, raging with destructive fury. It engulfed, encircled and shrugged him down, down, down toward Earth again. But Buddy Duke did not surrender easily. He struggled mightily against the Force, fought to take it within his grasp and destroy it; but there was nothing to touch, rip, shred, tear apart, even see; only to feel, inside himself, for it had no substance.

Color and beauty faded with the music. He began to sense earthly heat alternating with cold, becoming aware of his trembling body, the pain in his head, behind his eyes, in his throat, chest, bowels, groin, legs. His hand. Oh, Jesus! Trapped again! Trapped on the Earth he had almost escaped, enmeshed within its harshness and cruelties again.

Oh, God Jesus! Lemme stay! Keep me with You! Don't make me go back!

Why couldn't he have continued onward, outward, away from the taste of his desperations, the knowledge and fear and defeat that waited to tear at his insides, sear his brain?

And then, irrevocably, he was back. He knew it when the earthly voice called out to him.

"Buddy! Buddy! You all right?"

2

Reluctantly, Buddy Duke opened his eyes and stared straight ahead into the only break in the darkness he could make out, the panes of an uncurtained window, gray-struck with pale moonlight. The room was as unfamiliar to him as its shadowy furnishings, its strange shapes and odors. A deep, tormented sigh escaped his bruised lips and grew into a harsh groan as he became conscious of the agonizing pain in his left hand. When he tried to move it, shards of splintered bone stabbed across his knuckles, ran down into his fingers and relayed the pain upward into his wrist and upper arm. When he breathed, he became aware that at least several of his ribs were broken.

Jesus God, he thought, *them bastard mothers busted me to pieces.*

He groaned again, then heard the soft, anxious voice penetrate the blackness again. "You all right, Buddy?" And the voice, too, was strange to him.

He attempted an answer, but the words were strangulated in his throat. He tried to raise his head off the hard, lumpy pillow, but the effort set up another discharge of pain from the top of his head down into the nerves of his neck. He let himself go limp. Better this way. Only one huge ache, without the sharp pain.

Christ! One minute I was a man, a big man. Now I'm like a hunk of meat on a butcher's block. Where am I? It ain't home.

The small room was crowded with unfamiliar shapes, forms and shadows; its odor strange, yet not entirely unfamiliar. Something about the odor. Something. The smell of staleness. Tobacco. Alcohol. Food. With an overlay of cheap perfume. It reminded him of home. Laurelton. An-

136

geltown. His father, Sam Shackleford. His mother, Lutie. His younger sister, Elizabeth. Uncle Matt, who had died in Parkton Prison. And Ivy. Then it came to him; the perfume reminded him of his cousin Ivy. How could it be? They were in Laurelton, and he was in New York. But where in New York?

He felt the bed sag and almost screamed out in pain. The woman had knelt on its edge with both knees and leaned down over him. He could smell the musky flavor of her, the dampness of sweat, the overpowering, sickening sweetness of her cheap perfume.

"Who're you?" he asked in two croaking words.

"I'm Lorella. Lorella Turner."

The name meant nothing to him and she remained anonymous among the blending blacks and dark grays of the other shadows in the room. "Where'm I at?"

"You in my place," she replied with a hint of amusement in her voice. "Up on 118th Street, off'n Madison."

"How come I'm here?"

She giggled in a soft trill. "I brung you here in a cab. You kinda busted up some," she added needlessly.

"How bad?"

"Busted hand, somethin' fierce. Head's busted some an' you got a cut over your left eye. Cabby, he he'p me bring you in. You goin'a hafta get a doctor, man."

"I can't get to no doctor now. C'n I stay here for a while?"

"Shuh. Stay long's you like. Long's the money holds out." Money. "How much money I got?"

"Four hunnert'n ten dollars. It'll last a good while. You wan' a drink?"

"Yeah." She got off the bed and disappeared among the other shadows. "Hey!" he called after her.

"What?"

"You got anything stronger'n a drink?"

"Like what?"

"Like—H. Horse."

"Ain't got nothin' stronger'n pot. Four-five sticks. You want one?"

"Christ, no. I need somethin' with a blast. I hurt like hell all over."

"Cain't git it now. Come daylight, I c'n get you fixed up."

"Okay. Gimme the drink an' a stick."

He lay back, trying to relax. The woman had gone to the far side of the room and he heard a cupboard open, the tinkle of glass, then she came back with a tumbler of raw whiskey. He took it in his right hand and gulped at it, then felt the thrust of the marijuana cigarette between his lips and heard the scrape of a match as the woman lighted it for him. The room was still dark, but this close to him on the bed, he knew she was near-naked.

"Anything else I can do fo' you, Buddy?" she asked.

"What time is it?"

"Somewheres close to four o'clock."

"Morning?"

"Shuh nuff mornin'," she replied. "Man, you really hung up."

"How come I'm here, anyway?"

"Cabbyman, he brung you to the Blue Palace Bar where I work at las' night. He tellen Dave Blue you outside in his cab, all busted up. Dave, he tellen me to take you to my place. You a big name an' in some kinda trouble, beat up like you was. Cops find you, they makin' more trouble for you. Hey, you wanna sleep some more?"

"Yeah. Listen, Lorella, come time, you go get me that fix?"

"Shuh. No trouble. The whiskey hittin' you yet?"

"Not yet. Maybe soon. If I could get to my place, I be all right. Onliest thing, I don't think I c'd make it right now."

"You try to sleep an' I'll have it by nine, nine-thirty. That cat, he makes the street aroun' then."

"Okay. I'll try to sleep now."

She turned away from him and he lay quietly, trying to remember. Was it only last night that he had been reduced to a wreck in Al Saxon's office?

3

At ten o'clock he had marched proudly down the aisle with trainer and handlers flanking him, waving one gloved hand in response to the cheers and a scattering of boos from the Friday night crowd at the Garden. He nodded briefly to his opponent, Greek Sam Spyros, and turned away, listening for the first bell. Three rounds later he had been helped out of the ring, up the same aisle through a corridor of noise and into his dressing room. He remembered that while Sandy worked over him, Al Saxon had come in with Turk Longo and looked down at him with angry contempt on his face. He didn't speak to Buddy, but addressed Sandy.

"He all right?"

"Shuh," Sandy replied. "He be fine. Don' show hardly no marks a-tall."

"Too goddam bad. When you get him on his feet, tell

him I'll be in my office waitin' for him." Al and Turk turned and went out.

Buddy said, "What the hell he so uppity about? I done what I was supposed to, didn' I?"

"Yeah," Sandy said coldly, "you did. You sure did, Buddy."

Under the shower, getting dried down, dressing. What the hell's got into Sandy? he puzzled. And Al? I was supposed to take a dive and I did. All right. Now Al can get the rematch with Greek Spyros and I'll knock him from here to Harlem. All's I want is one real crack at that piece of cat meat. Just one. Then comes Joe Fletcher, Mike Kelleher and then Big Boy himself, Jim Bridges. I take him, I get a shot at the title. That was the deal if I hit the tank for Spyros. Then—

It was nearing midnight when he reached Saxon's office, a dingy two-room suite over a secondhand clothing shop. He recalled seeing the lighted clock through the window of the Western Union office that was in the same block.

In the ten years since he had left Laurelton, Buddy Duke, then Duke Shackleford, had come a long way. At 16, he had landed in New York with less than a hundred dollars in his pocket and a note from Ben-Joe Nichols to Sonny Poole, who had a piece of the policy territory in Harlem. The money lasted just long enough for Sonny to put Duke to work in the back room of a garage on 135th Street that was a numbers drop, delivery point for his runners. It had almost killed Duke to kick the habit he had brought with him, but he had lived through it somehow. For almost a year, Duke served as lookout and errand boy, then as runner, picking up bags of coins and crumpled dollar bills from other collection points—stores, poolrooms, filling stations, newsstands, and apartment house janitors—to bring back to the 135th Street drop; until Sonny reneged on a payoff somewhere along the line.

The syndicate, which took a very dim view of complaints of this nature, particularly when the payoff was to a plainclothes cop who picked up the weekly installment of protection money for the precinct, moved in swiftly. The least said of Sonny Poole's last hours on earth, the better; but the firsthand lesson in Sicilian justice was not lost on Duke Shackleford. He got out fast.

For a while, he worked as a dishwasher and pushed marijuana, but the latter job was too closely related to his first job and he deserted it for another as rack boy in a poolroom where he had once collected for Sonny. When he turned 18, he found a job at the Apex Gymnasium where he janitored and ran coffee and sandwiches for managers, promoters, fighters and sportswriters.

One day when there was a shortage of sparring partners, Duke asked Lips Dooley to give him a chance to fill in and show what he could do. Not only did Lips throw him some work after that first showing, but eventually substituted him in a preliminary bout when one of his boys quit cold. Impressed with Duke's handy win over his opponent, Lips became his manager and turned him over to Sweaty Davis, an old middleweight pro, to train. Strong, able and willing, Duke learned the hard way.

In his next three fights, outweighed and overmatched, he had taken fearful beatings, but managed to squeeze out a decision in the last bout. "You still wanna keep on in this racket?" Lips asked when he paid Duke his thirty dollars.

"Yeah, man. I'll go."

"You sure?"

"I said I'll go. I'm sure."

"Okay." Lips smiled at some unrevealed joke. "I'll tell you now. I threw you to three kids I knew could beat the livin' ass off you. You did all right. Not great, but all right. That Tony Moretti you win from, he was the best of the three. You beat him on guts, but you need some class. Sweaty's gonna give it to you. You lay down on him, you're through before you start. Okay?"

"Okay, man. I'll go with Sweaty."

"One thing I give you, kid. You sure ain't afraid in the ring."

"I been in the ring before, Lips."

"Where at?"

"Back home. Police Boys' Club."

"Well, this ain't no boys' club and it ain't no boy's game, Duke. You know that now, don't you?"

"I know it, man."

The climb upward had been hard. He won sixteen of his next eighteen bouts, twelve by knockout. Lips Dooley, succumbing to an unquenchable appetite for alcohol and women, eventually sold Duke's contract to Al Saxon, under whose guidance Duke began to move up faster, each fight carefully calculated to improve his stature. Win after win, knockout following knockout, he climbed from semifinals into main events. And into the money field.

The year before last had been his most active and best, and his greatest financial success. He knew Saxon was milking him for "extra expenses"; advertising buildup, entertaining sportswriters, a publicity firm run by Al's nephew, and "Goddam it, Buddy—" (at the start, his name had been changed from Duke Shackleford to Buddy Duke, more often, simply The Duke)—"you don't realize how much I got to spend to keep you in the spotlight so I can get you a good name fight."

But with all of Saxon's stealing and freeloading, there had still been plenty of money to live the good life. Enough to pay for the clothes, an expensive apartment, the Jaguar, women, liquor, friends. And to send an occasional money order home to Sam and Lutie and Elizabeth, who was now attending U.S.C. in Los Angeles. And then, the name fighters narrowed down. Managers had become cagy over the last six months, wary of Buddy Duke's impressive record. Sportswriters and sportscasters began carrying The Duke banner, calling for top names to give Buddy a shot at their ranking, but nervous middleweights suddenly became scarce, hitting the road circuit to build themselves up at the expense of unheard-of setups. Only when some fifth-rater's manager needed money would he permit his boy to come within range of The Duke's fists; and even these were becoming far and few between.

Buddy's money began to dwindle. His "cushion" of over $15,000 in cash had fallen to below $5,000. And then Al Saxon got a surprise call from Monk Esterbrook, who managed Sam (The Greek) Spyros, the number-five man in line for a title shot. Saxon and Esterbrook met in an out-of-the-way bar on Lexington Avenue and after an hour of talk and several drinks, a deal was set.

Buddy's first reaction was one of pure anger. "I'n goin'a do it, Al. I never hit the tank before an' I'n goin'a start now."

"It ain't the same, Buddy. We're doing it for the buildup."

"Whose buildup, his or mine?"

"Both of you. You play ball, you get a rematch with The Greek and we draw down a bigger gate. You stay eight rounds and that'll be good enough for a rematch. You win the rematch and move up closer to the top. I tell you, you'll look good."

"Not as good as The Greek's goin'a look. No, sir, I'n goin'a let that cat take me."

"Lissen, goddam you, you owe me—"

"I owe *you?*" Buddy laughed aloud. "Man, you been stealin' me blind. I been supportin' your whole family, your stable of bums—"

"And where the hell'd you be without Al Saxon's contacts, huh, boy? Back with Lips Dooley gettin' your stupid brains scrambled for peanuts. I'm tellin' you, Buddy, you

141

owe me. For the clothes you're wearing, for that fancy apartment, your slick broads. Where'n hell else could you have a couple of white broads—down in that hick Georgia town you come from?"

"Look, man, don't you ride this mule too hard—"

"You lissen to me, Buddy. You're on the slide and we both know it. You're on the stuff, hooked up to your eyeballs."

"What?"

"Don't try to kid me, boy. I've known it almost from the day you took your first shot. What I'm giving you is at least two cracks at some big dough. Without me—"

"You goddam ofay crook—"

"You calling me names, you junkie? I'm telling you now, you're goin'a fight Sam Spyros and dive in the eighth. Then we get a rematch. You beat him legit in the rematch and we'll take it from there. Now you wait a goddam minute before you say No. You run out on me now and I'll blow the whistle on you to the cops. All I have to do is give it to the papers why I'm dropping you and you'll be behind bars somewhere trying to wrestle that monkey off your back cold-turkey. You want it that way?"

Buddy Duke stared malevolently at Saxon. "I thought not. Now you pay attention to what I'm tellin' you. You cross me and you'll wind up in a gutter or in the East River, very goddam dead. Just you try takin' a powder on me, not the kind you been mainlinin'—"

"Okay, man," Buddy said resignedly. "You in the saddle."

But the year-long layoff and his excessive appetite for the pleasures of the flesh, good living and the need to feed his habit had taken its toll. The Duke trained badly. His timing was off, his footwork sloppy, and for the first time Al Saxon had him working behind closed doors, away from public and press. And for the first time Buddy keenly felt the disapproval of the only friend he had ever known in Saxon's circus—Sandy Morse, an old-time middleweight contender who had known when to quit the active ring and become trainer and handler.

"Whyn't you quit now, Buddy?" Sandy asked. "All's you doin', you takin' a downhill ride."

"I can't quit now, Sandy. I got to get me a good stake first. I only got a short way to go."

"You ain't never goin'a get there like this, Buddy."

"I got to try."

"What good's tryin' when you know you can't make it? I know you on the stuff, Buddy. You could get killed—"

"Shit, man, what good's livin' anyhow if you got to live like a pig?"

"Okay, son. I done my best."

In a season that had been notable for its lack of luster, the Duke-Spyros fight attracted considerable attention from the press, which pondered on the "new Buddy Duke strategy being perfected behind closed doors." The turnout by the ring aficionados was good, the television money even better. Buddy Duke was the 9-to-5 favorite at weighing-in time, and he had gotten a friend, Lucky Powers, to spread $4,000 of his last $5,000 around on Sam Spyros in exchange for the top-secret information that Spyros would win in the eighth.

For two rounds, Buddy looked like championship material. Then in the third, Spyros uncorked a series of left jabs and lethal rights that erased The Duke from his former standing among ring royalty. He went down three times within two minutes, the third time for the full count, unable to defend himself. As Buddy was being helped from the ring to his dressing room, no one was more surprised than Sam Spyros. Unless it was Al Saxon.

4

In his second-floor office, Al looked up from the circle of yellow light given off by the green-hooded bulb that hung over his scarred desk. In one corner, Jack Delaney sat thumbing an old, worn copy of *Playboy*. Turk Longo, his wooden chair leaning against the wall on two legs, stared emptily at his shoe tips from beneath a stained, wide-brimmed felt hat. The odors of rubbing liniment, stale coffee, tobacco, partially eaten sandwiches and beer merged with sweat and other unidentifiable smells. Calendars, nudes and discolored photographs of old fighters, with mangled autographs that looked as though they had been inscribed while wearing boxing gloves, stared down from the four walls. Buddy Duke was easily the cleanest, best-dressed man in the room.

"Siddown a minute, Buddy," Saxon said. Al pulled at his cigar and stared at a sheet of penciled figures. After a full three minutes of silence, Buddy said, "How about it, man?"

"You in a hurry, Buddy?"

"Yeah. I'm due up in Harlem for a party."

"You got time, boy. You saved a lot of time losin' in the third instead of the eighth like we set it up for."

Buddy said nothing and Saxon resumed studying the

143

figures. Another minute or two passed and Saxon put the sheet of paper away and said, "Well, big shot, you sure flung it away tonight, didn't you?"

Buddy stood up. "What the hell you talkin' about, man? I done just like I was told. I dived, didn't I?"

"You dived all right. You're supposed to put up a fight 'til the eighth and you get knocked on your ass in the third. Cold, stone dead."

"Well, hell, man, no use me gettin' all chopped up for eight rounds when I can do it in three, is there?"

"Bullshit, boy. You didn't dive and you know it. He took you like a prelim kid, fresh out his first time."

"So what? Next time—"

"Next time!" Saxon turned to Turk and Jack with a harsh laugh. "You guys hear that? Next time!" He turned back to Buddy with venom. "You think there's goin'a be a next time, you dumb black bastard? The Commission's holding up the purse. There's talk you was all hopped up and they're calling in people, talking to 'em. Sandy saw you mainlining one before the fight. Somebody talks and we won't get a goddam dime. And I could lose my license."

Buddy leaped across the short span with lightning fury. "Listen, you goddam white sonofabitchin' crook, you been robbin' me for years. I'm goin'a—" He reached Saxon's desk, grabbed his coat lapels and drew him halfway across the desk—"get my money if I got to beat it outa your lousy white hide, take you apart—"

At that moment, the ceiling fell in on him as Jack Delaney brought a sawed-off poolcue down on his head. Buddy's grip on Saxon loosened. He rolled over and turned his body upward to avoid a second blow that came crashing down, missing him by inches. He spun off the desk, only to take Turk Longo's knee in his groin and a two-handed chop on his throat. Then Delaney smashed the poolcue over his left eye, dropping him to the cigarette-littered floor. He tried to crawl away, but Saxon kicked him and the poolcue crunched against his side, then across his back. He reached for the edge of the desk to pull himself up. Longo, an ex-heavyweight, was waiting for him and caught him flush on the jaw with a hard right. Buddy bounced backward, rolled over twice and staggered drunkenly to his knees, bleeding from the mouth and the cut over his eye.

"You bastards!" he gasped. "You ofay motherf—"

Delaney swung the poolcue and caught him on the side of his neck. He fell into Longo's arms and felt Delaney's knee in his stomach. He vomited a bloody mass over Dela-

144

ney and laughed crazily as Delaney tried unsuccessfully to avoid it, dropping the poolcue.

Longo had Buddy in a full nelson then, and Delaney hit him twice, once in the stomach and a hard, solid right to the jaw. He sagged in Longo's grip, the fight gone out of him. Blood and words flowed in an uncontrolled jumble from Duke's mouth, unintelligble curses and filthy abuse for every white bastard and sonofabitch in the entire world.

The poolcue caught him along the jaw, cutting off his curses, stunning him. The room swayed, wavered, canted crazily, then went into a violent tailspin. He fell to his knees, reaching for the edge of the desk, waiting for the spinning room to come to a full stop. He felt the gummy vomit in his throat, swallowed hard and tried to claw his way up, but the overhead light began swimming. Then, someone was helping him up to his wobbly, rubbery feet, eyes running with tears, or blood, he couldn't tell which.

In a final act of brutality, Delaney and Longo forced him over the desk, face down, right arm crooked up behind his back, left arm extended along the desk. Saxon picked up the poolcue and brought it down twice across the knuckles of his left hand. Delaney and Longo released him and Duke dropped to the floor in a heap.

Saxon said, "Okay, boys, that's enough. Let the sonofabitch live." To Buddy Duke, less than half-conscious, cradling his broken left hand in his right, "All right, Boogie Boy, go to the cops. Tell 'em how you took a dive tonight. They'll check your arm and see the tracks on it, and you can rot in jail while you're taking the cold-turkey treatment. And the only thing you'll ever fight from now on is that monkey ridin' your back."

Buddy was kneeling in a sodden, bloody crouch, weeping. "All right, Jack, Turk," Saxon said. "Get him to hell outa here. Shove him in a cab and tell the cabby to dump him somewhere up in nigger heaven where he belongs."

5

He lay in the lumpy bed watching the dawn turn the windows from black to leaden gray to copper. His body ached, his head throbbed, and the pain in his left hand was almost unbearable. He tried to turn on his right side, but the slightest movement sent rivers of lightning shooting through him.

I'll kill those white bastards. All three of them. One at a time. Even if it takes me all my life. They ain't goin'a get away with it, so help me Jesus.

145

The sky had lightened. The woman stirred, raised herself on one elbow. "You feelin' bad, Buddy?" she asked.

"Real bad. What time is it?"

"Nearly nine. I'll put some coffee on, then I'll get dressed an' go out."

"Lissen. You go now. See if you c'n find that cat."

"All right. I'll try, but he don' ever come 'til aroun' nine-thirty."

She got out of the bed and he watched as she pulled the scanty nightgown off unashamedly and pulled a satiny slip over her naked body, wriggling into it. *Any other time,* he thought, *I'd— Oh, Jesus. Get movin', girl.*

She drew a short sheath over the slip, zipped it up, then put on a pair of low-heeled shoes. She ran a comb through her hair quickly and picked up her purse. "I'll need some—"

"Take it. Take what you need. Get enough for both of us for a couple days. When you come back—"

She took some bills from his wallet that lay on her night table. "I'll be back soon's I can," she called as she went out.

His nose was beginning to run and itch as the need came on him again, hammering at him through his physical pain. He felt the cramps and nausea, wiping at drops that were seeping down his bruised nose. How much time had passed, he couldn't calculate, but then she returned, preparing a fix for him, for herself. Her equipment was crude, unlike his glistening hypodermic and a dozen new needles to choose from in his apartment; a filed-down eye dropper and bent spoon. She straddled him, tied his necktie around his upper left arm, found a bulging vein and dug the end of the pointed dropper into it. "Theah. You got it now, Buddy. It'll take holt in a few seconds."

When he awoke, he felt better. He lay on top of the sheet, naked and cool, the breeze from a small fan caressing his hot body. She had bathed his hand and bandaged it loosely, painted his bruises with merthiolate, then washed him down with a cloth dipped in a basin of water, handling him as she would an infant. The room was hot and Lorella had stripped down to panties and bra, standing over him with the wet cloth in one hand.

"You a big cat, Buddy man," she said with an appreciative giggle. He stared at her nakedness with rising hunger, moving his thighs, sighing. She came closer to him, bent down so he could touch her with his right hand. The pain had been dulled by the heroin, but the sight of her stirred him. And then his hand dropped to his side and he closed his eyes. He was floating again.

In the waning afternoon, he was able to sip coffee from

146

the cup she held to his swollen mouth. Later, she spoon-fed some soup between his thickened lips. He asked for and received another shot and this time, when she stood over him, drew her down carefully and allowed her to minister to his sexual need. He slept again, his right arm around her, and later in the night, took her again.

Next morning, Lorella went out to buy food and returned with a tall, solemn Negro who carried a black medical bag. The man unwrapped Buddy's bandages and examined the knuckles of his left hand, then gave him an injection to kill the pain and taped his ribs tightly, sewed the cut over his left eye. To Lorella, he said, "He'll be all right soon. He's young and strong, but he ought to get that hand X-rayed. Don't you be taking too much out of him, Sis."

Buddy called out, "Doc—"

Lorella said, "He need a shot o' somethin' else, Doc."

The man said, "You got fifty for it?"

"Fifty? Got maybe twenny." Lorella saw the negative shake of his head. "Maybe thirty."

"Fifty. Buddy Duke can afford it."

"Doc," Lorella laughed, "you sure somethin'. You must have X-ray eyes."

"I take my chances, Sis, and I know Buddy Duke when I see him. I got to get paid."

From the bed, Buddy called out, "Give him the goddam fifty. Give it to him."

Lorella went to the night table and turned her back on the man while she counted out the fifty dollars. When she handed it to him, he said, "That's only for the shot, Lorella. Another fifty for fixing him up."

Sulkily, "Now you gettin' me mad, Doc. You ain't no different from them other whorerobbers."

He snapped with impatience, "I lost my license doing favors like this, Sis. You know what happens if somebody blows the whistle on me?"

"Sure. You'll work anyways, just like the rest o' the whores."

Again, Buddy called out, "Goddam it, give the sonofabitch the hundred an' let him get the hell out of here!"

The money changed hands quickly, the syringe was made ready, the solution injected into Buddy's vein. He expelled a deep breath and relaxed. The doctor left and Buddy heard the rush of water in the kitchen, the clatter of pots and dishes, the smell of food. He was hungry, his appetite stimulated. Lorella helped him up and he sat painfully at the table to eat, lost in Lorella's light chatter. She was a warm brown color, tall, with a well-fleshed body and hair that

147

hung at shoulder length. A good-looking, happy face, Buddy thought, well-kept for a small-time hustler.

She laughed with good humor at his question. "Me? Oh, a little of everything. Sing, dance, wait tables. When I hafta, I do a trick or two 'til a job comes up. Right now I'm 'tween jobs. Jus' hang around waitin' for somethin' to turn up. Jus' what I was doin' las' night when the cabby man come in." And then, "How about you? Can't do much fightin' with a busted hand, can you?"

"I'll make out. How high's your monkey ridin' you?"

"Not high. I'm a joy popper. I smoke some pot once in a while. I don't use much H, less'n things get real bad, but I'm one of the lucky ones. I c'n th'ow it off when I'm happy, when I got me a steady job or a steady man. Love singin'. I sing, I don' need nothin' else 'cept maybe a man once in a while."

"Like me?"

"Like you," she said with a happy grin. "Specially like you."

"Good. I need a woman like you for a while. How much money we got left?"

"Well, a hunnert yesterday, a hunnert for Doc, twenny for groceries. You had four hunnert'n ten. Say about a hunnert'n nine'y left."

"I had aroun' eight hundred on me last night."

"Eight hunnert! Sweet Jesus! Maybe the cabby—"

"Hell with it. Too late now. Lissen, it gets dark, you help me get to my place. I need clothes, a bath, and a real doctor. I got plenty of Horse stashed away there. You goin'a stay there with me a while 'til I c'n get myself squared away. Okay?"

"Sure, Buddy. Sounds great to me."

Once in his own apartment, he phoned Lucky Powers, who brought him his $11,000, representing his original $4,000 and the $7,200 in winnings at 9-to-5 odds, less Lucky's commission for having scattered the numerous bets among the bookmakers. During the next four weeks he remained in seclusion with Lorella except for two visits to his own doctor, who had examined him thoroughly, X-rayed his ribs and left hand, patching and setting the latter as best he could and placing it in a cast.

Lorella cooked for him, ran the errands he required, gave him a fix when he needed it, until he had his own doctor trim the plaster cast back far enough so that he could manipulate his fingers sufficiently to handle the hypodermic himself. It came to him then that to continue to live in New

148

York meant eventual financial ruin. Buddy had already accepted the fact that his ring career was over and he must make a decision about the future, and soon. He made it on the night he and Lorella lay in bed watching a televised sports broadcast on which it was announced that the State Boxing Commission had released the Spyros-Duke purse. Buddy knew he would never see a cent of his share of the money. To attempt to get it from Saxon would be courting physical disaster at the hands of Al's goons, even death.

The next day, he cleaned out his safety deposit box and closed out his bank account. Lorella packed his clothes and ring mementos and had the apartment house doorman lock them into the trunk and rear compartment of the Jaguar.

In a burst of generosity, Duke gave Lorella his furniture and $500 in cash. His last act was to lay in a supply of heroin that would last him until he could make a new connection elsewhere. This he carefully wrapped in cellophane packages, overwrapped with heavy brown paper and taped to the underside of the front and back seats of his car. With the balance of his cash in a money belt fastened around his waist, he began driving southward toward his father's home in Laurelton, Georgia.

He had taken the precaution to buy a chauffeur's uniform in case someone stopped him anywhere below Washington. In that event, he would pose as a chauffeur to a wealthy white family who had preceded him to their winter home in Florida by plane.

Adios, New York, scene of his greatest triumphs. And now, failure.

149

CHAPTER VI

1

The clearance and separation process at Fort Meade had moved routinely and endlessly, and finally Corey Armour found himself in a cab with three other officers, heading toward Washington to begin their period of terminal leave and transition into civilian life, still in uniform and unable to adjust to the idea of divorcement from the military.

His three companions were busy making plans for an evening celebration on the town and Corey found himself tempted to join them, but finally decided against it. What he had in mind was a preterminal-leave period of solitude, if only for twenty-four hours. He had made a reservation on the next day's early morning flight to Atlanta and was reluctant to change his plans. The other three seemed not to mind in the least, and when they reached Washington, Corey checked into the Statler, suddenly grateful to be alone and on his own.

He showered leisurely and toweled himself dry. In the full-length mirror, the first he had seen in over two years, he examined his body with care, noting the transformations since he had left home, lingering over the scar that would forever remind him of an unbelievable moment when a Viet Cong had leaped up out of a tangle of undergrowth and fired his rifle at point-blank range. At that precise moment, immobilized by the sight of a young, grim, determined face in front of him, Corey had frozen in his tracks, unable to squeeze the trigger of the carbine in his hands, thinking, "He's a child!" Feeling the impact of the bullet as it struck his chest and, falling, heard the fusillade of shots from a sub-machine gun behind him as the Viet Cong was cut down, a distant voice calling, "Medic! Medic! Here—" Then darkness.

Well, Corey thought as he fingered the now-thin line, they did a hell of a job. He remembered the serious, middle-aged surgeon who dropped by later to examine his own handiwork, the professional satisfaction in his voice as he said unsmilingly, "Well, Lieutenant, if you keep quiet about it and don't wear any low-cut formal gowns, only you, your wife, your girl friends and I will know about it."

The lung and wound had healed well. Medically, physically, he was sound as he had ever been. There were other changes, he noticed. His shoulders had broadened, his chest expanded, and the twelve or fifteen additional pounds he was carrying now, thankfully, were evenly distributed over his six-foot-one-inch frame. Except for the narrow band of white across his hips, his body was burned to a slightly deeper shade than his tawny hair. His gray eyes were more sober now, perhaps reflecting the memories of what they had seen during the combat portion of his stay in Viet Nam, the filth and misery in the villages, towns, in Saigon itself. A certain sober hardness had taken the place of boyishness in his 27-year-old face, giving him a more distinct resemblance to his father; firm, strong chin, straight nose, wide well-formed mouth, ears close to his head. His hair had a way of springing forward, extending over his forehead like a canopy, and he had long ago given up trying to train it to lie back.

There was little in his face, apart from the gray eyes, to remind him of his mother, Catherine, whom he had always called Caddy, and who had died when he was 19 and a sophomore at the University; Caddy, because she had encouraged him to call her "Cathy," but at that very early stage in his life, the best he could manage was "Caddy." And so Caddy she had become to her friends from that time until her death; but he recalled now that Kenneth had never addressed her by any name other than Catherine, nor could he remember any form of endearment coupled to, or substituted for, her name.

It seemed to Corey that his parents had always lived a life of formal estrangement, bound together by conventional vows of marriage, by invisible chains of necessity or convenience, without an open show of love, sentiment or the many obvious signs of affection normally exchanged between husbands and wives; a sudden unexpected kiss, a certain secret smile, a touch of hands that silently attested to their oneness. At home, there was little conversation between Kenneth and Catherine. More than often, table talk was between Catherine and Corey, or Kenneth and Corey, seldom between Kenneth and Catherine. Kenneth's business day was never discussed, nor was Catherine's work on her various clubs and committees.

The Armours entertained at small dinners and parties, but it seemed to Corey that on these occasions his parents were like actors playing out well-rehearsed parts as host and hostess. They circulated among their friends and engaged in lively conversations with various groups, but if one took careful note, Kenneth and Catherine were seldom together in the same group or involved in the same discussion.

It came to Corey later that his parents actually disliked each other and, apart from himself and material possessions, had very little in common. Alone with him, each had much to say, to discuss, but never when the three were together as a family unit. Each showered him with gifts for almost any reason, and even in this they seemed to be competing for his attention and love.

Corey grew into his high school years with the realization that his was a home without genuine love, warmth and devotion, a fact that became immediately obvious when he spent an occasional night at Polk Holderby's house, or stayed overnight with Sam Driscoll or Les Delevan, conscious of the ease between their parents, their interest in each other, their children, sharing bits of inconsequential information as though it were of utmost importance.

To postpone an inevitable act, Corey decided to shave, but so close to going home, he could not banish his thoughts. Since Caddy's death, he had actually had little contact with Kenneth. After her funeral, he had returned to the University and thrown himself into his studies, with tennis and swimming his major forms of relaxation. During the following summer, Kenneth had gone abroad on business for the Warren Company, and Corey had turned down his invitation to accompany him. Nor did he accept Bruce's invitation to spend a second summer at Loon Lake. Drew was 18 then, and was taking a guided tour of Europe, and Corey, remembering the summer before, decided the lake wouldn't be the same without her. Instead, he took his delayed driving trip through the COW states—California, Oregon and Washington—and made it back barely in time to return to the University.

When he finished shaving, he slipped into a robe and stretched out on the comfortable bed, smoked a cigarette to delay making the phone call. It was strange, he thought, how clearly he could see Kenneth now, remembering him only as a dictatorial, arbitrary and ambition-ridden man.

If, he asked himself now, I were asked to write my father's biography, what could I say of him? Principally, that I was never really acquainted with him; that we had never been more than intimate strangers, with decreasing intimacy from the time I discovered he was being unfaithful to Caddy with Shana Pierce. And again, as often in the past, he wondered how long Caddy had known about Shana before she died?

152

Corey's first knowledge of Kenneth's adulterous conduct had come when he was 15. The summer came to an end and he had entered his second year at Laurelton High, now the proud possessor of his very own imported Garland 12-gauge shotgun, a birthday present from Kenneth.

On a bright fall day, a Saturday, Kenneth had left the house early, purportedly on a business trip to Augusta. Corey and Polk, who was 16 and driving his own cutdown Ford, drove up into the Shadow Hills area to hunt for quail and doves. They ranged over the heavily wooded Halstead land, paused to rest and eat their lunch, then came down-slope onto Crane land without having sighted any game at all. They came over a rise and through a grove of thick pines and then spotted the sturdy hunting lodge Selwyn Crane had had built years ago.

"Hey! That belongs to us!" Corey exclaimed. "My Grandfather Selwyn left it to my mother. And all this stuff around it."

"Let's explore it," Polk suggested.

"Okay." They followed the valley through the pine trees and into the cleared area that immediately surrounded the lodge, now dense with tall grass and weeds. Polk tried the front door, but it proved to be locked. Corey said, "Wait here. I'll go around and try the back door. If it's open, I'll come through and open the front door for you."

To the right of the lodge, inside a small grove of trees, Corey saw the car parked, almost as though an attempt had been made to hide it. For a moment, he hesitated, then curiosity got the better of him. He mounted the back steps quietly.

The back door was unlocked. Corey entered the shade-drawn kitchen cautiously, feeling his way into the larger main room. He heard a sound of movement off in the bedroom on the right and tiptoed toward it noiselessly.

What confronted him when he pushed the door open with the barrel of his Garland was a scene he would never be able to wipe out of his mind—the blanched face of his father, arms outstretched in a vain effort to shield the naked body of Shana Pierce with a blanket.

"Corey!" Kenneth exclaimed. "My God, Corey, what are you doing up here?"

Corey stood frozen in the doorway, unable to speak, numbed all over, the shotgun still aimed ahead of him, directly at Kenneth's chest; and heard Kenneth's fearful cry, "Corey! For God's sake, don't—"

Then he recovered, turned and fled. He slammed the

153

back door, ran around to the front porch and called to Polk. "Come on, let's get out of here, quick!"

"What's up?" Polk asked excitedly. "Somebody's in there. I heard voices."

"Let's get away from here. Somebody busted in. Two men. They're drunk and have guns. One of 'em said he'd b-blow my head off."

"Hell, we've got guns, too," Polk declared bravely.

"Polk, they're mean as hell. They'll kill us."

"Well, let's hide in the woods and wait for 'em."

"No! I want to get home and tell m-my—d-dad."

"You said he was going to Augusta this weekend."

"I m-mean my m-mother. She'll call the sheriff."

"Hell, they'll be gone by then, Corey—"

"I don't give a d-damn. Let's get out of here. Now."

Corey, of course, said nothing to Caddy on his return home. Two hours later, Kenneth appeared, fully composed, and explained to Catherine that he had decided against going to Augusta and had taken care of the matter from his office by telephone. Catherine didn't seem to care one way or the other and rang for Tish, to tell her that Mr. Armour would be home for dinner.

"Where is Corey?" Kenneth asked.

"Upstairs in his room," Catherine replied and turned back to her book.

When he knocked on Corey's door, there was no reply. "Corey?"

No answer.

"Corey, please."

No answer.

"Corey, I know you're in there. I've got to talk with you."

Then Corey replied, "Go away! I don't want to talk to you!"

Kenneth went away.

Until Christmas of that year, Corey never spoke a word to his father unless a direct question was asked him, and to which he replied with the fewest words possible. He was spared the Thanksgiving holiday when Kenneth was called to New York during that week. At other times in Kenneth's presence, Corey made an overly display of affection for Caddy, which made her very happy; and if she took any notice of the strained feeling between son and father, she did not comment on the fact.

On Christmas morning, there was the usual exchange of gifts. Corey's to Kenneth was a suede hunting jacket which Catherine had chosen for him at Weinstock's Men's Shop.

154

Among Kenneth's gifts to Corey were a new Drummond rifle, a Spalding Champion racket, and a cashmere sweater. His final gift came at the breakfast table when Kenneth handed Corey a box that contained a miniature model of a Ford convertible. Corey's eyebrows raised upward, questioning a toy at his age. Then Kenneth said, "Lift the trunk lid, Corey."

In the trunk was a folded certificate for a new Ford convertible, adult size, to be delivered to him by Corbin Motors on his 16th birthday in March. Surprise overwhelmed his memory of that Saturday afternoon at Shadow Hills for the moment and he shouted, "H-holy c-cow! Thanks, Dad! Thanks, Caddy!" waving the certificate toward Catherine.

"Very nice," was Catherine's quiet remark, remaining aloof. "Thank your father, Corey. This was his own idea. I didn't know about it until this minute."

Corey turned back to Kenneth. "Thank you, Dad," he repeated, adding truthfully, "Gee, I don't know what to say."

"It's all right, Corey. Enjoy your presents for now. We can talk about it later."

"About what, sir?"

"Well—about—well, on your birthday, there will be a gasoline credit card to go with the car, an increase in your allowance—"

So Corey realized that this was not really a gift, but a bribe for his continued silence and, hopefully, an end to the breach between them.

He had finished the cigarette and the act of snuffing it out broke his train of thought. He reached for the telephone and placed the person-to-person call to let Kenneth Armour know he was back in the United States. He waited, listening to the dialogue between the local operator and the long distance information operator, then the Laurelton operator, feeling closer to home now than he had since he left it. Then he heard the familiar singsong cadence of Tish's voice. "Mist' Armour's raysidance," and "No, ma'am, you fin' Mist' Armour at his office this time-a day. Yes'm. South Laurelton 4000. You welcome."

A few minutes and three voices later, he heard one whose businesslike crispness had not been dimmed by absence. "Mr. Armour's office."

"I have a long distance call, person-to-person, from Washington, D.C., for Mr. Kenneth Armour."

"Who is calling, please?"

Corey waited, listening for the reaction. "Mr. Corey Armour," the operator said. "Is Mr. Kenneth Armour there, please?"

He heard the sharp intake of Shana Pierce's breath, as distinctly as if she were in his room, then, "Corey? Corey Armour? Please put him on, Operator."

"The call is for Mr. Kenneth Armour, Miss. Is he there?" the operator replied with a hint of restrained impatience in her voice.

"Mr. Armour is out of his office at the moment. I'll take the call. Tell Mr. Corey Armour it is—"

Corey broke in then. "Shana?" He heard a *click!* and Shana's voice was cut off. The operator said, "Mr. Kenneth Armour can't be reached, sir. Will you speak with anyone else?"

"Yes, Operator, to the person who answered." There was another *click!*-ing and he heard Shana saying, "—and please reverse the charges to this number, Operator."

"Hello, Shana?"

"Corey! Whatever in the world are you doing in *Washington?* We haven't heard from you for two months."

"Where is Dad, Shana?"

"He's in an important meeting with Mr. Theodore. Hold on and I'll put you through to him."

"If he's tied up with Mr. Warren, don't bother, Shana."

"I expect him back in his office in less than an hour. Let me ring you back then. Where are you staying?"

"The Statler, but I don't think I'll be here an hour from now—"

"Corey, please—" He could sense the rebuke in her voice, then, "When are you coming home? Are you still in the Army or out?"

"A little of both. I'm leaving here tomorrow morning for Atlanta and Laurelton."

"Wonderful! Give me your flight number and time of arrival. I'll have the company plane meet you at the airport in Atlanta and—"

"Don't bother, Shana. I'd much rather rent a car and drive up. If nothing else interferes, I should be home in time for dinner. Will you please give Dad the message. If he's free, I'll see him then."

"You know he will be." Again a shading of reproval. "I'll warn Tish. She'll want to prepare something special for your homecoming, I know."

"You do that, Shana, and thanks. Uh—tell Dad I'm sorry I missed him. I've got to hang up now. Good—"

"Wait, Corey, please. There are so many things your father will want to know—"

156

"They'll keep until tomorrow night."

"Is there anyone special you want me to call?"

"I think not. I'll take care of that when I get home. By the way, do you know if Wayne Taylor or John Curran is in town?"

"I ran into Mr. Taylor yesterday, but I don't know about Mr. Curran. Is there anything I can do, phone—?"

"No, thank you. That can wait, too. I've got to go now."

"Corey—"

He replaced the receiver with her voice still in his ears, wondering what his meeting with Kenneth would be like; speculating over Kenneth's anger and disappointment when he returned from Europe in the fall of '65 to learn that Corey had answered his induction call despite Kenneth's assurances that indefinite delays could be "arranged."

Home.

He thought of the hundreds of times he had heard the word on the lips of sons and fathers who had spoken it with holy reverence during his tour of duty. Home was Pittsburgh, Denver, Shoshone, Miami, Four Corners, New York, Tucson, Los Angeles, Salt Lake City. Home was a mansion, a farmhouse, a cottage, a shack on a mountainside, an apartment, a slum tenement. But it was home. Where love waited. Love in the vision of a wife, father, mother, sweetheart, mistress, brothers, sisters, children. Once, a pet.

Home for Corey was—what?

And then he remembered that he hadn't asked Shana if Lyle Emerson and Drew Warren were in Laurelton.

2

Again the morning heat was unseasonably oppressive, the gunmetal sky clear but for a few scattered clouds. The check-in clerk clamped a tag around the handles of Corey's heavy flight bag, stapled the claim check to his ticket envelope and pushed it across the counter toward him with a professional flourish, flashing a practiced mechanical smile. "Gate No. 20, Lieutenant," he said. "You'll be boarding in about ten minutes. Have a nice flight and thank you for flying Delta."

Corey pocketed the ticket, threw his light raincoat casually over one shoulder and walked toward the departure gate, stopping at the newsstand to pick up a copy of the Washington *Post*. The front page was divided between the war news in Viet Nam, several student clashes on various campuses, a Black Power demonstration in Oakland over

157

the arrest of a young militant who had shot a policeman, a pronouncement by a moderate civil rights leader that peace in the streets was becoming more difficult to maintain and predicting an extension of the long hot summer into winter.

He heard his flight announced over the public address system and followed the stream of passengers down the steps and across the smooth macadam to the plane, boarded at the forward section and trailed a shapely blonde stewardess along the aisle to a double seat in the first-class compartment. When the stewardess halted, an attractive young woman was already safety-belted into the window seat, staring out over the field. "I'm sorry, Miss," the stewardess said with a brilliant smile, "I'm afraid yours is the aisle seat. This gentleman—"

The young woman looked up, wide-eyed. Corey said, "Don't bother, please, it's not important."

The stewardess smiled, the young woman smiled, Corey smiled and the uniformed beauty who, Corey thought, reminded him of someone out of the past, took his raincoat and went about her duties. Corey sat in the aisle seat. His companion said, "Thank you very much, Lieutenant," and he replied briefly, "Don't mention it."

"This is my very first plane ride," she volunteered, "ever."

"It should be an experience to remember."

"Oh, I'm sure it will be. I—I'm nervous inside."

"There's really nothing to be nervous about," Corey said in his most reassuring voice, remembering other flights over water, jungles seeded with enemy guns, suspicious of every cloud in the sky, eyes alert for possible enemy antiaircraft guns and missiles. "The odds are a thousand to one in our favor."

"It's silly, I know." She laughed self-consciously. "My husband has just finished his flight training and is about to be shipped out for advanced training. I'm going to Atlanta to meet him."

He tuned her out while unfolding his *Post*, unwilling to be drawn into a conversation about the war, then her attention was drawn back to the window as the first of the motors was started. Moments later they were moving toward the long, flat black runway and took off without incident. Once aloft, seat belts unfastened, cigarettes lighted, Corey settled back in relaxed comfort and scanned the news from Viet Nam. Names of cities, towns and villages swam back through his mind, some remembered only by names invented for easier identification; Cut Plug, Flat Feet, Toe Crud, Bubo. From the page before him were more realistic

158

names he could identify with realistic places; Da Nang, Ia Drang, Haiphong, Pleiku, Hué. Aplong Hoi popped into his mind from nowhere, conjuring up the faces of Cord Waters and Lyle Emerson, of desperate men who hunted other desperate men through jungles and rice paddies.

Remembering.

Lyle's guilt over Cord's sacrifice.

"Back home," Lyle had said one day in the hospital, "I wasn't even aware he was alive. Even if I'd known him there, I don't know if I'd have given him much more than the time of day. And now—now—what's left of me, my life, I owe to him."

"He'd have done it for anyone, Lyle—" Corey began, but Lyle was too deeply immersed in guilt and self-pity to hear him.

"I wish he had been one of my pupils so I could have known him better," Emerson went on. "I didn't know him from Adam until he was sent down from the north as a replacement, but he damn well knew me, recognized me at first sight the day he reported in. I remember so little about the whole thing. I knew we were down and I'd been hit. I blacked out and came to while he was lugging me over to the pickup sling. I tried to warn him. 'Watch out, boy, they always leave one or two behind to pick off rescue crews,' something like that, and he just laughed and said, 'Hell, Mist' Emerson, just don't fuss and I'll have you out of here in no time.' I can't remember exactly. 'Can't leave no Laurelton man here to die. Ain't enough of us out here.' He called me *Mister* Emerson, not Lieutenant, as though we were back home."

Corey wondered now if Lyle had returned to Laurelton to his teaching job, still bitter and guilt-ridden, the artificial leg a lasting reminder of his assumed debt; or if he had gone to New York to try to find Jill Tinsley and try for a reconciliation. He hoped not. And turned his attention to the story of the death of a Negro in a jail cell in a town called Wetumpka in Alabama, wondering what the situation was like in Laurelton, recalling reading of recent riots in Atlanta, the most progressive Southern city of them all. And if Atlanta, why not Laurelton?

He was interrupted by a lunch tray passed across him to the young woman in the window seat, an orderly arrangement of food that looked like a colored advertisement in a magazine, each compartment neatly separated from the next to appeal to the eye, if not the taste. He declined politely, to the apparent disappointment of the pretty stewardess, and asked only for coffee. Out of the corner of his left eye he

159

watched his seat companion attack and devour her meal without any trace of nervousness.

He watched the blonde stewardess moving up and down the aisle, handling food trays expertly while her raven-haired partner served coffee. The blonde, whose name, according to the plastic strip she wore over her beautifully formed breast, was Dietrich, reminded him, when he saw her splendid figure from the back, of Paula Corbin, bringing back another memory; and he knew that from now on, no matter where, all scenes, people, colors, sounds and odors would forever remind him of similar or opposing scenes, people, colors, sounds and odors. The sound of pain, song, laughter, crying, wind, rain; the color of early dawn, sunset, a midnight sky, tree-green, rose-red, raw earth, land scorched by napalm, plowed by bombs, torn by mines, sown with artillery shells; the odors of flowers, animals, filth, human sweat, the perfume of young girls turned to an ancient war trade; of death.

The blonde Miss Dietrich, who reminded him of Paula Corbin, came back to remove the lunch trays—

September. The summer behind him, his freshman year at the University ahead, the hurry and bustle in preparation for departure and the adventure of living away from home. Catherine's endless fussing over his clothes; new suits, slacks, sports jackets, shirts, ties, shoes. From Kenneth, his own checking account. ("—and for heaven's sake, don't write a check unless there's enough to cover it. When you're down to $200 drop me a line and I'll have Sh— I'll deposit more to your account.") Tennis rackets being restrung. Last minute good-byes to friends leaving earlier for Duke, the University of North Carolina, Virginia, Pennsylvania and elsewhere. A complete "physical" for his car at Corbin Motors.

"Don't worry, Corey," Paul Corbin assured him. "We'll go over it from top to bottom, front and back. She'll be standing here waiting for you on Thursday afternoon. Sharp as new."

"Thanks, Mr. Corbin, I appreciate it. I've been away all summer—"

"I know. Great time in your life, Corey, going away to college. My Paula will be down there, too. You know Paula, don't you?"

"Yes, of course—" He remembered Paula vaguely, blonde, popular with her own crowd but had never been part of his own. Polk had dated her several times, he recalled.

"First time she's ever been away from home on her own. I'd appreciate it if you'd look in on her once in a while, just to get her over being homesick, you know."

"Uh—sure, Mr. Corbin, glad to. I'll check on where she'll be staying as soon as I get settled."

"Thanks. Grace is kind of upset about it, but somewhere, sometime, I keep telling her, you've got to turn loose of a child. To Grace, the outside world is a kind of big beartrap for a young girl, particularly when she's an only daughter."

"I understand—"

"You driving down to Athens alone?"

"Well, yes. The other fellows all want their cars with them, so—"

"For all of Corbin Motors, Grace can't see letting Paula have her own car there her first year. Claims it's a distraction from study, and a hundred other reasons. Would you mind driving her down? She won't have much luggage. I'm shipping most of her stuff."

Corey was reluctant, but could see no way out. "I'd be happy to have her. No trouble and there's plenty of room in the car."

"Thanks, Corey. One more thing. She's kind of an independent little cuss. If she thought I was arranging this—"

He phoned Paula that evening, mildly surprised that she remembered him at all, and received a delighted acceptance of his offer to drive her to Athens. The next morning, watching her bid farewell to a tearful Grace and self-conscious Paul Corbin, he was even more surprised by the sight of a very attractive young sophisticate who was dressed casually in an oatmeal-colored skirt with matching sweater, windblown honey-colored hair and exquisite legs. Perhaps a shade too tall, wearing alligator flats to cut her height.

"Too much wind for your hair, Paula? I can run the top up—"

"No, please don't. I love it on a day like this." She talked of her month at Nag's Head with Grace, the evidence of it showing in her even, golden tan. "You spent the summer up at Loon Lake with the Warren kids, didn't you?"

He was amused by her reference to Bruce and Drew as "kids," but let it pass. "Yes. How did you know?"

"Les Delevan is my cousin. He told me about the week he spent there. You didn't get back in time for the Labor Day Tennis Tournament at the Club."

"We didn't leave the Lake until the day after. Were you there?"

"Yes. We're not members, but Les invited me. Everybody

161

was disappointed that you weren't there. Are you going out for the Varsity Team?"

"If I can find the time."

"How about the swimming team?"

Corey laughed and said, "You know a lot more about me than I know about you. It's not fair."

"Well," Paula said slyly, "there are ways to correct that now that you're breaking away from your clique."

Corey passed it over and concentrated on the road. "I guess you'll be going for Law, won't you?" Paula said.

"Yes. How about you?"

"Liberal Arts. Mother's all for music, art or teaching. Dad suggested Sociology. What I'd like to do is take Business Ec and Administration."

"Are you planning to take over Corbin Motors some day?"

She laughed prettily. "Lord, no. I'd like to run a business of my own. A smart dress shop for teen-agers and young adults. I think my taste is good enough—"

"On that I agree."

"—for the buying end, but I'm short on how to *run* a business, the accounting and management. I'm sure I can sell—"

"Well, then, why not?"

"Mother. She's culture-conscious. She thinks a woman in business has got to be either queer or a whore."

Coming as it did, Corey was at first mildly shocked by Paula's outspokenness, then found that he was titillated by it. "I'll work it out some way when I get to Athens," Paula added. "If it comes to the worst, I can always hire somebody to handle that end of it for me."

An independent little cuss, Paul Corbin had said, and now Corey was in full agreement. He was sure Paula would one day have her dress shop. And almost anything else she wanted. He was further shocked when Paula said suddenly, "Dad set this up, didn't he? You calling to offer to drive me down, I mean."

"What makes you think that?"

"How else? All through Laurelton High you didn't know I was alive."

"I'm beginning to wonder how *that* happened."

"Well, you had your clique, I had mine. You divided your time between the Club and the Warrens, Willards and the rest of the social bigwigs. I guess there wasn't time enough. Anyway, Dad and Mother wouldn't let me have a car my first year, so I simply guessed that Dad put the bite on Mr. Eligible."

"It wasn't a bite, Paula. I'm glad he suggested it."

"That makes it much nicer."

As planned, Corey roomed with Polk Holderby, recently returned from abroad with a new bagful of incredibly stimulating, if true, sexual encounters that had erupted in England, inflamed France, blitzed Switzerland and left a blazing path through Italy. No one of their acquaintance could even approach Polk's claims of achievement and he was aptly christened Ding Dong Daddy.

By comparison, Corey's summer at Loon Lake, the incident with Lucas Warren omitted, was a brief, dull recital. "You mean you wasted a whole summer with those Warren creeps?" Polk asked in disbelief.

"That makes me a creep, Polk. I enjoyed every minute of it and got in a full summer of tennis and swimming."

"You get into Drew Warren, too?"

"You're out of line, Polk—"

"Boy, you're getting touchy in your old age, aren't you?"

"Let's just keep things in order, shall we?" To prevent further coolness, "You going out for anything this year?"

"If you mean athletics," Polk replied, "the answer is, hell, no. I've got to buckle down and come up with a minimum C-plus average."

"How come the sudden burst of scholastic interest for a swordsman like you?"

"A deal with Dad. Wait'll you see the new MG he bought me in London. A real nuclear bomb. It's coming over by boat sometime later this month. But I've got to sweat it out with a C-plus or better before I can call it mine, all mine. Hey, I'm counting on you for some help, chum."

"You think you'll be able to spare the time from your girl-watching?"

Until the MG arrived, Polk divided his open time between study and luring not unwilling campus queens into rewarding situations. After Thanksgiving, it became apparent that an F was more likely than a C-plus. Cutting a flashy figure in his fire-engine-red MG, Polk was heading for a straight A in Sex I, and in his own words, "Man, this is like turning a fox loose in a hen-house," offering Corey his choice among the conquered.

"Polk," Corey said emphatically, "will you for Christ's sake quit pimping for me? What's more, if you don't start burying your nose in a few books instead of maneuvering that thing of yours in questionable places—"

"Don't start running my life for me, Corey," Polk retorted. "The books, the classes, the lectures will all be here forever, but this *stuff*, man, it goes to seed fast if you don't tend to your weeding, hoeing and watering."

Corey, as promised, looked in on Paula, and found it no chore, but impossible to share Paul or Grace Corbin's concern over her possible homesickness. Paula had taken to college life with a zest and came up with a cordon of male and female friends, plus bids to the liveliest sororities.

In the Campus Coffee Shop one morning, Corey was reading a chatty letter he had received from Drew when Paula put a tray down on the table and slipped into the chair beside him. He put the letter away and helped her arrange the items from her tray.

"I saw you on the courts yesterday afternoon," Paula said. "You were terrific, taking Bill Hagen 6-0, 6-2. He's top-seeded."

"I was lucky. Next time, he'll probably take me."

"If he does, I'll lose the ten dollars I won on you yesterday."

"You *bet* on me?"

"Why not? I'm a sucker for a sure thing."

"Paula—"

"No lectures, Dad. I'm a bad enough winner, but a worse loser. I hate to lick my own wounds. Are you busy Saturday night?"

"Not particularly. Why?"

"I sort of promised the girls at the House I'd ask you to our party. They're dying to meet our next tennis champ close up."

"Did you bet on that, too?"

"Only with myself. Do I win or lose?"

Corey laughed. "You win. 6-0, 6-0."

Polk was there with a girl from Montgomery to whom he was paying adoring attention, broken only by Corey's entrance. From across the room Polk called out, "Hey, Corey! Come on over." With an arm intimately curled around Miss Montgomery's waist, "Meet my Southern-fried friend, Marybelle Gibson, Alabama's loss to the sovereign state of Georgia. Marybelle, this is Corey Armour, one of Laurelton's more notorious child molesters."

"My, my," Marybelle said in simulated awe, and which came out as, "Mah, mah," "how int'restin' to be with real celebrities. Are you as impo'tant as Poke heah?"

"Whah, Miss Gibson," Polk mimicked, "he's mo' impotent than—"

Corey cut him short. "No one here is as important as Polk, Marybelle. He's No. 2 on the Dean's Most Unwanted List, trying for the No. 1 spot."

"You know," Marybelle said, "I'm sure he'll make it befo' th' night is ovah."

"Well," Polk admitted, "I'm sure by God goin'a give it one hell of a try. Who you with, Corey?"

"Paula. See her around anywhere?"

"A few minutes ago, playing hostess. How come you're reduced to us common folks?"

"I'm doing a term paper on beatnik life among the underprivileged. See you-all later."

He found Paula and went through the ritual of introductions to the house mother and a bevy of Paula's sorority sisters, danced, had several spiked drinks being served from a car in the parking area, walked out with Paula to his car for a few experimental kisses and found the entire evening thoroughly enjoyable and refreshing.

He began seeing Paula more regularly, timing himself to meet her casually on campus, in the coffee shop, looking for her in the stands when he played tennis, inviting her to off-campus dinners that were eminently more satisfying than on-campus meals. When the football season got into full swing, they went to the games together, celebrated victories and comforted each other over defeats.

They drove from Athens to Atlanta for the Georgia-Georgia Tech game, which Georgia lost by a missed point after touchdown, 14 to 13, and ducked the post-game party at the home of a student friend to which they had been invited. Instead, they enjoyed a dinner at an excellent restaurant with two other couples, then slipped away to a movie and returned to their hotel before midnight. At Paula's door, something entirely unplanned, at least by Corey, occurred.

He unlocked the door, withdrew the key and handed it to Paula. She took it and said, "Thanks, Corey, it's been a wonderful day and evening. I'm glad we didn't go to the party."

"I am, too. I enjoyed—"

She leaned forward, offering her mouth, and he kissed her, but somehow, this was no ordinary kiss she returned. It was gentle, yet eager and lingering, unlike any kiss she had given him before. His arms tightened and drew her closer and she came willingly, then backed into the room, taking him with her. He closed the door while partly in Paula's embrace, knowing that tonight they would touch all bases, yet was hesitant to turn the first corner. The bed had been turned down and the bedside lamp threw a circle of light on pillows, blanket and exposed sheets, enhancing the picture

165

and mood. Her brief, silky nightgown lay across the bed, tempting, inviting.

"Paula—" Corey whispered, but the word was brushed aside by her lips on his. He responded avidly, hands exploring beneath the sweater under her suit jacket, caressing her firm breasts gently as Paula pressed toward him.

"Oh, Corey." A sigh with no hint of protest.

"What, Paula?"

"I want to tell you this. You're not forcing me to do anything I don't want to do. It's just that I made up my mind some time ago exactly who I wanted to do it with."

"You really know what you're saying?"

"I should. I've listened to others talk about it since I was fourteen. I've read all about it. Now I want to feel it for myself. With you."

"Paula, how could I not want to—"

"Look, I know it isn't love, but I've never really believed sex and love are necessarily one and the same thing. At times, yes, but not always. I don't like to sound too direct about it. All I want to do is find out for myself what it's all about."

Again, Corey was hearing Paul Corbin's voice, *"She's an independent little cuss"* as she went to the bed and removed her wool suit, blouse, shoes and stockings and stood in bra and half-slip. She took up her nightgown with an impish flicker of a smile and went to the bathroom door, turned and said, "Allow me this last show of modesty, which I expect to overcome very quickly."

Corey, midway between urgency and numbness, undressed and got into bed. When Paula appeared in the filmy gown, he asked, "Shall I turn the lights off?"

"No," Paula replied easily, "there's no point to it if I can't see what I'm doing." Corey held up the covers as she slipped in beside him, trembling lightly with anticipation, yet unafraid.

He discovered soon that there were two Paulas. The casual, on-campus Paula, and the charmingly rowdy, uninhibited Paula with whom he shared beds in a motel or an Atlanta hotel, where her character seemed to change completely. Alone and together, she was sensual and even her language became bawdily flavored without becoming coarse. She gave herself wantonly to the sex act, and at first Corey reacted with mild, puritanical shock to the small obscenities she uttered in uncontrolled passion.

On campus, their behavior was most circumspect; so proper that Polk suspected a blossoming serious romance.

Despite his numerous conquests, Polk seemed to resent Corey's takeover of Paula, whom Polk had dated occasionally at Laurelton High and felt he had some prior rights. He challenged Corey's position by trying to date Paula, who rejected him pleasantly, politely, and firmly.

"Hey, chum," Polk said one night from his study desk, "you got some kind of an Indian sign on Paula?"

Corey grinned. "In our society, son, the female of the species generally makes the choice of a mate."

"So much for the psychological horseshit. What I'm asking is, are you getting inside her pants?"

Corey closed a textbook and put his pen down. "You want to start a priest-confessor relationship with me, boy?"

"Well, Jesus Christ, what the hell are you getting so touchy about?"

"It's just that I don't like childish snap judgments or opinions. If we're going to continue rooming together, you can share my ties and socks and anything else that fits, but not my private life."

"Okay, okay," Polk grumbled. He got up and went out of the room, slamming the door behind him. From that point on, a certain coolness developed between them.

At Christmastime, Polk asked Paula if he could drive her home for the holiday and she turned him down. "I'm sorry, Polk," she lied, "I'm driving up with Corey. He asked me weeks ago."

She said it unconvincingly and Polk tried to trap Corey. "You driving anybody home next week, Corey?" he asked innocently.

"I haven't made any definite plans yet. You want a lift?"

"No, I'm driving the MG up. Just asking."

There was no reason for Corey to suspect Polk's idle curiosity until he compared notes with Paula and became aware that he had inadvertently allowed her to become trapped in a lie. He debated taking issue with Polk, but decided to let the matter drop. To mitigate the fact, Corey took on two more car-less passengers besides Paula to Laurelton. It was not until they were en route that he began thinking, not without some guilt, of Drew Warren. He knew that Paula would be involved with family, relatives and friends; that he would, as usual, be included with Kenneth and Catherine at Anderson Warren's annual Christmas dinner at Brookhill and the Warren New Year's Eve party at the country club.

Corey's reunion with Kenneth and Catherine was an enjoyable experience at the beginning, but after that first

167

night, everything returned to normal, the atmosphere between his parents as cool as ever, avoiding each other except when he was present. Catherine had seen to his dinner clothes and accessories for the two formal occasions. He drove out to see Drew, rode with her and was delighted, after nearly four months, to find an exciting maturity developing in her. It also surprised him to learn that Bruce, whom he had scarcely seen in Athens, had flown to Miami Beach for the holiday, breaking a family tradition of years. For some reason, Bruce's defection annoyed him, almost as much as his unaccountable guilt about Paula. He tried to make up for it by spending more time with Drew.

At the Brookhill Christmas dinner were the usual Company officers, members of the board of directors and their wives. The discussions were centered mainly on business, in which the men participated actively while their wives sat patiently and restlessly through it all, as they did every year. And as usual, Catherine sat stiffly aloof and withdrawn. At its end, Theodore, who had remained quiet throughout, disappeared upstairs. Drew took Corey to her sitting room on the second floor, a respite from the incessant talk below.

"Dreary, wasn't it?" Drew said.

"Deadly," Corey agreed.

"It doesn't seem like anything without Bruce home. I wish he hadn't gone off to Florida like that. She must really be something."

"Who?" he asked innocently.

"The girl, of course. It must be a girl. Don't you see much of Bruce at college?"

"Not often. We don't run in the same crowd. He lives off-campus and—"

"And what have you been doing for excitement?"

"Not much. Classes, study—" again guiltily—"and working out on the indoor courts."

"Did you make the team?"

"I'm not trying for it this year. I'll go out for it seriously next year. What's new in Laurelton?"

"Nothing new. You've been through that before—" She clapped a hand to her mouth and he saw the excitement in her eyes. "You'll never guess what's happened in a million years, Corey. Honestly, the most surprising thing—"

"What?"

"—became engaged a week before Thanksgiving Day," he heard her saying through the rush of words, "and are getting married—"

"Who?"

"—this New Year's Eve! Can you imagine that?"

168

"Great! Wonderful! If I only knew who you were talking about, I'd gladly give my consent."

"Didn't I tell you?"

"So far, you've kept that part of it a deep, dark secret."

Drew laughed, stood up and whirled around happily, her red dress billowing out and up above her splendid knees. Then she was close to him and he drew her down into his lap and kissed her. "Merry Christmas," he said. "Now who were you talking about?"

She burrowed closer, deeper into his arms. "Lucas and Laurellen Warren!" she exclaimed.

"What, those two? They're cousins, aren't they?"

"What difference does that make? They're in love, aren't they? Laurellen wrote me a long letter about it. Bruce and I asked Gran to give them the cottage at Loon Lake for a wedding present. I wanted to write you—"

"Why didn't you?"

"I expected you and Bruce home for Thanksgiving. After that it slipped my mind." She stood up and brushed her gown with her hands. "You'll be at the Club with us New Year's Eve, won't you?"

"I'm not sure of my plans, yet. But I'll see you before then."

"Come out and ride tomorrow? The horses need the exercise. So do I."

"It's a date. I'll check with Mother and Dad about New Year's Eve." Actually, he had planned to ask Paula.

"I can tell you that. They're going to the Club and will be at our table with the Drydens, the Hardings and all the others. The usual people. Please, Corey, I've never been to a real, grownup New Year's Eve party. And I've got a new gown from Atlanta—"

"I'll let you know tomorrow when I see you."

"Don't forget. I've been holding it open for you."

Next morning, he phoned Paula and learned that Grace had already accepted a New Year's Eve date for her with Bob Bennett, in from Columbia. The Bennetts and Corbins were old friends and each year took a table at the Club for that night. "I'll see you there," Corey said. "I'll be with the Warren table."

"With Drew?"

Corey laughed. "Not with Anderson or Theodore, honey."

"Mm-m-m. Is that little barracuda trying you on for size?"

"No more than that Bennett octopus you'll be with."

"Touché. What are you doing later today?"

"Riding at Brookhill with the barracuda. You?"

"I think I'll take a little karate practice to mix in with my judo lessons."

"What about tomorrow?"

"That's Thursday. I'm going shopping with Mother to replenish my beaten and battered wardrobe."

"Friday?"

"Maybe. We'll see."

The New Year's Eve affair at the Laurelton Country Club was, literally and figuratively, a crushing success. Extra tables reduced the dance floor to mere postage-stamp size, packed to sardine-can capacity so that the mass of bodies could move only as a unit. Corey and Paula managed to share two dances, crushed together, shuffling along with the crowd to music they could barely hear.

"Mass vertical sex," Paula whispered loudly into his ear. "It's disgusting."

"I haven't a complaint in the world," Corey replied. "In fact, I find it delightful. Everything so open and aboveboard."

"I wonder," she hazarded, "how many people, at this very moment, are getting laid in public this way?"

He leaned over closer to her ear. "You know, honey, for such a lovely girl, you've got a very dirty mind."

"Don't let it fool you, darling. I'll bet more than half the people in this room are wondering the same thing."

"So close to you, I don't have to wonder about it."

"That's our special chemistry. Mental chemistry and sexual attraction. *Le meme chose*. Do you think we could find a billiard table not in use?"

"Sh-h—don't be so obvious."

"Why not? It saves time."

"Just what do you do with all the time you save?"

"I save it up and squander it making love with you."

"And how are you making out with Bob Bennett?"

"He's trying, but he's only scrub-team material. What about the little barracuda who is eyeing us with daggers?"

"Not a chance. Are you free tomorrow?"

"Well, I'm glad I finally got through to you, but I'm sorry. Last day home. Family doings with relatives. Talk, dinner, talk, gather around the old television set, then off to bed. Pick me up early the day after?"

Corey groaned, remembering. "We'll have a full load going back."

"Oh, well, all is not lost. We'll be back in Athens soon enough. Weekends—"

"Yes."

Polk, Les Delevan, Perry Willard and Sam Driscoll arrived with their dates a few minutes before midnight, their party at the Marina Club having gone dull, adding to the general noise and confusion. Couples drifted back from the game room, library, trophy room, several ousted from the locker rooms by Club guards, wandering in from the parking area and golf course. At exactly midnight, the air was filled with confetti, balloons, screams, shrieks, tears over "Auld Lang Syne," kisses and wishes for the New Year. It seemed hardly to matter who was who or with whom.

Anderson Warren left shortly after midnight, Theodore a few moments later. The other Warren guests were scattered throughout the room. Champagne was flowing like water, the bar crowded six-deep and Corey said to Drew, "For God's sake, let's get out of this madhouse. I feel like I've got a pneumatic drill inside my skull, going full blast."

"Let's," Drew agreed. "This is where the horrible part of the year really begins."

They made their way to Corey's car and drove toward Brookhill. "It's awfully early to end a New Year's Eve, isn't it?" he said.

"New Year's Day," Drew corrected him, "by one hour and thirty-four—five—minutes. Happy New Year, Corey. Did I get to kiss you at midnight?"

"In all that hullabaloo with the lights out, I'm not too sure about you. I know a lot of others did, and vice versa."

"Paula, too?"

"Why not Paula, too?" he asked.

"No special reason, except that I watched you dancing together. Not exactly dancing," she amended. "It was more like a love affair set to music."

Corey felt the warmth of a blush on his face and was grateful for the darkness. "Isn't that a rather adult observation, Drew?"

"In case you haven't noticed lately, I'm a rather adult girl."

"Ah—yes—"

"Corey?"

"What?"

"Are you going to think of me always as a little girl, Bruce's kid sister who was always tagging along?"

"That would be almost impossible after last summer. And seeing you now."

"Then won't you please stop treating me like a child?"

"I wasn't aware I had been. Tell me, how does one not treat a girl as a child?"

171

"You're weaseling. Those last few weeks at Loon Lake, I thought you'd caught on."

"Ah—I don't know of any special way to treat you, Drew. After all, I've known you practically all your life."

"The way you treat Paula. The way you touch her, hold her, look at her."

"That's—uh—chemistry, Drew. I've seen you touch and look at your horse the same way."

"You're being deliberately insufferable. We're not talking about horses. People. You. Me. Paula. Do you see much of her at the University?"

"Your Honor," Corey pronounced mockingly, "I object to this line of questioning as irrelevant, immaterial and having no bearing—"

Drew sat up, her arms encircling his neck. "Don't do that! You want to get us killed?" he exclaimed.

"Then stop the car."

He pulled over to the side of the road and braked the car to a stop, and when he turned to her to remonstrate, Drew kissed him firmly on his lips. "There. Is that relevant and material to the case before the court, Mr. Lawyer?"

"Drew," he said, withdrawing, "you're not only reckless as hell, you're dangerous."

"I hope so."

He was staring into her eyes, the eyes of a woman. And the discovery was worrisome. She moved forward and there was little reluctance on his part this time. He kissed her, lingering, holding her, and finally pulled away silently, started the motor again and drove toward Brookhill swiftly, with Drew close beside him, one arm through his, clutching it tightly.

At the door, he took the key from her and opened it, then stood aside to allow her to enter. "Come in, Corey? New Year's Eves aren't anything without bacon and eggs and coffee—"

"I'd—I'd better not, Drew—"

"Please?"

"No, Drew. I can't."

Her disappointment was not well hidden. "All right, then. Kiss me good night?"

He kissed her lips lightly. "Good night, Drew."

"I love you, Corey," she said.

"Don't say that—"

"Why not? It's true. It's been true for a long time."

Wretchedly, "Drew, you don't know what love is. I think you're confusing it with something else. I'm not sure what—"

"The little sister business again," Drew said, and he saw

172

the glint of humor in her eyes and smile, making him feel young and awkward. "Just remember this, Corey. My grandmother was married to my grandfather when she was sixteen and her first son was born when she was seventeen. I'm eighteen and next year I'll be going down to Athens—"

He stood frozen in the doorway, listening stonily to her words. "Drew—"

"—and I'm going to be your girl. You won't need Paula Corbin or anybody else—"

"Drew, you're being hysterical."

"No, I'm not. Look at me. I'm completely calm and cool. I'm in love with you and you're in love with me and you know it's true."

He stared at her for a moment, then turned abruptly and ran down the steps to his car. As he drove away, he caught a brief glimpse of her in his rear-view mirror, a lovely wraith in her long white ball gown and fur jacket, standing in the dimly lighted doorway looking after him.

The stewardess who reminded him of Paula Corbin handed a jacket to his seat companion and thrust his travel-worn raincoat at him. "We'll be landing in about twenty minutes," she said to both. "Fasten your seat belts and no smoking, please." She was gone, buttocks fluttering provocatively under hip-hugging uniform skirt, the calves of her long, slender legs twinkling down the aisle.

Outside, the day had turned a murky gray with ragged, feathery wisps of cloud gusting about. As the plane banked toward the airport, Corey could barely make out the fuzzy dots of green that marked the black stretch of runway. The overcast became heavier and it was not until they were actually on the ground that the ghostly shapes on his right materialized into parked planes and mist-shrouded buildings. The time was 3:15, five minutes behind scheduled arrival time.

The air that hit him as he descended the mobile staircase was cold and heavily laden with moisture. Crossing the open area toward the arrivals gate, the wind swirled and whipped around his legs, chilling him. As he entered the building, a neatly dressed young Negro approached and asked, "Lieutenant Armour?"

"Yes."

"Got a car waiting outside for you, sir."

"Who are you?"

"Name's Toby. I work for the Warren office in Atlanta. Mr. Lynd got a call from the Laurelton office yesterday asking us to have every plane from Washington met today to look for you. The car is for you to drive up to Laurelton in, leave it there."

"Thank you, Toby."

"If you'll give me your checks, I'll get your baggage."

"Never mind. Suppose you get the car and meet me out front while I get the baggage."

"Yes, sir."

Shana Pierce, he thought, then wondered if it had been Kenneth who had thought to provide this service. He followed the other passengers into the baggage receiving area and a few minutes later claimed his flight bag. Outside, the sedan and Toby waited. Corey threw his flight bag on the rear seat. Toby said, "If you don't mind, Lieutenant, I'll drop off at the office and you can go on from there."

"I don't mind at all." He got in beside Toby, who expertly wheeled the car into the traffic flow. Twenty minutes later, they were at the Warren Atlanta office and Corey moved over to take the wheel. "You know your way, Lieutenant?" Toby asked.

"Yes, thank you, and thanks for meeting me."

"Not at all, sir. Have a good trip."

He found the highway to Fairview, lighted a cigarette and settled down for the drive, playing a quiet game of trying to identify old, familiar landmarks and spotting the new additions on a road he had traveled many times in the past. The mist thickened, the sky darkened and all moving vehicles were headlighted now as the mist turned to a light drizzle. He cracked the window on his left an inch or two to allow the air to dissipate the fog creeping up onto the windshield, then started his windshield wipers.

And fell to thinking of Paula and Drew again.

After that New Year's Eve, it was never the same again with Paula, as though a third person was with them on every date. Drew Warren. He looked at Paula and saw Drew's face, the intensity of her last words to him firm in his mind: *I'm in love with you and you're in love with me and you know it's true.* At the time, he had dismissed it as ridiculous adolescent nonsense. Later, he became less and less sure.

And he was aware that Paula had noticed the change in him; increasing silences between them, perhaps a lessening in ardor, a hesitation in deciding on their weekends. Paula's new self-assurance was so complete that he began to feel he was being *managed* by her, which gave him a deepening sense of immaturity. His work suffered and he used the need to study as an excuse to evade weekday dates and two weekends in succession. Paula did not press him until the third weekend, when he told her he needed to catch up on a term paper.

On that Saturday she watched him play two erratic practice sets of tennis, losing both to Tom Dennis, who hadn't been able to come close to making the team. She waited until he showered and they walked back toward the campus coffee shop.

"You made Tom look better than he is," Paula commented.

"Just an off day. Everybody has them."

"You seem to be having a lot of them, Corey. Is something wrong?"

"Wrong? Of course not," he replied quickly.

"I think we ought to talk about it, don't you?"

"What is there to talk about?"

"Us, for one thing. I think maybe we ought not see each other so—regularly."

"If that's the way you want it, Paula."

She laughed and said, "I gave you a beautiful opening, didn't I?"

"What do you mean?"

"That you pounced on it like a hawk on a chicken. Give me a cigarette."

"I don't have any with me. Wait a minute." He went to the cigarette machine and came back with a pack of Warren Imperials, opened them and held a match to the tip for her, saw her eyes examining his face closely. "Corey," she said, "it's all right with me if you want out. I won't die of a broken heart. What we've been having, I've enjoyed, but if we can't share that enjoyment, it isn't fun any more."

With the hurt of a small boy being spanked, "Paula, it's not that—"

"The way it was," Paula continued over his weak protest, "was fine. The way it is, is not. No ties, Corey. We're both free agents. Okay?"

He felt miserable, unable to look directly at her, hating his own cowardice. Paula said calmly, "Nothing lasts forever, but we'll always be friends because we shared something together, won't we?"

"Yes—"

She stood up and walked out slowly, head held high as she turned toward her sorority house. Corey sat in his chair, the cigarette dead, coffee cold, staring at the name Warren on the cigarette pack.

You're a goddamned fool, he told himself, *and a gutless louse.*

175

Until that New Year's Eve it had been going so well with Paula, so smoothly, unrushing, each yielding to the other's needs; so well, in fact, that Corey's mind turned to wonder if this was what the perfect marriage was intended to be like; undemanding, without pressures, the enjoyment of mature physical gratification and understanding between mature, understanding people on equal terms.

During that period with Paula, he had often considered the emptiness in his parents' lives and wondered how it would be between them today if they had shared a premarital union such as his and Paula's; if they would be sharing a bed instead of sleeping in separate bedrooms. Or if they would have married at all.

And now, with Drew firmly injected into the picture, dominating his mind so strongly, he had lost Paula. He saw her around the campus, more popular than ever, heightening his desire for her, unable to recapture the mood. They smiled at each other in passing, called a cheery "Hi!" at the coffee shop, waved during a class break; but she no longer came out to watch him on the courts. She was always with some new, anonymous face; and later, with Polk Holderby, flashing around in his fire-engine-red MG, at a dance, a game. He made no effort to replace her but threw himself into his studies and workouts on the courts and the indoor pool.

He sought out Bruce, but Bruce's older, faster crowd was lost on him, more interested in poker, drinking, dashing off to Atlanta for libidinous weekends. And in criticizing Polk and Bruce as libertines, it occurred to him that he was the pot who was calling the kettles black and had been no more moral than they; if anything, they were more open and honest about it than he had been.

He became a grind, a social loner, turning down Polk's and other offers to double date, fearful that one of those dates might include Paula and he would be unable to cope with her presence; then he fell to wondering how far she had gone with Polk or any of the others he saw her with. What made him suspicious was that Polk, not in keeping with his usual pattern, would never mention Paula to him as he had boasted of other conquests. And so, he grew cool toward his old friend Polk, who had begun to eye him with curiosity.

At the point where he was determined to change roommates, he realized that he could give Polk no logical reason for the move. They were approaching May and Corey decided to let it go until after the summer vacation, then do something about it in September.

Soon, he had another problem to occupy his mind; a letter from Kenneth mentioning perfunctorily that Caddy hadn't been feeling well and was at Laurelton Memorial for a checkup. Corey telephoned Caddy at the hospital at once and spoke with her and she calmed his fears. "It's nothing to be alarmed about, Corey, darling. They're simply giving me a complete series of checks and tests to try to find out what causes these abominable migraincs I've been having off and on during the winter. I'll be home in a few days."

He telephoned two days later, but she was in X-ray; the next day, undergoing other tests; the following day, asleep. With growing alarm, he called Dr. Worsham, who explained that the tests were normal routine. "She's fine, Corey, nothing to worry about," Worsham told him reassuringly, "except for the headaches, and we're tracking the cause down."

On the following Monday he had eaten his dinner and gone back to his room when Polk came in only a few moments behind him. "Phone for you, Corey. Long distance."

"Thanks." He ran down the steps to the wall phone and answered. "Corey?" It was Kenneth.

"Yes, Dad. What is it, Mother?"

"Corey, I'm afraid I have some bad news for you."

He could feel beads of cold sweat forming on his forehead. "Mother?" he asked again in a choked whisper.

"Yes, son."

"Well, *what?*" His voice became shrill, highly pitched with anxiety.

"It was a tumor on her brain. They operated this morning. They did their best, but she—didn't come out of it—"

He heard the rest of it in a silent daze, cold and numbed with shock, and without realizing what he was doing, hung the receiver up and leaned against the wall. Ed Wallach and Phil Drake were passing by just then, saw him standing there shaking like a drunken man, his lips working soundlessly, refusing, or unable, to answer them. Then Polk and several others were gathered around him, alarmed.

"Corey?" No answer.

"For God's sake, Corey, what is it? Who called?" No answer. Polk slapped him lightly, then again, harder, "Corey—"

Then he came awake suddenly and for no reason he could later account for, struck Polk cruelly in the mouth, knocking him back into the circle of faces that were hemming him in. He lashed out at Polk again, but other arms reached out, grabbed and held him, hustled him up to his room. And later, Polk came upstairs, a wet towel pressed to

177

his mouth, watered-down blood spots staining his shirt front.

"Polk, I'm sorry. Sorry as all hell. I didn't know what I was doing—"

"It's all right, Corey. Your dad called back a few minutes later, thought the connection had been broken. I'm sorry about your mother."

"I've got to pack—leave—"

"Not tonight. There's nothing you can do except kill yourself on that road—"

"Tonight. Now," Corey insisted.

"Well—all right, but not alone. I'll drive you up."

He wanted to do it alone, to be alone with his own thoughts, but Polk was equally determined. He threw a few of Corey's things together in a small bag and they went together in the MG, top down, wind rushing past them so that conversation was impossible. Polk dropped him at the house on Old Colony Lane, saw him into a weeping Tish's arms, then drove to his own house a hundred or so yards away to get a few hours of sleep before making the return trip alone.

There were so many at Caddy's funeral, well over a hundred people. Among them, Drew and Anderson Warren. Bruce and Polk, up from Athens. Wayne and Julie Taylor, John and Susan Curran, the Ellises, Willards, Harringtons. Aaron Weinstock and his son, Martin. Lee Durkin, Mayor Tom Cameron, the press, members of the City Council and County Commissioners, judges who had known Kenneth's father, Lewis, and Lewis's father, Marcus, judges themselves in another era; friends of the Cranes. Corey remembered standing beside Kenneth, looking at his stern, staring face, wondering what he really felt for his dead Catherine Crane Armour; pity, compassion, or relief that he was finally free of her?

Returned to the Armour house, callers streamed in all that weekend. Paula came with her parents, Polk with Mark and Sally Holderby, Anderson Warren with Drew and Bruce, Warren executives with their wives, an endless procession; so endless that Corey wondered with curiosity if Shana Pierce would eventually turn up. Finally it was over and on Monday morning, Kenneth said, "I hope you will stay on for a day or two, Corey."

"Why?" Corey asked.

"There are some things—your mother's will—"

"I don't think I'm up to it, Dad. I'm sure you will handle everything just as it should be. I've made arrangements to drive back this morning with Bruce Warren."

"As you wish. I'll write you."

"You do that."

They parted without sentiment or handshake; a simple "Good-bye, Dad."

"Good-bye, Corey. If you need anything, phone or drop me a line."

A week later, he learned in a letter from Kenneth that apart from some bequests of personal items to a few close friends, Caddy had left Corey the portfolio of stocks she had inherited from her father, Selwyn Crane, the house on Old Colony Lane, and the 600 acres of Shadow Hills land.

Corey spent the following summer on a solitary driving trip, aimlessly covering ground, crossing state lines, swimming at strange beaches, finding new high peaks, camping beside lakes, roaming through forests, in search of something lost and as yet undefined. He returned to Laurelton early in September to learn that Kenneth was away in South America with Duncan Collins, of the New York Warren office, on a contract matter. Drew had spent the summer with Bruce in Spain.

Until he was but one year away from finishing law school, Corey worked hard at his studies, practiced on the indoor and outdoor courts for his own release, and took little part in the social life around him. Polk, Paula, Bruce and the others of his undergraduate years were gone: Bruce into the Warren Tobacco Company, Polk to a Washington brokerage house for training, Paula to New York to be closer to the center of fashion design, manufacturing, buying and selling. Drew hadn't come to Athens as she had planned. Instead, she was spending her college years in schools abroad and only the last of those summer vacations at home on Brookhill.

Corey saw her shortly after her arrival. She was almost 22 then, and hardly the Drew he had known at any other age. In the quiet, antique elegance of her small sitting room on the second floor at Brookhill, she sat erect in the Louis XV chair, a good six inches away from its brocaded back, slender hands clasped in her lap, as close to regal as any word he could think of to describe her. The dress she wore was black and simple, with touches of white at the deep neckline and across the upper edges of its two false pockets; "fuss-less," as Tish would have described it. Rather than being worn, it had become a part of the body it covered and caressed.

Somewhere, someone had changed her hair style and she now wore it in an upsweeping crown for her exquisitely contoured head, exposing her graceful neck. Gentle shadows gave her eyes a near-Oriental slant and the faint hollows in her cheeks reduced the oval fullness of her face. She was slender as a model, full-breasted as few models are, slim-waisted and the somewhat short length of her dress placed a remarkable emphasis on her long, exquisite legs.

Yet her physical sophistication could not hide a certain strain beneath the practical calm of her face. "Sit here, Corey," she said, indicating the chair facing her. He went directly to her, took her extended hand into his own, then leaned down and kissed her proffered cheek lightly.

"Hello, Drew," he said softly. "It's wonderful seeing you again. It's been a long time."

"Yes, hasn't it."

"You look marvelous. Luscious. Damned near edible."

"Thank you. How have you been, Corey? And your father?"

"He's fine. Busy as ever."

"And you?"

"In law school. Out next year."

"And then?"

"I haven't decided yet. What about you? Back to Europe?"

She laughed prettily, breaking some of the tension in her. "I think not. I've got most of that out of my system. Frankly, I'm so happy to be back at Brookhill, I don't think I want to leave it. Ever."

"What about this summer?"

"Bruce promised to stay if I came back. He's with the Company, but you know that, of course."

"Yes. I don't think I've seen him more than once or twice since he graduated."

"Then maybe we can get together again this summer. Like old times. Tennis, swimming, riding. I can't tell you how much I've looked forward to it." Abruptly, "You're not planning on being away, are you?"

"No. I want to do some review work this summer."

"Where is everyone, Polk, Les, Perry—" a mere fragmentary pause, then—"Paula?"

"Les is working in a Richmond bank. Perry is with the Water and Power Company. Polk is up in Washington with a brokerage house for the summer. Paula, I hear, is managing a dress shop in New York, preparing to open one of her own some day—"

"Ah, Paula," Drew said with a smile that suddenly reduced him to feeling young, awkward and voiceless. She may have

180

noticed his embarrassment and said, "Stay for dinner, Corey? Bruce will be here."

"I—can't stay," Corey replied, but then, as though regretting his refusal, quickly added, "now, but I'll come back later, if I may."

"Please do. About seven-thirty?"

He left, not knowing exactly why, since there was nothing else he had to do; perhaps to recover from this new, splendid, sophisticated woman who had taken the place of the 18-year-old Drew Warren who had once said to him, *I love you and I know you love me.* And whom he had dismissed as a romantic, immature child.

The two months that followed were the most frustrating he had ever known. He saw Drew at Brookhill, but on Bruce's invitation and not hers. He took part of his pique out on Bruce, soft with inactivity, toying with him on the courts, attacking fiercely, driving him from side to side, from net to back court, forcing him to near-exhaustion. Occasionally, Drew would join them for a swim. Twice, she asked Corey to ride with her, but it was as though the past had never occurred. In July, she flew north to shop and visit with friends she had met abroad. When she returned, she was more available for a brief period, then was off to Sea Island for a week.

By mid-August, he was convinced he was in love with Drew, but the gap created by nearly four years abroad was too great to hurdle. She spoke of places and mentioned names that were familiar in the international sections of news magazines, her summer in Spain with Bruce, skiing weekends in Switzerland, visiting classmates at their summer homes, shopping in the world fashion capitals. Despite opportunities offered him by Kenneth, Corey had never been abroad, a fact he now regretted. He hoped for an opening that would take them back in time, to the summer at Loon Lake, the New Year's Eve at the country club, but somehow the subjects seemed too long ago and far away, a part of their youth that somehow eluded them.

Corey had been invited to the wedding of Sandy Morton, a former classmate at the University and a member of the tennis team. The wedding was to take place in Atlanta, the home of the bride, at noon on the third Sunday in August. With Sandy's permission, Corey asked Drew to the affair and when she accepted, his hopes rose again. On the Thursday prior to the wedding, he received a notice from the draft board to appear for examination the following week, but this was of little concern because policy dictated that he would be deferred until he had completed his final year at law school and taken his bar exams.

On Saturday, they drove to Atlanta for a prewedding party given by several of his former classmates at the hotel in which Corey and Drew were staying. The party turned out to be an old-fashioned fraternity get-together that lasted well into morning, so that both had to rush to get to the church by the noon hour. After the ceremony, there was an elaborate luncheon and by seven-thirty, Corey and Drew were on their way back to Laurelton.

Drew had never been more lovely or desirable. She had captivated every male at the Saturday night party and drew the attention of everyone at the wedding and luncheon, giving Corey little opportunity to be with her except for a dance or two, interrupted frequently by cut-ins.

On the drive home, Drew said, "It was such a lovely wedding, Corey. I had a wonderful time. Thank you for asking me."

He thought, I'd like to invite you to one more, ours. But there was the year of law school ahead, the notice from the draft board waiting for him, and a Drew Warren he was hardly sure about now. He said, "I could have seen more of you and talked more to you if I'd taken you to a movie."

"There'll be time for at least one movie before you go back to Athens."

"Also, the Labor Day tournament at the Club. Will you be free?"

"I'd forgotten. Will Bruce be in it?"

"Not this year. He's been dogging it. But I'm sure he'll be there as a spectator. Will you?"

"If you want me."

"Of course I do."

"Then it's a date. Are you going to win another cup?"

"If I do, it's yours."

"I couldn't accept a trophy you'd won, Corey." Then, "Where are we?"

"About twenty miles from Fairview."

"I'm done in. If you don't mind being alone, I think I'll try to take a nap."

He had meant to tell her about the draft notice and try to lead the conversation toward his plans, or hers, in some way link them together and thus introduce the subject of love and a future together; to press for an early wedding date, a year together in Athens before being called up for service. She was fast asleep, her head on his shoulder, one arm linked with his, the perfume of her a tantalizing effect on him. There was still time. The Labor Day weekend ahead

182

offering a means to recall another Labor Day weekend at Loon Lake.

It was shortly past eleven when they reached Laurelton. Drew awoke when Corey braked the car at a red light. She sat up and stared out at the quiet street scene. "So soon? I must have been asleep for hours," she exclaimed.

"You were. Through the worst Sunday night traffic I've seen in years."

"I'm sorry, Corey, what a beast to make you drive so far alone."

"You're forgiven in exchange for Wednesday night dinner at the Marina."

"Done."

As they approached the gateway to Brookhill, Drew said, "It's such a beautiful night. I'm sorry it's over— Those lights—the house—Corey—"

He had already seen them. The entire front of the house was lighted and several cars were parked in the driveway. As they pulled up to the front, they saw that one was a police car. They leaped out of the car and ran up the steps, Drew a few steps ahead of him. "Gran," Drew was saying, "something has happened—to Gran—"

Leona, weeping into one corner of her apron, opened the door as they reached it, dropped the apron to open her arms to Drew.

"What is it, Leona? Gran—"

"It's not Mist' Anderson, honey. It's Mist' Bruce——"

"Bruce? What, Leona? An accident?" She was shaking Leona's shoulders, her own composure totally shattered.

"He—he—" Then Chief of Police Durkin came out of Anderson Warren's ground-floor study to tell them. That Bruce's car had gone out of control while he was driving back to town from the Marina after a day on the Cottonwood and smashed into a tree. Sorry—.

Bruce was dead and his companion, Diana Cross, had died with him. Bruce Warren, 25, heir to the Warren tobacco fortune, the morning *Herald* described him. Diana Cross, 24, an accounting clerk at Warren Tobacco Company. Simple statements.

Omitted were other facts: Diana Cross was married; her husband, Louis Cross, had been overseas in Viet Nam for eleven months; Diana Cross was four months pregnant; and finally, Diana Cross was an octoroon, the daughter of a white man and a quadroon, who had come from Savannah to pass for white in a "white" job while her husband was overseas.

Two hours after Bruce's body was released by the County

183

Coroner, it was placed in his crypt in the Warren mausoleum, his soul prayed for by Reverend Wyatt Miller. By request of Anderson, there was no eulogy. Witnesses to the brief, solemn service were Anderson, Theodore and Drew Warren, Shad, Leona and Cord Waters, Kenneth and Corey Armour. When it was over and they returned to the house, Kenneth left at once to fly to Savannah to see the Cross family to offer sympathy, condolences, and a sum of money to soften their son's loss (and no doubt fend off a possible lawsuit).

Theodore disappeared into his own apartment. Anderson's concern now was for Drew. He sat beside her on the sofa in the large, formal living room, held her hand and spoke low, comforting words, but she showed no reaction to him or her surroundings. Her eyes were wide open, but she appeared to be in a completely dazed state, pale face showing deep shock, hands nervously twisting her handkerchief until it was torn into shreds; then a fold of her dress; breathing in short, shallow gasps, unaware of Corey's presence, unresponding to Leona's attempts to press a cold drink on her. Corey sent Leona for a glass of brandy and held it for Drew to drink, but the little she took seemed to have no effect.

Then Dr. Ballard arrived. He gave Drew a capsule to swallow and Corey helped Leona take her to her room while Ballard spoke to Anderson Warren. She refused to undress, and lay on her bed, corpse-like, her face streaked with tears.

"Lord, Lord," Leona prayed.

Drew seemed to be falling into a sleep and Leona left them, but then she began weeping, her body twisting from side to side with spasms of shuddering, whispering Bruce's name over and over again.

"Drew, darling—"

"Please—go away—"

"I'm going to call Dr. Ballard."

"No, don't, please. I'll—be—all right—"

"Drew, you've got to have something to help you, make you sleep."

"Oh, God, I don't ever want to sleep again."

"You've got to—"

"Leave me alone. Please—I don't want anything—anybody—I want Bruce—"

Corey grabbed her hands and held them together tightly. "Drew, stop it. Bruce is gone and you've got to keep on living."

184

She jerked away from him, shouting, "I don't! I don't have to go on living if I don't want to! I don't—"

Dr. Ballard entered the room then and Drew fell back on the bed, breathing hard, her head turned away from them. Ballard spoke to her, meaningless words. "Now, what's all this about, young lady. You're going to be all right."

"Go away, please," Drew moaned. "Please. Go away—"

Ballard busied himself with his black bag and prepared a hypodermic. Corey held her while Ballard injected the needle and within a few moments Drew showed signs of its effect, muttering drowsily, "Bruce—oh, Bruce—all I had left—"

Outside her door, Ballard said, "Stay with her, Corey. I'll send Leona in."

"How is Mr. Warren?"

"He's sleeping. I don't know about Theodore. I've sent for a nurse to stay for a day or two until the crisis period is over."

"Doctor, she—"

Ballard said firmly, "She's young and healthy. She should come out of it after a while. It will take her a little time to get used to the idea."

"If ever," Corey replied. "They were so close."

"Yes. Maybe too close, living out here in a small world of their own. Corey—"

"Yes, sir?"

"Be a good idea if you could be around for a while, let her transfer some of what she felt for Bruce to someone else. In a different way, I mean."

"Of course, if it will help."

"I can't say, Corey. Bruce was someone to hold on to, lean on, all the years she grew up without a real father, a mother she can't even remember. With her grandmother gone and Anderson seldom home, Bruce became a very important image to her. Losing him is like wiping out her entire family with one stroke. If you can take up the slack—"

Ballard went away and Corey returned to Drew's bed and leaned over her inert body. Her eyes were closed now, but her lips were moving, her body still trembling, and as he leaned closer to her mouth, he heard her whisper, "Don't leave me, Bruce, please—"

He postponed his return to the University for a full week and spent every day at Brookhill. Drew hardly left her room and his visits were like those to a person confined to a hospital room. At times she was almost catatonic, staring vacantly at a fixed object in the distance, unmoved by his

185

presence, unresponsive to Leona's efforts to get her to eat, taking her medication like an automaton. At other times, she rambled on compulsively, reminiscing over childhood incidents that involved Bruce. Then there were periods when she seemed to be able only to mention his name, leaving blanks in her monologue.

Labor Day came and passed. Another week moved by slowly and Corey, already overdue at the University, told Drew he must return to the University.

"Of course," she agreed at once. "I've been too selfish as it is."

Corey made a practice of calling her from Athens each evening for two weeks, but there was little to talk about. She was fine, Gran was busy, Theodore away in California on a business matter. Corey was fine, busy, eagerly awaiting his Thanksgiving holiday. Would she like to come down to Athens for a weekend? The answer was an unvaried, No, not at this time.

Early in November, caught up with his studies, he wrote Drew outlining his plans to return to Laurelton for Thanksgiving vacation. In mid-November he received a brief, almost incoherent note which ignored any mention of Thanksgiving. It spoke of "this vacuum I'm living in" and her intention of returning to Europe for a short visit. When he telephoned her that evening, she was already gone.

He heard nothing more until the end of February, a brief letter from Zurich, saying she would be staying on for a while. During the spring came three cards postmarked from London, Paris and Stockholm. Then a brief letter saying she would be spending the summer aboard the yacht of friends (unnamed) cruising the Mediterranean and the Greek Islands. Not once had she given him an address to which he could write her.

Corey finished law school, graduating fourth in his class. He took the bar examinations and was notified he had come out seventh on the long list of aspirants. A week later, he received a cable from Kenneth, in London on business, congratulating him, advising him he would return to Laurelton within a fortnight, bringing a gift with him. On that same day, Corey reported to the Army induction center and was sworn into service.

By the time he reached Fairview there was not the slightest trace of mist or rain. The sky had brightened and the outside air felt as though it was escaping from a furnace. Corey turned the air-conditioner on and closed the window. He found the turnoff to Laurelton and drove swiftly, past parched earth, trees and fields. And finally, he saw the Laurelton Memorial Hospital and a group of tall buildings on the east side of town, new since he had left, apartment houses that must be twelve or fourteen stories high. Then he came into the Civic Center, found Taylor Avenue and all at once, everything became familiar again. The rest of the way home was purely automatic.

CHAPTER VII

1

The nine years that separated Chase and Theodore Warren in age created a gap in their relationship that would continue for the rest of their lives. Chase's resentment began from the morning Anderson woke him to proudly announce the arrival of his brother during the previous night. At first, Chase gave the matter little thought, and later remembered back to the birth of the infant Clyde, who had died within two weeks.

"How long," he asked, "is this one going to stay?" Chase asked innocently, and for a moment, Anderson was struck dumb, unable to realize that Chase could recall that tragic event.

"For a long time, I hope," Anderson replied soberly. "He's a sound, healthy baby, Chase, your own brother. You'll grow up and play together. You'll learn together and some day both of you will work and share together. You'll watch our land grow, and grow with it, and some day you and your brother will do what I'm doing now, tell your own sons what'll be waiting for them when they grow up. You're the firstborn, Chase, so you'll be the leader until you step down to make room for your sons and nephews, the way I'll be doing one day—"

It came as Chase's greatest disappointment that Theodore, unlike the infant Clyde, continued to live; and his resentment grew stronger as the days, weeks, months and years passed. He drew closer to Anderson, this to his father's gratification. On those weekends when Anderson came home from New York after the Warren Tobacco Company had been formed, Chase remained close by his side, listening eagerly as Anderson explained in greatest detail the need to educate local factory workers, foremen and superintendents; problems that concerned labor, construction, equipment and the intricacies of financing. Chase never tired of Anderson's detailed explanations of the complicated plans he devised and pored over.

At school, Chase's favorite subject became mathematics, using Anderson's primitive shortcut methods to arrive at solutions to problems that were not consistent with existing book rules, impatient with his teacher because she required answers to the exact penny, fraction or decimal, all of which he considered unimportant. The dollars alone counted, according to Chase. At 14, he debated the value of literature and history with Mr. Longden, the principal, holding that these would play too little a part in his future and were therefore not important or necessary. This phase disturbed Cleo, but Anderson secretly chuckled with pride, seeing Chase's leaning toward "numbers" as an encouraging sign. He thereupon began introducing Chase to the mysteries of practical finance, using the Company's outstanding indebtedness, its financing, mortgaging programs and stock issues as a means to borrow for expansion, for increasing production and sales income, for eventual retirement of the debt.

Chase made few friends of his own age at school. He had very early developed clever trading habits and easily outwitted his classmates in the practice of swapping marbles, knives, spinning tops and other such miscellaneous pocket trivia, always at a profit to himself. Later, he matched coins with older boys, a game at which he seldom lost and, searching for a reason why, discovered a very important and lasting fact he would remember all his life: that apart from the luck factor, the law of averages was on the side of the participant who came into the game with the most money, simply because he could better outlast a temporary run of bad luck.

Theodore, meanwhile, grew up in a confused atmosphere of Cleo's overprotective love, Anderson's impatience for him to reach an age of understanding, and Chase's youthful resentment. In Cleo's and Anderson's presence, Chase's behavior ran between reluctant acceptance and indifference toward the intruder, a pattern his parents hoped would be short-lived. To Cleo's chagrin, the feeling deepened. Chase showed neither interest in, nor a sense of sharing with, his young brother.

It enraged Chase that toys he had long outgrown were given to Theodore and, stealthily, he twisted the tracks of his old train set so that at frequent intervals the train would jump the tracks. Later, he broke the clockwork mechanism that drove the engines. He ran his old tricycle into a wall so that its frame was sprung out of shape, set fire to his wooden wagon, rode his old two-wheeler bike down to the Cottonwood River and sank it, rather than see Theodore ride it. Yet, it bothered him not at all when Cleo replaced

189

these with a new tricycle, wagon and bicycle; he only resented Theodore's use of anything that had been his own.

Chase ridiculed Theodore's love of picture books, a ragged stuffed dog Theodore slept with, and later, his brother's devotion to his collection of coins and stamps in which Cleo had encouraged him. He was driven to attack Theodore physically only once. He was 15 at the time, Theodore 6, when he came upon Theodore playing with a group of Negro children in the servants' quarters. Matt, who was twelve, was teaching Theodore and Matt's brother, Oddy, who was four, to throw a knife at a target. Chase watched with disdain for a while, then approached the group and took the knife from Matt.

" 'At's my knife, Chase," Matt protested.

"Shut up, nigger," Chase retorted.

"Don't call him that," Theodore said. "That's a bad word."

"You gimme my knife, Chase," Matt demanded angrily. "My daddy gave me—"

Chase pointed the knife blade at Matt. "You call me *Mister* Chase, nigger, or you'll never see this knife again."

Matt stood with his two fists balled up, tears of anger welling up in his eyes. "Go ahead. *Mister* Chase. Say it."

"I'n goin'a say nothin' of the kin'. You a boy jus' like me. I'n callin' no boy *Mister*."

Chase turned and started toward the main house, the knife clutched in his hand. Matt ran behind him, leaped on his back, but Chase turned, twisted and Matt fell to the ground. Theodore ran to help Matt, crying, "You're mean! You're mean as a snake, Chase! You give Matt his knife!" Chase shook Theodore off and Theodore ran after Chase, hammering his two small fists ineffectually on Chase's middle. Then Matt came toward Chase and Chase shoved Theodore off with a blow from the hand that held the knife, and Theodore took a cut alongside his left eye that began bleeding profusely. Oddy and his two sisters let up a howl at the sight of the blood and their mother, Maudie, came on the run. She sent Chase off with hot words, ministered to Theodore's wound and took him to the main house where Chase was explaining the "accident" to Cleo.

Still later, during table talk at supper, Chase invariably chose subjects from which Theodore must necessarily be excluded; recalling with astonishing clarity certain details of the trip from Loudon to Laurelton which even Cleo and Anderson had forgotten, and events of the next five years before Theodore's birth; or school problems that were far over his brother's head. Away from the house, Chase

190

mocked Theodore in every possible way; for his inferior intelligence, youthful weaknesses, an unfortunate habit of nervous stammering when under stress, and the ultimate humiliation, advertising to his playmates the occasional failure of Theodore's bladder that caused him to wet his bed at night.

2

There was little change in the relationship of the two brothers when Anderson finally returned to Laurelton to build his first major producing plant. Offices had been established in New York to handle sales, distribution and advertising. The loft operation was placed in the hands of an assistant, leaving Anderson to concentrate on the new Laurelton factory. Within a year, it was in operation and the New York equipment was disassembled and shipped south to be installed as part of the overall operation. And Chase was there beside Anderson every moment he could spare from his school and studies.

And all in good time.

In 1914, the war abroad created a strong upsurge in tobacco consumption and cigarette sales forged ahead to an unprecedented popularity, making threatening inroads on plug and pipe tobacco as well as snuff. A second plant had been built and ground was broken for a third. Warehouses were springing up to handle raw materials and finished products awaiting shipment; WARREN'S BLEND for the muslin-sacked roll-your-own, WARREN'S DE LUXE, the regular machine-rolled cigarette, and WARREN IMPERIALS, the longer, cork-tipped brand.

Money poured in, but it poured out equally as fast to pay ever-mounting bills for construction, rising salaries and wages, for transportation, raw materials and an endless parade of necessities which cropped up continuously. Interest on loans grew to mountainous proportions and this was always paid with regularity, but the principal debt loomed larger than ever. It was Jonas Taylor's son, Ames, returned from Duke University and working in the Laurelton National Bank who, despite his youth, pointed the way one day when Anderson called at the bank.

"Mornin', Cousin," Anderson greeted.

"Good morning, Cousin Anderson," Ames replied.

"Uh—your daddy in?"

"No, sir. He's in Atlanta on business until Monday."

"Uh—Charlie Jarrett around, Ames?"

"No, sir. Mr. Jarrett is no longer with the bank."

"Eh? Uh—you taken over?"

Ames smiled self-consciously. "On a trial basis, I suppose."

"Well," Anderson said, "if Cousin Jonas is willin' to gamble on you, I don't think he can be far wrong. Congratulations."

"Thank you. If I can be of some help—?"

"I—well, maybe not. Just thought I'd drop this interest check off and maybe have a talk with your daddy over lunch. Uh—you busy?"

"Not too busy for one of our most important customers," Ames replied with a reserved smile.

"Then how about a bite? Never did enjoy eatin' by myself."

"I'd be delighted, Cousin."

Over lunch, Ames listened while Anderson talked. Construction, equipment, transportation, labor, raw materials— "Volume's up and keeps goin' up, but the danged costs keep goin' up right along with it. What happens if some day the costs get ahead of the sales volume, hey? Then I'm goin'a find myself wadin' in sweat up to my butt end."

"It poses an interesting problem, Cousin Anderson, but I'm sure there is a solution somewhere."

"I'd like to put one of my horny fingers on it before it eats me up alive."

"Let me study your last statement and give it some thought. I've a friend in Atlanta, an industrial engineer, and several others to whom I might put the problem. With your permission, of course. There may be a fee—"

"If it answers the problem, they'll earn the fee. You go ahead and see what you can come up with."

A month passed before Ames invited Anderson to a meeting in Atlanta. Present were Mark Holderby, the industrial engineer, William J. Carlisle, an attorney, and George Caswell, a stockbroker and financier, all young men, but knowledgeable in their respective fields. Ames had previously outlined Anderson's situation and the city men were ready with their advice. And Anderson began to learn how a big business must operate, all in one sentence.

Delegation of authority to competent, well-paid executives.

"No one man, Mr. Warren," Holderby said, "can possibly burden himself with thousands of details and still be able to view the overall picture. Others must function freely in their various supervisory capacities, each fully accountable to you, and allow you to devote your time to top-level management and direction without becoming too deeply involved with too many small details. Your interest must focus on inter-company communications. Frequent detailed reports that advise. Meetings between department heads that suggest. Operations that are free of your personal or emotional involvements in order to permit you to make quick, cold, effective decisions."

Anderson was taken aback. "I don't see how it can work," he declared. "I know every office man and clerk by name, every factory hand and foreman: I hired all of 'em myself. I know their wives and families. I work alongside—"

Holderby laughed lightly. "You have just placed your finger on the crux of the problem, Mr. Warren. Every time you appear on the job, be it construction, factory, or office, minutes that add up to man-hours are lost in purely personal involvement, hours that cost money. You pick up a shovel and fifty men stop working to watch the boss-man heave a few yards of dirt. You stop to inspect a machine and a dozen or more women stop working to watch the president doing a fifty-cents-an-hour job. When were you in New York last to check on your sales staff? When did you last call on a wholesaler or retailer to impress him with the presence of the president of Warren Tobacco come to chat with him, interested in *his* problems and incidentally to increase the size of his order? When —?"

It came to Anderson then that there was a business world far beyond Laurelton; in Philadelphia, Boston, Chicago, Denver, San Francisco, Dallas; and with the war in Europe, across the seas. Markets. Markets everywhere to capture.

The meeting came to a close with Anderson Warren hiring Mark Holderby as his consultant. Holderby would move to Laurelton with his wife, make a survey of the operation, go on to New York to do the same there, then return and write a final report, with recommendations.

By the end of the year, the character of the Company had changed completely. Holderby found the executives who, in turn, found the key operating personnel. People and equipment were shifted for maximum efficiency, linked to positions in which they were better suited. An office building was built in the center of the Warren complex and all administrative personnel brought closer together. The New York office saw drastic changes and a new executive director, Duncan Collins, was hired away from a larger tobacco company, at a higher salary, and installed in that key district.

"It's costin' me a mint of money," Anderson told Cleo,

"but I God, it's a dream come true. I got some travelin' to do, but I'll have more time to spend at home, too. And what it's costin' is a drop in the ocean compared to what's comin' in now."

And for Jonas Taylor, Warren's success meant increased production of paper, foil, cardboard, fiberboard shipping containers, muslin sacks and a broadening of his freight lines.

Very early, Mark Holderby forced Anderson to recognize the need for attractive packaging, point-of-sale display cards and window material to call attention to his products at the consumer level; and soon, Anderson was heavily involved in advertising and sales promotion. In his mind, he realized that this expensive form of publicity must be directed toward one goal: *Maximum Public Exposure*. Against profits and the raised eyebrows of his accountants, Anderson Warren plowed tens of thousands of dollars into keeping the name WARREN before the public eye; and when it seemed that he had saturated the available media beyond the efforts of his competitors, he dug deeper and spent more lavishly on premiums; not picture cards, flags, miniature rugs, cosmetics and toiletries offered by his fellow manufacturers. Instead, he devised a premium coupon savings plan that allowed his consumers to exchange coupons for useful household articles: pots, pans, dishes, table utensils, a variety of patterns in yard goods. The catalogue of such items he produced became a household guide in many urban and rural homes throughout the country.

Anderson experimented with new brand names, flavored and aromatic tobaccos, even colored paper. He popularized a number of his newer innovations, but never at the expense of his WARREN'S DE LUXE or WARREN IMPERIALS brands.

3

Early in 1917, Germany's unrestricted submarine warfare heightened American feelings and in March, after Congress refused President Wilson's request to permit merchant ships to be armed, he armed them by executive order. That act was followed, shortly afterward, by a note from the German foreign secretary to the Mexican government suggesting that Mexico enter the war against the United States to recover the U.S. Southwest; and on April 6th, the United States declared war on Germany.

Anderson was in New York on that fateful Friday and

was due to remain for another week. On the Monday following the declaration of war, he was surprised when Chase walked into his office unannounced. Anderson looked up from a letter he was reading, his eyes widening at the sight of his son, now a freshman at the University of Georgia, and sent his flustered secretary away.

"Chase, what on God's green earth you doin' in New York? Why the hell ain't you in school?"

"Father, I came up to tell you—"

He needn't have continued the explanation. It was there in his eyes, his proud bearing, the smile that sent Anderson's glow of love plunging into deep gloom. So soon, he thought, and the war not a week old.

"—that I've enlisted in the Army," Chase concluded.

"Chase! Enlisted! I God, with my contacts in Washington, I can get you a commission—"

"And keep me tied to a desk in Washington." Chase laughed easily at Anderson's dismay. "That's why I signed up this morning, just before I came in to say good-bye."

"Oh, God Almighty," Anderson groaned. "You just turned eighteen—"

"Father, please. I want to take a part in this war. I want to see what's over there. Almost half my class is going. I promise you I won't get hurt. I know it."

"And your mother, does she agree you won't be killed, or even hurt, because you promised her?"

"I don't know—"

"You mean she doesn't know about this yet?"

"She'll know in a little while. I sent her a telegram from downstairs just ten minutes ago. Besides," he added, "she'll have Theodore to comfort her while I'm gone."

So Anderson Warren worked harder and prayed longer and tried the impossible task of keeping himself sufficiently occupied to keep him from worrying about Chase. He returned home at once to comfort Cleo, but strangely enough, it was Cleo who comforted him instead.

"He'll be all right, Anderson. I know it. No harm will come to Chase. He's always been intelligent enough and had the knack to take care of himself," she said reassuringly.

But alone, she wept. Chase, on his way to New York, had given her hardly a thought. Only for his father.

The war boom skyrocketed cigarette production to unprecedented heights and Anderson Warren found himself hard pressed to balance supply with demand. Prime leaf prices shot up to a record 54 cents a pound. Warren not only absorbed the total crop around him, but called on Alistair and Benjamin to supply him, meanwhile sending his own buyers into North Carolina, Kentucky and Ohio to buy leaf while it was still in the ground.

Branch offices and warehouses were established from coast to coast. In South Laurelton, two new manufacturing plants were added to the growing complex of buildings, and Taylor facilities were expanded to supply more paper, foil, cardboard, fiberboard shipping containers and muslin sacks. Railroad spurs were built to link up with the main line and truck freighting operations increased. Homes sprang up overnight to provide living quarters for the new Warren employees brought into the area.

The war created a new form of excitement and desperation in Cairn County. The drain of eligible youth had left in its wake the old, the upper middle-aged and the very young. Wartime shortages and rationing created personal hardships despite the increase in personal wealth. Girls and women took the places of men who had gone off to the wars. Profiteering became a popular enterprise.

Cleo was caught up in the numerous committees formed to roll bandages, knit sweaters and gloves and scarves, sell war stamps and bonds, collect and send books to military camp and ship libraries, entertain soldiers and sailors en route or on furlough, scour remote areas for employables in war industries and other worthwhile occupations, this while Anderson traveled between Laurelton, Washington, New York and the various tobacco belts.

Meanwhile, Theodore grew into his ninth year feeling more lost than ever before. Chase was away at war, Anderson seldom in Laurelton, Cleo almost never at home, returning from her committee work after Theodore was in bed. And on those rare occasions when the three were together, Anderson's and Cleo's conversations invariably dealt with business, war activities, and Chase's most recent letters; a subject in which Theodore showed little interest. He would always look back upon that period as the loneliest he had ever known.

With keen prescience, Anderson made a bid to give lasting national recognition to his products. He became the first manufacturer, after America's declaration of war on Germany, to donate millions of cigarettes and sacks of roll-your-owns to the military forces at home and abroad. Trains and trucks, identified by banners, moved his gifts into camps, military hospitals, ports of embarkation, aboard ships and overseas. Each package and muslin sack bore a special label which read:

WARRENS
America's Finest Cigarette for
America's Finest Fighting Men
with Appreciation

It was a costly but rewarding gesture. Other manufacturers followed suit soon after, but Warrens had been first and more plentiful. Chase wrote from France that its first effect overseas had made a tremendous impact on officers and men alike, one that he predicted would be enduring. His prediction came true. At war's end, Warrens had moved up from 12th place into 6th and brought several offers of merger, even outright purchase, with Anderson to remain as president of the Warren branch. Anderson refused, looking upon all such offers as tributes to his personal success and eventual rise to first place.

Early in 1919 Chase, true to his promise, returned safe and sound, a first lieutenant of infantry with two decorations pinned over his left breast pocket which, with unusual reticence, he refused to discuss at length. He also refused the celebration party Cleo had planned to give on his return, anxious only to get out of uniform and back into civilian life. The greatest change Anderson noticed was in Chase's eyes, which seemed to have aged, perhaps by the battlefield horrors they had witnessed. Another was his impatience to make up for lost time

Chase's reunion with Theodore was a most puzzling one. On Chase's side there was now an adult willingness to let bygones be bygones and establish a closer, more intimate relationship, but amid Anderson's and Cleo's unbounded joy at Chase's return, Theodore remained cool and more estranged than ever. Their reintroduction to each other was as between total strangers. Chase soon gave up the effort.

After two weeks at home, Chase made it clear that he had no intention of returning to the University to resume his education. When Cleo gave up the struggle to keep him at home, Chase went off to New York with a pleased Anderson to begin serious training in the increasingly important sales and advertising divisions of the expanding company he was destined to head one day.

By 1920, Anderson achieved one of his major goals in life. He paid off his debt to Laurelton National Bank on June 15th. A year later, in that same month, the semiannual statement handed him by his chief accountant brought an even more exciting event to his attention.

He had become a millionaire

Time to build a fitting mansion for Cleo and his family. Time for many things he had never had time to indulge in before.

4

In 1920, although the price of leaf had dropped from a monumental wartime 54 cents to postwar 23 cents, it was still high by prewar standards. In that year came government controls, but the cigarette habit of the nation, swelled by the war and aided by Prohibition, kept a firm grip on the public taste and need.

Chase took to New York as though it had been built for him alone. The heavy emphasis now was on sales and its most effective and necessary ally and tool, advertising. After a brief talk with Duncan Collins, chief executive of the New York headquarters, Chase devoted his principal efforts in that direction. An army friend, Captain James Conwell, had returned to his former position as account executive with the Kilkarrick Advertising Agency. With the Warren account tucked under his belt, Jim Conwell became a junior partner in the advertising firm. Conwell was as imaginative as he was energetic and with Chase, proposed an extensive program of billboard, newspaper and magazine advertising that was bold and provocative, with beautiful, scantily clad women who seemed captivated by the aroma of Warrens, ready to succumb to the charms of handsome, cigarette-smoking male companions. There were complaints from decent, God-fearing citizens, which only heightened public interest. The old, art-cluttered cardboard containers were redesigned into legible, more readily identifiable packages. To the standard pack of ten, they added a paper-wrapped package of twenty, and sales soared. Warrens continued to maintain its grip firmly on 6th place nationally, no small accomplishment in a hard-fought, competitive market.

Ten years were to pass before Chase, now 30 and on a trip abroad to scrutinize and broaden foreign markets, met Marshall and Andrea Vanderkuyl while crossing from New York to Southhampton. The Vanderkuyls were enroute to the graduation of their daughter, Victoria, from a school in Zurich, then to spend the rest of the summer touring the continent. In August, he encountered the Vanderkuyls in

Rome and Victoria, whom he had pictured, from Andrea's conversation and an earlier picture, as a young, impossibly spoiled child, turned out to be a mature, charming and carefree young woman of 19.

They returned to New York together in early September and such was Chase's interest in Victoria that he at once drew a confidential McNally Report on her father and learned that Marshall Vanderkuyl had been born into great wealth and was indeed a man of considerable business stature and worth. Along with impressive New York real estate holdings, he owned a chain of three upstate newspapers, controlling interest in a Canadian paper mill, a bank in New Jersey, a small hotel in Manhattan and another in Florida. He was an investor in a Texas oil field, a cattle ranch, an orange grove and a vineyard in California, and was financially interested in an insurance company, based in Chicago. The Vanderkuyls owned a brownstone house in Manhattan, an estate in Palm Beach, a summer home at Sands Point and another in Bar Harbor.

Andrea Vanderkuyl, Chase soon learned, would be the parent he must please if he hoped to claim Victoria for his bride. He took note that Marshall Vanderkuyl seldom made a decision, business or familial, without discussing it with his wife. Andrea chose her husband's and daughter's meals, planned their days and evenings, as well as their traveling itinerary. Physically, she was tall and stately, at least two inches taller than her short, rather stout husband, perhaps ten years his junior. She could be charming to those she considered worthy, as in Chase Warren's case, and deliberately cool and inaccessible to others whom she classified as "climbers." No one, Chase knew, would ever be permitted intimate closeness to Victoria without the consent of her mother.

That Andrea was a complete snob and often hypocritical was not lost on Chase or Victoria, who excused her mother's behavior as a result of the elopement of the elder daughter, Vanessa, with a Chicago man she had met at college. Andrea's references to "poor Vanessa" verified Victoria's assessment and Chase thereupon made himself particularly pleasant and acquiescent to Andrea's whims and desires; at least for the moment.

He had no such problems with Marshall Vanderkuyl, whom Chase soon recognized as a crafty manipulator with little interest in any particular business he owned or in which he had controlling interest, only in acquiring, merging, or selling, always at a profit. It soon became obvious to Chase that Marshall's greatest disappointments to date were twofold: that he had never fathered a son with whom he

199

could share his complex dealings, and that Vanessa's husband, Leander Willis, had no greater ambition beyond his grubby job in Chicago. The situation, Chase felt, could hardly be more perfect.

Until the Vanderkuyls left for Palm Beach shortly after Christmas, Chase was a frequent visitor at the East 70th Street house, and in February spent two weeks at their Palm Beach estate. There, he met Victoria's sister, Vanessa, and her husband, Leander Willis, a colorless man who worked for a Chicago insurance company as an actuary. Before Chase returned to New York, he and Victoria had come to an "understanding" and eventually, after careful consideration, won the blessings of Andrea Vanderkuyl.

Chase and Victoria were married in October of 1931 in the ballroom of the Plaza, a lavish affair attended by a resplendent gathering of guests whose glitter and brilliance left Anderson and Cleo Warren almost speechless. Duncan Collins and other Warren executives and their wives were added to the guest list, if only to make a showing for the groom's side, but Theodore begged off at the last moment, citing a touch of influenza, and remained at the University.

Chase and Victoria spent their honeymoon sailing among the Caribbean islands and returned just before Christmas for a family reunion at Brookhill, where Marshall and Andrea Vanderkuyl joined them while enroute to Palm Beach. Vanessa and Leander Willis sent regrets. Theodore came up from Athens for the holiday and returned shortly after Christmas to attend a "very special New Year's Eve affair." He gave no sign of either approval or disapproval of the Vanderkuyls although Victoria made a special effort to be friendly, this somehow thwarted by the presence of Chase. After Theodore's departure and that of the Vanderkuyls the day after the New Year, Anderson asked Chase into his study for a discussion of the future, and suffered a vital blow.

"My father-in-law," Chase announced at the outset, "wants me to take an active interest in his business affairs."

Anderson grinned appreciatively. "So does *your* father in *his* business affairs."

"He's getting along in years, Father. He needs help. Leander Willis is too satisfied with his job to move out of Chicago."

Anderson cocked an eyebrow upward at Chase. "You—you telling me you're serious about this, son?"

"I've been—considering the proposition."

"For what? Money? I God, some day you'll have more'n you can spend—"

"It isn't the money alone, Father. Good Lord, Victoria goes through an annual allowance that more than matches my income. It's something bigger than that." Chase stood up and began pacing the floor of the study. "It's more than just one business. Corporations spread out across the country, interests in oil, land, cattle, newspapers, banks, hotels —the *variety*—"

"Wait a minute, Chase, wait a minute. You're moving too fast for me." Anderson paused and drew a deep breath, fighting for what he called "thinking time." "If it ain't the money, what about pride of ownership in something you're building with your own hands and brains—"

Chase stopped and stared at Anderson, then said coolly, "I don't own anything, Father. You built the Warren Tobacco Company. I don't own a single share of stock in it."

"Is that what you want, stock? Why, for God's sake? Hell, it'll all be yours and Theodore's some day anyway." His voice was tinged with indignation now as he added, "How much stock is Vanderkuyl offering you?"

Chase said it slowly. "I'm thirty-one years old. If I can do what Marshall Vanderkuyl thinks I'm capable of doing, I'll own one-third of his holdings by the time I'm thirty-five, to control, do with it as I see fit. I'm talking about one-third of something worth close to *seventy-two million dollars*. I can show you the McNally Report I drew—"

"I won't argue with your figures, Chase. I'm sure you wouldn't make a mistake about anything that important to you," Anderson said bluntly. "All right, when do you want to leave the Company?"

"Father, I—"

"When?"

"Probably in April, when he returns from Florida."

"All right. It's your decision to make and you've made it. There's no more for me to say." Anderson stood up, his tall body rigid, eagle's eyes glittering with angry disappointment.

"Father, every man needs his chance to do what he must —"

"I didn't marry my chance, Chase," Anderson said with bitterness. "I made it, and I God, it's there for any man to see in any McNally or other report he wants to draw on me. My name is spread all over the world, on every man's and woman's lips who smokes. I'm damn proud of what I've done and I hoped my son would be proud of his own accomplishments in the Company some day. You want to play around with real estate, newspapers, hotels and banks, you go ahead. I'll make out without you. Theodore and I—"

As Chase's eyes rose to meet his own, Anderson saw that

201

the mention of Theodore's name had only stiffened Chase's determination.

"All right, Father," he said shortly, "then you won't mind if Vicky and I leave at once. I think I'll go to Palm Beach and tell my father-in-law I'm ready to go in with him now."

At the beginning of his senior year at the University, Theodore Warren showed few signs of achieving academic prominence; in fact, it seemed very likely he would never be graduated, with or without honors. A listless student, he was more interested in the abundant social life, fraternity house poker games, and weekends in Atlanta. He had money, a powerful roadster and considerable personal appeal. Books and study bored him. He felt there was little purpose in straining to reach a goal that Chase, by virtue of his nine years seniority, would gain long before him.

Theodore's scholastic lapses had not gone entirely unnoticed. He had been frequently sent for by the Dean of Men for infractions of campus rules and for dangerously low marks. He had been arrested for multiple violations in town; speeding, reckless driving, once for operating a vehicle while under the influence of alcohol, associating with notorious women, taken into custody during a raid on a gambling house. However, as the son of Anderson Warren, whose philanthropies to the University were not inconsiderable, liberal tolerance was shown him by the authorities. Notified by the University's president, Anderson Warren paid a quiet visit to him and came away with a practical suggestion.

In his hotel suite, Anderson put it up to Theodore in a forthright manner. "Look, son," he said, "you got no choice. We sent you down here to get an education and I God, you're goin'a get it and bring home a diploma to prove it."

"I don't need a goddam watchdog, Father," Theodore protested hotly.

"Cussin' ain't goin'a help you out of it. You got the bit between your teeth these past three years, but I'm pullin' the rein in on you. You and this Ken Armour are goin'a live together, study together, and you're comin' back home with that sheepskin or I'll know the reason why."

"Why, for God's sake, do I need it to make money I've got no use for?"

"Well, let's say you need it to make me and your Mama happy. And if you don't get it, you're goin'a see what it's like tryin' to earn your keep on your own. Not one nickel from me, no fancy automobile, no—"

At that point, Theodore knew he had lost the battle.

Whereupon, he agreed to meet Kenneth Armour, the brilliant law student from Laurelton. Kenneth became Theodore's tutor, moved from his dormitory room into Theodore's rented house in town and settled down to his task.

The job of bringing Theodore's marks up to a satisfactory passing level by study was too much even for Kenneth, who then turned to manufacturing clever cribs and devices which Theodore used religiously and successfully. Theodore's academic status improved, but Kenneth was wise enough not to take him into the upper one-third of his class. The following June, Theodore was graduated and Kenneth Armour was well paid for accomplishing what had seemed a near-impossible task.

Theodore was twenty-two years old and the weight of the depression was being felt everywhere. He had planned a summer tour of Europe with several friends, but Anderson had other ideas in mind. Shortly after Theodore's diploma had been framed and hung on the wall in his room, Anderson asked him to accompany him to his office. There, Anderson said, "Sit down, Theodore. It's about time we had us a talk."

"Yes, sir," Theodore replied without relish or enthusiasm.

"Tomorrow morning, I'm taking the train to New York. You're going with me."

"Sir?"

Anderson plowed on, the furrows in his forehead deepening. "You'll be in good hands. Your brother Chase learned a lot from our people up there and you're going to learn the business from the selling and advertising end of it. A good place to start."

Theodore stared at his father with disbelief. "Me?"

"You. Advertising and selling go hand in hand and I got a hunch it's going to be more and more important as time goes along. Competition is gettin' tougher—"

But Theodore was neither interested nor was he paying close attention. "L-listen, F-Father," he said nervously, "I—I don't—don't—know—"

"You did good enough at college. What you don't know, you can learn from Duncan Collins, from our marketing people, our advertising agency. Chase learned it without four years at college and so can you. He's gone off on his own and there's only you left—"

He blurted the words out in rebuke. "I—I'm not—not—Chase."

Anderson studied Theodore for a moment. "All right," he said quietly, "we're both agreed on that. You're no Chase and maybe you'll never be a Chase, but you're a Warren and

203

I got to know that no matter what happens, there'll be a Warren at the head of the Company.

"I didn't build an empire to go to a passel of strangers when I die. I'm fifty-three years old, Chase is thirty-one, married, and he's disowned the Company. You're twenty-two. I don't know how many years I got left before my string runs out. I can't predict what will happen, but you got to get ready to take over this Company some day. And don't tell me 'No.' You got yourself an education and now you're goin'a put it to work."

When Theodore did not answer, his eyes glued to the tips of his polished shoes, Anderson said, "Best you go home and do some packin' and be ready by six o'clock tomorrow morning, you hear?"

5

At 6:00 o'clock the next morning when Anderson sat down to his usual scanty, solitary breakfast, he asked Maudie to send Leona to tell Theodore to stop dawdling and come to the table. A few minutes later, Leona returned wide-eyed with the news that not only was Mr. Theodore not in his room, but his bed had not been slept in. On investigation, Anderson found that none of Theodore's clothes was missing. His car was gone. He had left no note. None of the servants had seen him leave.

After an hour of deliberation, Anderson went back to Theodore's room for another closer look and a sudden thought struck him. He went to Theodore's coin collection cabinet and pulled the top drawer open, almost certain of what he would find. Or not find. The drawer was labeled *U.S. Gold Coins* and it was empty. He looked at Theodore's coin catalogue for those coins marked with an inked check mark, indicating those that had been bought for the collection years ago by Cleo. The checked coins totaled a little over $1,500 at face value and at collectors' prices were now valued at better than $4,000.

He could delay no longer. He shut the door, then went to Cleo's bedroom to waken her and break the news that Theodore had run away from home.

At two o'clock that morning, he had made his decision. He put on a pair of corduroy pants, hunting shirt and tennis shoes, and carried a light corduroy jacket over one arm. He counted $183 in his wallet, then went to his coin collection cabinet and emptied the top drawer of his U.S. gold coins of five-, ten- and twenty-dollar denominations, put them into three small chamois bags and tied them inside his trousers.

204

The house was asleep. He crept downstairs carefully and tiptoed to the front veranda. His Packard roadster stood in the driveway and, he noted with relief, on the downhill incline. He shifted the gear to neutral, released the hand brake and pushed, and when the car began to roll, jumped in. As he neared the bottom of the incline, he turned the ignition switch on, shifted into second gear. The motor caught, sputtered, held. Then he was out on the highway.

He drove south and east through Milledgeville and Macon, stopping only for gas, then continued on to Columbus and crossed into Alabama at Phenix City. He took a room in a ramshackle hotel and slept for four hours, then continued on to Montgomery. On the outskirts of town, he found a small hotel and decided to stay on a day or two while he formulated some sort of plan. Thus far, he had been too overwhelmed by his new sense of total freedom to consider the effect his disappearance might have on his mother. As for his father, all he could think of was that for the first time in his life, he had defeated him.

He made no definite plans except to keep moving. He was aware that by now Anderson might have notified the police or put private detectives out to search for him. Therefore, he reasoned, he must get rid of the Packard. He could not get in touch with anyone he had ever known. It was possible he might be traced by the trail of gold coins. He would have to change his appearance in some way. And above all, he must keep moving.

He remained in Montgomery long enough to change several of his gold coins into paper money, cashing each coin in a different bank. On the night before he decided to sell the Packard to a secondhand dealer, someone stole it. Afraid to report the theft to the police, he took his loss quietly, bought a bus ticket to Mobile and departed Montgomery. In Mobile, he cashed a few more of the gold coins and took a room in a cheap boarding house. By now, his clothes were rumpled and dirty and he added to the picture by not shaving or having his hair trimmed.

After a few days in Mobile, he caught a bus to New Orleans where he took a room in a shabby neighborhood frequented by seamen and workingmen for their entertainment. The house he roomed in was patronized by men of the sea, beached for the moment; men with a take-life-as-it-comes, happy-go-lucky attitude; men of varying ages who drank and whored the nights away and hung around the docks and Seaman's Hall by day, exchanging gossip, gambling, drinking to while the hours away.

Within two months, he became acclimated to the noise and dirt and the strange odors of unwashed humans and

205

cooking food, his ears attuned to seamen's rough talk, the tough, life-scarred and man-hardened girls and women who could hold their own in talk, drink, fight, or love-for-pay.

The men came and went to sea and they found him when they returned, and eventually came to accept him as one of their exclusive fraternity. The winter passed into spring and into summer and he now wore seamen's clothing, talked in their jargon, drank their brand of beer, wine and bootleg whiskey. He ate their food, gambled with them, slept with their women. And at summer's end, he caught a berth on a Rio-bound freighter and to the complete surprise of his seamen friends, who had vouched for him at the hiring hall, they discovered he knew nothing about ships or a seaman's duties. They took this as a huge joke, covered for him, protected him, taught him, and soon he was able to pass muster on his own.

There were fights in which he came off badly at first, but then learned to use his height and weight and soon began winning more than he lost, which gave him a deep and rewarding feeling. In Rio, he ran into his first wholesale brawl, a matter of barroom girls and the crew of a German freighter. The fight was broken up by a squadron of police and in the confusion, he and two others escaped through a window in a back room. He realized then that had he been caught, the remaining twenty-dollar gold pieces, eighteen of them, and his cash hoard of $265 would have been discovered and would certainly have been confiscated or stolen or paid out in fines.

Returned to New Orleans, he was beached for three months and this time took up with a young prostitute who had just begun her profession and much preferred one single, bearded giant to the catch-as-catch-can many and increasing competition in these hard times. At about the time he was tiring of her insatiable demands on him, he signed on again, this time to Port-au-Prince, through the Canal to San Pedro and eventually, San Francisco. Paid off in San Francisco, he jumped ship and enjoyed what pleasures the City by the Golden Gate offered for a month. In a moment of restlessness, he bought a near-wreck of a car for $80 and headed eastward toward Sacramento, then south through Stockton, Fresno and Bakersfield, barely able to coax the car over the mountain into the San Fernando Valley and Los Angeles, where the ailing wreck virtually fell apart. He abandoned it on a side street, found a room in the Mexican-Chinese section and holed up for a week of rest.

Gambling, drinking and shoddy women along Main Street's skid row brought his secret fund down to its lowest point, just below $100. Time to move along. He hitchhiked to Riverside, picked oranges, slept in the open, then caught a truck ride east that took him into El Paso. After a few days of unsuccessful job-hunting, he was picked up by a traveling man who was in a hurry to get to Chicago and wanted someone to help him drive. When he took over the wheel, the man slept, and then he noticed the .38 revolver in the man's shoulder holster. When they came to Nashville and stopped at a roadside restaurant, he excused himself to go to the rest room and vanished through a back door.

From Nashville, he drifted south, moving lazily, working at any odd job he could get in exchange for meals, sleeping in the open wrapped in a cheap blanket which had become his carryall. He came down through central Mississippi with New Orleans as his goal.

And having completed the circle, he found friends among the seamen and women he had known the year before. The depression had worsened, jobs were scarcer than ever, the docks and warehouses crowded with unemployed. He husbanded his remaining cash, doling it out carefully for food, a little drink, an occasional woman.

He had been running for two years and had seen much, and learned not to think in the past. And then, finally, he was broke and engulfed in his own insecurity. In that summer, without a roof over his head, he learned about hobo jungles and how to ride the rods. A bindlestiff. And on the outskirts of Jackson, in Mississippi, where he had gone for no special reason except that the wind had blown him in that direction, he and two other knights of the road were picked up by police and jailed as vagrants. He gave the name he had assumed at the outset of his great adventure, Tom Wilson, and spent the next ninety days as a guest of the County on the road gang. In chains, under the most unbelievably filthy conditions and the watchful eyes of the vilest, most inhuman, unspeakable vermin mankind had ever produced. By the time he was released, his back and arms bore lash marks he would carry for many years. It was his misfortune that he was tall and robust and muscular, and had thus become a prime target for the sadistic and brutal guards.

He was released in September and drifted south again, this time to Florida, where he was again jailed and served another ninety days in a turpentine camp. It was here that he was almost driven to kill a guard who had clubbed two Negro prisoners to near death for a minor infraction of a camp rule; but he was forcefully restrained by his white fellow prisoners who knew that hot revenge for the rash actions of one prisoner would fall upon all.

Eventually, his time passed and he gained his release. But

he had learned a valuable lesson. Now he kept off the roads by day and slept under protective cover of the woods. He traveled by night and begged food only from Negroes in their miserable shacks. They, among all people he encountered, were the kindest and most generous, since their plight and desperation formed a common bond of misery between them. They recognized his need and shared what little they had; cornbread, a piece of sowbelly, a stolen chicken, fish, thin soup, whatever could be gleaned or begged; and he was safe from arrest.

At one thin-boarded, tin-roofed, leaky hut, he slept on the dirt floor of its single room and wakened almost 24 hours later to find that the woman had scrubbed his mud-caked, weather-stained clothes clean. In late evening, he borrowed her scissors and trimmed his beard, then allowed her husband to cut his hair. The next day, they got him a ride on a produce truck headed for Jacksonville. He was paid thirty cents for his help in unloading, and was grateful to get it. That night he bought a loaf of stale bread for two cents and caught a freight north. He rode in the empty box car for three days and nights and the trip came to an end when they reached Richmond. In the Negro quarter near the yard, he spent fifteen cents for food and slept in the woods in a hobo jungle.

He was still drifting with the wind, directionless, without plan or reason, only with the need to keep moving, moving. He began walking north and came upon a large truck with a flat tire. It had begun to rain, driving hard with a strong wind behind it, and the truckman called to the tall, hunched, scarecrowish figure to help him with the huge tires. The job completed, the man offered him a lift. In the cab, still heading north, they shared the driver's sandwiches, a thermos of thick soup, another of hot coffee; the best, richest meal he had had in months.

Then the man held out a pack of cigarettes and he saw the name WARREN staring at him and he began to laugh quietly to himself.

"Lost a lot of time," the driver said. "Flat tire and rain slowed me down. You ever drive a rig like this?"

"Yes," he replied.

"You sure?"

"I'm sure."

"If we switch off, we can go straight through. I drive, you sleep. You drive, I sleep. I pay for the food. Okay?"

"Where are we heading?"

"New York."

New York. His destination three years ago when, in fear, he had cut out and run.

208

"Okay, friend," he said.

"You take over now. If you can handle it, I'll get me some shuteye."

On the last lap, he was asleep when the truck came to a halt in front of a warehouse in lower Manhattan. The driver peeled a single dollar bill from a thin wad and handed it to him. And having spent it for food and a pack of cigarettes an hour later, he was picked up within minutes on a vagrancy charge as he slept in a doorway. This time, uncaring, he gave his correct name to the precinct sergeant and was locked up in a large cell with other vagrants, sleeping drunks, fighting drunks, vociferous drunks.

In the morning, Walter Chambers, personnel director in the New York office of the Warren Company, thumbed idly through his newspaper. He was about to turn to the sports section when, for no accountable reason, a name leaped from the page toward him. He stared at it with incredulity; among a casual listing of arrests made the day before, one stood out like a beacon.

Chambers reached for his phone, then decided against it. He got up and strode down the hall to the office of Duncan Collins, vice-president in charge of the New York district. Collins looked up from a mass of statistical sales figures Trevor Richards brought him every Monday morning. "What is it, Wally?" he asked with restrained impatience.

"Something— May I see you privately, Mr. Collins?"

"It had better be important. I'm up to yon in the weekly sales figures."

"It's important, sir. I think it's very important."

Collins motioned Richards out with a nod of his head. "Give me five minutes, Trev."

Alone, Chambers put the newspaper down in front of Collins, his finger under the name. Collins was startled. "You don't think it can be a coincidence, do you, Wally?"

"It's worth a chance after three years, don't you think, Mr. Collins? Shall I get over there and check it out?"

"Ye— No. If it's only a coincidence, we'd look silly as hell, maybe rake up some unwanted publicity for nothing. I'll put Nate Ellis on it. He's more familiar with those people." Collins reached for the phone and asked his secretary to ring up Nate Ellis who had done some investigative work for the Warren organization in the past.

Ten minutes later, Nate Ellis presented himself at the police precinct and asked to see the man they were holding as a vagrant under the name of Theodore Warren.

Before noon, a tired and weary Theodore had been released and taken to Duncan Collins' athletic club where he was placed in the steam room, given a good scrubbing and rubdown, beard shaved, hair cut, nails manicured. Meanwhile, Collins' man at Brooks Brothers arrived to measure Theodore and by five o'clock returned with a suit, shirt, underwear, socks, shoes and necktie, with the promise of more to be delivered the following day. Dressed, Theodore accompanied Collins to his Fifth Avenue duplex where Diane Collins had prepared food for him. He was shown to the guest room where he put on a suit of Duncan's pajamas and slept the clock around.

He awoke the next day, ate a meal in bed and fell asleep again. Duncan Collins did not leave the apartment and, for added insurance, had an Ellis man standing guard in the hallway. On the third morning when Theodore awoke, he looked up to find Anderson Warren staring down at him with all the honest wrath of the Avenging Angel on his granite eagle's face; but there was no anger in the older man, only a somewhat curious relief.

"Theodore," he said.

"F-Father—"

"You all right, son?"

"Yes, sir."

"Your mother's been in a terrible state ever since you run off."

"I'm sorry for that part of it, Father. I had to—do it."

"All right, it's over and done with now. We're going home to her. I haven't told her yet. Shall I telephone her now?"

"Yes, sir," Theodore said with resignation.

"You did this thing you had to do. I hope it's out of your system," Anderson said a week after they had returned home from New York.

"I don't know," Theodore replied.

"You feel it coming on you again, you don't have to do it like a tramp."

"Father, don't talk to me the way you would to a child—"

"Then for God's sake, don't act like one."

"I've been a lot of places and seen many things," Theodore said slowly. "I've worked as a laborer, seaman, fruitpicker, truck driver and a hundred other menial jobs. I've been in jail, on a road gang, in a turpentine camp. I've been a hobo. I've stolen food in hunger and I was only inches away from killing a man once. I'm not boasting. All I'm telling you is this: I'm a man grown, so don't push me too hard.

"Right now, I don't know what I am or what I'll do. I

don't know whether I'm weak or strong. Sometimes I feel one, sometimes the other. It's going to take time for me to find out, but I'm going to find out in my own time, in my own way."

"All right, son. That was a long speech," Anderson said evenly. "Longest I ever heard from you. Now I'm going to make one. Far as what you been, what you think you are or what you're lookin' for, I don't give a hoot or a holler. Whether you're weak or strong, only time will tell, but I think you'll come out of it a man. All I'm askin' of you is this: don't do anything that'll send your mother to her grave before her time. It almost happened over these past three years, but you came back in time.

"There's a place waiting for you in the Company. I was wrong to push you, I know that now. But I want a Warren at the head of the Company when I die. There's just too much to leave behind for strangers. If you don't want it for yourself, get married and have sons who will want it. What's done is done. I'm big enough a man to forgive—"

"Any man can be big enough to forgive, Father," Theodore broke in. "The question is, are you big enough to forget? That's a lot harder to do."

"Aye. I don't know that yet, but I'll try if you will."

"Then let's leave it there for the time being. When I'm ready, I'll pick my own job. And Father—"

"What, son?"

"When the time comes, I'll pick my own wife."

Anderson Warren's lips clamped tightly together in a firm line. "Agreed," he said finally.

It occurred to Theodore that Chase's name had not been mentioned during his week at home and now he asked, "Where is Chase? What is he doing?"

Anderson sighed sadly. "Your brother is a goddamned bloated financier these days, got no time for any single company like Warren. He's in the stock market and real estate and God only knows what else. He won't be around to plague any of us. He don't seem to want anything unless he can control it by himself. Forget about him."

211

CHAPTER VIII

1

On that night in 1935 when Louise Drew, then 21, said farewell to her virginity, she did so with little more regret than a perceptive businessman would give up a block of blue chip stock, or cash, in exchange for a company in which he saw a possibility for growth and profit. That she could think in such terms, under the circumstances, she considered entirely reasonable, logical and practical, having come by her pragmatism early in life, and honestly. And in Chase Warren, Louise saw Opportunity.

When the two met for the first time that day in Duncan Collins' office, where Chase was lounging lazily on the sofa, cigarette and saucer in one hand, china coffee cup in the other, a spark seemed to have ignited between them. It was early in December of 1934, a dark, glowering morning after two stormy days that had deposited nearly twelve inches of snow on the streets of New York, near-paralyzing the city's traffic. The room Louise shared with another Warren Company clerk on West 79th Street was cold, the ancient furnace (and rooming-house janitor) so decrepit that both girls had been forced to sleep in their warmest underclothing and sweaters, using their outer coats for additional covers.

Louise came into Collins' office as usual on this and every Monday morning, carrying the six-day cumulative report of national sales totals which were telegraphed to New York from the seven Warren district offices and quickly compiled for the managing director's attention.

"Excuse me, Mr. Collins," she apologized, "I—"

"It's all right, Louise, come in," Collins said. To Chase Warren, "The weekly sales figures, Chase. Give me ten minutes to run through them and sign this so we can get it off to the home office."

"Go right ahead, by all means," his guest replied. "I'm in no particular hurry and this coffee hits the spot."

"Shall I wait, Mr. Collins?" Louise asked.

"Yes, please. I want this to go out before lunch time." Then noticing Warren's more than casual interest in the

212

girl, "Excuse me. Miss Drew, Mr. Warren. Mr. Warren, Louise Drew from our Statistical Analysis Department. Take a seat, Louise, while I look these over."

Chase Warren stood up, a smile on his dark, handsome face, and indicated the chair beside him which Collins had vacated. "Coffee, Miss Drew?" he asked. "Knocks off the chill—"

"Yes, please. I'll get it." She could feel Warren's eyes on her as she walked to the low cabinet and poured a cup for herself, something she had never been invited to do by Collins, now busy with the report and paying no attention to her. Warren was still standing when she returned and he again indicated the chair. She sat in it, unable to balance the cup and saucer and pull her skirt down over her knees. Warren took the cup and saucer from her, allowing her to make the adjustment, looking away as she made it. He opened the mahogany cigarette box on the low table and held it toward her, and once again she looked toward Collins, saw him preoccupied with the report, furrowed brow, making notes on a yellow pad. She accepted the cigarette and a light. "How long have you been with the Company?" Warren asked.

"A little less than a year," Louise replied.

"Enjoy your work?"

"It's fascinating. I like it very much."

He smiled and frowned at the same time. "Handling a lot of dull figures?"

"They're not at all dull if one injects a little imagination."

"Presupposing that you do have it, how does imagination help?"

She laughed lightly, uncertainly. "I suppose anyone else would think I'm silly—"

"Not at all. It's an interesting supposition. Tell me."

"Well, the figures are really only figures, of course, but each telegram is a *place* from where the figures are sent. Chicago, Denver, San Francisco, Dallas— I see the figures, but I imagine the cities, the people, the buildings, parks, theaters—"

"Beautiful," Chase Warren said. "Absolutely marvelous."

"Sir?"

"That you are able to translate hundreds of millions of cigarettes into cities, packages into people, cartons into buildings, bales and dollars into scenic beauty. I admire that very much. I wish I could learn to do that."

She crimsoned prettily and lacking an answer, sipped at her coffee, then drew on her cigarette while he continued to stare at her face. "You're not from New York, are you?" he

213

asked. "Originally, I mean. So few people I've met here are natives."

"No. I was born in Pennsylvania. My parents moved to Boston and later on to New Hampshire. My father is headmaster at Penchester, a preparatory school for boys."

"And I'm from the opposite direction. Laurelton, Georgia."

How strange, she thought later, that I hadn't considered the possibility that Mr. Chase Warren was one of *the* Tobacco Warrens. It came to her that she had never heard of *Chase* Warren and assumed that Anderson Warren, whom she had seen twice in the New York headquarters, was the only living Warren on earth. Now she gulped and said, "Then you're—"

"Anderson Warren's son. There's another besides me. My younger brother, Theodore."

"I didn't know. I've never seen you here before."

"I'm not active in the Company, Miss Drew. I have my own—interests—apart from this. I left the Company some years ago, but Mr. Collins and I have remained good friends."

Collins' phone rang then, drawing his attention away from the report. Chase Warren said, "Would you have lunch with me, Miss Drew? Dunc is tied up and I despise eating alone. I know a charming place nearby—"

She nodded her head without realizing how much she wanted to have lunch alone with Mr. Chase Warren, heir to the Warren tobacco fortune; without considering whether he was married or single; only that she would have accepted in any event.

"Beautiful," he said in a low voice, still smiling. He threw a quick glance in Collins' direction, still busy on the telephone. "I'll meet you in the entrance downstairs at—shall we say twelve-thirty?"

Louise nodded again. She got up and returned her cup and saucer to the cabinet, then went to the chair beside Duncan Collins' desk just as he was hanging up the receiver. He smiled at Louise, finished running down the recapitulation sheet of the report, initialed it and handed it back to her. "Fine, Louise. I'm glad to see those West Coast figures are picking up, particularly in the Los Angeles area. Such a large territory to cover. Send this off at once, will you?"

That night, Louise shared a light dinner with Rose Janowiecz, her dark beauty of a roommate, who was 28 years old and from Pittsburgh. They had met two years before at the Culver Business School where Rose, a clerk at the Warren Company, was taking night courses to become a secretary, the path she had chosen as the only possible and sensible one to meet "the right man." Rose had unashamedly admitted to a romantic attachment with Trevor Richards, who headed the Statistical Analysis Department, the admission coming after a class one night when she invited Louise to move in and share her room as a means of cutting living costs.

"What about your Mr. Richards?" Louise asked.

"Him? He never comes there. We go to a little hotel on 32nd Street once, sometimes twice a week, if he can get away from his wife."

"Rose, how can you—?" Louise began.

Rose laughed. "You're kind of cute, you know. Listen, Lou, there's a depression on. Jobs are damn hard to get, or to keep once you get one. You'll find that out when you start looking. And the office managers and personnel directors start sizing you up even before they hand you an application blank. A kid like you, no trouble at all if you play it right—"

"For a job?"

"For a job. When you're broke and the rent is due and you ate your last meal three days ago, yes, for a job."

"I would never—"

"Honey, wake up. So your old man sends you a few bucks every week and you don't have to worry about tomorrow. Okay. But if your old man's in Pittsburgh and is a goddam drunk who beats you and your old lady up and tells you, 'Goddam you, it's time you started bringin' in a buck or two,' and you say, 'I'm out tryin' to find a job every day. What do you want me to do, hustle on the streets, f'Chrissakes?' and he yells, 'Goddam you, if that's the only way you can make it, go ahead!' then what the hell? You scrape up enough for bus fare to New York and go in business for yourself, not for a drunken old man who's going to take every dime away and slap you around in the bargain.

"Okay, so I'm not what you would call a nice girl, but I got my own principles. If I hustled a little when I first got here, it was for me, nobody else. I got a job clerking. I'm going to Culver to better myself. A secretary's got a hell of a better chance."

Louise was fascinated by the petite Polish girl's honesty and open friendliness. She moved into the room on West 79th Street at a savings of several dollars a week and within three months, when Rose moved up from her clerking job to become Trevor Richards' secretary, she recommended Louise as her replacement.

"No strings attached, Lou," Rose told Louise excitedly.

"You think I can do it, Rose?"

"That job? Hell, it's nothing but figures. Anybody can do it if I can. It don't pay—"

"Rose, *doesn't*."

"Doesn't. Thanks. So it doesn't pay much, but Jesus—"

"Please, Rose, don't say 'hell' or 'Jesus.' "

"All right. Some other time. You want the job? It won't wait."

"I'll take it."

"Good. Play it smart and remember, Rosie will be there to help you. And don't tell your old man. Let him keep sending you that check every week so you can build up a rainy day fund."

Now, during the movie that followed her dinner with Rose Janowiecz, she thought of her lunch with Chase Warren, a success because he had the will and drive to succeed. Imagine giving up a chance to become head of the Warren Tobacco Company some day in order to go off on his own and become a multimillionaire in his own right. Courage. Or was it his suave effrontery, sheer arrogance, refusing to be stopped by people, depression, anything? This tall, confident, handsome—what? Perhaps *pirate* best described him. A man who knew what he wanted and took it.

Just then she realized, watching the blurred screen, that he wanted her and, when he was ready, would take her.

2

Louise had often wondered what, when that moment of decision came, her reaction would be. She thought of Rose Janowiecz's background, immigrant steel mill father, peasant mother, and compared it with her own.

Louise was the product of a curious combination, two humans who were as totally different as Mr. and Mrs. Janowiecz of Poland and Pittsburgh must surely be alike. Her father, Roland Edmonds Drew, had been an assistant economics professor at the University of Pennsylvania, an associate in economics at Harvard, a man with the underlying qualities of a 19th-century missionary. At a point in his life when he was about to receive a full professorship, he abruptly deserted Cambridge to become headmaster of Penchester Academy, a small, exclusive preparatory school for boys in New Hampshire.

Louise's mother, Martha, had always been the fighter in the Drew family. Long before that memorable Thursday, August 26th, in 1920, when Woman gained the hard-fought right to vote, Martha Drew had waged an unrelenting and continuing militant rebellion against the world of Man and his resistance toward giving her sex full equality, opportunity and rights in the professional, industrial, commercial, governmental and social world, with equal remuneration and recognition.

Endowed with a mind that eagerly absorbed the facts and fictions of life with a greed that bordered on physical hunger, as well as an ability to analyze and sort out the more desirable from its less favorable aspects, Louise Drew had, at an early age, come to certain precocious, albeit determined, confident conclusions.

She would, she decided, 1) graduate from college with honors, 2) be married by the time she reached her 25th birthday, 3) to a man of wealth (not *average*, but *extreme* wealth), and 4) she would, in some as yet undetermined way, gain control of a sufficient portion of that wealth to permit her to live as she damned well pleased and come and go as whim dictated. This, deeply imbedded in her young brain, became her carefully conceived Life Plan.

Her opinion of her father was no higher than that which she held of her mother. Roland's was a life of irony; Martha's one of desperate futility. The one common bond between them was a daughter neither seemed to appreciate or understand and who, in return, loved neither to any measurable depth.

Louise learned something from both. From Roland, that for all his superior wisdom and knowledge of money, he had been unable to accumulate any of it for himself and his family. From Martha, a sense of her mother's own inadequacy to face reality.

Love, Louise decided, was a complex confusion of ideas, depending largely on what misinformation one read or heard. To her father, Love was a dedication to work, something he accepted with totality and in which he found his deepest gratification.

To her mother, and communicated to Louise over the years in angry, bitter, one-way mother-to-daughter monologues, Love was a hideous, unfair trap conceived by Man, the conscious or unconscious rapist, and whether the former or the latter made little difference to the raped. The individuality of Woman in Man's world was a myth, a canard. Men were predatory beasts who seized pleasure and seldom, if ever, gave it. True equality was nonexistent, the bait in

217

the marriage trap; nor was it present in the sex act, which was highly overrated.

Life itself, continuing Martha's hypothesis, was a fraudulent partnership, else why was the burden of child-bearing and child-rearing placed upon the woman while the male animal remained free to roam the forests, posturing, preening, impregnating unsuspecting females?

And therefore, Louise, a woman must fight in any way she can for her just portion of the material benefits, her social security, her sanity. For trampling Woman into the ground in the way a vandalous boy tramples flowers in a garden, for the humiliation she must suffer, Man Must Pay.

Louise was wrong on at least two counts in her Life Plan. She was not graduated from college and she was not married at the age of 25.

When Louise was 17, Martha Drew gave up her unremitting struggle against a world of injustice to Womanhood and died in an apoplectic rage after reading an editorial in a Boston newspaper which had deeply offended her. In that year, Louise's boyishly adolescent figure had become enrobed with the delectable flesh and lovely contours of young womanhood, as feminine a creature as her mother had been unfeminine. Her hair was a soft bronze color, her eyes emerald green, her skin pink and creamy smooth. She was lithe in body and limb and a heady problem at Penchester, not only with the growing consciousness of the students, but with a good percentage of the faculty and more than a few of their observant wives. The situation, in time, brought multiple pressures, if not academic unrest and uneasiness, upon Roland Edmonds Drew, who finally agreed that steps should be taken.

At the close of that school year, Louise solved the problem of father, faculty and students by deciding to leave Penchester for New York. Roland, feeling deep relief, saw her properly enrolled at Barnard, found a room in a respectable boarding house for her and gave her an allowance that would insure her against the necessity of having to work in order to maintain herself.

Two years later, a bored Louise dropped out and enrolled at the Culver Business School, eager to escape her academic surroundings and embark on a career of her own choice. It was here she had met Rose Janowiecz and later took her first step into the business world by way of the Warren Tobacco Company.

On Chase Warren's return from Palm Beach the following spring, his marriage to Victoria was almost four years old and he considered that everything he had gained through his marital alliance with the Vanderkuyls had been well-earned.

Victoria's demands on his time, he felt, were unreasonable. His father-in-law, as Chase gradually extended active supervision over the Vanderkuyl holdings, relaxed into semi-retirement, traveling with Andrea for pure enjoyment, part of which included bombarding Chase with cablegrams from Bombay, Shanghai, Manila, Honolulu, Rome, London, Zurich, Havana, Caracas; telegrams from Palm Beach, Palm Springs, La Jolla, Carmel, Aspen.

There were stormy, painful scenes between Chase and Victoria, and a more serious threat of a separation (which brought Marshall and Andrea rushing home from Mexico City) and finally a desperate arrangement, on Chase's insistence, that he be free to move around at will, do as he pleased with the Vanderkuyl properties without Marshall's permission or interference—or else Vanderkuyl could return to harness and run his own empire and allow Chase to step out and divorce Victoria.

Chase, as he had assumed he would, won that battle. As to the final outcome of the war, he had not fully reckoned with Andrea Vanderkuyl.

So began a new era in Chase Warren's life. In those four years at the helm of a fortune during a heavily depressed economy, he bought and merged newspapers, picked up a Manhattan bank in considerable trouble, acquired several and various real estate parcels which included three office buildings in midtown and some apartment houses in Harlem. He went to Texas and picked up certain ranch lands his geologist believed to be in oil and natural gas territory, bought up a major truck line franchise to expand an existing line beyond the Mississippi, a small paper mill in New England to add to the Canadian output, and picked up a small aircraft plant in Southern California in whose land holdings alone he saw rich possibilities. In Oregon, he purchased timber lands, in Washington, an insurance company about to go broke, controlling interest in a paint and chemical plant in Ohio.

And back in New York between trips, the new and tempting prospect of Louise Drew.

He telephoned her one day in February and they went to dinner together. When he dropped her at her rooming house on West 79th, Louise read dismay and disapproval in his face. In March, with Rose Janowiecz's blessing, Louise moved into a small, tastefully furnished apartment on East 63rd, arranged and paid for by Chase Warren. She was 21, and Chase 35, when the affair began. He asked her to leave the Company, but Louise insisted on remaining, unable to visualize full days with nothing to occupy her time.

The arrangement, for Louise, was delightful and exciting. She dined in interesting, exotic, expensive restaurants and took unscheduled trips to cities she had only dreamed about, spent vacations in unbelievably luxurious surroundings. Her wardrobe included smart dresses, suits and evening gowns, lovely accessories, lingerie, and a pleasing collection of good furs and jewelry.

Equally rewarding was her introduction to sex, which she found not vile, ugly or shameful, as Martha had described it to her, but thrilling, exhilarating experiences with a man as well schooled in its art as the conductor of a symphony, to which she often related the act.

The affair went along smoothly for a full year, during which Roland Edmonds Drew and Marshall Vanderkuyl died within three months of each other, both of heart attacks. The first had little effect on Louise and Chase, but the second did. Marshall Vanderkuyl, from his grave, achieved a victory that hadn't been possible in life, no doubt inspired by Andrea Vanderkuyl.

Prior to the reading of the will, Victoria left the house early to keep an appointment with her mother at the Vanderkuyl home on East 70th Street, leaving word for Chase with their butler that she would meet him at the attorney's office at two o'clock. Chase suspected correctly that his mother-in-law and wife, with previous knowledge of the contents of Marshall's will, were meeting to plan some strategic move that would affect him, against which he would be helpless to plot a counter-move until the contents of his father-in-law's will would be made known to him.

Marshall Vanderkuyl's will came as a treacherous blow to Chase. As promised, he divided his wealth into thirds; one-third to his widow, Andrea; one-third to Leander and Vanessa Willis; the final third to his daughter, Victoria Vanderkuyl Warren. And to Chase Warren, "for his devotion to my daughter and my personal affection for him, one hundred thousand dollars, separate and apart from that one-third of my estate left to his wife." Chase looked into Andrea's cold eyes and knew that the war between them had only begun.

One hundred thousand dollars. No small amount in the depression year of 1935, but hardly the one-third of the nearly $100,000,000 estate he had expected to share with Victoria, now in her hands alone, placed there to keep Chase Warren in line.

As they left the Fifth Avenue offices of Marshall Vanderkuyl's attorneys, a silently triumphant Victoria slid into the waiting limousine while Chase stood on the curb as though trying to decide whether or not to join her.

"Coming, Chase?" Victoria called out, a light inscrutable smile on her carefully made-up face.

"I don't quite know." Chase replied with an attempt at casual indifference.

"Don't you think it would be better to talk it over at home than here on the street?"

"I don't know what there is to talk over."

"How will you ever know if you don't try?"

He shrugged and said, "All right." He got into the car and Victoria nodded to Thomas, their chauffeur. On the way uptown each looked out of his own side of the car, unwilling to begin a discussion which might have ended in disaster even before they could reach home. When they arrived, Chase went directly to the bar in the game room and poured a drink. Victoria came in a few moments later and said, "And one for me, Chase."

He pushed the engraved decanter and a glass toward her. "Help yourself," he said grittily.

Victoria's laughter infuriated him. "Poor Chase," she said. "Are you so disappointed?"

"All right, Vicky. You wanted to talk. You can't do that and sneer at the same time. Talk."

"Very well, Chase. There's a lot more than thirty-three million dollars involved, you know."

"Explain that to me, please."

"Chase, don't be stubborn or angry. You know why Father did it, don't you?"

"Of course. You and your mother influenced him."

"That's right. We influenced Father, but you can influence me."

He knew she was referring indirectly to Louise, that she had somehow known about her from the start and now had the power to put a stop to the affair. "I don't know that I want to, Vicky," he replied.

"Not for a hundred million dollars, Chase? Is she that important to you?"

"We were talking about your one-third of the estate—"

"Chase, don't be ridiculous. Mother can't do a damned thing with her one-third except turn it into cash or bonds and take a severe loss doing it. Leander Willis has about as much business sense as a ten-dollar-a-week office clerk, so he would do the same. And I'm certainly no brighter about finance and real estate than Mother or Leander."

"So?"

"So we'll never starve, or course, but wouldn't it be a pity to allow the Vanderkuyl estate to die when you could do so much with it? Think about it, Chase," she said temptingly, pausing while Chase poured another drink for himself. "Let's say that we let matters stand as they are. What happens then? You take a paltry hundred thousand dollars and go off somewhere to divorce me and start all over again. Who knows what will happen? You may even have to go crawling back to ask your father for a job and wait for him to die before you can inherit half of an estate. And who knows, Anderson may even outlive us all."

He was still unmoved by her speech. "But if you're reasonable," Victoria continued, "I know that I can persuade Mother, Leander and Vanessa to turn our shares over to you to do with as you have been doing all along."

He moved closer to the bait trying not to show his eagerness. "Full control?"

"Not as long as Mother is alive, but certainly more freedom than Father allowed you." She hesitated a split second to assess his reaction before sinking the hook deeper. "Meanwhile, you'll have almost a hundred million dollars worth of assorted properties to play with. Merge, buy, sell, trade. Stocks, real estate, banks, newspapers, oil—"

"What are your mother's terms, Vicky?"

"They're not unreasonable, Chase. To keep Mother informed monthly on all business deals, with her assurance that she will not be difficult, and that her own accountants will have audit access to the books. Second, your promise to be a faithful husband. No sneaking around the country with beautiful whores paid for with Vanderkuyl money. No apartments on East 63rd Street, expensive gifts or charge accounts included."

Despite his outward calm, Chase winced at his own reckless stupidity. "Anything else Andrea wants?" he asked.

"Yes. Grandchildren."

"Vicky—"

"Wait, Chase, before you decide. Most husbands give as part of the marriage bargain what I'm willing to pay millions for. I can assure you that I had to do a major bargaining job before Mother gave her consent this morning."

"Why, Vicky?"

"Because, as I told Mother, I'm a damned fool who loves her husband despite the things we know about him. You don't need to answer me now, Chase, I can live with my inglorious humiliation for a day or two longer to allow you to consider it. But when you do answer, one way or the other, you're going to have to live by that decision. Divorce, or a true marriage with children. Weigh it carefully, darling, and see if your precious Louise Drew is worth it."

He thought about it all that night and the next day. He thought of it in terms of Louise, of Anderson and Cleo, of Theodore. Of himself alone and free with a mere $100,000. And of Marshall Vanderkuyl, the gutless coward who had driven a stake into his heart before escaping into his own grave.

$100,000 was hardly enough to make a new start on his own, far less than he had taken annually in salary; nothing, really, when he compared it to what he could accomplish with himself in complete control of the entire estate. He had at that very moment a very private list of possible acquisitions in priority order, at the bottom of which, at some future date, was the Warren Tobacco Company; one he felt was rightfully his, or should be, when Anderson Warren passed on. With $100,000 he saw the end of that dream. He had lived too well and too high these last years, never counting the cost, seldom hesitating or quibbling over an extra hundred or two hundred thousand dollars to add a promising property to the Vanderkuyl holdings. Tremendous sums of money had passed through his hands without a single failure or loss and this, he knew full well, was because there was a huge fortune backing him, to give him confidence. What would happen to that personal reassurance with only $100,000?

Ergo, he must come to terms with Victoria and Andrea. On their terms. Resume the marriage, father Victoria's children. An occasional stepping out of bounds, certainly, but no Louise in a convenient apartment, an end to the youth she created in him by giving him her own youth.

Two days more passed. He hadn't left the house, nor had he seen Victoria. Only those most urgent business calls requiring his personal attention were transferred to him from his office, special mail relayed by messenger service. On the third day he went to see Louise and she needed no more than one look at his face to realize it was over between them. The parting was painful and she began to hear a distant voice, Martha's, recounting the evils in Man, the sufferings of Woman. It came to an end that day. Chase would pay the full amount of a new five-year lease on her apartment. He would deposit $10,000 to her bank account. Everything she already had was hers to keep.

"You are being more than generous, Chase," Louise said with cold, controlled anger.

223

"I wish it could be more, Louise," Chase replied. "I'm glad you understand how much this means to me."

"I do. Oh, I do, Chase."

"You're angry, of course, and I can't blame you."

"Shall I smile for you, dance, take off my clothes and throw myself at you with joy?"

"No, darling—"

"Please don't call me that."

"All right, Louise. I know you hate me now—"

"I don't hate you at all, Chase. I don't know why, but somehow I'm more easily reconciled to it than you think, even more than you seem to be. I'm sure I must have expected something like this would happen sooner or later."

"Louise—"

She turned and walked to the bedroom door. "Please go now, Chase. I don't know how much longer I can keep up this front."

"Louise, please—"

She went into the bedroom and closed the door behind her.

Thank God I was sensible enough to keep my job, she thought later. I think I'd go crazy without it.

She toyed with the idea of inviting Rose Janowiecz to move into the apartment with her, but decided against it. Rose wouldn't fit into the world where she had been living, one she intended to continue.

There were men in the Warren organization who were "possibles," but none in the Chase Warren class. The top-level executives were all safely married and the younger men, most of whom would never make it to the top, were eager for her company as always, but except for an occasional dinner and show or night club, hardly worth encouraging. And Louise was determined that the next time, a legal document and ring were mandatory. The legal right was always on the side of the wife; the only right.

There was one consoling thought. Chase's reconciliation with Victoria had eliminated the public notoriety of being named in court as an adulteress. Rose, she was sure, would keep quiet. She wondered if Duncan Collins knew, or suspected.

3

In the summer of 1937, a startling event took place. A year before, when Louise was at her lowest emotional point following Chase's rejection and return to Victoria, rumors about his brother, Theodore, had swept through the Warren building. It was common knowledge that Theodore Warren had quietly disappeared from his home in Laurelton several years before, and that Anderson Warren had engaged detectives to search the country for him; or his body. Theodore had left few traces behind: a Packard roadster the police had traced to a man in an Alabama city who turned out to be a car thief with a long record; some gold coins he had exchanged for bills in three or four southern cities. From that time on, nothing had been heard of him for three years, until Duncan Collins discovered Theodore in a jail in New York, arrested as a common vagrant, taken him home and held him there until Anderson Warren had come up from Laurelton to take his son home. The rumor didn't get very far after a quiet whisper circulated by Miss Federhoff, Collins' secretary, that anyone spreading the gossip would be immediately dismissed.

So it was, when Louise returned from a two-week July vacation in the White Mountains that Rose cornered her in the privacy of the ladies' room to tell her that none other than the mysterious Theodore Warren, after three years in Laurelton under old A.W.'s eyes, was not only back in New York, but would be working for the Company, going methodically through every division to learn how each functioned before deciding which interested him most.

"I'm terribly unimpressed," Louise said with apparent disinterest.

"He's *single,*" Rose emphasized. "And good looking."

"I couldn't care less."

"Oh, boy," Rose said knowingly, "he stung you harder than I thought."

"Who?"

"*Who?* Chase Warren, that's who."

"You're giving him too much credit, Rose."

"Oh, come *on*, Louise. This is Rosie you're talking to."

"Rose, if you don't mind, I'd rather not discuss it. Please."

Rose shrugged. "Okay, I just thought—"

"Well, don't. Chase Warren and I broke up over a year ago. I'm not a piece of merchandise or an—item!—that is handed down from one brother to another."

"All right, Louise, if you say so."

"I say so and I mean so. I fell once and that's as far as I intend to go. The next man I sleep with will be my husband."

225

Rose smiled and said, "Baby, I'm on your side. Only, don't turn down a good thing if it shows up."

It was Louise's turn to smile. "Are you suggesting I might marry Chase's *brother*, for God's sake?"

"So why not? You think Chase Warren would be stupid enough to tell a *brother*? A friend, maybe. A brother, never."

"Rose, I love you and now shut up, forget it, and let's get back to work before Mr. Richards accuses us of being a pair of lesbians."

"Anybody else, darling, maybe. Not Mr. Richards," Rose laughed.

On a bright, cheerful mid-September morning when Louise arrived at work wearing a particularly attractive new black suit that showed her vacation-tanned skin off to its best advantage, she encountered a small buzzing knot of Statistical Analysis clerks, male and female, huddled around Rose's desk; the water-cooler crowd, known as the swiftest gossip transmission belt in the building. She avoided the group and went directly to her desk where Rose joined her only moments later.

"Good morning, Louise," Rose greeted. "You look so nice this morning. Like you had advance information."

"About what?"

Rose's head inclined toward Trevor Richards' private office. "He's here," she whispered.

"Who's here?"

"Him. Theodore Warren. He'll be in the department for about a week or ten days. They just moved another desk into Trev's office for him."

"Is that what all the chatter was about?"

"It's enough, isn't it? Lou, he's *nice* looking, tall, smoky blue eyes, you should have seen how polite he was when Trev introduced him to everybody—"

"Rose, it's Monday and I've got the weekly recap to do. I'll get all the gossip later." Bag and gloves in a drawer, small, perky hat hung, she sat at her desk and began sorting the telegrams received over the weekend from each sales district.

Twenty minutes later, the door behind her opened and she heard Trevor Richards' voice: "—so we may just as well take a look at the report which originates every Monday morning at Miss Drew's desk and keeps us busy until Friday. Total sales nationally and, later on, a breakdown analysis of each district. By Wednesday, we'll have the foreign branch figures to add to our national figures—ah, Mr.

226

Warren, may I present Miss Drew? Miss Drew, Mr. Theodore Warren from Laurelton headquarters—"

Louise stood up and stared at Theodore Warren with coolly controlled appraisal and saw a tall, somber-faced man with blue eyes who seemed older than his approximately 30 years, a hawklike nose only a little less pronounced than Chase's. His frame was large, but his face was thin, as though it needed filling out, his hands firm, with slender, sensitive fingers. His clothes were conservatively dark, well-cut, his linen crisp and immaculate. Certainly he lacked Chase's quick, easy smile and vitality as he stood unsmiling and somewhat tense. He nodded briefly and acknowledged the introduction by simply parroting her name: "Miss Drew."

"If you'd like, Mr. Warren," Richards was saying, "this would be a good starting point—"

Louise said, "I think it would be better if I got the report out first, Mr. Richards, then I can use my file copy to explain the system we use. Mr. Collins likes to have his copy before eleven."

"Yes. Yes, perhaps you're right, Louise. All right, then, suppose we start at Reception where all district communications are received, time-logged and distributed to their proper sections. After lunch, Miss Drew can show you—"

Without further word, they moved off toward Reception.

After lunch, the Weekly Sales Analysis dispatched by messenger to Western Union for transmission to Laurelton, Richards was back with Theodore Warren. He gave Theodore a brief discourse on the analytical process and left him with Louise to have the details filled in. For over an hour, Louise brought out back files of reports, telegrams and cables, explained the four-page report, translated sales volume into percentages, broke down advertising costs to determine cost per thousand cigarettes. And through it all, Theodore sat and listened gravely and asked not a single question. At the end of the second hour, Louise said suddenly, "I'm afraid I'm not making this very clear or interesting for you, Mr. Warren."

"Oh, you are. Indeed you are, Miss Drew," Theodore said quickly. "I find it extremely interesting."

"You haven't shown it in the least. Perhaps Mr. Richards could—"

"No, no. I find it very engrossing, really." Then, for the first time, he smiled, "The actual details aren't terribly important for me to remember, are they, Miss Drew? The actual processing of figures to reach the end result, I mean."

"Then I think I've shown you as much as I can."

227

"Not entirely. As I get it, these figures are telegraphed to New York from each district. New York adds its own figures to the rest, and the final report is made up, approved by Mr. Richards, then Mr. Collins, then sent by telegraph to Laurelton. From that point, Laurelton is apprised of sales and remaining inventories in each district and initiates shipping orders to replenish stocks in our various warehousing facilities. Is that essentially correct?"

"Yes—"

"By Wednesday, you will receive similar figures by cable from every foreign branch and go through the same procedure."

"Yes—"

"Which proves that I have been an attentive student, doesn't it?"

"Yes—"

"Tell me, Miss Drew, do you ever go to Greenwich Village?"

The suddenness of the question took her by surprise. "Why—I have been there—several times. I don't know it very well."

"I don't know it at all. Would you like to be my guide on an evening in which you find yourself free?"

"I doubt if I'm familiar enough with the area to qualify as a guide, Mr. Warren."

"Nonsense. You explained this procedure so well I'm sure Greenwich Village will offer no challenge to you."

"I don't—know—if—"

"Mr. Richards? Mr. Collins? No cause for alarm, Miss Drew. I'm sure neither will object. In fact, we can keep it a dark secret between us, if you prefer."

She studied him for a moment and said, "I don't think I should, Mr. Warren. The Company frowns on office friendships—"

"Ah, friendship." Theodore said it with a sad smile. "With your religious devotion to Company rules, Miss Drew, I fail to see how a friendship could possibly begin, let alone develop."

"Mr. Warren, if you will excuse me—"

"If you are afraid I am a rich libertine, I can assure you—"

"It isn't that, Mr. Warren."

"You're not married, are you, Miss Drew?"

"No."

"Engaged?"

"No."

"Uh—romantically attached?"

228

"No. You can find the answers to most of those questions by looking at my file in Personnel."

Theodore sighed. "Then the only conclusion I can draw is that I am personally repugnant to you."

She smiled. "Hardly that."

"Or a colossal bore."

"Again, no."

"And you won't tell me why you won't allow me to see you after hours?"

"I don't enjoy being placed in that position, but—"

"But?" he pressed.

"It's simply that— Well, where can it possibly lead?"

"Ah," he sighed. "Why don't you give it a chance and see?"

"That's too much like gambling at a game you have no confidence in winning. Or breaking even."

"Are you using your statistical knowledge to influence your judgment?"

"There aren't any statistics I know of to cover that subject, only the laws of probability. And my own feelings."

"Your woman's intuition—or is it your New Yorker's natural distrust speaking?"

"Whatever it is, it is there. I can't help that, can I?"

"Do you mind if I keep trying?"

"I can't prevent that, can I?"

"Frankly, no." He stared at her for a moment, then said, "What is it, Miss Drew, a difference in social class? Believe me, I am not that conscious of—"

"Nor is it that, Mr. Warren. I am simply not interested and don't care to discuss it further."

He stood up then. "I understand. The choice is yours to make and you've made it. I can't blame you. I don't make friends easily. In fact, I don't know anyone whom I can honestly call a real friend." When she said nothing, "Isn't it strange," he continued musingly. "It only just occurred to me that I'm a wholly friendless man."

She turned and stared at him, disbelieving the words, but not the openly honest face that had spoken them. He was staring back at her, eyes frank and without guile. She said, "I can't believe you're without friends."

"A few acquaintances, of course," he replied, "but not one of whom I can honestly say, 'This is my friend.' That may sound odd to someone like you—"

"Mr. Warren—"

"No, never mind, Miss Drew. I am not asking for a sympathetic response. Thank you. You've been an excellent teacher in more ways than one. Very helpful."

Her face, she knew, was crimson, ashamed that she had treated a very gentle and lonely man in such cavalier fashion, yet there was nothing she could add at the moment to assuage his hurt. He turned then and went back into Mr. Richards' office and she saw Rose's face staring at her with a grin of curiosity.

An hour later, Richards came out with Theodore and walked him to the bank of elevators in the hall and returned alone. As he passed Louise's desk, he said with a smile, "Mr. Warren was highly complimentary of you. On Wednesday he would like to watch you from the start of your Foreign Sales Report."

"Thank you, Mr. Richards. I will be happy to show him the system."

Wednesday began as a bright and sunny morning, but shortly before noon became overcast, dark and drizzly. By noon, thunder roared, lightning rent the sky and New York was in a drenching autumn rainstorm. Louise had spent the morning with Theodore at her side as she collected cablegrams, transferred figures into orderly columns, added them to the previous Monday report and prepared the final analysis. When it was ready, Theodore stood up and said, "Thank you, Miss Drew. This has been very enlightening," and left.

When she was ready to leave for the day, the downpour was at its heaviest, the sky as dark at 5:30 P.M. as it would be at midnight. Employees, caught unawares without raincoats or umbrellas, huddled in the lobby of the Warren Building on East 42nd Street, hoping for a letup. Cabs, of course, were not available. Some few braver souls timed the arrival of city buses and ran to the corner, only to find them filled to capacity. With New Yorker resignation, they waited, complaining, for turns at the row of telephones in the lobby to notify families of the delay.

Louise stood in the doorway among a group of men and women watching cars and buses flash by, sending huge sprays of water onto the pavement, further saturating drenched pedestrians. And then, she felt a hand touch her elbow and moved to allow room for passage. It was Theodore Warren.

"Trapped?" he asked with a faint smile, towering over her.

"Aren't we all" Louise replied grimly.

"Not quite. I've a Carey limousine due in about three minutes. May I give you a lift? There's no telling how long this will last."

"I'd appreciate it very much if it won't be taking you out of your way," Louise replied.

230

"Of course not. No trouble at all. I'm going right past your place."

Quizzically, "Where, Mr. Warren?"

"Wherever your place happens to be, of course."

They both laughed and pushed their way to the outer fringe of the crowd just as the rented limousine pulled up to the curb. The chauffeur leaped out, opened an umbrella and ran toward the entrance as the doorman pushed into the envious crowd and announced, "Your car is here, Mr. Warren."

"Thank you." Partially protected by the umbrella, they got into the limousine and Theodore asked, "Where to, Miss Drew?"

She gave the address on East 63rd Street and Theodore relayed it to the chauffeur. "Do you live with your family, Miss— Do you mind if I call you Louise?"

"Not at all, Mr. Warren, since we work for the same employer. No, I live alone. My parents aren't alive."

"No family in New York?"

"No. A few scattered cousins through Pennsylvania, one or two in New England. I'm all alone here."

"That gives us two things in common. As you put it, we work for the same employer and we're both alone in New York. That's rather wasteful, isn't it?"

"That depends—"

"Look, Louise, if you have no other plans for this miserable night, would you have dinner with me?"

Hesitantly, "I—I'd planned on getting deeply involved in a new book I've been saving for such a night."

"Books are very lasting and there will be other rainy nights. Dinner and a show, if I can get tickets?"

Spontaneously, "All right. I'd like that very much, Mr. Warren."

"And outside the Warren Building, might I persuade you to call me Theodore?"

"Very well, Theodore."

After a moment, he said, "You know, I don't feel friendless any more."

4

During the next three months, Theodore managed, after leaving Statistical Analysis for other departmental briefing, to return on one pretext or another to talk with Trevor Richards and, at the same time, have a word with Louise. She had gone to dinner with him several times, to concerts, the theater, promising herself that each time would be the last. She had invited him to dinner at her apartment once and he came happily, bearing champagne, flowers and hothouse grapes. And they had gone to the Village once and to Harlem, and he had sent her small remembrances of the occasions: books, flowers and champagne.

Theodore had gone home to Laurelton before the Christmas holiday began and on Christmas morning she received a small package from Tiffany's by special messenger; a watch set in a gold mesh bracelet, elegantly and expensively simple. It wakened her to a certain sense of foreboding and she thought again of Chase, the apartment he was paying for in absentia, her comfortable bank balance as yet untouched by need. Chase, she knew, would be in Palm Beach with Victoria and their first child, a son named Marshall, after his grandfather.

In those passing months, she had not seen Chase. He had called once, not too long after his return to Victoria's bed, to ask if he might drop by for a visit, but she had refused him coldly, determined never to see him again, to erase him from her mind; and she wondered now if, when Theodore smiled at her, it was not Chase's smile she saw. So different in so many ways, these brothers. Chase's arrogant boldness, Theodore's timidity. Chase's strong, outspoken opinions, Theodore's quiet reflection on a question before answering. Chase's hard, driving ambitions, Theodore's patience. The differences were obvious. Only the lopsided smile was the same.

Recklessly, she began to think of Theodore in Rose Janowiecz's terms. *Baby, I'm on your side. Only, don't turn down a good thing if it shows up.* And, *So why not? You think Chase Warren would be stupid enough to tell a brother? A friend, maybe. A brother, never.* Would they see each other over the Christmas holiday? And if they did—? But she knew from Theodore that he and Chase were not close enough for exchanging either visits or confidences.

What were the odds? she wondered. Suppose she did marry Theodore, planned it to happen quickly, an elopement, without Chase's preknowledge or that of his parents? Love. Was she in love with Theodore as she had been with Chase? She thought long and as honestly as she was able on that question and decided she wasn't; and then wondered if, after a first love, the second can ever be as deep as the first. And what about discovery? Perhaps not from Chase, but surely Victoria knew and would she use her knowledge to take a belated revenge?

232

A big question. As big as the gamble itself. Marriage to Theodore. Children for insurance. The final step in her Life Plan. Was the risk worth the gamble?

Theodore came back to New York shortly after the New Year had begun and found the bracelet-watch had been returned by Louise to his apartment. He called her at once and the reception was cool. He sent flowers and an apology for having sent so costly and ostentatious a gift. She accepted the apology without enthusiasm. He called again the following week and she relented and accepted an invitation to dinner and the theater. On the following Saturday night, they ran into Darryl Jordan, the account executive on the Warren account from the Kilkarrick Advertising Agency, at the Cotton Club, and after having drunk a little too much, were persuaded to drive across to New Jersey to a brassy new night club that featured a back room gambling casino. Theodore was in a rare high mood. He gambled at the dice table and within minutes, playing for high stakes, had won over $8,000; but Louise knew that within minutes, his luck would change, a not unusual pattern to encourage high rollers. Let him win a few thousand, switch the dice and take him for all he is willing to pay or sign for while trying to win back his first gains.

When she saw the table crew change, Louise said, "Theodore, let's go. I'm—"

"I can't, Louise. I'm nearly $10,000 ahead—"

"Why give it back? You've won it, keep it."

"Louise, darling, I can't. I'm on a winning streak. It happens only once in a lifetime."

The hard-eyed stickman's voice droned, "Eight . . . point is eight . . . place your hard way bets . . . shooter's rolling . . . coming out for an eight . . . Seven! . . . pass line loses, pay the come bets . . . place your bets . . . pass line-bets . . . new shooter coming up . . . a hundred on any craps . . ."

"Theodore, please. I don't feel well."

Regretfully, Theodore gathered up his chips, the 25s, 50s and 100s. Louise went to the cashier's cage with him, where a dark, sullen man in a too-tight dinner jacket counted out 95 one-hundred-dollar bills and four twenties between thin, nimble fingers. "$9,580. Game'll be open all night, friend. Come back later, hey? Lots more where this comes from."

They said good night to Jordan, his companion and the other agency couple, apologized for leaving and went to Theodore's rented limousine. He sank back into the rear

233

seat and closed his eyes. "I'm glad we're leaving," he admitted. "You know, I'm more than just a little drunk."

On their way back, Louise became aware of the black car that had pulled out of the club grounds behind them and now seemed to be following them. She leaned forward and slid the glass partition aside. "I think someone is following us," she told the chauffeur.

"Mr. Warren a big winner?" the chauffeur asked.

"Yes."

"Clip joint," the chauffeur mumbled. "Okay, ma'am."

Theodore, dozing on the seat beside her, stirred. "What'sa matter, Louise?"

"Nothing, Theodore," she replied nervously. "Just relax and sleep."

The chauffeur, with the expertness of years at his work, found side roads and back streets Louise never dreamed existed. The car behind them trailed, then lagged, and was finally lost. By the time they reached the city, there was no doubt in the chauffeur's mind as he turned and asked, "Your place or his, ma'am?"

"Mine, please." The chauffeur nodded.

When they reached her apartment house on East 63rd, Theodore was either asleep or had passed out.

"Ma'am?" The chauffeur was standing at the curb, the apartment house doorman beside him. The lobby was as empty as the street at 3:30 on a Sunday morning.

"Please help him up to my apartment," she said.

Both men got Theodore out of the car and took him inside swiftly, then up to 17-D. Louise gave the chauffeur a hundred-dollar bill from the thick roll in Theodore's pocket and bought the doorman's silence with another. He helped her remove Theodore's outer coat, jacket, vest and shoes, then made up the sofa in the living room with extra sheets and a pillow she gave him. Theodore was in her bed and she made sure the doorman understood that she intended to sleep on the sofa.

The doorman disposed of, she went into the bedroom and removed Theodore's necktie, wrestled him out of his shirt and trousers, took off his socks and underwear. She covered his naked body with sheet and blanket, put the rest of his money on the dresser and weighted it down with a silver jewel box. She went back to the living room and dented the pillow, rumpled the covers, then went to the bathroom where she brushed her teeth, combed her hair out, stripped and got into bed with Theodore. She fell asleep at once.

When he awoke early in the afternoon, Louise was asleep. His mind was fogged and minutes passed before he

234

realized the enormity of the situation that found him in bed with the most beautiful woman he had ever known, both entirely naked, her back to his, arms encircled about her pillow. How, he wondered, had this come about? He remembered back to the Cotton Club, Darryl Jordan's invitation to follow his party to a night club in New Jersey, dim, noisy . . . table for six . . . the casino in the back room . . . drinks passed by scantily clad hostesses . . . the fevered excitement at the crap table . . . then, nothing. And now he was in Louise's apartment, her bed, Louise with him.

He got out of bed quietly, found his clothes, dressed to the waist and went to the bathroom. He found a razor and used toilet soap to shave, then returned to put on his shirt. He saw the money on the dresser, touched it, left it where it was. He went into the living room and saw the sofa made up as a bed, somewhat rumpled. In the kitchen, he found coffee and put the percolator on. When it was finished, he poured a cup of the black brew, sipped at it and lighted a cigarette. In the act of lifting the cup to his lips again, the kitchen door opened and Louise, her hair attractively tousled, stood there wearing a long, woolen robe, her face enigmatically calm.

He got to his feet. "Louise—"

"Pour another cup for me, please," she said simply.

As he did, and handed it to her, he said, "Louise, I don't know what happened last night—"

"Don't you? Don't you really, Theodore?"

"No. I swear it, Louise. I don't remember a thing."

She sat down at the table, staring at him over the rim of the coffee cup. "Do you want me to tell it to you, every little detail?"

"Louise, please. I wasn't responsible."

"That explains everything away very nicely, doesn't it? And excuses everything as well."

"Tell me—"

"All right. You won a lot of money last night and I persuaded you to leave so that you wouldn't lose it back. You passed out in the limousine on the way back. I was afraid to leave you alone with over $9,000 in cash in your pocket, and I didn't want to take it from you and send you home, leaving you to think you'd been robbed—"

"Louise, how—"

"Let me finish, please. I asked the chauffeur and Archie, the night doorman, to bring you up here. I gave them each $100 of your money for doing it. Archie made up a bed for you on the sofa and you were asleep even before your head hit the pillow. Then I went into my bedroom and got undressed." She paused to light a cigarette, showing emotion in her trembling fingers. "Shall I tell you what happened next, Theodore, or don't you really recall—"

"Tell me," he insisted.

"I was standing there putting my nightgown on when the door burst open and you were there, without a stitch on."

Theodore looked away and groaned, "Louise, I'm so desperately sorry—"

"It's a little too late for that. I couldn't scream without rousing the entire seventeenth floor. I could see people, police, news headlines—"

"Oh, my God, Louise, what must you think of me—feel—"

"Hurt. Bruised. Empty. But I suppose I'll get over it. The same thing has happened to other women and they lived." She waited for a moment through the dread silence, then said, "I once asked you where it could lead. I have the answer now." She drained the remains of the coffee in her cup, snuffed the cigarette out. "Well, your money is on the dresser. The rest of your clothes—"

He came around to her, knelt beside her. "Louise, listen to me. I love you. This isn't something I've just thought up. It's been with me for a long time, almost from the day we met." As she pulled away, he clutched at her arms and turned her back toward him. "Listen to me, Louise. I want you to marry me. Please say you will. I want you. I need you so much to have—have—done what I did last night. Louise?"

"What—what about your parents, Theodore?"

"They'll adore you the way I do. I know it. I'm long beyond the age of consent and my marriage is my affair and no one else's."

"Oh, Theodore, if I were only sure—"

"For God's sake, do you need it in writing, on a Company memorandum form, approved by the board of directors? Can't you see I love you? Surely, I've been obvious enough about it."

"I'm frightened, Theodore."

"About what?"

"Your parents. Your brother. A clerk in the Company and an heir to the Warren Tobacco fortune—"

"The question is neither my parents, my brother nor anyone else, Louise. Just you, and if you love me."

Louise did not answer at once. "For Christ's sweet sake, Louise, do you?"

She said it slowly, eyes cast downward. "Yes. If I wasn't sure before last night, I am now."

236

"Don't be ashamed, darling. I'll make it up to you." He drew her into his arms and kissed her hungrily, feeling her warm, yielding body beneath the robe. "Oh, Louise, Louise, I love you so much, so very much."

"Theodore, don't—I can't catch—my breath."

"Say you'll marry me. You haven't said it yet."

"Of—course," she gasped.

"When? How soon?"

"When do you want me to?"

"At once. As soon as we can dress and get away—"

"Theodore, my job—the office—"

His happy laugh boomed through the kitchen. "Job? To hell with it! Let Richards make up the report tomorrow, anybody, I don't care who! You're through working, Mrs. Warren!"

Early on that Monday morning in February of 1937, Theodore and Louise drove to Elkton, Maryland, in a hired car, where later that afternoon they were married in a ceremony neither would ever recall without distaste; a hurried commercial affair in a dreary living room, performed by a tall, cadaverous man who could have been the original of the famed caricature that represented Prohibition. His equally gaunt, unsmiling wife and a cabdriver, lurking outside for a fare, were the witnesses.

They drove southward during the cold night with the idea of spending their first night in Washington, but in the maze of heavy traffic through Baltimore, missed Route 1 and found themselves on State Highway No. 2, which took them past the Naval Academy on the Severn River into Annapolis. It had begun snowing when they arrived and they decided to stay the night at Carvel Hall. Theodore ordered food sent to their room and when the table and dishes had been removed, he took Louise into his arms. "You go first," he whispered.

She undressed in the bathroom and emerged in a negligee so spectacularly sheer that Theodore was robbed of his speech at the sight of her sensual beauty. When he came back wearing a silk robe over silk pajamas, she was in bed. "This won't be a repetition of the first time, Louise, I promise you," he said gently.

She looked up at him with an impish smile. "I'm sorry you missed it," she replied. "It wasn't really as awful as it must have sounded the next morning. I'll make it up to you now."

And she did. He was gentle, holding back until she began moving slowly beneath him, responding, aware of the com-

237

mingling of their arms and legs, gradually increasing thrust and counterthrust, eagerly receiving and giving, each drawing new strength from the other. He heard her moan softly, "Wait—wait—" and paused, luxuriating in her arms, staring into her fringed, half-closed eyes that were shaded by her tumbled hair, her flesh moist, lips parted in a lazy half-smile. Then he was incited as she began the gentle motion, reawakened, eagerly rising to deliver herself to him with unbelievable ferocity, fingers digging into his flesh, raking his back.

And finally, both at extreme peak, it came to an incredibly mad, wild conclusion, a furious attack that drained them completely. They lay spent, joined together, panting for breath.

It went well, Louise thought. I didn't need to pretend anything.

And Theodore thought, If this is what we will have over the years ahead, nothing can be better.

She got out of bed after a while, shamelessly naked, the fringe at her loins a sight Theodore would remember and cherish. And in Louise's mind there remained one thought only.

Chase.

Theodore sent wires the next morning to Anderson and Cleo, and to Duncan Collins, announcing the marriage. They drifted southward slowly toward Laurelton, stopping overnight in Richmond, Roanoke, Charlotte and Greenville before the last stage to Laurelton. They reached Brookhill at dusk, Theodore's first nervous moment, but after first introductions to Cleo and Anderson, and a drink mixed and served by an elated Shad, then dinner by a carefully dressed Leona and two serving girls, Theodore felt completely relaxed and saw that Louise was at ease with Cleo.

They slept in Theodore's room that night and next morning, Cleo and Louise began discussing plans to create a private apartment for their use on the second floor. There was no question of them living anywhere else but at Brookhill.

"Ah, Louise," Cleo said, "you've no idea how lonely a place as large as Brookhill can be. Of course you'll live here and have as much privacy as you want."

"Thank you, Mrs.—"

"No 'Mother'?" Cleo said suggestively with a warm smile.

"Mother," Louise responded firmly.

Cleo kissed her. "We'll be planning a nursery soon, I hope, Louise. Can you imagine how wonderful Brookhill will be to raise children—"

238

"Mother, aren't we being a little premature?"

"Not for your children, darling. You'll love it here. Laurelton is a wonderful town with wonderful, friendly people. And when I read about the weather up north, I declare I can't see why anybody would want to live there."

"It's not really so bad. Snow has its advantages, too. When it first falls, it hides so much of the dirt. Everything looks so clean, so new—"

"Louise?"

"Yes, Mother?"

"You do love Theodore, don't you?"

"Why—yes. Of course—"

"He does very much need someone to love him. Someone like you. He's a strange boy. He and his brother Chase never got along very well. They are nine years apart and there was resentment, jealousy—"

"That's understandable, Mother, but time—"

"Time never healed the rift between them. What you've done for Theodore already is remarkable. When we got the wire from Annapolis, I'll confess I was worried. So was Anderson, but now, you have our blessings." She smiled happily and added, "Finally, I've got the daughter I always wanted."

"Thank you, Mother. You're so sweet. And Papa Anderson, too. I want you both to know I'm very happy."

If Anderson was happy for the change Louise had made in Theodore, he was even more delighted with what Louise's presence was doing for Cleo. The two Warren women were caught up in a round of visiting and entertaining that occupied most of their waking hours. Louise joined the young married women's clubs and activities, and there was no end to the shopping to be done in Laurelton and Atlanta. Cleo planned and staged the most magnificent reception in years at the Laurelton Country Club, one that brought out-of-town guests flocking in to take up every spare room at Brookhill and in the downtown hotels, all of which touched off a series of gala dinner parties that lasted for two months. From Chase and Victoria Warren came a present of engraved crystal and a card with perfunctory congratulations. No more.

In November, after a difficult and painful labor she did not believe she would survive, Louise Warren gave birth to a 7½-pound son who was named Bruce. He was born just before nine o'clock on a Thursday morning and before he was three hours old, Anderson had sent for Kenneth Armour, now a member of the Warren legal staff, and ordered certain changes in his will which would include his newest grandson. At the same time, he set the wheels in motion to create a one-million-dollar trust fund in Bruce's name. While being driven to the hospital to be with Cleo, Louise and Theodore on that happy occasion, Anderson thought with regret, but not without some satisfaction, of Chase, Victoria and his first grandson, Marshall Vanderkuyl Warren, whom he and Cleo had seen only once when Chase and Victoria stopped off in Laurelton for an overnight stay while en route to winter at Palm Beach. He had made no such generous gift to Marshall who, because of Chase's voluntary estrangement and Victoria's coolness, he considered a Vanderkuyl and heir to the Vanderkuyl fortune.

On the back seat of his car, Anderson fondled the large velvet-lined box in which reposed a diamond-and-pearl necklace with matching bracelet and earrings which he had ordered while in New York a few months earlier, wondering if this were sufficient to show his appreciation to Louise for the gifts she had given him. New hopes, new plans for the future.

Louise's recovery was swift and soon Brookhill swarmed with gift-bearing visitors; and when the excitement finally died down, Theodore and Louise took a delayed honeymoon trip to Europe, leaving Bruce in Cleo's and Leona's more than willing hands. On their return, three months later, Theodore found that he had been elected to a vice-presidency and a place on the Warren board of directors. That night at a family celebration at Brookhill, Anderson handed him 25,000 shares of Warren common stock, reflecting that this was something he had never given to Chase, who had wanted it so much.

Theodore threw himself into his work with a vigor that astonished Anderson and surprised everyone else. His first major project, of his own making, was a recommendation that a teletype communications system to be installed in Laurelton that would put the home office in instant direct contact with each district office, eliminating the delay of going through New York.

This approved, Theodore was placed in charge of the project and went to New York to plan and coordinate the installations with Duncan Collins and Trevor Richards, then to move the Statistical Analysis Division to Laurelton.

Soon after, when it became apparent that the war in Europe must draw the United States into conflict with Germany, Anderson, remembering back to World War I, placed Theodore in charge of an expansion program to acquire land, construction materials and equipment to answer the hoped-for unprecedented demand for cigarettes the war period would require.

5

More and more, Anderson's reply to a question from a department head became standard: "Take it up with Theodore. He's handling the expansion program."

And so, in mid-1940, Kenneth Armour, his former tutor at the University, sat in Theodore Warren's office, holding a folder of papers in one hand, his usual bland legal expression overshadowed by annoyance.

"What is this, Ken?" Theodore asked.

"This option on the Carpenter place north of Tenboro."

"What about it?"

"I understand from Arthur Brimmer in our realty department that you ordered the option dropped. We've got $2,500 tied up in it—"

"That's right, Ken. I ordered it dropped and we're taking an option on the Harlan Tabor place instead."

"Would you mind telling me why? I haven't seen a memo —"

"There hasn't been one, and won't be until we get Tabor's signature on the agreement some time this afternoon."

"But why drop the Carpenter option?"

"Very simply, this, Ken. The Carpenter option is for 30 acres at a $980 an acre asking price. The Tabor place is only a few miles farther from there, 160 acres for $525 an acre and gives us access by water as well as highway. For $54,000 more, we can pick up 130 acres more, in a rising market."

"How?"

Theodore grinned. "I didn't go through our realty department. Spence Carpenter jacked up his price double when he learned he was dealing with Warren. I used Stannard Realty in town to get to Harlan Tabor. Lee Stannard offered him $50 an acre over the going price and Tabor jumped at it."

"Isn't that going out of the normal chain of command, Theodore?" Armour asked.

"Yes, it is, Ken, but we got faster action and a better deal that way."

"And is your father satisfied with a plant that will be built that much farther away from South Laurelton?"

"It's not going to be as far away as the Carpenter place, Ken. Nearer, in fact. Much nearer."

"I don't understand."

"I only put the idea to my father last night. What I'm planning to do, Ken, is move all our storage, inventory,

241

trucks and truck repair facilities down to the Tabor place, which will require about thirty acres. We'll move the present buildings down there intact and be set up and operating within sixty days at most. When all of it has been cleared out of this area, we'll have enough room right here for at least two new factories and plenty of land for any necessary expansion and employee parking—"

Kenneth Armour had lost an internal skirmish, was angered that he had been caught napping. He quickly dropped the matter and fell in with Theodore's plan, even praised it to Anderson at the next weekly staff meeting. And wondered how he could have underestimated Theodore so badly.

With the United States working desperately to come back from its devastating loss at Pearl Harbor while building the greatest war force in world history, Louise Warren gave birth to her second child, a daughter, who was given Louise's family name, Drew. And as he had done on the occasion of the birth of Bruce, Anderson Warren made another change in his will and asked Kenneth Armour to set up a million-dollar trust fund in his granddaughter's name.

Chase Warren learned of this disposition in a conversation over luncheon with Duncan Collins, with whom he continued to maintain social contact. What plagued Chase even more was the information that Anderson had rewarded Theodore with another 25,000 shares of stock. It was as though Anderson, who had never given Chase a single share of stock, was delivering a strong rebuke to Chase, using his generosity to Theodore as his instrument.

The birth of Chase's own son, Marshall, had elicited a telegram and a token gift from Anderson and Cleo, and no more, while each of Theodore's children had received million-dollar trust funds, and now Theodore held 50,000 shares of Warren Tobacco Company stock in his own name. Could this, Chase wondered, be the handwriting on the wall; that Anderson's intention was to cut him out of his will and leave everything to Theodore, Louise and their children?

In the privacy of his own office later, the implication grew stronger in Chase's mind, and as it grew, it became more untenable.

The war years gave Chase Warren the means to escape the direct surveillance of his mother-in-law. By now, neither sought out the other for any reason other than business. When Victoria brought her son to visit Andrea, it was always alone. At first, Andrea would send for Chase twice each year to be brought up to date on his administration of the Vanderkuyl business affairs. Once each year her auditors paid a visit to Chase's offices to inspect his books.

Now, her demands upon Chase had lessened. Andrea was spending more time in Palm Beach, as far out of range of the war news as possible. Leander and Vanessa came from Chicago to pick up Victoria and Marshall to accompany them to Palm Beach. When the Willises returned to Chicago, Andrea urged Victoria to remain through the winter and Victoria accepted.

Free of son, wife and mother-in-law, Chase began to explore newer possibilities for evading the yoke Andrea had placed around his neck. He began with a man he met through a business acquaintance in Texas. Kirk Dillingham was a shrewd man who lacked only one vital asset—money. He was 34, an engineer by training, but with an inborn restlessness that kept him moving around the country. He had been married and divorced twice and was on the make for any opportunity that could satisfy an ambitious appetite. After several meetings, Chase and Kirk felt a warm kinship and began discussing ways and means of becoming useful to each other. Kirk had ideas that were interesting, but Chase was reluctant to bring him or his ideas into the Vanderkuyl establishment.

Until Kirk Dillingham came up with an idea that Chase felt he could surreptitiously finance with Vanderkuyl funds.

Kirk talked of a minor phenomenon he had noticed on occasional visits to Mexico City. With thousands of used cars on the streets and roads, he told Chase, there was no place where the owner of a dilapidated car could buy other than new parts for his old car or truck. Only expensive new generators, carburetors, water pumps, distributors, starters and batteries were obtainable. Therefore, if it were possible to buy up these discarded items in the United States, ship them into Mexico, rebuild them into usable parts—

Chase became interested and sent Kirk to investigate its possibilities. There were, Kirk found, problems. The Mexican government frowned on alien operations unless Mexicans, in heavy majority, would be employed. Also, the red tape necessary for an alien firm to operate was of Herculean proportions.

But Chase's experience and contacts in such matters was far greater than Kirk's. Through an official in the Mexican embassy in Washington, whose son in Mexico City would be employed at a good salary and a 5% interest, the red tape disappeared as though touched by a magical wand.

Through advertising, Chase gathered a dozen auto mechanics, all beyond draft age, who would supervise an all-Mexican assembly line, each man and woman to be trained in a single operation. Procurement agencies were established in every major city in the United States to seek out discarded auto parts suitable for rebuilding, which were to be trucked into Mexico City.

Finally, a group of abandoned warehouses were leased, equipped and staffed and garages and auto parts stores contacted to distribute the rebuilt parts. At 50c and 60c an hour for Mexican labor over $2.00 to $2.50 an hour in the States, the supply was hardly able to keep up with the wartime demand.

Thus began AUTO-MEX, the first of a dozen or more companies that operated under the banner of Chase Warren's privately owned holding company, INTERCON, with Kirk Dillingham as his agent in order to keep his own identification with it from becoming public. As Intercon grew and prospered, Chase parlayed its profits into a large housing development in house-hungry Southern California and other holdings under the Intercon banner; and began to look forward to the day when he could disassociate himself from everything Vanderkuyl; business, Victoria, and his most truculent adversary, Andrea.

It was then that he began thinking of Anderson's slap and a means to destroy Theodore, no matter the cost. This achieved, his path to the Warren Tobacco Company would be cleared.

Despite the war that raged, the atmosphere in Palm Beach was benign, the weather amiable. There were many women of Victoria's age, and younger, who were husbandless, some already widowed by the first thrusts of combat. Sadly, these latter retired from social contact or returned to their permanent homes to mourn and pick up the remaining crumbs of their lives.

There was, too, a patriotic need to entertain the officers and men who were preparing to fight their country's battles from planes, the decks of ships, on the ground and below the seas; and Palm Beach showed no less enthusiasm or hospitality than other cities which took note of the vast number of displaced uniformed men. Homes were thrown open to officers who, in civilian life, could never have hoped to enter them socially. There were organized dances, beach and swimming parties, yachting and fishing trips to lessen the tensions of the horrors to come in distant theaters of malignance.

The Vanderkuyl home, a Palm Beach showplace, was one that was thrown open for the purpose of pure enjoyment. Bedrooms formerly occupied by distinguished social and industrial names were turned over to distinguished men in uniform. Meals were served at all hours, the bar open around the clock, the billiard hall, library and ballroom available for the pursuit of temporary happiness. Temporary was the keynote. As a face became familiar, it was suddenly replaced by one entirely new, fresh and eager. Generally, they were youthful and bright, adult, and showing little concern. Some were middle-aged and worried.

In 1943, Victoria was 32 years old. She had inherited Andrea's stateliness and good looks which made her appear far younger than her years. Always a well-mannered woman and despite Chase's flagrant infidelities, she had never given thought to a departure from normal, decent conduct which Andrea had instilled in her. And yet, it was because of the confidential reports which Andrea continued to receive from her private sources in New York that Victoria finally decided to bend her own resolves.

Lieutenant Commander Walter Cunningham was a quiet man in his early 30s, a graduate of the Naval Academy and captain of a destroyer since 1940, now on rest and rehabilitation leave. He was married, he told Victoria, but legally separated from his wife. Victoria and Walter met at a beach party given jointly with the Comstocks, who were the Vanderkuyl's neighbors, in order to enlarge the beach facilities and accommodate a larger crowd. Cunningham was staying in the smaller Comstock home where he shared a bedroom that had been made into a small dormitory by removing the canopied bed and replacing it with six cots. There was something terribly—even dangerously—appealing in Walter that, for the first time since she had met Chase, reached out and touched Victoria; to the point of becoming deeply curious about his life; boyhood, schooling, the Academy, marriage and career. Before the evening was over, Victoria had fallen victim to a force that was overwhelming.

Walter Cunningham walked Victoria home that night, accepted a nightcap and lingered over a cup of coffee. Victoria felt a reluctance to let him return to the Comstock bedroom he shared with five other men and showed him the room reserved in case Vanessa and Leander might choose to visit. She offered it to him and he studied Victoria's face carefully.

"I hardly know how to make the move without offending the Comstocks," Walt said apologetically. "They have really been wonderful to me."

"They'll never notice, Walt. Goodness, there must be at least thirty men crowded into that small place," she replied.

He said it slowly and meaningfully. "Vicky, do you want me here in your house?"

And just as meaningfully, she replied in a low, quick voice, "Yes, Walt, I really do."

"I'll be going back to my ship in less than a month."

"I know."

"Vicky—"

"Do it, Walt. I'm sure you're resourceful enough to find some plausible excuse."

He kissed her then and Victoria knew that nothing would ever be the same again. He left and returned within the hour, carrying a small suitcase and toilet kit. On the beach, the party was at its height, the bar and buffet tables crowded, officers dancing with vacationing debutantes, satisfied dowagers looking on happily, perhaps reliving a part of their World War I lives. And behind the locked door of one of the guest bedrooms in the Vanderkuyl home, Victoria Warren lay in Walter Cunningham's arms and wept; tears of happiness and release from tensions that had been stifled so long; tears for the happiness she could give a man like Walter Cunningham; tears for the marriage that had, until now, succeeded only in robbing her of her confidence as a woman.

During the remainder of Walt's leave, they spent as much time together as possible, sailing, swimming, playing golf, lunching at the club, driving to Miami Beach to dine and dance. They managed a three-day weekend aboard a borrowed cabin cruiser and offered no excuses or reasons for their absence. In the Vanderkuyl home, they slept together in Victoria's room or in Walt's.

Andrea, if anything else, was hardly a stupid woman. She knew from the very start that nothing short of total involvement could have brought about this revitalization in Victoria, and if she found the affair shocking, she was wisely determined to remain aloof and show not the slightest inclination to interfere. She had lost Vanessa through an unsuccessful campaign of carping criticism and had no intention of making the same mistake with Victoria. Also, she took a certain measure of secret delight in the vengeful thought that Chase Warren was being paid back for his continuing infidelities, of which she was well aware. At least, Andrea consoled herself further, Walter Cunningham was a man of good breeding and gentlemanly traits, a victim, like Victoria, of circumstances.

Andrea had never forgiven Chase for relegating her to a

voiceless role in the administration of the Vanderkuyl interests; no less than she had forgiven Leander Willis for his lack of ability in, or enthusiasm for, matters of complex finance. Reports from her attorney and accountant left her devoid of complaint or criticism of Chase Warren. The war had raised the value of, and income from, Vanderkuyl holdings to greater levels than ever before and the single irritating factor was that Chase Warren's stature and independence had grown far beyond Andrea's or Victoria's resources to control him.

Andrea's suspicions of her son-in-law had prompted her, alone and unabetted, to seek the services of a firm which specialized in industrial and corporate investigation. Each month, she received a report so meticulous in detail as to make it obvious that someone in Chase's employ was also in the pay of Atlas Research Associates, Inc. The reports were interesting, but inconclusive for her needs, so Andrea engaged a second firm of private investigators who dealt in a more personal nature with its clients and subjects. To Norton Harsh, head of Confidential, Inc., Andrea turned over a copy of every ARA report for follow-up and thereafter confirmed that her suspicions that Chase's business turpitude was strongly interwoven with his lack of moral character.

Norton Harsh had delved deeply into Chase's past affair with Louise Drew and thus learned of Louise's subsequent marriage to Theodore Warren. As the months and years followed, Andrea was able to follow Chase through various attachments and affairs with female employees and paid professionals used to entertain out-of-town business associates. Many of his trips reported by ARA for business reasons became the subject of counter-reports from CI indicating social activities, complete with photo copies of hotel registers and photographic evidence, all of which Andrea kept locked in her safe and to herself, awaiting the day when Victoria should decide she wanted to divorce Chase. She saw this possibility for the first time now in Walter Cunningham, but cautioned herself against any untoward move unless Victoria took her into confidence and asked for help.

With Walt's return to duty, Victoria lapsed into a state of lethargy. For days she took little or no interest in the gaiety that abounded and spent much of her time with Marshall, in guilt for having neglected him during Walt's stay. It helped little when he asked when "Uncle" Walt would return, or expressed his fondness for the man who had frequently romped with him on the beach. She slept badly, avoided Andrea and their neighbors, and seemed momentar ily happy when she received a letter from an undetermined A.P.O. address, then spent hours replying.

Then suddenly one day, she told Andrea she must return to New York. It was winter, the weather in the north was bad, yet she insisted and left with Marshall as quickly as transportation became available. Chase was in town when she arrived in New York and came home at once, making one stop at F.A.O. Schwartz to buy an elaborate set of lead soldiers, sailors, marines, ships, tanks and planes for Marshall, then flowers for Victoria.

That night, Victoria made a very special effort to be agreeable to Chase and succeeded in enticing him into an act of love she neither wanted nor felt, but which had now become imperative. For, during the preceding week, she had begun experiencing the well-remembered nausea of her first pregnancy.

6

The war, after the initial blow at Pearl Harbor, had moved westward and little-known names had become familiar household words to millions of Americans. Wake, Guam, Bataan, Corregidor, Sunda Strait, Guadalcanal; the electrifying Doolittle strike at Tokyo, the Battle of Midway. In the older war in Europe, England was bravely, desperately, standing off the Nazi war machine, but German subs in the Atlantic were taking a heavy toll of lives and shipping tonnage. In Africa, the names were Libya, Bengazi, Derna, Tobruk, Bardia. And Rommel. Montgomery. Then Sicily and the torturous move northward in Italy. In the spring of 1943, Miss Libby Cornell, Theodore Warren's secretary, found the envelope on her otherwise cleared and locked desk. A long, white envelope addressed to MR. THEODORE WARREN it had arrived before the regular morning mail by special delivery, postmarked from New York, and since there was nothing to indicate that its contents might be of a personal nature, Libby Cornell inserted her letter opener beneath the flap.

There were two sheets of single-spaced typed matter. The top sheet bore a printed legend in its upper left corner:

DIEBOLD INVESTIGATIVE SERVICE
CLIENT REPORT TO:
(CONFIDENTIAL)

The name of the client to whom the report was being made had been neatly cut out, probably with a razor. As Miss

248

Cornell began to read, she became fully aware of its confidential and horrifying nature, but nothing could prevent her from absorbing every word, occasionally muttering, "My Lord!" and "Good God!" And when she reached the bottom of the second page, she turned back to the first and re-read the entire report more carefully.

Finished, she refolded the two sheets of paper and inserted them in the envelope, resealed the flap firmly and sat at her desk envisioning the horror, far worse than the war news from the Pacific, Europe or Africa that morning, about to crash down upon Theodore Warren. And the Warren household. Anderson. Cleo. Those two lovely children, Bruce and Drew. And that awful, horrid woman, Louise Warren. That rotten *bitch!* How could she have—?

Libby Cornell's black thoughts were interrupted by the arrival of the mailroom truck and Ben Stedman, to deposit a tied bundle of mail for Mr. Theodore and his usual cheerful greeting.

"Good mornin', Miss Libby," Ben said with a display of old yellowing teeth. "War news gettin' a little better'n better every day, ain't it?"

Miss Cornell held the long white envelope up. Ben said, "You want that mailed, Miss Libby?"

"No. It's addressed to Mr. Theodore Warren. Have you seen this before, Ben?"

Ben took the envelope and studied it carefully through steel-rimmed glasses, shaking his gray woolly head. "No, ma'am. Musta come in before I did. Wasn't in the mailroom, else it'd have a time stamp on it and I'd of delivered it myself."

"You're sure, Ben?"

"Yes, ma'am, Miss Libby. I'n never seen it until this very minute."

"All right, Ben. Thank you."

"Nothin' wrong, is there, Miss Libby?"

"No. Nothing's wrong, Ben."

The old man shuffled out to the rubber-tired truck in the hall and closed the door. *Damn,* Libby Cornell thought. *I can't just hand it to him. I can't. And I can't slip it in with the other mail. He's got to see this first—*

A moment later she went into Theodore's office and placed the offending envelope on his desk, in the very center of the cleared desk pad where he could not miss it. Then she returned to her own desk and began slitting, reading and sorting the normal mail and interoffice memos according to category and importance. She was so engaged at 9:15 when Theodore Warren arrived.

"Good morning, Libby," he said, stopping at her desk. Indicating the mail, "Anything important?"

"Good morning, Mr. Warren," Libby replied. "Just routine, but there are several letters and memos I left in your correspondence tray last night that need to be signed."

"Thank you. I'll do that now and ring for you when they're ready. Will you see if Mr. Kendall will be available for lunch today, and bring your book, please. I've got a few things I want to get off before my first appointment. Mr. Welch, isn't it?"

"Yes, sir. I don't believe he's in yet, but I'll call. Coffee?" The question was a morning ritual.

"When I ring for you." He went into his office and closed the door.

Libby waited nervously for twenty minutes. She had taken calls from Mr. Welch, Mr. Harkness in Traffic, Mr. Funston in Construction, Mr. Addison in Real Estate and Mr. Clark in Sales, told them that Mr. Theodore was in an important conference. She placed their names on the call-back list in proper order, knowing the calls would never be returned. When a half hour passed and she hadn't heard from him, she went to the double doors, morning mail in hand, and knocked lightly. There was no reply. Fearfully, she opened the door.

Mr. Theodore was sitting at the large desk in the center of the room. The two pages were lying there in front of him, the envelope to one side. His eyes stared out at her from deep sockets, face blanched white, fists balled up as though ready to strike. He seemed to have aged by years, and she could have sworn he couldn't see her; a somnambulist.

She said, "Mr. Warren" three times before his eyes began to focus on her. He held up the envelope and said hoarsely, "Where did this come from?"

"I—I—d-don't know, sir," Libby replied. "I've never s-seen it b-before."

"It was lying here on my desk. You didn't put it there?"

She wished she hadn't lied and now it was too late. "N-no, sir. It must—somebody must have—put it there—after I left last night. I—haven't been in your office at all this morning."

He said nothing more. Libby walked to his desk with quaking knees and placed the mail in his incoming correspondence tray, waited for a moment, then went out. No longer able to stand the tension that had been building up in her over the past hour, she picked up her purse and went out of the room, down the hall to the rest room, relieved that no one was there. She leaned against the wall and began to cry. Later, she washed her face, refreshed her makeup and returned to her desk, more composed now. She went to Mr. Theodore's door, knocked and opened it. He had left, taking the two-page report with him.

He reached Brookhill at ten minutes past ten. Leona, hearing a car drive up, sent Shad, who was polishing the silver in the butler's pantry, to open the front door. He saw Theodore's car parked in the driveway and went to it when Theodore made no move to get out. Shad asked, "Somethin' wrong, Mist' Theodore?"

"No, Shad. Is Mrs. Warren home?"

"No, sir. Miz Warren an' Miz Cleo, they went into town together."

"The children?"

"They took them along."

"I see." He paused for a moment to take a deep breath, staring through the windshield with vacant eyes.

"Can I do somethin' for you, Mist' Theodore?" Shad asked, now concerned.

"No. Wait—" Theodore reached into his jacket pocket and took out the envelope, handed it to Shad. "I'm going in and pack a few things. I've got to go to New York. I want you to see that Mrs. Warren gets this envelope privately, Shad. I don't want anyone else to see it. Hand it to her when she is alone, you understand?"

"Yes, sir."

He held the door open for Theodore and watched him curiously as he walked somewhat drunkenly up the steps. Less than half an hour later, Theodore came down with a small bag, got into his car and drove away.

At noon, Cleo and Louise returned from their shopping trip in town. Handing Bruce and Drew over to Leona, Cleo asked Leona to bring a luncheon tray to her room, then went upstairs while Louise lingered in the hallway to check the morning mail, then started up toward her own room. Shad came into the hall and handed her the envelope. She read the name on it and asked, "Isn't this for Mr. Theodore, Shad?"

"Yes, ma'am. He come home a while ago and gave it to me, told me to be sure I gave it to you."

"Did he go back to his office?"

"No, ma'am. He packed him a bag, said he had to go to New York."

"What time was that?"

"He left about ten-thirty."

"Thank you."

251

"You be down for lunch, Miss Louise?"

"Yes, as soon as I freshen up and change."

"Yes, ma'am. I'll tell Leona."

She went to her room, sat on the side of her bed and opened the envelope. Two hours later, she was still pacing her room when Leona came for the third time to ask about lunch and for the third time was told, "I don't want any, Leona. And don't disturb me again, please."

The children were taking their naps. Cleo was asleep in her room. Louise went back to her own room, picked up the telephone and put in a call to Chase Warren's office in New York, was told he was not in and was not expected. She placed a second call to his home and was told that Mrs. Warren was out of the city. No, madam, Mr. Warren is with Mrs. Warren.

It was, she knew then, the end. Past had caught up with Present, with her Life Plan. Stupid, stupid, *stupid!* How could she not have known it had to happen some day. By whose hand, she wondered: Victoria's, revenging herself on Louise; or Chase, on the brother he had hated all his life?

And now, what? Pack up and leave? Wait and face Theodore? And Anderson? And Cleo?

The report, for all its length, was concise and to the ugly point, filled with facts about her parents, her school years, of Rose Janowiecz and how she had obtained her job at Warren in New York. It accurately detailed her first and subsequent meetings with Chase, the day he had leased the apartment on East 63rd Street, the name of the rental agent, the security deposit he had paid by check, the monthly checks sent to the rental agent by Chase. It listed charge accounts in her name and supplied the information that the bills were often paid by Mr. Warren's checks. It recorded the amounts of the checks he had given her and the name of the bank where she had deposited them. The amount he had paid for the five-year lease on the apartment, the check for $10,000 he had given her at the time of their final separation.

It supplied names of people who had known they were living together, and which the investigator had verified; a statement from the night and day doormen at the apartment house, both attesting to the fact that Mr. Chase Warren was a frequent overnight visitor in Miss Louise Drew's apartment; trips they had taken, photostatic copies of hotel registers where they had stayed together; gifts he had bought for her and had delivered to her apartment; flowers sent there, champagne, foods—

252

There was no mention of Duncan Collins, Trevor Richards, no statement from Rose Janowiecz. There was no need. The story was complete without their help.

And now, what?

Louise went through the next three days as though she had been drugged. Each time the telephone rang, an electric shock went through her. Each day when Anderson returned home from the office, she waited for the blow to fall. Each time Cleo spoke to her, it was the voice of doom reaching out to touch her. On the fourth day of Theodore's absence without any word, Anderson came home in midafternoon and went directly to his room to tell Cleo he was taking the night train to New York. He gave the same message to Louise.

"Is it about Theodore?" she asked.

"Yes, but I don't know exactly what it means."

"I don't understand—"

"I don't either. That's why I'm going to New York, Louise. I had a very strange call from Duncan Collins. I'll know more when I see him. I'll telephone you from there."

But he didn't call Louise, and if he called Cleo, Louise knew nothing about it. Anderson Warren returned to Brookhill after an absence of five days, but Theodore was not with him. Cleo seemed satisfied with his explanation that Theodore had taken a swing around the mid-West territory, but Louise knew from Anderson's cold appraising eye that he knew the truth; at least, Theodore's side of the story. When Cleo went up to bed, Anderson motioned to Louise to remain behind. "Come with me, Louise," he said, and led the way to his study where he closed and locked the doors. He sat in his favorite leather chair and indicated the chair opposite for Louise. She remained standing, arms folded across her breast.

"This won't be pleasant," Anderson said. "I think you'd best sit down."

"Where is Theodore?" she asked.

"He's still in New York. I couldn't force him to come home."

"Why should you need to?"

"Louise, don't let's play games. He told me he left the report with you. I know all about you and Chase, what you two have done to Theodore. What I can't figure out is, why Theodore went to the Diebold people to check out the report. They insisted it was accurate and could produce affidavits to substantiate it. I have reason to believe they can

253

do just that. The only thing they wouldn't tell was who had asked for the report, paid them to compile it."

"Why?" Louise ground the question out dully.

Anderson shrugged. "I don't know why, Louise. The why isn't important any longer. Only the truth, and we have that."

Again, "But why, why?"

"I told you, I don't know why and I don't care why. All I know is that Theodore had a right to go up there and blow his brother's head off. That is, if Chase hadn't gathered his wife and son up and left town for parts unknown. He had it coming to him. Question now is, what've you got coming to you?"

"I—have a—right to know where my husband is."

"All right, Louise, I'll tell you. Until the morning I got there, he was in the alcoholic ward at Bellevue Hospital. The police picked him up staggering drunk in a Bowery saloon. Somebody'd rolled him and stolen his shoes and coat. The police checked out a label on his suit coat and traced him from Brooks Brothers to Duncan Collins, who called me and asked me to come up. We got him out of Bellevue into a private hospital and as soon as Collins can make arrangements he'll be taken to a sanitarium in New Jersey. I stayed up there only long enough to get the story from him, what he could tell me of it."

Louise's face tightened under its pallor, her eyes pinched with pain. "When—will he be—able to come home?" she asked.

"No matter when, he won't come back here to you. And what happens to Cleo when she hears the truth, you've got that to carry on your conscience, too. If you've got one."

"Oh, God!" Louise's head drooped and her hands went up to cover her face. She dropped into the chair, sobbing.

"I take it," Anderson said finally, "that just between you and me you ain't denying any of this."

She didn't look up or answer the unasked question.

"How much, Louise?"

She looked up then. "How much?"

"How much. To clear out of here and never come back."

"Is that what Theodore wants?"

"Right now, Theodore ain't in any condition to know what he wants, except to kill Chase."

She took a full half minute before she spoke. "What about Bruce and Drew?"

"They stay. They're Theodore's children, Warrens. They stay and I can go into court and prove you're not a fit mother—"

254

"They're mine," she said angrily, "much more mine than his. I carried both of them—"

"You ain't going to give me a lecture on how children are conceived and born, are you, girl? Just what do you want to go quietly and leave us in peace? I'm not hard to bargain with. I'm sure you've got some kind of figure worked out in that businesslike head of yours."

She sat and stared at Anderson's unrelenting, granite-like face for a few moments and he waited patiently until she said, "All right. If you insist on a businesslike arrangement, a quiet divorce. The children. And enough to raise them properly and live comfortably."

He waited for more, but she remained silent. "How much?" he asked again. "And forget about the children. How much for you alone?"

"I don't know." She knitted her fingers together, unlaced them, balled them into fists. "I don't know. I'll have to discuss that with an attorney." And then, her voice tinged with anger and bitterness, "Of course, this won't be easy for either of us, the publicity, photographers—"

"Don't paint the picture for me, Louise. I can see blackmail better than you. I'll make you an offer instead." She looked up at him with cold eyes, lips drawn in a tight, thin line. "I'll be more than fair—generous—with you," he continued, "but when you leave Brookhill, you leave alone. Bruce and Drew stay here." He raised his hand when it appeared she would interrupt. "Don't let's start a fight we both know you can't win. You're entitled to a good settlement for your few years of marriage, for the two grandchildren you gave me and Cleo. They'll help heal the hurt a little bit for us. I don't know what'll help Theodore get over it.

"You're what now, 29, 30? You've got a lot of years of wear left in you. All right. You'll get your divorce, but on my terms. You fight me, bring this out in public and I'll fight you back with every cent I've got. I'll spend millions to keep you tied up in one court or another until your looks are gone and you're starved. I'll move Bruce and Drew out of the country where nobody can get within miles of 'em. I'll do anything—everything—to grind you down. You'll never sleep with another man again, eat with one, or even talk to one, that I won't have somebody watching you, lookin' over your shoulder, reading your mail. I'll dig up evidence, manufacture it if need be, to prove you're a whore and an unfit wife and mother.

"You know me, Louise, enough to know I'll do it. You've heard how I fought some of the biggest and most ruthless men in the country, chewed, bit and gouged to get where I am. Any way you may think, you've got to believe I never made a threat or promise I didn't live up to. You know I'm not bluffing you now. I swear it by the good God Almighty, I'll hound you into your grave long before your time comes."

She watched him tensely as he spoke his earnest and heated words and knew he was as totally sincere as he was ruthlessly determined. Her mind clung to crumbs of words, threads of gold among the dirty gray strings of menace and threat. *You're entitled to a good settlement—I'll be more than fair—generous—I'll spend millions—*

That her marriage was over, there was no longer any doubt in her mind. It struck her with a sickening thought and she was glad she was sitting down. Anderson's face had darkened, skin drawn taut on its bony skull, mouth pulled down in a grim, angry line, waiting silently for her reply. All she needed to bring this humiliation to an end was to speak the one word, Yes. Her mind lingered on the word "settlement" and she remembered two more that had lain dormant in her mind for a long time, almost forgotten since her marriage.

Security.

Independence.

Full and complete freedom and the means to enjoy it.

"Well, Louise?" Anderson asked finally.

"Yes," she said in a low voice.

She learned the terms of the settlement not from Anderson Warren, but from Kenneth Armour. Not at Brookhill. Not in his office.

By prearrangement, Kenneth Armour called for her on the following afternoon. They drove in his car to the Riverton Road and turned north, discussing the details, the terms, both eager to bring the unpleasant business to an end as quickly as possible. Kenneth Armour showed no more emotion over their discussion than if he were preparing a business contract, a lease for a parcel of land, a sales agreement. He spoke as he drove, looking directly ahead at the road and she thought to herself that he was so self-assured, the master's hired attorney dismissing a servant girl for stealing, dictating his terms coolly. But she could not look inside the man and know that he was suffering deep pain at this unwanted task.

Those terms, Louise admitted to herself, were generous; far more than she would have demanded had she been asked to name a figure.

Five million dollars. Plus.

256

She would leave immediately and quietly for Reno, take up her residence, remain in a house that would be rented for her, servants to minister to her needs, make no public appearances except in the company of the attorney who had already been chosen for her. She would, on arrival, be met by that attorney, who would assist her in filing for her divorce on grounds of incompatibility. The divorce would be heard in private chambers. At the time of filing the suit, she would receive a half million dollars. On the day she received the decree, she would receive another half million. The balance of four million dollars would be paid to her in annual amounts of a quarter of a million dollars, whether she remained single or remarried. At the end of the final installment, the sixteenth, which would come in her 45th year, if she were not remarried she would begin receiving annual payments of $50,000 until her death. This last was the Plus to her $5,000,000 settlement.

On the day after her decree was granted, she would find that arrangements had been made to fly her to Portugal, and from there to Switzerland. She would remain there in any city of her choice until the end of the war, after which she would be free to go where she pleased as long as she remained outside the United States of North America, Canada and Mexico. If at any time Louise disclosed any information, by carelessness or design, to any person or member of the press concerning this agreement or intimate details behind the divorce, other than the grounds on record, or in any other manner discussed any member of the Warren family that would reflect adversely upon the Warren name, payments would be stopped immediately.

She sat stiffly and grimly while Armour recited the terms, his hands steady on the wheel, his voice as firm as if he were reading from a prepared document. She saw, too, that he had timed their drive so that they were back inside the Brookhill grounds at the moment when she would be required to answer "Yes" or "No." An efficient man. As he pulled into the driveway and followed its curve to the front of the mansion, he glanced at her for the first time since she had gotten into the car, his look a question.

She said, "'You've been quite busy, haven't you, Kenneth?"

"Louise, I'm sorry, believe me. It all came as a shock—"

"Did it really?"

"Yes."

She took a deep breath and said, "Well, you can go back to your great Anderson Warren and tell him the whore said 'Yes.'"

Before he could reply, she got out of the car and ran up the steps and into the house.

Louise Warren left for Atlanta on the early train next morning without seeing Bruce or Drew, whom she had tearfully put to bed the night before; nor Cleo or Anderson. Only Leona, who gave her some coffee, and Shad, who drove her to the station. First step en route to her exile. She was not met by anyone in Atlanta, nor did she contact any of her friends or acquaintances there. She checked into a hotel and later that day caught a westbound plane. These movements, however, were reported to Kenneth Armour by telephone. She spent the next day in Los Angeles until she was able to catch a plane for San Francisco and there, another to Reno, arriving at dusk, met by the smiling, eager attorney who drove her to a servant-staffed house well outside the city limits.

That evening, the attorney telephoned Kenneth Armour to report the safe arrival of Mrs. Theodore Warren and that all necessary steps would be taken to put the divorce wheels in action at once. Moments later, Kenneth relayed the news to Anderson Warren.

And almost at the same time, a Diebold operative telephoned word of Louise's arrival in Reno to Chase Warren, who was at that moment in Salt Lake City.

7

Theodore did not return to Laurelton following his three-month stay in the New Jersey sanitarium nor, at the suggestion of his doctor, did Anderson visit him during that period of his mental collapse.

In Laurelton, Anderson was beset by problems of his own. Cleo had taken the breakup of Theodore's marriage with unnatural calm—or deep shock—when Anderson returned from New York with only a vague explanation that wartime demands required Theodore to remain in New York. He knew she did not believe this because she and Theodore had once again grown close together during his marriage, and she brooded over her son's absence and Louise's sudden departure. And one day soon after, Anderson came to her room and told her that Louise was gone and would not return, that it would be some time before Theodore would be able to come home.

Cleo received the news with her eyes fixed on the sky beyond the windows and when Anderson's voice stopped, she closed her eyes and lay back rigidly in bed, hardly moving a muscle. She remained in a semicomatose state, but during the night, when Anderson awoke, she was gone. He went in search of her and found she had brought Drew from her crib to Bruce's bed and was kneeling beside them whispering a story to them, calling one "Chase" and the other "Theodore," and he was frightened.

"Cleo!"

She did not answer. He knelt beside her, an arm around her thin shoulders. "Cleo, for God's sake, come back to bed."

There was no response. Anderson looked into her dull eyes, her expressionless face, then picked her up in his strong arms and carried her back to their room. As he put her down in the bed and drew the covers up over her, she smiled and said, "Good night, Daddy. Tell Mother to wake me early tomorrow. We're having a spelling test."

"Yes, honey, I'll remember," Anderson replied through his own tears. He sat in a chair beside her and held her hand and then he fell asleep, too. When he awoke next, it was still dark and Cleo was gone again. He went at once to Bruce's room and found her sitting up in his bed, Drew in her arms, crooning softly to her.

In the morning, Anderson and Carl Ballard took Cleo to the hospital and placed her in a suite with nurses to care for her around the clock. She had showed no reaction during the drive and did not respond to any questions put to her by Dr. Ballard, staring vacantly at the passing scenery, never curious about what was happening or where they were going.

Three days later, after Ballard's examination and a visit by Dr. David Chesler, a prominent Atlanta psychiatrist, Anderson asked Ballard, "What is it, Carl?"

"You heard Dr. Chesler, Anderson," Ballard said. "We can give it half a dozen names. Catatonic stupor, mutism, negativism, all forms of schizophrenia—"

"Boil it down to plain English, Carl."

"All right. This thing with Theodore and Louise is what triggered it. Other things that go 'way back. The death of her second child, the three years Theodore was missing, Chase's estrangement—"

"Most of it happened so long ago, Carl. Clyde's death, that was back in 1904. Chase, that happened when he got married back in '31—"

"In calendar time, yes, but the subconscious mind knows nothing about calendars, Anderson. Right now, Cleo has withdrawn herself from the world, rejecting everything in it, shutting herself away from humanity as far as it is possible

259

to do. It's going to take time and no results guaranteed. I wish I could be more optimistic—"

"You've seen others like this?"

Ballard nodded. "But no two the same because the basic causes are different. In this stage, there's no telling. It may be a few weeks, a few months before we see any signs, but it's only fair to tell you it could go on for a year, perhaps several years. How old is Cleo?"

"Sixty-four. Two years younger'n me."

Ballard's lips were pursed in a thin, sober line as he nodded. Anderson said, "If I brought Theodore home—"

"Chances are she wouldn't even recognize him. And all it could do to Theodore would be to increase his own guilt. Like his mother, he's got his own problems to whip."

"Carl—" It was a plea for help.

"I wish to God I could tell you more, Anderson, but these things are beyond me. Chesler is the best man I know in these parts. We could bring in carloads of specialists from all over the country, but I'm satisfied that Dave Chesler can do anything that needs to be done."

"What comes next? We don't have to move her to Atlanta, do we?"

"No. What needs to be done can be done here at Memorial. Chesler will give the orders to the therapists and come up from Atlanta as he's needed. She'll have the best possible care."

"Can I see her when I want?"

"Yes, but I would advise against it at present. For one thing, in her present state she won't be aware of your presence for a while. For another, it won't do you much good to look in and feel she's not showing progress."

"I God," Anderson said sadly. "I God. I was eighteen and she was barely seventeen when we got married. It's taken me all these years to do this to her, rob her of her senses—"

"Stop it, Anderson!" Ballard exclaimed sharply. And more softly, "You didn't do this to her any more than you are responsible for what happened to Theodore. Feeling sorry for yourself won't help any of you. I'm going to drive you home now and give you something to make you sleep. Tomorrow we'll talk some more."

"Carl—"

"What?"

"You think if we could bring Theodore home it would help?"

"I've told you, I don't know, Anderson. No one can say. I asked Dr. Chesler about that, but he didn't offer a comforting opinion. In her present condition, I doubt if it would help any."

Anderson had explained the situation to Dr. William Brenner and Brenner rubbed his pink jowls with fleshy pink fingers as he looked thoughtfully over the bleak New Jersey landscape through a broad expanse of glass. Finally, Brenner swiveled his chair back to face his visitor.

"You are asking questions, Mr. Warren, that only time alone can answer. How much we have accomplished thus far, I can't honestly say. Merely to describe the intensity of Theodore's paranoid schizophrenic tendencies—"

"You'll have to make it a lot more simple than that for me, Doctor," Anderson said. "Tell it to me in plain words I can understand."

"Ah, yes." Dr. Brenner pressed his fingertips together to form a steeple over his ample girth. "The results of your son's latest—ah—misfortune—had their beginning a long time ago. Jealousy of his older brother in childhood, resentment of Chase's achievements at an age when it was impossible for him to compete, perhaps a tendency on the part of his parents to overlook him while applauding or complimenting the elder son—many such acts, seemingly inconsequential at the time—"

Anderson nodded his head in unconscious agreement as Brenner pointed up examples of the development of the strained relationship between his sons.

"—so that when he was called upon suddenly to step into Chase's shoes, his instinct was to run as far away as possible from the idea of becoming his brother's shadow and perhaps showing himself to be a complete failure. Three years later, weary with self-admitted defeat, he allowed himself to be found. Then, believing it was his own choice, he entered the family business on what he believed were his own terms. With Chase absent, he performed well enough to gain confidence in himself and his abilities. He married and fathered two children. He accepted his family and business responsibilities and, in turn, was accepted in his own community of family, friends and associates.

"Then this terrible blow and the reemergence of his archenemy, Chase. You understand that it was Chase he blamed, not his wife—"

"You telling me—"

"I'm telling you he still loves his wife, Mr. Warren, whether he is aware of it or not."

"A woman who—?"

"Not a *woman* who, Mr. Warren, but a man, his own

261

brother, who deceived him, although at the time, she did not know Theodore, and later did not tell him she had ever known Chase. In his condition, Theodore willingly, gladly, transferred the entire blame to the one person he hates most, his enemy. His brother. Which is why his first impulse was not to punish Louise, but to come to New York to seek out Chase and kill him."

"And now, Doctor?"

"Again, I can't say. As far as we know, that impulse to kill Chase, at this moment, is dormant. I believe we have managed to make him understand that it would serve no purpose, that what took place between Louise and Chase occurred long before Theodore even knew, or became interested in, Louise. We believe he has, in some measure, accepted this."

"And Louise?"

"He realizes now that she was to blame for keeping her former alliance with Chase a secret from him, therefore his love and hate for her tip the scales back and forth."

"You think he wants her back?"

"Yes and no. The hurt he received, the damage to his ego, even to his very manhood, is deep and strong. So strong, he refuses to speak of it and until he can bring it out into the open voluntarily, there is little that can be done."

"If I took him home—?"

Brenner shook his head negatively. "Perhaps, but I think not. You must remember, Mr. Warren, that to return him too soon to the scene of his greatest emotional defeat, perhaps among curious eyes and whispered gossip, where everyone, you, his mother, his children and the servants are constant reminders, could have a harmful effect. Also, you, who arranged the divorce, will remain among those whom he believes harmed him, perhaps to be regarded as an ally of his enemy. An old quotation, if I may, sir. 'The friend of my enemy is my enemy.' If I may suggest—"

"What?"

"—that Theodore may be ready to leave here. He will not, I am sure, wish to go home, but I believe we can convince him to remain in New York, to do as and what he wishes to do. To keep him in this institution, which he regards as a prison, is now of declining value to him. He may, in desperation, choose to return to his work, but the decision must be his own. If he becomes interested in work again, it will perhaps diminish the tenseness, reduce the insecurity he feels and in some measure restore confidence in himself."

"I see. Did you tell him I was coming here today?"

"Yes. His reaction was negative. At this time, he still identifies you closely with the dissolution of his marriage to a woman with whom he was, and may still be, deeply in love. I think a confrontation with you at this time would be highly disturbing and damaging to him and do not recommend it. I am sorry to say this to you, his father, but—"

"Then—"

"Let me talk with him on the subject of leaving here. I think that would be the most effective means of handling the matter."

Anderson sighed deeply. "All right, Doctor. I'm going back to Laurelton. I think I can be more useful there than here. The children—"

"His, Theodore's children, you are referring to?"

"Yes. Has he mentioned Bruce or Drew in your talks with him?"

"No. He avoids the subject. Or any other that touches his wife. May I ask where Mrs. Warren is at present, Mrs. Theodore Warren, I mean?"

"She's living in Switzerland, the last I heard. I don't think she'll be moving around much with a shooting war going on." Apprehensively, "You don't really think he wants her back, do you?"

A shrug. "I don't really know what he wants, Mr. Warren. If I knew just that one thing, it would be tremendously helpful. As it is, we can only wait and see."

When Theodore chose to remain in New York, the burden fell upon Duncan Collins. Diane found an apartment in the East 80s and took great pains to have it decorated in bright, lively colors. The furniture she selected was modern, the draperies and rugs in light tones. She took extreme care to find an elderly married couple to take care of his needs without being intrusive and, at Dr. Brenner's suggestion, had Anderson ship his clothes, books and other familiar personal possessions from Laurelton, including his old stamp and coin collections and the pictures that had hung in his room before his marriage.

On the day of his arrival at the new apartment, he accepted everything without comment aside from a quiet, "Thank you, Diane. I think I would like to rest for a while."

For weeks, Theodore did not leave his apartment. He ate sparingly when meals were brought to him, slept when his mind and body required it, reread old favorites from his library of books, and showed little interest in the perpetual war news on radio and in the press. Much of his time was spent sitting in a comfortable chair on his balcony looking out on the East River while he listened to the collection of symphonic records Diane Collins had chosen for him. He made no effort to contact his father or mother or Collins, living in total unawareness of what had happened to Cleo, trying to shut Louise out of his mind.

As the weeks passed into months, he began taking walks, wandering along the river bank, then more boldly in a westerly direction. And one day, finding himself on East 42nd Street in front of the Warren Building, he went inside and took the elevator up to Duncan Collins' office, passing new faces in the hallway, busy people moving from office to office with purpose; but Collins' secretary of fifteen years recognized him at once and ushered him into the inner office.

Collins came forward to greet him. "Theodore, I'm delighted to see you. Come, sit down. It has been a long time." He ordered coffee brought to them and wrote a quick note, which he passed to Miss Federhoff, asking her to cancel his appointments for the balance of the day.

"You'll have lunch with me, won't you, Theodore?" Collins asked. "I've just had a lunch date cancelled on me."

"Yes."

It was a difficult, almost unnerving meeting for Collins, forcing him to great depths of ingenuity to pry some response from his dour, taciturn visitor. He touched on the war, increases in sales, New York's half-hearted dimout, an upcoming regional sales meeting during the following week, the weather, all without more than small, disinterested comment. During lunch at the Yale Club, Theodore's listlessness persisted and when it was over, he simply said, "Thank you for lunch, Dunc," and left Collins standing alone and bewildered on Vanderbilt Avenue.

In the weeks that followed, he took to dropping in more often, once during a conference between the Warren advertising director, Brock Abbott, and the Kilkarrick Agency's account executive, Darryl Jordan, which was taking place in Collins' office. Collins had questioned the need for so extensive a campaign at a time when supply could scarcely keep up with the demand.

"For the simple reason, Mr. Collins," Jordan replied, "that it is of paramount importance to keep our name before the public so that when civilian rationing ends, Warrens will be firmly fixed in the public mind."

"With millions of men in uniform who are taking up the slack?"

"Yes, even with that going for us. Remember that during these times of shortages at home, people are switching to

264

any brand that is available. Unless we keep reminding them that we are still in business, and will be when this is all over, we may find that we've slipped considerably later on. Automobile makers, refrigerator manufacturers who can't make or sell their products for civilian consumption are still spending heavily to remind the public that when the war is over, they will return from building tanks, guns and planes to automobiles, refrigerators, toasters and everything presently put aside for war production."

Collins was watching Theodore's reaction to the discussion and decided to take a small gamble. He said suddenly, "I would like to put the question to Mr. Warren and ask him how he feels on the subject."

There was total silence in the conference room as all eyes shifted to Theodore. Collins waited nervously, wondering if Theodore, having been so abruptly spotlighted, would simply get up and walk out, perhaps never to return. But his gamble had been a shrewd one. Theodore seemed to be thinking about his response, then said slowly, "I am in total accord with Mr. Jordan's viewpoint."

"Why, Mr. Warren?" Collins prodded a little deeper.

"Why?" Theodore pondered for a moment and Collins thought he had lost, but then Theodore said, "Because I can remember my father telling of his experiences during the last war. He was first among cigarette manufacturers to donate millions of cigarettes and roll-your-own makings to our troops, each sack and package carrying the Warren name. A lot of grateful men remembered when they came home and Warren became a strong factor in the industry. I think Mr. Jordan's suggestion to keep the name alive, even in the face of shortages, is imperative to the future of our product. We can't afford to allow our competitors to out-advertise us."

"Thank you, Mr. Warren." Collins said. Turning back to Jordan and Abbott, "Gentlemen, I think that settles the matter and I suggest you prepare the campaign as soon as possible."

Jordan and Abbott were elated and triumphant. They thanked Theodore and Collins. Jordan hinted that a celebration might be in order and the four went to lunch in high spirits which, for the first time, seemed to infect Theodore.

In the days that followed, Collins found a willing accomplice in Darryl Jordan. Jordan invited Theodore to visit the agency to watch the development and progress of the campaign, to offer suggestions. Theodore accepted and found himself in a new world of bright, witty, exciting writers, designers, artists and photographers; examining brisk, inspired

265

copy, provocative headlines, eye-catching pencil and color layouts, paintings and photographs. Luncheons became gala events, joined by others of the advertising fraternity, radio and stage actors and actresses, media representatives, a novelist or two. Spontaneous meetings ran from dinner well into the night, parties at Jordan's apartment, Abbott's tiny house in Greenwich Village, and later, the Kilkarrick place on Long Island.

At the Warren Building, Brock Abbott's office was enlarged to make room for Theodore who, without his formal consent, had become a part of the Warren advertising staff with title of Assistant Director. And before long, Theodore had entered into an affair with a young woman on the Kilkarrick art staff, drifted out of that into another with an actress who was playing second lead in a Broadway musical. Chase was becoming a dim shadow in Theodore's mind.

In Laurelton, Anderson Warren continued to go to his office each morning, but more and more he found himself shifting his work load onto Kenneth Armour's shoulders. His concern for Cleo was immense and she had shown little improvement since her state of withdrawal had begun, not much more than barely able to recognize Anderson. Carl Ballard eventually consented to her return home, in hope that the presence of Bruce and Drew, in familiar surroundings, might reawaken her interest in life. There was, however, little change and it soon became obvious that she had taken permanent refuge in her childhood, calling Leona and Shad by names of the Trimble servants of her youth. Bruce became a childhood companion, Glenn; and she renamed Drew for a doll she once owned, Gussie. Anderson shuddered when she smiled at him and called him "Daddy."

As for Theodore, Anderson received regular reports from Duncan Collins that showed a marked progress, but if Anderson was pleased, he gave no indication of his feelings.

The war came to an end and the next four years passed with few changes. Anderson gave his work only a half-hearted amount of attention and relied ever more heavily on Kenneth Armour to act in his stead, signing only the most important letters and contracts that required his personal attention as President.

In 1949, Cleo died peacefully in her sleep. Theodore learned of her death from Shana Pierce, who was Kenneth Armour's secretary, and was immediately engulfed in deep guilt and grief. Duncan and Diane Collins appeared at his apartment within the hour to help him pack, then flew with him to Atlanta where they were met by the Warren plane and flown to Laurelton. It was Theodore's first return in six years. Chase Warren was traveling in Saudi Arabia and could not be reached. Victoria sent her condolences.

His meeting with Anderson was no less awkward than his first sight of Drew, so much like Louise that he almost choked on his words of greeting, aching to take her into his arms, realizing that he was little more than a stranger to her. Bruce, at twelve, was tall and well filled out in the characteristic Warren tradition, blond and esthetically handsome. Both children regarded Theodore with the same polite, courteous "Hello" and handshake they gave to Duncan and Diane Collins. No more.

That first evening after dinner, Anderson excused himself and went to his study. A few minutes later, Shad entered and said in a low voice to Theodore, "Mist' Warren would like to see you in his study, Mist' Theodore."

The decanter of bourbon on Anderson's desk was uncapped, a small glass of the amber fluid in his hand when Theodore entered the room and stood waiting. Anderson indicated the decanter. "Help yourself," he invited.

"No, thank you," Theodore replied stiffly.

"Sit down, Theodore. Make yourself comfortable."

Theodore sat on the leather sofa against the far wall. Anderson finished his drink, then got up and crossed the room and sat in the side chair beside the sofa. "I didn't know whether to expect you or not," Anderson began.

"I came as soon as I got the word—from Kenneth Armour's secretary," Theodore added pointedly.

"If you're looking for an apology because I didn't call you myself, there won't be any." Anderson paused for a moment, then continued. "I don't want any wrangling between you and me, Theodore. Your mother's lying dead in her room and it ain't fitten that her husband and son start quarreling—"

"I have no intention of quarreling."

"So be it. We haven't been able to locate your brother. He's off in Saudi Arabia somewhere on business. His wife and son are in New York, but they won't be coming down." Anderson lit a cigarette, taking "thinking time" before resuming. "Before we bury your mother tomorrow, I want to remind you that you've got a son and daughter who don't know their father very well. I'm an old man and a twelve-year-old boy and a nine-year-old girl have got a right to have parents—"

"If you are about to suggest that I remarry, don't."

"All I'm suggesting is that you've got responsibilities and

267

obligations to two children of your own flesh and blood. Before you know it, they'll be full grown and you'll be a total stranger to both of them. I'm also suggesting that you come back to Brookhill to live and take your place in the Company where you belong, before that gets away from you, too."

Theodore studied Anderson's granite face without replying. "Last time we talked like this," Anderson continued, "you started running and didn't stop for three years. This thing with—Louise—that's taken you six long years to get over. You start running again, I'll tell you now there won't be anything for you to come back for."

"Are you blaming—?"

"Let's not start talking about blame, Theodore. From the time you were a toddler, there wasn't anything you ever wanted you couldn't have, but there was always something else you needed. On your own, you've been broke, hungry, in jail, but you were only half as old as you are now. At 40, it won't be easy this time and I won't be as forgiving as I was then."

"Why?" Theodore asked quietly. "Because you've got a grandson to take your place some day?"

Anderson nodded and Theodore could see some of the satisfaction in his father's eyes. "That's a good part of it," Anderson said. "Right now, you've got a chance to be a father to those two children. You walk out on them now and you'll never have the same chance again. Bruce and Drew will be mine to raise and keep. You think it over. You decide to go back to New York, or any place else, you let me know and I'll take what steps I need to take."

Theodore stood up and walked out of the study.

At noon the following day, with Jonas and Ames Taylor and a handful of close friends and servants to mourn, Cleo was carried from the house to the mausoleum and placed in her crypt to await her husband. There was only the briefest service and when it ended, Anderson said in simple eulogy, "She was a fine woman. No man ever had a more wonderful wife, no children blessed with a better mother, no grandchildren a more loving grandmother. I look to the day when the good Lord will let us be together again. Amen."

On the following morning, Duncan and Diane Collins returned to New York. Theodore remained in Laurelton.

8

In the ensuing years, Anderson Warren escaped the loneliness of his autumn years and Cleo's absence in travel. On business, for pleasure, there was no end to the number of scattered places in which he could fish, hunt or simply sightsee the days away; nor did he lack for company. There were friends, competitors, associates and branch executives at home and abroad who looked forward to an opportunity to be companion to the founder of the Warren Tobacco Company.

Theodore remained in Laurelton and slowly turned to the Company out of sheer need to keep himself occupied, interested principally in the advertising activities of the New York office, sending for Darryl Jordan and Brock Abbott occasionally to discuss current and upcoming campaigns, now reaching into the new world of television. More and more, he found himself returning home in time to meet Bruce and Drew at the end of their school day and on many mornings took over Shad's chore of driving them to school. He could scarcely look at Drew's face without remembering, not without some pain, Louise.

The process of ignoring Chase's part in the matter had been long, often unendurable, but now, time had begun to cure the erosion that had almost destroyed him. Gone were the fantasies in which he envisioned Chase at his mercy, inflicting the most vicious physical beatings, maiming, castrating him. He conjured up face-to-face encounters with Chase, conversations, always ending in violence in which Chase became the victim, he the victor; and later, simply refusing to acknowledge his presence. It was then that he remembered conversations with a now-forgotten young psychiatrist who had tried to force him to recognize that what had transpired before his marriage to Louise could have happened between her and any other man.

"No!" Theodore had stubbornly insisted, clinging to the idea that he had been deliberately persecuted by Chase.

"All right, Theodore," the doctor persisted, "I will reverse my opinion and come over to your side if you can explain to me how your brother could have divined that you and Louise would one day meet, fall in love and marry. You *do* admit she was a faithful and loving wife after your marriage, don't you?"

Grudgingly, "Ye-es—"

269

"Theodore, no man or woman is infallible to attraction to or from someone else. There are men and women who are secretly pleased, even smug, that they have remained physically faithful to their spouses, and yet, given the two right people in the right place at the right time and under the right circumstances, nothing could possibly prevent them from engaging in an affair, if single, in adultery if married."

And so in time, and perhaps from weariness of carrying that load on his shoulders and in his mind, the anger and tension lessened in him. There remained the need to draw closer to his children and this was more difficult than he had thought it would be. Bruce was occupied with the schoolmates he brought back to Brookhill to play, ride their ponies, eat and study together. Drew remained shy and distant, except with Bruce, whom she adored, and with certain of Bruce's friends. In order to encourage more company for them, Theodore ordered the swimming pool and tennis courts installed that summer, adding a country club atmosphere to Brookhill.

Inevitably, Theodore and Kenneth Armour came into closer contact, Kenneth so self-assured and confident in the face of Theodore's apparent insecurity. And Theodore saw some measure of defeat in the presence of his former tutor, the man who had arranged Louise's settlement and divorce. In Anderson's frequent absences, it was Armour who now held the reins and, despite resentment and distrust. Theodore found himself voting approval of Kenneth's proposals at staff and board meetings which he was forced, if only for the sake of ritual, to attend.

It took over a year before Theodore would move fully into the business world, attending luncheons, later small dinner parties at the homes of various Company executives or board members. The usual matchmaking games began, but he managed to evade these social entanglements, although he did engage in an occasional affair of short duration: a high school teacher, a widow in Atlanta over summer weekends, an assistant to the head of the Company's purchasing department, from whom he learned that the holier-than-thou Kenneth Armour was involved in a similar, longer-standing affair with the young, very attractive Shana Pierce, his secretary.

Satisfactorily, Bruce and Drew had come to accept him as a member of the Warren household, but his position, he knew, was still somewhere below that of Anderson and barely above that of Shad, Leona and Cord Waters, permanent fixtures as far back as both children could remember.

The war in Korea had stepped up Company activities and Anderson returned to take an active hand, now realizing for the first time that the organization was functioning smoothly under the direction of Kenneth Armour and, he hoped, Theodore. And for the first time since the founding of the Company, he began to think in terms of possible retirement; perhaps step up to the chairmanship of the board and move Theodore into the presidency, with Armour as executive vice-president. He decided to hold off, wait and see; and began spending more time with his cousin, Jonas Taylor, traveling about to various fishing and hunting preserves.

In 1956, Jonas Taylor was dead and Anderson had lost his oldest, dearest friend and financial adviser. Two years later, Jonas' son, Ames, of whom Anderson was genuinely fond, died of a stroke, leaving Stuart, who was married to Tracy Ellis's daughter, Coralee; Susan Taylor, who was married to John Curran; and Wayne, Susan's twin, in self-exile in Europe. What followed was distressing to Anderson; Wayne's return, too late for Ames' funeral; Coralee's tragic death when her car crashed into a stone gatepost at the entrance to the Curran estate, Betterton, and Stuart's subsequent death when his car broke through a guardrail on the bridge while being pursued by Deputy Chief of Police Lee Durkin, reawakening scandals that rocked Laurelton for months after.

Finally, in 1962, Anderson began to feel the years upon him and made only a few appearances at his office, occasional board meetings and the annual meeting of stockholders, which was more like a family gathering. The reins of the Company were more firmly in Kenneth Armour's hands and no one realized this more than Theodore.

9

In June of 1960, Victoria Warren and Andrea Vanderkuyl watched together with glowing pride as Victor Vanderkuyl Warren, 17, was graduated from MacComb Preparatory Academy with honors, and delivered the Class Prophecy with the same incisive, albeit good-humored, style that had won him the editorship of the MacComb *Sentinel*. Chase and Marshall, who had driven up separately and arrived somewhat late, were forced to sit at the rear of the auditorium during the ceremony.

Victor and Marshall were scheduled to spend the summer

abroad. In the fall, Marshall would return to Princeton for a year of post-graduate work, Victor to enter the freshman class there. Victoria drew great pleasure from the thought that Chase's son, Marshall, and Walter Cunningham's son, Victor, were the very best of friends despite the gap in their ages; and was saddened that Walter was not present to witness his son's graduation.

By the end of World War II, Walter had been divorced and decided to resign his commission as a Navy captain in order to accept a position with Com-Tex, an electronics firm specializing in the communications field. Walter had reorganized and strengthened Com-Tex's military division, which now accounted for nearly 65% of its sales to the armed services, and in 1959 had been elevated to the presidency of the firm. He had remained unmarried and the affair that had begun in Palm Beach with Victoria was resumed upon his return to New York.

Until Marshall and Victor were away at school, their meetings were circumspect and took place only when Chase was out of the city on his numerous business travels. Neither felt wholly safe or comfortable in the deception, and despite Walter's urgings that Victoria divorce Chase, there was the problem of the two children; also, the not unjustifiable fear that once Chase saw Victor and Walter together, Chase would immediately recognize Victor's parentage and thus add to Chase's power the threat of public exposure and scandal.

On their return to the city from MacComb, the four Warrens celebrated the occasion with a quiet, elegant dinner at Chase's club. The two boys later went off to join a more high-spirited celebration while Chase dropped Victoria at Andrea's house and went on to what had become known as "my weekly poker game."

Andrea had begun to show her age, but with no lessening of her grimness. Four servants took care of her daily requirements, but advancing age demanded the companionship of Victoria, upon which she had come to depend. Other than the monthly reports she received from Atlas Research and private meetings with Norton Harsh of CI, she had no contact with Chase Warren; the graduation exercises and dinner that followed were the first time she had seen him in the flesh in over five years and not more than the briefest of nods had passed between them.

Between ARA and CI, Andrea was fully aware of Auto-Mex and the subsequent companies bought, merged and formed into Intercon, yet she made no move to acquaint her attorneys or accountants with the separate corporate structure Chase had built at the expense of the Vanderkuyl interests. Each transaction was carefully documented in its separate file and when she was ready, she would align her sights and trigger her son-in-law's destruction. And here again, only the youth of her grandsons prevented her from detonating the final explosion. Yet, anticipation of that day seemed to give Andrea the strength and patience she required to pass her days. The taller Chase Warren grew, the more devastating and complete would be his defeat. Meanwhile, Victoria was happy with her Walter. Let Chase continue to build an empire that would eventually crumble, crushing him with humiliation and defeat beyond all endurance.

Noting Victoria's restlessness, Andrea asked, "Are you meeting Walter tonight?"

"I hadn't expected to, but this is a special occasion. I'd like to tell him about the graduation exercises. I'll take a taxi to his apartment in about a half hour. I'll be home long before Chase."

"How long do you intend to keep up this deception?"

"Mother, please don't—"

"I am not interfering, Victoria. You are giving up what could be the happiest of your mature years for that man—" Andrea seldom referred to Chase by name "—and heaven knows you deserve better than these occasional meetings. There's the risk—"

"We've been very discreet and I don't think Chase could care less. As long as Walter and I are satisfied— Let it rest, Mother."

"I only wish we could bring this thing to a head. I'm sure Walter could step in and take over our business affairs without any problems."

"I'm just as sure as you that he can, but I don't see why it is necessary. There's more than enough for all of us and I'm damned sick of the whole business. Walter and I have a satisfactory arrangement and as long as it pleases us, it will continue that way. The formality of marriage isn't a requisite for happiness and I'm beyond the need for it."

"And Walter?"

"Walter feels as I do. When the children are safely on their own, we will make our decision. Either way will suit us."

Andrea sighed and sipped at her wine while Victoria rang for Morris and asked him to arrange for a taxi. "Mother," she said when the butler left, "please don't worry about us. We haven't needed that for a long time."

"No, dear, you haven't." Nor, Andrea thought, me. But before I die, I will see Chase Warren brought to his knees and you will have nothing to say about that, dear Victoria.

BOOK II

CHAPTER I

1

The weather was warm and Buddy Duke, uniform cap tipped back on his nappy head, chauffeur's jacket lying across the back of the front seat, drove with extreme care, observing speed limits and road courtesy, keeping in the far right lane except when passing slow-moving trucks. Once past Wilmington, he stayed on Route 40 into Baltimore and blundered about until he found the York Hotel in a predominantly Negro neighborhood where he had once lived for a week preceding a ten-rounder he had won handily from a white boy, Denny—something—Schmidt, he recalled then, three years earlier. He chuckled with the recollection of the clumsy man who, in their very first clinch, had snarled, "Back off, boy. Keep your goddam nigger sweat off'n me."

Buddy had relived that fight many times with rare enjoyment. At the end of the first round, he knew he could take Schmidt any time he chose. A little too sloppy with fat, pink-faced, short-cropped blond hair; slow-footed and nothing going for him but strength. He punished Big Mouth Schmidt mercilessly for the next three rounds and even when Sandy and Al Saxon called for a knockout in the fifth, Buddy decided the blond German hadn't been punished enough. He taunted the white boy with his eyes and lips, stabbed and jabbed him off balance, rocked him back

275

on his heels with driving gut punches and danced out of danger easily.

And he clinched unnecessarily, rubbing his body sweat into Schmidt's precious pink skin, flicking it off his forehead into his opponent's face, rubbing it into his mouth with his wet gloves. And finally, as the tenth round drew to its final ninety seconds, Buddy became a slashing, ferocious tiger, jolting, body-punching the helpless white boy at will until, with twenty seconds left, he shot a hard left to his jaw, crossed with a right, and Schmidt went down to stay, a battered, bleeding hulk that hardly resembled anything human.

Then Sandy, chiding him in the dressing room. "You got no call to do nothin' like 'at to any man, Buddy."

"No? He got any call to tell me my nigger sweat is dirtier, stinkin' more'n his?"

"You crazy, takin' five-six rounds more to beat 'im than you hafta. Don't make no sense an' you don' make no more money lettin' 'im stay the whole ten, do you?"

"No, but I sure had me a good time sweatin' all over ole white boy."

"Yeah, well, you better start learnin' what's important an' what ain't," Sandy replied and continued the rubdown without further comment.

What's important, what ain't important. Something to ponder over in days to come.

He had had other opportunities to become "important," add to his public image and stature. He had been sought out by high-ranking aides of Malcolm X, Elijah Muhammad, of the NAACP, CORE, SNCC, and other groups, asked to join and lend his name to promote the cause of each, but he had given cash contributions only and none of his time, which he conserved for his career and pleasure. The money he had given had come easy. His time was far more valuable.

Now, seeing his ring career on the wane, he regretted his aloofness. With hatred coursing through him as never before, he saw merit in militancy and Black Nationalism. Negroes could not live with whites on any terms other than equal and no white man, even those involved in the civil rights movement, would ever permit him the ultimate equality. He had weighed the activities of the various Negro organizations and reasoned that the Muslims offered more than any other because it denied white participation. Then, Malcolm X had been gunned down, a martyr.

The Black Fez Movement had the right idea, he decided. Black men should join hands with other black men throughout the world to make their strength felt, because only in a unified effort could they win and hold what they won. Anything else was just so much shit. He had known and felt personal power until three white men deprived him of it. How long had it taken, ten, fifteen minutes? But with power multiplied by millions throughout the world—man, the mere thought of it was exhilarating. That was one thing was for damn sure important. Power.

In Richmond, Buddy decided to put his chauffeur's jacket on and wear his cap properly. He was in the real South now and old memories of prejudice returned. Ten years away from it hadn't robbed him of the knowledge of what could happen to him if he were picked up on so much as a charge of his brake lights not working properly. For a while he considered getting off Route 1, away from the heavy truck traffic, perhaps cut across on Route 60 onto 15 through Farmville and Clarksville, maybe west on 58 to South Boston, then southward to Durham, but the thought of possible arrest in a smaller town was even more repugnant to him.

Out of Petersburg he took 301 to Roanoke Rapids and continued southward, blending in with the traffic flow, stopping for food and sleep in the Negro sections of the larger towns, always aware, and not without some apprehension, of the undue attention his Jaguar was creating, fobbing it off as belonging to "my white boss, he an' his fam'ly, they in Miami Beach for the winter." It nettled him somewhat that among his own, no one had recognized him as The Duke; no Jackie Robinson, no Joe Louis, no Maury Wills he.

But he was homeward bound and felt an inner glow of warmth. Ten years had passed since he left Laurelton, but he knew that among his people there, his career would have been followed. One loss wouldn't make any difference to them; not to Sam, Lutie or Elizabeth, not to Banjo, Hobie, Jake and the others. He thought of the money he had sent home during his "hot" earning period, which had made it possible for Sam and Lutie to move out of the old shack on Paca Street to a better house on Wallace; made it possible to send Elizabeth to the University of Southern California in Los Angeles. She had sent him several snapshots along with letters, but he had almost failed to recognize her as the pretty, pig-tailed Elizabeth running off to school with her lunch under one arm, books clutched under the other. Elizabeth with a college degree. And why the hell she'd want to come back to Angeltown to teach in a rundown school was beyond him. He thought of Benny Tupper and wondered if Benny had ever finished his prison sentence for pushing.

277

Remembering Hobie Morris. Delia. Poor Dele, taken in the same raid with Benny.

And Ivy. He recalled Ivy with a special, erotic glow that made him squirm even now; wondering if she were still in Angeltown. Married? Children? And remembering, knew it would make no difference to him as long as she had kept her good looks and that fabulously sensual body. The mere thought of Ivy sent shivers coursing up and down his spine and he knew she would be among the first on his list to look up when he reached home. If she were there. Elizabeth had never, in any of her letters, mentioned Ivy.

At least, he had already solved the question of what he would do to replenish his money. A soft touch. No narcotics, no backroom gambling.

Numbers. Policy. Never before successfully operated in Angeltown on a large scale. Banjo, he was sure, would come in on a sweet deal like this one when he outlined it for him. Big city style. Banjo could front for him, help him get the runners while he set it up and nursed it into a big-time operation. Banjo would know who to contact, to pay off for protection, the goddam ofay fuzz who had their fat mitts out for any loose dollar they could pick up. They would need half a dozen good collection points in Angeltown, another four in South Laurelton, key men in the large industrial plants; men they could trust, bend the muscle on them if necessary, to keep them in line.

What changes would he find, he wondered. Not many, physically, in piss-poor Angeltown. Times were better, employment good when Sam scratched out a note two years ago to tell him they were in good shape and didn't need any more help from him. Goddam stiffnecked old man, proud as hell, independent as a rat in a corncrib.

He was still conscious of the cast that ran from just above his fingernails to his wrist, making his left hand practically useless in the most elementary functions: eating, dressing, washing, shaving. Fortunately, there was no pain; the heroin took care of that, but there was no way in which he could relieve the itching created by the perspiration that formed inside the cast, unable to touch or scratch the affected area, trying to concentrate on the scenery, car licenses, the radio; anything to keep his mind off it.

At Durham, he swung west again on Route 70 to Greensboro, then southwest on 601 to Charlotte, then to Gastonia and again south to Greenville, entering Georgia at Hartwell, beginning to *feel* home by the very smell of the soil. And then, *knowing* it when he reached Tenboro that evening at dusk, only 22 miles from Laurelton. In the Negro quarter along the west end of Commerce Street he found a small, malodorous restaurant and ordered a meal dictated by nostalgia. Brunswick stew. It came in a thick bowl with two slices of bread and a melting pat of butter, bubbling hot and looking marvelous, smelling like heaven; but a few spoonsful of the overly fat gravy, rancid meat and tired greens made him feel like throwing up. He pushed it aside and ordered a ham sandwich and coffee, then couldn't wait to get out of the place.

His battery was dead. Back in Durham, a filling station man had called his attention to the crack in his battery casing and the bluish-white corrosion around the terminals, but Buddy had dismissed it with indifference. Goddam service men were all alike, always trying to needle him into an unnecessary quart of oil, a lube job, new spark plugs, brake relining job, anything to squeeze an extra buck out of him. There was no arguing now. It was gone. No lights. Not even a peep out of the horn. Dead.

The restaurant man directed him to the nearest filling station, six blocks up on Commerce Street. He walked it, found an overgrown white youth, no more than 17, in charge, the owner off for supper. Everything about the boy was outsized; head, ears, hands, idiotic smile, even his dirty coveralls. The boy looked up from the hoodless Ford he was tinkering with, his torpid, acne-spotted face raised in question. And Buddy remembered. "Boss man around?"

"Nope. Home for supper. Somethin' you want, boy?"

Boy. Buddy Duke, *The* Duke, 26 years old. A "boy" to this ofay punk. "Yeah. You got a battery for a Jag?"

"Jag?" Insolently, "You got a Jag, or you on one?"

"Belongs to my boss. I'm takin' it to him in Florida."

"Jesus, some people got it soft." The youth's eyes fell on the cast and he pointed a grease-streaked hand toward it. "What you do, get your hand caught in your boss' pants pocket?"

Buddy raised the cast to above waist high, as though he would like to smash it into the adolescent face. "No," he said slowly, "I busted it on a man's jaw."

Scoffing, "Yeah, I'll bet."

"How about a battery? Mine conked out on me."

"We don't keep no batteries here, boy."

"How come?"

"No need to. Wholesaler's place is up the street, middle of the block. We need one, we pick it up on the spot."

"C'n you pick one up for me?"

"Sure. Tomorrow some time."

"I need it now."

279

"Well, you can't get it now. I can't leave the station by itself and besides, they close at five o'clock and it's almost five-thirty now."

"Any place else I can get one?"

"No place I know of. Come by tomorrow."

You faggy ofay bastard, Buddy said to himself. If we were anywhere up north I'd have your ass in a sling quick. "Okay," he said aloud, "thanks."

Without replying, the boy turned and resumed tinkering with the Ford. Buddy walked back to the restaurant. The last tinges of the dying sun flecked the sky with splashes of red as he checked the doors of the Jaguar to make sure it hadn't been tampered with. Standing beside it, trying to decide what to do. So close to home, forced to spend the night in Tenboro, tired of fleabag towns and fleabag rooms. Beginning to want another shot just to get rid of his mood of depression. Standing there banging his right fist lightly against the body of the Jag. He looked up and saw the thin, lanky restaurant man staring out of the dirty window at him, his short, fat wife bustling about behind the counter as she served three men sitting on stools. The rickety tables were empty. He went inside the restaurant again.

"You find the place I tellen you about?" the man asked.

"I found it. Can't get the battery 'til tomorrow."

The man nodded sympathetically. "They's the Blue Bell Cabins four blocks down the street where you c'n get a room——"

"They got a bus out of here for Laurelton anytime tonight?" Buddy asked suddenly.

"They's one around six-thirty." The man looked up at the fly-specked wall clock. "Got almost a whole hour. How about the car, you fixin' to leave it there on the street?"

"Listen. I got to be in Laurelton tonight. How about I leave the keys with you, you keep an eye on it for me? I be back maybe tomorrow or the next day. I'll pay you——"

The lanky man leaned across the counter, shielding his voice from the three customers. "You ain't runnin' from nothin', are you, son?"

Buddy smiled. "Hell, no. If I was, I'd just leave it and go. That car ain't hot. I'll be back, all right, and I'll give you five dollars to look out for it."

"Well— Not on the street. Them cops, they be in askin' questions, then haul it away. If they don't, the kids'll strip it clean. Tell you what, I'll get a coupla boys an' we push it aroun' in back. I got a shed back there——"

In the shed, Buddy paid the boys a dollar each. When

280

they left, planning their evening with broad grins, he got a suitcase out of the trunk, changed from the chauffeur's uniform into a neat dark gray suit. From under the seats he removed his cache of heroin and locked it in the suitcase, then carried it into the restaurant. The thin owner stared at him admiringly. "Man, that's some suit!" he exclaimed.

"Yeah. My boss give it to me. One of his old ones. We the same size."

"Mus' be a millionaire, your boss."

"That's just what he is." Buddy handed him a five-dollar bill. "I'll be back tomorrow, maybe the day after. Okay?"

"Shuh. Don't you worry your head about it. It'll be locked up there when you git back."

The bus depot was four blocks east on the edge of the commercial district. Buddy waited until 6:15 before leaving the restaurant, hoping his clothes and the glistening, streamlined two-suiter would be less noticeable with the sun all the way down. He walked quickly, keeping close to the building line on the shaded side of the street, praying no squad car would spot him, stop to ask questions, trip him on some technical contrivance, take him in on suspicion. And find the money on his body, the heroin in his suitcase. The thought of it caused him to break out into a sweat, cursing himself for stupidity. One more night wouldn't have mattered. And now it was too late. Some lousy ofay fuzz, envious of his English cut suit that had cost $180, the $35 shoes and $80 two-suiter could cancel everything. Suddenly conscious of his cast-bound hand, a perfect opener for a suspicious small-town cop.

The depot was half empty. He bought his ticket quickly, checked the bag through in order to get it out of his possession, remembering to add a polite "Sir" to every response to the graying, tooth-gapped, tobacco-chewing ticket clerk, then went out the side door to the boarding platform. Just as a foot patrolman entered the waiting room, sauntered around swinging his baton from its leather thong as he casually glanced over the white and Negro passengers lounging on their separate benches. Buddy watched from the platform area and when the patrolman started toward him, he went to the door marked "Colored" and waited in the reeking toilet until the bus arrived, its air brakes gasping asthmatically as it slid into its proper bay.

Several passengers debarked, leaving about a dozen on the bus. Another seven or eight waited in line to board. As they started to get on, Negroes first, by habit heading toward the rear, Buddy slipped out of the rest room and

281

climbed aboard, grateful that the patrolman had turned and was reentering the waiting room. He went to the back of the bus and sat in the far left corner, next to the offside window.

2

At five o'clock that afternoon, Angeltown's Velie Street, the hub of West Laurelton's night life, was relatively quiet. Not until full dark would it begin stirring with restless men, women, boys and girls, seeking escape from the heat and toil of their day among the taverns, cheap night clubs, their one movie house, The Goldfield, restaurants, pool parlors, hanging around corners or simply sitting out on wooden steps to watch the passing parade.

At the corner of Velie and Preston, the neon sign came on and began flashing, a huge banjo with a pair of moving hands that seemed to pluck at its strings and finger chords, the trademark of Ben-Joe Nichols' pool parlor, known as Banjo's Place. Through a loudspeaker, banjo music filled the air in the vicinity of the corner.

Inside, Mace Bodie lined up the angle, stroked his 20-ounce cuestick smoothly along the bridge formed by the thumb and index finger of his left hand. "Six-ball in the right side," he announced to his opponent, Eli Buller, and the half dozen loungers on the bench that ran along one wall.

"Man," one of the watchers said from the sideline, "with an open shot on the nine-ball." His voice indicated a subtle degree of admiration with which the low murmurs of the others concurred. Bodie straightened up.

"I got a dollar says I make it."

Buller walked around and stood beside Bodie, examined the angle and said, "You faded."

"Put your money where your mouth is at, boy," Bodie invited.

Buller withdrew a crumpled single dollar bill from his washworn blue jeans and stuffed it in the corner pocket of the pool table. Bodie added his matching dollar to it. Some small change passed hands among the watchers. Bodie bent over the table again, stroked the cuestick and gauged the difficult cut that might easily send the white ball into the upper left corner pocket for a scratch, then hit the white ball low and on the left side, drawing it slightly. The six-ball angled into the right side pocket and dropped with a solid *click!* on a ball that had been dropped in earlier. The cueball angled upward and to the left, hit the cushion and rolled to within an inch of where Bodie indicated with the tip of his cue that it would come to a stop. Only the nine-ball remained on the table.

"Rack!" Bodie called as he withdrew the two crumpled bills from the corner cache and shoved them triumphantly into his shirt pocket. "How you like them apples, baby?" he asked, not only of Buller, but of the watchers.

Amid murmurs of approval, Larry Powell racked the fourteen spent balls into the wooden triangle for the break shot. The score stood at five-to-nine in favor of Eli Buller. The balls racked, Bodie now lined up the cueball with the nine and the second ball from the top right corner of the triangle. "Nine in the right corner off the ten-ball," he announced. This time there were no challenges or bets.

The smoky room was long and narrow. There were four other tables spaced down the center of the room, unoccupied at the moment. Over each hung a low, shaded bulb that lighted the entire table and threw shadows on the grimy, paint-peeled buff walls that were marked with penciled names and telephone numbers, intermingled with occasional literary and poetic obscenities. At the front end of the room and to one side of the double doors was a lunch counter, over which sandwiches, cigarettes, soft drinks, beer and candy bars were dispensed

At the back of the room, Hinky Liggett, a large, slovenly, brutal-faced man, sat in a wooden chair that leaned against the wall on its two back legs, next to the door he seemed to be guarding, his narrow-brimmed felt hat pulled down over his eyes as though he were totally detached from what was going on at the rear table, a cigarette dangling from between his thick lips, a sawed-off cuestick resting against the wall beside him.

The door opened and a head projected itself through the narrow opening. Hinky looked up quickly and Jake Runnels said, "Tell the kid to bring five beers in." The door closed again.

Mace Bodie drove the nine-ball into the triangle. It glanced off the ten-ball and shot into the corner pocket like a bullet. The rest of the triangle broke wide open and Bodie grinned broadly at Buller's discomfiture, chalking his cue slowly. "You give up, Eli?" he taunted lightly.

"You just keep shootin', boy," Eli replied.

"Just what I'm about to do." Bodie leaned over the table again, preparing for a good run on the remaining balls.

"Hey, kid!"

Larry Powell turned from the table toward Liggett's bulky figure. "Five beers for the back room."

"Coming up." Larry walked to the front counter and gave the order to Noah Smith, the old man who presided over the sandwich and drink department. Noah placed five bottles of beer and five glasses on a tray, which Larry carried to the back door. Hinky stretched an arm behind him and rapped three times. Larry heard the grating of a bolt being drawn, then the door opened and Jake Runnels took the tray from him. This time, the aperture was wider and Larry saw the men who were inside the room, sitting at the round poker table. Ben-Joe Nichols, Jim Cuddy, and two strangers who wore black fezzes on their heads. "All right, kid," Runnels said, "beat it.'

Runnels drew back inside the room and kicked the door shut. The bolt grated into place again and Larry returned to the table to watch Mace Bodie drop the last ball of the rack to win the game and collect his scattered bets. Buller wanted no more of Bodie and another challenger took his place.

Larry untied the small green apron he wore and put it behind the sandwich counter. It was 5:30, time for his supper break. "Be back in an hour, Noah," he said to the old man. Noah simply nodded and continued to wrap sandwiches in wax paper for the pool shooters who would be coming in later. Larry slipped into his jacket and went out through the front door, turning west on Velie. As he passed the steps which led to the upper floors over Banjo's Place, a silky voice called out from the vestibule. "Hi you, Larry."

He turned toward the steps and saw the small red glow of a cigarette tip in the interior dimness. "That you, Rena?"

"It's me." He took a few steps closer to the shadows to where the slender, dark girl stood inside.

"What are you doing out here this early in the evening?"

"Came to get me some fresh air before things get goin' upstairs. You out for your supper?"

"Yeah. Going to be a long night downstairs, too. Well—"

"Cigarette, Larry? Sit a minute an' talk?"

"I'd like to, Rena, but I'm hungry. Got to be back in an hour. Give me a raincheck, huh?"

"Any time you want it. How about when you quit tonight?"

Larry laughed pleasantly. "Can't afford the prices, baby."

"No price if we go to your place."

He shook his head negatively. "I'd get thrown out of my room, bringing a girl there. Some other time, hey?"

"Sure. Some other time."

ination, one for minor insubordination; all spaced evenly in order not to permit his demerits to show up in a close group. In the middle of the fifth week, in a riot-control class, Sergeant Ralph Steckler, rotund and bullet-headed, was lecturing the class on procedure and, for purposes of demonstration, used two of the trainees as regular officers ostensibly coming upon a riot, or near-riot, situation. The rest of the class was acting the part of the mob.

"Somewhere in the crowd," Steckler was saying, "there is a leader. We hear a lot about those so-called spontaneous riots, but in my experience, that's a lot of psychological crap employed by people who've never been involved in a major riot. Somewhere, there's got to be a leader, the spark plug that sets the rest of them off.

"Until help comes, the idea is not—I repeat, NOT—to wade in and start cracking heads, trying to make arrests, no matter what. Keep trying to spot the leader, but in the meantime, call in a Code 9, request for assistance. Help will be on its way in a matter of seconds. The idea is to keep cool and detached, make no offensive moves except to protect yourselves, and keep your eyes open for that leader, so that when help arrives—"

From the outer rim of the class came a snort of dissent —"It'll be too late."

Steckler's shaven head bobbed upward in the moment of silence that followed the interruption. "Who said that?" he lashed out.

The silence continued, but several students turned in Larry Powell's direction. "All right," Steckler demanded again, "who said it?" His eyes, too, were now riveted on Recruit Powell.

"I did," Larry spoke up.

"You don't agree with that theory, Powell?" Steckler asked.

"No, I don't."

"On what basis, your broad experience against mine?" There were snickers from the white trainees and obvious embarrassment among the other four Negroes. Everyone knew Steckler, the ex-Army MP with 16 years on the force, who had been involved in the riots in Albany during his police service in that hotbed of earlier civil rights trouble.

"No, sir. It's just that you're employing the psychological aspect—"

"Just hold it. Come up here, Powell, and let's give the whole class the benefit of your superior knowledge," Steckler invited.

291

From beside him, Jim Davis whispered, "For Christ's sweet sake, Larry, cool it. Apologize—"

"You hear me, boy? Get up here. Fast."

This was a different tone for Steckler, that of an angry white man toward an inferior Negro, one that was most familiar, and detested, by all Negroes. Several white trainees laughed. Larry stood his ground. "I'll come up there when you address me with some respect, Sergeant," he replied coolly. "I'm not your boy or anybody else's."

"Respect?" Steckler shouted angrily. "You goddam nigger, when I tell you to move, you move!"

"Is that the kind of mob psychology people are supposed to respond to?" Larry asked. He was moving forward now, fists clenched belligerently, and before Steckler could answer, was facing him.

"Listen, Powell, this is a classroom—"

"Where we're supposed to learn what we're expected to do under certain conditions and in certain situations. Man, you can't teach anybody anything. You're just another hot-headed—"

Crack! Steckler was out of control. His fist shot out and caught Powell's chin, dropping him to the ground. The rest of the class, disbelieving the entire proceedings, began to form a circle around them. Larry got up slowly, shaking his head to clear his eyes. "White man," he said slowly, "I'm going to whip you and stomp you into the ground."

He lunged forward and lashed out at the bulky sergeant, who took two hard blows, hardly flinching. Steckler had backed off and rolled with both punches, drawing Powell in, then hammered him with a hard left and right to his middle. Larry buckled, but when the sergeant drove in to follow up his advantage, threw a shoulder block into Steckler, knocked him off balance and put across a hard left, flooring the bulky man. "Goddam nigger, am I?" Larry shouted as he stood back, waiting.

Steckler got up slowly and moved in, slashing away with his fists, giving more than he was getting and there was no doubt about the outcome now. Then, other officer-instructors were running toward the circle, breaking through it. The four Negroes in the class grabbed Powell and pulled him back, warding off his lunges and fists. "Boy," Ed Purvis said, "you sure screwed yourself this time. You don't quiet down, you going to screw the rest of us up. You're finished, you crazy fool. Don't finish us up with you."

Later that afternoon, Larry Powell was dismissed from the trainee school by Captain Walter Craig, its commander, who added, "—and you're damned lucky Sergeant Steckler didn't prefer charges against you. It's a shame, Powell. I don't understand you. You were doing fine, but you evidently aren't stable enough for police work. I know you'll resent the force for this, but you brought it all on yourself. If you're smart, you'll stay out of trouble, but I guess if you were as smart as you were supposed to be, this wouldn't have happened."

"May I go now, Captain?" Larry asked with some honest regret.

"Yes. I'm sorry, Powell."

"I'm not, Captain. I'm no white man's 'goddam nigger' and I'll never be."

The captain sighed unhappily.

By nightfall, the story of his expulsion had spread all over Angeltown. A number of people caught up with him to applaud his action, others to commiserate with him.

The first inkling Elizabeth Shackleford had of Larry Powell's trouble was when she returned from the school where she taught a third-grade class. It was four o'clock and her father hadn't yet gotten home from his job at the Warren plant. Lutie Shackleford was in the kitchen, hovering over the dinner on the stove when Elizabeth came in through the back door. Lutie was a tall, light-colored woman and it was not difficult to see from whom Elizabeth had inherited her good looks. When she kissed Lutie's cheek, she said, "Hi, Mom. Let me put these papers away and change my dress and I'll come help you."

"Don't you worry with it, baby. You just put your things away an' go to the parlor. You got comp'ny."

"Company? Who?"

"Larry Powell. I think he got somethin' troublin' him."

"Larry?"

Lutie nodded her head. "Somethin' got him by the tail. You c'n see it all over his face. Been waitin' almost an hour."

Elizabeth dropped the leather portfolio on her dresser and went to the parlor where Larry, who had heard her speaking to Lutie, stood waiting. They were nearly the same age, Elizabeth a strikingly handsome, well-formed girl with delicate facial features, shoulder-length hair and a skin the warm *café au lait* color.

She saw the pain of anguish in his eyes and went to him quickly. "Larry, what is it? What's wrong?"

"Beth, I lost my head today. Completely."

She laughed nervously, knowing it was more serious than he pretended to show. "Well, everyone does that at one time

293

or another. I lose mine half a dozen times a day, but it's not fatal." She peered closer at him in the dim, shade-drawn room. "Larry—"

"Mine was. I got kicked out of training school."

"Oh, Larry!"

"I'm sorry, Beth. I can't undo it. I came by to tell your father. He's been so good to me, I want to try to explain—"

"He'll help you, Larry. He's awfully fond of you. We all are."

"I didn't come by to ask for his help, Beth—"

"I didn't imply you had, but if he can, in some way—"

"It's no use. Look." He went to a window and drew the shade up. She saw the marks of battle on his face and stared at him uncomprehendingly.

"Larry, this isn't—"

"Like me?" he laughed tightly. "I guess it was exactly like me. I lost my head. A white man, Sergeant Steckler, called me 'boy,' then a 'goddam nigger' because I dared argue a point of psychology with him. It ended in a fight. There's no appeal."

"Dad will get you a job at the plant—"

"I told you I didn't come for help, only to explain how it happened. He's helped me enough already, Beth. I'm old enough to go out on my own."

"But where? What will you do?"

"I'll find something, somewhere."

"Pushing a wheelbarrow? Sweeping floors? Working on a construction gang? Driving a truck? Letting a college education go to waste? Larry, let me talk to Dr. Carter about a teaching job—"

"For the peanuts you make?"

"Larry!"

"I'm sorry, Beth. Right now, I guess I'm sore at the whole world. Look, I don't want you-all to take on my problems. I'll get a job on my own. I've got to learn how some time."

"Everyone needs help at one time or another, Larry. Please don't be too proud to accept it." She paused, then said, "Do you need any money?"

"No. I've got over two hundred dollars saved up."

They heard Sam Shackleford's old car drive in beside the house and into the backyard shed. "I've got to set the table for supper," Elizabeth said. "You'll stay, won't you?"

"Not for supper. I already told your mother I've got to see some man about a job, a possibility."

"I've got to run now. I'm teaching a class at the Center tonight. Larry?"

"What?"

"Please. If Dad or I can help, will you let us know?"

"Sure. Sure, Beth. You run along. I won't keep your dad long."

It occurred to him when he left the Shackleford house later that if he had given even a single thought to the effect it would have on these three prople, Sam, Lutie and Elizabeth, Elizabeth in particular, Inspector LaSalle could have taken his job and shoved it. From this moment on, he was on his own, unable to tell anyone his true purpose. He had a code number, a very special one. Two-Five. Undercover agent. That number could get him through to the inspector at once. If its significance were ever discovered in Angeltown, it could get him killed.

A loner.

At six o'clock, when he returned to Banjo's Place, there were more than a dozen people in the place. Hinky Liggett removed the small green apron he was wearing and threw it to Larry. "Git your ass on the job, boy," he growled.

"I'm on time, Hinky. It's exactly six o'clock."

"Don' back-mouth me, boy. Just tend to them tables." He went to the back of the room and resumed his favorite position, in the chair, leaning against the wall next to the door to the back room.

"Rack!"

"Coming up!" Larry responded and began his next shift.

3

The bus from Tenboro, after four or five brief stops along the way, reached Laurelton at 7:55. Buddy Duke claimed his suitcase and went quickly to the cab stand on the Willis Street side where the Negro cab drivers were allowed to line up. He took the first cab in line and, once inside, couldn't remember the number of the new address. Something-Wallace Street. The cab pulled away from the curb and the driver turned. "Where to, man?"

"Wallace," Buddy replied shortly, trying to remember.

"Wallace got lotsa numbers. Which one you want?"

"I—uh—hell, I forgot. Go ahead whilst I try to think of it."

"Shuh. Where you from, man?"

"From? I'm from here, Laurelton. Angeltown."

"You don' soun' like you from here."

"I been away up north. New York. You from here?"

295

"My whole life. I don't remember seein' you aroun'."

"Been a long time. You know the Shacklefords?"

"Sam? Miz Lutie? Elizabeth? Shuh, I know 'em."

"That where I want to go."

"Well, Jee-*zus*, man!" The driver braked his car, turned fully around to stare, his mouth open, two rows of white teeth gleaming. As he turned, he opened the door, which activated the dome light inside. "Now don' tell me you Th' *Duke!* Buddy Duke?"

He was home. He grinned with enjoyment and said, "That's me."

"Well, I be go to hell! Buddy Duke! Man!" He slammed the door shut and resumed his normal speed. "I'm Robbie Hewitt. Useta live five-six houses up the street from you-all when you-all lived over on Paca. Still live there. Your people, they on Wallace, just a few doors up from La Grange. They know you comin'?"

"No—"

"Didn' think so, else we'd-a knowed about it. Man, 'at's somethin'! Champ, I remember you when you just a bitty kid, hustlin' your newspaper route maybe a good ten years ago. Wait'll I tell it—"

"How about you keepin' it to yourself for a day or two, Robbie? I need to rest up for a couple-a days. Got to take care of this busted hand."

"Shuh, Buddy, shuh. It'll kill me, but I won't spill nothin'. Shuh good to have you home, man. What happen to your hand?"

"Busted it in an accident. Banjo's Place still runnin'?"

"Shuh. Full time. You know Banjo?"

"Shuh. Useta work for him." Buddy realized then that his northern accent was drifting away from him, as he picked up the local cadence to which he had been succumbing unconsciously since Richmond, becoming more pronounced here. "I know him, all right. Hey, is Benny Tupper aroun'?"

"Benny? Hell, no. That cat, man, he tried to bust outa Parkton long about four-five years ago. They got him in a swamp an' 'at's all she wrote. They give it to him good. Lanny Rooker come home, he say Benny died real hard."

Exit Benny. Murdered before they could get him back to the prison compound. "How about Jake Runnels, Hobie Morris?"

"Jake, he still aroun'. Hobie, he die two years ago come December, I think—" Robbie Hewitt continued the parade of names until he drew up to 708 Wallace Street, a larger house than the one on Paca Street in which Duke had been born and lived for sixteen years, but still a disappointment

him, turned and called out, "Jemmy! You Jemmy! Come get Mist' Corey's things! You hear me, Jemmy!"

For a moment, Corey stood there looking around at the neat grounds, as immaculate as ever, allowing its heat-laden, aromatic odors to penetrate deeply into his lungs, into his brain. He thought gratefully, *Everything is the same, nothing has changed,* knowing now for certain that this Georgia earth *was* different from all other earth anywhere else in the world, the special perfume of its trees and grass and flowers unlike that of any other; and perhaps the reason why men were so strongly attached to the land upon which they were born, be it farm, forest, or concrete pavement in a teeming city, to be argued over endlessly and uncompromisingly.

Even Tish looked the same, the few years difference in their ages leveled off by maturity, proud of her position as absolute mistress in a house of men, ruling over Jemmy and a part-time gardener, laundress, and the additional help brought in occasionally to do the heavy cleaning. He turned toward the house again and it, too, was the same. White brick, smooth columns that reached from the lower floor through the upper veranda to support the shingled roof. French window doors on both floors, the wide, fanlighted entrance door, the summer veranda furniture not yet removed and stored.

He was home; the home of poem, song, story, and man's constant thoughts when away in strange and distant lands. He carried the flight bag up the steps, dropped it to walk into Tish's welcoming arms, feeling her warmth, hearing her snuffling through tears of unrestrained joy.

"Lord, thank You!" she said prayerfully, then stood off for a better look. "My, my, you sure a sight to see, Mist' Corey. You lookin' just wonderful. You all right, ain't you?"

"I'm fine. Just fine. And you look wonderful to me, too. How are you, Tish?"

"Good's the good Lord 'lows a pore sinner." She indicated the flight bag and bent over to pick it up. "You want this in your room, don't you, Mist' Corey?"

"I'll carry it up, Tish. It's pretty heavy. Got everything I own in it."

She called out again, "Jemmy! Where you at, you worthless man, you?"

Corey hefted the bag and carried it inside the house just as Jemmy, the Armours' all-around handy man, came into the hall, smiling, panting, tying a striped apron over his black vest and trousers.

"Hello, Mist' Corey," he beamed toothily. "Bless this day. We shore happy to see you home in good health."

"Thanks, Jemmy. I'm mighty glad to be home."

Tish said, "You take Mist' Corey's bag up to his room right away, you shiftless Nigra, an' unpack it, hang his uniforms up an' press everything needs it. Go along now." To Corey, "Your room, it all ready for you, aired out an' freshened up. You hungry?"

"I'll wait for Dad, Tish."

"C'n I fix you a drink while Jemmy unpackin' you?"

"Fine. Bourbon and water, a little ice."

"Right away, Mist' Corey. You rest yourself. You home now. We goin' take care of you real good. After that ol' Army, I bet you c'n stand some good livin'."

"Yes, Tish, but no spoiling. You married yet?"

"No, *sir!*" she replied emphatically. "I'm just plain happy."

She looked it. Tish (short for the more fanciful Letitia) had always been a happy girl from his first memory of her, which was to say his first memory of almost anyone or anything. She was three years his senior and as children, they had played together until long after Corey had started to school. Tish had, in fact, been born in this very house.

Her father, George Lukens, had been the Armours' parttime gardener until he married Tish's mother, Rachel, their housekeeper-cook. Kenneth hired him as full-time butlerchauffeur-handyman when it appeared they might lose Rachel. When Tish was nine, George Lukens was killed in a car crash while returning from a visit to his brother Ed's house in South Laurelton on a rainy winter night. The entire Armour household mourned George's death and Tish was inconsolable for months after.

When Tish was 16, an almost fully matured young woman in her second year at West Laurelton High School, Rachel died. Kenneth and Caddy urged Tish to continue on in school, offered to bring in another woman until Tish was graduated, but Tish protested jealously, "It's my place. Mama always told me it was. I'n learnin' nothin' much nohow, so I might just as well quit an' take Mama's place now."

She had taken over Rachel's room and possessions and stepped into the job with a minimum of effort, happy to be in charge of the Armour household, and without complaint. Rachel had left her life's savings behind in a tin box in her trunk, a total of $2,100, which Kenneth invested for Tish and paid her the same weekly wage he had paid Rachel.

For a while, they thought Tish would be lost to them

when Willie Hastings, the new part-time gardener began a serious courtship, but after about six months, Willie disappeared and Tish became moody and sad. Only Corey knew how serious her affair with Willie had been. Knew that on frequent occasions, Willie had been slipping into Tish's first-floor bedroom after the Armours were asleep, or away. Her bedroom was directly beneath Corey's and he heard *sounds*, curious sounds that needed investigating.

From the outside back porch, he had peeked one night, but the lights were out and he could see nothing; but he knew Tish was not alone. And finally, one night, he crept downstairs in bare feet and listened to those mysterious sounds outside Tish's door. High-pitched, muffled sounds mingled with low, deep sounds. He turned the knob of the door noisily, knowing the door would be locked. And behind the door, all became suddenly quiet. Corey tiptoed upstairs again and watched as Willie crept silently away from the house to his room behind the garage. And next morning, as Tish served breakfast somewhat nervously, not knowing just *who* had been outside her door listening, expecting certain censure from either Mr. Kenneth or Miz Caddy, it was Corey who had thrown her the quick, sly, knowing grin, and Tish turned away, flushing angrily, yet comforted by the knowledge that it had been Corey, and that she would be safe.

He had his drink and chatted with Tish until he heard Jemmy come down, shirts, blouses and slacks over his arm, then went upstairs to his old room. It was hardly changed from when he had seen it last, over two years ago. The shelves and one glass-enclosed cabinet were crowded with cups, plaques and bronze figures, awards he had won at high school, the University and the Laurelton Country Club for his tennis and swimming victories. The walls were hung with banners, pennants, certificates of scholastic merit, diplomas, and the latest, his admission to the state bar. On a homemade rack were his rifle, shotgun, and half a dozen tennis rackets. In the closet, other bits and pieces of his youth: sports jackets, swim trunks, tennis shoes, swim fins, face masks and other memorabilia that had accumulated during those years.

One uniform in fair condition hung in the closet, shirts and underwear put away in the built-in chests, shoes racked beside those from his civilian life, other odds and ends from his flight bag laid out on the dresser top. On the bed, Jemmy had left the .45 automatic, four extra, loaded clips, and a leather map case he hadn't turned in before leaving Saigon. Spoils of war. From the closet, he took an old tow-

301

el-textured robe and terry cloth slippers, then stripped and took a cold, refreshing shower. He stretched out on the familiar, comfortable bed with a cigarette and thought again of Tish, back when she was 19, he 16 then, grown apart and not without some regret.

It was Polk Holderby, he recalled, who had encouraged the idea; Polk with his bagful of erotic experiences, possibly true, but even more probably, false. "Man," Polk said one day as Tish crossed the back yard carrying an armful of freshly cut flowers, "if that gal worked for us, I'd sure spend a lot more of my time home. Yes, sir. That high-yella is but stacked."

They were facing each other across the ping-pong table and Corey said, "Cut it out, Polk. Goddam it, Tish isn't—"

"She's a servant, isn't she? What the hell's a servant for except to serve?"

Remembering Willie Hastings, yet defending her, "You've got a real dirty mind and a mouth to match it. Tish isn't like that."

"Ah-h, nuts. They're all like that. Hell, they learn it by the time they start walking."

"Look, it's your serve. If you want to play, cut it out and let's play."

"Okay, okay. Jeez, anybody'd think she was *family* the way you take on. Ready?"

He had thought then, Well, maybe not family, but just about as close as anybody can come to it without being family.

And with the thought seeded in his mind by Polk, Corey found it difficult not to think of Tish in a way other than family. He began to watch her more consciously as she moved about the house, standing with the sun behind her when she was wearing nothing beneath her thin cotton dress; in the yard in one of Caddy's old bathing suits that was somewhat too large for her as she played the garden hose on her warm, toast-colored skin, bending over and unconsciously exposing generous, yet firm, breasts; coming upon her one day as she came from her bathroom after a shower, a towel tucked tightly around her hips, another over her shoulders, its ends dangling loosely down over her breasts, not in the least embarrassed at the sight of him.

Then came a Friday in July and Kenneth and Caddy were off to Augusta to attend a wedding, leaving Corey behind to participate in the junior tennis tournament to be played that Saturday and Sunday. On Friday night he had gone to an early movie with Wilson Baker in order to keep his mind off the upcoming tournament and was home and in bed by ten o'clock. On Saturday, Tish woke him early, gave him his breakfast and said, "Now you bring home that cup, you hear, Corey? Your daddy, he 'spectin' it."

That afternoon, he and Wil Baker teamed to win the junior doubles for Laurelton Country Club from the Homewood Country Club, 6-2, 6-1, and 6-2. On Sunday, he took on Dusty Alcock of the Marina Club and won the singles title 5-6, 6-4, 6-1 and 6-4. Two more cups for his shelf.

He came home to dress and went back to the Club for the Awards Dinner, chosen to represent Laurelton C.C. in the Labor Day Finals. Later, keyed up with success, he, Polk and Wil triple-dated. Corey's date was Holly-Ann Harrison, who was a year older than he. Polk and Wil were dating the Larkin cousins, Trudy and Ruth. They drove down to Fisher's Landing to dance to a new Dixieland Jazz combo in the outdoor grove, slipping back to Wil's car to sip at a bottle of bourbon Polk had filched from his father's supply. Trudy and Polk disappeared into the woods, Wil and Ruth wandered off toward the river's edge, leaving Corey somewhat nervously alone with Holly-Ann who, on Polk's assurance, was no novice on the back seat of a car.

They sipped more bourbon and Holly-Ann made no effort to resist Corey's feverish, awkward advances. In fact, she was not only eager, but considerably helpful. Overstimulated by his success on the courts, heated by the whiskey, and further inflamed by the sight of Holly-Ann's swelling thighs, ignition by the mere touch of his bare flesh upon hers led to a premature explosion that resulted in dark disappointment for both. Before the damage could be repaired and his desire rejuvenated, Wil and Ruth were back, laughing hilariously at their own disarray, followed shortly afterward by Polk and Trudy.

By the time Wil and Polk dropped Corey at his house, he was well under the influence of the bourbon, which helped somewhat to cover his disappointment. He made it up the front steps, the two trophies under his arms, then couldn't match his key to the keyhole. And suddenly, the door opened and there stood Tish, frowning her deep disapproval. Clothing disarranged, hair tousled, the two trophies clutched in his hands, extending them toward her, grinning foolishly. "Tish—look—look what—I won," he said triumphantly.

"You win it for drinkin', Corey?" Tish asked quietly.

He laughed explosively. "Hell, no. These are loving cups. Won 'em for loving."

"All right, Big Man, you better bring 'em inside. Lucky for you your daddy and mama ain't home."

303

He stumbled and the cups clanged to the floor. "Jesus," he said, "I'm drunk as a coot, Tish."

"You sure coulda fooled me," Tish replied coldly as she closed the door and picked the cups up and placed them on the hall table. She put an arm around Corey to support him. "C'mon now, let's get you upstairs."

She helped him up the steps, arms around each other, then into his room, guided him to the edge of the bed and sat him down, then took off his shoes and socks while he leaned forward, his head drooping over her shoulder. She stood up and he fell backward on the bed, eyes closed, arms flung out helplessly. Tish unbuttoned his jacket and shirt, sat him up and removed then, then loosened his trousers belt and pulled them off by the cuffs. His eyes opened as she was holding the trousers up to the light, examining the spotted cloth.

"Boy," she said, "you sure didn't get far with your lovin', did you? I don't know what you won them cups for."

"Oh, Jesus—help—me up—bathroom—"

She got him to the bathroom in time, supported him while he vomited into the toilet. When he had finished, she got him to the basin, squeezed some toothpaste on his brush. "Here. Get that taste outa your mouth. You smell like a moonshiner." As he held on to the edge of the basin and brushed his teeth weakly, she poured some pink mouthwash into a glass, held it for him. He swished it around in his mouth and let it drip out while Tish wet a washcloth and swabbed his face, neck and chest with it.

"Go ahead, Tish," he said finally, "I can do it myself."

"You can't do nothin' yourself. Not even take care of that girl you was with."

"Goddam it," he protested, "that was an accident—"

"Shuh." She laughed mockingly, scrubbing his face. "I bet it was your first time."

"Shut up—"

"Don't you tell me to shut up. You finished?"

He put the glass down, then raised it and gargled more of the mouthwash. Tish said, " 'At's enough. C'mon now, le's get you to bed."

Resentfully, "I can go to bed myself." But when he started for the door, he was unsteady and Tish took his arm, held it until he was back in his room. When he stumbled, she put an arm around him, led him to the bed. "Put your hands around that bedpost."

"Oh, for Christ's sake, Tish—"

"You stop your cussin' an' behave yourself. I'n got all night to be foolin' aroun' with you."

304

He was clinging to the bedpost and but for his shorts, he was naked. Tish went to the bed and got his pajamas out from under the pillow and came toward him. He saw her standing between himself and the bed lamp, wearing only her thin nightgown, holding the pajamas out to him, but he couldn't make the move to take them.

"Tish—"

She looked at him and saw the new, wide-awake look, heard his thickened voice, then saw the evidence of his sexual regeneration. "Look, Corey—"

"I'm looking—" He reached out, ignored the pajamas and took her forearm, gripping it tightly, drawing her to him.

"Corey, you better watch out."

"Tish, please—" His arms were around her, his head burrowing between her breasts, searching, his voice a plea. "Tish—"

"Corey, don't—"

"I need you, Tish—"

Her arms circled around him and his hips ground into her, lips seeking hers. She gave ground until she felt the edge of the bed against the backs of her knees, then turned suddenly, twisting out of his grasp. "You go along to bed, boy, you hear," she said in a voice that sounded stern, yet was strangely soft, "an' sleep it off."

"Goddam it, Tish," he said angrily, "it don't make any difference to you. What about Willie Hastings? I know about you and Willie, and you know I know it."

She stood in the doorway and said with curious dignity, "That's the last reason in the world I'd ever get in bed with you or anybody else." Then she turned and went downstairs to her own room.

Her reply shamed him then, and on several occasions later, when he remembered the incident, caused him to blush with embarrassment. What had passed between them that night was never mentioned again, nor did it ever recur. But he remembered it keenly sometime later when Tish was sent away suddenly to her Uncle Jeth and Aunt Idabelle Lukens in Angeltown where, some time later, she gave birth to an out-of-wedlock daughter, Marylee, fathered by Jemmy Dutton. A succession of women took her place while she was absent, but she returned eventually and it was some time later that Corey learned that Marylee had died of pneumonia.

On Tish's return, it puzzled Corey that she was adamant in her refusal to marry Jemmy, who had declared his willingness. Her reply to Kenneth was, "Well, I do like him some, Mist' Armour, but I don't know if I want to marry up with a shif'less Nigra like Jemmy."

A week later, Kenneth hired Jemmy as general handyman, and to this day, Tish hadn't been able to make up her mind about him.

5

"Corey?"

He stirred in his sleep and murmured, "Coming up."

"Son. Wake up." Corey felt the pressure on his shoulder. His eyes opened and he found himself looking up into Kenneth's grinning face.

"Oh. Hi, Dad. I guess I dozed off." He sat up, shaking the sleep out of his head, then took his father's hand and felt its strong grip. In two years, there were few changes in Kenneth, he noted. A little gray at the temples, but still lean and virile in appearance. "Glad to see you, Dad."

Kenneth smiled again. "You're looking fit. The golden warrior returned."

"Hardly that. You're looking very well yourself. Everything all right?"

"Yes, of course. What about that chest wound?"

"All healed and practically forgotten."

"That's good to hear. Gave me quite a hell of a shock when I first got the news from the Department of Defense. I tried to pull some strings to get out there, but they turned me down cold."

Corey made no move to open his robe to display the reddish scar. "Give me ten minutes to dress and I'll come down."

"Good. What are you drinking these days?"

"Anything you're having."

"Martini?"

"A martini will be fine. Dry, please."

"Ten-to-one. Almost powdery."

"Just about perfect."

His pre-Army slacks were too tight at the waistline, the sports jackets too confining around the shoulders. He put on a freshly pressed pair of Army slacks and shirt and went down to meet Kenneth. As he took the martini from his father, it occurred to him that this was the first social drink they had ever had together.

"Still in love with your uniform, Corey?" Kenneth said.

"Everything I left behind seems to have shrunk just hanging in the closet waiting for me to get back."

"Don't let it bother you. I'm sure your charge accounts are still active around town. Tomorrow you can start outfitting yourself from the skin out, from top to bottom. That's an opportunity a man seldom gets in his entire lifetime, an all-new, fresh start."

"I've never thought of it that way before. Thanks for having the car meet me in Atlanta."

"It was Shana's idea. She wanted to send the company plane, but the weather was too uncertain down there."

They sipped their drinks, finding it difficult to make small talk, and Corey knew the expected discussion of "the future" would come later. He was grateful when Tish interrupted to announce dinner and they went into the dining room. The table had been "set special" with Caddy's finest linens, china and silver, Tish's personal tribute to Corey's return.

The menu was a variety of his favorites: chicken that had been lightly dipped in batter and fried a crisp golden brown, a tender roast with a spicy mushroom and onion sauce, fluffy mashed potatoes with a hollow of melted butter, black-eyed peas, corn, stewed tomatoes, greens, hot cornbread with honey, and Corey's favorite among all desserts, a graham-crusted apple pie.

As they started on the salad, Kenneth asked, "What do you think of our chances over there, Corey?"

"I'm afraid I can't give you an expert assessment, Dad. Maybe I was too close to the forest to see the trees. My private opinion is that we're a very long way from losing, but nowhere close to anything resembling a clearcut victory."

Kenneth nodded, seeming to accept the neither-here, neither-there statement. "Not a very bright outlook, is it?"

"Not from my point of view. It isn't the kind of war I've read and heard about from men who fought in Europe, the Pacific and in Korea. This one is too much of a tongue-in-cheek thing, with heavy political overtones. We believe we're fighting for an important principle and need, but the wounded, crippled and dead can't care less about a principle that supports the civilian corruption you see all around you. You come off the firing line with the feeling that if those who make wars had to fight them physically, wars would be negotiated to death before they ever began.

"The whole thing is massive human degradation and no one can be trained to accept it for anything else, except a sadist. It's the lowest form of brutality and cruelty. Dirt, sweat, filth, disease, death, shame, and senseless, useless destruction. You get so you pray for one, all-out, massive attack on the enemy target to bring the damned thing to an end, but when you count the probable cost of lives lost on both sides, you shrivel up inside. It's rotten, immoral, but you're there. You're attacked and you kill to keep from being killed. If you point out that no one here wants it, that goes triple for the men who have to do the fighting."

So impassioned was Corey's indictment against war that Kenneth sat wordlessly for a few moments. Then, "You're right, I'm sure," he said finally. "It all brings home the possibility of thermonuclear attack, world censure, certain retaliation and the eventual destruction of the world itself."

"No one understands that better than those on the firing line, a war in which so few even know how we became involved. One thing for sure, it doesn't help much when you see a friend like Lyle Emerson get it, or one like Cord Waters get killed—"

"Emerson," Kenneth said. "Isn't he the one who lost his leg, the helicopter pilot?"

"Yes. The man Cord Waters was trying to rescue from the Viet Cong attack when he was killed. I want to look Lyle up the first moment I get. Is he back in town, do you know?"

"I'm not certain. I think I remember something about him returning. I'm sure any of your friends will know."

"And I'd like to get in touch with Cord's parents. I assume they're still at Brookhill."

"Yes. Of course. I don't know if you're aware of it, but there was some sort of a minor furor created around here after the ceremony in which Cord's Silver Star was presented to Shad and Leona."

"In what way?"

"I don't know how it got started. It seems that some northern liberal paper went beyond all others in dramatizing the heroism of a Southern Negro who gave his life to save his white hometown friend—"

Corey smiled. "They met for the first time in Viet Nam. Lyle never knew Cord back here, but Cord recognized him the very first time he saw Lyle in Viet Nam."

"Anyway, the writer either suggested, or reported as fact, that Cord's body, when it is eventually returned, will receive the highest military honors when he is buried here. It is very possible the writer didn't realize that Negroes here bury their dead in the all-Negro cemetery in West Laurelton. By the time the story was reprinted in other papers and news weeklies, it became an accepted fact that the burial would some day take place in the all-white Municipal Cemetery. Well, that started a flood of editorials citing Laurelton as the most progressive and enlightened Southern city in the matter of civil rights, which stirred up a storm of criticism from segregationist extremist groups from everywhere."

"It's hard to believe that people can begrudge any man his final resting place—"

"Corey, don't be naïve. By standards elsewhere, Laurelton has enjoyed comparative peace and harmony between its white and Negro communities, but it wouldn't take more than a light scratch to uncover deep animosities on both sides. I'm sure you can remember the demonstratons we had back in '54 after the Supreme Court decision was handed down, the work strike and rider strike and school strike against bus and school segregation, the economic boycott against merchants who were giving Negroes second-class service—"

"I remember them well. Also, that they were settled amicably by negotiation between the Negro and white members of the local civil rights committee."

"Amicable negotiation?" Kenneth laughed mirthlessly. "It was more than that, Corey, believe me. What made us unique was the fact that the Warren Tobacco Company and Taylor Industries controlled the largest payrolls in Cairn County. It was economic pressure brought about by Jonas Taylor and Anderson Warren that prevented a violent outbreak. Together, they threatened to back Amos Hart's economic boycott that would have crippled Laurelton's merchants if they refused to support the law of the land. Jonas Taylor had his fist around the necks of the police department, the City Council and County Commissioners. Those two men made this town see reason."

"I suppose the same pressure could be applied again, couldn't it?"

"I doubt it. Things aren't the same as they were in '54. For one thing, Jonas Taylor is gone. Anderson Warren is a very sick old man. And we're dealing with another element, the young people who have developed a new set of standards. In '54 you were—what?—fourteen or fifteen? Think of the changes you've seen since then."

"I guess I've been away too long."

"It will all come back to you soon enough. This restlessness under the surface—"

"It can come here the way it has come in other places," Corey said. "I've listened to the talk among Negroes in Viet Nam. When this thing is over and thousands who have been fighting for their country come back, they're not going to be satisfied with a second-class life after doing a first-class job over there. The lid could very well be blown off when they decide to fight for their own rights."

309

"Yes, that's what I was referring to."

"If it comes to that, I think I would find it hard to deny them."

"You can't be suggesting it will be beneficial, can you?"

"Perhaps not beneficial, but damn well deserved."

"Well——" Kenneth decided there could be no profit in pursuing the subject. He said, "If you go out to Brookhill, you'll see Drew Warren. She has asked about you a number of times. If I remember correctly——" Kenneth was smiling lightly—"you two were rather close before—before she left for Europe after——"

Corey's mind flashed back to the painful reminder of that night; their return from the wedding in Atlanta, Bruce's death, the funeral, Drew lost in the fog of personal tragedy. Over three years since he had seen her. He bypassed the reply that was expected of him by asking, "How is Drew?"

"Attractive as ever. Quite a mature young lady," Kenneth said.

"I'm looking forward to seeing her again. How is her grandfather?" And as an afterthought, "And her father?"

"Anderson is rather low. Terminal cancer. I'm surprised he's held up so well so long."

"I'm sorry to hear that——"

"And Theodore is—well. More active since Anderson's illness began, but——" Kenneth had finished eating and rang the bell for Jemmy. "Anderson handed over the presidency to Theodore some time ago, but I assume you know he's not very comfortable in that chair."

"Isn't there a brother, an uncle of Drew's I remember hearing about?"

"Chase? Yes, but Chase Warren has too many other important interests to keep him occupied. He turned his back on the Company years ago."

"It seems a shame."

"Yes——"

"Coffee in your study, Mist' Kenneth?" Jemmy asked.

"Ah, yes, Jemmy, thank you."

Tish bustled in seeking Corey's approval. "Tish," he said, "by the time I order my new clothes, I'll have grown two sizes. This has been the best welcome I could have had. Thank you."

"Shuh, go on, now. Ain' no more'n we always have, ain't that so, Mist' Kenneth?" Tish was beaming with open delight.

"No," Kenneth went along with her, "nothing more than we'd have for the President of the United States, the Prime

310

Minister of England or the King of Belgium. Just plain, everyday ordinary fare."

In Kenneth's study, they drank coffee over cigarettes. Jemmy brought a decanter of brandy for their post-dinner relaxation. It was a comfortable room where Kenneth did most of his after-hours work and reading, the room in which Corey had read his first adult books and later pored through his grandfather's and greatgrandfather's personal journals, memoirs of interesting cases, speeches, important landmark opinions handed down from the bench. Ancient leather-bound law volumes, decisions of higher courts, law reviews. Three walls were lined with such tomes, as complete a law library as any in professional use.

The fourth wall was almost entirely glass and looked out over a veranda into the garden, hedged-in for privacy. The desk was the old one which had served Kenneth's grandfather, an old, hand-crafted rolltop of dark walnut with dozens of fascinating cubbyholes and drawers, some open, some kept locked. The rug was an importation from the Middle East and the chairs and sofas were covered in rich, dark green leather with matching leather-topped tables which held tall, leather-hooded lamps upon them. The two lamps on the rolltop desk were of gaslight vintage which had been converted to electricity.

"You like this room, don't you, Corey," Kenneth said.

"I've always thought it was the most comfortable room I'd ever been in, Dad."

"I'm glad. Use it as often as you like. When it becomes yours some day, I hope you will preserve it and add to it as each generation of Armours before you has. There are books and documents here that go back as far as your English ancestry, old family records—"

"Of course I will," Corey said, and suddenly he wondered what had become of the silver-framed portrait of Caddy that had once stood on the top ledge of the desk between those of Lewis and Marcus Armour and their wives; and of Caddy's parents, Selwyn and Hannah Crane, also missing now. When, on which day since Corey had left, had Kenneth decided to remove his wife's photograph and those of the Cranes; perhaps his last reminder of them? He heard Kenneth's question as his mind turned to Shana Pierce—

"—plans?" was the last word he heard.

"I'm sorry, Dad, I was day-dreaming."

"I asked if you'd made any definite plans for your return to civilian life?"

Corey's mouth turned upward in a lazy smile. "About a thousand or more, but none definite beyond getting out of

311

uniform and into civilian clothes. That's what most of us did in Viet Nam, waited and made plans. Every conceivable sort of plan from going back to a farm, a ranch, desk job, filling station, bulldozer, executive—"

"And yours?"

"I think I'll take a little breather before I decide that."

"Of course. You're certainly entitled to a rest and vacation. But I naturally hope that when you do decide, it will be law."

He had expected that from Kenneth, so it came as no surprise. What did surprise him was that this was developing into an easy, mature discussion with the man he had always known to be so firmly dictatorial and arbitrary. A concession to my new maturity? Corey wondered. Kenneth was following up his last remark with quiet diplomacy. "Of course, you know there will always be a place for you on the legal staff at the Company."

"I appreciate that, Dad, but—"

"Don't discount the possibilities, Corey. I'm not at liberty to say more right now, but before long there may be some rather remarkable opportunities opening up which could insure your future."

"Thank you. I'll keep it in mind, but I'm not ready to make a decision at the moment."

It seemed that Kenneth would allow the subject to drop there, then he said with a slow smile, "Somehow, I get the impression you're being evasive. I'm sure you must have turned the possibility over in your mind."

"On a number of occasions, Dad, but I rejected it each time."

Kenneth flushed, knowing he should not have pressed the issue. "Corey—?"

"Sir?"

"That's another thing. Isn't it about time we dropped the 'sir,' Corey? It sounds awfully mid-Victorian between a father and son, doesn't it?" Kenneth was smiling, his eyes on Corey's face as though in appraisal.

"Of course, Dad. You know how Mother always insisted—"

"Yes. There were rules for everything, weren't there?"

There was no note of carping in the implied criticism and Corey acknowledged the truth in Kenneth's simple statement. A son always said "sir" to his father. In the presence of elders, he never spoke unless he was addressed first. He must ask permission before leaving the table or a room, apologize for being late for a meal or from an errand.

Rules. There were rules for Kenneth, for himself, for the servants, self-imposed rules for Caddy.

"Discipline," Caddy would say to Corey, "is more than a virtue. It is an art, a mark of civilized culture. Without it, there would be chaos, social anarchy. It begins at birth and ends with death." It was not, Corey knew, an original idea of Caddy's. He had heard it many times from his Grandfather Selwyn Crane, and had learned to couple discipline with respect. The Army had helped him to separate discipline, which must be enforced, from respect, which had to be earned.

When Corey did not reply, Kenneth said, "Corey, this isn't going to be easy for me to say, but I think it needs saying. I've always known you were closer to your mother than you were to me, quite naturally. There were certain influences I found difficult to overcome. When she—died—I thought perhaps things would change for the better between you and me, but you went back to the University and I was busy with my work. I expected that when you finished law school and returned home—but it never quite worked out that way. I was in Europe on business that summer and before I got back, you'd leaped into the Army—"

"I didn't exactly *leap* into the Army. I gave it a considerable amount of thought before I—"

"I'd expected you'd have discussed it with me first."

"Ordinarily, I'd agree. But we hadn't been discussing many things at the time, if you recall."

"You must have been aware that my responsibilities to the Company had been stepping up."

"Of course. It was one of the principal reasons why I acted on my own."

"Corey," Kenneth said heavily, "I know I've made mistakes in my lifetime that reflect the gap between us. I'd hoped some day to bridge that gap, just as I've always assumed you would one day take your place in the Company and guarantee your future here in Laurelton. Surely you can't afford to ignore the opportunities—"

"That you've made for me?"

"—that should naturally accrue—"

"Dad—"

With rising exasperation, "You can't resist interrupting me, can you?"

"Dad, we're not in a courtroom now. You ask for a waiver of formality and rules on one hand and demand them on the other. How can we have it both ways in a person-to-person discussion? Why can't we ever say what we

313

honestly feel without fear of a contempt-of-court citation hanging over us?"

Kenneth spread his hands, palms upward, out to either side of him. "All right, Counselor, have your say."

"Very well," Corey replied stiffly. "It's simply this. I don't want to become a law clerk for the Warren Tobacco Company. At one time I thought it would be a natural thing to follow in your footsteps and move up in line as opportunity permitted."

"When did you change your mind?"

"When I was about fifteen or sixteen—something happened—"

"What?" Kenneth asked the question sharply, but he already knew the answer. "Well, what happened, Corey?"

"I think you know, Dad."

"All right. If you can't bring yourself to say it, I'll say it for you. You're talking about Shana Pierce and me, aren't you?"

"That's one of the reasons."

"Corey, you were only fifteen years old when you accidentally found out about Shana and me. It was regrettable, I grant you, but what explanations could I have made then that would have been acceptable to you at that age, or made any difference in how you felt? Unfortunate as it was, I knew it would have to wait until you were old enough, reasonable enough, to understand and accept certain realities of life."

"Am I old enough, reasonable enough, now?"

"Old enough, yes."

A moment of silence, then, "Are you going to marry her?"

"I don't feel I need to answer that question, but if I should marry Shana, I wouldn't expect you to accept her as your mother. Naturally, I would hope you could be friends."

"That still doesn't explain anything I can understand."

"Why it happened, how it happened? At this time, it hardly seems worth the effort, but I'll try to make it clearer. I think the fact that you are financially independent of me will make it much easier. Apart from this house and the Shadow Hills property you inherited from your Grandfather Selwyn and your mother, you're worth close to a quarter of a million dollars. I'm sure you're aware of that."

"Generally. I don't know the exact figure. And that's something else I've always been curious about."

"In what way?"

"Well, why me? Why wasn't it left to you, or to you in trust for me?"

"There's no mystery about that, Corey. Your mother's father despised me. He thought I'd married Catherine for her money."

"Did you?"

Kenneth smiled wearily. "I suppose forthrightness comes naturally in the Army. Or perhaps with becoming an adult. To answer you just as openly, perhaps I did in some small way. I wanted to get married, I did need money, and I did love Catherine. Selwyn Crane was opposed to the marriage. He would have opposed anyone who came to rob him of his only daughter. But Hannah Crane approved and Selwyn eventually gave in. That didn't stop him from taking his revenge on me in his will. It was his distrust of me that made me accept the job Anderson Warren offered me when Harvey Makepeace retired."

"What about you and Mother?"

"You're back to the incident up at Shadow Hills, but I won't apologize for what happened, only that you saw Shana and me there together. To be honest about it, Corey, it began with Shana and me long after you were born, about five years later. Your mother had taken the attitude that having given me a son, she had served her purpose as a wife. She had been raised like a noble princess by two elderly parents, her mind filled with childish, unrealistic notions of what life was really like. Believe me, I didn't know that when I married Catherine, nor could I blame her for it later. But at that stage, I couldn't change all the curious beliefs her parents had put into her head."

"What kept you together, if that was so?" Corey asked.

"Again, simply, you. I offered Catherine a divorce when you were a baby, but divorce among very nice people like the Cranes was a filthy word, not to be mentioned in polite society. Catherine and I compromised and tried to make a go of it, because of you, as I said; but don't get the erroneous idea you weren't wanted. You were by both of us, and certainly by your grandparents.

"After you were born, there were no sexual intimacies between us. As far as Catherine was concerned, that part of our lives was dead. After Hannah died, Selwyn lived on in this house alone with two servants. When he died, I didn't want us to move into this house, but Catherine insisted. I gave in because of you. You'll remember, I'm sure, that Catherine and I never shared the same bedroom in this house. My bedroom and this study were the only two rooms considered to be exclusively mine."

315

Kenneth paused to light a cigarette and Corey said nothing. He sat in his chair and stared downward at the pattern in the rug. Kenneth began talking again.

"I was thirty-six, your mother thirty-eight, when Shana came into the picture. You were five, which made it more than five years since I had slept with a woman. Until I saw Shana, I had no need, no urge, in that direction. Five years of indifference and coolness had virtually castrated me, until I was reawakened by Shana."

He had stopped again and Corey asked, "Why didn't you marry her after Mother died? Wouldn't that have been the —uh—gentlemanly, honorable thing to do?"

"I detect a tinge of bitter cynicism in your voice, Corey, but I'll accept the question; and remember, you asked for this forthright discussion. I did ask Shana to marry me about a year later, but she refused, citing you as the reason, that she and I were secondary to the relationship between a father and his son. Believe that or not, it is true. If you and I can ever resolve our private differences, I'll be proud to ask Shana to marry me."

"At least," Corey said, "I can understand the situation a little better than before."

"The question, I think, is whether you can accept it."

"That's one I can't honestly answer at the moment." Then, as Kenneth stood up to leave, "Tell me, Dad, did you ever really mourn Mother's death?"

Kenneth turned and stared down at Corey for a moment. With some sadness in his voice, he said, "Truthfully, Corey, no. Only her life. It was so wasted by living it in a fantasy of the past while the present swept past her, trying to recreate her childhood with her mother and father."

Both knew that that phase of their conversation had come to an end. Kenneth walked to the door, opened it, then turned and said casually, "Interested in doing anything tonight, seeing any of your old friends? I imagine you'll be anxious to get in touch with them as soon as you can. Don't let me intrude. I've got to run into town for a while, a matter I want to discuss with Judge Holman."

"Not tonight, I think," Corey replied. "I've got a few things to think about before tomorrow, then get a full night's sleep. But don't let me keep you."

"Very well. If I don't see you later tonight, perhaps at breakfast?"

"Fine. By the way—"

"Yes?"

"Is there an accurate map of the Shadow Hills property around here anywhere?"

316

"I think so. There might be one in the large lower drawer of the desk. Why?"

"I have an idea I'd like to explore. One of those things that came across my mind in Viet Nam. Something I saw out there."

Kenneth went to the old rolltop desk and pulled out one of the bottom drawers. What he sought was not in it, and he tried the other side. He drew out a large folder, riffled through it and took a folded sheet from it, a blueprint, and opened it. "There it is, completely detailed and with the adjoining Halstead property."

"Thank you."

"And just in case you do decide to slip out for a while tonight, Corey, you'll find a new Thunderbird waiting in the garage for you. A sort of welcome home gift that Corbins' delivered this afternoon. I hope you like it."

Remembering the first car he had ever owned, given to him by Kenneth much this same way. "Dad—thanks—" he stammered.

"My pleasure, son. Enjoy it. Good night."

"Good night."

For a while he sat at the desk thinking over the immensity of the conversation he had had with Kenneth; this open and frank talk between them as men; and he knew that what Kenneth had said could only be the truth since he had had no time to prepare for a confrontation of this magnitude; and now, he suddenly felt that his loyalty to the memory of Caddy was shaken.

And then he heard Tish's voice from the dining room, and Jemmy's, humming in accompaniment to the old familiar spiritual:

"St. Peter be my witness
When I come to Kingdom Land
To be with my sweet Jesus
My soul is in Your hand—"

The telephone rang and he ignored it, knowing Tish or Jemmy would take it on the kitchen phone, too soon for anyone to be calling him. He reached up and turned on the two ancient lamps, sat in the well-worn, polished, leather-padded swivel chair and smoothed the folds of the blueprint flat. Some of the figures were small and faded, the draftsman's symbols obscure, but these, at the moment, were details he did not need.

Jemmy came in to remove the tray and coffee service. " 'Scuse me, Mist' Corey. You like some more coffee?"

"No, thank you, Jemmy. But will you go up to my room and bring me a brown envelope you'll find in the top drawer of my dresser?"

"Yes, sir. Right away."

He found a yellow lined legal tablet and began penciling a few notes when Jemmy returned with the manila envelope. From it, he removed a dozen or more sheets with notations and small rough sketches and began comparing them with the plan of his Shadow Hills land.

In the Tuyen Duc province northeast of Saigon, a protective ring had been thrown around the site and patrols established around the clock to keep the Viet Cong at a distance. Almost overnight, it seemed, the Seabees had moved in and occupied the area, bringing with them hundreds of truckloads of lumber, boxes, crates, bales and cases, which were turned into rough living quarters and shelter for the mass of materials and equipment that would go into clearing several thousand acres of jungle to establish a needed air base, complete with headquarters, administration buildings, warehouses, repair hangars, barracks and sanitary facilities.

As the clearing progressed, they brought in bulldozers, turn-a-pulls, graders, trenchers, diesel shovels, skip loaders and sheep's foot and compaction rollers. They erected two huge batch plants for mixing asphalt and concrete and brought in massive Barber-Greenes to lay the asphalt runways. By day, and under lights at night, these amazing, unbelievable men cleared, drained, filled, graded and compacted an area upon which carpenters, plumbers, electricians, painters and other artisans virtually created landing strips and a city where, only a short time before, a lush, treacherous jungle had flourished.

Then the fighters and fighter-bombers moved in and even before they began mounting air assaults, the Seabees were adding what someone called "the frosting on the birthday cake"; clubs for both enlisted men and officers, each with its own swimming pool, outdoor handball, volleyball, and tennis courts, softball and baseball diamonds.

One Sunday before the Seabees moved out, Corey and a Seabee commander, Hall Peterson, finished a set of singles which Corey had taken without much effort. Showered and sitting on the club porch in the shade of the overhang with cool drinks before them, Peterson said, "That goddamned serve of yours is like an armor-piercing shell. Jesus, how I bleed when you hardly work up a sweat."

Corey said, "How long have you been playing, Hall?"

"Six-eight years, at least."

"I've been playing more than twice that long. That serve is no accident. I've worked on it since I began playing."

"Amazing—"

"What I think is amazing is what you and your Seabees have built up here. Every time we came back from a patrol we couldn't recognize the place."

Peterson said deprecatingly, "With the right men and equipment, you can accomplish anything. Did pretty much the same thing back in Michigan a couple of years before I was called back into service. We took about fifteen hundred acres of raw land about thirty miles from Detroit, built a dam, created a lake and put up about two thousand homes for a developer and gave him a resort area within commuting distance of a metropolitan city. All the advantages of suburbia and none of the disadvantages, except driving to and from. We started with an idea, a vision— Hell, you're not interested in that. Let's—"

"Hall, I *am* interested. This thing has been on my mind ever since I began watching its progress. And you've just given me a little more than the itch of an idea. I'd like to hear more."

"Eh?"

"Hall, tell me more, will you? I'm terribly interested."

Peterson grinned. "Man, are you asking an old ham actor to show you through his scrapbook? You got a month to spare?"

"More, if necessary. You've got no idea how exciting this has been for me, watching a city grow out of a jungle. The lake idea makes it even more interesting. What does it take?"

"What I said before. Vision. And money. A hell of a lot of money. What we did back home cost about twelve million before the first house was built. This—" he waved a hand to include the entire base—"I haven't any idea. The government pays all the bills. Last of the gigantic spenders. Tell me, how come you're so interested? I thought you were a lawyer in civilian life."

"Only an unblooded one, Hall. But I own some land—"

It was nearing 9:30 when Corey threw his pencil down. The original notes he had made in Viet Nam had been transferred to the legal pad in a more orderly manner, the measurements he had guessed at now corrected to properly reflect those on the blueprint. The telephone rang and he waited to see if Tish or Jemmy would answer. It stopped ringing and he brushed a hand over his weary eyes, then

319

heard the soft knock on the door. "Come in, Tish," he called.

It was Jemmy. " 'Scuse me, Mist' Corey. Telephone for you."

Surprised, "Me?"

"Yes, sir. He say 'stinctly, 'Mist' *Corey* Armour.' "

"Thank you, Jemmy." He picked up the receiver and spoke into it. "Hello."

"Corey? Corey Armour?"

"Yes. Who is it, please?"

"Welcome home, you sneaky sonofagun! This is Ad Cameron—"

"Adam! Well, well. The first man on earth and the first to call me since I got home. How did you know?"

"I ran into your father and Judge Holman going into the Laurelton Hotel coffee shop. How are you?"

"Great, Ad. Good to hear your voice. How are you? Still mangling the news at the *Herald?*"

"Who's got a better right than the owner's son? That's number two reason for calling. Thought I'd run a little item in the morning edition to kind of warn mothers to get their daughters off the streets after dark."

"You haven't got me confused with Polk Holderby by any chance, have you, Ad?"

"The fox in the henhouse?" Adam laughed. "Jesus, it's good to hear your voice again. How are you feeling, boy?"

"Like the prodigal son trying to digest the fatted calf. And you? Married or anything?"

"Mostly anything. I don't suppose you brought a slant-eyed wife home with you, did you?"

"Now that would make a nice front-page item to brighten the lives of your readers, wouldn't it?"

"Well, how about something, anything I can include in the *Herald*'s welcome to its favorite tennis bum?"

"Not a thing, Ad. Only that I made it home from Atlanta through thickest traffic without incident or mishap."

"How about that Cong bullet—?"

"Soft-pedal it, will you? It's old hat and wouldn't interest anyone, not even clinically. I'd just as soon you didn't mention it. How about some news from you?"

"Like what?"

"Well, Lyle Emerson, for one thing. Is he in town?"

"Old Lyle? Sure enough. Came back from Walter Reed Medical Center about six-seven months ago. Been reinstated at Laurelton High and teaches night classes over at the R-V Center."

"How is he, Ad?"

320

"Well, pretty good, I'd guess. Don't see too much of him, but he gets around all right. Got one of those special cars through the V.A., fixed so he doesn't have to use his right leg to operate it. Gas pedal works from the left side—"

"I meant—"

"Jill? Nothing there. Far as I know, she's still in New York. It shows on him, but it's a closed subject. Hey! I've got work to do. Give me a ring for lunch soon?"

"First chance I get."

"Good enough. Look for your name in the local news section tomorrow. After that, stay close to your phone. All the guys—"

"That reminds me. Is Paula Corbin back in town?"

There was a brief pause. "Yeah, she's back. Came back about the time you left. Got her a dress shop in the new shopping center on the Mall. That's new, too, the Mall. It's mixed in with those high-rise apartment and office buildings east of the civic center. Caters to teenagers and the young married crowd—"

The reply struck Corey as too elaborate in detail and he interrupted. "She married?"

Hesitantly, "Yep. And divorced."

"Anybody I know?"

"Probably not, maybe yes. Some guy named Bob Bennett. His family lived here a long time ago before they moved to New York."

The name rang a bell and Corey tried to remember where he had heard it before, but Ad was saying, "—and that's the way the old wind sock blows."

"Any vital statistics on anyone else I know, Ad?"

"Not too many. Let's see. Hugh Brock and Caroline Robbins. Hugh's still at the Water and Power Company. Les Delevan's in a Richmond bank, married to a gal up there, Dale Something-or-other. Sam Driscoll and Peggy Masters, hatched a boy and a girl out of that one. The rest are all free-wheeling and dealing."

"What about Polk?"

"The old swordsman? You've got a surprise coming to you. He's with Archer and Moseley, the brokerage house, and damned near respectable. Hey, old son, I've got to hit the iron maiden if I want to get that item in the bulldog edition. See you soon, hey?"

"Sure, Ad." The line went dead.

The name Bob Bennett jiggled around in his mind, but he couldn't tie it up with anything concrete, leaving him adrift with other memories of Paula. Until Tish came in to interrupt his thoughts.

"I'm goin'a see the movie on tee-vee, Mist' Corey. Anything I c'n get you first?"

"No, Tish. I think I'll turn in. Would you have Jemmy wake me in time to have breakfast with Dad, please?"

"Shuh. You get a good night's sleep. You look awful tiresome." She smiled warmly and added, "It shuh goin'a be a fine thing havin' you home again, Mist' Corey. Been mighty lonesome, just the three of us raddlin' aroun' this big house."

6

He refolded the map, clipped his notations and sketches to it and was sliding them into the manila envelope when the phone rang. Rather than allow it to disturb Tish or Jemmy, Corey picked up the receiver at once. He no sooner spoke the word, "Hello," into it when he heard a soft, mellifluous voice. "Hello, lover."

"Hello?"

"Has it been *that* long, Corey?"

"Paula! For a moment, I— How are you? I asked about you less than half an hour ago."

"I know. Ad Cameron. I just ran across him at the *Herald*. I dropped by to make some corrections on my Saturday ad. I guess he told you about my shop—"

"Yes, he did, and I'm very impressed, although I know I shouldn't be. It's what you'd always planned."

"Well, yes, but I didn't call to talk shop. If you're not tied up—?"

He felt an old, strange pounding in his veins. "No, not at all, Paula."

"How about driving in for a little chit-chat over a cup of coffee? Or something with a little more authority in it."

"You took the words right out of my mouth. Pick you up at the *Herald?*"

"This boiler factory? I don't think that would add anything to a reunion. How about my place?"

"Same address?"

Her laugh was the same delightful trill he remembered so well. "Lord, no. You do need bringing up to date. I've got a pad of my own over my dress shop in the Mall. Paula's Casuals." She gave him directions and the address. "Drive around to the parking lot in the rear. The entrance to my apartment is next to the shop entrance. I'll meet you there."

"Twenty minutes." He hung up, went upstairs to freshen

up and get into a clean shirt and blouse, then went out by way of the kitchen to the garage. The gleaming white Thunderbird stood between the station wagon Jemmy used for errands and a Ford sedan, Tish's. The wider stall at the end, for Kenneth's big Mercedes, was empty and beside it stood a late model Chrysler Imperial. Jemmy's own convertible, which had been Corey's until he went into the Army, was outside in the carport area which was reserved for visitors. There were no keys in the T-bird and he was about to take the Imperial when Jemmy came out with the keys to the new car dangling from his fingers.

"You want these, Mist' Corey?"

"Thanks, Jemmy. I'm going into town to see a friend."

"Yes, sir. You got a house key, Mist' Corey?"

"No."

Jemmy extracted one from his trouser pocket. "I'll just put this one on the ring with the other ones." He slipped the house key onto the chain. "Night, Mist' Corey."

The motor kicked over smoothly. "Good night, Jemmy."

He found the Mall, a pleasant two-block-long street with wide pavements designed for leisurely window shopping, its curbs dotted by trees, alternating with boxes of flowering plants. Along the fronts of each display window were planter boxes filled with growing red and white geraniums, ivy and yellow pompoms. In the center of the street ran a long parkway with benches, across which the one- and two-storied shops faced each other—dress shops, men's haberdasheries, variety, millinery, jewelry and lingerie shops; a branch bank, a drugstore, ice cream and candy store, a restaurant and snack shop, book, stationery and gourmet food shops; at one corner a branch department store; on the other, a large supermarket. A real estate office, barbershop, sports car showroom, paint and wallpaper store, one with Danish furniture, silver and ceramics; a branch post office, savings and loan office, sporting goods shop, another for photographic supplies and cameras; a miscellany of other boutiques.

Beyond the Mall, two high-rise apartment houses and two tall office buildings stood like sentinels on guard. And behind the Mall, a huge parking lot. Corey drove into the lot and found the rear entrances to the ground-level shops similar to those in front, with similar display windows, trees and floral decorations. Above the shops, numerous windows were lighted, and these, he correctly assumed, were private living quarters. There were about two dozen cars parked close to the shop entrances as he drove in, searching for Paula's Casuals. Then a pair of headlights flashed off and on three times. He headed toward them and pulled in alongside as Paula got out of a smartly styled Ferrari roadster and stood waiting for him. He got out and stepped into her embrace for a resounding kiss. Then Paula drew back to examine his face.

"Let me look at you," she exclaimed. "God, you're still a beautiful man!"

"You're stealing my best lines, Paula."

"How *are* you, Corey? When I read you'd been wounded, I almost *died,* I was so upset. Then Lyle Emerson came back, but he acted so *queer,* didn't want to see anyone or talk to anyone. I wanted to ask him all about you, everything, but he— Why are we standing *here,* for heaven's sake? Come on up."

She had her keys out, chattering as she opened the door beside the darkened shop and snapped on upper and lower hall lights. He followed her up the flight of steps, reminded again of the airline stewardess, what's-her-name—Dietrich—the situation reversing itself; long legs, firm, lithe body, the summer dress a bit tighter and shorter, an above-the-knees view as she mounted the stairs. On the upper landing, she unlocked the door, using two keys, one for each lock, catching his inquiring look.

"Safety measure. One is a regular lock, the other something they call a dead bolt lock. Been too many burglaries around. I don't want to walk in some night and find an unexpected visitor waiting for me."

The apartment was like none he had ever seen in Laurelton. White, shaggy carpeting, low, modern, light-colored furniture, contoured chairs, elegant sofas that took up one entire wall, a squat, circular marble coffee table with huge cushions around it. "Make yourself comfortable and a couple of drinks," Paula said. "The bar is over there in the corner."

Paula disappeared into the bedroom. The floor-to-ceiling breakfront, when he discovered its secret, opened into a well-stocked bar, complete with its own refrigerator and sink. He found the ice compartment and poured two bourbon-on-rocks, remembered that Paula liked a dash of water in hers, added it; glanced over her collection of modern art in ultra-modern frames, shelves of books that were total strangers to him; and the long, low cabinet that surely must be a hi-fi-television combination.

Paula emerged in a deep-plunging green blouse and form-fitting slacks, kicked her loafers off and went to the cabinet. She lifted a panel, switched it on and he heard the first notes of Beethoven's *Appassionata,* one of her favorites from their days at the University. She came to the bar and took her drink, touched it to the rim of his glass, tasted it and said, "I see you still remember. Welcome home, Corey."

It was as though they had picked up where they had left off, the break, the cause of it. Drew Warren. He dismissed the thought at once. Paula was tracing her experiences after college; to Atlanta for a while, then New York—

"Then I ran into Bob Bennett. He was with a big ad agency there—" Corey remembered him now. Paula's date that New Year's Eve at the Laurelton Country Club when he had squired Drew—"and for some reason that escapes me now, we got married. I guess I forgot to tell Bob that I hadn't intended giving up my own career to bury myself in some woodsy Connecticut suburb designed for young pressure-cooked city executives, so—" an expressive shrug— "that blew up six months later. When I'd had enough of New York shops, I came back just as Johnny Curran was finishing the Mall. Bingo! That was really love at first sight."

"Happy, Paula?"

"Happier than I've ever been in my life! So free. Here, let me freshen your drink." She took Corey's glass to the bar. "What about you, Corey?"

"Most of what I've been through, you've read about or seen on television—"

"You were wounded. I didn't see *that* on television."

"Well, it wasn't much. But considering that Lyle Emerson lost a leg and Cord Waters lost his life, I got off rather easy."

She carried her drink to the sofa, handed him the other. "Take your jacket off and get comfortable, darling," she said, "you're home now. Relax." While he removed his blouse, Paula went to the air-conditioner controls and made an adjustment. Corey sank down into the sofa and Paula came to him, snuggled up beside him, pulled his tie down, slipped the knot, removed it, then unbuttoned three buttons of his shirt. "There, isn't that better?"

"Much. Much better."

Before she could draw back, one arm encircled her, drawing her closer. They kissed lightly, sampling, then harder, lingering over it. He felt her hand inside his shirt, running across his bare chest and was tempted by her shapely, unhaltered breasts straining against the material of her blouse.

"Corey—"

"What?"

"Like old times?"

"Not exactly. Better—"

"Mm—mm—don't talk—don't stop—"

"Paula, I don't think—"

"That's good, darling," she replied impishly, "just don't think."

"I can't—"

Suddenly, "There's nothing *wrong* with you, is there? That wound?"

He exploded into laughter. "My God, no! It was a *chest* wound."

"Then—"

"I mean it's not fair—right—"

Mildly aghast, yet smiling, "Was it less fair, more right, at college? What's with this nobility bit?"

"Paula, don't make me feel like a—"

"Or because I've been married? I told you we were divorced, didn't I?"

"Listen, Paula. I hurt you once. I don't want to repeat that. Maybe it doesn't make sense to you—"

"No, it doesn't." Firmly, with an obvious hurt in her voice. "Corey, I'm not used to *begging*. My God, it isn't still that oddball Drew Warren, is it?"

"If it were, why would I be here at all?" he replied lamely.

"I thought I had a good idea why. Corey, we aren't kids in school now. I'm a woman—"

"Don't I ever know it," he breathed.

"The Army didn't turn you queer, did it?"

Challenge? The sensuality she stirred in him? The memory of weekends in Atlanta, Gainesville, Madison, Union Point, Augusta—? He stood, bringing her up with him, then cradled her in his arms and carried her into the bedroom. There were no lights, no need for lights as they undressed, got into the bed and merged, young again, strong again, hearing her low whisper, "Oh, Corey, Corey, it hasn't been like this since—"

He awoke a little past four and dressed quietly, trying not to disturb her, but she stirred and sat up. "Polk?" she said sleepily.

He stopped in the act of zipping his trousers, heard her get out of bed and come toward him, bare feet shuffling on the carpeting. "Did you say Polk?"

Something muffled, said as though she had placed a hand over her mouth, then, "Now why would I have said a silly thing like that?"

326

"I wonder," he replied, not wondering at all as he resumed dressing.

"Corey, come back—"

"I've got to get home, Paula. You've got a shop to open in the morning." Tie on, pulled up. "I'll let myself out."

"You're angry."

"I'm not angry."

"Then— Corey, I'm having some people in Saturday night. You'll know most of them."

Silence.

"Please, Corey?"

"I don't know—"

"Eight-thirtyish—"

"I don't know—"

"Nothing formal. Dress sloppyish—"

"I—I'll let you know."

She was standing beside him in the dark, naked, one hand on his arm. "Good night, Corey." She reached up, pressed against him, kissed him. "I've missed you."

He didn't answer, but was even now moved by the closeness of her, aware of her nakedness, the feel of her body against his, the touch of her lips. "I'll look for you Saturday night," she said.

"Yes—well—good night—"

Driving homeward, he wondered just what the hell *that* was all about. Paula and Polk?

He put it out of his mind by thinking about Drew Warren.

CHAPTER II

1

The first day of October began just as the last day of September had ended—furnace-hot, humid, vaporous. For almost a month there had been no trace of rain nor was there now any indication of immediate relief. Hardly enough breeze to stir the drooping leaves, the earth thoroughly parched, macadam and pavements reflecting the penetrating heat of a relentless sun. Teachers, housewives and city workers joined farmers and planters in mute prayer for rain, but the skies remained defiantly cloudless, bronze-blue and empty of promise despite the hopeful prediction of an early morning news broadcaster that an upper level low (or was it a lower level high?) lying north and east of Laurelton might possibly push its way into the area.

Meanwhile, smoke from the industrial complex in West and South Laurelton drifted eastward and deposited its residual soot over homes, buildings, streets and vehicles. The placid Cottonwood rippled only when moving craft or bathers, seeking relief, stirred its mirrorlike surface. Overloaded air-conditioning plants and window units labored heroically the clock around, and many simply quit from sheer exhaustion.

Laurelton was in a condition variously described by police as "nervous" and "restless." At night, many were still sleeping in open parks, on porches, front lawns, in back yards or along both banks of the river in an effort to escape the oppressive heat. Burglary, robbery, car theft, rape and attempted rape were on the increase. Sporadic street fights and minor gang battles were common nightly occurrences and harassed police looked aside or winked at the after-hours joints, grateful that these had become a means of keeping more people off the streets and out of trouble.

At 5:15, Lee Durkin was startled out of a deep sleep into which he had fallen only after much restless tossing. Automatically, he reached out and shut the alarm clock off, but the clamor persisted. In the early morning dimness he saw a red Cyclopean eye blinking furiously and realized then that it was his telephone, the direct line to police headquarters. For a reluctant moment he glared back at the malevolent eye, then lifted the receiver and said gruffly, "Durkin."

"Good morning, Chief. Desk Sergeant Parrish. Your five-fifteen call."

"Thanks, Sergeant."

"Car's on its way, sir." A pause, then, "Temperature's eighty-eight and rising. There's a radio report of some slight chance of rain from the northeast by nightfall."

Durkin grunted a disbelieving, "Good," and hung up. He yawned sleepily, then sat up, swung his feet around to the floor, blindly searching for his bedroom slippers, one hand scratching his bare chest. For another moment or two he sat on the edge of the bed seeking wakefulness, then forced himself up. The curtains at the open windows hung still in the motionless, stagnant air and the outside sky to the east had just begun to show a few coppery streaks in advance warning of another day of unabated heat.

He went to the bathroom to shave, taking a little longer than usual under the cold shower, and was out in nineteen minutes, four over his best record, and began dressing his freshly perspiration-dampened body, wondering what new problems another day of record-breaking temperatures would bring. He pulled on a pair of dark gray trousers and tucked his short-sleeved white shirt inside, knotted a black tie loosely, remembering then that he hadn't put the water on to boil and decided there wouldn't be time for coffee. The car would wait for him, of course, but he had made it a fast rule never to keep any man on duty waiting needlessly.

He lit a cigarette and got out the dark gray matching jacket and carried it over one arm. Since taking over from Chet Ainsworth as Chief, Durkin no longer wore a uniform nor carried a service revolver. As he walked toward the front door, he heard the squad car pull into the narrow driveway, tires crunching on gravel. He put the jacket on, opened the door and stepped out on the porch.

A young officer leaped out of the car to open the rear door for him and Durkin waved him back, disliking any show of subservience to his rank; but the young man, properly attired in full uniform, held his ground and said, "Good morning, sir."

"Morning, Becker." As he stepped into the rear compartment, he added, "Harrison," to the older man at the wheel who had turned to greet him. Harrison, his beefy face wet with perspiration, also wore a jacket and tie. To both, when Becker got in beside the wheelman, "All right, boys, take

329

the jackets off. Ties, too. October first or not, it's too damn hot to stick to the rules."

Both men grinned gratefully as they removed the offending articles of clothing and opened the top buttons of their shirts. Harrison wheeled the squad car into South Drive as Durkin leaned back in his seat, more relaxed now, pleased that he could remember the names of every uniformed and plainclothesman on the force; in addition to which, he made a special point of knowing at least one item of personal information about each. He knew there would be no further conversation unless he generated it and asked, "Anything unusual going on, Harrison?"

The wheelman said, "Up to three-thirty we were running hard. These hot nights, nobody can sleep, seems like everybody's on the prowl. Half a dozen fights, nothing serious. Couple of muggings, kids—" His voice drifted off as he came into the main highway heading into West Laurelton, its industrial plants still shrouded in early morning sleep.

They listened to the crackling radio, the police communicator's time check, "oh-six-hundred," and a variety of call-ins and outgoing instructions to specific cars. Harrison reported Car No. 18 en route to headquarters and the communicator acknowledged the call.

They passed the turnoff that led to the vacant Androz' Club where Durkin's old friend, Cuban Joe Androz, had once hosted the finest and most expensive supper club in the area along with an honest, although illegal, gambling casino in the large private room at the rear. Cuban Joe was back in New Orleans again and Durkin was grateful that he had not had to force the Club to shut down after he had taken over as Chief. And with the memory of Androz came the aching nostalgia for Jessie-Belle, who had sung at the Club, the first and only woman he had ever loved deeply, lost to him by Stuart Taylor's murderous hand.

No. 18 stopped for a red light as they came into Velie Street, the hub of commercial activity in Angeltown. Lights were beginning to appear in the small houses, huddled together in their own shadows, as if drawing strength from one another. In full daylight they would show the ravages of time and neglect: peeling paint, loose boards, broken steps, missing pickets, littered yards. Four miles west lay the farm where Durkin had been born, a stony piece of land he, his father Grady, and mother Annie, had battled for years, barely able to keep alive on the little it gave up so grudgingly. After World War II, it had become part of a cheap housing development and over the passing years deteriorated into a blighted slum area.

He remembered those early years without bitterness now; when he had supplemented the family income by entering preliminary bouts at Collins' Arena on Friday nights, to the quiet pride of his father and despair of his mother; $20 for a four-rounder, later $30 for a six-rounder. Then his escape into the Army with the outbreak of World War II, a tough, work-hardened kid of 18, where, two Bronze Stars and a Silver Star later, he had won the heavyweight boxing championship of the ETO.

Came the news of Annie's death, and later, Grady's, while he was still in Europe. On his return to Laurelton, unable to bear the thought of resuming the battle with those few poor acres single-handed, he took off for New Orleans where, by prearrangement, he met Ernie Portola, the man who had trained him for his ETO title and encouraged him to continue his ring career in civilian life.

Fighting his way to within reach of the heavyweight title only to find the last few steps impossible to hurdle, unable to make deals with the big-time northern managers who feared for their boys. In New Orleans, he had met Jessie-Belle, the mulatto singer, fell in love with her, trained badly, then lost a bout to a younger man who was to have been no more than a routine tuneup for him; and quit the ring for good. His return to Laurelton for a brief visit, stunned by a magnificent citywide reception by a public that still regarded him as its first authentic war hero. Lee Durkin, the kid from Angeltown, the wrong side of the tracks, a celebrity!

It had been Jonas Taylor, Laurelton's most prominent and politically influential citizen, who had persuaded Lee to remain and accept the role of deputy chief of police in charge of the Angeltown district, most volatile trouble spot in all Laurelton, one that Chief Ainsworth had never been able to fully cope with. An Angeltowner himself, Lee was accepted here and the job became a reasonably easy one to run with full public support. And he had brought Jessie-Belle on from New Orleans to sing in Androz' Club, which eventually led to her tragic and untimely death.

And there, at Grand Avenue and Madison, he and Sergeant (now Captain) Jim Price, had shot down Turk Grunion and Nick Vincent, former New Orleans hoodlums who had moved in and sent defiant word they would never give up their lucrative hold on Angeltown's underworld. Four blocks to his left was the alley where Stuart Taylor had been brutally beaten by, Lee suspected privately, Clay Kendall, when Stuart tried to move in on Clay's wife, Shorey. And some ten blocks north, he remembered with an old pain the apartment where Jessie-Belle lived during those days when she sang at the Club.

Landmarks of his life.

The light turned green and No. 18 sped along Grand Avenue with its incredible conglomeration of stores, second-hand shops, restaurants, beer joints, pool parlors, small grocery stores, cheap night clubs, a gaudy new supermarket, used car lots. Dan Crystal's junkyard, still known by the old name, but Dan dead four years now. Everything closed down at this early hour; here and there a drunk asleep in a doorway, oblivious to the grim world and the hopelessness of the newborn day. A few women on their way to and from a small grocery store on the corner of Mercer. A horn salute and a wave from the wheelman in Car No. 12 as it waited for a light at Purcell. A tall, dark man with one bare arm around a young, giggling girl, weaving as they walked along the pavement. The shapes of sleeping forms on small, rickety porches.

A small dogleg on Grand Avenue brought them into the bridge entrance, the river below reflecting overhead and shore lights, a few barges and small craft beginning to stir. The Cottonwood River for years had proved itself a most advantageous geographical asset to the peace of the community. Approximately 65% of the white and Negro laboring class lived on the west side where most of Laurelton's heavier industry had been established in earlier days; the widespread Taylor Industries which included construction, manufacturing, transportation, engineering and land development; and the Warren Tobacco Company complex which lay immediately south of Angeltown.

There had been problems between the white and Negro communities, many of which still existed. Following the Supreme Court decision in 1954, and spurred by demonstrations elsewhere, there had been a show of civil disobedience, but no violent eruptions that had led to riots or deaths. Against heavy local opposition, Jonas Taylor and Anderson Warren, the two men who controlled over sixty per cent of the payroll in the area, had passed the word along to the County Commissioners, the City Council and School Board: *Go along or get out. We will not permit the economy of our community to be disrupted by militant segregationists, nor tolerate the senseless destruction of property. Oppose us and we will oppose you at the polls.*

However reluctantly, the majority of public officials and business leaders had come to grips with the problem and had cooperated. School desegregation had been orderly and newspapers throughout the state pointed to Laurelton

332

as an island of reason in a sea of insanity. The capitulation, it turned out, was only temporary.

It had taken demonstrations, beatings and arrests to de-segregate the buses; economic boycotts to permit Negroes to eat in a token number of formerly all-white restaurants and at lunch counters; to shop in white stores along Taylor Avenue; but not without hot resentment and some physical conflict. Movies, swimming pools and other public facilities were a more difficult problem to integrate, and housing a virtual impossibility. Teen-age gangs quickly formed on both sides of the bridge, each invading the territory of the other, provoking warfare with bicycle chains, baseball bats, switchblade knives and zip guns. Shop windows had been broken by bricks thrown from moving cars at night, tires slashed outside places of amusement; but generally, the violence failed to reach proportions beyond that which the police could control. There were arrests, charges hurled back and forth. Police were caught in the middle with protests of "police brutality," which might range from pushing, shoving and intemperate language, to broken heads and cracked ribs. There were hotheads and hard-noses on both sides and Durkin was well aware that his police were not entirely blameless. The force had its share of skull-breakers, men with low boiling points.

The situation had worsened progressively with the death of Jonas Taylor in 1956 and of his son, Ames, in 1958. Ames' son, Wayne, had taken over the chairmanship of the Laurelton Civil Rights Committee after his marriage to Julie Porter and return from a honeymoon trip in Europe. Shortly afterward, Mayor Max Hungerford, weary of trying to pour nonexistent oil on ever-present troubled waters, stepped aside to form an insurance agency. His brother-in-law and president of the City Council, Tom Cameron, became mayor. Police Chief Chet Ainsworth, without Hungerford's support now, tendered his resignation and accepted full retirement. Mayor Cameron then named Deputy Chief Durkin to become Chief and the nomination was passed with unanimous approval.

Car No. 18 passed the halfway mark on the bridge and Durkin's eyes instinctively picked up the spot in the rail where, in 1958, in pursuit of Stuart Taylor's car, he saw Stuart inadvertently forced to the right by a truck and crashed into the rail, his car hanging precariously on the edge for a few fateful moments until Lee screeched up behind him, braking his squad car, but not hard enough to prevent it from nudging the sports car over into the river. Lee had risked his own life to dive in after Stuart, but by the time he had searched for the car and body at the bottom of the Cottonwood, Stuart had drowned; thus saving a murder trial which Durkin believed would surely, in the hands of an all-white jury, have resulted in a futile effort to convict the wealthy heir to the Taylor fortune.

Progress was slowed by more traffic lights and the increase in truck traffic heading in both directions. Ahead and behind them came city buses and jalopy pool cars bringing the daily stream of maids, cooks, porters, delivery men and store employees over from West and South Laurelton; the city and county employees would come later. Harrison turned off Fuller into Taylor Avenue and fourteen blocks east pulled into the parking lot behind the police headquarters building.

2

Durkin entered the police building through the heavy steel door on the basement level, grateful for the blast of air-conditioned coolness, then walked along the empty corridor of steel-lined walls toward the stairway at the front of the building. Behind the thick walls were the felony and misdemeanor blocks, the drunk tank, and a special section for women prisoners. No matter the time of day or night or weather, there was always activity of some sort on this lower floor; moving bodies, groaning drunks, angry catcalls, curses and jeers at the duty officers who sauntered periodically past the barred cells; piercing screams born of nightmares; the whimpering fear of unknown, impending doom to come; the shocked white face of a benumbed, bewildered first offender.

A blue-shirted figure lumbered into the corridor from a cross-passage and Durkin nodded briefly to Fred Milhouser, the heavyset night sergeant in charge of the lower floor, now too old for more active duty and waiting out his retirement and pension on January first.

"Morning, Fred. How're Maggie and the kids?"

Milhouser snuffled. "They all doin' fine, Chief."

"Everything all right?" It was a useless, routine question to ask of a man with nearly forty years of service whose rheumy eyes had seen every ugly side of life and could no longer be surprised or dismayed by the vagaries of human behavior.

"Not too bad for a hot night. Couple knife fights, couple muggings, usual drunks."

"Well, take it easy, Fred."

334

"Shuh."

Durkin's nose twitched with the stench of air fouled by unwashed bodies, blood, drunken vomit, cell toilets, all blending with the overpowering odor of strong chemicals used by cleaning crews on each shift in a daily losing battle. A turnkey unlocked the barred door at the foot of the stairs and Durkin moved swiftly up the littered steps into the upper main lobby, almost deserted at this hour, then turned right, reaching for the key to the unmarked door to his private office. As he entered the room, he hung his hat and jacket on the clothes tree then switched on the overhead fluorescent lights which did little to dispel the usual gloominess of the large room.

As he expected, there was a light tap on the outer door and Peter LaSalle entered, carrying two mugs of coffee; expected because Durkin knew his arrival had been broadcast first by the communicator, next by the turnkey. "Old man's in the building."

"Morning, Pete." Durkin took the cup of coffee and his first sip. "Thanks." He moved to his desk and sat in the worn chair behind it.

Peter LaSalle was an inch taller than Durkin's even six feet, similarly lean and in the 190-pound class, with dark brown hair, an intelligent face that was reasonably attractive, and the kind of body on which all clothes, uniform, business suit or dinner jacket, would hang beautifully casual. He was the son of a retired police lieutenant and had, until his father's death at the hands of a panic-stricken narcotics addict, been pursuing an academic career at the University, one that changed abruptly in his senior year following Elliot LaSalle's funeral.

Now 34, of solid middle-class stock, married, interested in youth activities and athletics, LaSalle was dedicated to police work. He had devoted two years to postgraduate studies in police administration in Atlanta, attended the FBI Police Academy, taken night courses in law. There followed four years of active police work with a promotion to the Detective Bureau in his second year, again to sergeant, was top man in the examinations for his lieutenancy, and became the youngest captain in Laurelton's history, with two citations for bravery and numerous commendations for superior achievement. He now served as Durkin's special assistant with temporary rank of Inspector-at-Large.

"How's Nora?" Durkin asked.

"Feeling great. Well into her eighth month and not a complaint."

"Any cop's wife's got plenty to complain about. Nora's just smart enough, or Irish enough, to keep 'em to herself."

"At least, *I* can't complain."

"You're lucky, Pete. She's a mighty sweet girl. Anything important on the night report?"

"The usual run of the mill. Except for another police brutality accusation thrown at us."

Durkin reacted sharply, sensitive to the possibility of undesirable publicity. His head jerked upward, eyes on LaSalle's. "What is it this time?"

"Three kids picked up on a mugging job, apprehended in the act. Males, Negro, fourteen, sixteen and seventeen years old, the two older boys with previous make-sheets. Attacked and rolled a Negro grocery storekeeper after he closed up shop around midnight. They tackled him while he was walking to his house, three blocks away, probably waiting for him. He put up a fight and Officers Carr and Harper came on them while it was in progress.

"The kids broke and ran, but Carr nailed two and Harper got the third. Not much more than an hour later, their parents were clamoring at the 12th Precinct, charging police brutality. It seems that some housewife heard the disturbance and came to her window while the arrest was being made. She recognized one of the boys and ran to tell his parents—"

"Anything to it?"

"I doubt it very much. Carr and Harper have clean records. No marks on two of the boys. The older one has a scratch on his upper arm. Harper claims it was made when the boy, who was armed with a switchblade knife, tried to break away. The grocer claims he was too scared or busy to see what was going on."

"This damned heat," Durkin said. "A whole month of it and no sign of relief. I'm surprised it isn't a whole lot worse." He drained the last of the coffee and said, "What's the disposition?"

"I've set up a meeting with the parents and Reverend Amos Hart. I think they're going to bring their own doctor in with them to check out the boys."

"What time?"

"As close to noon as they can make it. At the 12th."

"I'm due at the Police Training Center for lunch. Craig thinks his class needs a little show of brass and a mild pep talk at the three-quarter mark."

"I was hoping you could look in on the investigation. It always helps when the Chief sits in as an observer."

"I'm sure you can handle it, Pete. This other thing is pretty important, too. Anything else?"

"Mostly routine. Hartman and Edwards picked up Stanley Shepherd and Frank Poole in the alley behind Lingell's Jewelry Store. They had four transistor radios, a tape recorder and half a dozen pen and pencil sets in their possession. Don Lingell identified the stuff as his property—"

"Shepherd. Edgar Shepherd's boy?"

"The same. The Poole boy is John Poole's kid. Just turned seventeen—"

"From Water and Power?"

"That's the one."

"Goddam it!" Durkin exploded. "Those two are going to scream like wounded ducks that we've got it in for their kids. That Shepherd boy's been in trouble twice before that I know of. Got more money than he can spend, a car of his own, and he's got to steal for kicks."

LaSalle sighed. A knock on the door. He got up and went to it, took a typed condensation of activities during the night shift, with less than two hours to go. He brought it to Durkin and looked over Lee's shoulder at it.

12:02 . . . Purse-snatching . . . Eddie Moberly, 19. Negro. Arresting officer, Nagle, Badge 442. Positive identification by Mrs. Laura White, Caucasian, age 53. Previous record . . .

12:12 . . . Attempted armed robbery . . . Roland's Owl Market, Post and 3rd . . . three unidentified Negroes, one female, two male . . . ages 18 to 24 . . . one armed with small automatic, two with knives . . . failed when Bernie Roland, Caucasian, 46, pulled .38 revolver and fired twice over their heads . . . Officers Connell and Dittman investigating . . .

12:27 . . . Burglary . . . Lingell's Jewelry Store . . .

Durkin flipped the sheet to the next item, the three Negro boys charged with the mugging LaSalle had already reported. Then on to the next items, running down the list quickly . . .

12:34 . . . Aggravated assault . . .

12:38 . . . Car theft reported by . . .

12:41 . . . Drunk and disorderly . . .

12:43 . . . Attempted rape . . . Lanier Park . . . 12:47 . . . Disturbing the peace . . . resisting arrest . . . 12:50 . . . Drunk, disorderly . . . 12:56 . . . Apprehended thief rifling glove compartment of car at . . . 12:59 . . . Hit-and-run on two parked cars . . . apprehended . . . 1:02 . . . Assault with deadly weapon . . . 1:03 . . . Assault,

337

disturbing peace . . . and so on until 5:40 where the report closed with the arrest of a vagrant found sleeping in Dr. Albert Gilpin's car in the County General Hospital parking lot.

Durkin tossed the report into one of the trays on his desk and took up a single sheet from another tray, his list of appointments for the day.

10:30—Meeting in Mayor's office.
12:00—Lunch at Police Training School.
 2:00—Meeting with City Attorney Andrew Cummings.
 2:45—Meeting with District Attorney Bolling West.
 2:30—Inspection new communications equipment.
 4:15—Conference, committee from Downtown Merchants Assn., Subject: Increase in Shoplifting.
 5:00—Visit County General; one sick, one wounded officer.
 6:15—Dinner meeting, Precinct Captains.

It would, Durkin thought, be another long day; and a hell of a job to squeeze in his normal work load between appointments. "Okay, Pete. Anything else?"

"I've been saving it for last, Lee."

Durkin looked up quickly. LaSalle, he knew, was not an alarmist and would not bother him with a routine problem. He pushed the appointment list to one side. "What's up?"

"The Black Fez is in town."

Durkin muttered an unintelligible oath. "When?"

"They showed up last night for the first time. Must have come in very quietly. Two of them. One, I'm fairly certain from the description, is the leader himself, Dr. Rhama. The other one must be one of his aides."

"Where'd you pick this up?"

"From my Two-Five over in West Laurelton. He spotted them in the back room of Banjo's Place, huddling in a private talk with Banjo. Jim Cuddy and Jake Runnels were there, too."

"They're in good company. Cuddy did two years at Parkton on an ADW. Runnels has been in twice, once as a narcotics pusher and once for car-boosting. We got anything more to go on?"

"Nothing definite, but we know the pattern. Rhama is a hard-core black nationalist who travels around the country preaching universal unification of all blacks against all whites. He's supported financially by militant extremist groups and wherever he stops, there's trouble. He moves in, incites local militants, encourages rioting among the young,

338

then moves on. He's a bone in the throats of the nonviolent Negro organizations and a paladin to the extremists."

"And it looks like he's picked us for his next target," Durkin said morosely.

"Very likely."

"Christ! With him showing up, we'll have to keep the whole force on standby around the clock, fingers on the trigger. We're shorthanded as it is."

"Not until something shows. I've been working on a plan to help stretch what we've got. It's not much, but it will help."

"How?"

"Well," LaSalle said, "the idea of pulling the second man out of approximately eighty per cent of our squad cars during daylight hours and assigning them to night patrol. It means we'll have to keep in closer contact with the day men in case of trouble, but we'll have more cars moving around at night, two men to the car. When and if trouble comes, chances are it will be during the night hours. The remaining twenty per cent of the cars would ride double by day in the West Laurelton area. The day men we shift won't like it, but we'll have to chance it."

"Get to work on it right away, Pete. I guess this won't be any different from the way the Black Fez works every place else."

"Probably not. It will start with some scattered minor incidents, a few smashed windows, a demonstration using teen-agers, hoping to work up a few cases of police brutality—"

"You think this one last night could be Rhama's doing?"

"I doubt it, considering that he only showed up last night. Chances are he may try to capitalize on it. Once he gets things stirred up, he'll get out on the streets and start preaching in public. That's where he does his best work. We'll begin seeing a lot more of the fezzes, cardboard imitations of the ones he and his people wear. Kids will wear them to school, teen-agers to high school. If the principals or teachers order them to take them off, they'll walk out and begin demonstrating. They'll show up on the streets—"

"I know," Durkin said with an unhappy frown. "We've seen enough of it on television. Chicago, Harlem, Cleveland, Detroit, the same old story all over again. A few busted heads, jails filled, outside militants coming in to spread it all over the air, in the papers and magazines. Worst of all, we can't put a finger on them until it happens."

"Well—we'll do what we can to keep on top of it. I'd like

to know just how deeply Banjo Nichols is involved in this thing, why the meeting at his place."

"Where's Rhama staying?"

"I'll know that a little later today. I've put two men over there checking quietly. Hotels, motels, rooming houses."

"I think maybe I'll have a talk with Amos Hart."

"That might help. He won't want any part of Rhama, nor will the other members of his civil rights group."

"Trouble is," Durkin said, "Rhama will probably bypass them and work with the younger people. And I'd better have a talk with the mayor this morning. We may have to bring the Sheriff's Department and State Police into this if it begins looking like a big-scale thing. I don't like it, but we'll need the extra help. The one thing I don't want is to have to bring in the National Guard."

"We may be forced into it. That's another part of Rhama's strategy, national publicity."

"Let's hope not." Durkin stood up. "I'll talk to Cameron this morning. Handle that brutality thing any way you think best, Pete, and let me know how it comes out."

"I'll keep in touch with the desk if you want to reach me."

3

At 708 Wallace Street, Lutie Shackleford stood at the gas stove in her worn cotton robe, forking thick slices of sizzling bacon around in a heavy black frying pan, one eye on a pot of oatmeal. Sam Shackleford came into the kitchen smacking his lips. "Sure smells good, Lutie. Coffee ready?"

"Everything's ready but you. Get you a dish of this oatmeal whilst I keep an eye on the bacon. How you want your eggs?"

"Eggs on a weekday? Duke come home, we all get in on the treat, huh?"

"Well, it don't happen every day." Sam ladled the steaming oatmeal into a bowl. "Gotta be crazy to stand over a hot stove, a day like this," Lutie said, "but— Sam, you think you could get the fan outa our room, or Lizabeth's, an' put it up in here?"

"Out of our room. Don't you remember, you put Lizabeth's fan in Duke's room last night?"

"Shuh, I did, didn' I? I hope she was able to get to sleep without it."

"Yes, I slept well. Good morning, Mom, Pa." Elizabeth came into the kitchen with a brimming smile. She went to the stove and kissed Lutie's moist cheek, then Sam's. "You go get the fan, Daddy. This room is like a furnace. Bacon *and* eggs, Mom? Is Duke up?"

"I'n heard a peep outen him. He must of been real tired. Go take a look and see."

"Sorry he was asleep by the time I got home last night. He really must have been done in. I was home before 10:30."

"Well, if you want to see him before you go off to school, you best wake him up now."

Sam returned with the fan, plugged it in at a counter outlet. The fan wheezed and ground into action, but only managed to circulate the hot air about. Elizabeth went down the hall and knocked on Duke's door. "Hey, Bubbal" she called. "You going to sleep the whole day away? Rise and shine, boy!" She heard him stir in bed. "You getting up?"

"What the hell! 'At you, Lizabeth?"

"Well, who else did you think it was?"

"Hey, hold it a minute."

"I'm in a hurry, Duke. Food's on. Come and get it."

"Soon's I throw some water on my face. Don't run off now."

He came into the kitchen a few minutes later, wearing nothing but a wide-sleeved silk maroon robe with the words BUDDY (THE) DUKE in large white letters sewed on its back. Elizabeth was sitting at the table with her back toward him. He took two quick steps, wrapped his right arm around her waist and lifted her, chair and all, off the floor. She dropped her fork and a slice of bread, squealing, "Put me down, King Kong!"

Lutie turned from the stove and laughed at the hilarious sight of Elizabeth struggling to free herself, evidently enjoying the rough-housing from her strong brother. "Put her down," Sam said. "She got no time to be foolin' aroun'. I got to drop her to school on my way."

"Shuh." Duke lowered the chair to the floor. Elizabeth stood up, embraced and kissed him. "My, my, my, you sure growed up a sweet-lookin' gal, even without the pigtails hangin' down."

"Oh, Duke. I'm so glad to see you again. I don't know how to thank you for all you—"

"Hush up, pretty gal. It's worth it an' more, seein' you like this. You sure enough a smart college gal?"

"Sure enough. If I weren't, I wouldn't be teaching now, would I?"

"My, my," Duke marveled, examining her with admiration. "Jus' lissen to how nice that sister of mine talks. Good

341

lookin' *an'* brainy. What a hell of a combination. Hey, Little Sis, how many boys you got runnin' after you, huh?"

Airily, "Oh, I guess about as many as you've got girls chasing after you, Buddy."

Sam glowered and said, "His name is Duke, not Buddy. That Buddy is somethin' he got up north. In his home, he's Duke Shackleford."

"Hey, now, Pops, you got a blue meanie on this mornin'?" Duke asked with a laugh.

"I don' know about blue meanies, but you was Duke 'til you left home an' you're still Duke in this house."

"Okay, okay—"

"Stop you-all's fussin'," Lutie said as she came from the stove to fill Duke's plate. "Now don' gulp your food down, son."

"Mom, that was ten years ago. I'm twenty-six years old an' I been eatin' high on the hog a long time now."

"That's real good," Lutie replied with rare good humor. "Jus' don' eat like one."

"Well," Elizabeth said, "it's beginning to sound like home used to be. All we need is Ivy swishing her hips around—"

"You ready, Lizabeth?" Sam asked abruptly.

"Almost, Dad."

"Lunch pail ready, Lutie?"

"Any time you are, Sam. Lizabeth's lunch, too. Let her finish without gulpin', can't you? What's your hurry this mornin'?"

"If I'm goin' get back here after lunch to run Duke down to Tenboro, I got to get in early an' get my people started."

"Listen, Pop," Duke said, "iffen it put you out, forget it. I c'n pick me up somebody to drive me down—"

"Boy, ain't you ever learned not to throw your money around?" Sam asked.

"Take it easy, Pop. It's my money an' that's what it's for. Spend it or waste it, there's more where it all come from."

"For heaven's sake!" Elizabeth exclaimed. "What's going on around here? Duke isn't home a full day and we're already bickering about nothing. That's one hell of a welcome home—"

"You stop usin' that kinda talk in this house, young lady," Sam snapped.

"Oh, brother! Let's go, Dad, before a riot breaks out." Elizabeth got up from the table, took her wrapped lunch from the counter. Sam got his lunch pail and started for the door. Duke sat hunched over his plate. "See you later, Duke?" Elizabeth said as she passed him, one hand running across his shoulders.

"Sure, sweetie. I'll be back by supper time."

"*A rivederci.*"

"Hey?"

"That's Italian for 'so long.' "

Duke grinned. "Okay. *Hasta luego.* That's Puerto Rican for the same thing. Like our leader says, Keep the Faith, Baby."

They were gone. The old Ford coughed itself into life and its gears crunched and growled in protest, then finally ground its way out of the open garage and into the street.

"What's buggin' the old man, Mom?" Duke asked. Lutie put her own plate of food on the table and sat wearily in the chair opposite him, poured a cup of coffee into her oversized cup.

"Duke, maybe you done forgot your own Papa."

"How come you think I do a thing like that, Mom?"

"Well, you know he is a religious man. He don' like swear words. He don' like people comin' to the table half undressed. An' he don' like big talk about money. It make him feel like you th'owin' somethin' up to him."

"Oh, sweet Jesus, Mom——"

"Like that. Sweet Jesus, lessen you singin' about Him or you in church prayin' to Him, he don' like it."

Duke laughed light-heartedly. This was all so—comical —so idiotic. "Okay, Mom. I'll try to remember, but it won't be easy."

"Duke, don' take on so. Your Papa, he got his problems, too."

"Pa? At the plant?"

"No. Just aroun'. People stirrin' things up, ruckusin' aroun', chil'ren don' show no respect for their elders. You know, this civil rights thing——"

"Well, they got a right to, ain't they, Mom?"

"Shuh. Long's they don't go tearin' aroun' in white people's business, tryin' to undo what's bein' done for us——"

"Like what, Mom? Who's doin' what for you?"

"Lots of things, Duke. We got more money'n we ever had. We got a good home—I know we wouldn' had it without you helpin' with Lizabeth's education out in California, but thing's are better'n they ever was before. We sit anywhere on our buses, lot of our chil'ren goin' to white schools 'cross the bridge now——"

"Any white kids come over here to go to our schools, Mom?"

Lutie looked up in surprise. "Well, no. What for?"

"So you think because a few colored kids are 'lowed to go to a poor white trash school, we equals at last, hey?

343

Mom, you jus' dreamin'. Them goddam ofays, they got their feet on our necks jus' like they always did an' all we got to do is wiggle a little, they stomp us to death."

"I guess that's what Pa's afraid of, Duke. You come home an' talk biggety that way, the way you talkin' now, you goin' stir up things."

"Maybe they need stirrin' up."

"Duke," Lutie said pleadingly, "this ain't New York. Down here, you *some*body to the young people. They goin' look up to you. You talk like you doin', they'll listen to you and all's they need is somebody like you to set 'em off, then there's goin'a be trouble."

"What trouble?"

"All kindsa trouble. The young people jus' lookin' for some excuse to go rammagin' aroun' the way they been doin' in other cities, breakin' store windows, settin' fires, stealin'."

"Takin' what they shoulda took a long time ago—"

"Duke, you hush that kinda talk up. Them boys go 'cross the bridge an' riot, what you think's goin' happen over here when the white people come lookin' to get even? They start one fire, we can all go up like wood shavin's. Fire department take its time gettin' here, most of Angeltown could burn to the groun'. They go hollerin' 'Burn, baby, burn!' but you know who's goin'a burn faster an' quicker an' longer, don't you?"

"Mom, don't be scared, for Christ's sweet sake. Bein' scared is what's been wrong with us for hundreds of years. We got rights we entitled to. The highest court cats in the country say so. Onliest thing is, if we don't act like we want it, we ain't never goin'a get it."

"Duke, please, son—"

"Don' worry, Mom. I don' think there's enough guts here to fill a tin can. These Uncle Tom cats ain't goin'a get off their black asses to do a damn thing. It'll pass the way it always passes, with the honkies sittin' in the saddle whippin' us mules." He stood up. "Gotta take a shower an' get some clothes on."

Lutie sighed and weakly poked a fork into a piece of bacon, feeling the weight of the defeat that engulfed her.

Twenty-six years old an' he still can't fool his ol' Mama. He ain't foolin' me with his big talk. An' about that hand, neither. I seen the scar over his eye where the stitches been pulled out. An' all that tape wrapped aroun' his body I seen after he was in bed sleepin' las' night. He didn' get that hittin' no ring post. I don' think he fool Sam none, neither.

344

*How does a man wearin' them big gloves hit even a brick
wall an' bust his knuckles up so bad?*

It hadn't happened in the ring at all, she knew. Duke was
running from trouble. And heading into more of it. The
way he had run from home ten years ago, without a word
to her or Sam, not hearing from him for over three years,
not until he was in the ring and on his way up. And they
still didn't know why he had run away that time. The police
had come asking questions, giving no answers. Just want to
ask him a few things, Mrs. Shackleford, they had said, volunteering nothing.

She was sure Sam felt it, too. Duke was hiding something, from someone. Talking big. Talking trouble. This was
no simple visit, else why was he bringing all his belongings
with him? All the clothes he said he had in the trunk of his
car.

Thank you, Lord, she said in silent prayer. *Thank you
there wasn't no cuttin', wasn't worse than it is. Thank you
again, Lord, an' keep an eye out he don't get into nothin' he
can't get out of. Amen.*

She stood up, wiped her eyes and face with her apron
and began carrying the dishes to the sink.

4

Kenneth was finishing his breakfast when Corey came
down, freshly shaven, dressed in shirt, tie and slacks, ener-
vated by the lack of sleep. Kenneth cocked a half-question-
ing eye toward him and said with a smile, "Good morning,
Corey. Sleep well?"

"Like I haven't slept in years. Good morning, Dad." He
slipped into his chair and reached for the large glass of orange juice that was nestled in a bed of crushed ice. "Mm-
m-m—just what the doctor ordered." As he drank it, Corey
thought that if this were only a few years ago, Kenneth,
after a discussion as sober as the one they had had the night
before, would have sat here grim-faced and silent, accus-
ingly, as some form of punishment.

Corey put the glass down as Kenneth folded his copy of
the *Herald* and passed it across the table. "You seem to
have broken into print," he said. "I ran into Adam Cameron last night and told him you were home."

"I know. He called me a short while after." He picked up
the paper and found the brief item at once, on the front
page.

345

COREY ARMOUR BACK FROM VIETNAM DUTY

After two years of active duty with the U.S. Armed Forces, 18 months of which were served in Viet Nam, Lieutenant Corey Armour, son of Kenneth and the late Catherine Armour, of 22 Old Colony Lane, returned to Laurelton yesterday. Holder of the Purple Heart which he won in combat, Lieutenant Armour, after a period of terminal leave, will return to civilian life. The *Herald* joins his many friends in saying, "Welcome home, Corey."

"That," Kenneth observed, "should start the phone ringing."

"It will save me a lot of time looking up phone numbers," Corey replied.

"If you aren't busy for lunch, you might like to drive down—"

"I don't know yet, Dad. I want to go into town and do something about some new clothes. I thought I might take a run out to Brookhill after that."

"It's just as well, I suppose. Will I see you here for dinner?"

"I'm sure I'll be free by then. And Dad—"

"Yes?"

"Thanks again for the new car. I changed my mind and tried it out last night. It was too tempting not to. It's just perfect."

"I assumed so when I came home and found it gone. Enjoy it, Corey. It's my way of telling you how glad I am to have you home again." The smile evaporated. "This has been a very empty house during the past two years." He touched his napkin to his lips and stood up. "Did you find the map helpful last night?"

"Yes. Very much so."

"I can't help wondering what you have in mind."

"It may be nothing at all, but if it looks as though it might come to something, I'll go over the whole thing with you."

"Well—any time. See you at dinner. Have a good day. You'll appreciate the air-conditioner in your car. It feels like another scorcher."

Kenneth went out just as Tish bustled in bearing a platter of scrambled eggs, bacon and pancakes. She poured coffee for Corey and, satisfied that he was content, went out again. Corey finished his breakfast with thoughts of Paula now, and Paula then. And Polk, drawn into a triangle by a careless mention of his name. After a second cup of coffee, he

346

went into Kenneth's study where he made a list of "musts" for the day. Call Lyle. Call Polk. Brookhill: Shad and Leona. Drew. (This last underscored twice, unconsciously, frowning when he realized he had placed special emphasis here.) At the top of the list, he inserted the name Weinstock's Men Shop. The phone rang. He ignored it and continued studying his list, having added the names: Wayne Taylor? John Curran?

From the doorway, he heard Jemmy's voice. "For you, Mist' Corey." He picked up the telephone. "Hello?"

"Corey!" It was Polk Holderby's unmistakable voice. "Jesus, Corey, I—I—"

"Hi, Polk—"

"Man, if I'd known sooner, I'd've kicked you out of bed this morning. I passed your house on the way in only twenty minutes ago."

"Don't tell me you're at work already?"

"Sure enough. Market opens in eight minutes. I'm with Archer & Moseley—"

"I know. Ad Cameron told me last night. And the job?"

"Between you and me, it's such a soft touch, I almost feel guilty. But the hell with that. When am I going to see you? How about lunch?"

"What about it?"

"Noon?"

"Check."

"We're on the ground floor of the Taylor Building."

"I know. See you at noon. Go back to your ticker tape."

Polk laughed. "Ticker tape? Boy, you *are* behind the times. We do it with radar now. Opening round coming up. Look for you at noon."

He hung up, added "Lunch, noon," beside Polk's name. He got the phone book out and checked it for Lyle Emerson's number and found the name listed, the address an unfamiliar street. He dialed the number and got no answer, then realized that at nine o'clock Lyle would be on the job at Laurelton High. He considered calling Brookhill, then decided against it. Shad and Leona would be home at any time he got there. He didn't want to talk to Drew just yet, knew that Leona would insist that he do; or she might still be asleep at this time of the morning. And thinking of sleep, he toyed with the tempting thought of sacking out for another hour or two. The phone rang again and he lifted the receiver. "Corey?"

He knew the voice at once. Somehow changed, yet somehow the same. "Hello, Drew. It's wonderful to hear your voice again."

347

"And to hear yours. I just finished reading the item in the paper about your return and wanted to welcome you home."

"Thank you, Drew. How are you?"

"Very well. And you?"

"Never better. My father told me about Gran. I'm terribly sorry, Drew."

"We—we're getting reconciled to it. I'm sure he'd love to see you. He's mentioned you several times recently."

And you? Corey wondered. Aloud, "As a matter of fact, I intended driving out to Brookhill—"

He caught the sudden lift in her voice. "Today?"

"—to see Shad and Leona. I thought it might help a little if I told them of the few times I'd seen and talked with Cord before it happened."

Was there a dip of disappointment in her quiet, "Oh." Then, "I know it will make them happy."

"Will you be home this afternoon?"

"Yes. I don't get away from here much. Bring some swim trunks and we can take a dip. It's so dreadfully hot and our air-conditioning plant is having its usual case of heat prostration. How about coming out for lunch?"

"I'm sorry, Drew. I've got to get into town and do something about some civilian clothes to replace these uniforms—"

"Not before I see you in yours," she exclaimed.

"There's every chance for that. The changeover will take a few days at least."

"This afternoon, then?"

"Yes. I promised to have lunch with Polk. I'll drive out as soon as I can break away."

He gave up the idea of going back to sleep and started upstairs to finish dressing. He got to the kitchen just as Tish was reaching for the phone. "Tish, I'm not in. Take any messages and say I won't be in until dinner time."

He parked the white Thunderbird on the lot behind Weinstock's and spent the next two hours picking out four suits, several pairs of slacks, a topcoat, shirts, two hats, a raincoat and other accessories. Listening to Aaron Weinstock's chatter while being measured for alterations. Of new styles and fabrics, his son Martin's progress in his own law office (Martin had been a classmate at law school), the effect of the prolonged heat wave on fall and winter clothing sales. "By Thursday, half will be ready. I'll have the rest delivered to you on Saturday," Aaron said finally.

"That will be fine, thank you. I've got to run now. I'll be in some time next week to fill out the rest of what I want.

And give Martin my best. Tell him I'll look in on him as soon as I get squared away."

The uniform marked him as a target for curious glances, waves and calls from passersby, to which he responded in kind as he walked along the street to the Taylor Building. He entered the lobby, found the ground-level entrance to the brokerage firm and went inside. Beyond several rows of desks and a long line of glassed-in cubicles, he entered the large room which resembled a small theater of upholstered armchairs, its screen a huge electronically operated board that flashed symbols and figures on moving tape and automatically registered the latest prices in white figures on a black background that took up the rest of the wall. Gone were the bustling board boys who formerly posted the price changes, victims of automation.

In one of the glass-enclosed offices that ran along the back wall, Corey saw Polk leaning over an executive's shoulder as both examined a report of some kind. The smiling executive looked up, nodded Polk on his way and turned back to answer his telephone. Polk gathered up the report, went out and almost collided with Corey before he saw him.

"Watch it, Polk—"

"Corey!" There was genuine warmth in Polk's face as his eyes scanned Corey from head to foot, their hands locked in a firm clasp. "Man, you look—wonderful! How are you?"

"Great, Polk. What's the good word?"

"Seeing you, old son. You look fabulous in that outfit. Listen, I've got Weed Carpenter waiting for me. Give me five minutes to hand this financial statement to him and I'll be free. Ready for lunch?"

"Any time you are. Don't rush it. I've plenty of time."

"Back in a couple of minutes."

Polk disposed of his business with his client neatly and with all the smiling, confident aplomb of a used-car salesman. Within five minutes he and Corey were out on Taylor Avenue, heading toward the Civic Center. "Boy," Polk exclaimed, "you're a relief to my aching old eyes in that soldier suit. Is that your Purple Heart?"

"That's it—"

"Christ, what a hell of a conversation piece—"

"What about that Madison Avenue uniform you've got on?"

"*Wall* Street, man. Madison Avenue is sincere gray. This is good old sincere, conservative black, inspires confidence, with the accent on the *con*. You know, like a pipe-smoker.

Nobody ever thinks of a pipe-smoker as being anything but sincere and honest."

"Polk, you haven't changed a bit."

"Don't you ever believe that, Corey. Ah, here we are, let's turn in here." They had reached Davis Street. "There it is, Marco's. Let's get with it and drink up a storm. Courtesy of A & M."

"Why A & M?"

"Why the hell not? As of this moment, you've become a prospective client and one of my jobs is to entertain clients." Polk noticed Corey's eyes staring toward the east area. "All new during the past two years. Progress. High-rise apartments and a big shopping center, the Mall. One of Johnny Curran's projects. We're bustin' out all over. Here we are, Marco's. This is new, too."

At the door, a dinner-jacketed host looked at Corey quizzically. Polk said, "My guest, Louis. Lieutenant Corey Armour, just home from Viet Nam. Have a card made out for him before we leave, will you? Corey Armour, Mr. Kenneth Armour's son."

"Ah, yes, of course. With pleasure, Mr. Holderby." Louis unhooked the velvet-covered chain. On the way to the bar, Corey said, "I haven't joined some sort of subversive society, have I? I thought all that jazz happened during the twenties, long before we were born."

Polk grinned slyly. "Time brings changes, son. Marco's isn't a public restaurant. It's a private dining club. Keeps the niggers out."

Hearing that offensive word from Polk for the first time since he had known him, Corey reacted with shock. Time had indeed brought change.

He recalled a time in January of 1961 when Charlayne Hunter and Hamilton Holmes, on an order from a federal district judge, were enrolled and attending their first classes at the University. That he and Polk, among others, had staunchly refused to join the demonstrations and openly denounced any student action that would prevent the two Negroes from attending. Then he suddenly recalled that neither he nor Polk had joined a smaller group, headed by Martin Weinstock, to counter-demonstrate against the demonstrators.

Polk missed Corey's look of concern as they threaded their way through groups of members waiting to be seated, a small number of women among them. They found a place at the crowded bar and squeezed into it. Some of the faces around them were familiar, others difficult to match with names, many totally strange; the latter were recognizable as the breed of young executives and scientists imported by Taylor Industries and the Warren Company; transplanted, degree-bearing men from distant universities who were specialists in electronics, economics, marketing, sociology, agronomy, plant physiology, engineering and administration. Permanent and transient employees in slim Continental suits not unlike that of Polk's, who spoke in terms and accents foreign to native ears; clannish at lunch, parties, the country club and Marina; standoffish, yet politely careful not to offend local traditions and customs. Corey's uniform attracted the attention of a number of men who came up to greet and welcome him home, among them a member of the City Council; and Paul Corbin, who asked how he was enjoying his new car; men of his father's generation and a few of his own. After several greetings were exchanged, he heard Polk saying, "—and with this heat spell hanging on, you're liable to see a little excitement around here before it cools off."

"Polk, I've had just about all the excitement I want to see for a long time. Besides, I don't understand what's going on. We've never had that much of a problem here before."

"Boy, you've been away too long. In the past two years, they've gotten pushy as hell, screaming for more welfare handouts, an end to the poverty they themselves created, wanting niggers on the jury, even on the bench, for God's sake. Let 'em, they'll push us to hell out of the city. We give an inch, they want a yard. Our front yard. Always crying for more, no matter how much they get."

"Well, you've got to admit there's a hell of a lot of room for improvement, that there is a Constitution that guarantees—"

"Oh, come off it, Corey. Don't wave the flag in my face. They want full equality, but they want it on a silver platter without doing a goddamned thing to earn it. You know it can't work that way."

"Not unless people give it a chance to work. And you might be surprised to know I've seen it work when all things were equal."

"Where?"

"In Viet Nam."

Disdainfully, "Oh. The Army. By force of regulations. You don't call that *working,* for God's sake, having it rammed down your throat, do you?"

There was no point, at the moment and in a hostile environment, in trying to convince Polk. The bar and waiting room were crowding up with more patrons. "Looks like you

351

could stand a few more restaurants, judging from this mob," Corey observed.

"Private eating clubs, yes. Nobody wants to open a public restaurant. First customers they'd get would be nigger integrationists trying to christen the place, just for the hell of it." Polk's voice was abrasive to Corey's ears and he showed it in his own tone.

"Polk, I don't get it. You were never a red hot white-sheeter before. What's happened?"

Polk studied Corey quietly over the rim of his glass, eyes narrowed slightly, his mouth unsmiling. "I guess you *have* been away too long, old son. Back in school, I felt the way you do, but you get to where you can take only so much of it. We used to feel, hell, let a few in and lose 'em in the crowd, they'll drop out from loneliness. Okay, let 'em ride anywhere they please on the buses. A lot of shops opened up to 'em and never did make up what they lost in white customers. We integrated the schools and it didn't amount to a hill of beans after a while. But, goddamn it, when school's out and they start crowding in everywhere else, taking white men's jobs, trying to move into elective offices, live next door to you—"

"And marry our sisters?"

Polk ignored the ancient jibe. "—that's when you go looking for that white sheet yourself. Time was we all got along fine, as long as they kept in their place, but then they started this goddamned pushing and crowding us, hollering for black power. Look around you next time you walk the streets. They don't even walk the same any more, they march. You stand in their way, they'd just as soon spit in your eye, knock you to one side."

"After four hundred years of slavery and a hundred of humiliation, can we expect much less?" Corey asked.

"Don't you start swallowing that propaganda bullshit, Corey. They're like the goddam unions when they started to move in some years ago. They came in smiling, bowing and scraping, asking just to get a foot in the door. As soon as they got that much, they began to crowd in until they took over and just about shoved management out the back door—"

"I think that's an over-exaggeration, Polk."

"You think so? Biggest mistake ever made was letting 'em in in the first place. We can't keep giving in to everybody who wants what somebody else worked damned hard to get. There's no end to it. Let me tell you, Corey, if these niggers try to break out around here, you're going to see the god-damnedest—"

They heard "Mr. Holderby's table" announced on the paging system and carried their drinks to a table for two in the main dining room, ordered their meal and another drink. When Corey tried to reintroduce the subject that had been interrupted, Polk flashed his impish grin and said, "Forget it. You'll change your attitude when you see it for yourself. We've got other things to talk about. Hey, you in for a piece of this crazy market?"

"Whatever it is, Dad's been keeping an eye on it for me. He doesn't seem to be too concerned about it, so I'm not. I suppose that sooner or later I'll take over my own portfolio."

"He's right. The market is kind of crazy right now, but stocks are paying their regular dividends despite the drop in the averages. Nobody knows where the interest rate will be tomorrow. Gross national product is up and a lot of people are taking some profits and there's a normal leveling off, but the trading volume has been spectacular. I'll be glad to look over your portfolio any time and give it my personal attention and the benefit of my vast and expert knowledge."

"Thanks, Polk. I'll keep it foremost in my mind."

"Any time. What about now? What can I do to help brighten your combat-hardened life? You ready to try out the hometown fleshpots? Tell you, there've been some right nice additions—"

Corey grinned. "Ad Cameron hinted that you were sort of settling down into respectability."

"As far as my job is concerned, naturally, but I haven't stopped living or taken any chastity vows. Did he tell you Paula's back in town?"

Reservedly, "Yes."

"He tell you she got married in New York?"

"Yes—"

"And divorced?"

"Yes."

"Well—" Some of the steam seemed to have gone out of Polk, late with his news. "She's got a shop of her own in the Mall, doing a big job with the younger crowd. Lives in an apartment over the shop. Listen. She's having a crowd over Saturday night. How about I call her and set it up—"

"I—no, I'd rather you didn't, Polk," Corey said evasively. "I've got her on my list of calls to make. If she asks me, fine."

"If? Sure she will. Hell, you and Paula had a good thing going in Athens, didn't you?"

Aware suddenly that this was something more than casual conversation now, suspicious that Polk was trying to elicit

353

information about which he seemed uncertain, Corey said, "It's no secret that we were friends, if that's what you mean by 'a good thing going.' "

"Ah, come off it, old son. This is Polk you're talking to."

"Polk, that's a rather slimy thing to imply, isn't it? I had other friends besides Paula, so did you. If I remember, you were pretty strong with her for a while, weren't you?"

"After you and she broke off, yes." More soberly now, "Matter of fact, I still am."

So the reason was out in the open now. "Seriously?"

"You could call it that. Only thing is, I don't know how serious it is with Paula. Maybe it was being married to Bob Bennett. It didn't work out between them. Lasted only six months. Once burned—"

"It happens, Polk, but doesn't always leave permanent scars."

"Maybe." Polk's mood changed again, just as suddenly. "You see Drew Warren yet?"

"No. I talked with her for a few minutes this morning. Have you seen her lately?"

"I don't think anybody has. Keeps pretty much to herself out at Brookhill. Rumors, though—"

"What kind of rumors?"

"Well—that she's been doing some heavy drinking. Not in public, of course. She came home from Europe not long after you left and had some kind of problem. Nervous breakdown or something, alcohol maybe, nobody knows for sure. Her old man was a drinker—"

"Where did the rumors come from?"

"Hell, you know how it is around here, Corey. Part-time nigger help, one of Doc Ballard's nurses shooting her mouth off. You can't keep much quiet in a town like this, particularly about somebody like the Warrens. I hear that Old Anderson is about to go. Everybody's waiting to see which way Theodore's going to jump—"

Admitting to himself that this much, at least, was true, Corey felt a deep revulsion sweep through him. "I'm just as sure there isn't a damned thing to the gossip about Drew," he said. "I think I'd have caught it, even over the phone."

"Sure. As I said, it's only rumor." At that moment, Louis came to the table and handed Corey an elegantly printed glossy card, his membership in Marco's Dining Club. Corey thanked him and pocketed the card. Polk said, "Time a working man got back to his job, old son. You want me to stake out a date for you for Saturday night?"

"No, thanks, Polk. I think I'd rather look the field over first, if you don't mind."

The waiter brought the check and Polk signed it. "I've missed you like all hell, Corey," Polk said on the way out. "You know, I got called up after you left, but they turned me down on eyesight. Sometimes, I used to wish I were with you over there." There was a poignant sincerity in Polk's words and Corey felt a sudden sense of inadequacy; or perhaps guilt, over his sexual reunion with Paula, now less than twenty-four hours old.

"Thanks for the lunch, Polk. We'll do it again soon."

"My pleasure, old son."

Leaving Polk at Archer & Moseley, Corey walked back to Weinstock's parking lot, pondering over the rumor of Drew's drinking; over Polk's declared attachment to Paula; and that Paula, in bringing him up to date on their mutual friends and acquaintances, had mentioned Polk's name but once, and accidentally.

And again, he realized that time had indeed brought changes; and with it, a gap he might not be able to bridge.

5

On his way to Brookhill. Remembering. Trying to visualize Drew as he had last seen her, a not comfortable picture. Tear-filled eyes, mourning for Bruce, inconsolable. Ashen-faced, incredibly lovely even in grief, hardly aware of anyone or anything about her, living in a fenced-in, walled-up cell of her own. Anderson, bowed in his own sadness. Theodore, graven-imaged, escaping to his own room and the solitude of his personal hell. Dr. Ballard, more concerned with Anderson than with Drew. ("She's young and healthy. She'll come out of it.")

Leona, weeping for Bruce and perhaps for her son, Cord, a helicopter gunner just arrived in Viet Nam. Shad, walking around disconsolate, immersed in the tragedy that surrounded him.

And with Drew, two weeks later, as she slumped in a brocaded chair in her own sitting room, looking so tiny, white-knuckled hands clenched tightly in her lap. Wanting so much to comfort her, unable to penetrate the wall of wretchedness that enclosed her. "Drew—"

She continued to stare down at her clenched hands. "Drew, won't you talk to me—"

Looking up for a brief moment, eyes brimming, looking away. "I know you feel it, too, Corey. Bruce was so fond of you. You were his friend."

"I wanted to be. I tried to be."

"Oh, Corey." She put the damp handkerchief to her eyes and he took a larger one from his breast pocket and handed it to her. "I don't know—I can't stand it. We were so close. I loved him so—"

"I know, Drew. You meant everything to him."

"How can a thing like this—happen? So much to live for —his whole life ahead—all thrown away uselessly—without reason—for a col—colored girl—married—pregnant—"

"Drew, it can't matter any more, the why, the how. It happened and it's over. You've got to accept it, get over it."

Flashing a pained look at him. "I'll never get over it. Never."

And the last time, the day before he returned to the University. Her face hollow-cheeked from loss of appetite and sleep, face strained, nervously twisting her handkerchief. "I've got to get back to Athens, Drew."

"I understand, Corey."

"I'll write, come up the first weekend after I get caught up. I'm two weeks overdue—"

"I know. It was kind of you to stay. Thank you."

"Don't thank me. I wanted to." Then, "Would you come down to Athens for a weekend soon, Drew?"

"I couldn't—I wouldn't want to leave Gran—he needs me."

"Yes. Well—I'll try to get up soon."

"Don't neglect your work, Corey. This is your last year—"

Then, less than a month later, the brief note telling him she was going to Europe. The few cards from abroad, each from another capital, none with a return address. No indication when, or even if, she would return. Her summer spent partly in Switzerland, then a card from Paris telling him she was leaving on a Mediterranean cruise with a group of friends. No more cards. A letter, brief, when he was wounded.

Alone in Laurelton that summer with Kenneth abroad on business, devoting his time to preparing for and taking his bar exams. And in September, having passed the bar, deciding to take his Army service. Army. Infantry. OCS. Viet Nam. Angrily indifferent to the news of Drew's eventual return to Brookhill. Answering her indifference with indifference of his own, yet longing for her.

The entrance to Brookhill came up on his right and he turned into the open driveway. Moments later, he pulled up in front of the broad steps. A strange young Negro girl, immaculately dressed in black with a small white apron, opened the door.

356

"Miss Warren, please," Corey said. "Mr. Corey Armour."

"Miss Warren is expecting you, sir. Will you please step in? I'll tell Miss Warren you're here."

He waited in the large formal living room with its old, finely carved mantel and French mirror, yellowed with age now; two Flemish tapestries hanging on either side of it. On its glistening parquet floor, a 19th-century Persian rug.

Corey was standing in front of a small cabinet of carved ivory figurines when he heard Drew's heels on the bare portion of the floor. He turned and his first impression was that this was Drew Warren as he remembered her, smiling, both hands extended, walking gracefully toward him. Her dress was a simple sheath that hung from her shoulders and ended two inches above her kneecaps, covering, at the same time revealing, her magnificently contoured body and flashing legs. There was an intangible air of shyness in her manner and expression, at once warm and cool, and as she drew closer he noticed the shadows that gave the illusion of added depth to her eyes and accented the hollows of her cheeks. She seemed tired, under strain, examining his face and finding it difficult to place him in his natural place.

When she spoke finally, her voice sounded lower and huskier than he remembered it. "Hello, Corey. How nice to see you again."

The desire to sweep her into his arms was overwhelming, but he detected a certain reticence in her and waited. As his hands clasped hers. Drew halted, leaned forward slightly and offered her cheek, which he brushed lightly with his lips. "And wonderful to see you, Drew."

Simultaneously, they said, "It's been a long time," and burst into laughter together, somewhat relieving what was becoming a moment of awkwardness. Then Drew said, "Shall we go up to the smaller sitting room? I feel lost in this—barn."

Corey was at once conscious of the odor of alcohol on her breath and, as he mounted the stairs beside her, thought it would not be easy, as it had been with Paula, to pick up where they had left off three years before. In the second-floor sitting room, they sat in facing chairs across a low marble-topped coffee table which was at right angles to the fireplace.

"Would you like a drink, Corey?" Drew asked.

"Not at the moment, thanks, but don't let me stop you—"

"No." She said it quickly, too decisively, then, "You look absolutely marvelous, Corey. Your shoulders are broader—"

"The uniform has a lot to do with it. I'll have to put up

357

with it for a few more days. Tell me about you, Drew. I've heard so little—"

She bit her lower lip. "I'm sorry about not writing. I've always been a notoriously poor correspondent, you know, and there was really so little to say. I did send some cards and wrote when we received word you'd been wounded—"

"I remember. And I understand, Drew. So much had happened in so short a time." He felt even more strongly now that he could not take her back to the night of their return from Atlanta and the weeks that followed immediately after. If it came at all, it must come from her. "And the Viet Cong were keeping us pretty busy."

"It must have been horrible—"

"All wars must be. Let's not talk about Viet Nam. I'd rather catch up first. And my breath, now that I've seen you."

The implied flattery drew a quick flash of a smile, her head thrown up and back, showing the confidence of a flawlessly beautiful woman who can afford the luxury of simplicity. "I hardly know where to begin," she said. "You know about Gran—"

"Yes."

Matter-of-factly now, "One can't expect to hold on forever to those one loves. I'm getting used to the idea of parting with— Anyway, Gran, poor thing, is old. We had a little celebration on his birthday, the 19th of last month. Gran, the nurse, Dr. Ballard and I. It wasn't very cheerful." She gave a little sigh and said, "It's all so strange. He's lived for just eleven years short of a whole century and I've only known him for about a quarter of that. I've often wished I were much older so I could have known him longer, when he was younger—"

The words ran on, almost compulsively. No mention of Bruce or Theodore, too close to the first, too distant from the other. And then, surprisingly, she spoke of the mother she had been too young to remember, the first time he had ever heard her speak of Louise Warren at length. "—and when I got to Rome," he heard her saying, "I tried to get in touch with her. She is the Countess di Edda now. I went to her home, but she and her husband were in Venice. In Venice, I was told they were spending several weeks at their home in Santa Marguerita. I drove there, but when I arrived, their houseman told me they were out. I came back the next day and a maid told me they had left for Nice. So I gave up and returned to Rome. Later on, in Paris, I joined some friends for a yachting trip among the Greek islands—"

How curious, Corey thought, that her words were without depth or feeling, an almost mechanical recitation in which she had become detached from the story, as if it were about someone other than herself, seeking to understand it as she told it, groping in a dark cavern, trying to find a way out. And then she stopped abruptly, checking herself, once again alert. "That's enough about me, Corey. What about you? I'm sure you must have a million plans." She was smiling, but there was little animation in her smile.

"Hardly. Not more than one or two at the most."

"Are you—going to stay in Laurelton?"

"For the time being, if something I have in mind works out."

Her forehead wrinkled slightly. "What about law? You did pass the bar exams, didn't you?"

"Yes, just before I went into the Army."

"Then—" Puzzled, "I'm sure there is a place waiting for you in the Company's legal department."

"I've already had that offered me by Dad, but I haven't come to any decision yet."

"Or in the New York office if you don't want to stay here."

"Or New York. I've one other thing I want to look into before I commit myself."

"Somehow, I never imagined there would be any question —" Drew began, when the interruption came.

"Excuse me, Miss Warren." It was the maid who had admitted him half an hour before.

"Yes, Sue-Ann."

"Mr. Anderson asked if he could see Mr. Armour, Miss Warren."

Drew turned to Corey. "I was with Gran when Sue-Ann told me you were here. Would you mind—?"

"Of course not. I'd like very much to see him," Corey said.

Nor, Corey thought as he looked down on Anderson Warren's thin, wrinkled face, had he been prepared for this. The Anderson Warren of even a little over three years ago, despite his advancing age, had been erect, his face burned deeply by the sun, full-fleshed and hearty. Now, he seemed small and shriveled, his face gray and pinched beneath a network of fine lines that resembled a relief map. Everything around him seemed massively oversized: the bed, furniture, even the pillows, the pajama jacket that hung loosely from his shrunken form. His coloring was sallow, the whites of his eyes discolored, his mouth a gaping cave of near emptiness, thin strands of white hair standing away from his head, revealing the bony structure of his skull.

When Corey entered the room he was sitting up in bed, resting against two large pillows. Beside the bed, a nurse sat in a chair, reading. She rose at once, nodded, and went out on the veranda, taking a small transistor radio with her. Anderson Warren smiled and reached for Corey's hand with a fragile, bony claw. "You've grown a lot," he said. "If I'd seen you on the street, I don't think I'd've known you."

"I'm sure you would if I were in civilian clothes, sir. I'm delighted to see you again."

"Welcome home, son. Sit down, sit down. You, too, Drew."

"If you'll excuse me for a few minutes, I'll send Sue-Ann up with something cold to drink," Drew said. "Besides, I know you'll be talking about the war and I don't particularly want to hear about it." To Corey, "Don't go away before I come back."

"I won't."

The war talk was held to a minimum, broken by the arrival of Sue-Ann with a clinking pitcher of iced lemonade. When she left Anderson said, "Bright as a shiny penny, Sue-Ann. She's Leona's niece. Brother works on the place, too. Kind of makes up for the loss of Cord in a little way. Ah. This old house is too much for Shad and Leona. Always was, no matter how many we had working around here." He sighed deeply. "Cleo and I, we always had an idea there'd be at least a couple dozen grandchildren and greatgrandchildren to fill it." Anderson's trembling hand raised the glass to his thin lips for a sip, then handed it to Corey to place on the night stand. "You get to see Leona's boy over there, Corey?" the old man asked.

"Several times. Cord was one of the best crew chiefs and gunners in his helicopter squadron. His pilot and crew thought the world of him."

"You tell that to his papa and mama?"

"I haven't seen them yet, but I intend to before I leave."

"You tell 'em. Do 'em a lot more good to hear it from somebody they know, who knew him, instead of some stranger come down from Washington, reading it off a piece of paper."

"Did Lyle Emerson come out to see them?"

"The fellow Cord saved? He came out. Tell me he cried like they were his own close kin. Blamed himself for it, but Shad and Leona, they understood. Told him it was the good Lord's doin', and not to try to carry the burden on himself. Good man."

360

"The best."

"Well, what about you, son? Goin' into the Company? We can always make room for a smart young lawyer."

"Not at the moment, sir. I've got something I want to try before I come to any decision."

"Anything you need help with?"

"I don't think so, thanks. It's something I have to work out on my own."

"Ah, that's the best, on your own. No bigger satisfaction in life. Corey?"

"Sir?"

"Do something for an old man?"

"Anything I can."

Anderson twisted his thin body around and Corey lent an arm to help him sit up more erectly in bed, then lie back against the pillows, exhausted by the effort. He took several deep breaths then said, "I don't have any more problems to face before I go, Corey. The business—well, what happens there will happen, no matter what. That's out of my hands now." He paused and took another deep breath. "It's Drew." He turned pale, watery eyes on Corey. "Ever since Bruce died, she's been lost. I've tried to reach her, but there's too big a span between us for her to get any comfort from me.

"Theodore, he's always had too many of his own problems to get close to his own children, recognize that they had needs, too. I guess you've been as close to Bruce and Drew as anybody, closer than most—"

His words hung there as though waiting for an answer. "We were—very good friends," Corey said simply.

Anderson nodded. "I know. She'll need somebody. I'd like to feel that when I go, she'll have—somebody close to her—will be around if she needs—" His voice broke, but the plea in those few words made further effort unnecessary.

"I'll be here, sir, if she wants or needs me."

"She will. She's been lonely ever since we buried him. She couldn't stand it here without him. Ran off to Europe and stayed away over a year, running. Came back when there wasn't any place left to run to, half alive. It was a terrible thing to see. Even now, she hardly leaves the place, just moons around—"

"I'll try, Gran," Corey said, trying to bring the conversation to an end.

"She needs a friend, Corey, somebody she can trust. She'll have other problems, complicated ones. People will always be after her, for good or evil, and without somebody

361

to lean on, she'll be confused. I don't want her running—
like her father—been too damn much running in this family. She'll have a lot to stand up to—legal matters—personal
things—this place." A pause. "She always liked you, son—"

"You're overtaxing yourself, Gran."

Anderson smiled wearily. "Every time I get to the nub
and hub of something, somebody's always telling me I'm
overdoing or overtaxing." He put out a hand and grasped
Corey's arm. "All right, son, I am a mite tired now, but I'm
glad I got to speak my piece to you. It relieves me a lot—"

"I promise you, Gran, I'll be here when and if Drew
needs me."

"Thank you. That's all I'm asking."

Corey saw Leona alone in the kitchen. Tears sprang into
her eyes at the sight of him in uniform and he comforted
her by relating his few meetings with Cord in Saigon, the
few meals they had shared.

"You et with him at the same table, you and Cord, Mist'
Corey?" she asked open-eyed.

"Of course, Leona. It's a lot different in Viet Nam than it
is here."

"No wonder he write how much he like it there. Shad an'
me, we couldn't understand how a good boy like Cord,
raised to believe in God, could like bein' where people were
gettin' killed, Cord doin' some of the killin' himself, when
he useta cry at the sight of a dog killin' a fox, a rabbit in a
trap—"

"It wasn't the killing, Leona, believe me. Very few men
enjoy seeing others die, even an enemy. The thing Cord
liked was the freedom he found in the Army, where what
counts most is the kind of man you are."

"Tell me again what he said, what his pilot man say
about him. Mist' Emerson, he tellin' us lots of fine things,
poor man, but he cry so when he talk about it."

Shad came in then, overalled, red earth clinging to his
hands, face wet with sweat, refusing to take Corey's hand.
"'Scuse me, Mist' Corey, 'til I wash up an' change into
clean clothes, please. Gardener, he sick today."

They talked. Sue-Ann came in and hovered nearby, hanging on to every word, until Drew came in to take him away.
"Thank you for talking to Gran, Corey," she said. "It
meant so much to him. He's sleeping quietly now."

They walked through the house toward the front veranda
and down the steps to his car, nothing passing between
them until he opened the door on the driver's side. For a
moment, he looked down over the carefully tended garden,

the rows of majestic oaks, across the fields they had ridden together. To his right, the pool and tennis courts, nets down. Beyond, the stable with its doors closed. No sign of dogs, no grazing horses or cows. Not another human in sight. Brookhill, he felt, was dying with Anderson Warren. When they placed him in his crypt beside Cleo, how long before the two remaining Warrens would abandon Brookhill and its memories; except for occasional visits to the mausoleum and the decaying house?

"Drew?"

"What, Corey?"

"I didn't ask about your plans."

Her face turned away from him, "I haven't any. I've stopped making plans."

"No one ever stops making plans," he said.

"They do when there's nothing to plan for. What happens will happen, plans or not. Someone once said the best plan is to live one day at a time."

"That's fatalism, a philosophy for the old, the tired, and those involved in a war."

"I haven't found a better one to replace it."

"Drew, what is it?"

"What is what?"

"This change in you."

"We all change, Corey. Time, circumstances—"

He took her by her arms and turned her toward him. "Drew, stop talking nonsense," he said firmly. "You're not old enough to be through with living. We had something together once, you and I. How can an accident that happened to someone else, no matter who, have destroyed it? How?"

She pulled out of his grasp. "I said time and circumstances change people, Corey. I'm not the same Drew Warren you knew—"

"Who once said she loved me?"

"That was another time, the circumstances were different—"

"Because Bruce died?"

"I don't want to talk about it."

"What about me, Drew?"

"I—I don't know, Corey. I'm confused. Please don't be angry." Tears were welling up in her eyes as she swung around to face him again. "Whatever it was, I can't—couldn't—" She turned suddenly and ran up the steps and into the house. For a moment he stood looking into the open doorway, then got into the car and drove home.

At the 12th Precinct in West Laurelton, Inspector Peter La-Salle and Police Surgeon Dr. Thomas Gorman walked toward the interrogation room. Inside, Captain Jim Price, wearing a frown of deep concern, sat at one end of the table, bracketed by Officers Lloyd Carr and John Harper. Price tapped a long, yellow pencil against the edge of the table. Carr, about 24, sat stiffly in a wooden chair, fingers tightly interlocked, showing his obvious nervousness. Harper, with twelve years on the force, lounged nonchalantly in his chair, one leg crossed over the other, smoking a cigarette.

Grouped at the opposite end of the table in a semicircle of chairs were Dr. Royal Betts, the Reverend Amos Hart, of the African-Zion Baptist Church, two irate fathers and one mother, who muttered angrily under her breath, this to the visible annoyance of Betts and Hart. All but the police officers were Negroes.

As LaSalle and Gorman entered the room, Captain Price lifted a receiver and spoke into it. LaSalle was shaking hands with Hart and Betts, whom he knew, then with the two male parents. The woman looked away and refused his extended hand.

A moment later, the door opened and a Negro officer ushered in three youngsters, then backed out. The boys were 14, 16, and 17 years old and wore what appeared to be a uniform of sorts; tight blue denim pants, short-sleeve dark blue T-shirts, canvas tennis sneakers. The older boy's upper left arm had a small bandage on it. The two older boys showed open and sullen defiance and contempt for the gathering, but the 14-year-old was struck dumb at the sight of his father. His eyes opened wide and his lips trembled in fear, near tears, as the three moved hesitatingly across the room toward their parents. The woman stood up and slapped the 16-year-old boy across his face as hard as she could with an open hand.

Dr. Gorman stepped in between them, shielding the boy. "Mrs. Ransom," he said, "the charges of brutality here are against these two officers. You don't want the same charge applied to you, do you?"

"He ain' no good," Mrs. Ransom raged angrily, "no damn good at all. He like his papa. I don' see him twixt one day an' the nex'. He taken every cent he c'n find or steal from me, spend it on girls. All's he think of is girls. He on'y sixteen an'—"

Reverend Hart tried to pacify her, but she shook him off. Dr. Betts talked to her sternly and on his threat to have her expelled from the room, she slumped dejectedly in her chair, glaring balefully at her son, seeming to accept the charges against him, willing to punish him herself, yet here to press charges of brutality against the two white arresting officers. Her son returned her stare with angry disdain. When a police photographer entered the room, Mrs. Ransom sat up, pointing at the complicated equipment he carried.

"What for he in here?" she demanded in alarm.

LaSalle said, "Let me explain, Mrs. Ransom, gentlemen. This is not a hearing to establish the guilt or innocence of your sons. That hearing will be held later by the juvenile authorities. Two officers have been accused by you and these two gentlemen of unnecessary violence while arresting your sons for an alleged crime—"

"They always beatin' Nigra boys," Mrs. Ransom declared emphatically.

"Which is what we are going to try to determine here. Dr. Betts and Dr. Gorman will take the boys into the next room. The boys will strip down to their skins and be examined for any marks of violence and their conditions generally. Any parent and Reverend Hart may, if he wishes, be present If any bruises or other marks of alleged brutality are found, they will be photographed for evidence, and used in a court of law to prosecute the officers—"

"Your courts, your laws," one father charged.

"And yours, Mr. Foster," LaSalle said quietly.

" 'Till we got Nigra judges, it don't mean nothin'," the other father interjected.

"That is not within the province of the police, Mr. Rogers," LaSalle said. "Are you agreed on the procedure I have outlined?"

"We are," Amos Hart said before anyone else could speak. To the parents, he added, "These gentlemen are doing their best to satisfy us on your charges. If you obstruct them, I can't stay here with you."

"You ain't talkin' for me, Rev'ren'," Mrs. Ransom said.

"I'm not speaking for anyone but myself, Mrs. Ransom," Hart replied. "Mr. Foster and Mr. Rogers and Dr. Betts asked me to be present as an observer. Inspector LaSalle agreed. What he proposes is honest and fair to everyone, in my opinion. How about you, Dr. Betts?"

"I agree," the doctor said with deepening impatience. "We're wasting time that I can put to much better use."

"Then I'd suggest we get on with it," LaSalle replied.

Foster and Rogers nodded. Mrs. Ransom, in her perverse mood, said, "My boy don' need no 'zamination. All's he need is for me to wear his backside thin with a broom handle."

The doctors, parents, LaSalle and Captain Price went into the next room with the three boys. The two officers remained in the interrogation room, smoking. "Take it easy, kid," Harper said.

"Jesus, John, if one of those kids has an earlier bruise on him somewhere, we're dead."

Harper laughed lightly. "Don't worry. Doc Gorman can tell an old bruise from a new one. Hell, the only mark we put on them is the little scratch on the Rogers kid's arm."

"I'd still like to be in there. Don't you—?"

"Hell, no. I don't want to bust out laughing when Gorman and that coon doctor find the needle marks on the Foster and Rogers kids "

"Needle marks?"

"Sure. Old and new ones. I spotted 'em when I put the flashlight on 'em last night. Junkies. Mugging to get money to pay one of Banjo's goddamned pushers."

"I didn't see—"

"You'll catch on, Lloyd. First chance you get with a pickup, you roll up his sleeves and look for the wormholes. On a nigger, they'll be harder to find. Hell, even in this light nobody saw 'em, but Gorman will find 'em. So will the nigger doctor."

"Jesus, just kids!"

"Kids, my ass, buddy. No such thing as a kid when he's hopped up and carrying a switchblade or a zip gun. Just remember, a fix makes a man out of a kid in five minutes. Don't ever forget it if you want to see your wife at the end of your watch." Harper winked over his grin. "Relax. This is today's going price for picking up a mugger, junkie or a black power juvey. Police brutality. Shit."

The examination had taken less than twenty minutes. When the adult group emerged, Amos Hart was apologizing to LaSalle for the inconvenience the police had been put to. The elder Rogers and Foster were stonily silent and eager to leave. Mrs. Ransom was saying, "—an' you don' slap the fear of God into their hides, 'at's what comes of it; dope, robbin', dope, prison, dope, murder—"

"Can we go now?" Foster asked.

366

"Yes, sir," LaSalle replied softly. "I'm sorry we'll have to detain the boys for further questioning—"

The five Negroes turned and went out. Harper stood up and said, "How about it, Captain?"

Price said, "You're clear. The kids admitted it was a hoax in order to take the sting out of the charges."

"What about the wormholes?"

"The two older boys admitted mainlining, but wouldn't tell where they've been getting it. The younger boy is on marijuana."

"Niggers," Harper sniffed with contempt.

LaSalle turned on him abruptly. "Harper, I don't ever want to hear you use that word again. It is in direct violation of a departmental order and you'll draw a suspension without pay for it."

"Yes, sir."

"It might also interest you to know that our statistics for white addicts have been on the increase as well, young people from good middle- and upper-class families. Keep that in mind."

"Yes, sir."

"You and Officer Carr are excused now."

Both men said, "Thank you, sir," and left. The young Negro officer who had brought the boys into the room reentered and Price nodded his head in the direction of the examination room.

In Dr. Royal Betts' Pontiac sedan, Amos Hart turned to the three passengers on the back seat and said sternly, "I hope you're satisfied with what you-all heard and saw. Nobody laid a hand on any of your boys except to arrest them during a holdup, and you can't blame the police for that. Sister Ransom, who told you the police beat up your Eli unnecessarily?"

Rose Ransom said, "Miz Clark, she tellen me the yellin' an' scufflin' waken her up an' she seen it from her window, they beatin' Eli an' Davey an' Chick something awful."

"And you, Linus?"

"Miz Ransom tole me," Linus Rogers replied. "An' I tole Andy Foster, then we all went to see you, Reveren'."

"The way I got it from you three, it was as though you were there and saw it yourselves. So I got riled up and got Dr. Betts to go with us to examine the boys and we saw and we heard and we know the truth now, don't we?"

No one answered.

"All right. Don't you be faulting me when I bring this up in church on Sunday, and I want to see you three there. I

367

know I'll be called an Uncle Tom or a hanky-head for sid-ing with the police against three Negro boys, but being Negro doesn't automatically make us right all the time. I'll fight brutality, evil and wrong all day and all night, but I don't like to be made a fool of by prejudiced people, black or white.

"Your problems with your children are no different than anybody else's. You let 'em run wild, you don't even try to exercise any control over 'em, they get in trouble and you try to throw the blame on everybody but yourselves. You turn 'em loose and expect the church and school to raise them properly. We try to do our part, but unless you do yours, it won't work."

"I can't watch Eli an' work all day, too, Revern'," Rose Ransom whined.

"If you'd taken hold of him from the first, maybe he'd be spending most of his time after school at the R-V Center instead of in poolrooms or roaming the streets at night. My Lord, dope and marijuana. You, too, Andrew, and you, Linus. Both of you work and your wives don't. What's your excuse?"

Both men shook their heads, eyes unable to meet Hart's. "I don' know, Amos," Foster said. "I jus' don' know. I beat the livin' sh—excuse me—I beat him, I tellen him, Sarah do the same, it don' he'p none. A beatin', it don' mean nothin', it wear off an' he's out looking aroun' for trouble to git into, hookin' school, stayin' away three-four days at a time, cat-tin' around', gettin' into somethin'. Beats me."

"Maybe if you'd done more talking a long time ago and set better examples for your boys, you wouldn't be needing to beat them and drive them out into the streets. The church, the schools, can't do anything without you, and blaming white people for your own shortcomings won't help one bit. The home is where it's got to start from a child's first day, but you can't drink or ruckus around and expect him not to see and do the same."

"Yeah," Rose Ransom agreed. "Shuh," Linus Rogers added. "Amen," Andrew Foster nodded

Amos Hart and Dr. Betts sighed resignedly.

CHAPTER III

1

Kenneth Armour's father, Lewis, and grandfather, Marcus, had paved the way toward his career as a lawyer long before he was born. Judge Marcus Armour, whose brilliant legal mind, honesty and integrity had gained him much public prominence, was rewarded with an appointment to the State Supreme Court where he became Chief Justice, to remain there until he died. Marcus' son, Lewis, no less brilliant than his father, was equally a defender of human and civil rights, a strong champion of equal justice for all, long before it became a popular attitude to adopt. His crisp, outspoken opinions and decisions sparkled with honest wit and irony and were treasured in the memories of many jurists and attorneys, frequently dusted off by newspaper editorialists seeking to make a particularly pertinent legal point. Eventually, Lewis was elevated to the Court of Appeals where he became its ranking member until his death. At the time, Kenneth was a junior at the University

If honesty, integrity and dedication to their chosen profession brought lasting honors to Marcus and Lewis Armour, it had produced little wealth to be inherited by Kenneth. Both jurists had often refused tempting investment suggestions and offers made them by good friends, fearing such favors might some day place them in embarrassingly unethical positions, subject to charges of conflict of interests. Instead, they invested their money in the soaring stock market and during the 20s, became "paper millionaires." Marcus died in 1928, a paper millionaire, but unfortunately, the crash of 1929 wiped Lewis out completely and Kenneth, after his father's death the following year, found himself the owner of a small house, another small piece of commercial property where his father and grandfather had practiced law before moving to Atlanta, and very little else; in fact, hardly enough to pay the taxes due or his way through his first year of law school.

Thereafter, Kenneth waited tables, tutored, took Saturday selling jobs, and delivered whiskey for a local bootlegger. When a campus cop picked him up while delivering a Saturday night cargo to a fraternity house, he believed this was the end of his career. However, after he was questioned by the Dean of Men, the matter was quietly brought to the attention of a jurist friend of both Lewis and Marcus who, in turn, brought the case to the attention of Anderson Warren. Anderson turned the matter over to his personnel director who found that a recent addition to the Warren executive staff, a man from Gainesville with a family, was in need of a house. The executive was persuaded to rent the Armour house and Kenneth's financial plight became less threatening, enabling him to sever his connection with his bootlegger source. Also, Anderson later engaged Kenneth as a tutor for Theodore Warren, who was in scholastic difficulties, for a generous fee.

Tutoring Theodore Warren was a boring necessity to Kenneth, a task that called on his ingenuity to provide unorthodox means to insure that Theodore would graduate with a bare average grade. Meanwhile, living with the young tobacco heir in his rented house in Athens, Kenneth became a member of Theodore's regular poker sessions and found it no great feat, with a little application, to win enough money each week to add a few luxuries to ease his burdens. There were other benefits; rent and food were free, the supply of cigarettes, liquor and female companionship almost endless. And with their simultaneous graduations, Kenneth and Theodore returned to Laurelton and the close, forced association came to a temporary end.

Kenneth's return to Laurelton had not gone unheralded. As the grandson and son of famous jurists, it was expected that Kenneth would emerge high on the honors list. In this respect, he disappointed no one, graduating No. 1 in his class, a fact duly noted by the statewide press. Later, on passing his bar examinations in that same position, it was generally conceded that he was destined to occupy the seat his grandfather held at the time of his death, if not one on the United States Supreme bench.

Kenneth had much going in his favor. Certainly, he had social status, and with it, a brilliant future in his profession. Added to these credits, he was personally attractive. No athlete, he was nevertheless blessed with height and excellent physical proportions. He exercised with daily regularity. His clothes, however few, were good and fit him properly. He chose them carefully in solid grays, blues and blacks for interchangeability. No browns or tans, which would require shoes, shirts, ties and socks in complementary colors at an added and unnecessary expense.

Kenneth was similarly meticulous in choosing his friends,

370

male and female. He accepted or rejected social invitations
according to their rank of importance and opportunity to
meet someone who could become professionally important
to him later. He turned down offers from several Atlanta
firms, politely declined a job on the Warren legal staff, rejected an offer as junior associate in the office of Tracy
Ellis, who was chief counsel for Taylor Industries and the
Laurelton National Bank; this in the very depressed year of
1933.

Boldly, he reopened the old office on Fuller Avenue in
which Lewis and Marcus had practiced; long unused, but
with a most complete law library. And beneath the faded
sign that read:

ARMOUR & ARMOUR
Counselors-at-Law

he hung his gleaming new shingle with the simple legend

KENNETH ARMOUR
Attorney-at-Law

Kenneth recognized that he had no such noble thoughts
that had endowed Marcus and Lewis with greatness; and
not the slightest intention of beggaring himself in the name
of the Brotherhood of Man. In fact, the state of genteel,
borderline poverty was extremely strong and distasteful in
his mouth. He accepted any and all cases, however small,
which came to him as a natural inheritance to the name Armour, but he insisted on full payment for each service performed, even in small weekly or monthly payments. In
court, he was no less ardent than the Armours who had
preceded him and had left their indelible marks in Laurelton's Hall of Justice before moving on to greater rewards.

Kenneth's first financial break came when a bricklayer
named Cassett was seriously injured by a truck owned by
the Taylor Construction Company. The Taylor attorney,
Tracy Ellis, called on Mrs. Cassett that same evening with a
sheaf of ten-dollar bills that totaled $500, in exchange for a
release from Paul Cassett. In fact, he drove Mrs. Cassett to
the hospital a short while later, only to find that Kenneth
Armour was already at Paul Cassett's bedside. Kenneth, to
Ellis' surprise, was representing the Cassett family. Further,
he was informed by Kenneth, it was now the doctor's opinion that Paul might never walk—or work—again; that the
cost of an operation on his spine, perhaps others to follow,

necessary care, medication and hospitalization, would run into a very considerable amount of money.

With nervous determination, Paul Cassett refused the $500, which looked as big and thick as a sheaf of newly ripened wheat, and as rich. Nor was Ellis later able to convince Kenneth that a settlement out of court, for as much as $2,500, would be to the best interests of all concerned. Kenneth listened and coolly turned down the offer, his mind dwelling on what kind of a picture he could present to a jury in a packed courtroom while he pleaded his father's theory of full and equal justice for his poor client.

Kenneth promptly sued Taylor Construction for $100,000, an outrageous amount for those times, and considering that Paul Cassett had never earned more than $30 a week in his life. The case gained much attention in local legal circles where Kenneth was regarded by some as either stupid, immature, or leaning far too heavily on the reputations established by his father and grandfather. Kenneth remained resolute and the case came to trial.

In the matter of jury selection, Kenneth outmaneuvered Ellis and managed to get six jurors who were themselves working men, married, and with families. For the first day of the trial, only Mrs. Cassett sat beside Kenneth Armour. On the second day, the four Cassett children, ranging in age from two to eight, freshly scrubbed and wearing clean clothes which showed signs of age and neat repairs, were added to the scene. And on the third day, Kenneth played his trump card by having Paul Cassett brought from the Country Hospital on a stretcher, borne by two white-clad attendants and placed on the floor in full view of the jury, to testify on his own behalf, the eyes of his wife and children visibly dimmed with tears.

The jury was out for less than two hours and returned with a verdict of $57,000, the largest such award in the entire history of Cairn County. The *Herald* gave the story the front-page prominence it merited and featured a picture of Kenneth Armour. Tracy Ellis filed a notice of appeal, but Jonas Taylor ordered the appeal withdrawn.

For his share, Kenneth took $19,000, leaving $38,000 for the grateful Cassetts. Notably, Paul Cassett required no further surgery and was up and about, fully recovered, within three months.

Six months and many small cases passed through Kenneth Armour's hands before Opportunity knocked again, this time in the person of Edgar Garnet, a respectable Negro farmer in South Laurelton and a man of more than modest wealth. A quiet, industrious and intelligent man,

Edgar Garnet had for years invested his hard-earned money in small parcels of land that became available from time to time, including some that were now a part of Angeltown's bustling business district along Velie Street and Grand Avenue. In several of his negotiations, Garnet had taken a part ownership in the businesses occupying his properties in lieu of rent, sharing in later profits.

Kenneth's complaint was against the Warren Tobacco Company and alleged that in acquiring numerous tracts of land, it had inadvertently trespassed upon a piece owned by Garnet, and upon which now stood a generous portion of a large building. Implausible as the story had at first seemed, Kenneth first checked the deed carefully and told Garnet to keep quiet about the matter. Next, he thoroughly examined records in the County Land Office. He called in a team of surveyors to verify the legal description as shown by the recorded deed and was satisfied that in some inexplicable manner, an error had been committed, no doubt honestly, but nevertheless clearly a case of trespass.

Kenneth then called on Harvey Makepeace, Anderson Warren's attorney, who at first hooted at the idea, then began making his own inquiries into the matter; only to discover that a discrepancy, made by their civil engineering department, had indeed occurred; a careless clerical transposition of figures from another legal description in putting the original tract of land together from a group of small farms.

Makepeace tried desperately to squirm out of his dilemma, but Kenneth blocked every exit. Eventually, the matter, no small one now, was brought to Anderson Warren's attention. Reluctantly, Warren was forced into an out-of-court settlement with Garnet, which cost the Company ten times the original value of the land. The settlement was made in Warren's office where Anderson had invited Kenneth to lunch with him. The meal was served from the special kitchen next to Warren's private dining room on the top floor of the building and when it was concluded, Anderson lighted a cigarette as Kenneth waited for what he surely guessed was coming.

"I knew your grandfather and father very well, Kenneth," Anderson said, opening the door.

"I know, sir. I've heard them speak of you in most flattering terms."

Warren waved that aside with his cigarette, using it as one would a baton. "Matter of fact, before he moved to Atlanta, Marcus handled some of my law business. Later on Lewis took it over from him until he went down to the city. Now—" Warren paused and Kenneth knew his assumption was correct. "—it looks like there's a third generation to reckon with. Yes, sir. I liked the way you helped out with Theodore. Fact is, I had Harvey make you an offer when you first came back, but you turned him down. Now, you just cost me $20,000 for a skinny piece of dirt I could've bought for less'n $2,000—"

"If," Kenneth interjected, "you hadn't built your building on another man's property first."

"—if my people'd been on their toes like you were, instead of sittin' on their fat rumps. Anyway, what's done is done and I've made it a policy never to look backwards except to profit by an old mistake. It's forgotten. No hard feelings. Damn' waste of time."

"I agree, sir."

"I like what I see in you, Kenneth. Always was impressed with you. How about coming in and joining my law boys?"

"And give up my private practice, sir?"

"In time, hell, son, you'll more than make up anything you lose now, I promise you."

Kenneth's response was immediate. "Your offer is very flattering, sir, but I'm afraid I can't accept."

Warren blinked in surprise. "You figgerin' on a judgeship, too?"

"No, sir I'm planning on remaining in private practice here in Laurelton. I expect to do my financial best as Number One in my own law firm rather than as Number Five on your legal staff."

"Now hold it, son. You don't expect me to run you in over the heads of Harvey Makepeace and the others, do you?"

"No, sir, I wouldn't expect that at all. In fact, I couldn't be a party to any such thought," Kenneth replied with tongue in cheek.

Through eyes that squinted almost to the point of closing, Warren said, "You a loner, son?"

"No, sir. It's simply that I function best when I formulate my own plans and strategies and see that they are executed properly."

"In other words, you want a free hand."

"It amounts to that, Mr. Warren. At least, that's what I'm building toward. A staff organized by me to do things the way I want them done. I'll live by my own successes and die by my own failures, but they'll be mine."

"I see. No use tryin' to talk you out of that, I guess."

"I don't think so, sir." A pause, then, "However—"

"However?" Warren encouraged.

"—I wouldn't be adverse to acting for you on a consulting basis."

"Just what does that mean?"

"That I would retain my own offices and identity and make myself available to you when and if my services were required."

"I see." Warren pushed himself away from the table and stood up. "I'll think on it, Kenneth. Good-bye."

It soon became apparent that the magic of two generations of Armours had been visited upon the third. Other cases found their way to Kenneth's door, mostly civil matters (and a few criminal, in which he was careful to assess his chances for victory before laying his reputation on the block), but in each case, his fee was established by his client's ability to pay. And just as he was selective in his choice of cases, so was he diagnostic and discretionary in his selection of a wife soon after.

2

In his ultraplush office now, Kenneth Armour sat at his desk reading a personal letter from Tom Shelby that had been mailed from Richmond on the day before. He was jotting down a few notes to which he intended to refer in his reply when Shana Pierce, the only person permitted to do so, knocked on the door lightly and entered. As she did, Armour looked up and watched as she walked toward him, a light smile on her face that warmed him with appreciation. His eyes followed her as her shapely legs flashed beneath a knee-length light blue dress, carrying her elegantly contoured body across the room with a fluid grace that never failed to stir him; even after the years they had been together as employer and confidential secretary.

As she reached the desk, his private phone rang. Shana walked behind the desk to the sill-high cabinet and picked up the receiver. "Mr. Armour's office."

"Mr. Kenneth Armour, please. Long distance from Richmond."

"Who is calling, please?"

"Mr. Thomas Shelby."

"One moment." To Kenneth, whose eyes were still upon her, "Tom Shelby, calling from Richmond." He nodded and took the receiver from her. "Tom? Ken here." A pause. "I got it only this morning. As a matter of fact, I was just about to answer—"

He listened for a few moments, his eyes running over Shelby's letter, then, "Well, if you're flying back to New York today— No, the situation is still the same. Yes. Well, Kirk doesn't expect me to push this now, does he?" Another listening pause. "Tom, tell Kirk for me that there isn't anything anyone can do until—well, it happens. I'm sure it can't be much longer. When it does, I'm just as sure that T.W. will come around to the proposal. Let's not nag at it now, Tom. I've been through all that with Kirk a number of times. Yes. Of course. Yes. And my regards to him. Goodbye." He handed the receiver back to Shana, who cradled it. "They're like hounds getting close to the fox, aren't they?" Shana said.

"I honestly think they blame me because the old man isn't dead yet," Kenneth replied.

"Then there's no need to answer his letter?"

"No." He picked up Shelby's letter and tore it into small pieces. "Kirk Dillingham wants him back in New York tonight."

"Ken, do you really think Theodore will give in to Intercon?"

"From what you've already seen and know, do you doubt it? He's never wanted the Company from the very start. The only reason he's sitting in Anderson's chair right now is because his name is Warren and Anderson forced the presidency on him. When the old man goes, Theodore will be free, really free, for the first time in his life. He'll run, and this time, there won't be anything to come back for. That leaves Drew, and there's no reason to believe she would want to hold on to the Company."

"What about Chase Warren? Won't he somehow be involved when his father dies?"

Kenneth frowned at the mention of Chase. "Chase?" he said. "Chase Warren hasn't shown any interest in the Company for years. When he walked out on Anderson to take over the handling of the Vanderkuyl affairs, that finished him here. Anderson may remember him in his will with a cash gift, but I doubt he'll do any more than that. Certainly he won't leave him any stock."

"What about you?"

Kenneth leaned back in his chair and took a deep breath. "Me?"

"I mean as far as the Company is concerned. If Theodore accepts Intercon's offer."

"Part of the deal is that I will go along with it. As president. Dillingham has big plans, Shana. With Intercon money, Warren can expand, pick up several smaller compa-

376

nies, add a dozen new brands to the line, get into the full modernization program we need so badly, the new automated experimental plant—"

"What if Theodore should finally refuse their offer?"

"There are other ways, Shana. It would mean a fight, of course."

"A proxy fight?" Her lips puckered up in distaste.

"Possibly, but I doubt if it will come to that. Some other form of pressure, perhaps."

"That's rather dirty and underhanded, isn't it?"

Kenneth shrugged. "You don't get where Kirk Dillingham is without using pressure where it needs to be applied."

"It *is* a dirty business, isn't it?"

"Shana, once you're involved in big business, you play the game by the rules that were established many years ago, so far back that they've become today's norm. Anderson Warren could tell you more about the men who made the rules back in his heyday, the old barons whose children and grandchildren are most respectable today. You go along or you go your own solitary way."

"It's a pity, isn't it?"

"Depending on where you sit. Look at it from my point of view. If I were to persuade Theodore to reject Intercon's offer, I remain here as a salaried employee, what I've been ever since I started here. I don't own a single share of Warren stock except what I bought and paid for on the open market. If I go along with Intercon, on the other hand, I come in on the ground floor. The presidency at double my present salary, stock options along with many other benefits. I'm not as wealthy as most people believe, Shana. Comfortable, yes, by Laurelton standards. Even more than comfortable. But I can't afford to look down my nose at a proposition that will give me security for life."

"Your going with Intercon will mean leaving Laurelton, won't it, Ken?" Shana asked.

"It will mean *we* will leave Laurelton, Shana. Any plans I make will include you. You know that. We'll headquarter in New York. Wouldn't you like that?" When she didn't answer, he added, "If conditions were different?"

"What conditions?"

"Us. In New York there wouldn't be any obstacles in our way. We'd be free of local prejudices. We could get married—"

"What about Corey?"

"Shana, darling, Corey is a full-grown man now. I hadn't realized it until he came home. I'm sure he understands now, much more clearly than before, and if he doesn't, it

377

really won't matter. By his grandfather's and mother's wills, he's worth close to a quarter of a million dollars. He's ready to go out and practice law at any moment he decides. If he's sensible, I'm sure he can marry Drew Warren and never have to concern himself with money again as long as he lives, as long as his children and grandchildren live. That's his decision to make and he's old enough now to make it for himself. I'm more interested in your future and mine, together."

"Ken—"

"What, Shana?"

"I—"

"Say it. Don't hold back now."

"I hope it can work out. I want what you want for both of us, but—"

"But what?"

"I hope it can be done without this—this dirtiness, this underhanded business with Dillingham and Intercon. It's sordid—"

Sordid, Kenneth thought. A harsh word, but it's the kind of world we live in, the kind of people we live and work with. And what about us, these past years? Aloud he said, "Shana, if Theodore were really interested in the Company, it would be different, but he's simply detached from it, as he has always been, living in a world of his own. Actually, he's much better off out of it, wealthy beyond any normal man's dreams and without the responsibility that could only become an anchor around his neck, a burden—"

"I don't know, Ken, but I just wish it didn't have to be this way. Intercon's way."

"Once it's over, Shana, we'll be living in New York and away from the pettiness we've had to put up with all these years. It will be a new life, a new start in an entirely new society—"

"Yes, I suppose so."

"I wish you acted more happily about it, darling."

"It takes a little time to get used to the idea now that it's so close to happening."

He said nothing then. She picked up a few papers from his correspondence tray and went out as Kenneth's eyes lingered on her retreating form, remembering.

Shana Pierce was 38 years old, but could easily have passed for 30. Medium in height and slender, she had a waist so small that it tended to exaggerate her breasts and hips. Her legs were long and beautifully formed, and her eyes, perhaps her most attractive feature, were large and blue-black, the color of her long lashes and hair. Her nose was short and impishly tip-tilted, her mouth a fraction too wide and quick to smile, displaying brilliantly white, perfectly formed teeth.

Even Kenneth admitted privately that Shana was not beautiful, yet there was a rare, vital quality about her that produced a strong sensual effect. In movement, she was gracefully poised and dynamically provocative, but beyond all else, she was intelligent, quick-witted and showed a dedicated interest in her work. There was little about Kenneth's position as executive vice-president—or Kenneth—that was strange to her.

Often, when she was away from him, Kenneth spent much time thinking how it had begun with Shana. And when. Which, however reluctantly, must revive memories of his wife, Catherine.

Catherine Crane.

Two years older than Kenneth, Catherine had been born late in the lives of Hannah and Selwyn Crane, at a time when both had long given up any hope or thought of issue. Nor had they ever recovered from the phenomenon of their daughter's arrival on earth, which, despite an extraordinary amount of love and devotion squandered lavishly upon her, was not without certain problems of understanding.

Catherine's friends, not unlike her food and clothing, were chosen with infinite care. Destined to inherit a more than modest estate, she had been overly protected from boys who might one day grow up to become fortune hunters or defilers of female flesh, as well as from girls whose social backgrounds and standing would not bear close scrutiny. Raised in an atmosphere that was antiseptic, if not sterile, Catherine grew up in a sheltered world of carefully chosen nurses and tutors, screened from the realities of normal everyday life.

Although there was about Catherine a certain appealing wistfulness and childish charm, the watchfulness of Selwyn and Hannah made it extremely difficult for her to make and keep close or lasting friendships among either sex. One by one, she watched her few acquaintances become engaged, marry, commence families, take part in community life and activities from which she was excluded; somehow remaining in the foreground, yet as remarkably anonymous as a ball boy during a tennis match. That she was decidedly plain and dressed in a manner more in accord with her mother's rather than her own contemporaries, failed to help matters.

When Kenneth Armour returned from Athens to Laurelton, it was Hannah Crane who decided the time was ripe to do something about Catherine. Kenneth's position and reputation were impeccable, his deportment exemplary. The first step in Hannah's determined campaign was to discuss the matter with Selwyn who, after being pushed, cajoled, coerced and finally bullied by Hannah, consented to move certain of his legal affairs from Stickles, Buckley & Towle to Kenneth Armour's law office.

Since Selwyn directed his business affairs from his home at 22 Old Colony Lane, it became necessary for Kenneth to visit the house frequently, often remaining, at Hannah's invitation, to dine. As time passed, Selwyn began to see a certain pattern of quiet ruthlessness in Kenneth's manner of conducting the Crane affairs which, although eminently successful, he did not particularly admire; and when Hannah began hinting of a closer relationship between Catherine and Kenneth, Selwyn showed firm disapproval and resistance to such an alliance.

Selwyn's feelings were not entirely unfelt by Kenneth, made more obvious by the fact that in more recent months Crane had begun calling at Kenneth's office to discuss legal matters, thus removing the necessity for his attorney to call at the Crane home; but Selwyn suspected he was playing a losing game when Hannah began inviting Kenneth to supper apart from legal or business considerations. Nor, when the motives of Hannah Crane became clear, was Kenneth averse to the possibilities that lay in a marriage to Catherine. She was quiet and shy, a good listener. Away from her parents' watchful eyes, he was certain that many improvements could be made in Catherine. Hannah was his staunchest ally. Catherine, whatever else, would make fewer social and personal demands on his time than a younger, more attractive, more social-minded wife would.

Selwyn was the last of the land-holding, cotton-growing Cranes, a name that held considerable esteem, prestige and respect in the County, although it was well known that Selwyn had played no part in building the wealth he had inherited.

Catherine was not unwilling. Enlivened by Kenneth's attention, urged by Hannah, encouraged by her few friends, but aware of her father's opposition to Kenneth, she eventually decided to take the only positive step left to overcome that final obstacle. She allowed Kenneth to seduce her, a harrowing, degrading episode that almost destroyed her emotionally when it was finally over. And not too long after, Hannah quietly informed Selwyn that nature had reduced resistance to a matter of expedience. Catherine was pregnant.

Kenneth and Catherine were married in what was announced as a quiet elopement and, while he lived, Selwyn Crane never spoke another word, civil or otherside, to his son-in-law, not even on the occasion of the birth of Catherine's son, Corey, the following year.

Selwyn had made no major contribution to the financial welfare of Armour's business. Instead, he went back to Stickles, Buckley & Towle and revised his will, leaving everything he owned to Catherine, to be held in trust for her son, with no mention of Kenneth. He made this known to Catherine in a letter which precluded any hope for a reconciliation.

With a wife and son to support, Kenneth was happy to receive a message from Anderson Warren one day, asking him to call. After lunching together, Anderson turned over to Kenneth all legal affairs pertaining to his personal estate. In addition to certain tax and insurance matters, there were the wills of Anderson and Cleo to revise, in which he took note that Theodore Warren, recently married to Louise Drew, and father of an infant son, Bruce, had deposed Chase Warren as the prime inheritor. Also, there was a million-dollar trust to be established for Bruce and, notable by its absence, no mention of Chase's son, Marshall.

Kenneth Armour, leaving Anderson Warren's office that day, did so with the knowledge that he was finally on his way up. In time, he was certain, he would replace the aging Harvey Makepeace as chief counsel for Warren Tobacco Company.

Hannah Crane died in 1943 and four years later, Selwyn followed her to his grave. His will remained unchanged. Everything was left to Catherine to enjoy during her lifetime, and in trust for her son, Corey. It came as a shocking blow to Kenneth to learn that Selwyn had quietly sold off most of his property, excepting the 600 acres in Shadow Hills and the six-acre estate on Old Colony Lane where he had continued to live alone, with two servants, until his death. Most of the money had been put into stocks whose value, in the post-World War II years, had depreciated considerably, and Kenneth almost convinced himself that Selwyn had planned this loss deliberately in order to thwart his son-in-law.

Kenneth urged Catherine to sell the Old Colony Lane property, but Catherine refused. "I was born and raised in that house and lived there until I married you, Kenneth," she stated firmly. "My father left it to me and Corey so that he could grow up in it. I intend that he will."

"Catherine," Kenneth replied, "you are being stubborn

381

and foolish. We can sell the property now for a small fortune and—"

"Stop it, Kenneth. I have no intention of selling it now or ever. If you don't want to live there, you still own this house, but Corey and I are moving next month."

The battle lines had been drawn. Kenneth knew then that he would never command a penny or have any say in Catherine's inheritance which, despite Selwyn's lack of investment sense, still amounted to a respectable sum. However, Catherine's determination marked a deep rupture between them that would never be healed. For the time being, Catherine held the upper hand.

She had somehow always understood that, in time, Kenneth would be unfaithful to her, and accepted that possibility with stoical equanimity. Considering their unsatisfactory sex relationship, she suspected that he was guilty of infidelity even though she had no positive proof upon which to pin her suspicions. She was even more convinced when, on moving into the Old Colony Lane home, he refused to share Selwyn's and Hannah's bedroom (the largest and coolest of all) with her. Catherine accepted his decision without complaint or accusation.

However, she was wrong to have suspected Kenneth of extramarital activity at that time. She was, in fact, wrong by a full year.

3

Shana Pierce's father, Henry Driscoll, died when she was 16, leaving her to the care of her hypochondriac mother, Cora (or perhaps it was the other way around), who had never enjoyed a day of good health from the day she learned she was pregnant. Fortunately, there were no major financial problems. Henry ran a small, but fairly successful insurance agency and had quite properly left a substantial amount of insurance to provide for Cora and Shana. After Henry's death, the Driscoll Insurance Agency continued operation at the direction of Simon Pierce, Henry's capable young assistant, who had been given a 10% interest as long as he remained to manage the firm.

Shana's proximity to her perpetually ailing mother created an ever-increasingly intolerable situation for the attractive 16-year-old daughter. On being graduated from Laurelton High School two years later, Cora arbitrarily denied Shana her long-dreamed plan to go away to college, a promise made her by Henry long before his death.

Thus, on the morning following graduation exercises and the long-awaited celebration dance (which Shana missed because of Cora's sudden gallbladder attack), Shana boldly marched into the office of the Warren Company's director of personnel and came away with a job as a filing clerk. Cora wept bitter tears and pleaded with Shana to give up the job and, if she must work, take a position with the Driscoll Agency; but Shana firmly refused on the basis that the insurance office offered no challenge and would necessitate firing someone who needed a job in order to make room for her.

To give herself an even greater freedom from Cora's constant complaining, Shana devoted three nights a week to a secretarial and business administration school. A fourth night was spent before her radio, recording news and conversational programs to improve her shorthand. It took two years before she moved from filing into the secretarial pool at the Warren Company.

A short time later, Cora Driscoll surprised Shana and her current doctor by dying peacefully in her sleep. After the funeral and a brief period of mourning, Shana returned to her job, despite Simon Pierce's insistence that she no longer needed to work and, if she wanted something with which to occupy herself, could come into the agency in an executive capacity. Shana refused, but increased Simon's interest to 15%. She continued to live in the cottage with a devoted maid, Elsie, to look after her needs and comforts.

Some months afterward, Miss Thatcher, who had been Anderson Warren's secretary for 25 years, failed to show up for work, this on a day when the board of directors was meeting. Mrs. Armistead, head of the secretarial pool, assigned Shana to record the minutes of that meeting. It was on this morning that Kenneth Armour, legal adviser to the board, first saw and became aware of Shana Driscoll.

Kenneth was reaching for his 36th year on that morning. The sight of Shana, then 20, demure and with complete confidence and zestful youth and refreshing beauty, made him think of his tasteless marriage, empty of joy except for his son, Corey. During the meeting, he found it almost impossible to keep his mind entirely on the agenda matters under discussion, concentrating on Shana's clean, fresh looks and the manner in which she seemed able to record simultaneous and multiple conversations and interruptions without becoming flustered in the slightest; certainly a vast improvement over Miss Thatcher.

When he received his copy of the proceedings on the following day, his memory of Shana was rekindled, added to

383

by the extreme clarity of the transcript. Within a fortnight, he had maneuvered his own secretary into the office of a member of his staff and asked Mrs. Armistead to recommend someone to take her place.

"Any preferences, Mr. Armour?" Mrs. Armistead asked.

"Eh? No. No, none whatever," he replied as casually indifferent as he could make himself sound. "Just as long as she is efficient and quick to learn."

Mrs. Armistead, always fair and impartial about assignments, sent him four secretaries, on probation and by seniority of service, within as many weeks. All were helpful and eager for the prestigious position, but somehow failed to meet Armour's exacting requirements. The fifth trial applicant was Shana Driscoll.

For several months, Shana worked extremely hard to hold the job which would mean elevation to near-executive status among her colleagues and a substantial raise in pay. And Kenneth quietly reveled not only in her complete ability to please him, but at the sight of her in his office, touching those things he touched, having her near him, complimenting her work, occasionally sharing lunch sent down from the executive dining room when he was pressed for time.

It began one spring night when they had worked late to finalize a brief that must be placed on the 10:35 train to New York. They had dined in Kenneth's office together, then made corrections and insertions in the thick document ("Wherever did they get the name 'brief' for a 170-page document like this, Mr. Armour?" Shana had asked with a good-humored smile. The question caught him without an answer and they shared a laugh together). When the brief was finally reassembled, checked, stapled and packed for mailing, they left the building together.

It had been raining most of the day and now was pouring. Shana's car refused to start. "Leave it and come along with me, Shana," Kenneth said. "I'll drop this at the station and take you home."

Although she knew that with a little more encouragement her car could be persuaded to start, Shana accepted his offer. The package disposed of, Kenneth drove her to her small cottage. It was a Thursday night and Elsie was spending her day off, as usual, with her family in West Laurelton. At her house, Shana said, "Good night, Mr. Armour, and thank you so much for the lift. I'm afraid I've been a terrible nuisance."

"Of course not, Shana. I'm deeply grateful to you for staying. You needn't bother coming in early tomorrow.

Take a cab to the office and put through a petty cash voucher. Also, a memo for overtime. We will have someone in the garage take a look at your carburetor or starter, or whatever the problem is."

Still, she made no move to get out of the Cadillac. "Such a beastly night, isn't it?" she said, then as though the thought had only just struck her, "Would you like to come in for a drink? Or coffee?"

It was an opening he had hoped for, one that, among others, he had often speculated on, wondering what he would say or do if it were given him. "Yes," he replied almost too quickly, "I would very much like a drink."

"Then why don't you drive the car around to the garage? It's much closer to the back door from there and we won't get so wet."

The car concealed, they entered the house through the kitchen and went into the living room where Kenneth started a fire in the fireplace. "Bourbon, scotch, rye? I may even have the makings of a martini—"

"Bourbon with a little water, please," Kenneth ordered.

They sat on the sofa before the fireplace and talked of many things; business, which led to his travels to other cities, foreign countries he had visited, expanding markets. She got up to refresh his drink as he talked, an unusual experience and far different from any such conversations at home. She returned and sat beside him on the sofa, knees drawn up beneath her, listening with deep, wide-eyed interest. And then suddenly, he stopped talking and stared at her for a moment. He reached up to cup her chin in his hand and said very quietly, "Shana, I'm not very good at this sort of thing, but even at the risk of losing you, I want to hold you in my arms and kiss you."

Her face, for all her readiness to accept a proposal from him, flushed as she drew back and stared down into the drink she was still holding.

"Shana, if I've shocked you, I'm very sorry. If you want to transfer to another job, I'll understand and arrange—"

"No," she said in a low voice and, unsure that he had heard her, repeated it more firmly. "No."

"Shana, it's a lot to ask of a young woman, to involve herself with a man sixteen years her senior, married and with a son, but I haven't been able to stop thinking about you since the first day I saw you."

"I know—I mean, myself. I've felt it, too, something—" Her words were a mere whisper.

"Then look up at me." He took the glass from her and put it on the end table with his own. He put an arm around

385

her shoulder and turned her toward him, drew her closer. Her skin was warm to his touch, her mouth yielding to his as he held her in a tight embrace.

In her bedroom they were two shadows as they undressed and crept silently into bed. They made love hungrily, with the electrifying fierceness of a sudden war, with few words, later in peace and contentment. Shana slept in exhaustion, but Kenneth lay awake staring at the dim outlines of her exquisite body, the mound of her breast, the curving line of waist and hip, a lovely confection of young womanhood who had restored a shaken belief in his own manhood and reduced his years to her own. And finally, he slipped his arms under and around her and held her tightly, joyously, against himself. She awoke then and turned to face him, touching his face, neck and chest. "What time is it?" she asked drowsily.

"Nearly three-thirty." He could hear the faint rustling of the hairs on his chest as her hand caressed him, the softness of her breathing. "I've got to leave you now."

"Is it still raining?"

"Yes. Can't you hear it?"

"I can't hear or see, only feel. I never knew what a blessing rain could be to anyone other than a farmer."

"Shana—"

"I know. You get dressed. Don't turn the lights on. And kiss me before you leave."

He embraced and kissed her, feeling her warmth, again drawing youth from it. "You'd better go now," she said softly, "or I'll keep you here forever."

He withdrew reluctantly. "There won't be any—" she began.

"Difficulty? No. I often work late. Very late. Catherine and I haven't shared the same bedroom for years."

He dressed quickly, kissed her, pulled the covers over her and left.

By the end of 1949, the two-year-old affair began to deteriorate. Shana charged that Kenneth was complacent, taking her for granted. Kenneth countered that Shana was expecting more attention than he could show without allowing their true relationship to become public property. Shana cried and said, "I don't give a damn," and Kenneth replied, "I've got to give a damn. I have a son to protect." To which Shana responded, "What about my protection, my rights?"

When Kenneth asked, "What rights?" the affair began to show the strain. Not only the affair, but their office association began to suffer.

There were ways out for Shana. More attractive than

ever, she had discouraged a good number of interested, but not interesting aspirants. Youth, of which she possessed ample at 22, was not particularly important to her after the stable maturity of Kenneth Armour. Then Simon Pierce, who was 31, single and intelligent, moved into the arena as a contender. And one night, after a serious and lengthy argument with Kenneth, Shana resigned her position and shortly afterward accepted Simon's proposal of marriage.

They were married on New Year's Day of 1950. Simon moved from his bachelor apartment into Shana's house. Out of sheer boredom, she became interested in the Driscoll Agency and within a short time realized that both her marriage and job were what she had once described to her mother as unchallenging. It was even less, she discovered. Dull and a complete bore.

In early June of 1950, Simon, who was patient, generous and gentle, shocked her to her very core. They had gone to bed and he drew her toward him, intent on stimulating her into the act of love, when she turned away and said, "Not tonight, Si. I'm tired."

Simon lay back on his pillow, hands locked behind his head and said nothing. "You're not angry, are you?" Shana said.

He uttered a brief and unconvincing, "No."

"Look, Si, there are times when—"

"Don't bother to explain, Shana. I know."

"Then why are you acting as though—as though—"

"Shana," he said quietly, "I know I'm not as glamorous or dynamic a figure as Ken Armour—"

She sat upright in bed. "What? What did you say?"

"I don't know how many people you've fooled, Shana," Si said calmly, "but I'm not one of them."

"You—"

"I know. I've known it for a long time. Hell, it was written all over you. I even saw you with him one night in Atlanta, long before we were married. He was supposed to be in Washington, I think you told me, and you were spending the weekend, where was it, Augusta? I had to be in Atlanta on business that Monday morning, so I drove down on Sunday night. I saw you at the hotel, just getting into his Cadillac and thought it was funny as hell, you in Atlanta when you were supposed to be in Augusta. Then I saw him at the desk, checking out. I waited and saw him get into the Cadillac with you.

"It so happens I always stay at that hotel and know the desk clerks. I said to this one, 'Wasn't that Ira Cannon just

387

checked out?' and he said, 'Nope. Mr. and Mrs. Charles Barnes from Savannah.'"

"Si, for God's sake, why—if you knew, why did you marry me?"

He said simply, "Hell, Shana, I thought I'd told you, I was in love with you."

Si left the emotional tangle for Shana to wrestle with, but she could find no way out of this new predicament. In late June, the invasion of South Korea came and Si arose early one July morning, left a letter for Shana telling her where she could find the car, then drove to the Army recruiting station and enlisted.

She waited to hear from him, a reply already prewritten in her mind, begging his forgiveness, promising that she would continue to run the agency until he returned, that they would make a fresh start. His letter never came. In October, she received word that Si was dead. Not in combat, but of a heart attack brought on by overexertion while helping push a truck out of a mudhole in a place called Pusan.

What truly amazed her then was that Si had so many friends she had never known or heard of. They came to call, offering condolences. She answered a surprising number of telegrams, cards and letters. And there were two business letters, after a while, inquiring if she would be interested in selling the Driscoll Agency.

Kenneth Armour came back into her life then, to ask if she needed help in any way. She turned the two letters over to him and two months later, took his advice and sold the agency to one of the firms with whom he had been negotiating on her behalf. He then advised her how to invest her money to get the maximum income from it. She was now financially secure, but when he asked her to take her old job back again, she leaped at the opportunity.

A month later, she returned. There was never another break between them, although their discovery in Shadow Hills by Corey, some years later, created an uncomfortable situation that carried over after Catherine's death. Corey's knowledge of their intimacy had became the obstacle to the possibility of their marriage.

Face it, Kenneth told his reflection in the mirror while washing his hands before leaving for the day. You're 55, getting closer to the 60-mark every day. Your son is a grown man, on his own now, ready to make his own future without you. The only person who really cares a damn about you is Shana, who is sixteen years your junior and who has spent her best years on you. You're past middle age. There's still time to marry her, live the rest of your life with her. A month, a year from now, she could just as easily say, "No, old man."

Face it. You've lost Corey and you know it. Can you afford to lose Shana now? Financially, she is secure, made secure by your investments of her money in solid blue chips. What need for an old man when she can still pick and choose from a dozen or more younger men?

He toweled his hands dry and adjusted his necktie. This Intercon thing. I wish to God she felt better about it. If it comes off, we can go off to some quiet place and get married, move to New York, a large apartment, good address, entertaining, president of a newer, bigger, stronger Warren Tobacco Company. What more could a woman want? God, I'm shaking, trembling like a nervous kid, just thinking about it. What if she were to say, "No"? What good would it all be then, living in New York alone, beginning from the very start by myself—without her—without Corey—

4

Sam Shackleford checked his daily work sheet, made sure his crews were back from lunch, then turned the balance of the day's work orders over to his assistant. He punched out at the same moment the echo of the one o'clock whistle died, got into his Ford and drove home. Duke was lounging on the front porch, dressed in form-fitting slacks and a short-sleeved knit shirt which exhibited the muscularity of his broad chest and arms. He stood up when Sam came up on the porch. "Soon's I change, Duke," Sam said.

"Take your time, Pop. I'n in no hurry."

Sam went inside and returned fifteen minutes later, dressed in his black Sunday suit, white shirt, dark tie and hat. Duke witheld the flip remark he had on the tip of his tongue about going to a funeral. Funny, he thought, the cool reaction of Sam to his return, almost grudging; but then Sam had never been much for showing his true feelings or open affection. Duke remembered that time long ago when they had received word that Sam's brother, Matt, had died in the Parkton Prison and his father's cold, stony acceptance of the news, shaking off the weeping Lutie's efforts to comfort him. "He's dead," Sam had said without emotion. "Ain' no amount of cryin' goin'a change that." Remembering his own futile anger that Sam could take the outrage so calmly.

Lutie came out wiping her hands on her apron, her face,

389

neck and arms moist with perspiration, smiling at the sight of her husband and son together. "You-all be careful an' enjoy your trip," she said, "an' be home before six. I got a good supper on the stove."

Duke kissed her and said, "We be there before three an' home long before six, Mom. You take it easy."

Lutie laughed. "I got a million things to do, but it get done, little by little. You drive slowsome, Sam, you hear?"

"Shuh," Sam replied laconically.

"Mom, we get back, I'm goin'a look into gettin' you a real air-conditioner—"

"Le's go, Duke. Talk about that later."

"Sure, Pop."

They followed the river road south to Tenboro, and there was no coolness in the heavy air that enveloped them, yet Sam refused to stop to remove his coat. Outside his home and away from work, Sam wouldn't think of dressing less formally. Big hands gripping the wheel, eyes fastened on the road ahead, he finally broke the silence. "How much that thing you got on cost, Duke?" he asked.

"This?" Duke pinched the fabric of the knit shirt. "I don' remember exactly. About twenty-two fifty, maybe twenty-five."

"An' them pants?"

"They slacks, Pop. About fifty-sixty dollars. Why?"

"I don' know. Never seen any like it. Just askin'."

"They good stuff. The best."

"It's a awful lot of money."

"Yeah, but it makes a man feel good jus' knowin' what he's got on is as good as it comes. These shoes, they alligator. Cost seventy-five a pair. I got me maybe ten pair."

"Seven hundred and fifty dollars, jus' for shoes?"

Duke laughed, enjoying himself. "Pop, it's only money. You got it to spend, you spend it. That's what it's for."

"Where it goin'a come from now you can't fight no more?"

"I'n worryin'. Soon's my hand heal up, I'll go back—"

"To where, Duke? New York, where you run away from? Just like you run away from here ten years ago?"

They rode in silence for a few moments and Sam said, "Well, Duke?"

"Lemme tell you, Pop. I was in a fight, yeah, but it wasn't in no ring. An ofay crook—"

"A what?"

"Ofay. It mean Whitey. Mr. Charley. A white man. Anyways, he was my manager. He work for me, just like my trainer, sparrin' partners, an' all. But he robbin' me blind

390

for a long time. This last time, I catch him at it. He got two of his goon honkies to bust me up, usin' a poolcue on me. Okay, maybe I won' fight no more, but I got other ideas I learn up there, an' I got money, don't you fret none about that."

For a while, Sam concentrated on driving through the huddle of traffic approaching Fisher's Landing, then they were out in the open again. "Pop," Duke said suddenly, "you worried about somethin'?"

"I don' know, Duke."

"You don't act happy about me comin' home. Not like Mom or Lizabeth."

"It ain't that I ain't happy. It just—well, what you goin'a do now you home?"

"Do? I tol' you. I got ideas—"

"That's what's bothersome, Duke. You come home broke, I could get you a job at the plant. A good, steady job—"

"Pop, you sorry I come home with some money, good clothes, a car of my own? You rather see me hitchhike from New York, beggin' handouts, sleepin' in barns or in a field somewheres?"

"No. You know I don' mean that, Duke. I mean, you comin' back, talkin' big, actin' big, showy clothes. That's fine up in New York, maybe, but down here, people don' take to New York ways. In a big city, Atlanta, Savannah, maybe. We got people with money here in Laurelton, but they don't wear no twenty-five-dollar shirts, seventy-five-dollar shoes or fifty-dollar pants. Henry Clark, the funeral parlor man, Milo Roose from the insurance society, Walter Lynch, the real estate man, a dozen others, they got money, live in good houses, good as any white man's, but they don't act showy with what they got. Their children, they go to our schools—"

"Pop, that's so much shit you been takin' all your life. White man's shit. You got money, you got a right to do the same as any white man do with his money. You got a right to better houses, better clothes, a better car, better things for your kids. His money ain't no better'n yours, yours no worse'n his. Money is money. It buys the same things, if he'll let you buy it. On'iest thing is, sometimes he won't."

Sam's lips tightened. "That's what I'm worried about, Duke."

"What?"

"That kind of talk. It spells trouble. You got some money, fine. You take a job, save your money, get married, that's fine, too. But you aimin' to loaf aroun', showin' off your fancy clothes, talkin' to boys who ain't got no money, givin' them ideas. Boys who can't hold a job longer'n two weeks. First thing you know, they gettin' your biggety ideas. That's the kind of trouble I mean. We got a lot of good people around here, Duke, an' we're gettin' along. Maybe not as fast as we want, but we gettin' there. We livin' better every year. We buildin' up community respect—"

"Oh, Pop, you buildin' up nothin'. You just dreamin'. Mist' Charley, when you get somethin' built up, he jus' put his foot down on it an' squoosh it right down again. He got his foot on your neck an' tell you, 'Move, nigger,' an' you move. He tell you, 'Hold it, nigger, right where you at,' an' you hold it right where you at. It ain't no different today than it was ten years ago, a hundred years ago. You live in a better house, sure, but it still ain't as good as Mist' Charley's house. You ride anywhere on a bus, sure. A few colored kids go to some poor white schools. Big deal. What you don't see is, they Mist' Charley's buses, Mist' Charley's houses, Mist' Charley's schools. His stores, eatin' places, his everything. He th'ow you a few more scraps when you bark, you think you own the doghouse an' got it made. Well, you ain't an' you know it. You still a slave like your gran'-pappy was, livin' by white man's laws an' white man's judges. One set of laws for him, one set for niggers."

Sam expelled the breath he had been holding back, fearful of his own rising anger. He said finally, "Duke, maybe it be better if you go away, go back up north somewhere. We don't need nobody comin' in to stir things up. We got enough of that here already, 'thout addin' more to it. This hot spell, it like matches an' gasoline lyin' side by side, waitin' for somebody—"

Duke laughed loudly. "Pop, you know what? You a white nigger, damn' if you ain't. You playin' Uncle Tom just the way Mist' Charley wants you to play it. Cool. Do what he says, the way he wants it, he let you live. For every nigger got a job like yours, for every Henry Clark, Milo Roose, Walter Lynch, how many niggers just barely makin' out, hey? How many not makin' out at all? How many niggers on the street havin' to make it by stealin', girls screwin' to make a dollar—"

"Shut up, Duke."

"You mad now, ain't you, Pop, but it's the truth an' you know it. Whitey, he keeps colored kids out of school so they can't learn nothin' except field work, laborin', janitorin', sweepin' up, tote that barge, lift that bale. Even if he gets a good education, you think he's goin'a hold down a decent job, get the same money for the same work? Why else you think niggers are better fighters, better baseball players, better basketball players? Because they hungrier, got to do better'n Whitey to make it, that's why. The ones can't make it, they got to steal or starve. You c'n only mash your nose up against a store window so long before you pick up a rock an' break the glass an' grab what's in there makin' your mouth water. Nigger crime rate's high, sure. Why the hell not? What other chance they got?"

"Duke, I'm tellin' you, all you talkin' is trouble. We movin' ahead. More children goin' to school, learnin' trades at the R-V Center—"

"So's they can get less pay for doin' the same job."

"Not no more. Not in the Warren plant, not in the Taylor factories."

"What about in the stores? In the offices?"

"Nothin' happens overnight, Duke. It takes time, but we movin' ahead in the right direction, I'm tellin' you again. I don' want you startin' anything with your big talk."

"You afraid the Kluxers'll get me, bomb the house out, set us on fire? The White This an' the White That?"

"We got none of that trash in Laurelton, Duke."

"No? Just because they don't parade on the streets in white sheets an' hoods. You got 'em, Pop. You just make one wrong move, they come out of hidin' like roaches, a whole goddam army of 'em."

Sam's head shook from side to side in disconsolate defeat, seeing no way in which he could reach his son's extremist-oriented mind. He concentrated on driving then and no more conversation passed between them until they pulled into Tenboro just before three o'clock. Duke directed Sam to the West End Lunchroom. After checking the Jaguar to make sure no one had tampered with it, Duke went back to where Sam waited in the Ford. "Up the street, Pop. I'll show you where it is."

They found the filling station. An older man had replaced the youth of the night before and Duke explained his need.

"Yeah, my boy tellen me about you last night. I'll send up the street for it." They waited until the mechanic returned with the battery and Duke paid the money into the man's hand as Sam stood by wincing at the sight of so much money for a new battery; paying for it with no more care than if it were a loaf of yesterday's bread, knowing he could get it for much less in Laurelton.

"You know how to put this in?" the owner asked.

"I know how, Mister," Sam said.

"Okay. I c'd send a mechanic with you—"

"Don' need no mechanic. I c'n handle it," Sam insisted.

They drove back to the shed behind the restaurant. Duke took note of Sam's quiet appraisal of the maroon Jaguar with amusement. "This—uh—this yours, Duke?"

"It's mine. An' all paid for, Pop. Took me all of five minutes to buy it. For cash money."

"You got any tools?"

"Right here." Duke opened a panel in the door and revealed a set of tools, glittering like new. "Comes built in, special for this car." Sam removed the old battery, jockeyed the new one into place, hooked it up and tightened it. Duke turned the key in the ignition switch and the motor turned over at the first touch. "Okay, Pop. You need any gas? I got to fill up. You follow me up the street an' we fill 'em both up, hey?"

Sam's tank was filled first. He pulled out a flat, worn wallet, but Duke waved him off. "You go ahead, Pop. I'll get this one."

"You don't want me to wait for you?"

"No need, Pop. I'll catch up on the road."

The owner was putting the gas hose into the Jaguar's tank when Sam pulled out. Already, the mechanic and two hangers-on were looking under the Jag's hood, examining the motor. Then two customers came out to inspect it, appreciation for the imported car showing in their eyes and manner. Duke paid for the gas and got in behind the wheel, feeling a sense of gratification. The hood was still up.

Look it over, he thought with deep pleasure. Let your goddam ofay tongues hang out, you bastards.

One of the white customers said, "Whose is it, boy?"

Duke started the motor, allowing it to idle. One of the mechanics closed the hood and Duke dropped the shift lever from neutral into drive and released the emergency brake. "I said, whose is it, boy?" the man repeated.

Foot on gas pedal, he allowed the Jaguar to drift up beside the man who had asked the question. "It's mine, that's whose it is," he replied with a note of belligerence in his voice.

"Yeah? Who'd you steal it from, nigger?"

Duke depressed the gas pedal slowly. "Not from no trash like you, Whitey." As the car moved out, he called back, "You come up where I live I might give you a dollar to wash it for me." He was out in the street, the knot of indignant white men behind, heard one voice shout, "You sonofabitchin' nigger bastard! You better run less'n you want to get buried in that—"

Foolhardy, he knew. Feeling a slight trembling in his

394

hands. Recalling Sam's warning words. Checking his rear-view mirror to make sure no one was pursuing him. How long before a Whitey cop would be on his tail, hauling him in on some trumped-up charge? Big talk. Trouble talk.

In the more crowded business section, he drove cautiously, gliding into the traffic pattern, drinking in the admiration he saw in the eyes of other motorists and pedestrians when he came to a stop. No resentment. As though they *knew* the driver was somebody's houseboy or chauffeur. Screw you, all you white bastards. It's mine. All mine.

Once out on the open road, he began breathing easier, one careful eye on the mirror as he let it out a little more, watching for the red knob on top of any car behind him, the tell-tale mark of a county police car. Within a few miles, he saw Sam's Ford up ahead. He came up quickly, beating out a tattoo on his horn, waving as he passed the Ford, hitting 95, wondering what Sam was thinking. Within a few moments, the Ford was a vague dot on the streak of brilliant road far behind him and he glowed with pride and satisfaction.

When Sam reached home, Lutie was waiting supper for him. There was no sign of the maroon Jaguar. "Where's Duke?" he asked.

"Duke?" Lutie looked out behind him. "Ain't he with you?"

"No. He pass me just outside Tenboro, goin' like one of them big jet airplanes. Pass me so fast, I thought I was standin' still. Supper ready?"

"We waitin' on you an' Duke."

"Well, don' wait no more. He prob'ly had to go in town to show off his fancy car."

"We ain't goin'a wait for him?"

"We ain't goin'a wait. We got a time to eat, sleep, an' wake up aroun' here an' we ain't goin'a change our ways to suit anybody else."

Elizabeth came out on the front porch. "Where's the champ?"

"Somewheres showin' off his pretty new car in his twenty-five dollar shirt, fifty-dollar pants an' seventy-five-dollar shoes," Sam retorted sharply. "You teachin' a class tonight?"

"Yes."

"Then we goin'a eat right now an' I'll drive you over to the Center. One thing, our Duke ain't goin'a starve."

Corey reached home by five o'clock, greeted by Jemmy with a sheaf of telephone messages from old friends, casual acquaintances, well-wishing neighbors, including the Holderbys. But none from Lyle Emerson. He fixed a drink for himself in Kenneth's study, found Lyle's number and dialed it, but there was no answer. He went to the kitchen and spoke with Tish for a few moments, tried Lyle's number again from the kitchen phone, then went upstairs to shower and change.

When he came down, Kenneth was home, having a martini in his study while looking over the closing market prices in the evening edition of the *Herald*. He put the paper aside when Corey entered. "Join me, Corey?"

"Thank you." Corey poured a drink for himself.

"Interesting day?"

"Yes, very. I ordered some new clothes at Weinstock's, had lunch with Polk and just got back from Brookhill."

"You saw Drew, then."

"Yes. Also, Anderson Warren and the Waters."

Kenneth said, "It won't be easy for Drew when her grandfather dies."

"I suppose not. She never had many friends, even as a child. I don't know whether she was naturally shy, or if the Warren money created so much of a barrier that—"

"She'll need what few friends she has."

Corey did not reply, feeling that this was Kenneth's sense of opportunism rising to the surface; a lonely heiress in need of a friend. Marriage. So simply pat. To stem that line of conversation, Corey said, "Dad, the Shadow Hills land—"

"What about it?"

Corey withdrew the map from the envelope and spread it out on the desk. "I put the Crane tract at 603.76 acres, here." His finger outlined the limits of the tract. "Now here, surrounding it on the north, east and west borders, is the Halstead tract, approximately 1,200 acres. Four miles west, here, is the Cottonwood River. Two and one-half miles east is the Laurelton-Riverton highway."

Kenneth nodded, following Corey's finger as it moved across the map. "I don't suppose you're ready to tell me what you have in mind."

"It may be only a waste of time, Dad. I need some more information before I can be sure. This Halstead land. Do

396

you think there is any chance of buying it, or taking an option on it?"

"I think there's a very good chance of either or both. When Tom Halstead died about six or seven years ago, he left the property to his two sons and a daughter. They're all married. The daughter, if I remember correctly, lives in Valdosta and the two sons in Macon. Some time ago, I was approached by their attorney who was trying to sell it off for the heirs."

"What would you guess it is worth?"

"The same as yours. As raw land, between $250 and $275 an acre. I think your Grandfather Selwyn bought it years ago for about $60 an acre, or less. So yours is worth about $165,000 tops, if you could find a buyer. I guess the Halstead land would go for around $300,000."

"Do you know who is handling the property for them?"

"At the time I was approached, I think it was Lee Stannard who was working with the attorney. Are you serious about this, Corey? I mean optioning those 1,200 acres. If you are, I can put someone on it to work it out for you. I think Stannard would give you a six-month option for about $2,500 or $3,000."

"It would be a pure gamble."

Kenneth smiled. "If whatever you have in mind is sound enough, it's worth a $3,000 gamble. You can't get hurt too badly."

"You're right. I think I'll drop in and talk with Stannard myself."

"Why not? If you're going to get mixed up in a business deal of some sort, you might as well get your feet wet at the start."

"Dad, I'm not holding back. This thing I have in mind is based on a conversation I had with a top Seabee engineer in Viet Nam. I need to have it checked out. If the idea isn't practical, I'll drop the $3,000 and forget it. If it is workable, and I believe it is, or at least there's a chance that it could be, it could be a very interesting and profitable project. And if it is, I'll tell you all about it. I'll need your advice."

"All I can say, Corey, is good luck. I hope it works out for you. If you'll excuse me, I think I'll get ready for dinner."

Corey scanned his map and figures for a few minutes, then checked the phone book for Wayne Taylor's number and dialed it. A servant answered. Mr. Taylor was not in. Mrs. Taylor? Who was calling? "Yessir, Mist' Armour, I tell Miss Julie."

"Corey? How nice to hear your voice. We saw the item in the morning paper. How are you?"

"Wonderful, Julie. And you?"

"We're all fine. Wayne, little Ames and Charlotte. She's new since you've been gone."

"My belated and warmest congratulations. I hadn't heard. Is Wayne in town, Julie?"

"Yes. I spoke with him only ten minutes ago. He's at the office and won't be leaving for another half hour. He's in some sort of conference with Johnny."

"How are Susan and Johnny?"

"Just wonderful. You know about their two, don't you?"

"Yes, of course."

"When are we going to see you, Corey? We haven't had any decent tennis competition around here while you've been away."

"Soon, I hope. Just as fast as I can convert to civilian life and get some practice on the courts."

"On, or in?"

"Perhaps both. Nice talking with you, Julie. I may try to ring Wayne at his office."

He looked up the Taylor Industries number and dialed it, caught Wayne's secretary as she was leaving for the day. She put him through and he went through the home-welcoming process again, one that was beginning to bore him. "Wayne, I called to ask if you could spare me a few moments sometime soon. Something I'd like to discuss with you. And Johnny, if he's available."

"Let me check my calendar, Corey. Hold it a moment." Wayne came back on. "How about tomorrow? I'm free at two-thirty for about half an hour, and that's an open time for Johnny."

"That's perfect. I'll be there at two-thirty."

"We'll look for you then."

At seven, dinner was announced. Corey and Kenneth talked as they ate, covering local subjects; business in general, the housing shortage, names familiar and unfamiliar. Over coffee in the study, Corey dialed Lyle's number again, again there was no answer, and the disappointment showed on his face.

"Trouble locating someone?" Kenneth asked.

"Lyle Emerson. I can't seem to find him in. I think—" He dialed Information and got the number of the Recreational-Vocational Center, dialed that number. No, Mr. Emerson was not there, but was expected. Any message?

"No, thank you. I'll try to drop by. What time is his class over?"

"Nine-thirty, sir."
"Thank you."

The Laurelton Recreational-Vocational Center was a privately sponsored and operated institution that had been organized in 1955 by Miss Katie Willard, who had been regarded for over four decades, and not without some fondness, as a genial oddball do-gooder. In 1918, then 24, her fiancé had been killed in the Argonne and from that day until her death at age 70 in 1964, she had never been known to wear anything but black.

Recovered from her initial shock in 1918, Miss Katie resigned her memberships on the Beautify Laurelton Committee, Zoo Fund, Library and Music Commissions, Garden Club and Historical Society, and embarked on numerous programs to help the needy. A member of the wealthy Willard clan, she organized drives to accumulate old clothes, furniture and household goods and appliances, for which she paid to have cleaned, repaired and reconditioned, then quietly distributed to poor white and Negro families. She donated a playground, had an old hearse converted into a mobile library, stocked it with books and drove it from neighborhood to neighborhood encouraging the poor to read and make greater use of the City Library system. During the depression years, the store from which she operated her charitable program became a food distribution center as well, and in 1942, she crusaded actively for a much-needed recreation and social center for neglected Negro soldiers and sailors, patterned after the U.S.O.

In 1955, while city, county and state officials and commissions still studied, planned, discarded, discussed, argued and fought bitterly over allocation, distribution and use of Federal and State funds to improve conditions by providing vocational training for the underprivileged and unemployed, the wiry, energetic Miss Katie decided to take the bull by its own horns and point it in the proper direction.

She donated a 30-acre piece of unused Willard land in West Laurelton for her project. On it stood a large frame house, two barns and three warehouse buildings, one a double-decked affair, which were once used to store baled cotton. With donations solicited from private citizens and business establishments, notably the Taylors and Warrens, the house was converted into classrooms, one barn into an assembly-dance hall, one into a gymnasium. Two warehouses were divided into vocational training classrooms and outfitted with motors, tools, paint-spraying equipment, sewing machines, generators, carpentry, electrical and bricklaying

399

equipment. Donated lumber was fashioned into work benches and tables which held metal and wood lathes and other tools. The two-storied building became the administration building and classrooms. By the end of 1955, the R-V Center had become an established fact.

School teachers, nurses, mechanics, painters, carpenters, bricklayers and handymen gave of their spare time to instruct those who were eager to learn; a job placement service was organized to find employment for those ready to take on a new occupation.

The young were not ignored. For every age group there were indoor and outdoor athletics, games, dance groups, art and music classes. Lew Benziger's Camera Shop donated used cameras, film and darkroom equipment, and Lew's son, Michael, taught classes in picture taking and film processing.

By day, a nursery was established so that working mothers could leave their children while they went to their jobs as day-workers in homes, stores and factories. On a rotation plan, nonworking or temporarily unemployed mothers supervised and tended the nursery.

In time, the project expanded by sheer demand. Older children came after normal school hours to expend their pentup energies at games, forming teams known as the Titans, Falcons, Angels, Tigers, Leopards, and one, with a touch of perverse humor, Yankees. Later, when Lee Durkin, an active supporter of the project, became Chief of Police, he led his own personally supported and sponsored Police Boys' Club and Band to become a part of what was often called "Miss Katie's Center."

But one aspect saddened Miss Katie's heart. From the first, she had planned her project for the underprivileged white and Negro children and adults alike, but only the Negroes came to play and work and learn. White children looked on, often with envy, forbidden by their parents to enter and participate in "Nigger Heaven." When Miss Katie died, most of what was left of her money was willed to the Center.

Eventually, most of the white volunteer instructors left the Center. The nursery school and playgrounds were heavily patronized by day, but adult and youth night classes had fallen off greatly. There were only a few paid employees; an office manager, a nightwatchman, a groundskeeper, a woman to prepare and serve food and snacks, and one to supervise the volunteers.

At nine o'clock, Corey Armour slipped into his uniform

jacket and drove into town, cruising through the traffic flow along Taylor Avenue as far as Fuller, then took the cutoff leading into the bridge. Crossing into West Laurelton, he could see numerous pleasure boats and several loaded barges moving north and south on the Cottonwood River. On the west bank and south, the Marina Club was flood-lighted, member craft tied up to a dozen or more finger piers, a few already canvas-covered for the coming fall weather, much too soon with the present heat wave that persisted. And this sight, too, evoked memories of days and nights spent cruising on the Cottonwood, countless swim-ming and fishing parties, outings and picnics, all a part of him forever.

Once across the bridge, he turned off Grand Avenue onto Cottonwood Road, then left into Division Street, which sep-arated the commercial from the residential sections. For six blocks, the homes were owned by medium-income white working families, for eight more by lower-income whites. At the corner of Division and Washington, known locally as Deadline, the shabby homes of the Negro workers began, running west for more than twenty blocks. The name Dead-line was oppressively meaningful—few Negroes or whites ever crossed into alien territory on foot by day, never at night. An unwritten law permitted passage in a car as long as it kept moving.

Six blocks beyond Washington, Corey pulled into an open driveway, under a sign that read:

WEST LAURELTON

RECREATIONAL AND VOCATIONAL

CENTER

Everybody Welcome!

6

The adult night class Lyle Emerson taught was called "Basic English," but its purpose was, in reality, to teach men and women to write and read the most elementary words, sign their names legibly, learn the requirements and procedures by which they would be permitted to register and cast their votes. The class, less than four weeks old, had already been pared down to exactly half its original 36 members, and

Lyle knew there would be more defections as first enthu-
siasms waned and work-gnarled, aged hands grew tired of
clutching unfamiliar ballpoint pens to scrawl childlike hiero-
glyphics on sheets of cheap, lined paper. Too many years of
laboring in the fields and at housework had passed to keep
their first determination to learn at any sort of a peak, despite being nagged and harassed by their own children, the
Reverend Amos Hart and others to keep at it. There were
fewer problems with the generations of children and grandchildren these oldsters had brought into the world, but they
too, must learn, keep learning, encouraging the young in
their homes.

"Nine-thirty," Lyle Emerson announced from behind the
battered table that served as his desk. "That's it for tonight,
ladies and gentlemen. I am very happy with the results I've
seen in these few short weeks and I hope you will all practice and complete your homework for the Thursday night
class. Thank you for coming and I hope each of you will
talk to those of your friends who were absent tonight and
encourage them to come back. Good night."

The class broke from silence into low murmurs of relief,
heads shaking with doubt at the scratchings on the papers
they folded into pockets and purses, commenting on their
own shortcomings.

"Shuh," one woman said with a low, self-conscious laugh,
"I c'n see right now I'n never goin'a write no better'n these
chicken tracks I been makin'."

A glum-faced man replied, "I done tole my gal it hain't
no use tryin' to learn no field hand nothin'. You know what
she tellen me? 'You lissen to me, Granpa,' she say, 'iffen
you don't do it, I'n goin'a do it, neither. Th' day you quits
the Center, I quits high school so's we'll bothen us be dumb
niggers who cain't vote or work in a decent job.' Shuh nuf,
she tellen me to my own face."

Lyle Emerson limped down from the platform and joined
the group. "She's right, Mr. Harris," he said gently. "If her
grandfather and father refuse to set an example for her,
why should she care or bother? If you don't register and
vote, why should she when she reaches voting age?" The
group had turned quiet again, listening. "One of today's biggest problems between white and Negro is the lack of understanding and communication. What your granddaughter
is trying to say to you, is, 'If you show no interest in keeping up with me, very soon there won't be anything between
us, and if we can't communicate with or understand each
other, how can we ever hope to understand anyone else,
white *or* Negro?' "

Chili Dunlap said, "How come you think you understands us so good, Mist' Emerson?"

Lyle said with a smile, "I don't flatter myself that I do, Mr. Dunlap, not as much as I'd like to. The point is, if I'm willing to make the effort to understand and know you better in order to help you, I think you should be willing to help me understand and know you better."

"But what *fo'?*" a voice on the edge of the group asked.

"Let's say for the benefit of both of us, Mr. Gannett. Also, because whether we like it or not, want it or not, we're here on the same earth and living side by side in this community. If we're going to live together and work together in peace, we've got to be able to communicate with and understand each other. Two years ago, you remember, I am sure, almost no Negroes were voting in this county. Today there is a sixteen per cent Negro vote here, by registration count, which should make it clear that there is a greater need for more Negroes on the rolls. A few years ago, there were no Negroes sitting on juries. Today there are some, but not nearly enough.

"I know it seems like a very slow process to you, but education has always been a slow process. There are those who are crying out for black power, urging others to defy the nation's laws, inciting them to violence, but reasonable men will know that if you and enough of your people become registered voters, you can change discriminating local laws and ordinances by peaceful means instead of trying to change them by violence.

"It won't come overnight. It may not come for years. But if we both work at it, perhaps it may come in your children's time, in their children's time, and only if we start trying to make it work now, today. Think about it. Think what it would be like today if that start had been made at the end of the War Between the States."

There was some head-shaking and one or two voices murmured, "Amen."

"Seems like it long overdue," Mr. Gannett said dispiritedly.

"I agree," Lyle said, "but the start must be made and it must come from you, encouraging the youth." He sought for another way to explain it, in words that would be more meaningful. "Mr. Gannett, you've spent years working in tobacco fields, haven't you?"

"A'most from the time I c'd walk," Gannett replied.

"Then you know you've never seen fine, golden, cured tobacco that didn't start out as well-cared-for seedlings in a bed that had been planned and tended carefully from the very start. You saw those seedlings replanted in a row out in the field and hoed, weeded and worried over for weeks until they were able to stand up and start growing straight and strong. Then you watched over them, examined them for blight and other diseases, pulled the suckers off, guarded them from too much sun until they became tall and broad-leafed prime tobacco leaves, ready to be cured. And then the curing.

"Well, those children and grandchildren of yours aren't any different from seedlings, Mr. Gannett. They are born and loved and raised until the time comes for them to be transplanted into a school, encouraged to study and learn and become educated voters some day, making their place in the kind of world they will have to build cooperatively with others. It's a fight, yes, but so is growing tobacco.

"And it isn't all hopeless. Today, there are Negro boys and girls working in jobs they could never have hoped to hold years ago. Take a look next time you go into the County Building, the Federal Building, the City Hall, and see how many young Negro men and women are working behind desks, how many young, strong Negroes have been added to the police department over the past five or six years. Why?

"Because they received enough education to pass the tests that all applicants must pass, white or Negro. There aren't many, I'll agree, but the start has been made and a few more are added every year. So when you think there is no purpose to what you are doing here, think of them before you decide it isn't worth the effort."

By their nodding heads, Emerson saw a measure of agreement and for the moment he was satisfied that he had gotten through to them. The group broke up slowly and headed for the door. Emerson hobbled back to his table-desk. The stump of his right leg had been paining him for several days and he wondered if he might not need another operation, dreading the thought of further hospitalization. Since he had begun wearing the artificial limb, he had never become fully adjusted to the strangeness of it, irked by the harness. The padding that felt so soft in the morning turned hard and abrasive as the day wore on, and he could hardly approximate the effortless movement of the experts at the Army hospital who had demonstrated their amazing free-dom of movement and agility. Yet, he thought gratefully, he had never experienced the fantasy pains in his missing foot or kneecap which other amputees had claimed plagued them constantly.

He cleared the table of the few papers and a textbook,

locked them in the single center drawer, lit a cigarette and went out, switching the lights off and closing the door. Because of his leg problem, he had been assigned to a ground-level classroom. At first, he had taken the Monday, Wednesday and Friday night classes in English, taught to a younger group of working adults, but then, as he saw the need grow, had asked for the Tuesday and Thursday night classes to prepare the older generation for voter registration, something to fill his hours of loneliness. But, he thought grimly now, the wear and tear on that goddamned stump—

He limped down the long hallway toward the front of the building. The other classrooms had already emptied and only the lights in the Administration Office and the room next to it, which held a refreshment bar for instructors, were on. Teachers from the vocational classes on the upper floor and other buildings were arriving, pouring coffee, helping themselves from the platters of freshly made sandwiches and a variety of doughnuts and sweet rolls, chattering among themselves, animated over their successes, deploring their failures.

Emerson paused in the doorway, trying to decide whether to go in or go on. As usual, the two other white instructors had left the moment their classes were over. Only the Negro teachers remained and his hesitation was evidence of his own doubts over their acceptance of him. He saw Elizabeth Shackleford turn away from the counter, a cup of coffee in one hand, a paper-wrapped sweet roll in the other. As their eyes met, she smiled and came toward him.

Among the entire staff of voluntary instructors, Elizabeth Shackleford was perhaps the only one who showed more than a passing awareness of Lyle Emerson's presence. The others were polite and respected his knowledge and ability, but were distant; and unless their conversation was conducted on a purely academic level, he was offered no part in it. When he first came to the Center, there were five other white instructors, but their number had dwindled to two women, former teachers who had indicated they would serve until someone could be procured to take over their duties. Among those present now, he was scarcely noticed except by Elizabeth.

Tonight, she wore a white sleeveless dress with a short, matching jacket that ended just below her waist. She was fair, the color of light toast, her features elegantly patrician. Her hair fell straight to a soft roll that curled inward at the base of her neck, with a feathering of bangs over her forehead. As she came toward him, he stiffened, conscious of his

405

artificial leg. To turn and walk down the hall to the doorway, from this position, was not an easy maneuver. He stood stock-still and waited, "Hello," she said, "how about some coffee?"

"I think I'd like some very much," he replied, and came inside the room.

"Why don't you take these and I'll get some more for myself?"

"No," he said too quickly, then added, "Thank you, Elizabeth, I'll get my own."

Her face clouded for a moment as she realized that this was his sensitivity toward his artificial leg. Then she smiled and said, "Come back. I'll save a chair for you."

The chairs were regulation lecture room chairs with a broad right arm on which to rest a notebook or, in this case, a cup of coffee and plate. Her eyes followed his progress to the counter, focused on the way he swung his body from the hips to mitigate his limp, thinking of the hardship he had endured, the suffering brought on by his great loss. They had had a number of conversations in the past and she was satisfied that, unlike the other white instructors who had left, Lyle Emerson was deeply and sincerely devoted to his chosen work among her people. When he turned back from the counter, she looked away from him so that her interest in his lack of full maneuverability would not be noticeable. He returned with a large mug of coffee and a sandwich and eased himself into the chair next to hers. "How was your class tonight?" he asked.

Elizabeth grinned, then grimaced. "Rough. I'm down to twenty-two from forty-eight, better than fifty per cent dropoff in less than four weeks."

"Mine is exactly fifty per cent, eighteen left out of thirty-six. I hope I can pick up a few of the dropouts through the others who are sticking it out."

"I may get a few of mine back by getting around to see them in person."

"If you run across any of mine, give them a pep talk for me, will you?"

"Sure, glad to. Incidentally, thanks for that study outline you gave me. I think it's beginning to show some results. I never saw one like it at U.S.C. Is it the same one you use at Laurelton High?"

"Not exactly. I modify my study outlines to fit the needs of the majority. I did the same on the one I gave you."

"Well, I appreciate it. It's made things much easier."

Someone called out to Elizabeth, an offer to drive her

home. "Not tonight, Ben," she replied, "I've got a lift." Ben nodded, waved and went out.

"I don't want to keep you, Elizabeth——" Lyle began.

"You're not, and I don't really have a lift. That was a fib. I just don't want one from Ben." She said it in such a way that made Lyle ask, "He got long arms?"

"Too long and too many."

"My, my. The respectable Ben Naylor."

"And married to a nice woman with two children."

"But you may have missed a ride. Everybody else heard you."

"No matter. I can take the bus home or even call——"

"I feel responsible, Elizabeth. Would you accept a lift from me?"

Without hesitation, she said, "Of course." It was the first time in the six or seven months she had known him that he had made such an offer, one she would not have considered under other circumstances. That he was aware of the connotation was made clear with his next question: "Do we leave together?"

"Why not?" she said, perhaps a little too casually. "We work together, don't we?"

More relaxed, he replied, "Of course. Are you in a hurry?"

"Not particularly. It's still early. I'd like another cup of coffee." She was on her feet before he could make the move upward. "One for you?"

This time he accepted without any show of independence. "Yes. Thank you."

When she returned there were fewer than half a dozen others in the room. Elizabeth and Lyle sipped their coffee and smoked cigarettes in silence for a while, then Lyle said, "Elizabeth, you've been at this longer than I have. Do you sometimes wonder if we're getting through to the people, that they believe what they are doing is worthwhile?"

"Yes, I do. I have the advantage of living over here with them and I pick up a lot of feedback. What you don't know is that they're as self-conscious as they are because of their ages and ignorance, but you should hear them boast to their neighbors about their progress. Not a day goes by that I don't see some evidence of it, hear it from the children I teach every day."

Emerson sighed. "I wish I could see it. At the end of each class I find myself needing to resell them on coming back to the next one. I get that almost helpless feeling of not being able to reach them."

407

"Some day you will if you believe that what we're doing is really important."

"Yes, it could be—"

"It *is*. I know it is."

"Sometimes, I—this may sound crazy to you, but I almost wish I could change my color in order to get closer to them, inside, deep into their minds, the way you can, know what they think and feel. This mistrust of a white man, any white man, I can see it in their faces, in their response, or their lack of it."

"It isn't that. Not mistrust. They're simply wary. Out of all the white people who originally took part in this program actively you're about the only one left who has shown he intends to stay with it. Some dropped out for legitimate reasons, others by pressures brought on them by other circumstances. I think they're waiting to see just when you give up and drop out."

"I won't. You know I won't, don't you, Elizabeth? Not under any kind of pressure."

"I know it, Lyle, but they don't. Or why you're doing it at all."

"Why?"

"Yes. They wonder why a white man is so involved in their problems."

"Do you feel the same way?"

She laughed lightly. "No. Not in the least."

"Why not?"

"Because I know why. At least, I think I do."

"Tell me what you think you know about why I'm doing it."

"Lyle, I don't want to get into a personal discussion—"

"You started it, Elizabeth. I'd like to know why. Tell me."

"All right." She took another sip of coffee and a deep pull on her cigarette, then exhaled slowly. "Because of Cord Waters. What he did for you. I know that when you got back here you asked the School Board to let you teach over here at Sidney Lanier High. They refused because it was an all-Negro school. You appealed the decision to the County Commissioners and they upheld the School Board. The only other way you had of paying off your debt to Cord was to teach at the Center on your own time. Not just three nights a week, but five. That guilt burden must be very heavy to carry."

"It wasn't guilt, Elizabeth. I really wanted—"

"Stop it, Lyle. You couldn't offer yourself to Shad and
408

Leona Waters as a replacement for Cord, so you did the next best thing."

"I'm not doing it for that reason."

"You *are*, Lyle, whether you want to realize it or not. Everybody expiates guilt in his own way. This is your way."

"Assuming that guilt is a part of it, he did save my life and lost his own doing it. Am I supposed to discard that, forget it?"

"No, of course not. It's a wonderful thing to remember. And what you're doing here is a wonderful thing, too, but what happened to Cord shouldn't become the primary reason for doing what you are doing here. If it does, then the burden is too great. If you do it because it's the right thing to do—"

"Don't you believe that all debts inevitably become burdens?"

"Not if you don't really owe them. Not to Cord, not to his parents, not to my people. He did what he was trained to do, what became instinct, second nature, just as you would have done the same thing for him if your situations had been reversed. Men have been known to throw themselves on live grenades to protect others, taken other risks that endangered their own lives."

Lyle smiled wryly. "I'm getting quite a liberal education tonight," he said.

"I didn't mean to lecture, Lyle. I know it must be a horrible experience to have lived through, but in one way or another, we all have them. Sooner or later, the luckier ones are able to accept things as they are and go on living in peace."

"Thank you, Teacher. I hope I can remember your words of wisdom." He looked around the room and discovered that they were alone. The woman behind the counter was putting the last of the food away. "Hey! The world has walked out on us. Shall we go?"

When they reached the parking lot, they saw the white Thunderbird pull in, heading across the paved parking lot toward them, the head thrust through the window on the driver's side, calling, "Lyle!"

Lyle paused and peered toward it. "Who is it?"

"It's me, Lyle. Corey Armour."

"Corey! By God, is that really you, Corey?"

"Nobody else."

"Good Lord! Where did you come from?" Lyle was hobbling awkwardly toward the T-bird as Corey got out and went quickly to meet him. A shake of hands, a tight embrace.

409

"Man, I've been trying to get in touch with you for two days now. Don't you read the paper any more, see anybody?" He looked beyond Lyle to Elizabeth

Lyle recovered and said, "Corey, this is Miss Shackleford, one of the Center instructors. Elizabeth, Corey Armour."

"How do you do, Miss— Are you related to Sam Shackleford?"

"He's my father."

"It's a pleasure, Miss Shackleford. I remember your father and knew your Uncle Matt a long time ago. I hope you'll forgive me for barging in like this. I've been very anxious to see Lyle—"

Elizabeth said quickly, "Of course. This isn't a date, Mr. Armour. I missed my ride home and Mr. Emerson kindly offered—"

"If you don't mind, then, may I ride along with you?"

"Of course," Lyle said. "Let's use my car. It'll hold three on the front seat. Leave yours here, Corey, and I'll bring you back to it." Moving toward the Dodge now, "I'm sorry I missed the item in the paper, Corey. I really hadn't heard you were back. I've been kept so busy—"

Trapped between them, Elizabeth had little to contribute to the impromptu reunion. She sat quietly, conscious above their conversation of the pressure of her left thigh against the bulky harness and the rigid artificial leg, making no move to draw away in order not to add to Lyle's sensitivity. She looked directly ahead through the windshield, almost feeling their breath on her cheeks when they turned toward each other to ask and respond to questions of how? when? and where? And suddenly, she wished she had refused the ride, walked the four blocks to the bus stop, although she was justifiably afraid to walk alone at night in this forbidding section. And what if she were seen, respectable Sam and Lutie Shackleford's teacher-daughter, riding in a car at night with two white men? Idiocy to its nth degree.

She allowed her mind to dwell on other things, remembering.

When the first money came from Duke, a money order for $300, it was the very first word they had had that Duke was even alive. The laborious, involved letter that came with it was on hotel stationery and told of his new profession, his most recent important victory, and enclosed clippings from three newspapers hailing "Buddy Duke" as a "comer." One clipping featured his picture, a smiling face, one gloved hand raised in triumph, titled "Gladiator."

410

They felt a mixture of pride, misgivings, doubt and some fear that there was something morally wrong, somehow, in a boy, their young son, earning so much money for destroying another within "one minute and thirteen seconds of the second round." Elizabeth, who was 17 then, was agog with excitement. "How long is a round, Pa?" she asked.

"I don' know, honey. Maybe three-four minutes."

"A whole hundred dollars a round?"

"Well, coulda been more if he send us three hundred. Say so in the paper, don't it, done it in the second round?"

The money order lay on the kitchen table around which they sat staring in wonderment. "Read that last part of the letter again, Lizabeth," Sam said

"It says, 'They be more comin soon. You git another hous to liv in an use the res to Lizabeths schoolin. I al rite don wrry bout me. Love Duke. Buddy Duke.' Lord, what spelling!"

Fiercely protective, Lutie said, "You hush. He didn' have the same chances you had." In the solemn quiet that ensued, they continued to stare at the moncy order that represented so much money. Then Lutie said, "We do it."

"Do what?" Sam asked.

"We send Lizabeth to college. We use the money we been savin' for a new house, the money we was savin' to send her to college."

"College," Sam grunted.

"No, Ma," Elizabeth said. "I graduate high school in June and that's enough. Time I got a job——"

"Waitin' tables, housework, wearin' yourse'f thin before your time?" Lutie snapped. "This your chance your brother givin' you, girl. You go away someplace where you can learn, be somebody. You can't do nothin' here. Come next fall, you go make somethin' of yourself." She paused, more at ease now that Sam and Elizabeth seemed to accept her statement. "Where c'n you find out about colleges?"

"Mr. Masters, the principal——"

"Your Pa and me go see him."

"You can't, Ma."

"Who can't?" Sam said. "I know Stanley Masters. His pa drives a truck at the plant. We go see Stanley to his house tonight. Your brother given you a chance to better yourself, Lizabeth, you got to take it."

Before she left for Los Angeles, there were two more money orders, one for $550, another for $800, with the promise of more. Buddy Duke was moving up fast and his manager, Al Saxon, according to the press clippings, was predicting a championship match for Buddy Duke within

411

two years. Mr. Masters had helped her with the arrangements, even writing ahead to find suitable living quarters near the campus.

She boarded with a Negro family in a clean house less than a mile from campus, Negroes who were native to California and didn't fully understand the struggle of a Southern Negro trying to adjust to a new way of life in a world that was bright and new and marvelously alive with clean, bright faces, white and black, sparkling with intelligence, life, and hope. She was shy, even among her own, and kept to herself, all the while aching to be a part of her surroundings; the excitement over basketball and football, track meets, baseball; but somehow she couldn't let go. She swam in the Olympic-sized pool where there were no color bars, went to an occasional movie and sat among the white patrons, ate in restaurants where no one took issue because of her color.

She was more responsive in class; eager, perceptive, studious; and in her second year, after a summer at home, she returned to California more desperate than ever to do even better. She was 19 then, and he was a youngish 40, an associate professor in English who had given her some reassurance during her freshman year when she needed it most. More, in fact, than she had gotten from her own people here.

She learned that Alec Holcomb, to her deep surprise, was also from the South. "Ten years away from Charleston," as he put it. He encouraged her to participate in outside class activities; a literary society, art shows, music recitals, lectures. He was delighted that she leaned toward a teaching career and urged her to continue in that direction. "Nothing," he said, "could be of greater need or value to your people. Education will do more toward their liberation than all the welfare money or menial jobs can produce. Knowledge brings the understanding needed to strike the chains from them, and education at the earliest stages of learning is the foundation of knowledge."

In time, Elizabeth gained the confidence she needed. She attended Alec's recommended lecture courses, took active part in a literary society, joined a drama class. Under his guidance, she felt there was nothing she could not face. Alec drew her into a writing group he had formed and for a while she was totally absorbed with the idea of becoming a writer.

She began to make friends and learned that white male students were no more or no less interested in forming a

412

sexual relationship with her than they were with white girls, and although she brushed off these efforts, she took joy in the feeling that there was a brand of equality that placed her on the same level of acceptance with her contemporaries, black and white. She was tempted to experiment, but steeled herself against temptation.

It was at the start of her junior year that she came to believe she was in love with Alec Holcomb, that he was attracted to her. She found excuses to remain behind when others in his informal writing group were gone, but he made no attempt to take advantage of the opportunities she gave him. He lived alone in a small, neat house, cared for by a woman who came in twice each week to do his laundry, clean, and prepare the only two cooked dinners he ate at home.

Elizabeth admired him tremendously. She began dressing with greater care, spending her carefully husbanded money to make herself more attractive to him. Alec not only noticed, but commented with admiration on her emergence from the chrysalis of youth into nubile womanhood.

On a Saturday afternoon, she went with a group to view the Matisse exhibition at the Los Angeles County Museum and saw Alec there, alone. He joined her group, discussed Matisse in his usual easy, informal manner, with anecdotes and sparkling comments that were the reasons his class lectures were so popular. Later, as the crowd grew denser, Elizabeth saw him examining a display of bronzes and left the group to join him. They continued through the rest of the exhibition together and when they had seen it all, walked through the grounds in the late afternoon, past the stadium to the parking lot where his car stood. "Home?" he asked.

"No. I can't bear the thought of being inside four walls on an evening like this. Drop me—"

"Dinner?"

"I'd love it. Some place different. New and exciting."

"My choice?"

"Your choice is my choice."

He drove out toward the coastline and cruised along miles of beach as the westering sun drowned in the Pacific and night began to take over. He kept on until they reached Laguna Beach. "Hungry?" he asked.

"Starving."

"How about some Mexican food?"

"Beautiful thought."

The evening had turned cool and they ate at Arturo's, in an outdoor patio which looked across the broad, empty

413

beach and the wide, empty ocean, seeing it from behind sheets of glass used to keep the wind out. A huge fireplace in the center of the patio, candlelight; tortillas, tacos, frijoles, salad and cerveza. The patio became crowded, but they were alone and content on their small island of peace.

"Alec?"

"What?"

"Why aren't you married?"

"I was."

"Divorced?"

"No." She waited. "She was Japanese," he said. "We were married in Tokyo and there were delays in getting permission to bring her back to the States. Army regulations were very strict. By the time the red tape was cut and cleared away, she was dead. A traffic accident."

"I'm sorry."

"Among the world's great tragedies, a mere incident in life."

"You must have loved her very much not to have married again."

"Don't read a great romance into it, Elizabeth."

"You can't be that detached, can you?"

"Detached? No." He sat for a while looking directly into her eyes, smiling at her with his eyes, but not with his lips. "I was a coward," he said finally. "I loved her, yes. But when I returned to Charleston and she was still in Tokyo, I realized the enormity of bringing a Japanese woman home. My family was outraged. There were my mother and father, two married sisters and a married brother, their children, aunts and uncles. I delayed the procedures several times because of my own fears. Finally, when permission came through, I delayed again. I had only to sign one piece of paper, then send her the money to come to America. But I held back, steeped in my own cowardice. And then I received word that she was dead.

"I suffered from the loss and my own guilt. That was when I left Charleston and came out here. I blamed society, my family, the South, the world. Until I realized that I alone had to bear the blame and penalty." He looked up sadly and said. "I shouldn't have told you what an ugly man I am inside."

"You aren't ugly, Alec. You were young—"

"And you are young, but you understand. I was young and I was a damned fool."

"Alec—"

"What?"

"Let's go now. I'm getting chilled."

414

They drove back to Los Angeles by the freeway and she dozed with her head on his shoulder. When they reached her house, she said sleepily, "No, Alec. I don't want to go in there. It depresses me."

He took her to his house. A month later, she moved in with him. That summer, after a brief visit home, she returned "to make up some extra credits." In mid-July, Alec loaded his car with camping gear and they roamed the Sierras like two gypsies, sleeping in bedrolls beside camp fires that overlooked lakes, hiking, swimming, cooking their own meals out of doors, alone with a kind, understanding Mother Nature to look on without censure.

Toward the end, she knew more about Alec than he knew about himself; and that they were mired in a hopeless romance and it would come to nothing. What she had learned was that Alec was still a coward, that his first marriage and his defection from it was stronger than his professed love for her. And as she had come to know, it ended with her graduation. They said good-bye one morning at the downtown bus depot and there were actual tears in his eyes when he said his last words to her. "I'm sorry, Elizabeth. I told you once what an ugly man I am inside. Be a good teacher."

Sayonara. Return to Laurelton.

She sank back against the seat of the Dodge, trying to shrink herself into some smaller form as they rode along Division Street to Mercer, where Lyle started to turn in. "Not here," Elizabeth said. "The next block."

"I thought you—"

"The next block, please," she insisted.

Lyle understood then and drove past Mercer to La Grange, turned left until they were approaching Wallace. In the middle of the block, she said, "Here. I'll get out here, please."

La Grange Street was narrow, its houses small. Only one or two showed lights. At the far corner was a lamp post with a dimly lighted bulb, its outer shade broken. "Elizabeth—" Lyle started, but she cut him off with, "It's all right. My house is just around the corner on Wallace. Thank you very much for the lift."

Corey got out, helped Elizabeth to the pavement. They bid each other good night and she began walking, but Lyle waited until she had reached the corner, then drifted slowly toward Wallace, saw her mount the steps to the porch of her house and headed back toward the Center and Corey's car.

415

Elizabeth came up the walk, fumbling among the odds and ends in her purse for her house key. As she mounted the steps, Sam Shackleford called to her softly from where he sat in a wicker chair at the far end of the porch. "Honey?"

For a moment she was startled and froze. Only three weeks before, Mrs. Elder, who lived two doors away, had come home alone to find someone hiding, crouching in the shadows on her porch, a man who struck her, dragged her into the house, raped and robbed her. Her husband was at work on his night maintenance shift in the textile plant.

"Pa?" she said with relief. "Mom with you?"

"No, she's asleep, all tuckered out with the heat. How come you walkin' home? I told you a hundred times, you got no ride, you telephone me."

"I had a ride, Pa. They dropped me at the corner. What are you doing up?"

"Too hot to sleep. It's a little better out here. You hungry?"

"No. I had something to eat after class."

"Sit with me?"

"Sure, Pa. Let me put my things away." She went inside and returned a few minutes later. She had changed into pajamas and wore a lightweight robe. "This heat," she complained. "Will we ever get any cooler weather this fall?"

"We always do. Once this spell breaks, we start complainin' how cold it is. School all right?"

"Yes and no. If we could just keep the night attendance up. The older people just don't seem to care about learning."

"Can't fault 'em too much, can you, honey? You take a man laborin' hard all his life, a woman raisin' her own children an' somebody else's, washin', scrubbin' all day long, it take a lot to make 'em want to learn to read an' write this late in the day."

"I know, Pa, and I understand, but they've got to show their children and grandchildren that they're making the effort, that it's important to their futures."

"You right, Lizabeth, but it just proves nothin' happens overnight. It takes the Lord's own patience in every one of us to work at what we want. Seems like nobody's got enough of it, patience, I mean, specially among the young people. Want everything been goin' wrong for years to change overnight. Like Duke."

"Is Duke home?"

"No. He come home after you left. Come breezin' in, change his clo'es an' go right out again."

"Pa?"

"What, honey?"

"Pa, don't be too upset by Duke. You've got to remember he's been away from here for ten years, living up north under different circumstances, in better surroundings, where people looked up to him—"

"An' turn his head—"

"And respected him because he was among the best in his field."

"I know that, honey. Other colored boys done the same thing in the same field, boxin', baseball, football, basketball. They do it in business an' law an' medicine, too. When they do, they got to set a good example for others, show 'em it ain't out of their reach to get someplace, not talkin' about grabbin' what they want just by reachin' out an' takin' it by force, threatenin' to burn an' destroy. Fire, anger, wrath, that's the way to destruction of everybody."

"Pa, don't take it so seriously. I don't think Duke wants to start any civil war here. He's young and he wants the right to feel free and equal. The same as I do."

"You different, Lizabeth. You teachin' people how to do it the right way. By learnin' to write an' read so they can register an' vote. Enough people vote right, they get the right laws. It takes time, but it's comin'."

"Oh, Pa—" She realized there was little use in prolonging the discussion, to explain the differences between his generation and hers and Duke's, and the one coming up behind them. "I think I'll go in and try to get some sleep."

"Go ahead, honey. No use waitin' up for him. He prob'ly be out most of the night anyway. Sleep good."

8

Several times, before they reached Lyle's apartment, Corey had felt impelled to reach out to assist him, but restrained the reflexive instinct; to offer an arm when Lyle got out of his car; on the way up the four steps to the lobby, taking them one at a time as Lyle stumbled once, caught the rail to regain his balance; opening the lobby door; adjusting his step to the thickness of the carpeting along the hallway; finally, inside the apartment, again slightly off balance while removing his jacket and tie.

Now, over a year since the operation, Lyle was less reticent to talk about the experience. The hospital, an "AK amp," or above-the-knee amputee, among other "amps"; the second operation to prepare the stump properly for the prosthesis, as the artificial replacement was called, to come; the first days and nights of pain and depression, bordering on paranoia; withdrawal from the professional and amateur instructors and cheerer-uppers who had themselves been through the same mill; the intense, shattering self-pity, the agonizing hopelessness of tomorrow.

"Christ, they were everywhere, the amps. BK's, AK's, BE's, the hip disarticulations. No matter the degree, there was always somebody with something worse, all the way to a quadruple amp, no arms, no legs, only a torso, the poor, sad bastard."

"How long—"

"After the final surgery about ten or twelve weeks before they began. Kept me busy with crutches until the shrinkage was uniform and the wound safely healed. Then the measuring, the plaster cast to form the socket for the prosthesis and the harness." Lyle rapped knuckles against the artificial limb, then hobbled to the kitchen counter to fix drinks.

"I won't try to tell you what I went through until I could begin to accept this Daddy's Dandy Little Helper; the mental hurdles and gymnastics, the therapists, the visiting amps who can do everything from riding and jumping horses to playing eighteen holes of golf. All it adds up to is this: no matter how good it is, it's not the same and won't ever be the same because, come bedtime, you've still got to unstrap the sonofabitch and stand it beside the bed to remind you of what you lost. That's when you tally up the personal cost of war and realize that there's nothing else to do but try to live with it."

"Lyle, can it be worse than—"

"Death? Sometimes, yes. There are some things you never get used to living with. Or without. This is one of them. At night, seeing it standing there before you fall asleep, seeing it the first thing when you wake up, waiting. Or when I've been on it too long. I may come to accept it more graciously some day. At least, I hope so." He broke off, then said, "But off or on, the sonofabitch is always there, reminding you."

"How is the job?"

Lyle handed Corey his drink, put his own on an end table and maneuvered himself into the lounge chair beside it and hand-adjusted his leg onto the ottoman. He sipped his drink deeply, then said, "Fair. Pay is still far below the national average, but my monthly retirement check helps me get by. Lucky I wasn't a postman or track-walker before I got it."

"Lyle, I—" Corey thought then, *How can anyone with two legs possibly make it easier for a man with only one?*

"What?"

"Uh—" He needed a new subject in a hurry. "I was thinking—Saturday night—"

"What about it?"

"You remember Paula Corbin, don't you? She's having some people in. I wonder if you'd like to come along with me? I'm sure you'll know most of them."

"Thanks, Corey, but no. I don't swing with your crowd. They're younger than mine was. Some day, maybe. I use my weekends to rest up. A drive somewhere, read, and get some sleep."

"You haven't become that anti-social, have you?"

"Call it what you want. I teach history five days a week. I teach at the R-V Center five nights a week. That doesn't leave me much time for socializing."

Corey said it quietly, gambling on its effect. "She really hit you one hell of a blow, didn't she?"

Twisting around in his chair suddenly, "Who?"

"Jill Tinsley."

"Oh. Her." Lyle tossed off the rest of his drink. "I think I'm damned well over *that.*" He said it convincingly, without anger. Then he got up and went to the kitchen and poured another stiff straight bourbon and came back to the chair. "You know, as soon as I could make it out of the hospital, I went up to New York looking for Jill. She'd switched jobs to an advertising agency, working in a little cubbyhole, knocking out brilliant, sparkling prose for some underarm deodorant account. Christ, what a scene when I stood in the doorway looking at her, actually sweating out that stomach-turning crap we have forced on us.

"There she was, grinding out that filthy garbage, too busy at her typewriter even to look up. I guess she thought I was one of the copy boys standing there. Didn't look up at me. She called out, 'Yes, what is it?' I didn't answer, so she turned around and saw me. She went absolutely white and I thought she'd faint. Then she stood up and said 'Lyle.' Just that one word.

"I said, 'Hello, Jill,' and she looked around like a trapped animal trying to find a way out, but there was only the single door and one window, thirty-two stories above Lexington Avenue. Then she said, 'Lyle, please excuse me—I need some water.' Hell, there wasn't any doubt about that. She brushed past me and disappeared down the hall. A little later, a girl came in and told me 'Miss Tinsley was taken ill and had to leave. She's sorry.' That was the last I saw of Miss Jill Tinsley."

"Lyle, you knew it would probably happen—"

"Sure. I guess I had to taste the whip firsthand before I could make myself believe it."

"Try to forget it. I know that's easy for me to say, but you can't waste the rest of your life on a dream."

"I know that, too, Corey, but they both come back. Awake, during a class, asleep, they keep coming back."

"Both?"

"The leg and Jill, the two I lost when that goddamned Cong bastard got me. And Cord Waters. He's there, too. I went up to Brookhill to see his father and mother first thing after I got back. That was an experience. The two of them sat there listening quietly, politely, trying not to cry. And I wondered how much they hated me for being alive. And then Mrs. Waters got up and came to me and said, 'You poor man. How you must be suffering.' Imagine that. *She* was sorry for *me*."

"I'll buy that."

"But he's dead, Corey. Their son is dead and I'm here. No father, no mother, no wife or children to be happy I'm alive, and they're mourning an only son who'll come back in a box they won't even be allowed to open."

"Lyle—"

"I know, Corey. It's been said before and often. It wasn't my fault. I didn't ask him to help me. But I can't forget that he did and he died for it."

"And that's why you're working at the Center."

"It helps. Not much, but I need it."

He asked the question before he realized he had spoken it. "And Elizabeth Shackleford?"

Lyle's head jerked upward. "Don't read anything into that, Corey. We just talk and that's all. Tonight was the first time she's been in my car, and only because it was my fault she missed her ride. But since you mentioned it, she's a hell of a girl. Bright as a whip. Got her teaching credentials at U.S.C. in Los Angeles."

"How?"

"She has an older brother, Duke, who's something of a middleweight contender up in New York. When he hit the big time, he sent some money home and the family used it to send her away to college."

"Good for her. She seems very intelligent."

"Oh, she is that. A good kid, but that's it."

Corey finished his drink and put his glass down on the table and stood up.

"How about one for the road? I'll fix them." Lyle was up, hobbling toward the kitchen now and called out, "How about you, Corey?"

"The same. Bourbon on the rocks, and hit me light."

Lyle laughed. "I meant, what about your plans?"

"I haven't decided anything definitely yet."

"Aren't you going to step into the Warren setup?"

"I don't know. I may go out on my own, but I've got another thing up my sleeve before I make up my mind. At any rate, I'm going to use my terminal leave up before I commit myself."

"Cheers and good luck."

"Cheers, and thanks."

9

Riverside was a small community lying west and north of Angeltown, where the Negro business and professional elite lived. Men like Henry Clark (Clark's Funeral Home), Milo Roose (Afro-American Insurance), Walter Lynch (Lynch Real Estate), and Dr. Royal Betts (Physician and Surgeon), the more prosperous store-owners and entrepreneurs who dealt exclusively with Negroes in West Laurelton. Although Riverside was within Laurelton's city limits, few Negroes, except those from Angeltown who worked as maids, laundresses, gardeners and handymen, knew the area well. Its social restrictions were almost as rigid as those between Negro and white, with color the only common bond.

Riverside homes were substantially built, of brick or frame, yet consciously unpretentious, spaced well apart from their neighbors and subtly hidden by trees and hedges, seeking privacy from passing eyes; yet with the suspicion that each was cleverly designed to keep the curious at a distance. Beyond the hedges, lawns and gardens were neatly tended, porch and lawn furniture as good as any in Laurelton's upper-middle-class home, late-model cars in their garages. Their children were well-mannered, clean and neatly, although not ostentatiously, dressed, and were taught never to discuss material possessions and to restrict social contact to their Riverside companions.

The section had once been an agricultural area of small, Negro-owned or rented farms that had become rundown, later sold or abandoned when Laurelton's growing industrialization siphoned off the manpower required to plant, weed, hoe, harvest and market its yield. Gambling correctly on a continuing prosperity after World War II, Walter Lynch and Milo Roose had gathered a number of prosperous Negroes together and proposed their plan to create the Riverside community, restrict it to residential property and keep the commercial where it was, in Angeltown. Quietly, Lynch took options on the desired land and shortly thereafter broke ground for two homes—for Lynch and Roose —with the others following soon afterward. Afro-American Insurance and Laurelton National Bank financed the development, Taylor Industries supplied materials, equipment and supervisory labor, and Riverside was born. Lots were large and expensive; home plans had to be approved by The Committee. Only those financially secure could afford to live in Riverside.

People here lived quietly and graciously. Most were church-goers and there was no police problem. Quarrels were solved privately among themselves and if one threatened to grow out of hand and attract public attention, The Committee was generally strong enough to bring sufficient pressures on the offenders.

Riverside supported all charities as a group. Its own Committee representative analyzed requests from various organized church and charity groups, discussed the need and, if approved, checks were written. It supported the Recreational-Vocational Center and the Laurelton Civil Rights Committee and refused to recognize the militant wing. Its residents were no more or less honest or dishonest, ethical or unethical, reverent or hypocritical than their white brethren east of the Cottonwood River.

On the basis of his wealth alone, Ben-Joe Nichols owned a house in Riverside.

In the comfortable, low-ceilinged den of his sprawling one-storied house, Ben-Joe Nichols, dressed in crisp yellow slacks and an apple-green silk sports shirt, poured two glasses of bourbon, dropped in some ice cubes, added a splash of water. He slid one of the glasses across the bar counter to Duke Shackleford and raised the other in silent salute. Duke touched the rim of his glass to Ben-Joe's and sipped the cold drink with relish.

Banjo, Duke thought, was really an ugly cat, getting old and flabby, but a smart operator. The front section of Banjo's Place, the poolroom, was a legitimate coverup for whatever illegitimate enterprises he directed from the back room, and there were few in South and West Laurelton from which he did not receive a substantial cut. And that, Duke knew, was more than rumor.

When Lee Durkin moved across the bridge to become Chief of Police, Ben-Joe Nichols gathered the haphazard vice element together and organized it under his own leadership, using "protection" as his lever. It had cost him a lot to buy his way into the police organization, but it was worth it as long as the word didn't reach high enough to find its way to Durkin's ears.

The process, under proper supervision from the "other side," had been refined down to simplicity. Instead of paying off to any and every cop who dropped in on him, he now paid off to a single man who passed the cash along to another echelon and who, in turn, sent it along to where the orders were handed down. Banjo's hold on "protection" gave him the iron fist he needed to expand and develop his suzerainity over gambling operators, after-hours joints, whorehouse operations, the importation and distribution of tax-free bootleg whiskey that was poured into refillable bottles, and bookmaking establishments. For himself, he claimed all rights to the distribution of marijuana and heroin.

Let one operator fall into his disfavor and the word would be passed to the proper man and a raid would put the defector out of business. Otherwise, when the word of an imminent raid was passed down to Ben-Joe, he would make sure the police would not be disappointed, but they would find no major vice operations in progress; a small crap game or poker game, a pair of cheap hustlers, a small-time lawbreaker wanted for a misdemeanor, or a pusher would be offered up as a sacrifice. The police would be satisfied for the time being and Banjo's lawyer, Gale Reed. would put up bail, pay the fine for the apprehended, or one or two would be permitted to serve a short jail sentence. Business would return to normal within a few days, in a new location, if necessary.

Banjo, now past his mid-50s, showed every sign of good living. In the ten years since Duke had seen him last, Banjo's body had become almost corpulent, thickened with the fat of prosperity. He was a very dark man with heavy Negroid features: thickly hooded eyes, a flat, bridgeless nose over wide, pink-tinted lips. His hair was nappy, shorn close to the skull, more gray than black. A five-inch, twenty-year-old scar ran from the corner of his right eye to his lower jawline, which gave him a perpetually grim, sinister look. His wife and three children were seldom seen in town, preferring to remain among their own in Riverside.

From his side of the bar, Ben-Joe saw in Duke everything he had always wanted, envied and never had: a lean, lithe figure, well-muscled, young and hard, light brown in color, and facial features that were clean and straight. And mixed with the envy, a certain amount of resentment and contempt for this "nothin' lucky kid who couldn't play it cool, busted out before he made it to the top, trying to copper his bets before he hit the skids."

"Yeah, Duke, you lookin' real good," Banjo said. "You been aroun' an' seen a lot, done things, had the best of it. We followed you a long time, right down to your last fight." Duke caught the emphasis on that "right down to your last fight" and winced slightly. "What you got in mind to do now?"

"Just visitin' the folks, lookin' up old friends 'til my hand heals up. Kind of restin' up a while."

"Shuh. Well, you enjoy your visitin'. Most of your old friends, they still aroun'. A few of 'em gone. Been about ten years now, ain't it? But people aroun' here still know Buddy Duke even if they don't remember Duke Shackleford."

"Yeah, I guess." Duke took another sip of his drink. "Banjo—"

Frigidly, "Banjo, that's my business name, Duke. Here in my own house say it Ben-Joe."

"Sure, you want it that way, Ben-Joe."

"That's how I want it. What you got on your mind?"

"Well, I been thinkin', suppose I was to decide I had enough of fightin', want to come back an' settle down, go into somethin'—"

"Like what?"

"Somethin' I got in mind, been thinkin' on."

Ben-Joe shrugged. "You got somethin' in mind, what you need anybody else for?"

Cagy bastard, Duke thought. Aloud, "Well, what I got in mind it needs a partner."

"There's plenty people aroun' to listen to you if you got a good business proposition."

"You the kind of people I need for the business I got in mind, Ben-Joe."

"Son, you got a proposition to make me, stop beatin' aroun' the bush an' lay it on the line. I like it, I say so. Likewise I don't, I say so."

"All right. Policy."

"Policy. You mean insurance?"

"No insurance, Ben-Joe. Numbers."

"Numbers." Ben-Joe took a long pull at his glass while staring over the rim from under his lizard-like eyes. *He looks cool,* Ben-Joe thought, *but he's sweatin'. This all he got to hang his hat on. He th'ough in the ring an' if he don't sell this, he got nothin' else goin' for him.*

Ben-Joe put his glass down slowly. "Not a chance, Duke," he said, shaking the large globe of head from side to side. "Not a snowball's chance in hell."

"How come?"

"Tell you why. Numbers ain't nothin' new to me. In a big city, they fine, run smooth. You got people spread out all over to put up pennies, nickels, dimes and quarters to hit a 600-to-1 shot straight, or a 100-to-1 shot on the boxed numbers. Okay, you divide a big city in a hundred drops, maybe more. One, two, three get knocked over, you got ninety-seven more workin' for you. Place this size, you can't have more'n a dozen or so drops. You lose a few an' maybe take a big hit the same time, you out of business."

"There'd be enough to pay protection, an' plenty left to split two ways," Duke argued. "You take just the big plants alone—"

"Can't see it, Duke, else I'd been in it long time ago. Too many details, too many runners, too many mouths talkin'. You start takin' small change from the little people, you robbin' the church collection boxes. Amos Hart, the other preachers, they start raisin' hell from the pulpit, ain't no amount of money goin'a be enough to keep the cops off'n your back. Churches, they got to have their own little rackets, collect the little money with their bingo games, lotteries, suppers. They too strong to fight once they get riled up."

"You ain't never tried it?"

"No. They try it here long ago, but it didn' work out too good. I don't try nothin' ain't got no chance to make it."

"Ben-Joe, lissen. This thing, it's worth the chance. I know. I seen money flowin' like it rainin' down from the sky. This ain't chickenshit, man. It's a five-billion-dollar-a-year business in this country. Not million, Ben-Joe, *billion.* You know how much a billion dollars is?"

"That's Harlem, Chicago, Los Angeles, every big city in the country you talkin' about, Duke. Even Atlanta an' New Orleans, but not Laurelton. It's tough enough to pay off as it is. Come cold weather, it gets tougher. Police got more time to stick their noses into other things. The answer is No. N-O, no."

"Suppose I go on my own?"

"You can't make it, boy."

"I can try."

"Shuh. You blow what little bitty money you got to set

425

yourself up an' the first day you in business, somebody blow the whistle on you, you dead."

"Yeah." Duke's eyes narrowed to slits. "Like the time somebody blow the whistle on Benny Tupper, the time they pick him up. An' almost got me the same time." He said it slowly, trying to gauge Ben-Joe's reaction, watching the flicker of annoyance, the movement of his lips and the twisting of the ugly scar.

"All right," Ben-Joe said finally. "Benny, he needed a lesson. He was talkin' too much, flashin' too big a roll, foolin' with too many broads. Tryin' to take over, too. He put you on to help him, a sixteen-year-old kid, without askin' me. When I run somethin', Duke, I run it. My own way. I'm The Man. An' I ain't about to let you or nobody else bust up what it taken me years to build up. Lemme put you straight, boy, what I got is mine an' nobody walks in an' takes a piece of the action just for askin'."

"I got money to buy in."

"What you call money?"

"Five-six thousand."

"You call that money? Shit, man, you ain't much bigger'n you was ten years ago. You a busted-down fighter with a busted hand an' no way to go except down. You on the stuff, too. You got the smell of it on you right now, an' a user spells nothin' but trouble. That was Benny's trouble, fallin' for the stuff he was pushin'. You nothin' but a name, an' that don't buy you nothin' more'n a drink or a cup of coffee 'till they stop printin' your name in the papers an' it all wears off. You take your numbers thing an' go back up north with it, or down to Atlanta, see if they let you break in. This is my town, an' I say who do an' who don't, an' you remember that."

"All's I'm askin' for, Ben-Joe, is a piece of your action for a piece of mine. Partners."

Ben-Joe stared with incredulity. *"Partners?"* he exclaimed. "With what? Man, you ain't *got* no action." He fell silent and Duke had no answer. He squirmed on the bar stool, fingering the glass in his hand, running one finger around its rim in a continuous circle, lips drawn in a tight line. Ben-Joe said, "Benny tell you he was workin' for me?"

"Hell, no. When I said it before, I was only guessin'. You was the one admitted it."

Ben-Joe relaxed. Even smiled. "That was pretty smart, Duke."

"All fighters ain't got their brains scrambled, Ben-Joe, and I ain't walkin' aroun' on my heels yet."

"Come to think of it, maybe you could learn. Maybe."

"What?"

"Whatever it is, first thing you got to know, you got to know who's boss."

"You already showed me. I know it."

"You busy tonight?"

"Nothin' I can't shake loose of."

"Come aroun' to the Place, say about eleven?"

"Shuh."

"I'll see you there. We'll talk over a few things, see if you fit in with what I got in mind. Okay?"

"I'll be there."

10

His anger finally dissipated, Duke returned to Angeltown. He drove the length of Velie Street, then along Grand Avenue, senses reawakened and sharpened by old memories dating back to his newspaper route. Now, many modern fronts disguised ancient and decrepit stores and taverns, restaurants, Freely Jones' shoe-shine parlor, Hinkle's Dry Cleaning and Laundry, Pal's Barber Shop, Oasis Tavern and the Angeltown branch delivery stop where he used to line up to get his papers early every morning. There were two fairly decent office buildings for accountants, doctors, real estate agents, a sign shop, carpet and furniture store, hardware emporium, a garage and several used-car lots he had never seen before.

At nine o'clock the streets were brilliant with neon, noisy with rock-and-roll jazz, heavy with pedestrian and vehicular traffic. Hipsters and swingers and their mini-skirted girls sauntered along toward favorite hangouts or simply stood in groups in front of the one movie house, The Goldfield, a popular restaurant, a tavern, and around the garishly lit night clubs that featured swing or rock combos and scantily clad dancers.

Little Harlem, Duke thought. And that scared chickenshit two-bit Banjo, hugging his rackets like a miser counting his gold; living out there in Riverside among the Uncle Toms, afraid to come out from under the white man's yoke. Don't upset nothin'. Keep everything just the way it is. We rake in our share, pay off, they won't touch us. Goddam hankyheads, they know the onliest thing makes a nigger's world go 'round is money and as long as they get theirs, everything is okay and the rest of the world can go to hell. Well, Mist' Ben-Joe Nichols, we play it your way for a little bit an' see what goes.

Duke turned back into Velie Street and caught sight of a tall, loose-jointed man who glided along as though he were on skates rather than walking. Oley—no, Odie Bell—Bilson. Odie Bilson. Recalling that Odie had worked at his father's filling station, one of Benny Tupper's delivery points ten years ago. He pulled up ahead of Odie, found a parking space at the curb and waited for him to catch up.

"Odie!"

Bilson stopped short, swiveled his hips around, stared at the Jaguar from under the inch-wide brim of his dapper hat, then approached cautiously. At curbside, he leaned over and thrust his head into the car, eyes blinking without recognition at its occupant.

"Don't you remember me, Odie?" Duke said.

"No—can't say—"

"Duke Shackleford, man, remember? Buddy Duke?"

Odie's brain worked slowly, the two names confusing him momentarily. Then they seemed to blend together in his mind and with it, recognition. "Duke? You *Buddy* Duke?"

"One an' the same. How you, Odie?"

"Me? Fine, fine. Jee-*sus*, man! You Buddy Duke, shuh nuf?"

"Shuh nuf. Come on, get in."

"Uh—this your wagon?"

"Nobody else's. Get in."

"Well, goddam!" Odie opened the door, telescoped his body into the seat, one arm extended along the back, facing Duke. "Man, what you doin' back here?"

"Well, what the hell, Odie, it's home, ain't it? Back to visit the folks an' old friends."

"Well, I'll be go to hell! You seen any the other guys?"

"I seen a couple over at Banjo's Place last night. What else is aroun'?"

"Mosta the old cats. Willy Eggert, Booker Dance, Dave Sharkey, Luke Tolbert—le's see, Wilma French, Adah Loomis—man, lotsa new faces aroun'."

"How about some of the old ones? Like Ivy Shackleford?"

"Ivy? She's aroun'. Hangs out mostly at the 2-2-2 Club."

"Must be a new one. Is that *the* place?"

"That's the place, for sure. I'm on my way there now. It just down the street. How about comin' along with me, meet the guys—"

"Show me the way to go home, boy."

They drove along Velie beyond Jeff Davis Avenue and

turned in where Odie directed him, a narrow, cobble-stoned street. "This is it. Peach Alley."

From Velie he could see the lightning flashes of neon coming from the east side of Peach Alley, lighting up the entire area. On both sides, narrow brick pavements fronted its rickety, one-storied brick houses which had evidently been taken over by the swing set. Each house was painted in weird, colorful abstract designs that resembled a block-long mural of an extended nightmare. In the center of the block, an immense neon sign blinked out the figures

2

2   2

2

The horizontal figures were in yellow, white and orange, the vertical in green, white and purple, splashing the painted houses nearby with brilliant hues of light. A uniformed doorman opened the door of the Jaguar and signaled one of the several boys from a bench to take the car to the parking lot next door.

Inside, the noise of raised voices almost drowned out the din of the combo which was on a small stage blaring out a cacophony of disharmony. A chorus line of six girls jogged, swayed and bobbed across the stage and on the small dance floor, male and female bodies performed the same dance, crouching, wiggling and bouncing independently, rhythmically and wildly. The bar was crowded, the air fetid with smoke, body sweat and perfume. And no one seemed to mind in the least.

And there, after pushing his way through the narrow aisle created by Odie Bilson, Duke saw Ivy Shackleford. In the dimness of what passed for lighting, she sat on a stool at the far end of the bar, a man on either side of her, leaning into and over her. But there could be no mistake on Duke's part. She was Ivy, almost as he remembered her from ten years ago. A little more filled out, hair styled exotically different, makeup changed to include something Oriental about the eyes, satiny brown skin showing from a white strapless dress, bare arms resting on the bar, a tall, well-iced drink before her. But she was Ivy, all right. She did not see him at the other end of the bar, nor did he make any effort to go to her at once. But he felt the effect of her presence, excited by the sight of her.

Dave Sharkey, and Luke Tolbert were at the bar and welcomed Duke warmly with shouts that attracted others and drew a circle of enthusiastic admirers around him. Drinks were ordered and passed over heads to the outer fringe who were trying to press closer. The combo signaled a break and returning dancers added to the crush. Booker Dance and Willy Eggert joined them with much shouting and back-slapping while others, too young to remember but knowing Buddy Duke from radio, television and newspaper accounts of his ring victories, hung about the edges of the circle.

And then an arm curled around his neck from behind and he knew from the first touch that it was Ivy. Before he could turn fully around, he heard her silky voice. "You want to get out of this mess, Bubba?"

He was electrified by the familiar name, used by no one else but Elizabeth and Ivy when they all lived together in the old shack on Paca Street. He turned and looked into her smile and said, "Yeah, baby. Gimme ten minutes."

"The door alongside the stage. Hallway to the left. Ten minutes." She drew back into the crowd and was gone.

He finally broke through to the bar. "I'm Buddy Duke," he said to the perspiring bartender. "Give my friends here somethin' to drink. Up to twenty dollars worth an' charge it to me. I'll be back in a little while."

Those within hearing squealed, shouted delightedly and began ordering. Odie cleared an aisle and Duke backed out, promising to return later. He made it to the curtained doorway next to the stage and threw an elaborate wink at Odie. "Be back in maybe an hour, Odie. Somethin' needs tendin' to. See all you cats later."

"Shuh, man. We be here."

Passing musicians and girls in tights with kitten head-dresses, open rooms with relaxing musicians, he moved quickly down the hallway and found Ivy waiting at the exit door which opened into the parking lot. "Where to?" he asked.

"My place," Ivy replied. "You sure look handsome, Bubba. You coulda knocked me over with a breath of air when I look up and see you standin' there."

"I need my car?"

"No. It's just down the street a few doors."

From the outside, the house was the same as the other one-storied houses, a small structure common to the residential area just off, but still a part of, the commercial section. Ivy told Duke that Connie Clark, who ran the 2-2-2, had bought up the block and promoted it into a retreat for the upcoming young who could afford the traffic.

The inside of the house was hardly what he had expected.

430

"Okay." He drew deeply on his cigarette and exhaled. "Where you gettin' your H?" he asked.

"Me?"

"Yeah, you. I seen the marks on you."

"You still turned on?"

"Yeah. I kick it twice, but I'm turned on again."

"Don't worry. I can get it for both of us."

"I want the contact."

"I can't give you no contact except me. It ain't like it used to be. Everything's tightened up hard."

"I got to know, Ivy. I got to get into it, somethin', while I got some money. I brung some stuff down with me from New York. Good an' clean. But I got to get in before I use it up."

"You mean pushin'?"

"Shit, no. I mean at the top."

"You can't make it, Duke. It's a closed shop."

"It's always a closed shop 'til somebody opens the door."

"You can't, I tell you. It's closed, locked. The way it is, you could get killed tryin'."

"I could get killed a hundred different ways. Listen, Ivy, what you gettin' out of it? A little cheap house, some clothes, your food, a guy you sleep with who prob'ly can't give you enough, you so hungry for a real man. With me, we split down the middle—"

Her head rolled from side to side. "Baby," he said, "look at me. I'm twenty-six years old. You what, twenty-eight, twenty-nine? In this business, nobody lasts long. Everybody washes up fast 'cept the ones on top. You don't make it whilst it there, you don't never make it. But if I'm goin'a make it for bothen us, I got to know things."

"I can't, Duke—"

"Okay, then, your contact. Who's your pusher?"

"Duke—"

"Come on, baby, quit stallin'. Who?"

Resignedly, "All right. Connie Clark, he runs the 2-2-2, other houses an' stores in this block. But he ain't The Man. The Man gets it to Connie, Connie, he hands it out to the pushers. I'm the one works this territory, the 2-2-2 Club. I get it from Connie, I push it, I pay off to Connie. That's where all this is comin' from."

"You sleepin' with this Connie?"

"I told you enough already."

Duke smiled across the table at her. "Okay, sugar, just to show you I ain't stupid, I'll tell you. Banjo Nichols is The Man."

She wouldn't deny or acknowledge, and sat completely

433

still, staring at him. "Fat Banjo Nichols," he repeated. "So you sleepin' with him or Connie Clark. Okay, either way, you givin' a lot more'n you gettin'. I won't bust things up for you, baby, but don't you be surprised if I don't get in my own way."

"Duke—"

"Don't be afraid, Ivy. You said it yourself, I ain't no little boy now."

She laughed wryly. Duke snuffed out his cigarette and stood up. "Help me get dressed, baby. I got to go see The Man."

11

At 10 P.M., Banjo Nichols sat alone at the green-baize-covered poker table in the back room of the poolroom, poring over a much-thumbed pocket-sized notebook, flipping its frayed pages back and forth. Occasionally, he checked a figure on one of a number of small slips of paper he took from his shirt pocket, and made an entry in the notebook. The notebook was his total record of every one of his business transactions outside of the poolroom. For tax and accounting purposes, another more formal set of records were kept in a safe in one corner of the room and handled only by his accountant.

The room was hot and airless and Banjo's face, arms and body were soaked with sweat. He made a final entry in the notebook, then took the sheaf of small notes to the toilet in a small closet, touched a match to them. When the flames had consumed the paper to within half an inch of his fingers, he dropped them into the bowl and flushed them away.

"Got to get me some air-conditionin' in here," he muttered to himself. "Room's like a goddam oven." He had had the same complaints from the men who gathered in the back room twice a week to play high-stakes poker, but he knew that Velora, who managed the eight rooms on the two upper floors, would be after him again to provide the same comfort for her girls. ("They whores, Banjo, but they ain't animals. You tighter'n a monkey's ass, man. Cool the place off, we can double our business.")

Always something to run up the expenses. Knocked over Benny Acton's horse parlor and Eddie Corner's poker room last week, picked up two pushers and closed down Rosie Wilder's, all in one month, but the goddam payoff still the same. No use talking to the collector. Wasn't none of his

434

boys done it. Now, for the one air-conditioner he wanted, he'd have to buy eight more to satisfy that bitch Velora.

Banjo wiped his face and neck with a towel, walked to the door that led into the poolroom, pulled the heavy bolt back and opened it. The room was filled with players and the usual watchers and bettors, every table in use, with action at the food counter. Immediately outside the door, Hinky Liggett, sitting in a chair that was tilted against the wall, raised his head in Banjo's direction. "Want somethin', Banjo?"

"Tell the boy to bring me a cold beer. Two," Banjo amended. He closed the door and returned to his chair at the poker table, the only one of six that featured arms.

"Hey, kid!"

Larry Powell had just racked up at the No. 4 table and looked toward Hinky, who signaled to him by waving the sawed-off poolcue that always stood beside the chair. Larry walked briskly to him. "You want me, Hinky?"

"Yeah. Two beers for the back room. Cold. One glass."

"Right away."

When he returned from the front counter with two bottles of beer and a refrigerated glass on the tray, Hinky rapped the poolcue against the door. Banjo unlocked and opened the door. "Put it on the table," he told Larry.

Larry entered the room and went to the table, where he opened one bottle and poured the beer. "You want me to open the other bottle now, Mr. Nichols, or leave the opener with you?"

Banjo slid his massive body into the armchair, a tight fit. "Open it," he grunted. Larry did so, picked up the tray and started to leave. Banjo had already downed the first glass and was pouring the second. "How long you been workin' for me, Larry?" he asked suddenly.

Larry turned back to the table. "Almost six months, Mr. Nichols."

"Long enough for you to start callin' me Banjo, ain't it?"

"If you say so."

Banjo smiled and the ugly facial scar widened and lengthened. "You a real polite boy, ain't you? They learn you that in college? Or when you was on the cops?"

"I don't know. I guess it just happened that way."

"You learn anything while you in training there?"

"Not much besides basic police routine. I wasn't on the force, only in training school."

"How long?"

"Almost four months. Two weeks to go to finish and go on probation."

435

"You know anything about that inside special detail they got?"

"You mean the Internal Security Squad? I know there is one, but I never knew who was on it. Nobody knows except Chief Durkin and Inspector LaSalle. It operates to keep a close check on the force itself."

"I know how it works."

"I guess I can't help you with that. They work under cover."

"Yeah. Well—"

There was a soft knock on the only other door in the room, the one opening into the alley, used by Banjo's poker-playing friends and business visitors. Banjo seemed not to hear the knock. He said, "Okay, Larry, you c'n go back to work now." He followed Larry to the door to the poolroom, closed and bolted it behind him. Then he went to the back door, pulled the bolts and opened it. A heavy-set man, hat-brim down over his eyes, entered the room. Banjo bolted the door again.

The man said, "Jesus, what a sweatbox."

"You don't have to stay in it as long as I do, Sergeant," Banjo replied laconically. "Sit down."

At 10:20, the action at the center table had grown tense. Mace Bodie was shooting a five-dollar game with his favorite opponent, Eli Buller, who was ahead 42 to 28 in a 100-point game, with the side bets from the watchers running close to $100. Larry was waiting for the call. "Rack!" as Eli banked the four-ball into the lower left corner pocket and sighted in on the six-ball, which would leave the remaining twelve-ball in perfect position for a break shot.

The pay telephone that hung on the wall next to the food and drink counter rang. Noah Smith answered it and called to Larry, "It's for Hinky."

Larry nodded. Eli stroked, shot, pocketed the six-ball and pounded the butt end of the cue stick on the floor. "Rack!" As Larry racked the fourteen balls into his wooden triangle, he turned his head toward the back wall and called out, "Telephone for you, Hinky."

The legs of the chair came forward. Hinky picked up the sawed-off poolcue and started toward the front of the room. "Keep an eye on the door," he said as he passed Larry and lumbered toward the telephone. At that moment, there was the rasping sound of the inside bolt. The door opened no more than two inches and Banjo said, "Where's Hinky?"

"Gone to answer the phone," Larry replied. "Something I can do for you?"

436

"Yeah. Bring me two cold beers. An' two glasses."

"Right away." The door closed, but Larry did not hear the bolt grate into place. He took the two bottles of beer and glasses from Noah and put them on a tray. Hinky was still on the phone. When Larry reached the back door, he took a wild gamble. He held the tray on his left palm, knocked twice quickly, then turned the knob. The door opened and he entered the room.

Banjo and his visitor looked toward him, both faces showing surprise and anger. On the table was a pile of greenbacks which the man had been stuffing into an envelope. The visitor leaped up quickly and turned his back on Larry. Banjo snapped, "Goddam it, you know better'n walk in here like that—"

"I'm sorry, Mr. Nichols. Hinky wasn't there, and I knocked—"

"Next time, you knock an' *wait*. Where the hell is Hinky?"

"He's still on the phone."

"All right. Put it on the table an' get out."

Larry put the tray on the table, snapped the caps off and went out. The visitor had walked to the dark corner and stood at a small, littered oblong table that Banjo used as a desk, his back still toward Larry, one finger spinning the dial of the telephone, an idle gesture, since the receiver lay in place in its cradle.

The visitor said, "That sonofabitch saw me."

"He didn't have time to get a good look at you, Sergeant. I got in his way—"

The visitor wasn't satisfied. "I don't give a good goddam, he saw me. Get rid of the bastard. Tonight."

"I can't do that, Sergeant. He's a good boy. Been with me six months. He could steal as much as he makes every week in that room an' he ain't takin' as much as a dime. I been watchin' him an' I got use for him."

"That won't save my ass if he talks. Or yours."

"He won't talk. I guarantee you. What I got in mind for him, he can't afford to talk. You leave him to me."

The visitor was not entirely convinced. "You better by a goddam sight make sure or else he could blow the works, and that means you, too."

"Okay. I said I'd take care of him. You got your loot—"

Grudgingly, "Okay. Next week."

"Next week, but see what you can do about them places."

"What the hell. We got to make a showing, else they'll change the whole vice squad. Take it easy. You can open 'em up again next week."

"Shuh. Meantime, I got to pay lawyers, fines—"

"You can afford it."

Banjo walked to the alley door. White sonofabitchin' bastard. One of these days I'll screw you, too. He unlocked the door, looked up and down the unlighted alley and nodded. The visitor stepped out, head down, and disappeared into the darkness.

12

At 11:15, Duck Shackleford sat across the poker table from Banjo Nichols, his eyes fixed on the scar-faced older man's spatulate fingers as they skillfully shuffled a deck of cards, held and cut them neatly with one hand. Riffle . . . cut . . . riffle . . . cut . . .

"You want in, Duke, I can make a place for you. I got a use for a smart boy, but nobody comes in on top an' I don't need no partners. You do one job good, you get a better one to do next time. Everybody gets tested the same way. He belongs up, he get moved up."

"Lay it out for me, Banjo."

"All right. This civil rights thing. All summer long, we had some troubles. Little stuff, nothin' like Selma or Birmingham or Atlanta. Just some kids tryin' to integrate the swimmin' pools in Oglethorpe Park an' the beach out there at Laurel. Didn' come to nothin'. The County give in some more on voter registration after the Atlanta thing, handed out a few more jobs in the County Building, the City Hall. Chief Durkin puttin' twenty, twenty-five colored boys on his force, but the fire department still keepin' it lily white.

"We got Amos Hart preachin' how we movin' ahead, but he an' the people know we movin' slower'n molasses in January. Hart, Roose, Clark, Lynch an' Doc Betts, they all on the Joint Civil Rights Committee, but they go along, scared to stir anything up. They don' want no outsiders comin' in to wake up our people. That's bad for business.

"All right. But the young people up to your age, they know what's goin' on in other places an' they don' like what they see. Black people get less pay than white people for the same work, like drivin' milk wagons and bread trucks. Rest of the jobs don't count because our people can't get the same jobs white people get.

"Okay. Them young people, they like sheep, too. Learned it from their daddies an' mamas. What they need, they need somebody to look up to. A leader they c'n respect. He say, 'Do,' they do. He say, 'Cool it, baby,' they cool it."

438

Banjo stopped to finish his glass of beer. "Am I gettin' through to you, Duke?"

Duke nodded. "You comin' in clear, but you ain't said nothin' yet."

"All right. You're Buddy Duke, big-time fighter, big shot. They'll look up to you, do what you say. I call the shots, you pass it along, organize it, let 'em do it. We goin'a take this civil rights thing an' put it to work for us. You understan'?"

Again a nod from Duke. "I understand fine, Banjo, an' I'm all for it, but this ain't the kind of thing I had in mind—"

"I *know* what you got in mind."

"Well, where do I come in?"

"Doin' what I tell you to do. Like I say, you do one job good, you move up to the next job. One day, maybe you find yourself runnin' that numbers thing with me."

"Partners?"

"Partners. Pay expenses, you take forty per cent, I take sixty. We got a deal?"

Duke hesitated for a moment, then said, "We got a deal, Banjo. When do we start?"

"We already started. You know the Black Fez?"

"I seen somethin' of 'em in Harlem. Little potatoes next to the Muslims."

"Yeah, but they mean business. What they want, they tryin' to bring all black people into one camp, make us strong in every city an' state, move an army of black soldiers from one place to another. This Dr. Rhama, he the leader of the movement. His man, Brother Leonard, he the head man in Georgia, the one started the last ruckus in Atlanta. They been lookin' for a town like this one, ain't had no big trouble before, to start somethin' goin' for 'em, but Amos Hart an' his church crowd, they workin' with the white Civil Rights people to keep the Black Fez out.

"Dr. Rhama an' Brother Leonard, I brung 'em in here. They want me to work with 'em, but I got to stay clear. That's where you come in. You work with Dr. Rhama for me. You my representative. We got to work with the young people, nobody older'n twenty-five, thirty, an' as young as you c'n get 'em. Police think the trouble ends when the heat spell is over, but they got another think comin'. We goin'a keep 'em busy all winter, run 'em off their feet 'til they know what an' who they got to deal with. That's it."

"What about me?"

"You line up the people to work with you, Dr. Rhama, an' Brother Leonard. You still got friends here, ain't you?"

439

"Some."

"Like who?"

"Oh. Like Odie Bilson, Dave Sharkey, Booker Dance, Luke Tolbert."

"I know 'em all. Take Luke, he drivin' for the Ainslee Farms Dairy. He in a good spot. Booker Dance, he do the same for Cloverland Bakery. Dave Sharkey, what he do?"

"He drives a truck for the Warren people. Works for my old man."

"They all in good spots. Could be useful."

"Okay, Banjo, what's my cut?"

"Time bein', you get paid by me. Expenses an' a little somethin' over."

"What about the boys?"

"They get paid, too. I pay you, you pay them. An' you keep me out of it. I'll give you a couple more boys. Jim Cuddy. Jake Runnels, Mace Bodie, one or two more I got in mind. They'll be your organizers, stir up the kids you need to do the marchin', singin', the demonstratin'. The kids don't get nothin' cept a license to carry the signs you give 'em an' raise hell when you say. They don' want nothin' more'n that."

"What comes next?"

"Time comes, I'll tell you. Thing to do is get organized quick as you can an' get busy on the first steps. Okay?"

"Okay. We'll try it, see how it works out."

Banjo showed two rows of large teeth in his smile. "Okay. Dr. Rhama an' Brother Leonard, they stayin' in a motel out on Pierce Road. Clean an' quiet. You find some reason to move out of your daddy's house. The Nigerian Motel. See Vern Webb, the manager, he take care of you. Nex' thing, you got to get your own people an' have a meetin'. What's most important, you keep my name out of it. All's they know is you, nobody else. That means you don't hang around here, maybe drop in once in a while, natural-like. You want to see me, call me first. I want to see you, I send you word. We fix a time an' you come in through this back door."

"I got to have some place to meet the boys. Won't be smart bringin' 'em to a motel."

"No. You know the 2-2-2 Club?"

"I been there."

"Safe place. Police don't bother it much. I'll pass the word to Connie Clark to give you—uh—privileges, let you use a back room for your meetings. Connie an' me, we old friends."

"I'll bet on it."

"You bet, you'll win. Just one more thing, Duke. Don't try to outsmart me. It's been tried before an' ain't worked yet." Banjo squared the deck and laid them aside. "You understan' me?"

"I understand you, Banjo."

"Let's drink on it. My throat's dry from talkin' too much. Go to the door an' tell Hinky have the boy bring us some beer."

Duke flushed at the change of tone, now a direct employer-employee order. He looked up and saw Banjo's eyes watching for his reaction and recognized that the order, like its tone, was deliberate. After the brief exchange of glances, Duke got up, went to the door and shot the bolt back, opened it. Hinky Liggett turned his head toward him.

"Tell the boy to bring two beers," Duke ordered, using the same tone Banjo had used on him moments ago. Liggett's response was one of belligerence.

"Yeah? Who say?"

"Banjo say." It was enough. As Hinky called for the rack boy, Duke closed the door and shot the bolt again. A few moments later, he opened it when Hinky knocked. The boy carried a tray with two bottles of beer and two glasses. At the table, he uncapped the bottles and poured the beer into the glasses. Banjo said, "Duke, this our rack boy, Larry Powell. Larry, this Duke Shackleford. Buddy Duke."

Larry smiled and nodded. "The famous middleweight?"

Duke nodded and returned a brief, brittle smile. "I know your family, Duke. Elizabeth and your mother and father. Elizabeth has told me a lot about you, talked about you all the time."

"How you know Lizabeth?"

"I used to be in charge of an athletic class at the Center. Baseball, basketball—"

Banjo said, "Larry was on the cops about six months ago. Got kicked out of trainin' school for bustin' a ofay sergeant, called him a goddam nigger. Larry's been to college."

"Yeah? How come you doin' a rack boy's work?"

"Not much else I could get around here."

"You try the big towns, Atlanta?"

"All I could get was clerking jobs or labor work."

"Well—"

Larry picked up the tray and the empty bottles. Duke fished a roll of bills out of his pocket and found a dollar bill. "Here, Larry," he said.

"Put your money away, Duke, it's on me," Banjo said.

"This ain't for the beer. It's a tip," Duke replied. He dropped the bill on the tray and Larry said, "Thanks," in a

441

low voice, then went out, feeling humiliation, put down by Duke because he had dared mention his friendship for Elizabeth. Put down by one of his own.

Duke reached the 2-2-2 at one o'clock, closing time, and found Odie inside at the bar with Booker Dance, having a last beer. At a table, Dave Sharkey, Willy Eggert and Luke Tolbert sat with three girls, finishing their final drinks. Dave leaped up and introduced Duke to Wilma French, Adah Loomis and Cherry Miller, mini-skirted, bright-faced girls who looked young enough to be high-school students. A scantily clad waitress stood by with the check on a small tray, waiting. Duke took the check from her tray, glanced at it and dropped a ten-dollar bill on the tray with the check. "On me," he said, and to the waitress, "Keep the change, honey."

The girls were ready to leave. Duke called, "So long," and went to the bar to talk with Odie, who then shuffled over to whisper a message to Dave Sharkey. A huddle formed at the table and Willie Eggert was elected to drive the girls home while the others remained behind with Duke and Odie. Then Connie Clark came out of his office to check the cash register tapes, a tall, very dark man with the good-natured smile of a genial host, but with cold, piercing eyes. "Hey! You Buddy Duke, ain't you?"

Duke left his group and walked toward the tall man. Banjo's man. The Man's man. "You Connie Clark?" he asked.

"None other. Heard you'd been in earlier. Glad to welcome you to the 2-2-2. Come as my guest next time."

"Thanks, Connie. I was talkin' to a friend of yours a little while ago."

"Yeah. He call and tell me. Say he appreciate any courtesy I show you."

"Thanks. How about a room where me an' my friends can talk in private, maybe play a little after-hours poker?"

"Sure. No sweat. Billy!" The waitress Duke had tipped before came hurrying up and Clark enveloped her in a one-armed embrace.

"Billy, honey, this the famous Buddy Duke. You show him and his friends to room number twelve, huh?"

"Yes, Mr. Clark. Right away."

"Like I been sayin'," Duke said, "you go along with me, you start gettin' somethin' out of your lives for a change, somethin' you got comin' to you but ain't never got. On'iest thing is, you go in, you go in all the way. No holdin' back.

442

You do what you told an' you keep your mouths shut tight."

The room was only large enough to hold a round table and six chairs, used for conference purposes. The single window was locked and shuttered, the walls of painted plasterboard, the floor bare.

"Time's come when we got to stand up an' take what belongs to us, the way our people been doin' in other places. You got to learn one thing, it's there for the gettin', only nobody's goin'a do your gettin' for you. You want to sit on your asses 'til you too old to do anything about it, you never get nothin' because them ofay bastards, they'll never stop holdin' you down long's you show 'em you won't fight for what's yours, belongs to you. We show 'em we'll fight, do 'em the same way they done us since the beginnin', that's when we start livin'. It's goin' on all over the North an' other parts of the South right now, today. You fight hate with hate."

On their faces, he saw doubt. When he spoke of "they" and "them," they seemed to lose interest. When he spoke about "me" and "I" and "you," they regained interest. He decided to switch to the "I" and "me" line.

"They try to screw me good up there, but I wasn't about to let 'em get away with it. Long's I was a gold mine, they let me live, goddam 'em, but when I had this accident an' busted my hand, they come at me, tryin' to suck me dry. Well, I screwed 'em first an' got out 'til my hand heals up. An' I ain't finished with 'em. Same thing here. You gotta screw 'em before they screw you. You show fight, you mean business, they give in. They got to learn the hard way, with a fist in the belly, a smash in the jaw. Do unto 'em what they been doin' to us, only we got to do it first. And now."

"Shuh," Booker Dance said. "Make sense to me."

"How we go about doin' it, Buddy?" Luke asked.

"Any way we can find. Fight, steal, burn the ofay bastards out, if we got to."

"They ain't all that bad, is they?" Odie asked.

"You think they ain't? You ever see any of the good ones comin' 'roun' to do anything for you, Odie?"

"Well, there was Ol' Miss Katie at the R-V, there was Ol' Mist' Jonas Taylor. An' Mist' Ames—"

"They all dead—"

"An' Mist' Anderson Warren—"

"They tell me he's dyin'. Go ahead, rattle me off some more."

Odie fell silent.

"An' what they ever give you? You live like they do, eat

443

like they do, ride in fancy cars like they do?" No one answered. "All they do, they give you a hind tit to suck on for a little bit, make you think you somebody. On top. All you on top of is nothin'. Shit, man, down here, you live with rats an' roaches an' eat hog sloppin's. You don't even know what a real thick prime steak taste like, a fresh Maine lobster, Maryland blue crabs, Long Island ducklin', juicy lamb chops, an' cherrystone clams."

"Well," Dave Sharkey said, "question is, how we do it, get what we got comin', like you say?"

"Well, you-all with me, we can do somethin' to stir these hanky-heads aroun' here up, show 'em the way to go. Get *our* people in the action, not them white niggers over in Riverside. How about it, you with me?"

To a man, the others nodded. "We with you, Buddy."

"All right. Long's you with me, I'll work somethin' out. You in, you got to stay in. One of you drops out, flaps his mouth aroun', the others goin'a take care of him. That understood?"

Again the bobbing of heads in assent. Luke leaned back in his chair, tipped away from the table. "Buddy, tell us some more about Harlem."

"Yeah, Harlem," Duke said, smiling. "Man, ain't no place like it on earth, if you can go the right way. It got plenty of bad about it, too. The slums, the rats, the roaches, the garbage, it ain't no different than any place else, the South Side of Chicago, Detroit, Los Angeles, New Orleans. A nigger's still got to pay more than an ofay to live an' eat worse an' less. But they fightin', an' that's what counts. They'll get what they fightin' for, just like us will.

"For me, it was different. I had money. An' don't think there ain't a lot like me with money, men in all kinds of business. Everyone of 'em'll tell you. Ain't nothin' like bein' on top, livin' on top. I been there an' I know. On top their women, too, come beggin' for more. Eat with 'em, drink with 'em, dance with 'em, an' sleep with 'em. That's bein' on top, ain't it?"

"Man!" Odie exclaimed. "How them white gals, Buddy?"

"Odie, boy, they ain't no better, no different from oui gals, less'n better. All's they do, they dress it up, show it off better. In bed, they nothin' much, go crazy with a real man. They tellin' me I spoil 'em for the ofays. That's what it mean, bein' on top. No more drinkin' the skim milk after the cream's been licked off, like sloppin' hogs after they take the best part for themselves."

"I got to go, Buddy," Dave said. "It's past two and I got to work tomorrow."

444

"Okay, let's break it up for now. Luke, you an' Booker stay behind for a few minutes. The rest of you, keep what I been sayin' in mind an' to yourselves. We be in touch."

A little before one o'clock, Hinky Liggett rapped his sawed-off poolcue on the leg of his chair and called, "Last game before closin'." Larry had brushed and covered two tables, waited for the games on the others to come to their end. Up front, Noah Smith was placing the perishables in the refrigerator when Banjo came out of the back room and called to Larry. "You finish up the tables, Hinky," he added. Hinky got up glowering. In the back room, Banjo motioned Larry to a chair at the poker table. "Sit down, Larry."

"Yes, sir." Banjo smiled again. This was the po*lite*st boy. He squeezed his bulk into the armchair.

"Larry, that man was in there before you walk in on us—"

"Yes, sir?"

"You get a look at him?"

"Just barely."

"You recognize him?"

"No, sir."

"You sure, Larry? It's important for me to know. You seen him at the table in the light, didn't you?"

"Tell you the truth, I wasn't paying much attention to him. I had my eyes on you."

"Tell me what did you see?"

"Well—" the situation was getting touchy now— "I saw he was a white man—"

"What else?"

Go for broke, Larry told himself. "He was putting some money in an envelope."

"You know what the money was for, don't you?"

"I don't know, but I can guess."

"Go ahead, guess."

"Well, I'd say it was some kind of a payoff. For something you bought, a service." A pause, then, "A payoff. For protection, maybe."

"That's a smart guess. How much you make here, Larry?"

"My take-home is $31.70 a week. Plus a couple of tips now and then from a winner."

"Can't have much left after you eat, sleep an' step out a little, hey?"

Larry grinned. "I don't do much stepping out, but you're right. It takes just about all of it to get by."

445

"You got a car?"

"No, sir."

"Girl?"

Larry thought of Elizabeth Shackleford as he shook his head from side to side and said, "No girl."

"Shuh. You don't have much fun, do you?"

"Later on, maybe. I can't afford it now." Quickly, "I'm not complaining, Mr.—Banjo."

"That's better." Banjo sipped his beer, put his glass down. "You a pretty smart boy, ain't you?"

"Well—my marks at college were good."

"But you got yourself kicked off the cops. That wasn't so smart."

"No," Larry admitted sheepishly. "I lost my head that one time."

"Yeah. It only takes one time to get all screwed up." A pause, then, "Larry, I can use a good smart boy like you if he know the score, keep his mouth shut an' his head screwed on tight. You interested?"

"Well—"

"I'll tell you. You been to college, you been on the cops, an' it didn't get you a goddam thing 'cept a job as a rack boy takin' home $31.70 every Sat'dy night and most of it owed before you can get to spend it. Right?"

Larry nodded in smiling agreement.

"All right. I know you know a lot more than you're sayin', an' that's a good thing. Bein' roun' here six days an' nights a week for six months, you got to have some ideas of what's goin' on in this room."

"Well, I know about the big poker games—"

"What else?"

Larry squirmed in his chair and the oppressive heat was little or no help to him. "I'd say you use it to conduct your outside business interests—"

"What business interests?"

"Banjo, I—uh— It's none of my business—"

"I'm askin' you to tell me, boy."

"Well, I'd have to guess at prostitution."

"You mean whorehouses, say so."

"All right, whorehouses. I'd guess you get payoffs from several other gambling houses you own, from bootleg whiskey brought into the county."

"What else?"

"I can't guess at anything else. It's not my—"

"Then you pretty dumb, ain't you, boy?"

"All right," Larry snapped. "I'll guess marijuana and heroin along with the rest of it."

446

Banjo laughed and slapped a fat hand on the table. "God-dam it, boy, that's the way to speak up. I know you're smart now. All right, you keep your mouth shut like you been doin'. Pretty soon I'll have a job for you that'll raise your pay some, give you enough to even buy you a car. You interested?"

Enthusiastically now, "Yes, *sir!*"

"Okay. Go back to your work an' keep this to yourself."

When he left the Place half an hour later, Larry walked to Grand Avenue, making sure he was not being followed. At Grand and Central, he went into the public phone booth at Creston's service station, which was closed for the night. There was no one in sight. He reached up and unscrewed the light bulb several turns before closing the door, then used a small pencil-type flashlight and dialed Inspector La-Salle's home number.

"LaSalle here," came the sleep-filled voice.

"Inspector, it's Larry."

"What's up?"

"Something new. I think we'd better set up a meeting."

"Can you give me an idea now?"

"Well, for one thing, Buddy Duke, the middleweight fighter. His real name is Duke Shackleford, a local boy—"

"Sam Shackleford's son?"

"Yes, sir."

"I didn't know they were one and the same. What about him?"

"He's come back to town within the last day or two. From New York. With one hand in a cast. Tonight, he was locked in the back room with Banjo for over an hour. I'd guess they're putting some kind of a deal together."

"All right, Larry. I'll do what I can to check him out first thing in the morning. Anything else?"

"Yes, sir. Banjo called me in twice to talk along confidential lines. I think he'll be moving me into something soon. Also, he had a caller earlier, a white man, to whom he was making a sizable payoff—"

Eagerly, "Who?"

"I don't know, but I think I'd recognize him if I saw him again."

"All right, Larry. I'll set up a meeting as soon as I can. Keep in touch with me."

"Yes, sir. Good night."

Larry hung up, opened the door, screwed the light bulb tightly into the overhead socket and headed home to his single room.

447

CHAPTER IV

1

Corey awoke early on Thursday, remembering that this was the day he would exchange uniforms for civilian clothes. He heard some movement in Kenneth's room and checked his clock. Seven-forty. He decided to forgo breakfast with his father and avoid a possible discussion of future plans—and "plans" brought Shadow Hills back to his mind. A call to make on Lee Stannard. His 2:30 appointment with Wayne Taylor and John Curran.

Then, the mystery of Drew Warren. Rich, lonely, desirable. And empty. It was as though she had died on the night Bruce was killed, that a new person had taken over her mind.

Death came into the life of everyone; of a parent, a brother, sister, relative, friend. It was everywhere. Viet Nam, downtown, next door, at the nearest cross street, in every house where people lived. Bruce had been someone special, of course, but even the most special people were not immune to death and went to their graves alone; mourned, yes, and mourned deeply, but not beyond reason. Corey had mourned Caddy's death and hated Kenneth for the unhappiness she had endured, whether or not of her own making. And he had mourned for Bruce as a friend. Bruce's death was hardly comparable to Caddy's, but in time, both wounds had healed and become bearable. And the deaths he had witnessed in combat—

His thoughts turned to the abnormal, even to the mild suspicion of incest and its subsequent guilt, but he dismissed this as entirely ridiculous. Then he recalled how often, from his earliest memory, Drew had leaned upon Bruce for the comfort she had never known from her father, the mother she hardly knew and couldn't remember. The close, intimate matters girls discussed with other girls, Drew discussed with Bruce: school problems, choice of clothes, homework, horses, dogs. Bruce's patience was remarkable. She tagged along behind him, always welcome. Bruce had first taught her to swim, and dance, play tennis, other games to while away her time. His friends had become her friends until she began forming her own friendships, none hard or fast. Bruce had remained Drew's closest confidant.

Remembering once when Bruce told Corey, not without some embarrassment, that Drew had questioned him about certain bodily functions that were disturbing to her; that he had sent her to Dr. Ballard for the explanations.

Corey could understand, under these circumstances, this extraordinary closeness between them, products of a broken marriage, indulged by their grandparents—but Drew's prolonged *obsession* with Bruce's death remained shadowy and caliginous. And disturbing. Perhaps in time, with a renewal of association—

He fell into a light doze, then heard Kenneth's car as it drove away from the house. He got up, showered, shaved, dressed and came down to breakfast, fussed over by Tish and Jemmy, enjoying their attention.

Lee Stannard, despite a casual façade, could not entirely conceal his interest in Corey's inquiry, placing a $10,000 figure on a one-year option for the 1,200-acre Halstead land. It was a starting point for the bargaining which followed.

"Fifteen hundred for six months," Corey countered, "with an option for another six months at the same price."

"Tom, Jr. won't go for less than one year at ten thousand."

Corey stood up. "Then suppose we forget it, Mr. Stannard. I'm sorry to have taken up your time."

"Now hold on, son. That land up in Shadow Hills—"

"Is raw, unimproved land that has been sitting up there since the beginning of time, used only by trespassing hunters, bird-watchers and picnickers—"

"How about seventy-five hundred for one year if Tom, Jr. will stand for it?"

"—and is no more valuable than the six-hundred-plus acres of Crane land. I'll come up to two thousand for six months with the same option. I'll know then whether an idea I have is worth going into deeper."

"Six thousand."

Corey shook his head negatively. Still standing, half-turned toward the door, "My final offer, Mr. Stannard, is two thousand for six months with an option for another six months at two thousand." He turned the knob on the door.

Stannard got up and put a hand out to stay him. "You're a hard man to dicker with, Lieutenant. Tell you what. Let me call Tom, Jr. down in Macon. What Tom says, Roger and Miss Emma will go along with. You mind stepping into the outer office for a couple of minutes?"

Corey sat on a bench turning the pages of a much-

449

thumbed vintage copy of *Look* Magazine, glancing occasionally through the glass partition as Lee Stannard put in his call and began talking with Tom Halstead, Jr., using his pencil to make notations and quick calculations, gray head bobbing, arguing, gesticulating with his free hand, finally nodding in agreement. He hung up and signaled Corey to come back into his office. "All right, Lieutenant. Tom, Jr. says six months is okay, so is the option for another six, but he wants twenty-four hundred, eight hundred each for Roger, Miss Emma and himself."

"How soon can I have the option?"

"I've got his power of attorney. Soon's I see the color of your money."

"Will a light green check on Laurelton National do?"

"Good as cash any day in the week."

Stannard called in his secretary and dictated a short-form option agreement and receipt while Corey wrote his check. "I don't guess you'd care to give me a hint as to what you got in mind, would you, Lieutenant?" Stannard asked.

"I'm afraid not at the moment, Mr. Stannard. I will tell you this much, however—"

Stannard leaned forward with interest. "What?"

"It may all come to exactly nothing," Corey replied. Twenty minutes later he walked out with the option in his pocket and a smile of satisfaction on his face.

At exactly 2:30 Corey was shown into Wayne Taylor's private office and found Johnny Curran, Wayne's brother-in-law, with him. Only Johnny, dressed in an open-throated khaki shirt, work trousers to match, shod in boondocker boots, seemed out of place in the atmosphere of opulence. From hand-rubbed cypress walls, oil portraits of Jonas and Ames Taylor looked on, Ames with a gentle half-smile on his benign countenance, Jonas with a characteristic frown, seeming to disapprove of the world he had left behind.

Wayne and Johnny rose to greet Corey when he entered and after the personal questions had been asked and answered, Wayne said, "Johnny is on his way to one of our construction projects, Corey—"

"I'll try to give this to you as briefly as I can." He sat in the chair beside Johnny, facing Wayne across the broad, gleaming desk top. "I own 600-plus acres up in Shadow Hills." Out of the corner of one eye, he saw Johnny sit up more erectly in his chair, evincing interest. Corey opened the manila envelope, withdrew his map and spread it out on the desk in front of Wayne as Johnny moved in and leaned over for closer examination.

450

"You will notice the blocked-in area marked CRANE TRACT, which is the part I own. Exactly 603.76 acres. I'm sure you're both familiar with the area."

"Generally," Wayne said without looking up. "I guess we've all done some hunting up there at one time or another." Johnny merely nodded.

"This idea came to me in Viet Nam when I remembered that for a long time the housing situation in Laurelton had been more or less critical. In the few days I've been back, I've seen a number of new developments, high-rise office and apartment buildings—"

"If you're talking about housing, Corey," Johnny interrupted, "there is something of a shortage of available land, true, but Shadow Hills is twenty to twenty-five miles away from the center of Laurelton, a good three or four miles off the Riverton Highway, raw, undeveloped land—"

"I'm not talking about an ordinary housing development, Johnny," Corey replied. "Over a year ago, I ran into a Seabee engineer who was in charge of digging up thousands of acres of jungle and swamp to create an operational base and airstrip. I watched them carve up land like you would slice a turkey, bring in earth, compact it, build administration buildings, barracks, warehouses and, in a short time, created a city for several thousand men. They piped in water, ran power lines—"

"Whoa. Slow down, Corey," Johnny said. "Don't forget we're not at war in Laurelton and we don't operate with Defense Department budgets or military labor."

"I've got that in mind, but I'm only using the Army to illustrate a point. If I were talking about an ordinary housing development, I could anticipate those objections and forget the whole thing, but as I said before, this isn't an average or commonplace project I'm talking about."

Wayne said, "Let Corey line it out for us, Johnny, or you'll never get out of here today."

"Shoot, Corey. Sorry I interrupted," Johnny apologized.

"On the map, you'll see something like 1,200 acres that are owned by the Halstead family. That land, and mine, have a current value of somewhere between $250 and $275 an acre. That would make Halstead's 1,200 worth about—"

"Three hundred and thirty thousand tops, a few thousand more or less," Johnny said.

"Yes. To get to the point, the Halstead 1,200 plus my 600 would give us more than we need for what I have in mind. The idea is to create a combination home-and-vacation resort development, an all-year-around—"

451

"Hold it," Johnny began, but Wayne waved him off. "Let him go ahead, Johnny. We can discuss the details later."

"Take another look at the map," Corey continued. "The Halstead tract is directly north of mine and surrounds it on the north, east and west sides. Where it ends to the south and mine begins, the land resembles a bowl. Now—" with a finger, Corey began tracing several irregular lines through the center of the bowl area—"visualize in here a lake running from this point to this one in length and from here to approximately there in width—" He heard Johnny whistle lightly under his breath at the mention of "lake"—"a resort lake with homes along its irregular shore line, access roads from the main highway, streets, and all utilities. Think of it in terms of from 2,000 to 2,500 homes, schools, plus villages to accommodate stores, a hotel, motels, movie house and in short, an entire community. It would attract not only permanent residents from both Riverton and Laurelton, but summer vacationers from miles around for swimming, fishing, boating, tennis, everything anyone would want in a resort atmosphere.

"I know there are hundreds of loose ends I haven't touched on and I'm going largely on a discussion with my Seabee friend, based on his experience in civilian life. Much of it depends on certain key factors, principally our ability to bring water in from the Cottonwood, to build the dam we would need to create the lake."

Wayne said, "What you're suggesting here, Corey, doesn't conform with our normal type of operation. This is no small undertaking."

"I realize that. In fact, my friend proposed that I present the idea to a big development company, one with large-scale financial resources and backing. My own thought is to keep it under local control, the jobs and payroll, materials, supplies, equipment and services. Taylor Industries has its own bank, architectural, engineering, construction organization, the manpower sources—"

"You know, Corey, we've never gone into deals with partners before. If you were interested in selling your land—?"

"I think not, Wayne. I'm more interested in taking an active part in the overall project."

"Johnny," Wayne said, "have you got any thoughts on this?"

"Only the roughest. I think we're talking about fifteen to twenty million dollars before the first house is built. After the dam, roads, streets, utilities—"

"And," Corey added, "a residential community of between 2,000 and 2,500 homes, perhaps 5,000 to 7,500 people, with all necessary services provided. Schools, stores, hospitals, libraries, churches, police and fire protection, year-around recreation. This isn't a development one builds, sells and walks away from, but a permanent, continuing—"

"Have you discussed this with anyone else, Corey?" Wayne asked.

"No. Only Lieutenant Commander Hall Peterson, my Seabee friend."

"Do you know if he was talking off the top of his head or from experience?"

"He told me he was involved in a similar and successful development in Michigan, about thirty miles from Detroit. With all the crowding in this area, drawing on other communities around us, and talking with Dad and others about the need for more housing, I think this might have a good chance. I'm not talking solely about luxury housing. Some choice acre, half-acre and quarter-acre lots, yes, but mainly, adequate homes on average-sized lots, all with access to the lake, several beach areas, public marina and private boat slips. The location is ideal for commuting, twenty-two miles north of Laurelton and twenty-six miles south of Riverton, almost the halfway mark—"

"What about the Halstead land, the heirs?"

Fon an answer, Corey pulled out the option with Lee Stannard's signature as legal agent for the three remaining Halsteads, and passed it over for Wayne and Johnny's scrutiny.

"You're pretty sold on this project, aren't you?" Wayne asked.

"I am. I'm not up on cost details, but from what I've seen, I'm convinced it can be done."

"What do you think, Johnny?"

Curran laid his scale rule down. "If it's feasible, I like it. This would be the biggest single thing we've ever tackled. We're talking big money—"

"Very big money," Wayne agreed.

"Sure, but why not? There've been bigger projects elsewhere. It's a hell of a challenge. We'll need to get into basic concept, design, layout, engineering and construction surveys, the water and dam problems, zoning, subdivision, utilities, the whole bloody works."

"Then suppose we get our people together and discuss it and give Corey an answer of some kind, preliminary, of course. Say by the middle of next week?"

"We can't have too much by then," Johnny said.

"Enough to know whether we're interested in pursuing the idea further?"

"That much, yes. At least, we can get a vote of confidence or no confidence from our various department heads."

453

Wayne turned to Corey. "What about next Wednesday?"
Corey said, "Fine. Thank you. Any special time?"
"Noon. Make it for lunch here."

2

At least on the surface, Mayor Tom Cameron's reaction was an amazing exhibition of total calm. During the half hour of Lee Durkin's summation of the situation, Cameron had taken four telephone calls ("Go right ahead, Lee, I'm listening"), signed several letters his secretary brought to him ("This will take only a few seconds, Lee, keep talking"), called a clerk on the intercom to bring some coffee ("I'm entitled to a coffee break, too, even if I'm only the mayor"), and got up to go to the large window to look down on the civic center park ("We've got to do something about people eating their lunches down there and leaving their damn litter behind").

Durkin had finished his briefing. Cameron continued to stare out of the window for another thirty seconds, then returned to his desk. "Just who in hell is this Dr. Rhama?" he asked finally.

"As far as we know, he's a self-appointed Saviour of the Black Race. He's for everything black and against everything white. We've got reason to believe he's trying to merge every black extremist group into one big coast-to-coast movement with himself as its leader. Pete LaSalle's put a file together on him, with information from New York, Newark, Detroit, Cleveland, Atlanta, Los Angeles, everywhere there's been any major rioting, looting and burning. Pete believes he's being financed by organized groups in other cities who are just as anxious to put a national organization together."

"It'll never work," Cameron stated with emphasis.

"Maybe not, but in the meantime, we've got to face up to the fact that wherever he shows up, there's trouble, and he's already in town with at least one of his men. We know he's checked into the Nigerian Motel out on Pierce Road and he's had at least one meeting with Banjo Nichols. Also, Nichols owns a piece of the Nigerian."

"Well, Lee, it's more or less in your lap, isn't it? What are you planning to do about it?"

"I don't rightly know, Tom. Cause is one thing, effect is something else. We've got several plans to cover certain situations, but we've never had to worry about outsiders before. There ain't a lot we can do unless he makes a move."

454

"Well—can't we do something to head him off, pick those two up on some charge, vagrancy—"

"We could, if we want to speed things up. We pick him up and he'll be out on a writ in no time, with a good reason to bring more of his people in to organize demonstrations, picketing, needle the police into making arrests, charge us with police brutality, and the next thing you know, we've got what he's looking for—a full-scale riot, complete with burning, looting, the National Guard and curfews, with everything on national TV, in every newspaper and picture magazine."

Cameron muttered an oath.

"Before I left my office," Durkin continued, "I called Reverend Hart and asked him to meet me here to talk things over. I don't know how much good it will do, but I'm taking a gamble that he don't want Dr. Rhama agitating over in 'Angeltown. Besides, he's the only man with any kind of influence on the other side of the bridge."

"I wouldn't count on him too much, Lee. People over there don't listen to him the way they used to."

"Don't blame that on Hart, Tom. If the City and County had shown good faith and lived up to the promises they made long ago, a Dr. Rhama wouldn't stand a chance. The situation's been getting riper every year over there—"

At that moment, the intercom announced Hart's presence in the outer office. "Show him in," Cameron said.

Amos Hart entered the large office and came toward the desk. Lee Durkin rose and extended a hand, which Hart took, pressed, and released. Tom Cameron stood up, nodded without smiling, but did not offer his hand, using it to indicate a chair. Hart sat down and clasped his hands over his stomach.

Hart was a man of impressive stature, tall, with large, deepset eyes. His head was massive, but not out of proportion to his exceptionally broad shoulders, barrel chest, thick arms and legs. He was an intelligent man, well-educated and with a knowledge of national and international events upon which he often drew as text matter for his sermons. His voice was deep and cultured, that of a man with much practice in public speaking.

He was different from many of his chosen profession in that he recognized the inequities and wrongs of the past, but seldom dwelt long on past history, pushing on to the future. He believed sincerely that the best and most effective results could be obtained for the Negro by reasonable demands and open discussion with reasonable white leaders; and that violence, arrogant demands, and the desire to force the nation

455

to change its attitudes of several centuries overnight could only create counter-resentment, more violence and arrogance.

But he knew that despite the gains that had been made, and the backing he had among his own generation, he was rapidly losing his audience of tomorrow, the young adult and teen-age groups who demanded full equality and opportunity today—now—and in their haste, were falling prey to the advocates of violence. They refused to heed his pleas for strength through peaceful unity instead of weakness through divisive tactics and had openly accused him of "selling out" to the white community, thrown him into the general classification of "Uncle Tom" and "handkerchief head," euphemisms that suggested treason toward his own people.

Yet, in the early days of the civil rights movement, he had forcefully led demonstrations that were successful in desegregating Laurelton's schools and buses. He had been arrested more than a dozen times during restaurant sit-ins, broken merchant resistance against equal service to Negroes by organizing a boycott ("Don't Buy Where You Can't Work or Get Service"). He had led strikes where minimum wage laws were ignored and overtime went unpaid. In those days, his church was packed to capacity, his words applauded and cheered, his advice sought and heeded.

But with the gradual changes and minimal improvements had come dissatisfaction. The young had become impatient and increased their demands. Machines were driving Negroes out of the fields and new problems were created—what to do with illiterate, uneducated, unskilled field hands who flooded into Angeltown seeking jobs that were not available. Negro-owned stores, garages, contracting firms, sign shops, junkyard and secondhand stores, cleaning services, barbershops could find no use for them. They became a part of the unemployed and unemployables who "hung around," a brooding, disenchanted people who were directionless and without means of support other than meager welfare funds.

Amos Hart pleaded their case before the County Welfare Commission, but there could never be enough money to satisfy all the needs. He encouraged them to attend free day and night classes at the R-V Center to learn new skills and trades, to read and write, but the movement failed by natural inertia.

So, the crime rate rose. Petty thefts, holdups, muggings, burglaries. Violence in the streets rose. Drunkenness. Homicides. A white policeman was shot and killed while apprehending a stolen car. A Negro officer was mortally wounded

456

while trying to break up a minor street fight. An unattended police car was turned over and set afire while the officer entered a house to investigate a family disorder. The younger element, seeking outlet for pentup energies, committed acts of violence against white property and people that they could never have gotten away with in their own community, often applauded by their elders. Vandalism became rampant in schools and police were tied up over weekends guarding public buildings. The only real crime, it seemed, was in being caught.

White militants came out into the open and bitterly condemned the Negroes, lashing the good and evil with the same whip, castigating the police for inaction. White youths, eager as the Negro youths to flex their muscles, retaliated in kind. They drove across the bridge in groups looking for revenge and found willing and eager opponents. Rocks were flung from speeding cars, breaking windows, neon signs, striking down pedestrians. Negro girls were molested. Negroes complained that the number of whites arrested was disproportionate to the number of Negro arrests for the same crimes. Gangs were formed. Black Bobcats, Tigers, Alligators. Pythons, Hawks, Falcons, Eagles, Panthers. Red Devils fought Black Devils. Junior KKK's battled Junior XXX's. Bicycle chains, baseball bats, switchblade knives, beer cans loaded with sand, filled and empty pop bottles and zip guns became the standard battle weapons.

White and Negro pulpits rang with protests and pleas, but to the youths, their parents were doormats and squares, Uncle Toms and hanky-heads, has-beens. In their own councils, they decided that the problems of the young could be solved only by the young, and in their own way. Yet, there was disunity among them and no single leader to pull them together. Until now.

Amos Hart was aware of Dr. Rhama's presence in Laurelton. "I heard about him just last night," he informed Cameron and Durkin.

"You think he'll call on you?" Durkin asked.

"I doubt it. Dr. Rhama knows that he and I are miles apart philosophically. I met him during the trouble in Atlanta last year. I made my feelings known to him then."

"What if he should contact you?" Cameron asked.

"He won't, Mr. Mayor."

"Do you think we—there would be any good if, uh, you were to contact him?"

"I think not. He would take it as a sign of weakness on my part and capitalize on it."

"Can you suggest what his next move will be?"

Hart smiled. "He's very predictable, Mr. Mayor. Laurelton is a fertile field for his type of operation. First, you'll see the young people running around wearing black fezzes. You'll start seeing posters on walls and fences with a picture of a black fez and the word JOIN! in white letters on it. Then he'll organize a mass public meeting and voice his demands openly, preach from street corners—"

"He'll never get a permit," Cameron predicted with certainty.

"He won't need one, Tom," Lee Durkin said. "He'll apply for one and hope the City will deny it. Then he'll appeal and make statements to the press, radio and television reporters. By the time they get through promoting it, it will be picked up by the papers and stations everywhere in the South, then break nationally. Laurelton will become the target with everybody's eyes on us. Reporters and cameramen will come running, smelling blood. Then, Dr. Rhama will stage an illegal rally of some sort and dare us to stop him. We'll try and there'll be a few dozen arrests. In will come the outsiders, militant organizations, students, black power, flower power and professional do-gooders, with the ACLU waiting to defend them in court. Next, Rhama will call for a march on the Courthouse or City Hall. You know the rest, Tom."

"That's an accurate picture, Mr. Mayor, but it will only be the beginning. We've never had a full-scale riot here, but I think we're seeing the start of one. My group has preached against violence, and you know it, but I'm afraid time is on Dr. Rhama's side. He knows how to stimulate riot better than the rest of us know how to prevent it, and he'll have plenty of ammunition to incite the people who will listen to him willingly."

"What ammunition?" Cameron demanded.

"Mr. Mayor, you know the answer to that as well as I do. The Civil Rights Committee you appointed has come up with lists of grievances and some means to overcome them, but nothing has been done except to congratulate the Committee for its good work, then table the reports. I'm getting weary of trying to answer 'Why?' when my people ask the question. Or, 'When?'"

"Mr. Hart, these things—" Cameron began, when Hart impatiently interrupted.

"Mr. Mayor, these things are the things we have brought up repeatedly only to have them ignored." Showing anger now, "When was the last time you or any member of the City Council walked down some of the unpaved, unlighted streets over in West Laurelton? Do you know how many

458

houses still have outside privies, dirt floors, no sanitary facilities? How many are heated by kerosene stoves or wood-burning ovens? How few sewers there are across the bridge? How many children are bitten by rats while they sleep at night? All of what you call 'these things' are covered in the Committee report, but tell me one thing that has been done to correct—"

"For God's sake, it can't all be corrected overnight. You can't expect that, can you?" Cameron exclaimed.

"No, I don't, but if even one small move had been made to show good faith, there would be something to point to with some hope. And if you're weary of listening to the same old complaints, I'm just as tired of hearing the same old answers. Ten years ago, Mayor Hungerford was telling us 'It can't be done overnight. Have patience.' Today, you're repeating his words. We hear about the high rate of employment and thousands of Negroes in Cairn County are out of work. We hear and read about the affluence around us, and thousands of grown folks and children in Cairn County go to bed hungry every night. We're told that Washington is spending billions on welfare and food programs, but this state puts one roadblock after another in the way of that money and food getting to the people who need it most. I've never held with violence to achieve equality, and my public record is clear on that, Mr. Mayor. I like to think of myself as a man of God, but I can't produce miracles. If the City and County won't pick up their share of the burden, I'm afraid that those of us who are carrying the full load will have to lay it down."

Cameron threw a quick glance at Durkin, but saw no relief, aid or comfort there. Adopting a light, although uncertain, tone, he said, "You're not threatening to abandon the Committee, are you, Mr. Hart?"

"There's nothing to abandon, Mr. Mayor, and I'm not the threat. Dr. Rhama and his kind are. Let the TV cameras expose our poverty to the rest of the country and Dr. Rhama will have all the excuse he needs to justify his charges of inequality, deliberate rejection of federal education, welfare and food programs, calculated inhumane treatment, that white landlords are getting rich on slum shacks—"

"And what about Negro merchants and landlords who are equally as guilty?"

Hart smiled and said slyly, "Dr. Rhama won't even whisper that. Everybody knows that only white landlords, merchants and officials exploit Negroes." Hart smiled grimly, sighed, then rose. "Mr. Mayor, we're in for a troublesome period, but not enough people have the clear vision to see it.

I hope it doesn't happen, but that's like asking for a miracle, too. Good day, gentlemen."

When Hart left, Cameron turned to Durkin. "Well, Lee?" His voice was that of a man who had been betrayed.

Durkin shrugged. "I don't know, Tom. He's a good, decent man. And he's a lot more right than he is wrong. I hope we haven't lost him."

"What do we do now?"

"I guess we stand by and watch for the next move. We're like a fire department waiting for a fire to break out, but don't know where it's going to happen. I'll get my strategy board together and see what we can come up with."

Corey hadn't realized that the meeting had taken over an hour and decided to drive directly home, his mind cluttered with unfamiliar details remembered from points made by Wayne and Johnny during the discussion. When he reached home, Jemmy informed him that his new clothes had arrived and he went to his room at once to make the transition to civilian life official.

Wearing light blue slacks, white sports shirt and dark blue sports jacket, Corey won Kenneth's instant approval at dinner. The conversation was general until Corey told Kenneth that he had taken the six-month option on the Halstead land. He outlined his project and related the discussion with Wayne and Johnny. He saw in Kenneth's interest instant approbation and normal legal restraint and underwent a lengthy questioning that made him at once aware of his father's superior knowledge in matters of high finance, construction, general values and, in particular, the legalities involved. He discussed urban densities, land use, public services, zoning, schools and junior colleges, state and federal participation, all with the ease of a man especially skilled in such matters.

Mini-bus routes at token fees, even if subsidized, to connect all areas, golf courses, bridle paths, community recreational zones. Financing, tax structures, public maintenance, local government, minimum standards in house plans, sales organization, advertising and promotion. Corey's head swam with subjects that had not yet arisen or occurred to him, until he suddenly laughed and cried, "Uncle!"

"Uncle?"

"Yes. I give up, Dad. Until I get some definite word from Wayne on Wednesday, I'm not going to fill my head with details that may never materialize."

Kenneth agreed. "Of course, you know you'll need much more money than you have available. Remember, the price of your land shouldn't go in at current market value, but at the escalated rate. How you will share depends on how much your personal financial involvement adds up to. I think I can help you there, to some extent—"

It was a generous offer and Corey was reluctant to turn it down, knowing his refusal to accept would hurt Kenneth.

"—but," Kenneth continued, "in terms of a project of this magnitude, it wouldn't amount to nearly enough. However, I'm sure you can borrow—"

"I? Where.?"

"If the idea is sound, there are sources. Private—ah—personal—"

There was only one such private, personal source Corey could think of. Warren money. Drew? He said, "I don't want to think about that now, Dad. Let's see what Wednesday brings."

"Of course. That would be best," Kenneth agreed.

3

It was nearing noon when Duke awoke with a sudden start. He raised himself on one elbow and allowed his mind to clear itself of the dream that had startled him into consciousness, its details already evaporating in a cloud of wispy threads. He shook his head and it was gone. The bed creaked under his weight as he sat up and swung his legs over the side. The blinds were drawn, but the sun was strong and provided light enough for him to make out the three leather bags, two as yet unpacked, standing against the wall. He twisted his torso under the corset of tape. Uncomfortable, but no pain. Today he would see the doctor and have it removed; maybe the cast on his hand as well.

Goddam heat. Jesus. Noon. He got up, slipped the silk maroon robe on his naked body and went to the bathroom, stopping to poke his head into the kitchen to call, "Hi, Mom," to Lutie, who sat at the table with a pan in her lap, shelling peas.

"Hello, son. You ready to eat?"

"Soon's I take a shower an' wake up. I be out soon."

"You take your time."

He had shaved the night before and his face was still smooth. He brushed his teeth and stepped under the revivifying cold shower, recalling the events of the night before. Ivy, the woman. Nothing he had known in New York could top Ivy. The meeting with Banjo and the one that followed with Odie, Booker, Dave and Luke. Willy Eggert would come in with the others, he was certain. Not much by New York standards, but if he could put them through the paces on this thing Banjo wanted done, he could use them later on when he organized his numbers setup, Banjo or no Banjo. Things were beginning to look better. Much better. At least, he was next to the man on top. The Man. And before it was over, Buddy Duke would emerge as The Man.

In a high mood, he toweled himself dry, dressed in silk lime-colored slacks, a sports shirt to match, with lime-toned loafers.

"Duke? You ready, son?"

"Comin', Mom." He unlocked the largest suitcase, removed ten one-hundred-dollar bills from his hoard, checked the pliofilm bags that contained his cache of small cellophane envelopes and the hypodermic outfit, then locked the suitcase again and stacked the two others on top of it.

His breakfast was on the table, a stack of buckwheat cakes, sizzling hot sausages, Lutie pouring coffee for him. He attacked the meal with zest as Lutie resumed her seat opposite him, quietly absorbed in her pea-shelling chore.

"What'sa matter, Mom, ain't you feelin' good?"

"I'm all right, I guess. Didn't sleep so good. Neither did Pa. He sat up mosta the night, listenin' for you."

"Hell, no need for him to do that, Mom. I'n no kid."

She sighed sadly. "No, you ain't, that's the Lord's own truth." She paused for a moment, looking directly into his eyes. "Your Pa's a good man, Duke—"

"You ain't tellin' me somethin' I don' know, Mom."

"— but you rilin' him with your wild talk."

"Time somebody down here done some talkin'. And did some doin' along with it."

"Not the way you doin', Duke. You still young an' you been away a long time, maybe too long. You forgettin' this is a good town."

"Good," Duke snorted derisively. "You don' know what good is because you never had nothin' better. What he an' you got for all the years he work hard? Just a low-payin' job herdin' a bunch of lower-paid labor hands aroun' a warehouse. He's a good, hard-workin' man, sure, only he never made enough to live any place except in a shack over on Paca Street, or even send his daughter to college. He—"

"You remindin' me what we owes you, Duke?"

"You don' owe me nothin'. Who owes you is the people he been sweatin' for, gettin' old for, gettin' nothin' except the food to keep alive so he c'n work himself to death. Mom, you want somethin' better, you got to do somethin' to get it whilst you young enough to enjoy it."

462

"Lordy, you think we don't know that? But son, you goin' about it the wrong way. You actin' like you the onliest one ever thought about better livin', better jobs, better schools an' all the rest. Well, you ain't. We know what's goin' on other places. We got a C'mittee—"

"C'mittee," Duke sneered.

"—been studyin' our problems, talkin' with people who been to other places, talkin' to leaders there. We ain't asleep. We just don't want no wars, no bloodshed here."

"You don' get nothin' just talkin', Mom. It's worth gettin', it's worth fightin' for, takin' it."

"Maybe, if need be, but we got more by talkin' than most of the others got by fightin' an' ruckusin' aroun'. We done good without it so far. If we need it, we got to wait for people who know how to fight the right way to come help us, not wild smashin', settin' fires, hurtin', killin', turnin' our friends against us."

"When they comin', Mom, the people who know how to fight the right way, peaceful, so nobody gets hurt?"

"When we need 'em. When they get the time."

"I'll tell you when they come. Never. You know why? Because you don't want 'em to come. You an' them white-scared hanky-head Riverside niggers don' want nobody to do nothin'. They ain't goin'a come because they go where people are ready to fight for what they got comin' to 'em. 'Til you make a move, nobody'll come. You ain't important enough. You'll wait 'til you dead."

Lutie took her pan of peas to the sink and ran some water over them. "You an' your big city ideas ain't makin' things any easier. You home two days an' you got your Pa all upset. We been happy a long time—"

"Sure, Mom. You-all happy. You happy because you don' know no better. You jus' *think* you happy because you don' know what it is to *be* happy. You never had it, so you don' know what it is."

"Duke, son, you jus' bringin' sorrow an' trouble for us, stirrin' things up this way."

"Mom, I'm bringin' you a look at freedom from slavery, is what I'm bringin', and goddam it, you so blind you can't see it. Pa can't see it. But I bet Lizabeth can see it. She been away from here an' she knows what's good an' what ain't. You still slaves, like your grandpappies were, only you got it jus' a little better'n they had it, so you think you right up there on top. *You jus' don' know*, Mom. I been out of here an' up there, an' I *been* on top. I seen it. I lived it. I had it real good—"

"You had it so good, why you come back here, talkin'

463

trouble like you doin'? You had your freedom up there, then why didn't you stay there an' keep it?"

Duke pushed himself away from the table and stood up, legs apart as though facing an adversary in the ring, eyes blazing with anger. "You want me to go back, say so, god-dam it! You an' Pa, like hosses a man is tryin' to pull out of a burnin' stable, keep runnin' back inside. Jesus, you *want* slavery, don't you? It's more comfortable to be a slave, ain't it?"

"Duke, Duke—" Lutie turned toward him, her eyes brimming. "All's I know, son, we want some peace an' quiet like we been havin' it. I want your Pa walkin' aroun' with a smile on his face, happy with his work, proud of his job an' his family, the good talk between him an' Lizabeth."

"Oh, Jesus, Mom—"

"An' you takin' the Lord's name in vain, cussin'—"

Duke turned and went out. He returned moments later while Lutie was washing his breakfast dishes at the sink. She didn't turn when he came in, not until he called, "Mom?"

She put the plate down, wiped her hands on the apron, then touched an end to her eyes. Duke was counting off five one-hundred-dollar bills from the sheaf. "They's five hundred dollars—"

It was more cash than she had ever seen at one time in her entire life, fascinated by the sight of the five bills that fluttered down to the oilcloth covering on the table. "F-Five hundred—"

"Yeah, Mom. Use it any way you want. Clothes for you an' Lizabeth, anything." He folded the rest of the bills and put them back into his pocket. "I see you later, Mom. I got to go to the doctor an' get my hand looked at. May be time to take this cast off."

4

"Corey?"

"Good morning, Paula."

"I've got only a moment. It's a busy Friday. How about tomorrow night? If you make it definite, I'll invite a few more people. The old crowd, or what's left of them. You can kill half a dozen birds with one stone."

"What time?"

"Anytime from seven-thirty on. If you're early, we can have a quiet drink together."

"Seven-thirty it is."

"Over and out, lover."

464

He hung up. Curiously, there was nothing for him to do. He had gone over the Shadow Hills figures in his mind, checked the notations he had made in Viet Nam, remembering vividly the air base he had watched being born in the Tuyen Duc province; Hall Peterson's description of the lake community in Michigan; reliving his meeting with Wayne and Johnny. Johnny, he was sure, would be for it; a challenge to his energy. The way he had said, *"This would be the biggest thing we've ever tackled. We're talking big money."* How much money? Fifteen, twenty, thirty million?

It was one o'clock and he toyed with the idea of calling Kenneth to see if he were free for lunch, but decided against it since neither could add to their conversation of the night before. Six days until Wednesday. Tough it out. He thought of driving up to Shadow Hills to take a hard look at the land again, and discarded that idea. He wouldn't have time to walk over the entire area. If he got an early start tomorrow, Saturday—

The phone rang and it was Drew. "You forgot to bring your bathing suit the other day," she said after the preliminary greetings. "Have you had lunch?"

"No, but I didn't have breakfast until late."

"Then you're invited for a swim and a late lunch. Do you feel up to it?"

"I do, with thanks. In thirty minutes?"

"Meet me at the pool."

He went directly from his car to poolside where Drew sat dangling her legs in the water. She wore a black one-piece suit that glistened like the pelt of a seal, cut to give her maximum freedom, wearing sunglasses to lessen the glare of sun on water. She waved and pointed toward the guest bathhouse and a few minutes later he joined her at the pool.

"Ready for a dozen laps?" he asked.

"I'm not in that good shape."

"If it were anyone else but you, I'd believe them."

"Let's give it a try, shall we?"

She slipped a rubber cap on and slid into the pool. Corey dived shallow and came up beyond mid-pool, energized by the sudden shock of cool water, using his overhand stroke, keeping even pace with Drew. Her form was still good, but at the end of four full laps, she pulled up and sat on the coping, shaking her hair ends free of water droplets. Corey continued for three more laps before quitting.

"I wonder if I'll be as wobbly on the tennis court," he said between breaths.

"We can test that after lunch if you like."

"Nothing more strenuous than this." He dried himself with the large bath towel. "Ah, it's great, isn't it?"

"Yes. It hasn't had much use for a long time. I had the men working on the courts all day yesterday and today. They were practically going back to the jungle."

"We can't let that happen, can we?"

"I've been doing a lot of thinking about the stables, restocking them. The kennels, too. Would you help me, Corey?"

"I'll be happy to, Drew, as soon as I get a few things squared away."

"I was thinking how nice it would be, almost like old times."

Almost. Never again the same. But nothing, he thought, is ever the same and why should she or anyone else expect it. Everything, everyone changes, goes, leaves an indelible imprint for others to look back upon happily or unhappily, trying to cover the unpleasant, relive the pleasant. "Yes," he agreed. "Drew?"

"What?"

"Busy tomorrow?"

"No, why?"

"I was thinking of driving up to Shadow Hills early to look over a piece of land I own up there—"

"I remember it. We picnicked up there a few times long ago. I could have Leona pack a lunch— Corey, it's a wonderful idea. What time shall we leave?"

"Suppose I pick you up between seven and seven-thirty."

"I haven't been up that early in years."

"I'll want to do a lot of walking."

"We won't be away too long, will we? Gran—"

"I think about four o'clock."

"I'm sure it will be all right. Shall we have lunch now and talk about it?"

5

Dr. Royal Betts concluded the examination and said, "Well, Duke, there's no need to tape you up again. You're what we call a good healer. And I won't have to replace the cast on your hand, but I'd suggest you favor it for a while. Just as a reminder, I'm going to bandage and tape it, knuckles and wrist. It'll give you room to exercise it a little. You shouldn't have any problem if you keep it out of trouble. Anything else?"

"No, Doc. I had a complete checkup before I left New

York." Duke buttoned his shirt with little difficulty, tied his tie, put on the dark green linen jacket. "Pay you now, Doc?"

"You can pay the young lady at the desk outside. Twenty dollars."

"Prices gone up aroun' here, ain't they?"

Betts grinned toothily. "Some. Like everything else. Half of it will go toward medicine for the next man or woman who can't afford it. Sort of robbing Peter to pay Paul."

"Thanks, Doc. See you."

"Good luck. And say hello to Sam and Lutie and Elizabeth."

The absence of the tape gave him a strange new freedom. He twisted his body experimentally, testing for twinges that never came. He balled the fingers of his left hand up, but they were too stiff from inactivity to form a firm fist. Soon, with exercise, the nightmare of Al Saxon and his goons would be a thing of the past. He got into his Jaguar and drove to within a block of Ivy's house and parked. It was just after two o'clock and the memory of her was still exciting. He walked up the empty, narrow street to 203 and knocked on her door. No answer. He knocked again and a third time before the knob turned from the inside. The door opened as far as the guard chain would permit and he heard Ivy's sleepy voice ask petulantly, "Who is it?"

"It's me. Duke. Open up."

"Duke? God, man, what you doin' wakin' me up at the crack of dawn?"

"Come on, baby, it's after two o'clock. Open up."

The door closed, the chain rattled, the door opened again. All the shades were drawn and the interior was dim, less hot than the outside air. Ivy, her hair tousled in sleepy disorder, wore only a pair of very brief panties. "Man, I didn't get to bed 'til after daylight. I don't get some more sleep, I'll be a zombie all night long."

"Go on back to bed. I'll come with you."

"How much sleep you think that'll get me?"

"Much as you want. We'll both sleep."

She got back into her rumpled bed and watched him undress, stimulated by the sight of his perfectly formed body, raising her hips to slip off the wisp of garment in preparation for the inevitable act. He got into bed and they merged into one being. "What happened to all the tape you had on last night?"

"No more. Doc gave me a clean bill of health. Looka here. Cast gone, too. Just a li'l ol' bandage."

She snuggled against him, squirming into his embrace. "How's Uncle Sam an' Aunt Lutie? An' Elizabeth?"

"You really interested in how they are?" Duke asked with a light laugh.

"No. Just being polite."

"Well, skip the politeness an' let's get to the hospitality." He kissed and fondled her awake and heard her moan softly as they began to move in concert, increasing the tempo until both were soaked with perspiration, yet uncaring, each straining to receive the maximum of what the other had to give. And finally sated, they slept in each other's arms. At four, Ivy awoke and took a cooling tub bath, put on a light robe and began to fix a normal breakfast, her first meal of the day. She woke Duke in time to shower and join her. Later, they lounged in chairs in the living room.

"You goin' to stay on with your people?" Ivy asked.

"Not too long. Just long enough for 'em to get used to the idea, then I'm gettin' a place of my own. We be a lot more comfortable there, wherever it is."

"That sounds good. When?"

"When somethin' I got in mind works out."

"You still talkin' about that—"

"What I'm talkin' about, it started last night. I got a piece of news for you, Ivy baby."

"What?" She said it with apprehension, almost fear.

"You an' me, we workin' for the same man."

"Connie Clark?"

"No. Banjo Nichols."

"Duke—"

"Don't be afraid, baby. He lettin' me in, but just over the doorstep. Later on, I be all the way inside. Then you an' me, we goin'a be ridin' high an' wide."

"Duke, don't get mixed up with Banjo. He's trouble."

"Hell, honey, anything worthwhile is worth the trouble it takes to get it. You jus' don't worry an' leave things to me."

Duke arrived home at six, just as Sam and Elizabeth answered Lutie's call, "It's ready." Sam went inside while Elizabeth, freshly bathed, wearing a cool white dress, waited for Duke to park his car and run up the steps to the porch. He put his arms around her waist, lifted and kissed her.

"Hey, Bubba! I got to thinking I'd never see you again. What have you been doing?"

"Lookin' up old friends an' mindin' my own business, mostly."

"Well, thanks for putting your nosy sister in her place."

He put her down and grinned. "Just love the way you talk, baby. Real educated class."

"I worked at it, Duke. I still practice every day. If I didn't, I'd get sloppy lazy and forget."

"An' waste four years of college?"

"Duke! Lizabeth!' It was Sam's booming voice coming at them from the kitchen.

"Coming!" Elizabeth called out. To Duke, "I don't know what's happened to Pop these past two days. He's gotten cross as a bear with a sore nose."

In the kitchen, the oilcloth had been replaced by a fresh white tablecloth and in the center was a low vase of cut flowers from Lutie's garden. Over the roast loin of pork, Lutie threw short, nervous glances back and forth between husband and son. Dinner was a time set aside for exchanging general news each had gathered during the day: Elizabeth's students, Sam's warehouse crew, Lutie's neighbors and the gossip picked up while shopping; but tonight, only Elizabeth spoke of her day.

"How about you, Pa?" Elizabeth asked.

"Just another day. Nothin' much happened. Had to drive a truck over to Rexford first thing this mornin' 'cause one of my drivers didn' show up 'til past noon. Dave Sharkey."

Duke looked up and said nothing.

"Said he seen you last night down at the 2–2–2 Club, Duke," Sam continued.

"I guess he's right. I dropped in there for a while."

"You find anything upliftin' there?"

Elizabeth said, "Pa, for heaven's sake!"

"Wasn't lookin' for no revival meetin', Pa. Just had a couple-a drinks with old friends."

"Anybody I know?" Elizabeth asked to break the silence.

"Don't know who you know or don't know, sugar. Las' time I saw you, you still wearin' pigtails an' playin' with dolls. Hey! I did see somebody say he knows you, later on over to Banjo's Place. Boy name of Powers."

"Powell. Larry Powell."

"That's the one. Rack boy there—"

"Yes. It's a shame, letting a good education go to waste."

"Didn't do him any good on the cops. I hear he got kicked out of the trainin' school."

"Not for lack of intelligence. It was personal."

"Sure. He step on some white man's toes an' got kicked out."

"It was a matter of principle, Duke."

"I bet it was. I wonder how many Negroes with principle got a lot of us plain niggers lynched the past hundred years."

"That's enough of that kinda talk," Sam said sternly.

"That's freedom of speech for you," Duke retorted. "Not even amongst ourselves do we talk the truth."

"Was that truth you was talkin', boy?"

"An' don't call me 'boy' like the ofays do."

"I guess you think you somethin' special now, hey?"

"Listen, Pa, you ridin' the wrong mule. You want to ride somethin', ride your white bosses who been puttin' niggers down since we born."

"I don't like that kind of talk, Duke."

"Duke! Pa! What is this all about?" Elizabeth pleaded. "For heaven's sake—"

"Your brother's got to be too big, too good, for his fellow Negroes," Sam replied.

"Fellow Negroes," Duke said deprecatingly. "Poor cruds, never been nowhere, done nothin', see nothin'. I'd like to—"

With practiced restraint, Sam said, "Maybe it's best. Leastways, they don't get no biggety ideas in their heads. Mostly, they good boys with steady jobs an' that's better'n most have in lots of other places."

Duke snickered. "Sure, sure. That's the way to look at it, Pa. If you too dumb to know anything, you better off. Born a nigger, stay a nigger all your life. Don't come out from under the manure pile less'n some ofay tells you it's all right to come up for a little smell of fresh air. Then, back under again."

"How much fresh air you get hangin' aroun' beer joints an' poolrooms tellin' other people how bad they got it?" Sam retorted. "There's things we want different, true enough, but they're comin'. Maybe they better up there in New York, but not so much from what we hear. Or Chicago, Detroit or Philadelphia, either."

"In New York," Duke began expansively, "I had me—" but Sam interrupted with a tinge of annoyance and sarcasm.

"In New York, you got what you had because you had the money to pay for it. How many more like you up there wearin' expensive clothes an' drivin' Jaggers? You think you doin' anybody any good makin' 'em feel all they got to do is go out an' take what they want?"

"Pa, it's people like you is what's the matter down here. The trouble is, you satisfied. You work in overalls, take a white man's leavin's all week long. Then you put on your one suit on Sunday an' go to church to thank the Lord for lettin' you live. You an' everybody else like you. You no different'n the slaves in Lincoln's time, takin' a few crumbs from the white massa an' lickin' his hand to say, 'Thankee, suh, thankee, mastuh.' It ain't no better now, only thing is, you *think* it is 'cause you out of the fields an' in a factory."

But it was Mist' Charley's fields then an' Mist' Charley's factory now."

"More big talk," Sam said. "We been gettin' along all right with you away, Duke. What you come home to do, start trouble for everybody?"

"You call it trouble to want what's right?"

"An' I guess you the onliest one knows what's right, what's best for everybody else, huh?"

Lutie, saddened by the turn of the conversation, apprehensive of impending escalation of the disagreement, rose abruptly and went out of the kitchen, toward the living room. Elizabeth followed her, anxious to calm her fears.

"I know better'n you do, Pa. It's right for us to have better houses, better schools, better streets, same as over in East Laurelton. An' it's right for colored folks to go to the same movies, eat in the same restaurants, swim in the same swimmin' pools, go where we damn' well please without askin' Mist' Charley's permission. An' it's wrong for us to have to do most of our buyin' here where we pay more for cheaper stuff. That's what's right an' if you can't see it or understand it, then you wrong an' I'm right. Colored people in other parts of the country, even in the South, know I'm right an' they doin' somethin' about it, or tryin' to. It time somebody waken up Angeltown to do somethin' about it, too."

"An' I'm tellin' you, Duke, it ain't goin'a be done by people like you blowing your hot breath in other people's faces. There's a time an' a place, a better way to do what needs be done—"

"Ain't no better time or place than right now an' right here. You wait, an' a hundred years from now, they still be waitin' for somebody to do what needs doin', just like we waited for a hundred years after we was turned free. Free? Hah!" Duke kicked his chair back and stood up. "Ain't no point talkin' to a deaf man. I'm goin' out."

Sam stood up, taller and broader than his son. He pushed a hand into his pocket and withdrew the small fold of bills Duke had given Lutie earlier, dropped them on the table. "You better take this with you, Duke. With nothin' comin' in, you'll be needin' it soon enough."

"Keep it," Duke snapped. "They's plenty more where it come from." And snidely, "You know how long it taken me to make five hundred dollars in New York? Sometimes as little as a minute."

"We don't need it," Sam said firmly. "An' you miss the whole point of this talk. Mainly, you ain't in New York now."

471

"All right, Pa. I guess if my money ain't welcome, I ain't either. I'll find me a place of my own to live."

"If you want, I can't stop you. You welcome here long's you want to stay. It your home, too. But if you stay, get you a job an' don't make no trouble—"

Duke laughed and went out, leaving the $500 on the table and Sam to stare balefully at it.

He found the Nigeria Motel on Pierce Road, a U-shaped building set back from the road and surrounded on three sides by trees, well-illuminated by a large neon sign and each individual unit identified by a single light beside its doorway. The twenty units ran together and were disappointingly small, with narrow bathrooms and limited closet space, each with its own window air-conditioning unit. Vern Webb read Duke's disapproving silence correctly and said, "All people want just for staying the night, maybe two. Unless you want one of the cottages—"

"Cottages?"

"Back of these. 'Course, they come higher, family size."

"Let's take a look."

A brick path led from the open parking area to a gentle rise behind the larger building to where four cottages stood in a row, about fifteen yards apart, each with its own private porch. In the cottage on the west end, lights showed, but the other three were dark. Duke headed toward the one next to the lighted cabin and Webb unlocked the door, switched on the overhead light and started the air-conditioner going to kill the musty odor. It contained a living room that was convertible into sleeping quarters, bedroom with twin beds, a larger bathroom with tub and shower, efficiency kitchen and more generous closet space.

"How much?"

"Fifteen a day."

"How much by the week?"

"Knock off a whole day. Ninety."

"An' by the month?"

"Well, let's see. Never had anybody that long." A moment of silent calculation, then, "Make it three-twenty-five a month. Includes maid service every day, change linens twice a week. Telephone is extra. No pets, no loud music or TV, no big parties or ruckusin'—"

"Three hundred," Duke countered.

Webb shook his head. "Don't see how I can."

"Ain't gettin' you nothin' stayin' empty, is it?"

"Well—as long as Ben-Joe send you, all right. Three hundred."

472

"Okay. You got somebody to bring my stuff in?"

"I'll get my boy."

Within half an hour, he was settled, his clothes distributed in the closets and bureau. He drew the blinds and curtains in the bedroom, took the waist belt of money from the remaining locked bag and counted his money slowly, carefully. Of the $8,200, only $5,100 remained. He tried to account for the difference, remembering only the larger sums: $500 to Lorella in a burst of overgenerosity. $500 left on the table when he walked out on his family. Adding to his supply of heroin had taken a good chunk, traveling expenses, the new battery, the $300 advance to Vern Webb for rent. Cautioning himself mentally to husband his $5,100 more carefully until he could get set up, he took another $100 to add to the $440 he had in his pocket and stored the $5,000 in the money belt and locked it up again. He then removed one of the cellophane packets, got out the hypodermic outfit, reduced the powder to liquid in the bent spoon and gave himself a fix. When it began to take, he locked the closet, disrobed and got into bed, dozed, thinking of Ivy, dreaming of the hundred Ivys in his future once his plans came into being.

An hour later, Duke got up and showered, then began to dress. Sam had given him the perfect opening to make his move, but he felt some remorse over Lutie's tears when, after Sam left to drive Elizabeth to the Center, she came into his room and saw him packing. But he knew he could not remain there and work with Banjo. He was slipping into his jacket when the phone rang.

"Mr. Shackleford?"

"Yeah."

"This is Dr. Rhama. I'm in the cabin next to yours with Brother Leonard. Mr. Nichols told me to expect you."

"Yeah—well—"

"Would you mind stopping by before you leave?"

"Be there in a minute."

Duke turned the lights off, double-checked his door and went to the cottage next to his. When he knocked, a light-colored man opened the door, introduced himself as Brother Leonard and indicated Dr. Rhama, seated in the one upholstered armchair as though it were a throne, a black fez perched on his head.

"Welcome, brother," Dr. Rhama greeted with a light smile and a wave toward the sofa. "This is my chief aide, Brother Leonard." Duke and Brother Leonard exchanged brief, unsmiling nods. "I understand we will be working together for our cause."

473

Duke nodded. "You understand, of course, that you will be working directly under my orders, or those transmitted to you by Brother Leonard?"

Duke nodded again. It was the man's diction, his clear enunciation of each syllable, that was disconcerting. "Our plan is a simple one, Brother Shackleford. First, and as quickly as possible, we must let the white authority know that there is local resistance, awaken them to the possibility of increasing disturbances by our dissatisfied people. When we have implanted that in their minds, then we will hold a meeting to make our greater demands known—"

At 10:30, Duke drove back to Banjo's Place where he found Odie Bilson and Willy Eggert engaged in a game of pool. Within moments, every patron in the place had gathered to greet Buddy Duke, disrupting the action at every table. After a few minutes, he ordered a beer for everyone and waited for Odie and Willy to complete their game. He signaled Odie, who racked his cue, spoke to Willy, and the three left together.

"You know where we can find the other guys, Booker, Dave an' Luke?" Duke asked Odie.

"If they ain't at the 2–2–2, they'll come along soon."

"Good. We got a job to do a little later tonight. We need maybe three-four cars, old ones nobody knows. Long about midnight, one o'clock, we goin'a meet across the bridge—"

6

Weather and the small terror along Taylor Avenue were the topics of discussion throughout Laurelton on Saturday morning. Corey and Drew heard it on the car radio during their drive north to Shadow Hills.

Four cars filled with Negro youths had, during the early morning hours, raced simultaneously down Taylor Avenue and Mason Drive, heading westward, throwing rocks through plate-glass windows of commercial establishments. Twenty-two windows were smashed before the cars separated and disappeared. Police cars circled the area and threw roadblocks up across the bridge, but no traces of the vandals were found. It was presumed that they had fled south along the east bank of the Cottonwood, probably as far as Fairview, perhaps north to Riverton, crossed over to the west bank, and eventually drifted back to South or West Laurelton.

The commentator blamed the action on the extended pe-

turned and displayed a warm, beautiful smile. Although her waist was tiny, her breasts and hips were full and every movement emphasized a supernal litheness and vitality that detracted from her clean, fresh looks. "Thanks so much for the lift," she said. "I'm probably the only girl in town who doesn't own a car. For one thing, I hate driving and for another, I'm so close to everything, I don't really need one, so why bother. You're just back from Viet Nam, Joyce told me."

"Well—yes—"

"Here, let me take this and let's get out of this messy kitchen. My girl doesn't come in on Saturdays." Leading the way to the living room, Corey was momentarily titillated by the swing of her figure in the close-fitting dress that ended a good two inches above her knees and suggested that she was wearing absolutely nothing under it; she sat on one of the two small sofas and smiled up at him. "Cheers."

"Cheers." He touched the rim of his glass to hers, then raised it to his lips. "You're staring," she said with a deepening smile.

"There's so much worthwhile to stare at."

"A compliment, I hope."

"A compliment, very definitely."

In reply, she winked and sipped her drink. "Sit down," she said, "there's loads of time. Tell me about you."

"I'm a very dull story, but a good listener. You're not from Laurelton, of course."

"Since fourteen months ago. I came here with my husband, Greg Fields. From New York, although I'm originally from Dallas. Greg was in charge of installing a bank of computers at the Warren Company. You'll hear about it soon enough, so let me be the first to tell you about it. We were on the thin edge of a divorce before we left New York. For a while it looked as though the change might work, but once we got used to the scenery here, the old problems came on again and a year later we separated. Greg went back to New York and I took a secretarial job in the copy department of the Fuller and Conwell advertising agency and I've been there ever since. End story. What's yours?"

"Even less than yours. Born and raised here, college, law school, Army, home again. End story."

"That's *all?*"

"Sum and total."

Pouring a second drink for them, Hilary said, "I didn't think it was possible to condense so many years into so few short sentences. You should be a scissors man."

"A what?"

"A news editor. Cutting copy for the front men, the announcers. You could probably cut an hour news program down to two minutes flat. But I've heard lots about you from Joyce and Perry. And Paula."

"That should be enough to bankrupt me with anybody."

"No, no. I liked what I heard."

"And I like what I see."

"Very gallant."

"Very honest."

"That deserves another drink."

He poured the third drink and handed one to her, but she was staring at him, smiling with her lips parted slightly. She moved closer to him. He put his glass down and kissed her lightly on her lips. She drew back for a moment and said, "That was nice." She tilted her head slightly to one side and kissed him harder and his arm went around her, touching the nakedness of her back, feeling the force of her lips on his own. He broke, kissed her cheek, nuzzled her ear and she pulled back and said, "You know, we may never make it to the party."

"Joyce and Paula would never forgive us."

"No, they wouldn't. Shall we go?"

They were the first to arrive at nine. Paula, wearing a short robe over very little else, answered the door, her head turned away, calling instructions to someone named Josie to tell someone else named Hadley to for God's sake stop fiddling around and finish setting the bar up, company was beginning to arrive; then to Corey and Hilary, "My, my, how did you two manage to team up?" She brushed her lips across Hilary's cheek and gave Corey a resounding kiss as she embraced him. "A spanking-fresh, brand new civilian man. And such a beautiful one." Another kiss. "Nothing to wipe off, lover, I haven't put my lipstick on yet." To Hilary, "I'm so glad you could come, darling. Entertain Corey for me while I get some last minute things done."

Hadley, a tall, thin Negro in a short white jacket, came to take the bottle of bourbon from Corey. Paula, calling ahead to Josie, went back to the bedroom. Hilary and Corey went to the bar where Hadley beamed toothily and awaited an order. "I'll stay with the martinis," Hilary said, adding, "Very dry, Hadley."

"Yes'm. An' you, sir?"

"Bourbon over ice."

They sipped their drinks while Hadley produced bowls of nuts and other nibblers. Then Paula was back, wearing a daring mini-skirted dress in white and gold that resembled something out of a Hollywood spectacular of the Roman era. Hilary's immediate reaction was, "I love it, Paula. I wish I had the figure for it. And the courage."

Corey's response was a low whistle. "That," he said, "has got to be the all-time champion all-girl dress."

Paula twirled in a complete circle. "The newest thing from New York by way of London. It's called a No-cheater."

"For very obvious reasons. No girl with anything to hide would dare wear it."

"I'm introducing it tonight. By next week every young over-weight fatty in town will be bursting seams to get into one. Hadley, a bourbon on the rocks and make it strong. I've got to catch up."

Josie, a short, dark woman, bustled in from the kitchen with trays of crackers, cheese, smoked oysters, artichoke hearts and mystery dips. No sooner were they placed on the long oval coffee table than the doorbell rang. Hugh and Caroline Brock with Sam and Peggy Driscoll, who had driven with them. Kisses, handshaking, back-slapping and arm-grasping, everyone talking at once. The room became boisterous and Perry and Joyce Willard came in, Joyce at once seeking out Hilary for a brief inquisition. Hadley was busy at the bar, Josie passing hot hors d'oeuvres. Then Ad Cameron with Melaine Todd, Wyatt Harper and Cissis Clark.

Corey turned to the momentarily vacant bar to refresh his drink and Paula materialized beside him. "Make it two, Hadley," she ordered.

"Yes'm, Miss Paula."

Drinks in hand, watching the others, Paula said, "Just like the old days, isn't it, Corey?"

He laughed, his spirits raised by the excitement around him. "Not quite, but it's wonderful to see them all together again. I miss Les, but seeing Melanie and Cissie as grown women, Lord—"

"And you. You look just like what you are, the newest thing in town."

"Not quite as new as your dress."

"You really like it?"

"Love it, but for God's sake, keep off the streets in it. The rape rate would be astronomical."

She took his left arm and placed it around her waist. "Kiss?"

He kissed her lips lightly and withdrew, catching a glimpse of Hilary, a quizzical smile on her lips. He raised his glass to Paula. "Cheers," she toasted.

"Shalom," Corey replied.

"Sha-what?"

481

"Shalom. Peace. It's Hebrew. Israeli."

"I'm surprised. Think of that. Shalom, peace. I thought it was Vietnamese."

"I wish they had it."

"Corey—"

"What?"

"Tonight, when the others go, you stay. I want to talk to you."

"Something special?"

"Just talk. You know, boy-girl talk."

"What we're doing now. Over a very fine drink."

Someone called to Paula and midway across the room, the door was pushed open. New faces. Jim and Gabrielle Stone, transplanted Chicagoans, Gabrielle a stunning Latin type who might have stepped off a Broadway stage or from a movie screen. Then Ellery Thomas, who was pushing 40, with Hope Ford. Hope no more than 18, mini-skirted, net stockings, with breasts protruding to near-miraculous proportions, kissing every male lustily, much to Ellery's annoyance. And immediately on their heels, John Prestman and Valerie Stedman. Valerie at once threw her arms around Corey and he recalled vaguely that she was two years behind him at the University. Prestman, a recent arrival from Augusta, an engineer with the Water and Power Company, lost among these old friends. More introductions over the high clamor, drinks passed on a tray by Hadley, Josie racing to keep up with the demand for the fast-disappearing food.

After the initial confusion, Corey managed to escape the center of the huddle and followed Hilary to the bar, but within moments they were surrounded by Adam, Hugh and Sam, Corey answering the "How was it over there?" grilling, the "Remember the time down in Athens when—" reminders. The talk was a hodgepodge of cars, recent vacations, homes, the weather, civil rights, antiwar feelings; Corey's battle wound. Lyle Emerson, turned loner.

Subjects began, were interrupted, and soon lost. The temperature, competing with the air-conditioning system, rose with the decibel volume. Jackets were removed, ties loosened, guests sprawled on sofas, chairs, on the floor, splintering off into groups; the girls volleying between dress and hair styles, the men exchanging salacious jokes reserved for party occasions.

By ten-thirty, when Polk Holderby arrived, alone, the party had mellowed somewhat. Everyone but Paula, Hadley and Josie listening to Jim Stone's psychedelic experience at an LSD party on a recent trip to San Francisco. "Man, it was the weirdest of weirdies, the wildest—"

"Was that a *business* trip you took, Jim?"

"Purely business, but the *trip,* that was thrown in."

"You took the LSD?"

"Took it? It was damn near rammed down my throat."

"What was it like, the effect—"

"I don't really know. Weird it was, but to pin it down would be like trying to describe the color red to someone who's been blind since birth. Sometimes I feel like I'm still on the same trip."

"Then how in hell—"

Paula was greeting Polk, taking a wrapped bottle from him, a brief kiss on her cheek. He waved and called an all-inclusive, "Hi, everybody!" went to the bar with Paula for his first drink. Corey left Hilary's side and joined them as Paula returned to the group.

"Polk," Corey greeted.

"Hey, old buddy. I see you made it. How about this layout?"

"Wonderful. Particularly with so many of the old gang. What held you up?"

Polk grinned and winked mischievously. "Come last, leave last."

So much, Corey thought, for Paula's invitation to remain after the others were gone.

Ad Cameron came to the bar for a fresh drink. "How's old Merrill, Lynch, Pierce, Fenner, Smith and Holderby?"

"Rising firmer and stronger every day," Polk replied.

"You get it up to respectable strength, we may be able to do some business together again."

"Boy, I get it up to respectable strength, who needs you? I'll have plenty of takers," Polk said loudly.

This last, overheard by most, turned the mood of the moment back to suggestive quips and innuendo in which others joined, accompanied by high giggles and shrill laughter. And now Corey began to feel somewhat out of it. Everything was coming on too fast. The girls were sitting, kneeling or lying stretched out on the floor, heads pillowed on male laps, seemingly unconscious of the blatant display of their sex. Hope Ford was lying on her back, shoes off, feet raised and braced against the edge of the coffee table, her mini-skirt hiked up so high that the edges of her panties showed. Gabrielle Stone leaned forward giving everyone a splendid view of her exquisitely molded breasts, her hair carelessly covering one entire side of her olive-toned face.

It was a new form of open exhibitionism and Corey, observing closely, was confused by it. And he suddenly thought of Drew, no doubt alone at Brookhill, or sitting beside Anderson Warren's bed as he lay in drugged sleep, waiting for the end to come.

"Penny?"

It was Paula, coming from the kitchen, taking the bar stool beside him. "You'd be overpaying me," he said.

"You get used to it, Corey. Everything is moving faster these days."

"A little too fast for me. That Ford kid should be out on a movie date with a boy her own age, then some ice cream at Stocker's and home to bed."

"She's eighteen, Corey, and probably started dating at thirteen."

"And Ellery is at least forty—"

"Married and divorced twice."

"It's obscene. What chance has she got?"

"What chance did you or I have in Athens?"

"At least we were the same age, in college—"

Paula laughed then. "Look at her. Would you turn her down?"

"I'm not thinking so much of that as I am what her parents must be thinking about right now."

"Harry and Jen Ford? I think they'd even settle for Ellery to get Hope safely off their hands."

"Even at that, the odds are lousy."

"Don't moralize, Corey. The important thing would be to get them married off and get their basic training legally. After that, they're on their own. The modern way—"

"Paula!" It was Polk calling.

"Got to play hostess, Corey. Don't forget, you're staying."

"You forgot. I brought Hilary—"

"I didn't forget. She can go home with the Willards who were supposed to bring her. That was a piece of Joyce's manipulating."

"Paula! C'mere!" Polk's voice was insistent, possessive.

"What about Polk?" Corey asked.

"Oh, Polk." Paula dismissed Polk with smiling disdain. "You stay. We'll be serving soon and they'll begin leaving around one, those with baby-sitters—"

"I asked you what about Polk."

"Forget Polk. He's been going for me like a little boy after a lollipop ever since I've been back."

"He's serious about you, isn't he?"

"I don't think Polk has ever been serious about anything. You remember him at Athens. All talk and action until he got what he wanted, then it was all over as soon as he saw a new face or an interesting wiggle. More than anything else, he talks too much, and I can't stand men-talkers. They're

484

more dangerous than bombs." She leaned forward and kissed him, knowing, as he knew, that Polk's eyes were on them. She winked and said conspiratorily, "That's only for now," and went to join the others, sitting beside Polk. Corey poured a stiff drink for himself.

Hilary was involved in a four-way discussion with Sam, Valerie and Hugh. Corey wondered if there were some way he could slip away into the night, wondering where Lyle Emerson was at this moment, what he was doing to lessen his emotional anguish. He saw Polk with his arm around Paula, one hand caressing her as he talked across the chatter to Hugh Brock, an almost sexual fondling. Corey took a fresh drink to Ad Cameron's chair and sat on its arm, not listening to Melanie Todd's inconsequential debate with Ad, caught Hilary's smile, the motion of her hand indicating the empty place on the sofa beside her, and refused to yield to the temptation, now wondering what the hell had come over him; an anger he could not define.

He heard the tolling of the bell in the City Hall tower and counted the twelve strokes. Paula left Polk's side and went to the dining area where the table had been set with plates, silver, napkins, china, and a large silver coffee urn, its single red eye signaling readiness.

The buffet of cold ham, thinly sliced roast beef and smoked salmon. Potato salad, slaw, fresh tomatoes mixed with cucumber slices. Hot biscuits. Small chocolate eclairs. Hot and iced coffee, hot and iced tea. Corey ate lightly, but managed two drinks with his food. Again, seated in groups on the floor around the coffee table, on sofas and chairs, balancing plates and cups, an occasional spilling or dropping on a dress, suit or the carpet.

At 1:15 the Brocks left apologetically, taking the Driscolls with them. Corey saw Joyce Willard in a brief whispered conference with Hilary, then Joyce and Perry left, Ad Cameron and Melanie Todd tagging along for a nightcap. Good nights were called and invitations pressed on Corey as each couple left, leaving Polk, Hilary and Corey behind; and it was obvious that Polk was waiting for Corey to leave with Hilary. Paula kissed Jim and Gabrielle Stone at the door, closed it and said, "Polk, you won't mind giving Hilary a lift, will you?"

Polk's mouth opened and his face became flushed. "I—ah—"

Corey saved him from further embarrassment. He said to Polk, "I think Paula forgot that I brought Hilary. If you don't mind—"

Polk quickly said, "No. Not at all, Corey."

Paula darted a swift flash of anger at Corey, then reassumed command. "Of course. I'm sorry. Do forgive me, Hilary, it's been such a hectic evening."

There was only coolness in Paula's "good night" to both Hilary and Corey, no embrace, no kiss.

Not until they were in his car did Hilary speak. "Corey, I'm sorry if I've created a—situation—with Paula."

"Don't be silly. There's no involvement there."

"No? I thought it was pretty obvious you were to stay behind."

"You're imagining things."

"I'm glad of that. I wouldn't want to cause any—disruption."

"You're not, so forget it." He started the car and drove slowly toward Phillips Drive, almost with an unwillingness to reach their destination; but the few blocks took only as many minutes. He parked and got out to hold the door on Hilary's side open and when she emerged, turned toward him with a bright smile and said, "Nightcap? It's the only saloon open in town this time of night."

"I—yes, thanks."

She handed him her key and he unlocked the door, stood aside as she entered and hit the light switch which turned three lamps on in the living room. "Bourbon, scotch—or coffee?" she asked.

"Bourbon now, coffee after."

"I'll put the coffee on and you pour the bourbon. Togetherness in the kitchen. Come along."

He got the tray of cubes out of the refrigerator, poured the bourbon. Hilary had the coffee on, sipped at her drink. "Back in a moment," she said. "Take our drinks out to the living room?"

He finished the one he had, poured another and went into the larger room, placed the drinks side by side on the table by the sofa. He lit a cigarette and stood up, removed his jacket and loosened his tie, begining to feel the effects of the whiskey he had consumed.

"Take the tie off, too," Hilary said. He turned, slipped the tie off and dropped it on a chair. She had changed into a short robe, no longer than the dress she had worn earlier, but more flared at the bottom. Her legs were bare, suggesting that the robe was all she had on and he could feel the stirring, a churning as she came toward him, smiling, and sat beside him on the sofa. He handed her the drink, lit a cigarette for her as she leaned back, kicked off her slippers and rested her bare heels on the low table.

"This is the nicest, most relaxing time of any day," Hilary said. "I can feel as though the rest of the world is asleep and mine to do with as I please."

"You don't happen to have a God-like complex, do you?"

She laughed teasingly. "No, nor any other complexes. I'm an amazingly simple and uncomplex woman."

"That's a rare admission."

"I am, really."

"Would your husband—uh—"

"Greg," she supplied.

"Greg. Would Greg think so, that you're simple and uncomplex?"

"He should know that best of all. Greg was a bundle of nervous convolutions, coiled up in a business corkscrew, lost in a labyrinth of despair and drowning in emotional swamps. He needed a psychiatrist more than he needed a wife and when he discovered that, he was finally happy."

"That sounds like the findings of a psychiatrist as written by a clever copywriter," Corey said.

"Aren't we all? Amateur psychiatrists, I mean."

"In a way, yes. I suppose we all turn to some form of analysis to get rid of our own problems."

"What are yours?"

"I don't really know, except that I don't want to add to them."

"Is that—are you trying to make some kind of a point?"

"I don't even know that." He stood up then and said, "I think I've had a little too much to drink. If you don't mind —" He picked up his tie and jacket.

Hilary's mouth had become a pout. "As you wish."

Corey walked toward the door, turned and said, "Good night. And thanks." She didn't answer and he went out.

He drove home slowly in the quiet night thinking of Paula and Polk, of Hilary Fields. Of Kenneth and Caddy and Shana Pierce. Of Lyle Emerson and Elizabeth Shackleford. And of the complexities of everyday living. One step either way and he could have become permanently reinvolved with Paula or immersed in Hilary, two attractive, desirable women. And then he wondered how much Drew Warren had played in his unconscious resolution not to become involved with either.

8

On that Saturday night, Brookhill lay quietly in sleep. Drew, after having dinner on a tray in her grandfather's room in order to try to stimulate the old man's appetite,

487

gave up the effort when he showed little response to her presence beyond holding her hand until sleep overcame him. She went out, leaving him in the care of Mrs. Thompson, an elderly, motherly woman who had returned to nursing after she became widowed. By prearrangement with Ada Elgin, the four-to-midnight nurse, Mrs. Thompson had come on duty at eight o'clock prepared to remain until eight in the morning, when Erna Keller would take over.

At 11:30 Theodore Warren had come home, gone up to Anderson's room and found him asleep. Mrs. Thompson roused herself, came into the bedroom from the veranda, exchanged a few whispered sentences with Theodore, who left and went to his room. Moments later, Anderson awoke. Mrs. Thompson went to him at once, took his temperature, pulse and blood pressure, made notes on the clipboarded chart, then gave him his midnight medication. He refused the sleeping pill and she did not insist, knowing that it would be a wasted effort.

Anderson asked her to turn the lights off, which Mrs. Thompson did, then went to the adjoining room and turned on the television set to see the late movie, using a headpiece that confined the sound to her ears. Before long, she was fast asleep.

The night, like the day it had followed, was hot, the humid air stagnant, the leaves on the trees hanging limp and noiseless, all the normal night sounds, the creakings of the old house stilled. It was, Anderson thought, as though he were the last living thing on earth.

He raised himself up on his elbows and felt a trembling from his own slight weight. He sat up then, wondering if he could make the trip without disturbing anyone. His daily exercise, upon which he insisted, was restricted to several minutes out of bed to go to the bathroom, this on the arm of a nurse who would remain outside the slightly opened door in case he needed help. During the past two weeks, he had devised a ruse to impress his weakness on the nurse and Dr. Ballard by calling for assistance to return him to his bed; but Anderson's purpose in this deception was known to himself alone. Yet he knew, because of his growing weakness, he could no longer put off what he must do.

Since leaving the hospital in Baltimore, Anderson had decided he would die when he chose the day, the time and place—and in dignity. Not lying like a helpless vegetable for the ultimate moment of death. More than anything else, he wanted to spare Drew this final agony of watching him disintegrate, the final decay of human flesh.

He lifted himself slightly, swung his long, almost fleshless

488

legs to the floor and stood up, holding on to a bedpost, then released it experimentally. Slowly, step by step, he went to the door, stopped to listen for the nurse. No sound came from her room. He opened the door, stepped out into the lighted hallway, closed the door softly. One hand touching the wall, he made his way to the back stairway and in the same manner, step by step, he descended the stairs. On the ground level, he shuffled through the butler's pantry, into the kitchen and out on the back veranda. Four steps down, clinging to the rail, brought him to the cemented walk, where he rested for several minutes.

He turned right and walked slowly along the path, undismayed by the darkness, knowing well the route to the mausoleum. He moved haltingly, cautiously, resting every few yards until he came to the enclosure. Once inside the gate, he sat on a bench for a while to recoup his expended strength, then got up and followed the path to the door of the marble resting place of the Georgia Warrens. Little Clyde, beloved Cleo, adored Bruce.

The Italian bronze doors swung open at his touch and he stepped into the marble cloister, at once feeling some cooling relief from the heavy air outside. Four small night lights burned dimly, but with sufficient illumination to guide him to the bench before the three bronze plaques that identified the occupants, the crypt beside Cleo's empty and unmarked, awaiting him.

For a few minutes he sat on the bench thinking back in time to their life together, the young years of love, of hardship, of success. Of Alistair and Benjamin. Of Chase and Theodore. Of Louise, who had changed Theodore's life; wondering if he had been right to drive her away; and how much he had contributed to Theodore's failure as a man. Then finally realizing that there were no second chances.

"Cleo," he said, "I don't know if what I'm doing is right, but I've got the need in me to do it. I don't know what lies beyond. If there's life after death, I'll know it soon enough. If there's nothing but darkness, I'm not giving up too much to get there. I can't do any more for Theodore. Or Drew. I'm old, I'm tired, I'm dying. There's no more use for me here. I want to sleep beside you like I once did, with Clyde and Bruce, among my own."

Tears rolled down his cheeks and he brushed them aside with a hand, and when the turbulence in him subsided, he got up and went to the urn where he had hidden the plastic tube he had stolen from his private car the morning he had returned from Baltimore. In one corner, he found the faucet and a glass container used by the gardener to water the

489

flowers he cut fresh each day. He filled the container and went back to the marble bench.

He put the first pill in his mouth and took a sip of water. Another. Another. Until they were all gone.

At 4:15 on Sunday morning, Mollie Thompson awoke with a start. The television set was dark, the earphones hanging down from her neck, a red light on the set indicating that the current was still on. She glanced at her watch and was startled, then went quickly into the next room. Her patient was gone, his robe left behind on the bed. She ran to the bathroom, knocked softly, called out hopefully, then went inside. In nervous turmoil, she went to the bedroom door and looked out into the hallway, but it was empty. She checked the veranda and peered over its rail.

Crying over her helplessness, she ran to Drew's room, hesitated, then went swiftly downstairs and rapped on Shad and Leona's bedroom door and told them Anderson Warren was missing. Leona ran upstairs to verify his absence, while Shad telephoned Dr. Ballard, who was out on an emergency call. When he hung up, he went upstairs where Drew, Theodore, Leona and Mrs. Thompson were gathered in the old man's room. When Shad entered, Drew said calmly, "Shad, please get a flashlight and come with me. I think I know where he is." To the others, "Wait here, please."

They found him where Drew was certain he would be, lying on the floor in front of the marble bench, the plastic pill tube clutched tightly in one hand, the container of water overturned on its side. He had a small purplish bruise on the side of his head where he had fallen to the floor in his last moments of consciousness, but otherwise seemed to be in normal sleep.

Shad picked Anderson Warren up and carried him back to the house, Drew beside him, holding one of Gran's hands between her own, as though to keep it warm. Shad placed Anderson on his bed gently and the weeping Mollie Thompson drew the sheet over his chest, then confirmed the fact of his death. The plastic container was in the pocket of Drew's robe.

Leona wept disconsolately, murmuring, "Poor man, poor man." Shad went downstairs to light the driveway and lower floor, and remained there to wait for Dr. Ballard's arrival. Theodore, his eyes moist, had the least to say and went downstairs, taking Leona with him to put some coffee on. Drew, dry-eyed and remote, sat beside Anderson's bed, ordered Mrs. Thompson to go downstairs and wait.

Drew was still with Gran when Dr. Ballard arrived a little before six o'clock. He examined Anderson briefly, drew the sheet over the old man's head, then went to Drew and helped her up.

"Drew—"

"It was a blessing, Dr. Carl," she said. "He died peacefully in his sleep."

"Drew—"

She took the container from her robe pocket and handed it to him. "No one will know, will they, Dr. Carl?"

"No, Drew," he replied gently, "no one will know."

In the Armour household, Jemmy shook Corey awake at 6:45. "Telephone for you, Mist' Corey."

Corey struggled awake, having fallen asleep, it seemed, only minutes ago. "What time is it?"

"Most seven. It Dr. Ballard, Mist' Corey. He say it most impo'tant."

Corey thought first of Kenneth, an accident, and sat up quickly, apprehensively, taking the receiver from Jemmy. "Hello."

"Corey? Dr. Ballard here. Sorry to get you out of bed this early—"

"What is it, Dr. Ballard?"

"Anderson Warren is dead. I wanted to reach your father, but your man tells me he's in Atlanta. I wonder if you can reach him there?"

"I'll try. What about Drew, Doctor?"

"For the moment, she's holding up. I don't think it has fully hit her yet."

"Is there anything I can do? Anything?"

"She may need someone—"

"I'll be there as soon as I can get dressed. I'll try to reach Father from Brookhill."

"I'd rather you didn't tie up the phone here, Corey."

"What about Mr. Theodore?"

"He's here, but— Corey, try to locate your father, then come out here. I'll try to reach Chase Warren in New York. There are other calls I've got to make—"

In Kenneth's study, he found a personal telephone directory, got the Atlanta branch manager at his home and located Kenneth at his hotel. Kenneth asked Corey to call the Laurelton airport and order the Warren plane to Atlanta to pick him up and a Company car to meet him on arrival. Corey did so, showered himself into full wakefulness, gulped at a cup of coffee while he dressed, then drove to Brookhill.

The mortuary people had taken Anderson Warren's body away for final preparation before interment. Wayne and

Julie Taylor had arrived with Susan and John Curran. Julie and Susan sat on either side of Drew in the large downstairs living room. Wayne and Johnny were speaking to Dr. Ballard and Leona and Shad were arranging a table with cups and saucers beside the large coffee urn.

Corey went to Drew at once. "I'm sorry, Drew—"

"Thank you for coming, Corey," she said simply. She sat still as if she had been carved from marble, tense, yet appearing calm. Julie and Susan got up and went to the study to answer the telephone calls that were beginning to come in, at first a few, then a steady inpouring as the word was spread by frequent radio announcements.

Later, Reverend Wyatt Miller appeared, apologizing for his late appearance, occasioned by early Sunday services. He spoke briefly to Drew, then at greater length to Theodore and Wayne Taylor and departed. Ballard's call to Chase Warren was returned and the two men spoke for a few minutes. Chase asked to speak to his brother Theodore, but Theodore refused to take the call; then to Kenneth Armour, who had not yet appeared. Ballard told Wayne that Chase would arrive in Laurelton on Wednesday, in time for his father's funeral. Still later, Dr. Ballard accompanied Drew to her room, taking Leona with them. When he reappeared, he informed the others that Drew was asleep and was not to be disturbed. Drew did not come downstairs again that day.

Corey was home when Kenneth arrived there during the afternoon. Kenneth at once began to make numerous telephone calls, talked with Company officials in various cities and several abroad. Over dinner, he told Corey the funeral, scheduled for Wednesday at 3 P.M., would be private for the immediate members of the family and only a handful of outsiders; the Armours, Shad and Leona Waters, Duncan and Diane Collins, the Mayor, a representative of the Governor, and those of the Maryland and Virginia Warrens who might come in response to his notification by telephone. The service would, on Anderson's previous instructions, be brief and without eulogy, and interment would follow immediately in the Warren mausoleum.

9

All of Laurelton and Cairn County felt cheated that so few of the thousands whose lives had, directly or indirectly, white and Negro alike, been touched by Anderson Warren, would be permitted a final glimpse or to pay a last tribute to his many contributions to the community and their own well-being. On the Sunday of his death, prayers were said by the congregations of every church in East, South and West Laurelton. Later, representatives of each faith met and agreed to conduct a special memorial service on Wednesday to coincide with the hour of his funeral.

From all over the state, the nation and abroad came wires and cables of condolence. The local and national press and electronic media praised Anderson Warren as a humanitarian and for his financial grants to hospitals, medical and scientific research organizations, schools, colleges, universities and private charities. The industry of which he had been for so long a part lauded his business integrity, citing him as an example by which all men could live. The State Legislature passed a commendatory resolution testifying to his greatness, and on the day of his interment, this was read by the Governor before television cameras. From the White House came a warmly worded expression of regret for the nation's great loss.

On Tuesday, Duncan and Diane Collins arrived from New York. From Richmond, Alistair Warren's son Austin flew in with his wife, Rhoda, and son Lucas, who brought his wife, Laurellen. From Baltimore came Ralph, the son of Benjamin Warren, and his wife, Mary, the parents of Laurellen. Austin's other children, Bradford and Charlotte, were in Europe and Ralph's Clyde and Christian were in New York and Los Angeles; all wired or cabled their regrets and condolences. These Warrens were driven to Brookhill where they would remain until after the funeral.

It was Theodore who remarked to Kenneth Armour that this was the first time in memory that Brookhill was filled to near capacity, the first time so many Warrens were gathered under one roof; and added the ironical observation, "My father would have enjoyed this very much."

Chase Warren arrived early on Wednesday morning and went directly to the Laurelton House. He came alone, making excuses for his wife, Victoria, and two sons, Marshall and Victor.

Locally, business came to a virtual halt on that day, which was officially proclaimed a day of mourning. Civic buildings and schools displayed their flags at half mast. Churches on both sides of the bridge were filled that afternoon and loudspeaker systems were installed so that the overflow of worshipers could hear the offered prayers and praises for Anderson Warren. Along the public road that paralleled the western edge of Brookhill, a steady flow of cars bearing the curious drove back and forth, hoping to catch a glimpse beyond the bronze gates, normally kept open, now closed and guarded by uniformed police.

Promptly at three o'clock, Reverend Wyatt Miller commenced the private service in the large downstairs parlor. It lasted twenty minutes and at its conclusion, Anderson Warren's coffin was carried by ten estate employees down the narrow path that led to the mausoleum. Behind the coffin walked Reverend Miller, alone, and behind him, Drew Warren beside her father, pale and solemn, her eyes on the coffin; then Leona and Shad Waters. Chase Warren walked alone, then came Austin and Rhoda, Lucas and Laurellen, Ralph and Mary, Kenneth and Corey Armour, followed by Wayne and Julie Taylor, John and Susan Curran, the Collinses, Mayor Tom Cameron, County Commissioner Dale Anderson, the Governor's aide from Atlanta, and finally, Dr. Carl Ballard.

En route, estate workers and their families stood with heads bared and bowed as the procession passed by, murmuring prayers, offering blessings, wiping away an occasional tear. As the funeral party reached the mausoleum and entered, the field employees gathered outside the enclosure to wait until the final service would be concluded.

Inside, the casket was placed upon a dolly and rolled up in front of the single opening in the wall. Reverend Miller spoke a brief service commending the body to God. The casket was lifted from the dolly and placed into its crypt and an unmarked bronze plaque was temporarily bolted into place, to be replaced later by one more suitably engraved.

It was over. The funeral party returned to the house and Mayor Cameron, Commissioner Anderson and the Governor's aide left at once, followed shortly afterward by the Taylors, Currans, and the Reverend Miller, who was driven into town by Kenneth Armour.

Except for Laurellen, the Maryland and Virginia Warrens showed grave solemnity, if not uneasiness, as representatives at the funeral of the legendary man none had ever seen, and knew of only from their parents and grandparents. Austin, a dour, thin-faced man, frequently glanced at his watch as though eagerly awaiting a decent departure hour. Ralph busied himself exploring paintings, bronzes, glass and ivory art objects, nodding his approval and commenting favorably to Mary, who was seldom far from his side.

Chase Warren stood, sat, and drank whiskey alone, to all intents and purposes an outsider. He conferred with Duncan Collins for a brief moment, spoke a few words with Austin,

494

then Ralph. Theodore had excused himself early and left the room.

Drew sat on a small settee at the far end of the room, Laurellen Warren beside her, their facial resemblance quite noticeable. Dr. Ballard had followed Theodore from the room, then returned and signaled Corey into the hallway, asked him to accompany him to his car. Once outside, Ballard said, "You in any hurry to leave, Corey?"

"No, not if I can be of any help."

Ballard "hm-m-m-ed" and said, "I'm concerned about Drew. The others will be leaving soon and I'd feel better if she had someone close to her around, just in case."

"Of course—"

"She loved that old man, almost as much as she loved Bruce. She's holding back, hasn'd shed a tear yet. That bothers me more than a little. I remember back when Bruce died—"

"Doctor—"

"It's all locked up inside her, tearing her apart emotionally. The reaction could create a serious problem."

"A drinking problem, Doctor?"

Ballard shot him a quick side glance. "Doesn't take long to get the word around, does it? Well, she's had that problem and another beside it. A sleeping pill habit. Don't ask me how it happens, Corey, but I can tell you this much. Drew Warren isn't a chronic alcoholic. She drank a lot, yes, for the same reason she became addicted to barbiturates, out of loneliness, trying to forget the painful things of her life."

"What about psychiatry?"

"She tried that when she went to Europe after Bruce died, but the pain was stronger than her desire to cure it. I sent her to a good man there, but she dropped out of sight after a few visits. I don't really know what happened over there. She came back here one day and wouldn't talk about it.

"Since she was three, Drew has lived a kind of fantasy life. Louise disappeared, Theodore became a wandering stranger, Anderson and Cleo were already old. Bruce was the only one left to hang on to, give her a sense of identification. When Bruce was killed there wasn't anyone left and her world fell apart. She's had more sorrow in her life than happiness and I don't know any medical cure for that. I'd guess you come as close to— Do you understand what I'm trying to say, Corey?"

"I think I do and I want to help. If she'll let me."

"It may take a little time, but she will. Eventually. You're

495

still a firm link with the happier times she's known. Make the effort, Corey, even if she resists. She's worth it."

Ballard got into his car, started it, waved a hand and drove off. Corey returned to the house. Leona told him that Drew had gone to her room, that Laurellen was with her.

"And Mr. Theodore?"

"He's in the study with Mr. Chase."

"Do you think I might see Miss Drew for a few minutes, Leona?"

"I'll send Sue-Ann up to see, Mr. Corey."

He waited downstairs. Through the window, he watched the other Warrens strolling about the formal gardens of Brookhill.

In Anderson Warren's study, Theodore sat in the leather chair at his father's desk, Chase in an armchair facing him. There was a certain sameness about them, yet the contrasts were equally remarkable. Chase, nine years older, looked fifteen years younger than Theodore. His hair showed very little gray, his eyes were clearer and he was at least twenty pounds lighter. Of equal height and bone structure, Chase was the more slender, and the richness of his clothes and linen, his manicure and carefully chosen jewelry all integrated with his suave, superior manner of cold indifference and quiet insolence.

The years of estrangement, resentment and hatred that lay between them were too difficult a gulf to bridge, unpronounced yet apparent as Theodore waited with marked impatience for Chase to be gone once again, forever out of his life, hands clenched into tight fists, head averted to avoid Chase's eyes. Chase was saying, "You mean to tell me he never discussed the disposition of his estate with you? That's incredible."

"Incredible as it may seem—"

"I don't believe you, Theodore."

For the first time, Theodore swung around and faced Chase directly. "I don't give a good goddam what you choose to believe or not believe, Chase, and I don't intend to discuss Father, his estate, or anything else with you," Theodore replied in cold, clipped words.

"What about the Company?" Chase demanded.

"You'll find out everything you want to know when the will is read."

"When?"

"I'd suggest you ask Ken Armour." Theodore swiveled his chair to his right, away from Chase, in an act that im-

496

plied their conversation was over, but Chase made yet another attempt to keep it alive.

"Sooner or later, Theodore, you'll have to discuss this."

"If I do, it will be through our attorneys."

"Goddam you, why do you have to be so infantile about this? I don't like you any more than you like me, but I still think enough about the Warren name not to want to see a family fight in open court. If we—"

"And I'm not interested in your belated feelings about the family name."

"You miserable sonofabitch," Chase snarled. "You got hung up on a tart, married her and blamed me for your own stupid mistake. Carrying on in this idiotic way all these years. What kind of an ass are you?"

"That sounds more like the way I've always remembered you," Theodore said. "You've never cared a damn about anything or anyone but yourself, not for Mother, Father, the business, the world. I've told you before, Father never discussed the disposition of his estate, but I've got an idea you won't like what you hear when his will is read. If you have any idea of moving back into the Company, I'll fight you with everything I've got. You walked out on it once and I'll do my best to see you in hell before you step back into it. I never wanted it for myself, but I'll fight you every way I can. Does that make my position clear?"

"If that's the way you want it—"

"That's exactly the way I want it."

"That's your final say?"

"I have nothing more to say to you, now or ever."

Chase stood up and walked to the door. He opened it, paused, turned back as though he would speak, then thought better of it and went out, closing the door behind him. Theodore did not look in Chase's direction but sat at the desk, eyes staring vacantly at the green desk blotter.

Drew had removed her mourning black and lay on her bed in a yellow robe. Laurellen sat on the edge of the bed, the pretty girlishness of a few years ago matured into soft beauty and warmth. At Loon Lake, there had been a greater closeness between Drew and Laurellen than with their other cousins, one that had prompted Laurellen's revelation of the intimacy between herself and Lucas.

"Drew, I'm so sorry," Laurellen said.

Drew smiled wanly. "Don't be, Laurellen. Gran lived a long, full life. He didn't want anyone to mourn him or be sad."

"That's what we're always told, but when you love some-one—"

"What about you and Luke, Laurellen?"

Laurellen's smile was one of full happiness. "It's wonder-ful, Drew. I was worried at first, but Luke settled down at once. He went into his father's contracting firm and did wonders. Then his brother Brad came in and now Daddy Austin is talking about retiring and making Luke president."

"How nice that it all worked out so well."

"The thing I'm sorry about is that we're so far apart, we Warrens. After Bruce—I so much wanted to come down when we heard, but— I never really thanked you and Bruce for the house at Loon Lake, just a letter, but Luke and I ex-pected you and Bruce to visit us there summers. Then Bruce died and—I guess that ended Loon Lake for you."

"Yes—I—went abroad for a year—"

"Drew, would you like to come up to Baltimore for a visit? We'd love to have you, all of us. We've got this big place out in the Worthington Valley, with horses, a pool—"

"Thank you, Laurellen, but not for a while. There will be so many things here to settle, the estate and the Company, before I can start making plans for myself."

"Well, the invitation is always open. I—don't think I'm butting in, but the invitation includes Corey Armour." Has-tily, she added, "If you want him, of course."

Drew smiled again. "He's nice, isn't he?"

"Absolutely darling. I hope you include him in your plans. I liked him the first time I saw him at Loon Lake, the time with Luke out on the dock that night."

"I remember. I hope Luke's forgotten it."

Laurellen laughed prettily. "Only when I let him. Some-times it's useful to remind him that he had a real letch for you. He insists that it was only because you reminded him of me."

"That's a very pretty compliment. Thank you."

"Drew—if I can ever do anything to help—in any way —anything—will you let me know?"

"Of course, but—"

"May I tell you something in confidence?"

Puzzled, "Certainly—"

"Then tell your daddy to watch out for his brother Chase."

"Chase? For heaven's sake, why?"

"I don't know exactly, but I do know he's made it a point to come down to Baltimore to see Luke's father several times. And mine, too. Luke never got involved in whatever it is, but he told me it has something to do with your father.
498

I know there's some bad blood between them and Luke doesn't like Chase Warren, but I think my father and Luke's respect Chase because he's so rich and successful."

"So are Uncle Austin and Uncle Ralph, aren't they?"

"Lord, yes, but not in the big flamboyant way Uncle Chase is. Uncle Austin is something of a snob about people who are richer than he is, even though a lot of his own wealth came from the stock his father bought from your Grandfather Anderson a long time ago. I'd guess Uncle Chase's visits have something to do with the Warren Tobacco Company."

"I don't think Uncle Chase can hurt the Company, Laurellen. I do know he and Father aren't close, but that's about all."

There was a light tap on the door and Leona came in apologetically. "Mr. Corey asked if he could see you for just a minute, Miss Drew."

Laurellen got up. "I'll leave now, Drew. I think the families want to start back for Atlanta before dark. Our reservations are on the early plane tomorrow morning."

"I do hate to see you leave so soon," Drew said.

"Uncle Austin and Luke," Laurellen said. "I don't think they're sure enough of Brad to want to leave him alone too long. Will you think about coming up for a visit soon?"

"Yes. Good-bye, darling. Thank you for coming, and give my love to Brad and Charlotte, and to Clyde and Chris." They embraced, kissed, and Laurellen left.

Corey knocked on Drew's door and, on her invitation, entered the room. She was sitting up in bed and now her facial muscles had grown taut, seeming to draw most of the color from her face.

"Drew," he said softly.

"I'm all right, Corey. Please don't look so concerned."

"Have you taken the pills Dr. Ballard left?"

"No. I've been visiting with Laurellen. I don't want to sleep yet."

Her hands were gripping a small handkerchief, twisting it. "How about taking one now? They'll relax you. You're tight as a drum."

"Corey, please don't baby me—please don't."

"All right, Drew. Do you want me to leave?"

She hesitated. "No. But I don't want to talk." She closed her eyes then and he took her hand into his own, feeling strength, or hardness in it. After a while her fingers went limp and he looked at her face and saw it was relaxed, either dozing or asleep. When he tried to remove his hand, her eyes opened and they were tear-filled. He caught the

499

odor of brandy and knew she had braced herself liberally for the funeral service and procession to the mausoleum, had seen it in her faltering walk; and perhaps again since she had come up to her room. Her voice, he noted, was low, almost harsh.

Drew closed her eyes again and said, "Corey, bring me a drink, please. The bottle is on my dresser."

There was no point in refusing. He went to the dresser and poured brandy into the glass and brought it to her. She drank most of it and held the glass with its remaining quarter of an inch. "Something I've taken up since you've been gone, Corey," she said. "Shocked?"

"No. But it's not an answer to anything."

"It helps," she said simply.

"For how long?"

"Until the next time."

"There can be too many next times, Drew."

She finished the brandy and laughed mirthlessly. "Oh, Corey, Corey. If you only knew how many times I've wished the next time was the last time."

"For God's sake, Drew, do you know what you're saying?"

"I know. They're all gone now. Grandmother Cleo, Bruce, Gran—"

"There's you. And your father—"

"Yes," she said, "there's my father," and Corey could sense the scorn in her words.

"Drew, this isn't at all like you."

"I told you, Corey. Time brings change. I'm not the same girl you knew a hundred million years ago. I'm different in many ways."

"No one can change that much in so short a time," he protested. "Goddamn it, Drew, stop talking to me in abstract terms, will you?"

She said, "I think I like you much better when you're angry. You *are* angry, aren't you?"

"Only because you're behaving like a child. A silly, immature child."

Drew was at once contrite. "That's what I am, can't you see, what I've become? A silly child with a silly, immature child's feelings—emotions—" Abruptly, she turned away from him and lay on her side. "Corey, please go. Please go now. Now—"

BOOK III

CHAPTER I

1

At 8:40 P.M. Officers Ben Hammond, white, and Paul Green, Negro, were on routine patrol in Car No. 8 out of the 12th Precinct, which was the headquarters station of West Laurelton, Captain Jim Price, commanding. They had made one complete turn of their area of responsibility and answered one radio call, a 415 (Disturbance), which turned out to be a minor argument between an elderly man and his younger sister, and which was quickly settled by a few calming words from Officer Green.

There had been little conversation between the two officers since they had commenced their tour of duty at four o'clock, other than a few ice-breaking words concerning Anderson Warren's funeral and the prolonged heat spell. It was their first time out together, Green's first tour in a squad car. Green was a rookie with two months of his probationary term remaining. Hammond's regular partner, Walt Coleman, had been reported sick by his wife a few hours before the tour began and after several hours together, and against regulations, Hammond pulled out a pack of cigarettes, lit one and offered the pack to Green, who refused. "Go ahead, kid," Hammond urged amiably, "nobody'll see you. Just keep it below the dashboard between puffs."

"It's not that," Green replied softly. "I don't smoke."

Hammond grunted and pocketed the pack, hiding the lighted cigarette from view by cupping his hand over it. He was a dapper man of about 30, a bachelor with a reputation as a "swinger" who had been involved with the attractive wife of a prominent attorney in East Laurelton who, without convincing proof of his wife's misconduct, settled for Hammond's transfer to West Laurelton. An ex-Marine, Ben was extremely careful of his appearance, his uniforms meticulously tailored to precise fit. The word among the Negro officers, Walt Coleman in particular, was that Ben was an "all-right guy to ride with, for an ofay." Yet, Paul Green was wary. On introduction, Ben had smiled, extended a hand and said, "Hi, partner," but Paul could not bring himself to call Hammond by his first name and to call him "Mister Hammond" seemed overly formal and awkward. He solved the problem by not addressing him by name at all.

"You like riding a car, Paul?" Hammond asked.

"This is my first time out."

"I know."

"I kind of liked riding the bike for four weeks, you know, all that power between your legs, just you, it's great. I guess either one is better than inside work or walking a beat."

"Well, you get a taste of everything your first six months out of training. You do your plainclothes yet?"

"First month. I teamed with Sergeant Pohlman." Green shook his head from side to side and laughed lightly with the memory. "Man, that's one tough cat."

"Pohlman? Strictly G.I. Kind of a sonofabitch, but you learn a hell of a lot in a hurry from him. He's up for detective lieutenant first opening turns up."

Green found it comfortable to talk with Hammond, an entirely new experience for him. Like talking to almost anybody, one of his own people; and a little confusing. "Then I had a couple weeks with Sergeant Carter, vice detail—"

"Now there's a real prick for my money," Hammond said. "I'd hate like hell to get stuck with him for a partner."

"Well, I sure didn't learn anything from him," Green said. "Man, he won't let you do nothin'. You answer a call with him, you wait outside while he goes in, does all the talkin', makes the report, everything himself. Give him one thing, though, he sure knows every rathole over here, every gambler, whore, con man."

"Yeah, and you can bet a month's pay they all know him, too."

It was a cryptic remark that Green couldn't quite under-

502

stand and since it was highly critical of another white man, and a ranking superior, he decided to drop the subject. At that moment, the radio sputtered a message for Car No. 8, another 415 at the 2-2-2 Club. Hammond swung right into Patterson Street, past Mason, Livingston, Barry and another right into Velie for four blocks. When they reached Peach Alley, Hammond turned in and slowed down for the traffic that was streaming toward the 2-2-2 Club, all pedestrian. Green had one hand on the door handle, ready to leap out, baton in left hand. Up ahead in the center of the block, a small crowd had gathered around the two young men, about 19 or 20, who were arguing loudly and brandishing fists without making actual contact. To one side stood an angry, tearful girl of indeterminate age, holding the upper part of her torn dress with one hand to cover her somewhat flat chest, shouting at one of the two boys. Around them, a circle of their contemporaries were shouting encouragement to the antagonists and others were joining the altercation from the 2-2-2 lobby.

As Green got out of the car, he said to Hammond, "Let me see if I can handle this alone, huh?" Hammond nodded agreement since this was routine procedure in an all-Negro involvement where the presence of a white officer might precipitate matters; and Green had done well with the earlier 415.

Green pressed through the outer rim of the group gently, smiling, calling, "Let me through, please," and "Excuse me, please," until he reached the inner circle. He stepped in between the two belligerents and said, "All right, fellows, let's knock if off. What's the complaint here?"

The girl with the torn dress pointed to the taller of the two boys and shouted, "Looka what he done to my dress, like to rip it right off my back, black bastard."

"All right, all right, miss," Green said placatingly, "let's keep it quiet. Hollering won't get it sewed up for you. Come on," turning to the crowd, "it's all over, folks. Let's clear the pavement and street. Move along, please—"

From the outer rim of the circle, someone called, "Shuh. Do like the white man's nigger say, else he bust your head in with his big club."

Green stiffened, fighting off the temptation to turn on the heckler, remembering the order to keep his mind on the matter at hand. Always one big mouth looking for trouble, itching to start something. He ignored the jibe. The shorter of the two belligerents was saying, "He's drunk, man. He tore her dress right off'n her, right inside the Club. All's I was tryin' to do was keep him from strippin' her naked."

503

Green turned an appraising eye on the taller youth, one hand on his arm, then turned him loose for a moment. The boy was wavering, lips slack, eyes clouded glassily. "You been drinkin' in there, son?" Green asked.

"I ain't your son and it ain't none-a your goddam business," the boy replied. Shouts of approval and laughter from the crowd. "Tell 'im, man! 'At's tellin' 'im!"

Green was in a quandary. He had never been in this kind of situation before except in training school with his classmates acting out the part of a mob. This, he knew instinctively, was recognizably different, no classroom problem; just as he was aware that Hammond was required to turn in a check-report on his conduct at the end of the tour, as witness to his professional behavior. He knew the book: Keep calm at all costs, no matter what happens. When you act, act firmly and decisively.

The 415 (Disturbance) had become a 390 (Drunk and Disorderly), could very quickly escalate into a 700 (Resisting Arrest) or erupt into a— What the hell was the code for Striking an Officer in the Performance of his Duty?

Take charge, Green. Take positive action. No point in trying to settle anything here. He would have to get them away somehow, settle it out of the hearing and eyes of the growing crowd. He stepped in, took the taller boy's wrist, wheeled him around in the direction of the police car. To the other boy and the aggrieved girl, "Come along with us to the car. We'll straighten this out." But the crowd began pressing in toward them. "All right," Green said firmly, "make way and let us through, please."

The crowd directly in front of him gave a little, but made no aisle for him. From the rear, he could feel them pressing closer, shouting, "Let 'im go! He ain't hurt nobody! Turn 'im loose, you white nigger!"

Green felt, rather than saw, the press behind him. Someone grabbed for his baton from behind. He swung around, the tall boy in front of him, and poked the baton toward the thickset man who had one hand on it, then pulled it back. The man set up a howl and the curses began.

"Black sonofabitchin' cop—"

"Nigger ofay—"

"White man's black bastard—"

"You no-good motherfu—"

Lord, help me, Green prayed, help me from my own! His back was toward the street, retreating toward it slowly, feeling the bodies of the crowd pressing against him, knowing that any moment he might feel a knife, an arm around his neck, thinking, "Jesus, Lord, I'm blowing this one, real

504

good." And then he heard the strong, authoritative voice of Ben Hammond behind him.

"All right, folks, let's cool it. Break it up before the other cars get here and take you all in. You don't want that, do you? This way, Paul."

Green turned and with amazement saw a clear aisle to the car, both doors open on the curb side, waiting to receive him and his prisoner. Without undue haste, he moved toward it, put the fumble-footed boy inside while Hammond talked with the girl and other boy involved and led them toward the car. The tall boy, still feeling a sense of security in the crowd encircling the car, made a grab for Green's service revolver, but was no match for the officer, who slapped handcuffs on his wrist and through a ringbolt anchored to the floor. The girl slipped into the car's front seat, the other boy on the far side of Green on the back seat. Then Hammond was behind the wheel, cool as ice, smiling, starting the motor. The shouts became louder, waving fists, cursing, pounding on the metal sides and rear. Hammond eased the car into gear, switched on the twirling red light and siren. The crowd gave way and No. 8 moved out slowly.

"You okay, Paul?" Hammond asked.

"Just shook a little. Thanks."

"Don't thank me. You were doing fine."

"Not 'til you came in."

"Just like I was supposed to. It was a two-man job. What's with the boy?"

"He's a 390 all right. Wobbly. Smells like a brewery. Ought to close that joint, selling beer to minors—"

"Yeah. You see your friend Carter, tell him about it. We'll check him out at the station. No evidence on that yet."

Hammond was right. There should be no discussion in front of the prisoner and witnesses. If the girl preferred charges, they'd have something more, but he knew that by the time they reached the 12th, she and the other boy might very easily change their minds.

Green's body and shirt were wet with perspiration. It angered him that the crowd, his own people, showed more resistance toward him than to Hammond, a white man. For all the complaints that there weren't enough Negro policemen in Angeltown, this was almost positive proof that white officers were more effective than Negroes, despite the arguments of Negro civic leaders to the contrary. Curse and abuse their own—or was it that they knew he was a rookie? Or that one of their own should be more lax toward arresting a Negro? And what if this were a white neighborhood,

505

would he have been able to back up Hammond as Hammond had backed him up? He doubted it.

As he guessed, the girl and the other boy, once they stood before the desk sergeant in the 12th Precinct, refused to prefer charges, insisted the tall boy had not been drinking beer in the 2-2-2, that the whole thing was a friendly argument and her dress had been torn accidentally. The desk sergeant, having been through similar cases many times before, simply shrugged it off. All were turned loose.

At 9:20 P.M., Car No. 8 was back on patrol, now cruising along Grand Avenue to the approach of the bridge, where they saw Car No. 12, Officers Peterson and Urey parked. Urey flicked his lights twice and Hammond pulled up alongside, got out and talked with Dale Peterson for a few moments, then came back, got into No. 8 and made a U-turn back into Grand Avenue.

"Keep an eye out, Paul," he said

"Something up?"

"Maybe. Pete told me he and Urey spotted four cars, one right behind the other, came across the bridge about ten minutes ago. Four or five kids in each one. Could be looking for trouble, maybe because of that rumpus over in East Laurelton last Friday night."

"Oh, my. He call it in?"

"No. Nothing to go on, just suspicion. He told Wells and Barton in No. 4 and Marshall and Quinn in No. 14. We'd better cover Velie Street first——"

At 9:40, they were heading south on Granby approaching Velie, when a blue sedan with four white youths in it shot into Granby from Velie, turning south. Hammond stepped on the gas and got as far as Velie, blocked by a stream of traffic proceeding on a green light. He hit his light and siren buttons, but by the time the way was cleared, the blue sedan was out of sight. As they crossed Velie in pursuit, Green said, "Hold it. Somethin' to your left. Look——"

Hammond braked, backed, turned east on Velie. Up ahead, another crowd had formed in front of a store-fronted building. Smoke was pouring out of the smashed show window, laced with small tails of red-orange flame. Green had the radio mike in his hand, reporting it to the 12th. The communicator acknowledged with, "We've got it already. Assistance is on the way."

"Give him the description of the blue sedan. Get a roadblock up at the bridge——"

But Green was already supplying the information. He checked out just as No. 8 arrived on the chaotic scene. Negroes of all ages were milling around the burning store.

506

The lower floor of the Apex Credit Furniture Company was ablaze. There were two upper floors, two apartments on each floor. Two men and one woman emerged from the narrow side doorway, carrying personal belongings, clothing on hangers, a barking dog, a cage with a parakeet. A young girl came out next, stumbling, coughing, clutching an armload of clothing and some school books. Smoke poured heavily from the two smashed display windows.

Green and Hammond leaped out and ran toward the steps. Up ahead on Velie, they could see the lights of fire vehicles approaching. "Anybody else in there?" Green asked the two men who had just emerged. Both seemed dazed, almost overcome by the smoke. One nodded affirmatively. Green and Hammond entered and ran up the stairs, flashlights almost useless in the smoky corridor. Hammond stopped at the second floor while Green ran on ahead to the third to make his search.

Below, the fire trucks were drawn up, a chemical wagon, pumper and ladder truck. Wells and Barton in No. 4 were behind them. Marshall and Quinn were blocking the street off with No. 14, diverting traffic. Hammond emerged from the building with an old woman and her grandson, the boy carrying an infant in his arms. Then Green appeared, leading a young woman who was carrying her two-year-old daughter, assisting a young man who was on crutches. The building was clear of occupants, the firemen already swarming into it with hoses, scrambling up ladders, fighting to control the blaze and keep it from spreading. Two more fire trucks pulled up, then Peterson and Urey were there to keep control on the gathering crowd. A car with a *Herald* reporter and photographer followed one with radio reporters. The wet street had become a litter of hoses and communications wiring.

Talking with eager witnesses. "White boys . . . blue car . . . two cars . . . one dark gray . . . Ford . . . Chevy . . . Dodge . . . threw rocks . . . bottles with a burning wick . . . bomb . . . first car threw the rocks . . . no, wasn't the first one, second one . . . the blue car . . . five white boys . . . four boys an' a girl . . . no license numbers, it happen so fast . . ."

Hammond checked in. The roadblock had picked up a dark gray Pontiac sedan, four white youths, no evidence of gasoline, no rocks, but found two lengths of tire chain, a baseball bat, two six-packs of beer, one empty, and a pint bottle with an inch of whiskey in it. Taken in for questioning. No blue car.

By 10:30, the fire was smoldering, but well under control. Angry crowds milled around nearby, venting their fury into radio and television microphones, indicting the police.

"Where the cops *before* it happen, you tell me. Plenty of 'em *after* them Whiteys bomb the store. Looka there. Three police cars, six cops. Whyn't they out lookin' for them white boys, 'stead-a loafin' aroun' here? They think them Whiteys still aroun' here, for Chrissakes?"

" 'Taliation? 'Taliation for what? Nobody livin' over them stores acrost the bridge, was they? On'iest thing was some broken windows. Nobody set no buildin's on fire, did they?"

"Lord, they *mean*. Killin' mean. Comin 'over here, burnin' us out, tryin' to kill people. Well, you wait. Just you wait an' see. What? Sure, man. You better believe it, Mist' Charley. They ain't goin'a get off for free. I'm tellin' *you*, man!"

Lieutenant Doug Lynch, Captain Price, and Inspector LaSalle were on the scene when Lee Durkin arrived. All but two fire trucks were gone. Cars No. 4, 14 and 8 were replaced by Car No. 16 at midnight. The dispossessed tenants of the burned building had found temporary refuge among neighbors, and most of the crowd, the radio, television and newspaper people were gone, but neighbors sat out on their stoops, too outraged to go to sleep. Elsewhere, Angeltown was in an unsettled, angry state as the story spread and the people seethed with fury. At the bridge, police cars refused to allow Negro youths, in cars and small trucks, to cross into East Laurelton without sufficient reason. Search of the vehicles turned up tire irons, bicycle chains and other possible weapons. The police confiscated the weapons and turned the cars back. No arrests were made.

In Laurelton, similar roadblocks had been set up informally on the road from Fairview south and Riverton north, but there was no evidence of any attempt from those avenues.

2

At 12:30 A.M. there were less than 50 people milling around the scene of the fire. The roof and third floor of the Apex Building had collapsed. Only the rear portion of the roof remained, supported by half a dozen blackened uprights. Firemen were working from the scorched buildings on either side to remove the hazardous remains. Thankfully, the fire had been contained to the single building. Captain Price, Sergeant Boley Carter and several 12th Precinct officers were on watch while another dozen officers, under Lieutenant Lynch, patrolled the area quietly on foot in case of a sudden outbreak of violence.

Everything seemed under control when Lee Durkin left the scene and drove west, rather than east, until he came to the large white clapboard church of Reverend Amos Hart in the 2200 block of Division Street. He parked in front of Hart's residence, which stood next door to the church. There were lights showing on the first floor. Durkin got out, went up the paved walk and knocked on the front door. Amos Hart opened it and invited the chief in. "I almost expected you would call, Chief," Hart said in greeting.

"Well—I thought maybe a little talk might do us both some good."

Mrs. Hart insisted that Durkin take the large wooden rocking chair, bustled out to the kitchen and returned with a pot of tea ("It settles you down nicely, much better than coffee"), despite Durkin's protest that she go to no bother.

Emily Hart was a small birdlike woman, the daughter of the retired Baptist minister whose place Amos had been sent to fill in 1952 on his return to his home base in Atlanta, fresh from war service in Korea. Emily had been born in this house and took over its management when her mother died, had been married to Amos here in 1954, and seen her father buried from it only a year later.

Durkin sipped at his cup of unwanted tea and longed to smoke a cigarette, but the living room was so antiseptically clean and Amos so ecclesiastically solemn and proper, that the introduction of tobacco smoke and ashes would seem almost irreligious. The furniture was old, but each piece of wood looked as if it had been polished, the upholstery cleaned, the rug vacuumed, the curtains freshly ironed only moments ago. There were two paintings (by Emily), three Haitian primitives, dozens of framed, autographed photographs on the wall, the most prominent among them of Reverend Martin Luther King, Jr., Roy Wilkins, and the deceased Medgar Evers. In one corner was an upright piano (Mrs. Hart's) and beside it, a golden-hued harp (Reverend Hart's). Each chair and the sofa had its own crocheted antimacassar pinned in place, each lampshade its own transparent dust cover.

For all his build, Amos Hart seemed smaller in his huge leather-covered reading chair, sunken in the deep groove made by his father-in-law years before, further deepened by Hart's 240 pounds. The cup and saucer seemed tiny in his massive hands as he raised it to his lips, drained it, put it down on a napkin Emily had placed on the table next to him.

"I was working on my Sunday sermon when Emily came in and told me it was on the radio, then later the direct telecast from the scene. I was tempted to go there, but it it was almost over and I thought my presence might stir up more harm than do good. Bad. Very bad, Chief."

Durkin nodded in agreement. "We picked up four boys we suspect might have been a part of the whole thing, but don't have anything to tie them into what happened. I guess you know this was in retaliation for the damage those Angeltown boys did over on Taylor Avenue last Friday night. Then, it was just rocks. Tonight it was a gasoline bomb."

"That could have killed several people."

"And next time, it could be zip guns, rifles or shotguns. The question is, how do we prevent it from happening, instead of sitting around adding up the cost of lives and property after it happens?"

Hart sighed. "I wish the good Lord had given me the wisdom to answer that, Mr. Durkin. There's wrong on both sides, in the hearts of your people and mine. Mostly, they're good people on both sides, but it takes only a few bad ones to create havoc for all. You can't curb your young and we can't curb ours."

"Well, Reverend, we'd better start realizing we've got a pretty nervous situation on our hands."

"Yes. Yes. Only a few years ago, you and I faced each other in heat and anger, but we managed somehow to settle a few basic problems as long as there was some sign of progress being made. Trouble is, what we older people see as progress, the young ones see as stagnation. They accuse us of selling out to the whites when the fact is that parents on both sides have lost control and authority over their children. Our young can't remember back far enough to recognize there's been improvement, so they're impatient. They want full quality and equal opportunity today, now, not tomorrow or next month or next year. The law of the land says it's their legal right and we know it's their moral right, and they want it. And I can't find it in my heart to say they're wrong."

Durkin twisted uncomfortably in his rocking chair and Emily Hart said, "Why don't you smoke if you want to, Mr. Durkin?"

Lee smiled and pulled his pack of cigarettes from a pocket and Mrs. Hart brought an ashtray to him. He said, "Thank you," and turned back to Hart. "I'm not disagreeing with you, Reverend," he said, "but there's got to be some way other than violence to settle the problem." He sighed and added, "First time we met was when you led the 'Don't Buy' boycott, wasn't it?"

"Yes. Right after the Supreme Court decision in '54. We had our share of sit-in demonstrations. We got spat on, beat up, went to jail and some to prison, but the upper courts freed us. Only the boycotts seemed to work. First, the Don't Buy Where You Can't Work boycott, then the Don't Ride the Buses—Walk to Freedom campaign. You remember." Durkin nodded, Hart smiled. "We pooled cars and trucks and rode people to their jobs free until the bus line almost went broke driving empties. They found out for the first time that more Negroes rode the buses than white people. We won out in the schools, too, but we know it's not enough.

"There's still no equal pay for equal work except in a few places. There's no equal or decent housing except for those who own their businesses and can afford a cleaner ghetto in Riverside. There are no Negroes laying bricks, carpentering, plastering, painting or doing electrical work on any white building jobs. We've got thirty or forty Negroes doing clerical work for the city and county, a few more in the Federal post office, and you've got about fifteen or twenty men on your force—"

"Twenty-six, and more in training," Durkin interjected.

"—but Chief Gary Hobbs hasn't got one Negro in his fire department. They apply, go into training, and not one lasts more than three or four weeks."

"That'll change too, Reverend."

"When, Mr. Durkin? In time to curb our people's impatience? What can we tell our young men, out of work and just hanging around on the streets, in poolrooms and bars? That some day they'll get it all in one lump sum? Today, we've just about lost them. They don't believe anybody. They look at their parents with disgust and arrogance, forget that when we were young today's civil rights laws weren't even on the books. They remember stories of lynchings, but they forget it was the older generation that lived through the physical beatings, lynchings and humiliations long before they were born, that we took the worst of it for them.

"But they learn quickly, the young ones, and now they're talking about taking matters into their own hands, and that's why I've got no answers for you, Mr. Durkin."

"You're getting more people registered on the voting rolls, Reverend—"

"Not enough and not fast enough. The requirements are

still too high, too rigid for the older people. Not enough of them are learning, and the whole process takes too long."

"The question is, what do we do now, tomorrow, to keep all hell from breaking loose?"

Hart looked up and stared into Durkin's eyes. "You're a good man, Mr. Durkin. You were born and raised over on this side of the bridge and you understand our problems. You've been more than fair in your treatment of our people. Inspector LaSalle, Captain Price, they're good men, too, but there are others—" Hart's huge hands came up, pink palms turned outward in a gesture of resignation. "In the long run, nothing happens to correct the evils we live with."

"I know, Reverend. I've argued before the City Council and the County Commissioners for better streets, lighting, tighter laws against the owners of slum housing, for more job opportunities and equal pay—but I'm only one man. There are others who realize how much good comes from social improvements, but we're outnumbered. We've got to have help from your side of the bridge, too, people willing to do more than just sit around and wait for their welfare money."

"I know that, too, Mr. Durkin. There's a lethargy that's like poison going through their systems and it won't be cured until they can see some purpose to working at a job that's going to pay them less than the welfare money they get. We both need help."

"Yes." Durkin agreed. "But right now we're going to need a little more from your people."

"In what way?"

"Well, this Dr. Rhama thing."

"You can't blame tonight's doings on the Black Fez, Mr. Durkin. That came from your side of the bridge."

"I admit that, but I've got to guess that he'll try to cash in on what happened. And soon. It gives him what he needs, an incident he can blame on all white people, use it to create more dissension. He does, and there won't be enough police to handle it, not even if I call in every county sheriff's deputy. It could mean the National Guard, Federal marshals, property damage, lives lost, work stoppage. Payrolls cut off, schools closed. I'm not trying to be deliberately pessimistic, but this has all the earmarks of big trouble, outsiders coming in to stir both sides up. N-double-ACP, SNICK, CORE, the Black Fez, Ku Klux Klan, White Camellias, White Citizens Council, everybody trying to cut himself in for a piece of the action."

"I know. I know," Hart breathed, then, "All right, Mr. Durkin, you've made a kind of point. I'll do the best I can. I'll talk to my people Sunday. I'll try to make them see

512

right from wrong, but it won't be easy because I've already lost most of my younger people. The teen-agers, those in their twenties, they don't come to church any more and they're the ones we've got to reach. To them, I, their parents, are Uncle Toms and Aunt Janes. We're despised as hanky-heads. I won't preach hate, so they pick up their hate wherever they can find it. But I'll try."

Durkin sighed and stood up. "That's all we can both do."

"There's something else," Hart said. "I've heard that across the bridge a vigilante committee or group is being formed. I don't know how true that it, but the word is being spread over here. Something like that can become the match that lights the fuse."

"You got anything to go on except rumor?"

"No, but the talk is all around. They see signs of it in the white plants where they work. A white man tells a Negro, 'Watch your step, boy, else I'll put you on the list.' You know what being put on the list means, don't you, Mr. Durkin?" Over Durkin's quick nod, Hart continued. "It means he's a marked man. Marked as a victim for a Ku Klux attack some night. Let four or five Negroes hear that from different sources and there's good reason to believe it."

"Yes," Durkin admitted. "I haven't picked up any of that, but I'll alert my men to be on their toes for any signs. Meanwhile—"

3

She was not, Corey was forced to admit, the Drew Warren he had known as a child, as a girl romping happily with Bruce and his friends at Brookhill, as the shy, self-conscious adolescent with whom he had worked to improve her swim stroke and taught to play tennis so she could give Bruce a decent game; nor the emerging beauty in whom he had begun to develop a more than casual interest after the summer at Loon Lake.

Reflectively, he remembered that she had never encouraged friendships among her own comtemporaries and was happiest when she was somewhere near Bruce. In high school, at Loon Lake, she had always preferred dates with boys from her brother's group; and Corey wondered if this was not the reason why she had chosen himself above the others—because he was closer to Bruce.

Now it seemed as if the Drew of the past was hiding behind a mask of dull pain; that the mask had become the face, showing the insularity of a lonely, barren existence, preferring solitude and memories to reshaping her life and future. Dr. Ballard had told him she had tried psychiatry, but there was no sign that it had done anything for her; and he realized that one must want and agree to be helped before psychiatry could be effective. Then, he reasoned, it was more important to her to be tied to whatever it was that held her in bondage to Bruce.

Anderson Warren had known. The old man had told Corey in so many words. *She'll need somebody. I'd like to feel that when I go, she'll have somebody close to her, someone who will be around if she needs—*

Then, *She's been lonely ever since we buried Bruce. Couldn't stand it here without him. Ran off to Europe and stayed away over a year, running. Came back when there wasn't any place left to run to, half alive.*

And his own commitment, *I'll try, Gran.*

She needs a friend, somebody she can trust. She'll have other problems, more complicated ones—I don't want her running—like her father—she'll have a lot to stand up to—

And again, his own words, *I promise you, Gran. I'll be here when and if Drew needs me.*

But, he thought now, how does one help someone he can't reach?

There were messages for him when he reached home. Polk. Ad Cameron. Paula (two from Paula). He shuffled through the notes, then dialed Polk's number and talked with his mother, who told him Polk was out, a dinner engagement. Ad Cameron was not at home or at his office. He made no effort to reach Paula, now consigned, in his mind, to Polk.

It was too early for dinner. He talked with Tish, who was eager for more details of Anderson Warren's funeral, then went upstairs, showered and changed into slacks and sports shirt. Kenneth came home and went upstairs to refresh himself, then joined Corey in the study for a drink.

"A sad day," Kenneth observed.

"Yes," Corey replied. "Dad?" Kenneth looked up inquiringly. "Dad, what is it with Drew?"

"In what way?"

"I mean her drinking."

"Was it that obvious to you?"

"Not only obvious, she admitted it to me."

"If she did, you know more about it than I do. I've heard about it, but the reason for it escapes me. I suspected she stayed away in Europe because of a personal problem, obviously Bruce's death, but I wasn't aware of the drinking

514

part of it until quite some time after she returned. She's always been an introverted type, you know, and I suppose there's some psychological or psychiatric reason that goes back to the difficulty between Theodore and Louise, but— Well, she's not the sort of person one can get close to, talk with seriously. Perhaps you—"

"I tried today, but I struck out, badly."

"Then—"

"Have there been any other signs, rumors?"

"None that have reached my ears."

"Anderson Warren knew, Dad. He as much as told me so in the one talk I had with him the first day I went up to Brookhill after I got back."

Kenneth sipped his drink thoughtfully, then said, "Corey, I haven't tried to interfere with any decisions you may be making, nor do I intend to crowd you with fatherly advice or guidance—"

"But—?"

Kenneth smiled. "Yes, there's always a 'but.' Later perhaps. I'd like to say this to you first. You may already have guessed that I would like to put my own life in order. I'm speaking of Shana Pierce."

He paused and Corey said, "Go ahead, Dad."

"Very well. I intend to ask Shana to marry me. I'm not asking for your approval. Until now, I've always managed to keep you in front of that question, but I realize that you're your own man now and although I would like a favorable reaction from you, I can't wait much longer."

"If that's all you want from me, Dad, you have it. I've no objection, even to Shana moving into—"

"No, not that, Corey. I believe we will be moving to New York soon. We would be married there."

"New York?"

"Yes. I'm sure that with Anderson Warren dead, Theodore will accept a generous offer to sell out to the Intercon Corporation. The offer has been made through me by an Intercon emissary and I had advised Theodore, for good reason, to accept. I think he will. In which case, I have Intercon's assurance that I will become the new president of Warren Tobacco with my headquarters in New York as part of the parent corporation."

Corey was genuinely taken aback. "I—I don't know what to say, Dad," he said finally, "except that, well, I hope it all works out for you."

"And Shana?"

"And Shana. If congratulations are in order, you have mine."

515

"Sincerely, Corey?"

"Openly and sincerely. I remember you once told me that the reason you couldn't explain—ah—certain things—was that I was too young to understand at the time. I think I'm old enough now to understand that, and many other things."

"That's your maturity speaking and I'm very grateful, Corey. Things happen unaccountably to everyone, fortunately or unfortunately. How a person evaluates them, and decides, determines his future happiness or sorrow."

"And if one finds an evaluation or decision too hard to make?"

"Then he deserves to be pitied because he'll find himself trapped in a hell he can't hope to escape."

"Drew Warren, for instance?"

Kenneth nodded. "Drew Warren as a point in fact. Perhaps you can understand and accept this now. Drew Warren has been victimized all her life; inadvertently by her father and mother, by the deaths of Cleo, Bruce and now Anderson Warren. When Bruce died, there were only Theodore, a self-made recluse, and Anderson, an old man preoccupied with his own need to forget. You went back to the University—"

"If I had known then," Corey said.

"It may have helped matters, and again, it may not. Don't blame yourself. Anyway, it seems that everyone had something to turn to except Drew. Then she left for Europe. I can't tell you any more than that. I don't think she confided in anyone. She came back and kept to herself at Brookhill, almost the sort of recluse Theodore had become, making no effort to resume any previous friendships.

"I had hoped, with your return, that— What I'm trying to say without giving you a wrong impression—"

"Is that Drew and I would fall into each other's arms?"

"Well, at least, resume on your former friendly basis. A —marriage—could solve many problems for both of you, and why not—"

"Or add to our problems, possibly?"

"I can't say. It has been said that it's just as reasonable for a man to fall in love with a wealthy girl as a poor one."

"An ancient and abused bromide, and a hell of a reason for getting married, isn't it?"

"Perhaps. But you and Drew were once more than a cliché."

"That's true, but as Drew pointed out to me, she's not the same person she was even three years ago."

"Ah, Corey, who ever is? Are you the same person you

were three years ago? Perhaps if you could get her to explain that bit of cryptic nonsense, you may solve the puzzle of Drew Warren."

They answered Jemmy's summons to dinner and somehow Corey felt closer to Kenneth than ever before in his life. He realized that what had gone between his father and mother had been between them and not between Caddy and himself, nor between himself and Kenneth. Each man lives his own life, marries, reaps his pains and sorrows, his joys and happiness. His Caddy was not Kenneth's Catherine and each would remember her in his own way.

Kenneth went out after dinner and Corey assumed he would spend the evening with Shana. He returned to the study to look over his Shadow Hills plan.

Later, a troubled Tish came in to tell him to turn on the radio and he heard a firsthand account of the fire and near-riot in Angeltown. He thought again of Lyle Emerson at the R-V Center and heard Mayor Tom Cameron's warning to all to stay out of the area, that no one would be allowed to cross the bridge in either direction unless he had proper business there. He listened until it was announced that all was under control, then went to bed.

4

On Thursday morning, apart from a one-column report of Anderson Warren's funeral (the complete story of his death, a two-page obituary and suitable editorial tribute had been published earlier in the week), the front page of the morning *Herald* was dominated by the news of the vandalism in West Laurelton, with a four-column picture of the blaze and smaller shots of the victims who had lost most of their possessions.

In the center of the page, with a heavy black border around it, was the *Herald*'s featured editorial:

BLACK POWER . . .
WHITE RACISM . . .
Neither can be tolerated

The ever-present threat of lawlessness, destruction and senseless violence must end at once or the Civil Rights movement will be set back to the post-Civil War era. There can be no contest of strength between Black Power and White Racism. Both are morally evil and wrong. Either means a break with law and order and can only result in anarchy. The problems of living

517

together in a community, working together, must be solved by both sides, willingly or reluctantly, but necessarily, lest violence take the place of peace and decency and become the order of the day. We say to both sides, Neither of you has won, nor can either win except by reasonable thought and conduct. Back off now and consider carefully your actions and motivations. You elders must exercise control over your young or accept the responsibility for their deeds. You must allow your own tempers to cool and evaluate the possible results of failure. History will tell you: Neither side has ever "won" a war. All of us, citizens and civic leaders, must work together, side by side, to right existing wrongs and differences. Of 200,000,000 people in the United States, ninety per cent cannot sleep, work or live in comfort with its guilt; nor can ten per cent win by force.

Join hands now.

All else is tragic folly.

On page 2, the *Herald* reported it had received over $300 in cash and checks from individual citizens, to be distributed among the needy victims, this apart from telephone calls asking where clothing, food and other necessities could be sent. The *Herald* suggested that additional monies and goods be sent to the R-V Center in West Laurelton for distribution and would send its own delivery trucks to homes without transportation means to gather the donated items.

5

It was nine o'clock when Leona Waters, carrying a tray with a cup of hot black coffee, knocked lightly on Drew Warren's bedroom door and entered. The bed was empty, sheets and pillows in disarray, her nightgown and slippers on the floor. Leona went to the veranda and found her young mistress lying curled up on the chaise, head almost touching her drawn-up knees. She placed the tray on a wicker table, picked up the empty brandy bottle and glass from the floor and went back into the bedroom. She found a light robe and brought it back to the veranda, then shook Drew awake.

"Huh—oh—Leona—"

"Good morning, Miss Drew. I brought you some coffee. Here, sit up an' put this robe on." She put an arm around

518

Drew and helped her to sit up. "There, that's better, now drink this—"

Drew suppressed a groan, rubbed her eyes, brushed her hair back with her hands. "God—" The word escaped her involuntarily, then, "Won't it ever cool off—" The rest was a mumble.

"I didn't hear you," Leona said.

"Nothing. It wasn't anything, Leona." She swung around and put her feet on the floor, saw Leona holding the cup toward her, then looked down at the floor searchingly.

"I put it away, Miss Drew." A pause. "It was empty."

Drew took the cup and sipped at the coffee without replying, no longer embarrassed that Leona, Shad and Sue-Ann knew how much she depended on alcohol to help her get through her sleepless nights. The days were easier, but the long, quiet nights—

"Have they all gone, Leona?" Drew asked.

"The last of 'em left yesterday, honey."

"Now there were two—"

"What?"

"Remember the Ten Little Indians we used to sing about when we were children? One little, two little, three little Indians—Grandmother Cleo, Bruce, Cord—" She saw the sudden tears well up in Leona's eyes at the mention of Cord's name. "I'm sorry, Leona, I didn't mean—"

"Child, child, what you doin' to yourself?"

"Leona—"

"Lord, Lord, child, I helped raise you from the day you was born, like I helped raise your brother Bruce and my own Cord. I couldn't love you no less'n I loved my own and it just killin' me to see what's happenin' to you. Honey, you got to let the dead rest with God. You can't keep livin' with 'em once they gone."

The cup rattled in the saucer and before Leona could reach for them, had fallen into Drew's lap, spilling the rest of the coffee over her robe, splashing the white cover of the chaise. "Leona, for God's sake, stop it!" She turned away from the weeping woman and buried her face in her arms.

Leona picked up the cup and saucer, dabbed at Drew's robe with her white apron. "Honey, honey," she crooned, "I wish I could take it off your shoulders, carry it for you—"

"Go away, please, Leona—"

"All right, Miss Drew. I came to tell you—Mist' Theodore ask after you. He say he'd like to talk to you if you awake."

"My father?" Drew asked dully.

"He say not to bother you if you don't feel well."

"What time is it? Is he still at home?"

"It's a little past nine-thirty. He say he'll wait in the study."

For a moment, Drew sat in silence, then said, "Help me get dressed, Leona, then tell my father I'll be down soon. And bring me some more coffee, please."

She found Theodore in the first floor study, a room that was completely Anderson's. Everything in it was old. The massive leather chairs, furniture, rug, books, personal journals, yellowed photographs of his and Cleo's families in Loudon, his first home; the early Warren tobacco fields and first manufacturing plant. The first advertisements for Warren's roll-your-own and machine-made cigarettes, posters; model drawings of various pieces of equipment, new and unique for their time, plans and sketches of newer improvements, patents. Photographs of Anderson and Cleo; with Chase, with Theodore, of Bruce and Drew; but nowhere was there a photograph or snapshot of her mother, Louise, perhaps removed when her oil portrait disappeared from the formal living room.

Theodore was sitting on a two-seated leather sofa when Drew entered and stood up now to greet her silently. His face seemed tired and more lined than before and his shoulders sagged forward wearily.

"You wanted to see me, Father?"

"Good morning, Drew. Yes, if you feel up to it. There are some matters we should discuss, but if you are—indisposed—it can be put off."

"I think it might be better to talk now."

"Yes, well—won't you sit down." There was a knock on the door. Theodore called out, "Come in." Sue-Ann came in apologetically, carrying a tray with a silver coffee service, cups and saucers. She put it down on the table beside Drew's chair and left. Theodore sat on the small sofa again, showing his uneasiness. "This is something we've never really done before, isn't it?" he said.

"Not that I can remember." Drew busied herself with the coffee. "Would you care for some?"

"No. Thank you." He lighted a cigarette. "Drew, it's rather late for me to be apologizing or mending fences. I know how deeply you loved your grandfather, that his loss will, if it hasn't yet, hit you quite hard. If you would like to take a trip somewhere, a change of scenery—"

"I think I'll be quite all right, Father. For the time being, I'd rather stay on at Brookhill. Perhaps later—"

"That possibility occurred to me, but—" Theodore was

finding it difficult to talk through the stifling formality. He turned his head away from her stare, unable to meet her eyes, feeling awkwardness in this new role. "Drew," he said finally, "There will be a formal reading of your grandfather's will very soon. I haven't seen a copy of it, but he indicated to me some time ago that you and I will inherit the bulk of the estate. That is, everything apart from certain personal bequests to servants, key employees, charities, and educational institu—"

"What about the Company, Father?"

"That is what I wanted to discuss with you, learn what your feelings are about it. I don't like to touch on the subject of Bruce—" he saw her wince, her hands clench into tight fists—"but had he lived, there would be no question of my retaining control. For him. I think your grandfather would have provided conditions for that eventuality."

"Is there some question about it now, control of the Company, I mean?"

"That depends. I have had tentative offers from a New York corporation with widespread holdings, Intercon, to sell the Company at a price reflecting its current market value. Before I make my own decision, I would like to know how you feel about it."

"I—don't really—know. Except that I can't visualize the Company in someone else's hands, strangers. Who is, or are, Intercon?"

"The Intercontinental Corporation. I don't know them personally, Drew. The offer has come through Ken Armour. A man named Kirk Dillingham is head of Intercon. I've never met him."

A moment or two of silence passed before Drew said, "Doesn't the Company mean anything to you, anything at all?"

Theodore swallowed hard. "I don't know exactly how to answer that, Drew. Once, a long time ago, it meant a lot to me. Then something happened—"

"You mean between you and Mother, of course."

"Yes," he said hoarsely. "You were too young then to know—you couldn't have been more than three—"

"That was when you went away, after she left."

"Yes. I went away. Or rather, I ran away. From Brookhill, my father, the Company—"

"And your children."

"Yes. From you and your brother, everything. Drew. I know how you must despise me. I can't blame you. You have every right and reason for hating me."

"I don't despise or hate you, Father. I don't even know
521

you. I grew up believing that your mother and father were Bruce's and my parents. You were somebody—strange. Someone who came, stayed a while, disappeared, then came back from time to time. A few years ago, you returned and stayed on. How can I hate a stranger?"

"Drew, I don't expect you to forgive me. I was a sick man. I may even be sick now. Not physically, sick from need of something I lost, was taken from me, when I needed it most."

"Did you ever try to find her, get her back?"

"It was too late. I didn't know where she had gone. Before I could gather my wits, it was too late. I woke up in a sanitarium, under restraint. It was five years before I came back here. You were three when I left. Your brother and you were in school when I returned, a stranger, as you said. I was never able to overcome the years I had lost.

"You're right, of course. I came and went, unable to live without Louise. There were times when I thought I would go mad, and meanwhile, you and Bruce were becoming adult. I saw Louise in your face and body, heard her voice in yours. I didn't even know if she was dead or alive until about ten years ago when I asked your grandfather and he told me she was living in Italy, remarried."

Now hearing him tell of his anguish, seeing it upon him, Drew could feel compassion. "Oh, Father—'"

"When Bruce died, I began to see something of what I had lived through in you. I wanted very much to reach out and comfort you, but I didn't know how. Then you went off to Europe—"

"Ran, is a better word for it. I ran because I didn't want to live here without Bruce. I understood about you and mother by that time, that Grandmother Cleo and Gran were *your* parents, not Bruce's or mine. Bruce was the one person closest to me and when he died, I wanted to die, too. So I ran away. But like you, I eventually came back. Now, with Gran gone, where do we run, Father?"

"I don't know, Drew. I keep asking myself, If not here, where?"

"Then why not stay and run the Company?"

"Why, Drew? For you? Do you want it?"

"Maybe for both of us. Something we need to hold on to."

"Does it mean that much to you?"

"I hadn't thought about it much until you started talking in terms of selling it. I remember—it's childish—when I was in Europe. Switzerland, Denmark, England, France, everywhere I went, times when I was desperately alone and despondent, I would pass a tobacconist's shop somewhere and see the name WARREN on a bright red or gold package in a window. I would go in and buy a pack, several, just to feel them in my hands and know for one short moment that I was somehow touching Brookhill, walking down a street in Laurelton, that we were all together again, Grandmother Cleo, Gran, Bruce, home—"

"Drew, you said 'maybe for both of us.' If I thought that—"

"Why not, Father?"

"You've called me 'Father' several times this morning. If the word had more meaning than a title that identifies me as your sire, it could be worth the effort."

"There are only the two of us left. That might make it worth the effort."

"If you believe that, Drew, yes."

"And the Company?"

"Yes, of course, if it will make things better between us. You'll marry one day, have children—"

"Father—"

"Yes, Drew."

She rose and went to him. He stood up with eyes bright, towering over her and she put one hand around his neck, drew his head downward and kissed his cheek lightly. "I want it very much, Father," she said, "for both of us now, and for your grandchildren later, if there are any."

Theodore made no move to return her kiss. He felt her gentle touch, the first tenderness he had known between them in years, saw the sadness and hope in her face. He said softly, "Drew, I was never much of a son to my father and mother, nor a father to Bruce and you. If I had been, everything might have turned out differently, better—"

"Please don't say any more."

"Only this. If I stay, will you? Do you think there's a chance for us?"

Drew sighed. "I think so, Father. For both our sakes, I hope so."

523

CHAPTER II

1

The meeting scheduled for Wednesday had been postponed because of Anderson Warren's funeral and took place at 2:30 on Thursday. Corey arrived at Wayne Taylor's office on time and until John Curran joined them, they talked of the fire and near-riot the night before and the possibility of further problems that might come in the wake of Dr. Rhama's presence, now generally known.

Today, Johnny was dressed more formally and carried several rolls of map paper and a file of notes, evidencing considerable preliminary examination of the Shadow Hills proposal. The sight of larger, more detailed maps of the region, covered with tissue overlays and penciled diagrams, was heartening to Corey.

When they were seated, Wayne opened the meeting. "Corey, we've given your idea quite a lot of thought and discussion since we last met. We've brought in our engineering, construction, design and operational brains for opinions, suggestions and advice. On Tuesday night, they gave us their initial findings, subject to further examination and inspection. We're still waiting to hear from the financial feelers we've put out.

"First reactions, on the whole, are favorable, although tentative. Our real estate survey indicates the desirability of such a project. It could relieve housing pressure here, create many jobs, skilled and unskilled, utilize our own supply sources as well as others in Laurelton and farther away. We're looking into the question of zoning, but I don't believe that will present any problem since the tax structure will benefit the County on land that is now producing practically nothing in the way of tax revenue. There's still quite a bit to look into, but at the moment, Taylor Industries is willing to undertake a major survey of the water and power situation, which is the key to the whole project. Johnny?"

Johnny opened and spread out another and larger map of the two tracts in question, Crane and Halstead, covering 1,800 acres. The tissue overlay depicted a more carefully drawn sketch of the lake, showing an irregular shoreline that would provide a maximum number of waterfront lots. At the north end was a sketch of the dam, approximately 1,200 feet long, 40 feet high and 500 feet wide at the base, with a mechanical spillway structure and a circular open drop inlet gate-well to control overflow. There were complicated drain systems and sluice gates and other devices that were totally foreign to Corey.

The drawing showed lakeside roads, streets, homesites, areas set aside for public use; three villages for commercial purposes, play areas, a nine- and an eighteen-hole golf course, country club, churches, schools, library, fire and police stations; a residential community outlined to the last detail, even to its 30-mile network of communicating streets, the roads which linked up to the Riverton-Laurelton highway lying to the east.

The sense of appreciation and thrill Corey felt was indescribable as his eyes scanned the master drawing, broken only when Johnny said, "Of course, we haven't gotten into analyzing costs. We've checked the County land maps and believe it feasible to run a pipe line in from the river. This subdivision indicates about 2,000 homesites, but we think it can be stretched to another 500, apart from the commercial and public areas. We don't intend, naturally, to develop the entire area at once, you understand, but to bring it in one section at a time, as needed."

There was more discussion that concerned concept, design, building restrictions, geological findings, sanitation controls; and many possibilities and probabilities which were far over Corey's head.

Wayne said finally, "Before we go deeper into this, Corey, if at all, the question of the extent of your participation will have to be settled. As raw land, you already know its value. Since you own six-hundred-plus acres outright and hold option to twelve hundred acres, which I assume you are prepared to execute and buy if the project becomes fact, that much, at a fair increase in value, would be your contribution to the overall cost, plus what additional amount you would want to put into the project to increase your proportionate share. As to the extent of your further participation, the details on the legal end should be worked out in conjunction with the legal staff before we proceed—"

"I'm sure you will find me cooperative," Corey said. "I'll want to discuss this with my father, and I would want to participate in the overall project, rather than as a mere investor. As to additional investment, I'll need some extra time to consider that."

"Then," Wayne said, "suppose we prepare an agreement

525

that will indicate a limited partnership based on a newly appraised value of those eighteen hundred acres, deliverable by you to the new corporation, plus any amount of additional capital you can raise, with stock issued at par value and further options."

"That will be entirely agreeable," Corey said.

Wayne stood up and smiled for the first time since the meeting had begun. To Johnny, "Well, Redhead, it looks like we've got ourselves a partner."

To which Johnny smiled in return, extended a hand to Corey and said, "Welcome into the family, Corey. We're not too difficult to live with."

They shook hands all around and went to the bar where Wayne poured drinks for the ceremonial toast to the new alliance. "Julie and Susan came up with a name last night, so if it's satisfactory to you, Corey, here's to TAY-MOUR, INC., developers of Shadow Hills Holiday Homes."

Corey's grin could only be interpreted as one of complete approval.

2

As Theodore Warren had anticipated and was in fact expecting, Kenneth Armour's secretary telephoned to ask if he could spare some time for a brief conference. Theodore gave himself a full hour by setting the appointment for three o'clock and promptly on the hour, Armour appeared.

Theodore saved him the trouble of a preliminary introduction of the subject. "I suppose you want to discuss the Intercon proposal, Ken," he said.

"Essentially, yes."

"Yes," Theodore repeated, but Armour could see neither approval nor disapproval in his face. There was no enthusiasm he could detect in Theodore's manner or voice. "I've been weighing advantages against disadvantages, Ken—" He paused, found a cigarette and lighted it.

"You were saying—" Kenneth prompted.

"I've concluded that the disadvantages outweigh the advantages considerably."

Armour said confidently, "I am sure Intercon will agree to any reasonable modifications in their proposal. I'd like to suggest a meeting—"

"Ken, I don't think it would be advisable. I'm not interested. I believe you should break off contact and discontinue any further discussions with Intercon."

"Isn't that a rather complete reversal of your previous

feelings, Theodore?" Armour asked with some strain in his voice.

"Perhaps, but I have a definite reason now. Say a change of heart. I intend to keep the Company within family control and remain at its head."

Now Armour began to feel a pounding inside his skull, as though small pneumatic drills had been implanted there and were at work. "This places me in a rather embarrassing position, Theodore. I have kept you fully informed. You know I've been quietly talking with Kirk Dillingham on the assumption that—"

"If you will recall, Ken, I gave you no assurances."

"No, but—" He paused to wet his dry lips with his tongue. "I wonder if you are aware of the physical improvements the Company will require in order to fully modernize—"

"I've been reviewing the Plant Requirements Report very carefully and see no reason why we shouldn't undertake it ourselves; the new experimental plant, data processing equipment, automation of certain facilities wherever it is practicable."

"Theodore—"

"Yes, Ken?"

"I think I should advise you there is more to this than what appears in that study."

"For instance?"

"My primary reason for entertaining Intercon's offer when it was first made was because I was given to understand that we might, if the offer was firmly refused, become involved in a proxy fight."

"A proxy fight? Ridiculous."

"A proxy fight, Theodore. Let me call to your attention that we have not increased our dividend of two dollars per share in quite a few years, and if you will examine the most recent stockholders' list, you will find that Intercon holds about twenty-two per cent of Warren common stock."

"What can they hope to do with that? The Warren Foundation holds twenty-five per cent, Taylor Industries another ten per cent. There are eight per cent more here in Laurelton and another twenty per cent in the hands of the Warren families in Virginia and Maryland. That adds up to well over fifty per cent, sixty-three per cent in fact—"

"Your arithmetic is accurate, if you can be sure of the northern Warren twenty percent, plus the balance outstanding elsewhere. It could be a battle and Intercon not only has the financial resources but hard experience in these matters. They've never lost a proxy fight in their entire history."

527

The silence became oppressive. It had never occurred to Theodore that he could *not* count on the twenty percent held by the descendants of Benjamin and Alistair Warren, both long dead now. He asked himself now what loyalty he could expect from Austin and Ralph Warren whom he scarcely knew; at best, a question he could not answer. And now he was left with Kenneth Armour's suggestion—or was it more?—that Dillingham, with a generous offer, could very well have that twenty per cent committed to Intercon. Also, he wasn't entirely certain why dividends hadn't been increased for the past six or eight years. Profits had risen, the stock was up—something about accumulating reserves for needed improvements, modernization.

"—and I have it on excellent authority," he heard Kenneth's voice over his thoughts, "that prior to engaging in a costly proxy fight, Intercon is prepared to make a tender offer to pick up the nine per cent at a substantial price over market value to give them at least fifty-one per cent."

"As chief counsel and executive vice-president, Ken, on what basis could Intercon institute a proxy fight?"

Armour shrugged. "Going by past performances, it would deal, generally, with gross mismanagement and neglect, holding dividends to a bare minimum over the past years—"

"On your recommendation, as I recall, for purposes of accumulating reserves for improvements and expansion."

"Of which we were, and still are, in need. Also, of operating inefficiently so as to raise costs and lower Company profits, refusal to diversify into other fields as competing firms have in recent years. There is also the possibility they might attack the Warren Foundation—"

"On what grounds?"

"As a tax dodge, or purely for publicity value. Remember, Theodore, the Foundation has in the past paid very handsome salaries to its officers, members of the Warren family among them. Anderson, Cleo, yourself, Bruce and Drew. Look back into the records and you will find years when those combined salaries totaled more than the funds disbursed for charitable and educational purposes. There are explanations, of course, but in public print, we might find our explanations too weak to stand against the charges Intercon's experts will have made."

"And your recommendation, I take it, is to accept Intercon's offer."

"That has been my considered judgment from the start. I must add, considering past history, that I came to that opinion in the honest belief that it would meet your full approval."

528

"When do you think Intercon would start to—make its move?"

Kenneth shrugged. "My opinion is that it would come the moment they receive your definite refusal to deal with them."

Theodore stood up and walked to the window. He looked down at the activity in the forecourt parking lot for a few moments. Without turning around, he said, "Very well, let it stand where it is at the moment, Ken."

"Dillingham will be pressing harder for an answer, now that the funeral is over."

"Let him press. When I make my final decision, I'll let you know. Stall him until then, if necessary. It won't be much longer."

3

As the school day ended, police switchboards began lighting up and numerous reports of street fighting poured in. Squad cars scurried to school yards and athletic grounds, but the moment they left, warfare broke out again. Several male teachers became involved and others remained in the buildings for fear of encouraging escalation in the muscle-flexing between white and Negro students. Some windows were broken, tires slashed, radio aerials on parked cars bent or broken as gangs quickly formed to defend and retaliate. In one predominantly Negro school, rags and waste were set afire in the basement and firemen answering the call were pelted with rocks. In all, 22 arrests were made, Negro youths in the majority.

In Angeltown's 12th Precinct, Captain Price called in all off-duty Negro officers and asked for the five Negro trainees from the training school to be assigned to him temporarily. White businessmen reported roving gangs of six to twelve members who were entering their establishments and openly stealing small items of merchandise from tables and counters, threatening the owners with violence if they dared to interfere. Several white-owned stores had closed down voluntarily. Many of the young participants were wearing black fezzes.

On the streets, arguments between older people and the shouting, jeering youngsters broke out, the latter blatantly defiant of any authority, police or parental. By five o'clock, over 30 arrests had been made.

At 12th Precinct Headquarters, Captain Price and Lieutenant Lynch studied the revised emergency plan with

Inspector LaSalle and held off a decision to advise Chief Durkin to place it into effect, hoping that by six o'clock hungry appetites would clear most of the youngsters from the streets. If the minor violence began spreading, the city could well be facing major civil disobedience, even riot conditions, and necessitate alerting the fire department, Sheriff Apperson's deputies, possibly State Police and National Guard. Apperson had called on Durkin during the afternoon, proposing direct action, but Durkin and LaSalle had agreed on a "wait and see" attitude. To go in swinging could only accelerate minor violence into full riot proportions.

At least, LaSalle thought, Larry Powell is on the inside now. Larry's last call, at noontime, had supplied the information concerning the demonstration planned for Friday night at the Arcadia Theater which might easily be a diversionary tactic to draw much of the night force away from another scene of planned major vandalism.

A special "torpedo squadron" had been formed and schooled in a locked classroom. LaSalle's earlier proposal was already in effect—a single officer in each prowl car by day, putting more cars into use, doubled up at night. Each car carried helmets, gas masks, tear gas shells and riot guns. One officer at the wheel at all times, in constant communication with Central Communications in case of a general outbreak. And above all, caution in approaching any conflict.

Shortly after six o'clock, quiet was temporarily restored on both sides of the bridge. Now the waiting began.

His class over, Lyle Emerson arranged books and papers in the drawer of his table and closed it. He picked up a manila file of homework that had been turned in this evening to take home and mark before going to sleep, then decided to do it now, there was so little of it. He counted the sheets. Fourteen, each containing ten words laboriously scrawled, slanted, staggered, running off the pages. But it was something, each in some way showing small improvement. He underscored the misspelled words in blue, wrote the final gradings, 40, 50, 60, and one 70, in red at the top of the paper, adding where he could a congratulatory, "Much better," "Very neat," and in the case of the 70 grade, "You're doing fine. Keep it up."

He slid the file into the drawer and turned his desk lamp off, then went to the door and hit the wall switch that controlled the overhead lights. When he stood up, the pain was there again, the dull ache running upward from the stump into his hip, the needlelike stabbing along the edge. The air was hot and densely humid and he thought again that perhaps a drier climate, Arizona, California, would be helpful.

Then, as it had been happening more and more frequently, he thought of Elizabeth and wondered if she had come down from her second-floor classroom; if she would stop for a cup of coffee before leaving. For the last two nights, she hadn't, and he had felt a keen sense of loss in having missed her; and wondered if she were angry because Corey Armour had seen them together. Remembering her sharp change of tone when she said with pointed emphasis, *"This isn't a date, Mr. Armour."*

He locked the door and walked down the hall toward the snack room, stood for a moment in the doorway searching for her among the men and women who stood or sat in groups talking seriously, knowing their discussions tonight were centered more on the fire and near-riot than the performance of their students. He felt out of it, far out of it; that if he walked in, the conversations would lapse and turn to some other subject. He was saved from entering the room by Elizabeth's absence, and continued past the lighted Administration Office toward the front door. As he passed the stairway to the upper floor he heard footsteps, her footsteps, and waited. She came down and around the turn and he looked up, saw her splendidly formed legs flashing silkily as she descended step by step, wearing a dark brown skirt with a sleeveless beige blouse, thin enough to show a lighter-toned bra beneath it as she slipped the lightweight jacket over her bare arms, switching her purse from hand to hand.

"Hello, Elizabeth," he called.

"Hi, Lyle." She was at floor level now.

"I've missed you the last two sessions."

"I had some things to do." She was fumbling through her opened purse.

"Coffee?" he asked.

"Too hot." She came up with a quarter. "Can you change this for me, Lyle? I need a dime or two nickels to make a phone call."

"I think so." He burrowed in his pocket and found a nickel, a quarter and three pennies. "Sorry. That's all the change I have."

"Damn it. I hate to bother them in the office."

"Important?"

"Well—I wanted to call Dad and ask him to pick me up."

"Don't bother, Elizabeth. I'll be more than happy to—"

531

"No." She said it quickly, perhaps too quickly, and saw the reaction of hurt in his eyes. He turned away abruptly and said, "I'm sorry. Good night."

"Lyle, please——"

"It's all right, Elizabeth."

She caught up with him and walked to and out the front door. "I didn't mean anything by it, Lyle. I appreciate your asking me."

"Sure. I know." He started toward the parking lot, then stopped. "The way I'm appreciated for the time I contribute at the Center, but just keep in your place, white man."

"I tell you, it isn't that, Lyle."

"Isn't it? Jesus good Christ, you people have the most peculiar ideas. You rant, rave and protest against segregation and you're not one goddamned bit different or less intolerant than those you attack."

"Oh, Lyle, don't—please—I apologize, deeply and sincerely. Cross my heart." She drew a finger in the symbolic cross and he smiled at this childish superstition. "Sure. I understand, Elizabeth. Good night."

"Does that mean you're not going to give me a lift home?" she asked.

His smile erupted into a laugh. "Come on," he said, holding out a hand toward her elbow. In the car, they avoided the subject of the possible race conflict in town, talked of the heat and progress among their students, but as both knew, they were talking around the subject they must inevitably return to, the human tensions involved. "It doesn't look good, does it, Lyle?"

"Not very. It's a damned shame."

"Why can't they see it, both sides?"

"Because it's been allowed to go on too long. I think the worst thing that ever happened to the Negro, except slavery itself, was Lincoln's assassination. If he'd lived he would have tried harder than Johnson, the other Johnson, not LBJ. I'd like to think he would have given it a good start toward eventual equality."

"I don't believe it would have happened that way, Lyle."

"Why not?"

"You couldn't believe it yourself if you were a Negro. That generation was too close to the paternalism of slavery, too dependent on their owners for food, clothing, shelter, someone to care for them when they were sick. When they got their legal freedom, they didn't know how to accept it, what to do with it. Everything came too swiftly, promises of land and mules, education, training, but they didn't get anything more than the Indians got. Promises."

"Then you believe it was hopeless from the start?"

"It takes a Negro to know the real meaning of hopelessness."

"Do you think I haven't been there, that others haven't felt and known hopelessness?"

"Yours was physical."

"*And* emotional, believe me."

"Well—it's still not the same. Born black, born loser," she said.

"That is defeatism at its very worst. I don't believe that and I don't think you do either, deep down. Sure, it looks bad now, but it can't last. People are more aware now, whites as well as blacks. We're seeing it happen elsewhere."

"But this is happening here, now. I'm afraid we're born losers."

"Losers don't go through college the way you did, just to come back to what they were fighting to escape. You could have stayed out west and taught in Los Angeles and enjoyed a different, better life, intellectually, financially and emotionally."

"Then you tell me: why did I come back?"

"Because there was a need and you could fill that need. You've proved it to yourself a hundred times. I've heard you say so in many different ways. Don't let this thing make you lose your hope."

"Maybe. But I feel so—blah—about everything."

"How about a ride in the country to blow some fresh air through your mind?"

"I can't."

"Papa waiting up for you?"

"No, but I shouldn't. I shouldn't have come with you now."

"I'm glad you did."

"It's no good, Lyle."

"We're back to color again, aren't we?"

"Lyle, this isn't Los Angeles, New York or Brazil. A Negro girl and a white man can only add up to trouble. Even murder. You know that, don't you?"

"But you came anyway. Why?"

"Don't make me say things I shouldn't."

"Why shouldn't you if you feel them? At least, so far, we've been honest with each other, haven't we?"

"Not entirely. I think we *think* we're being honest, but all the while we're covering our true feelings with words that say something else."

They were beyond the turnoff to Elizabeth's house, heading for Riverside Drive. Lyle turned left and followed it south to where it would take them along the Cottonwood River Road. Elizabeth made no effort to dissuade him. Instead, she leaned forward and slipped her suit jacket off. "I don't understand," Lyle said.

"I'll try to explain. I can't get it out of my head that you're treating me like a white girl because—because of what happened to you in Viet Nam, something, a debt you owe to the Negro race because a Negro boy saved your life."

His hands gripped the wheel tighter, but he said nothing. "I'm sorry, Lyle. I've made you angry again."

"You're damed right you have. Or should I be happy because you feel that I'm no different—that—"

"I'm terribly sorry, Lyle. I had to say it."

"I don't need that. I've had enough pity. Especially from you, and not because you're a Negro."

"Please don't be hurt, Lyle, but why me?"

"Why you? Because you're a fine, intelligent young woman. Because I—admire you very much, as a person, what you stand for, work for, live for." He took a deep breath.

"Go ahead, finish it," Elizabeth said.

"There's nothing to finish. I've said it all for the moment. Except- -except that we're human beings and the least we can do is behave like what we are, not like frightened animals, scurrying away into hiding at the sound of a footstep."

They had come to a side road that led down to the water's edge. Lyle turned the car into it and dropped into low gear because of the bumps and ruts in the dirt road. He eased the car forward toward the river, then felt Elizabeth's hand on his forearm, gripping it tightly. Up ahead, his headlights had picked up several parked cars. He stopped and they could hear voices; shrill, happy young male and female voices, enjoying a night dip in the river. Lyle threw the car in reverse and backed out, turned the car north again.

"Does that answer your question, Lyle?" Elizabeth said wryly. "Whatever they are, Negroes or whites, it makes no difference. We couldn't share with them. Together, we're bigger losers than we are apart."

Lyle said nothing. He was remembering an old expression heard years ago. *Whether the hammer hits the egg or the egg falls upon the hammer, the egg loses every time.*

A creed for losers.

On Friday morning, Corey lounged in Kenneth's study poring over half a dozen magazines he had picked up the day before at Stocker's, dealing with home design, interior and exterior architecture, area planning and developing. The night before, he had told Kenneth of his talk with Wayne Taylor and John Curran and Kenneth showed vivid interest in the project and the encouragement of Taylor Industries backing. There had followed a long discussion of the extent of Corey's financial participation.

"And you know, of course, that this house and property are also in your name, Corey." Kenneth added.

"I've never thought of it as mine, Dad. It's ours."

"You should start considering it. If my plans to move to New York work out, this would become a rather expensive establishment for you to maintain. Considering its value, the house and acreage are easily worth a good hundred and twenty-five to a hundred and fifty thousand dollars, a considerable part of your net worth. Of course, I don't recommend putting all your eggs in one basket, but it would provide a comfortable cushion for you to lean on until income from the Holiday Homes development starts coming in."

The thought of disposing of the Old Colony Lane property, the only home he could remember, disturbed Corey more than a little. It was large and roomy and comfortable and he could recall Caddy's complaint that it was too large for the amount of help she had; and when Kenneth had suggested selling it and moving into a smaller house, or an apartment, her reply was an imperious toss of her head. "When Corey marries—" became her standard reply.

When Corey marries.

How many times had she used that expression to him. "When you marry, Corey, this will be your home, where you and your wife will watch your children grow up."

There had always been the subtle suggestion, an implication, that she and Kenneth would live elsewhere; or perhaps Caddy and Kenneth would simply disappear into thin air. Also, there were Tish and Jemmy to consider.

Kenneth's remark about his own plans to move to New York was also disturbing as was the thought that the Warren Company would pass into strange hands, its headquarters far removed, become one of a number of subsidiaries of a faceless, bloodless, unknown octopus named Intercon;

with Kenneth directing its operation by means of some complicated, automated pushbutton device.

If only Theodore Warren—

He turned back to his magazines, exploring floor plans, exterior brick, redwood siding, stone, cedar shake roofs; Georgian, Plantation, Bermuda and Ranch; interior paneling in mahogany, walnut, cypress, wormy chestnut, knotty pine; traditional and modern. Depending on size, the prices of lots might run from $6,000 to $20,000, the cost of building a house from $14 to $18 a square foot. The excursion was futile and he gave up trying to compute values in favor of the enjoyment of merely looking at the color photographs.

And what part would he play at the legal end? Titles, agreements, contracts, leases. He thought of Lewis and Marcus Armour then and doubts began to appear. Was this the kind of law to which he had applied himself so assiduously at the University? he wondered. The project, he felt, and his financial participation in it, were sound enough, would be amply rewarding. Why not let it go at that and open his own offices for the practice of general law, civil and criminal, the career he had envisioned throughout his school years?

He threw aside the magazines and went upstairs to shower and shave. 10:30. A hell of a thing, he thought. Army routine had its way of keeping a man busy, on duty or off, during every moment of the day and night. Home and unoccupied, time hung appallingly heavy on his hands. He was free, but everyone he knew was busy at a job. Adam, Polk, Hugh, even Paula. He thought of Hilary Fields, but knew that she, too, had a job to do.

There was Drew, but he was reluctant to call again. He had phoned twice. First, Leona, then Sue-Ann, reported that "Miss Drew is asleep." She hadn't returned his calls.

He drove into town and stopped at the *Herald* office, but Adam Cameron was too busy to stop for lunch, apologized as he ate a sandwich at his desk. "I'd like to, Corey, but I've got to stick close to the pot. Damned thing could boil over any minute now."

"Seriously, Ad?"

"You'd better believe it, son. The kids are out in force, looking for trouble. Damned juvenile holding pens are filling up like crazy, police trying to get 'em released in custody of their parents, just to make room for more. That fire didn't help things much and if it keeps up, the sky could fall in. And if I were you, I'd tip Lyle Emerson off to stay

536

the hell out of there until this thing is over. He'll make a perfect target. Let's try to get together soon."

He phoned Hugh Brock from Ad's office but Hugh was in a luncheon meeting. Perry Willard had already had his lunch. Polk was out with a customer. He thought of dropping in on Martin Weinstock, his former classmate at law school, phoned and learned that Marty was in court. He walked over to Stocker's and had a sandwich at the counter.

5

In Kenneth Armour's office, Shana Pierce picked up the receiver of the white phone, his private line. "Hello." She listened for a moment, then said, "One moment, please, Mr. Shelby," and handed the receiver to Kenneth.

"Ken Armour here, Tom. Yes, go ahead." As he listened, Shana saw the frown lines in his forehead deepen, his lips tighten, signs of impatience or reluctance. Then, "Fairview? Why Fairview? You're only thirty-two miles away. You could be here in less than an hour." After a full minute of listening, he said, "Very well," and hung up. To Shana, "For some mysterious but important reason, he wants me to meet him at a motel on the outskirts of Fairview. Some vital word from Dillingham and he doesn't want to be seen in Laurelton."

Shana shrugged and shook her head in small quick jerks from side to side. "Ken, isn't this whole thing taking on an atmosphere of peculiar intrigue? If they have a business matter to discuss, why is everything so hush-hush and hidden, meetings in out-of-the-way motels—"

Kenneth smiled and said, "Shana, God and Intercon perform their miracles in mysterious ways. Big Business may seem ridiculous and childish at times, but in the long run, they do manage somehow to produce results."

"He'll want answers you can't give him."

"I'll give him what I can. If Theodore persists in refusing Intercon's offer, there's only one alternative and I'm sure Dillingham will take it and turn his guns loose. With Anderson Warren out of the picture, he wants action before the guessing games start. Any rumor that Intercon is interested in acquiring Warren Tobacco could stimulate offers from other competitors who would no doubt want to keep Warren Company out of the hands of a raider like Kirk Dillingham. With Intercon in the magic circle, there might be a number of radical changes that would upset the present power structure, and the Industry can't afford an upheaval."

"I'd so much rather, if it comes to that, see it go to a legitimate competitor."

"Except that I couldn't expect the same offer I've had from Intercon, Shana."

"Do you want it so much, Ken? New York, under Dillingham's thumb?"

He winced slightly at the phrase "under Dillingham's thumb," which suggested the role of a puppet; but then, he thought, had he been more than that under Anderson Warren's control? Not quite, no. He had given much of his own to the Company, particularly since Anderson's illness had begun and operational power had been almost totally in his own hands. If there was a puppet, it was Theodore, not himself.

Aloud, he said, "I want— Honestly, Shana?"

"Honestly, Ken."

"All right. I'd rather stay right here, doing the job I've been doing all these years, even with Theodore as a figurehead president. If he is serious about keeping the Company intact, even facing the threat of a tender offer or a proxy fight, knowing that with a powerful, experienced opponent in that field we might very well lose, I would still put forth my best effort. The problem is, I'm not sure about Theodore. He's weak and in the middle of a fight, he could break and decide to give up.

"Also, I have reason to believe that Dillingham has more up his sleeve than I know about. I'd guess that he has in some way got hold of the proxies of the northern Warrens and with that in his hip pocket, he could make a generous public offer for enough of the outstanding stock to gain control. All he would need is nine per cent."

"Couldn't Warren make the same fight for that stock?"

"There may not be time. I'm sure Intercon has the stockholders' letters, newspaper and financial journal ads ready to go. By the time we could even get into low gear, the battle would be over."

Shana bit her lower lip. "I hope Theodore decides to put up the fight," she said.

At the Fairview-Broadmoor, Kenneth went directly to Bungalow 12, set apart from the regular units and hidden from view of the swimming pool by a row of tall hedges. He knocked and was admitted by Tom Shelby, urbane, smiling and apologetic. "Sorry I forced you to come all the way down here, Ken, but this is terribly important."

"It had better be, Tom. I'm being deeply inconvenienced."

538

The door to the inner bedroom opened and Chase Warren entered the living room, smiling blandly, one hand extended toward Kenneth. "I hope not, Ken," he said.

If Chase had been trying for a supreme surprise effect, he had succeeded. Armour's eyes opened wide and his mouth dropped open, but he remained speechless for moments as Chase crossed the room and came to him. "Chase!" He looked from Chase to Shelby, back to Chase, then dropped his hat on a chair. "I think I'm beginning to see that I've been played for a first-class idiot," he said stiffly.

"Don't take it that way, Ken." To Shelby, "Let's have a drink in here, shall we? I can use one."

"Bourbon over ice," Kenneth said weakly. "Chase—"

"Relax, Ken." Chase sat in an armchair. "Sit down, please." When Kenneth dropped into the other armchair, "I won't waste time apologizing, Ken. You know the truth now. I'm Intercon. Kirk Dillingham is my front man."

"Chase, I don't think I want any part of this," Kenneth said more firmly.

"Let the shock wear off for a few minutes." Shelby returned with the two drinks, handed them to Chase and Kenneth. "Tom, I want to talk with Mr. Armour in privacy. Suppose you give us about an hour." Shelby nodded without speaking and left the bungalow. Chase turned back to Kenneth, his glass raised in salute.

"Chase," Kenneth said, "I won't be a party to your take-over scheme. In fact, I—"

"Ken, except for my sudden appearance, nothing has changed. You were ready to do it for Kirk Dillingham, for Intercon and the presidency of the new Warren Company. Everything is the same as it was yesterday, a month ago, a year ago."

"I disagree. This puts another face on the matter."

"How?"

"The whole thing becomes a family matter and I couldn't allow myself to take your side against—"

"Unethical, Ken? Is it any more unethical to deal with me than with Dillingham?"

"Call it anything you will. I haven't been exactly happy over my own bargain with Kirk, but that was largely because I assumed Theodore was only waiting for your father's death in order to get out from under."

"You assumed that. Has anything changed?"

"Yes. Theodore wants to stay with the Company, keep and exercise control."

"Why, for Christ's sweet sake? He's never wanted it be-

539

fore, you know damned well he hasn't. Why the sudden change now?"

"I don't know why, but I'll guess it's for Drew's sake. Maybe to try to rebuild the father-daughter relationship he never had. Maybe to some day leave the family Company to her children. Whatever his reasons, I think he's entitled to them."

"Why more than me?"

"Because you walked out on it and Anderson years ago. You could have had it all, handed to you on a silver platter. But you wanted something bigger and gave the Company up. What's more, I largely suspect you were responsible for that report on Louise—"

"You don't know that, Ken."

"Anderson believed it, and so do I. Because Theodore had begun showing signs of deep interest in the Company, you decided to pull the rug out from under him. It's obvious now. You wrecked his marriage and drove him to the brink of insanity so he wouldn't be standing in your way when Anderson died."

Chase's face had hardened, yet he continued to exercise control over his voice. "Ken, you know it's useless to fight me. Theodore can't possibly win. I'm prepared to take every means available to me to take the Company over, and you know I'll win."

That, Kenneth thought with anger, is true. Throw in or get out. Take your choice now. Five minutes from now will be too late.

"Be reasonable, Ken," Chase was saying. "Why play on the losing side when you've got so much more to gain with me?"

"With everything else you have, Chase, why this? Why splatter the Warren name with filth?"

"Because I've got two sons of my own who will some day take over the firm that has borne their grandfather's and father's name and will bear their sons' names some day. Because I intend it will become the number-one name in the tobacco industry some day. And finally, because I think it's due me."

"Your father didn't think so."

"If you think I'd expected to be mentioned in his will, except for that jingoistic legal phrase, 'my son, Chase Warren, for whom I have provided amply during his lifetime,' I hadn't. I knew I was taking a calculated risk when I walked out on the Company, but make no mistake, Ken, with your help or without it, I intend to take over the Company. Whether you share in its fortunes or not is up to you."

540

Chase stood up, took Kenneth's and his own empty glass to the kitchen. Kenneth heard the bourbon pouring, the clink of ice cubes being added. Chase was taking his time and Kenneth knew he must answer the question, *"Well, Ken?"* on Chase's return. He sat in the chair, his eyes on the doorway to the kitchen and then Chase came through it, two glasses in his hands, walked to him and placed Kenneth's drink on the table beside him.

"Well, Ken?"

Kenneth did not touch the glass. He looked up into Chase's eyes and said, "The answer is still no."

6

On the return drive to Laurelton, Kenneth experienced the reawakening of a strange but not entirely unfamiliar sensation. Fear. Fear which bordered on mild panic. Not in years had he questioned his own business wisdom or ability to analyze a situation quickly and make a swift decision. So low had been his error ratio that he had moved out of the domain of pure legal work into the upper strata of corporate leadership. Now, with so much at stake, his decision to divorce himself from Intercon—and Chase Warren—had become a strong challenge to his self-confidence.

Every step along the way since law school had been planned with patience and care. He had turned down lucrative offers in order to open his own law office, a dangerous decision for a fledgling attorney, but had gambled on the reputations of Lewis and Marcus Armour to see him through. His marriage to Catherine, despite Selwyn Crane's objections, had helped to some extent. On his own, he had won decisions against the Taylor and Warren attorneys and, when the time was ripe, finally accepted Anderson Warren's offer to head the tobacco firm's legal staff when Harvey Makepeace retired.

With pragmatic mind and eye, Kenneth had planned his progress cautiously, his eye on the top corporate level. There were then five attorneys on the Warren legal staff in Laurelton, three older, two younger than himself in years, all senior to him in service. There was a New York firm of legal consultants, others in key cities. These presented few problems for him. Kenneth made no radical changes. He asked for suggestions and opinions, but left no doubt that the ultimate decisions were his own. Meanwhile, he studied the background history of the industry, pored over countless cases and court decisions, and managed to make his presence known and felt throughout the widespread organization.

In time, Kenneth moved into the area of general policy, touching all bases in administration, finance, operations, sales, advertising, public relations and expansion, becoming knowledgeable in every phase. He received copies of all departmental and branch reports, examined and approved financial statements, balance sheets, communications to stockholders, agreements and contracts. He traveled between key branches, accompanied Anderson abroad to assist in foreign alignments, studied tax laws and found numerous methods of escape. At board and executive meetings, he frequently acted as spokesman for Anderson and it soon became an accepted fact that Ken Armour was "the man to see."

Moving upward and forward rapidly with flawless skill and suave confidence, Kenneth was aware that despite his deficiencies, Theodore Warren would, in Anderson's lifetime, remain No. 2 in the Company family and eventually succeed his father, but had never remotely considered the moody, unpredictable Theodore as a threat, assuming he could manipulate the unstable son into the chairmanship of the board while he, Kenneth, would take over the presidency.

When Intercon first entered the picture, Kenneth had turned a deaf ear to its proposal, but when the pot was sweetened by increased financial benefits, opportunism overcame loyalty. He listened, analyzed, rationalized, justified and finally accepted Kirk Dillingham's offer with the understanding that no action would be taken during Anderson's lifetime. He reviewed the rewards with satisfaction—presidency, generously increased salary, liberal stock options, enlarged fringe and retirement benefits, his headquarters in New York, away from the scene of his defection. And Shana. Marriage without local social condemnation.

Once definitely committed, it was later that he felt some doubts, created by the difficulty he experienced in screwing up enough courage to tell Shana; a first hint that his secret maneuvering had an unclean blemish about it, further emphasized by Shana's unspoken disapproval.

"If that's what you want, Ken," she had said when he pressed her, rejecting his reasoning that when Anderson died, there was every likelihood that his death would signal the certain end of Warren Tobacco; and that if he went along with Intercon, its life would not only be prolonged, but grow fat with expansion.

Until today, when the injection of Chase Warren made

542

clear his own deceit and self-aggrandizement. The decision to say no to Chase had been difficult, but Kenneth knew he could not justify his acceptance of Theodore's long-time enemy. Not to Shana. Not to Corey.

Not to himself.

And so, as he drove slowly homeward, he felt as close to defeat as he had ever been, but not without a certain sense of cleansing the taint on his conscience. He could take satisfaction in his accomplishments. He had manipulated people, outmaneuvered antagonists and competitors. When he spoke, he did so with Anderson Warren's authority. His directives were heeded as though they were the law itself. He had been given whip and reins and sat firmly in the corporate saddle.

Until now, when all could be lost to the one man he, like Anderson, Theodore, Duncan Collins, everyone, had underestimated. Chase Warren. And now the scent of defeat was recognizably invidious.

Kenneth thought of Corey again with an inner smile of approval that was without reservation. He had never been really close to his son. Catherine had seen to that, using Corey as a weapon against him. Long ago, this had caused Kenneth many worrisome, even sleepless, hours. It had always been Catherine to whom Corey turned when in need of advice or approval; reasonable enough because Kenneth was too often away, too frequently involved in business problems. So the child had become a youth, grew into adolescence, then into young adulthood without his father.

Kenneth had often regretted that there had never been time to spend with his son, hunting, fishing or sailing, vacationing together. Always, there was something to interfere; school, Catherine's refusal to be uprooted from her comfortable world to "traipse around." He recalled sadly that he had never helped Corey with his lessons, his build-your-own planes, ships, automobiles. Corey's own friends, or their fathers, had taught him to swim, to shoot a rifle and shotgun with accuracy. The Club pro had encouraged him to play tennis, to perfect his natural bent for the game. And he had often wondered from whom Corey had received his sex instruction; certainly not from Catherine or himself.

Now he saw Corey, the man, the war veteran, as a healthy, intelligent being, a son to be proud of; with a mind and convictions of his own, undoubtedly possessed of a fine sense of values. And this, Kenneth believed, had played no small part in his own firm decision to choose the Company, the side of Theodore against Chase, despite formidable odds. Thus he felt a sense of perhaps futile, yet incorruptible courage, in the sure knowledge of Corey's and Shana's approval of his action today.

And in Corey, perhaps he saw himself at that age; what he should have become—a Lewis or Marcus Armour; but if the truth was to be faced, he was a man of ripened years who had cast no shadow and thus left nothing noteworthy behind as his father and grandfather had. He told himself that none of a man's past ever dies, can never die because it lives on within his mind; and he consoled himself that for every ending there is a beginning. Today was such an ending, and thus, a beginning. How it would grow or flourish must be carefully planned, worked at.

Inevitably, he began to remember how it all started, the manner in which he had been used and duped by Chase Warren, through his emissaries.

It had come one day in 1965 in the person of Tom Shelby, an engaging man then in his middle thirties, who arrived in Laurelton to sound Kenneth Armour out, bringing with him an impressive financial report on Intercon, the principal he represented. In the main, Shelby spoke of the advantages in a Warren linkup with a huge corporation which had ample resources to expand, modernize and, hopefully, move Warren into closer, more direct competition with the nation's leading cigarette manufacturers. Shelby was an expert at drawing attractive pictures.

"How did Mr. Dillingham come to choose me to approach?" Kenneth asked.

Shelby's smile was flattering in itself. "Mr. Dillingham leaves very little to chance, Mr. Armour," he replied, continuing with an outline of some of the personal rewards Kenneth might expect to gain if he would side with Intercon; a "finder's fee" for valuable services rendered, stock options, his retention as president of the *new* Warren Tobacco Company at double his present salary, increased retirement and other fringe benefits.

The expected reaction did not come off. Armour hedged. "I can't think why Warren Tobacco should be so high on Intercon's acquisition list, Mr. Shelby. There are others, perhaps smaller—"

Shelby merely smiled and replied, "In your place, Mr. Armour, if you will forgive me, I should regard Mr. Dillingham's interest as a sincere form of flattery toward your leadership and guidance since you became executive vice-president under Anderson Warren."

"Thank you for your vote of confidence, Mr. Shelby, but I don't think there can be any further use or purpose in discussing this subject. Certainly not while Anderson Warren is President."

"I am fully aware of that, Mr. Armour. What we have been discussing are mere preliminaries. Intercon has no set target date, except in the—ah—future. Mr. Warren is now over 86—"

Kenneth smiled thinly. "And Mr. Kirk Dillingham probably receives regular intelligence reports on the state of Mr. Warren's health, which he no doubt checks against actuarial statistics. As for my leadship and guidance in the Company, I don't think I would be interested in turning it over to—"

"I assure you, sir, there is no plan to replace—"

"—to a group of Intercon's field examiners. As it stands, we are quite a happy and harmonious family, a fact, I am sure, which has not gone unnoticed by Mr. Dillingham."

"Mr. Dillingham is a very resourceful man."

"I am quite certain he is, Mr. Shelby, but I don't think I am interested in prolonging a useless discussion, and I'm afraid I have a number of other matters calling for my attention. If you will excuse me—" Armour was rising to his feet.

"A moment, please, Mr. Armour. May I make one request, that you not make a definite decision in this matter. Why not let it rest for the time being while you think it over in leisure?"

"And would that relieve you of the necessity of reporting complete failure to Mr. Dillingham?"

Shelby laughed pleasantly. "That, too, perhaps, but I would rather suggest that you may, in thinking the proposal over, find some engaging advantages you may have overlooked in this brief chat. I would like to leave the door open in case you change your mind."

Armour did stand up now. Smiling affably, he extended a hand, which Shelby took into his own. "In that event, I have your card. Thank you, and thank Mr. Dillingham for his interest."

"My pleasure, Mr. Armour," Shelby replied, and left.

Armour kept Shelby's card, but did not call him. He was not overly surprised to see Shelby during a convention of tobacco manufacturers in Miami Beach the following winter, although Shelby made no effort to persuade him further at that time. Nor did Armour avail himself of Shelby's proffered hospitality; an invitation to dinner, another on an all-day cruise aboard a 60-foot yacht with a small group of Intercon (Kenneth guessed) executives and an exciting selection of seemingly congenial young women. On the morning of Kenneth's departure from Miami Beach, Shelby dropped by his suite. Armour was breakfasting and invited Shelby to join him. Over coffee, the younger man said, "I expect to be in Atlanta sometime during March, Mr. Armour. I wonder if I might come to Laurelton for a little talk."

Kenneth said, "I can assure you that Anderson Warren is enjoying excellent health, Mr. Shelby, but if you still care to come, I'd suggest you telephone ahead to make sure I'm in town. I might add that I haven't changed my mind."

"I'll look forward to my visit with pleasure nonetheless," Shelby replied. "I have a limousine downstairs, if I may offer you a lift to the airport—"

"No, thank you. My man has made all necessary arrangements for transportation."

Shelby's reminder had influenced Kenneth to give some further thought to the Intercon offer. By March of 1966, he received Shelby more cordially and finally agreed to meet Kirk Dillingham the following month as a house guest at Dillingham's home in Pinehurst; to, he told himself, put an end to the matter once and for all. Once there, however, the two men relaxed with several other guests and talked privately as a twosome while playing golf on the private nine-hole course. Dillingham was a man of obvious culture and great wealth and did not press the issue to the extent Armour had expected, which came almost as a disappointment. The weekend was pleasant and enjoyable, but came to naught.

Nor, on a subsequent visit to New York in May, was Kenneth surprised to receive a personal call from Dillingham, inviting him to his penthouse apartment for dinner. Kenneth expected to find other guests, but within moments of his arrival became aware that he and Dillingham would be dining alone; and this, he assumed, would be the night for a definite offer and a decision.

The food was superb, the wines rare, the brandy warming. Dillingham was, as he already knew, a marvelous host and entertaining conversationalist, and now he discovered that the older man's investigative resources were far more extensive than he had imagined, as certain facts began to unfold subtly. His knowledge of Anderson Warren was amazingly complete and thorough, as was his information of Theodore's background, Chase Warren's desertion of the Company to direct the Vanderkuyl fortunes; he was just as minutely informed on Kenneth's life, going back to his father, Lewis, and grandfather, Marcus, his marriage to Catherine Crane, of his son, Corey.

By the time he left, shortly after eleven, Kenneth was convinced there would be little to gain, and much to lose, if he decided against the Intercon takeover; and he was more certain that complete takeover was exactly what Kirk Dillingham had in mind. Flying back to Atlanta the following morning, Kenneth began charting his future to coincide with the death of Anderson Warren.

Midway between Fairview and Laurelton, Kenneth noted the time: 4:15. He stopped at the next service station and telephoned Shana to tell her he would not return to the office, but would meet her at her house. Shana asked no questions. Kenneth then telephoned Tish and told her he would be delayed on a business matter and would not be home for dinner.

At Shana's house, he took the chilled martini she had prepared and relaxed with it as she joined him. Elsie was in the kitchen singing over the preparation of dinner.

"Well, aren't you curious?" Kenneth asked with a smile.

"I'm a patient woman, darling."

"Yes. You are that." The double meaning was not lost on Shana. "I'm not holding back. I've been trying to frame it properly in my mind since I left Fairview."

"Why bother? Just tell it as it happened. What did Shelby say to make you turn so serious?"

"Shelby?" Kenneth laughed now at the thought of Tom Shelby's fawning and at the memory of Kirk Dillingham. "There is no Shelby, there is no Dillingham, there is no Intercon, Shana. They are all mere cobwebs that disappear when you breathe on them."

"Ken?"

"I'm all right, Shana. Let me ask you this: suppose I had made no plans, that there was no New York in my future, that I were to leave the Company, that I asked you to marry me and continue to live in Laurelton."

"I'll suppose only the first three parts of the question, Ken. I think you already know the answer to the fourth."

"Then, will you marry me, soon?"

"Yes. Yes. Yes."

"Ah, love, thank you." He took her in his arms and kissed her. "Now I can tell you more freely. Chase Warren is Intercon and Intercon is Chase Warren. The two are interchangeable, but inseparable."

Shana almost spilled her drink. *"What!* Chase Warren?"

"In a nutshell. Over the years, it would appear that Chase created Intercon, using Kirk Dillingham as his front man,

547

no doubt to disguise, for his own purposes, his own participation. It may be that he has been planning for a long time
to one day take over what he has always believed to be his
rightful inheritance, the Warren Tobacco Company, sometime after Anderson's death. He put Shelby, then Dillingham, on to me to dangle the carrot in front of my nose, but
when he moved it within reach today, the thought of taking
the first bite made me quite ill."

"Ken—"

"Wait, Shana, there's more to it."

"I can't wait to say it. How glad I am, how proud of
you—"

"Don't become overwhelmed, Shana. You know I've been
giving it a lot of thought. It was no more right to go over to
Dillingham than it was to Chase, you know."

Shana remained quiet, looking at his face. "So," he continued, "no New York, no big dreams of a presidency, a
new life—"

"Hush, Ken. What has been worrying me sick is how I
could possibly move into that new life and still be myself.
We belong here."

"It isn't over, of course. Chase will probably declare war
very soon and he has every reason to believe he will win.
We're too far behind to put up a good fight. It would appear that he will win and Theodore and Drew will lose the
Company. And I will have lost, too."

"You've often said it was only a job."

"Yes, I know. But I'd grown into it, worked at it, and
I've left nothing behind, just something for Chase Warren
to step into and take over. I've been thinking on the way
home what I would have built if I had never gone into the
Company, had stayed with my own law office, like my father and grandfather before me, to practice law with my
son and leave that behind for him."

The mention of "my son" evoked Shana's next question.
"What about Corey, Ken? And us?"

"Corey and I have talked more since he's returned than
in all the years we lived together before he left. He's no
longer a boy, Shana. He's been a lot closer to life—and
death—than most, and he understands many things about
me he couldn't have known before. I think it will work out
between us. I hope it will. I've told him about you and me,
but I think I'll wait a while, give him more time to adjust to
the idea before I discuss it with him again."

"And in the meantime?"

"I want to think it out a little more before I tell Theodore that Chase is the enemy."

From the dining room, Elsie's voice called, "Time for one drink before supper's on, Miz Pierce!"

"One for the future," Shana said as she poured the last of the martinis.

7

At 8:00 P.M. Inspector LaSalle instructed the headquarters communicator to announce that a modified version of the emergency plan was in effect. Car No. 23 moved into the prescribed area and began cruising the immediate vicinity of the Arcadia Theater at normal operational speed. Cars 19 and 12, each carrying two uniformed officers, began slowly cruising to the south, six and eight blocks from the theater. Cars 28 and 17, each with two men from the Detective Bureau, took similar stations four and six blocks to the north. The last four cars, forming Unit A of the Torpedo Squadron, were prepared to move in swiftly on receiving the Code 9 (Assistance) call from Car No. 23. A second unit of four cars had been assigned to be prepared to throw a roadblock across the west end of the bridge if necessary. From the east, patrol cars were cautioned to be on the outlook for any outbreak of vandalism in the commercial area. All off-duty officers and police trainees had been placed on standby alert.

At 8:16 Officers Ben Hammond, and his partner, Officer Paul Green, made their fourth circle of the six-block area, bringing them back to Taylor Avenue within sixty yards of the Arcadia, where Hammond parked No. 23 with a clear view of the lighted pavement beneath the Arcadia's marquee.

In late afternoon, the sky had become overcast and shortly before deep dusk there had been a rumbling of thunder with the promise of possible relief to the sweltering city. Humidity was oppressively high and the faces of the two men in No. 23 glistened with moisture as they waited. Shortly after they parked, there was the reflection of a quick flash and Ben Hammond said with a grunt, "Lightning."

Paul Green nodded. "Hope it brings some rain. A lot of it. We could sure use it."

"Fat chance. It'll probably blow over."

Green, now that the long silence was broken, said to the older man, "You think maybe this tip came from some kind of a kook, a crank?"

Hammond replied with an indistinguishable snort, then

said, "Call in and tell 'em there ain't a damn' thing stir-ring—"

"There they are!" Green's voice mounted with excitement as he pointed to the light-bathed patch under the marquee where a middle-aged couple, four teen-aged boys in slim pants and tight, short-sleeved shirts, two women, and two young couples were formed in a loose queue near the ticket office. Another group of about eight or ten young boys and girls idled in the open lobby, chattering, laughing, examining the stills and posters on display while they waited for the supper show to break.

"Where?" Hammond hunched forward over the wheel.

"Other side of the theater, coming out of the alley. Five, six, seven—" He counted as they emerged from the alley and came into the light.

There were 14 Negroes in all, 10 boys and 4 girls ranging in age from 14 to 17, some grinning self-consciously, all nervously determined. More to himself than to Green, Hammond muttered, "Goddam stupid id—" The last word was lost in an under-the-breath mumble.

"They got a right," Green said defensively.

"They got no right to take it in their own hands. All these damn kids are doin', they're agitatin' for trouble, beg-gin' for it."

"Well, trouble's the only way they ever got to ride up front of the buses. Trouble's the only way they got the schools to desegregate. Trouble's the only way they got to eat in a few places they never could walk in before—"

"Okay, kid," Hammond said without impatience or ran-cor, "what I don't need right now is a goddam civil rights lecture from you."

The placard-bearing group reached the front of the Arca-dia and the white ticket-buyers and loungers turned to stare in bristling hostility at the invading pickets. The amateurish lettering on the signs spelled out their demands:

WE PAY TAXES — WE'RE ENTITLED
TO TAXPAYER PRIVILEGES!

DESEGREGATE WHITE THEATERS!

WE SHALL OVERCOME THIS, TOO!

It was the final sign, held by an older picket bringing up the rear, that almost precipitated a head-on collision with one of the white loungers. It read:

550

BLACK POWER WILL CRUSH YOU!
DESEGREGATE OR BURN!

Green reached for the car mike and Hammond took it from him. He spoke with the headquarters communicator and told him that the demonstration had begun, adding, "No, not yet. If it starts, I'll give it to you fast enough."

A burly white youth, about 19, lunged forward, but was restrained by his three companions and a frightened, pleading girl who wore a loose jumper and hip-hugging denim slacks. The pickets began moving in a circle, singing the familiar *"We shall overcome,"* in defiant response. The white youths began chanting, "White Power! White Power! White Power!" The middle-aged couple stared at the scene with open-mouthed disbelief and mild horror, then moved quickly inside the theater. The two older women and several of the young girls moved farther into the lobby, but the others remained to stare, hoot, and reply to the singers, waiting expectantly for the impending clash.

The girl in the ticket booth pressed a button frantically and summoned a black-suited man from inside the theater, who came at once and ordered the elderly doorman and the boy and girl behind the refreshment counter at the back of the lobby to close up shop. Together, they hurriedly put up a heavy wire protective screen to completely enclose the counter. The manager hurried back to his office to use the telephone.

In No. 23, Paul Green wet his dry lips and said, "What do we do now, move in?"

Hammond, wiping his forehead with an already moist handkerchief, showed exaggerated nonchalance in the presence of his less experienced partner. "Don't wet your pants, kid," he said. "We move in now, all we do is pull the pin on the grenade. You heard the orders. Anything starts, we move, but only to block that alley. The support cars will come in and take care of the kids while we take out the reserves supposed to be in the alley." He checked his watch with the dashboard clock. "Eight minutes before the show breaks." A pause, then, "You been in one of these before?"

"No."

"Well, maybe you'll get a taste of real action for a change. Either side of the bridge, it's a lousy show. What we do now is—" Hammond reached for the radio mike. "Car 23 to Station One," he announced.

The response was immediate. "Come in, 23."

"Quent, it's started, but no ruckusing yet. The show won't

break for another seven and a half minutes. You'd better alert the others, but don't give 'em the Code 9 yet. Still fourteen demonstrators, about sixteen watchers, and a few more gathering. We're positioned on the north side of Taylor, east of Pine, in front of Webster's Office Equipment."

"Okay. Ben. Inspector LaSalle's standing by. I'll alert him. Stay where you are for orders. Over."

"Out, and pleasant dreams, you desk jockey."

Across the street from the theater, a group of Negro men, women and youths had suddenly materialized, standing back against the store fronts and in doorways, eyes locked on the pickets and onlookers in front of the Arcadia. Among them was Duke Shackleford, watching. More white passersby had joined the taunters in the lobby, some of the older men evidently trying to persuade the teen-agers to go inside and leave the pickets to themselves, but with little success.

And then, with exactly four minutes remaining before the show was due to break and empty perhaps another 150 to 200 more whites into the lobby, nature lent a welcome, helping hand. With an ear-shattering explosion accompanied by angry flashes of lightning, the skies opened and sent a torrential downpour on the heat-stricken city that was very close to cloudburst proportions. Across the street the Negroes scattered toward their cars and into doorways that offered little protection.

The whites in front of the theater drew back inside the lobby, most of them in high glee at the fate of the drenched, sodden pickets who stubbornly clung to their signs and continued to march in the circle beyond the marquee, their singing voices drowned out by the noise of the downpour and rumbling thunder. Within three minutes, the cardboard signs were rendered totally illegible by water damage, some torn away completely from their staffs. Sensing imminent desertion, their leader gave the signal and the fourteen dispirited marchers disappeared into the alley from which they had come.

In No. 23, Ben Hammond, sweating profusely in the enclosed sedan, picked up the radio mike and relayed the good news, saying to Green, "Well, Paul, chalk one up for the Rain God. the policeman's best friend."

Green predicted gloomily, "They'll be back. Four movie houses in Laurelton and only one stinking, crummy joint in Angeltown. Yeah, they'll be back all right."

The streets were cleared by the time the show broke. The initial intensity of the rain slackened somewhat and became more of a gentle "farmer's rain." People in the lobby ran for their cars in the parking lot adjacent to the theater and along the street curbs, and soon, only a few youngsters, indifferent to the rain, huddled together in pairs and foursomes on their way to Stocker's Drug Store and the pleasures of its soda fountain. Others braved the longer distance, a full block west, to Huber's Hamburger Heaven for added sustenance and the privilege of dancing to juke box music.

And at Police Headquarters, Inspector LaSalle relayed the word to Police Chief Durkin, who received it without any sign of elation, knowing that whoever had planned this demonstration and the backup crew in the alley would soon be busy again, probably on the next clear night.

8

The rain, welcomed by most as a signal that the prolonged heat spell had finally run its course and that normal fall weather would take over, was not as well received in other quarters. To the poor whites on both sides of the bridge, to the West and South Laureltonians, it meant winter would be on its way, with cold and rain, the Cottonwood flooding at times, the need for heavier clothing, the added expense of wood, coal and kerosene to feed stoves for heating purposes, shoes to buy, more food to be consumed. And certainly it had interfered with Dr. Rhama's plans for the demonstration at the Arcadia.

Also, the rain had disrupted the very private activities of Tibby Rollins and Tucker Morris, who had been scouting around for a likely house to burglarize. Tibby and Tucker had done well throughout the extended summer, finding many open doors and windows to make their labors lighter.

During the early hours of this Friday night, they had broken into one house whose white occupants were out seeking relief from the heat, a house in a not too affluent white neighborhood close to the east end of the bridge, and their effort had been unrewarding beyond a small palmful of change from a china piggy bank and a small camera of dubious value. When the rain came crashing down, they ran to Tuck's dilapidated Ford, pulled its leaky top up and headed across the bridge toward Angeltown and home.

"A lousy fifty-seven cents," Tibby complained.

"Well, just so it wasn't a total loss," Tuck said brightly.

"Shit, man! I'd sure like to get inside one of 'em big white houses on the east end for once."

"Oh, cut it out, man. I tellin' you before, I'n gettin'

caught in the east end of town. Get caught there, you ain' never goin'a see the outside of Parkton."

"Goddam, that's where it is!"

"Shuh. An' that's where the ofay cops are, too. They'll be other nights, boy. We hit us a couple good ones last month, ain't we?"

They crossed the bridge, which looked as though it had become part of the river itself, with the wind whipping the rain eastward, obscuring the lane markers. In Angeltown, Tuck continued along deserted Grand Avenue, and Tibby asked, "Where to?"

"Ain' much we can do with fifty-seven cents, is there. Home?"

"Hell, I show up home, my ol' lady think I'm sick."

"Okay, where to?"

"Cut up to Division. Maybe we find somethin' there."

"Man, we ain' goin'a find nothin' else tonight. Ever'body ain't home already, they runnin' home to shut windows." Tuck turned into Division Street nevertheless and cruised along the pedestrian-free street. At Washington, they spotted a cruising police car and continued on, Tibby checking to see that they were not being followed. Reassured when the prowl car turned into a side street, they reached the entrance to the Recreational-Vocational Center. Tibby said suddenly, "Hold it, man. Pull in here."

"What for?"

"Pull in, man. I'll tell you what for."

Tuck entered the driveway. Classes were still in session, cars dotted around the parking lot. Tibby said, "Pull aroun' to the right an' cut your lights off. Up there, alongside the two-story building—here, at the back. Stop here."

Tuck cut the motor. "Man, what's buggin' you? Ain' nothin' in there worth the trouble to take."

"I just thought about it. Lissen, when my ol' man had me goin' here, I taken shop trainin'. The shop room is on the second floor. They got all kinds of tools, motors an' stuff we can keep for a while and sell."

"Oh, man, you flipped. We get caught sellin' stuff like 'at—"

"Didn' we sell off all the clo'es we picked up before? This stuff'll bring in a lot more'n rags. Now come on, Tuck, what else we got to do? Nobody'll see us in this rain here, will they? We just wait 'til classes start breakin' up an' them squares gone home. Ain' nobody aroun' 'cept one ol' night-watchman."

"Okay," Tuck said finally. "If you say so, Tib, okay, but I don' like it much."

554

Lyle Emerson's class on this night was reduced to twelve; the Hibbards, the Watkinses, the two elderly Harmon sisters, Albert Warner, Ephraim Crowley and four whose names he couldn't remember offhand. Lyle was reviewing requirements for registrant voters, reading the sentences slowly, the class repeating the words after him. The passage had been both written and printed on the blackboard to impress it on their memories, to remind them later when they would see it in printed form in the Voting Registrar's Office.

Suddenly, Albert Warner, the janitor from the African Zion Baptist Church, threw his pencil down and closed his eyes. Lyle looked up and said, "Mr. Warner?"

Warner shook his gray woolly head. "It ain't no use, Mist' Emerson. It just ain't no use. I can't learn it, get it inside my head. I'm just a dumb Nigra—"

The others stared at Albert with sympathy and understanding and Lyle knew he would either win or lose them all here and now. He moved down among them and sat on the arm of one of the student chairs, his artificial leg stretched out straight in a more comfortable position.

"Mr. Warner," Lyle said with kind patience, "you *can* learn it. It's *important* that you learn it, if not for your sake, for the sake of the others here, for your children, to make them proud of you. What you are doing here, learning here, is great—"

"What so great about it, Mist' Emerson? I goin'a be anything but a janitor if I learn to read an' write a few li'l ol' words?"

"Mr. Warner, anything new that a man learns is great, if he gains by it. And any job can be as great as you want it to be, if you do that job right. Janitor, truck driver, running a bench saw, painting a house or a fence, operating some complicated machine, it's all the same. Why? Because when you do a thing well, or better than the next man, you build pride in yourself, into your work, and no matter what it is, you've got to have pride in what you do before you can have it in yourself, whether it's gardening, doing odd jobs, hauling—"

Eph Crowley said slyly, "Or shootin' a game of pool?"

The Harmon sisters giggled. "Or shooting a game of pool," Lyle said soberly. "If you study the game, the angles, the bank shots, and try to be the best there is, yes. That takes a certain kind of skill, and pride, too, pride in accomplishment. If you don't look higher, Mr. Warner, all you'll ever see is the rut you're in and you'll never be able to climb out of it. That's why you've been coming back to these classes the way you have, to learn. To look higher. To build pride in yourself." In the silence that ensued, he said softly, "Shall we start it again from the beginning?"

Albert Warner nodded.

At the first sign of rain, four men in Elizabeth Shackleford's class on the second floor went to the windows and pulled them down. Elizabeth sat at the table which served as her desk, waiting for her class to copy the words she had written in large, bold script, her mind on the disruption Duke had created within her family during his first few days at home. Now, Sam walked around moodily, angry with himself for having precipitated her brother's abrupt departure from home. Lutie moved about dejectedly, like an automaton. And there was nothing Elizabeth could do to break the tension, restore the laughter and conversations they had once enjoyed together as a family. She wanted to seek Duke out and have a long talk with him, but had no way of knowing where he was living or how to reach him.

She thought of calling Larry Powell, of walking along the center of activity, Grand, Velie, trying to find Duke's Jaguar. In fact, she had planned this last for tonight; now the rain forced her to change her mind. And suddenly the memory of last night and her disturbing ride with Lyle Emerson popped into her head and she was determined to put an end to *that*. More complications in her life she most certainly did not need.

A young student came into the room with a note and left it on her desk. She picked it up, read it, then rapped her ruler on the edge of the table to gain attention. "I have a note from the office downstairs suggesting that we cut our classes short tonight because of the heavy rain, which may make it difficult for some of you to get home. There's less than an hour left, so if anyone wants to leave, we'll continue on Monday night where we leave off now."

The class, as one, was agreeable to the suggestion. While they gathered up papers and textbooks, Elizabeth added, "I want to tell you that you are doing very well. I'm especially pleased with Mr. and Mrs. Tilden's work, and for Miss Abby, who caught up so quickly after being out sick for two whole weeks. I'll expect you back on Monday night for our next class, so don't disappoint me."

There were uncertain smiles and comments of gratification from the three students she had singled out for praise. "A few more weeks," Elizabeth continued, "and I'll be proud to personally lead every one of you into the Voting Registrar's Office and watch each of you register."

They went out singly and in pairs, thanking her; and

when they were gone, Elizabeth erased the chalked instructions and individual names from the blackboard, doing the unnecessary job slowly in order to miss Lyle Emerson and his expected offer to drive her home. She took her purse from the table drawer, refreshed her makeup, ran a comb through her thick hair, then walked the length of the room to pull the four light cords, plunging the room into darkness. The long corridor was dimly lit as she stepped into it, turning toward the front of the building and the stairway to the first floor.

Until she reached the manual training room, all the other classrooms were dark. Through the door pane, she saw that at least one light had been left on, and hesitated, wondering if she should go in and turn it off, conscious of the constant flow of memos about expenses exceeding budgets, cautioning instructors to effect every possible economy.

She opened the door and stepped inside. All the wood- and metal-working equipment, power and hand tools, lathes, drills, were already covered or locked away in their cabinets. She started toward the light cord at the farthest end of the room when she heard a noise of movement. Startled, she called out, "Who's there?"

There was no answer, but she heard a shuffling noise that came from behind her, to her right side. Tremulously, she said, "I know there's somebody behind that bench who has no business there. Who is it? Come out, now, or else I'll——"

An arm flashed up from behind her and a hand was cupped over her mouth. At that moment, the single light went out. She struggled, trying to twist away, but the second arm caught and pinned her as it curled tightly around her waist. Then she heard the desperate whisper in her ear, "Don't you try to holler, lady, or it's your ass."

Suddenly, she discovered fright as she had never known it in her entire life, and even if the rough hand had not prevented, Elizabeth later doubted that she could have called out. In the darkness, she felt the strength of the man as he drew her back against him without effort. She heard his voice call softly, "You okay, man?"

And the other voice replied, "Okay." She heard the second man approach, then felt one of his hands touch her, pawing lightly. The man holding her said, "Goddam it, I tol' you don' turn no lights on, didn' I?"

"How the hell was I goin'a unbolt that thing without no light, just this li'l two-bit flashlight?"

"Well, do it now whilst I hold her. She hollers, we dead."

"She won't holler, will you, Sis? 'Cause if you do, I got

this here knife goin'a make your face look like ten cents worth of cat-meat, you hear?"

Elizabeth nodded through her terror, knowing the man could not see the motion, but that the one whose hand was over her mouth could feel it. She tried to say, "Yes. Yes," unable to under the pressure of the evil-smelling hand.

"Lissen, Sis. We goin'a take an' unbolt a piece of 'quipment here, take us about five-ten minutes. We don' want to hurt you none—"

For God's sake, go ahead, she said silently. Do what you have to do, take what you want and get out, turn me loose.

The man holding her, now assured of her lack of resistance, had begun exploring her body with his left hand, both below and above her waist. She was pulled backward, slightly off balance, her legs apart, feeling the clammy perspiration of her own fear. She felt his hand running along her thigh, then her skirt was being raised, his hand inside her thigh, moving upward—

With a sudden violent thrust, she pulled away. Both his arms clamped around her and still she could not cry out. He spun her around and pulled her toward him and she brought her knee up and forward sharply, finding his groin. He expelled a sharp gasp of pain and the second man called out, "What the hell, Tuck, can't you keep a gal quiet, f'Chrissakes?"

"She kneed me—git the bitch—"

Elizabeth had torn loose from him, stumbled, fell to her knees and began crawling frantically away. The second man almost fell over her as he grabbed and held on to her, his hand searching for and finding her mouth, slapping a palm over it, his rough nails digging into her flesh. The first man, floundering around, hissed sharply, "Knock her out an' let's get the hell out of here. This thing ain't no goddam good at all. I tol' you—"

"Shut up! We gone to this much trouble, we take what we came for. All's it needs is one more bolt to come off. It loose now. Go get it whilst I hold her."

It was useless for her to struggle against his strength. Sitting on the floor, the man had his legs and one arm clamped around her body, his other hand tightly over her mouth. Her skirt was ripped and had slipped upward so that if he touched her—. Twist as she may, he moved with her. She lay in his grasp quietly, almost relaxed, and then she felt his arm creeping downward touching her, gripping the triangle— She moved her head backward, butting his chin and he loosened his grip on her mouth, and as he did, she bit into his hand, deeply, feeling something tear, the taste of his blood in her mouth. He hit her then, twice, using his fist in anger, and it loosened her tongue. She screamed, a piercing cry for help.

On the floor below in the snack room, Lyle Emerson sat with a cup of coffee, waiting. The other instructors had come from their classes and most had formed passenger pools at once and left. Besides himself, there were only three left in the room; the woman behind the counter who had served them; Ralph Atkins, the manual training instructor who was also the night superintendent; and the caretaker. Lyle, whose class was on the first floor because of his difficulty with stairs, had been among the first to come into the snack room, waiting to see if Elizabeth had a ride home.

As the others left, he was puzzled by her absence, and wondered if she had gone directly out from her class, joined a pool group in the hallway. Or if she had been absent tonight. He finished his coffee and hobbled out into the hallway, now beginning to feel the first twinges of pain in the stump of his leg, remembering another amputee who had told him that one advantage of losing a leg or an arm was that one became an accurate weather forecaster; and now it appeared that the man had not been joking at all. He had been pain-free most of the day, but suspected it had been because he had taken an extra pain capsule at dinner time. Now it was beginning again. He walked to the front part of the building and as he passed the stairway, looked upward, hoping to see Elizabeth coming down. Then he turned toward the door, feeling a deep sense of disappointment. He looked out into the heavy downpour and assessed the amount of water he would take on before he could limp to his car, a good thirty yards away on the parking lot. He reached for the doorknob when he heard Elizabeth's scream.

They hadn't taught him the method he now used to climb stairs, nor could he remember later how he had accomplished it. At the first sound, he flung himself toward the steps, took hold of the rail and hopped up the steps, dragging his artificial leg behind him, making no conscious effort to use it. He got to the second floor and hopped, hobbled and leaped in bounds along the hallway until he reached the manual training room. Far behind him, he heard another pair of footsteps on the stairs but for the moment, he was intent only on getting inside that room. The first scream had been followed by a second and a third, guiding him, urging him on, and he burst into the room with such force that the door broke from its upper hinge and swung loosely.

Someone hit him, but the glancing blow slid off his chest. He grabbed for the hand, found it and held on with his left while he threw a hard punch with his right, missing. He threw it again and felt it connect with solid flesh. Withdrawing his fist only a few inches, he attached his target again, found it, heard a cry of pain. "Tuck—Tuck—he'p me—"

He struck again and again, brutally, madly, then felt a blow along the side of his head. And another. But he would not let go his grip on the man's wrist, fighting him, and now the second man with every effort he possessed. He took a kick on his artificial leg and it threw him off balance, and falling, he took one man with him. He heard the stomp of a shoe beside his head and rolled to one side, away from it.

And then someone else burst into the room, fell over the tangle, pulled himself up. It was Atkins, calling, "Lyle, Lyle, where—?" A light went on, the cord pulled by Elizabeth, and Atkins went after the man who was trying to raise the window, caught him by his trouser belt and hauled him backward. Lyle could barely distinguish his man now, young, heavily built, about 20. He threw a hard, slashing blow to the side of the youth's head, catching him along the neck, but the man shifted at the last moment and the blow was not effective. He pushed himself away, got to his feet, found the doorway clear and ran out of the room into the hallway. The man fighting Ralph Atkins swung rights and lefts into the manual-training instructor's middle, broke away, leaped over Lyle Emerson and disappeared after his companion.

Then he saw Elizabeth kneeling over him, helping him, her face bruised. She crept into his arms and he held her, soothing her. "It's all right, Elizabeth, it's all right. They've gone now. They won't be back. It's all right."

Atkins helped them up. The old caretaker appeared now, asking what he could do. Lyle couldn't stand up. Something had twisted his leg apparatus and he needed to remove the whole thing in order to straighten the harness out. He asked Elizabeth to go with Atkins and the caretaker so that he could make the adjustment, but she insisted on remaining with him. He got a handkerchief out of his pocket to wipe some blood from her chin, then realized that it was not her blood, but that of the man whose hand she had bitten.

Atkins said to the caretaker, "You got a first-aid kit downstairs?"

The caretaker, almost benumbed by what had happened, nodded. "Bring it up here," Atkins said.

"Go along with him, Ralph," Elizabeth said. "I'll help

Lyle, then we'll both come down. You'd better phone the police, too."

When they were alone, Lyle leaned against the side of one of the work benches and unloosened his trousers belt. "Elizabeth," he pleaded, "please go downstairs and have your face attended to. Put some alcohol on it. It's swelling. I can do this by myself."

"I want to help. Your face is bruised, too. Oh, Lyle, I'm sorry—"

"You couldn't help it, Elizabeth. Now run along. I'm fine."

"No. I'm going to help you. It wouldn't have happened if I—"

"You had nothing to do with it. I heard a scream. I didn't know who it was, somebody in trouble—"

"But it was me. Now stop being foolish and let me help."

He lowered his trousers. The stump was half-twisted out of the padded socket. He unloosened the belted harness arrangement, adjusted the stump properly in the socket, then buckled it up properly. Elizabeth bent and raised his trousers, helped him belt it. Then, together, they went down the hallway and to the stairs, taking them one at a time, her arm supporting him around his waist.

Atkins had called the 12th Precinct and by the time Elizabeth had brewed and poured fresh coffee, a prowl car arrived. Each told his story, answered questions, gave descriptions, and finally, after taking a last look around, the officers left. Atkins went out a few minutes later, after helping the caretaker lock all the doors and windows. As Lyle and Elizabeth went out, she put an arm around his waist again and although he did not need her help, he did not object.

They were drenched by the time they reached Lyle's Dodge and, once inside, he said, "Your folks are going to be very upset when they see you coming in like this, Elizabeth. If you'd like, I'll go along and explain—"

"No." She said it quickly, sharply. "I don't want to go home like this. God knows what my folks would think."

"Where?"

"Could we ride around a little until I dry out some?"

"It's turned cool, Elizabeth. We could both catch pneumonia." Lyle reached forward and turned the car heater on. "You should get an ice pack on your cheek before it begins to swell up more. Look, would you mind very much going to my place? I could let you have something to wear while your clothes dry. I've got an ice pack and you could even

561

iron your dress to get the wrinkles out, sew up that rip. You could telephone home and reassure your father and mother."

"What time is it?"

He turned the overhead light on and checked the dashboard clock. "Just nine-twenty."

"Good Lord," Elizabeth exclaimed. "So much happened, I'd have thought it was past midnight."

"It happens quickly. Shall we go to my place?"

She turned shy, hesitant. "Won't it cause—trouble?"

"No. I always park on the back lot, close to the rear entrance. I've got permission to use the freight elevator when my leg bothers me. Saves me walking steps and the long hallway. No one will see us this time of night."

While she telephoned and told Lutie she was at the home of one of the other instructors and would remain until the rain eased up a little, Lyle found a warm robe for her to wear. She changed in his bedroom, then hung up her dress, stockings and undergarments on the shower curtain rod in the bathroom. Lyle changed into dry clothes and found her in the kitchen putting a pot of coffee on, marveling over the small, efficient kitchen and its conveniences.

"I seldom use it," Lyle told her. "Quick breakfasts and frozen meals over weekends. Lunches at school, dinners out."

"What a horrible waste. Lordy, if I had a place like this, what I couldn't do with it. I'd almost never leave it."

"You'll have one some day."

"Here?" She laughed skeptically. "I doubt that very much and I think you do, too. I've seen places like this in Los Angeles. I might even have had one if I'd stayed there."

"Why didn't you, Elizabeth? Why did you come back to —this—after four years out there?"

"Why did you, Lyle? You don't have a family here like I do, so much less to come back to." When he didn't answer, she said, "Because it's home. My family is here and there's a need to educate our children, maybe teach them to grow up without the hate they learn soon enough."

"Was that all?"

"I don't know what you mean."

"I—I've always thought there was something strange."

"What?"

"In you. An attractive, even beautiful girl, well-educated —it seems that you would have met someone out there, fallen in love, married."

Elizabeth turned away from his eyes, went to the stove

562

and moved the percolator more directly over the flame, then said, "Where are the cups and saucers?"

He ignored the question. "There was someone, wasn't there?"

She reached up, opened a cabinet door and found the cups and saucers, her back turned toward him. "I apologize, Elizabeth. It's none of my business. I'm sorry."

"Why?" she said with a light tinge of bitterness. "Because you've suddenly discovered that I'm like anyone else? That I'm capable of love and emotions and can bleed when I'm cut, the same as a white girl?"

"Elizabeth!" He pressed his hands down on the table and pushed himself upward clumsily, limped to the stove counter and turned her around to face him. "You know me better than that, don't you?" he said. "I wouldn't hurt you for anything in the world. I'm sorry. I asked that stupid question without thinking. I had no right to pry."

She turned toward him, the cups and saucers in her hands, and he saw the well of tears in her eyes. "Don't, Elizabeth. I know what it's like. I've been there, too."

"You?" It was a mere whisper.

"Yes. I was engaged before I went to Viet Nam. We were going to be married as soon as I got back. When this—happened to me, she went to New York and dear-Johned me."

She was at once contrite. She put the chinaware down and touched his arm. "Oh, Lyle—"

"It's all right. I'm over it."

She looked up at him with a tight smile. "Does anyone ever get over it?"

"We try. And if we try hard enough, eventually we do."

"I guess that's another difference between whites and Negroes. I believe a part of it always stays with us, no matter how much we try to forget. As far back as Psych I, we were taught that we never forget anything we've learned, that it's always there in our conscious or subconscious, waiting for something to trigger it awake. I suppose that's why the white-black barrier is always there, because neither race can forget, the whites who put it there, the blacks who can't break it down."

"Barriers have been broken or climbed before, Elizabeth."

"Not here, Lyle. Not yet. And they won't for a long, long time to come."

The coffee was ready and Elizabeth served it. He stared at her in the overlarge robe, but saw only the lean, exquisitely formed body beneath it, the loose V that formed just

563

above her breasts, revealing the upper mounds as she sat down at the table in the breakfast nook. She looked up at him and saw his face, and drew the edges of the robe together, almost apologetically.

"I didn't realize how small you were until now," Lyle said. "You're almost tiny."

Elizabeth said, "As soon as I've finished this, I've got to run."

"Your things can't be dry yet," Lyle protested. "Besides, you ought to get some more ice on that cheek."

"They'll be dry enough."

"Finish your coffee." He said it firmly, a command, and she sat down again, one hand clenching the edges of the robe, then drained her cup.

"You aren't afraid of me, are you, Elizabeth?"

"No—"

"Then why the sudden hurry to leave?"

"Lyle, don't make me answer that. I'm a damned fool and you know it's wrong for me to be here."

"What sin have we committed?"

"None." she replied. then added, "yet."

"Yet," he repeated with a wry laugh. "Do you expect me to attack you, rape you? Is that one of the things you learned as a child and can't forget, that all white men rape colored women?"

"Lyle, let's not start that."

"All right." He pressed the palms of his hands down and levered himself up again. "Get dressed and I'll drive you back to Angeltown. I'll even drop you two or three blocks away from your house, in the dark where no one can see us."

She came to him then and said, "Lyle, don't be angry, please. You're an intelligent man. You should be able to understand."

"I understand this, Elizabeth. I'm a man and you're a woman and color doesn't change that fact. I haven't made any indecent advances, but you're acting as though I've asked you to spend the night with me. Right now, you're trembling with fear, actually crying."

"Lyle, don't, for Christ's sweet sake, don't!"

She was crying openly, resting one hand on the table, the other covering her eyes. Lyle reached for her, took her into his arms and she made no move to evade him. He put a hand under her chin and raised her face, then kissed her and she did not pull away, but clung to him, her arms tightening around him. He kissed her bruised cheek, mouth, chin

564

and throat, then lower, where the robe formed the loose V. He felt her stir in his arms, then became aware of the need that was rising in him, conscious that Elizabeth, so close to him, was aware of it, yet did not move away from him.

"Elizabeth—"

"Lyle, don't make me want to do something I don't want to do," she whispered.

"Is it because I'm—"

"Don't say that. It's not true. You're a whole man, as whole as any other. That's how I see you, know you."

"I can't let go of you."

"Lyle, it's hopeless. It can't be."

"Somewhere else—far and to hell away from here—"

She kissed his lips to stop the flow of words. "Don't, Lyle. It's crazy, impossible. Please, I can't take any more of this."

He drew back and stared at her sad, lovely face and kissed her bruised cheek lightly. "All right, Elizabeth. Let's get you home safely."

He found a steam iron which he had never used and while Elizabeth set up the collapsible ironing board, found a sewing kit for her. She ironed her underthings, put them on in the bathroom, brought the dress back and pressed the wrinkles from it and sewed the ripped seam. She had no outer coat and Lyle found a raincoat and hat for her, a top-coat to drape over his own shoulders. They left the apartment, again using the freight elevator at the rear.

In his car, he said, "This doesn't solve or end anything, Elizabeth."

She said stolidly, "It can't come to anything, Lyle."

"Why not? Aren't we human beings with normal desires and appetites?"

"Yes, but we're also capable of reasoning, which makes us different from other animals."

"And what does your human-being reasoning tell you?"

"It makes me wonder how much of this is real, and how much is—rebound. For both of us, I mean. And how much is guilt?"

"Yours or mine?"

"Both of us."

"Rebound?"

"Think, Lyle. Your girl dear-Johned you in Viet Nam. I got mine in California. An assistant professor. He was white—"

The words struck him like cubes of ice. "Let's not talk about it now."

"We've got to." A pause, then, "There may not be another time."

He expelled a lungful of breath he had been holding. "Lyle," she said, "do you know what my people, the other instructors at the Center, think, actually say about you?"

No answer.

"They say that because of Cord Waters, you're doing your level best, everything you know how, to become a Negro, to pay off your debt to him."

"That's a goddamned stupid, senseless thing to say. Do you believe that?"

"I don't know what to believe. Psychologically, there may be a lot of truth in it."

He said then, "Does it bother you that I'm in love with you, that you may be in love with me?"

She turned toward him quickly, unable to deny the possibility, yet feeling that she should. She looked away again and stared at the lights of the bridge and those in West Laurelton, seeing them through tears and the heavy fall of rain, the splashes created by the windshield wipers. "I don't know, Lyle. I honestly don't. What does bother me is—"

"What? Say it."

"—what will happen on the day you get rid of your guilt and decide to become a white man again. What happens to me then? I'll still be a Negro, won't I?"

He drove the rest of the way in silence, by turns angry, cynical, bitter, even amused. He refused to drop her near the corner in the pounding rain and stopped in front of the house, which was in darkness except for a dim light beside the door, shrouded by the night and the rain, the street empty of moving vehicles or people.

"Good night, Lyle," Elizabeth said. "May I thank you once more?"

"I don't want thanks from you. I'll look for you at the Center Monday night."

"One favor, Lyle, please. Don't make anything appear obvious in front of the others. They're a lot more perceptive than you think."

"So I gather from what you've told me. All right, as long as you don't deliberately avoid me."

She turned to stare into his face, then leaned forward and kissed him gently. "I'm sorry," she said softly, "really sorry. I wish there could be more." She moved toward the door, one hand on the handle, then remembered and shrugged out of the raincoat, removed the rain hat and laid them on the seat.

"Keep it," he said, "you'll get soaked again."

She opened the door an inch and said, "You see how hopeless it is, Lyle. I can't even do that because I wouldn't be able to explain it. No more than I could explain you. Good night."

The rain had cast a damper on the city. On both sides of the bridge, the streets were empty of pedestrians and few moving cars were abroad. Buses made their final runs with the exception of the two "owls" that operated all night. Patrol cars moved slowly, watchfully, constantly alert for the "quiet cats" who operated in the commercial areas, burglarizing retail stores when they believed the police would be less vigilant. But street and barroom disturbances, muggings, street holdups and similar offenses would be at a low ebb. It was not a night conducive to outdoor activity.

There were only two pool players and two onlookers at Banjo's Place as midnight drew close. In the back room, Duke Shackleford sat at the poker table with Banjo, mesmerized by the man's fantastic dexterity as he shuffled a deck of cards and made one-handed cuts.

"A bust, you say?" Banjo said. "Not so much as you think, Duke. One thing we showin' 'em, they ain't through with us. It's only a beginning. They got suspicions now they goin'a have problems, that we ain't layin' down an' takin' what they dish out. The thing last Saturday night, you got no idea how many people over here liked it. The rain broke up the demonstration tonight, but our people, they're for it. We got to keep up the pressure."

Duke shrugged. "Even if it didn't rain, it wouldn' of come to nothin' much. Chickenshit, that's all. A few kids would've been rousted by the cops, no more. What I like, I like to see somethin' big happen, real big, let the ofay bastards know we got plenty of muscle an' ain't afraid to use it."

"You wrong, boy. You pull somethin' like that, we get the county cops, highway patrol, state police, even the National Guard on our necks. Martial law. They on every street over here, order a curfew, an' we can't even move without they knowin' it. Idea is, give 'em just enough to keep 'em busy without callin' in outside help."

By now it had become obvious to Duke why Banjo Nichols had so suddenly become interested in civil rights. He reasoned, correctly, that since no gambling joint, whore-house or other illegal operation could exist for long without detection by the police, Banjo was adding insurance to his bought protection in order to keep his various operational outlets from being knocked over. Therefore, his need to keep the police busy, off balance, their hands filled with civil rights problems and off Banjo's operations. And what better use could he make of civil rights than this?

It made sense. Laurelton supported a police force of about 180 for day and night work, including traffic duties. About 30 men worked in plainclothes; 32 squad cars, 26 motorcycles. Take one affair, the window-smashing thing in East Laurelton, or the Arcadia Theater demonstration, and just about the whole force became involved. Loss of time, loss of sleep. Pick up a few kids and another demonstration would start up to release "our children"; unwanted publicity in the press, on radio, television; charges of police brutality.

And when the Mayor, the Chief of Police, and City Council came searching for ways and means to end the strife, who could better guarantee peace than Banjo Nichols? For a price. Lay off me, I lay off you.

But, Duke wondered, was what was good for Banjo Nichols good for Duke Shackleford?

"If you say so, Banjo," Duke said with false amiability.

"I say so. Don't get too impatient, else you screw up the whole thing. Keep it in mind, just enough an' not too much. Like the thing tomorrow mornin'."

"It's all set up an' ready to go."

"No problems?"

"No problems." Duke yawned. "Ain't no use hangin' aroun'. Guess I'll get me some sleep."

"Another beer?"

"Sure."

Larry Powell brought the two beers to them again and Duke eyed him with curiosity. There had been little conversation between them and no further mention of Larry's acquaintance with the other members of the Shackleford family. And again, Duke threw a tip on Larry's tray, emphasizing the customer-waiter relationship. Duke drank his beer and Banjo let him out by the alley door, locking it behind him.

In the poolroom area, the game had come to an end, the players through for the night. Larry brushed and covered this last table, then checked out with Hinky Liggett and Noah Smith, the counter man. Outside, he turned up the collar of his jacket and walked north on Preston, west on Elmira to Jackson, then south on Jackson mid-block to the alley. Larry looked around cautiously, saw no vehicles in motion, no pedestrians afoot. The unmarked police car was parked just inside the alley and Larry hurried toward it and got in, grateful to be out of the rain.

Inspector LaSalle said, "Everything okay, Larry?"

"If you can call being wet as a herring okay, I guess so. The best break we got tonight was this rainstorm, came like the hand of God—"

"We never look a gift horse in the mouth," LaSalle said, "even a temporary break. Let's get to where we can talk in peace and dry you out a little." LaSalle drove eastward, crossed the bridge and headed for the garage next to the headquarters building, waving to the night man at the entrance while Larry turned his head to one side to avoid the attendant's eyes and retain his anonymity. At the rear of the building, they got out of the car and went into a small office, where LaSalle locked the door behind them. From a locker, he removed a pair of mechanic's coveralls, which he handed to Larry, who shucked down to his underwear and pulled them on, then sat at the table and accepted a cigarette from LaSalle.

"What's up, Larry?"

"The 'who' will be a lot easier to answer, Inspector. Since I talked with you last, Banjo has been huddling with Dr. Rhama and his number-one boy, at least two times that I know about. Tonight, Banjo was locked in with Duke Shackleford for almost two hours, probably discussing the aborted demonstration at the Arcadia or some other strategy. I'd be willing to guess that Duke is on Banjo's payroll, for whatever that amounts to. And I've watched Duke collecting a group of his own hangers-on, maybe because he's a major celebrity where celebrities don't come easy or often.

"Odie Bilson, Dave Sharkey, Luke Tolbert, Booker Dance, Mace Bodie. Then there's Eli Buller, Jake Runnels and Jim Cuddy. Dave, Booker, Luke and Mace all have jobs. Jake, Eli and Jim are Banjo's boys, hustlers, pushers, pimps, or whatever. I don't know exactly, but they're always in on Friday nights, payday. Just about all of them, except for Dave and Booker, have some kind of record, but you'd know more about that than I do."

LaSalle nodded. "Bodie has a long juvenile record, nothing recent. Sharkey is clean, but Odie Bilson's been up for car boosting, Luke Tolbert for an old mugging rap and an ADW—"

"Anyway, they're all palling around together now, generally at the 2-2-2 Club, once in a while at Banjo's. Tonight, Duke came in with Luke and Booker, about ten-thirty.

Hinky took Duke into the back room and the other two drifted out a little later. Duke was there until just before I left."

There was a knock on the door and LaSalle answered it. Lee Durkin, in shiny black rain hat and slicker came in. He nodded to LaSalle and said, "Hello, Powell," to Larry, who stood up. "Sit down, sit down," Durkin urged, removing his hat and raincoat. "Well, Powell, the inspector tells me you're doing a fine job over in my old territory."

"Thank you, sir, but I can't say I enjoy it."

"I guess not, no more than any of us enjoy doing some of the things we've got to do. You're not asking for out, are you?"

"N-no, sir. I guess not."

"Good. Bring me up to date on what's going on over there."

Larry repeated what he had told LaSalle.

To Lee Durkin, the story of Banjo Nichols was as old as the story of gambling, vice and narcotics on both sides of the Cottonwood River. No laws devised by man could prevent or eliminate prostitution, bookmaking and other forms of gambling; all one could hope to do was effect some control, try to keep outside syndicates from coming in, and make enough arrests to warn the wrongdoers that the laws would be backed up. Major crime such as premeditated murder was rare. There were occasional shootings, stabbings and cuttings resulting from private brawling, but there were no unsolved murders on the books.

Statistics on marijuana and heroin use showed a gradual increase in each successive year and this concerned Durkin very deeply. Despite all the intellectual opinion that marijuana was not in itself a dangerous drug, in that it was not addictive, records showed that marijuana users later turned up as heroin addicts; generally in the case of habitual users who needed more "blast" than marijuana could provide.

The arrest of pushers was seldom rewarding. If the pusher refused to talk, there was generally a lawyer present to offer bail or do his legal best to secure the lightest possible sentence, plead for probation. If the pusher talked, an intermediate supplier or subdistributor would be picked up; but the pusher could count on no outside legal aid. Therefore, few talked, preferring to "go" with The Man. None had ever pointed a finger directly to The Man, and Durkin was positive that pushers and subdistributors had no idea who The Man was, although he suspected that Banjo Nichols fitted into that slot.

Which presented him with the age-old police problem:

that somewhere inside the Department, a small core of men was on the take, one profitable enough and reaching high enough to protect Nichols.

As Deputy Chief, he had been aware that most of the force, at one time or another, in one way or another, were on the take; from well-meaning, grateful citizens at Christmastime; from grocers, liquor dealers, clothing merchants, auto dealers, house painters, carpenters, electricians, television dealers and others always ready to "give a cop a break." There were restaurants where cops "ate free," newsstands where papers and paperback books— But these were not Durkin's major concern. The "take" that lay uppermost in his mind was the cash payoff taken in exchange for protection to the operators of vice.

On becoming Chief, Durkin had instituted an Internal Security Squad, but soon learned that not only did these specially chosen men resent being known as "cop-stoolies," but in three cases were themselves indicted for accepting bribes and dismissed after departmental trials.

When he returned from New Orleans in 1953 to accept the post of Deputy Police Chief in charge of West and South Laurelton Districts, Durkin had learned certain basic facts about police work from Jonas Taylor, his sponsor. He had never forgotten.

In Jonas' study on Laurel, the Taylor plantation, he listened intently to the influential older man's counsel. "You got to learn to compromise, Lee," Jonas had said, "just like a man's got to compromise all his life with one thing or another. Not you nor any man living can whip this problem a hundred per cent. An Army couldn't do it, so you'd have to be an idiot to expect you could do it all by yourself with maybe a dozen honest men to help you.

"With gambling, prostitution, moonshining, you've got to take a reasonable attitude; like I said, compromise. Why? Because in most cases, what you compromise with, you can control—if you're smart. You got to live with a few gamblers, bootleggers and madams, but if you work with 'em, you've got to make 'em work for you. Don't give anything unless you get something better back for it."

There had been more, but essentially, that was the important philosophy behind it; and it had worked *outside* the Department. The rogue cops *inside*, however few the takers, were the problem. One of the problems.

Following the Supreme Court's civil rights decision in 1954, old relationships between white and black were virtually destroyed. Cooperation with Durkin's old, close contacts across the bridge fell so low that communication was almost nonexistent and former pipelines into the heart of the black community disappeared. He had become The Enemy.

Durkin knew that Banjo Nichols, the one-time small poolroom operator, had become ruler of the small underworld that existed but the man had grown clever with age and experience. His only possible source of information could come from a Larry Powell.

When Larry concluded, Durkin said, "So far we've been able to keep on top of things. We've been lucky, but we can't count on our luck holding up too much longer. Dr. Rhama spells trouble and we've got nothing yet to go up against him with. Until we know just what he's up to and can pin something on him, our hands are tied.

"We haven't got any more on that fire-bomb thing and had to release the four kids we picked up on suspicion. It wasn't their car that was involved, so we've got nothing to go on, and naturally, the kids won't talk. The scattered street fighting the next day was spontaneous. We've let most of the kids go, put 'em on probation in custody of their parents. There's no particular pattern we can follow, so we're guessing and running around in the dark after a lot of shadows, trying to be ready when something bigger breaks out.

"I don't have to tell you what could happen if both sides start tossing gasoline bombs around. Anybody, even kids, can make the damned things and there isn't enough fire equipment in all of Cairn County could keep the whole city from being burned out once it got started."

LaSalle said, "All we've got to go on are the two leads, Dr. Rhama and Banjo Nichols—"

"And nothing positive there," Durkin interjected. "Any ideas or suggestions, Larry?"

Larry shrugged. "No, sir. Only what I've reported so far. I'm sure it ties in with the arrests Captain Price's men have been making over there, picking up some of Banjo's pushers, knocking off his gambling joints and closing down on two of his whorehouses."

"And we still can't get anybody to point the finger directly at Banjo," Durkin said. "What about this white man you saw in the back room the other night?"

"I told the Inspector I couldn't make a positive sight identification at the time. He was wearing civilian clothes, a dark blue suit, white shirt, plain blue or black tie, dark gray hat with the brim pulled down over his eyes. He looked to be about forty or forty-five, I'd say five-feet-nine or -ten, stocky, about a hundred and ninety pounds. I got only a glimpse of his face, and it was in the shadow of his hat, then he got up and walked to the back of the room and stood with his back to me. I'm sure he was being paid off. I saw the money, the bills he was shoving into an envelope, and he didn't like it a bit when I barged in suddenly. Neither did Banjo, who gave me hell, coming in the way I did, without knocking."

"And which bothers me as much, if not more, than anything else," LaSalle said. "Keep your eyes open for him, Larry. He could be important to us."

"Then," Larry continued, "there's still Duke Shackleford to keep an eye on. One thing, I don't think he's in this for nickels or dimes, nor getting mixed into it for the love of humanity and equal rights alone. He's a sport with a big spender's appetites and habits, and that takes money to support."

"Shackleford," Lee Durkin said musingly. "His sister's name turned up tonight—"

The mention of Elizabeth brought Larry to his feet in an involuntary move. "What? Elizabeth?"

Durkin said, "You know her?"

"Yes. What was it?"

"She interrupted a 459 earlier tonight—"

"Where? Is she all right?"

"There was a tussle. At the Center. She got a minor bruise on her cheek, okay otherwise, except shaken up a little. Two other instructors ran the two men off, but we've got fairly good descriptions and part of one name. Tuck. Familiar?"

"Tuck? No. This was at the Center?" Larry asked.

Durkin filled him in on the details filed in the official report. "We're bringing them all in tomorrow morning to go through the mug shot files. Damned shame. I've known Sam and Lutie for years. Watched Elizabeth grow up and go off to college. I even had something to do with Duke becoming a fighter, used to train a group of kid boxers at the Center when I was operating out of the 12th—"

Larry Powell's earlier composure was shattered. He started pacing the room nervously. "What about police protection for the Center?" he asked. "They sure can use it."

"First incident of its kind in years, Larry. It's over now, but we'll have a prowl car covering it more closely in the future." A pause, then, "She important to you, Larry? Elizabeth?"

"Yes, sir. She's very important to me."

"Well, I'd say it won't happen again. Lucky those two instructors were handy."

574

LaSalle said, "If we're finished for now, maybe I'd better drive Larry back to West Laurelton."

"All right, Pete. You do that, and Larry, keep the Inspector up on anything new with Dr. Rhama, Duke Shackleford and Banjo Nichols."

"Yes, sir."

2

The intensity of the storm had diminished during the night and Laurelton woke to a gloomy Saturday morning of steady rain and heavy overcast with light, gusting winds. The temperature had dropped to the low 60s and practically everyone but the merchant class breathed with relief. In order of importance, the morning *Herald* headlined its three most important stories:

RAINSTORM BREAKS LONG DROUGHT
Expected to Continue
Through Weekend

RAIN WASHES OUT THEATER
DEMONSTRATION
Foils Effort to Desegregate
Arcadia Treater

BURGLARY ATTEMPT AT R-V CENTER
Two Men Routed by Viet Vet
Lyle Emerson

Not noted in the *Herald* because of secrecy and timing were two other events of importance. At 5:30 that morning, 12 of the 18 Negro drivers for Ainslee Farm Dairy reported at the milk distribution center on Pall Mall Road carrying signs protesting "Unequal Pay For Equal Work" and demanding better working hours and conditions. The remaining six drivers were quickly persuaded to join the majority and no milk trucks left the loading docks to serve Laurelton's supermarkets, grocery stores and homes. Luke Tolbert was the strike leader at Ainslee.

At Cloverland Bakeries, Booker Dance led the walkout of drivers who were making similar demands. Twenty-two drivers and maintenance men refused to enter the building on Green Haven Avenue, choosing to parade in a slow circle, carrying rain-soaked placards.

By 8:00 o'clock, the strikers remained adamant and Ainslee's and Cloverland's executive and office personnel began phoning their major outlets to inform them that no deliveries could be made. As time wore on, their switchboards were flooded by calls from independent stores, hospitals, the city jail, milk vending stations and home delivery customers. At ten o'clock the first private trucks and cars began arriving to pick up individual orders of bread and milk, but the picket lines had been strengthened by other Negroes wearing black fezzes and carrying DON'T PATRONIZE placards.

In town, houseworkers, janitors, delivery boys, maintenance workers at the Water and Power Company and truck drivers were calling in "sick" and harassed retail merchants, druggists, restaurant owners, parking lot and service station operators cursed angrily and tried to set resentful white employees at "Nigra work." Sons and daughters were pressed into service and calls made to neighbors to allow their teenage sons to come to work at increased wages on this non-school day.

The one-day work stoppage was a grave, but not crippling, inconvenience. Taylor Industries, the Warren Company and other industrial plants were the least affected since they did not operate full staffs on Saturdays, except for long distance trucking operations and maintenance; nor were the walkouts here as complete as they were in the retail service areas.

There were numerous reports of clashes, particularly at Ainslee and Cloverland, when customers brushed past the pickets, but these were handled by the police who had been called in early and were standing by in the event of such outbreaks.

In the Shackleford home, Lutie hadn't seen the story until Sam, a habitual early riser, brought the paper in from the porch to the kitchen table. When he had read the news of the storm and opened the paper to expose the bottom half, the cup of coffee he held clattered into the saucer. There was the story, naming Elizabeth as a principal participant, along with Ralph Atkins and Lyle Emerson, with a two-column picture of Emerson.

"Lutie! God Almighty—"

Lutie, standing at the stove, turned, startled. "What is it, Sam? What's wrong?"

"Lizabeth. *Our* Lizabeth!" He got up and swept past Lutie toward Elizabeth's room. She was asleep, covered to the neck by a blanket, lying so that her left cheek was exposed. He knelt beside the bed, touched the bruise gently.

From the doorway, Lutie asked in a frightened whisper, "What, Sam? What's wrong?"

Elizabeth woke then and sat up in bed. "Pa—what—?"

"The paper, honey. I just read about it. Last night—"

"Oh. They put it in the *paper?*"

"On the first page. You all right, baby?"

Lutie reached the bed and held one of Elizabeth's hands. "For the love of God, what—what happened to your face?"

"It's nothing, Mom. Please don't be worried. I'm all right. I'll tell you all about it if you'll let me get up and put something on. Is the coffee ready?"

"It's ready. Get up, Sam. Let the child get dressed."

In the kitchen, Elizabeth read as she sipped her coffee, blessing Lyle's foresight in using the ice pack on her cheek. The swelling had disappeared and only the slight discoloration on her cheek was evident. The details of the story were vague and confused, but essentially correct, and it annoyed her that the story had been printed at all; particularly with Lyle's picture featured so prominently, and bare mention of Ralph Atkins, whom Sam knew.

She told them the story as it had happened, minimizing Lyle's part, emphasizing that of Ralph, making it seem that Ralph had reached her first and frightened the two men off, Lyle behind him.

"Then why they put that white man's picture in the paper 'stead of Ralph's?" Lutie asked.

"Because the *Herald* already had his picture in their files and none of Ralph. See, he's still wearing his uniform. If they'd had one of me or Ralph, we'd be in there, too."

Sam said, "Then when you talkin' to your Mama last night, where you callin' from?"

"I told Mom. It was raining so hard and I was upset. One of the instructors drove me to her house. I drank some coffee and waited until I was calmer, then she drove me home. I didn't want to come right home and scare the daylights out of you."

"If you'da told Mama, I coulda drove over to get you," Sam protested.

"There wasn't any point in upsetting you."

"I'm upset now, thinkin' you'd go to some stranger 'stead of your own Papa an' Mama."

"Pa, I'm sorry. I was too unnerved to be thinking straight at the time. She suggested it and it sounded like a good idea."

"Sam, you let Lizabeth alone now. You jus' fussin' an' upsettin' her all the more—" The doorbell rang. "Go answer the door," Lutie commanded, her arms around Elizabeth, hugging her to her breast. Sam went to the front of the house and returned a few moments later. "Policeman wants to talk to you, Lizabeth."

"Police—?"

"Somethin' about goin' down to police headquarters to look at some pictures, see can you 'dentify the two men from las' night."

The three went to the front room where a Negro officer introduced himself and explained his errand. Elizabeth at once agreed, but Sam insisted she finish her breakfast and that he would drive her to Police Headquarters and be present during the search. The officer thanked them and left. Moments later, carrying a copy of the *Herald* in his hand, Duke arrived, storming into the kitchen. "Mom, Pa. You all right, Lizabeth?"

"I'm fine, Duke, really I am. I'm so glad to see you."

He touched the bruise on her cheek then removed his rubber-silk raincoat and hat and sat down at the table. Lutie, reacting to this impromptu family reunion, said happily, "Now we all goin'a have us a good breakfas', family style, like it ought to be, all together."

Bacon, eggs, grits, cornbread with molasses, topped off by steaming cups of coffee, the conversation guided away from Duke's activities and Elizabeth's experience of the night before. Duke brought them word of the Negro strikes in town and told them of his cottage at the Nigerian, hinting mysteriously of an offer of a job he might be taking, giving few details. Even Sam was drawn into the conversation, wondering if the strike would be prolonged and if it would be extended into the following week and thus affect his warehouse operation. Duke reassured him that it was probably a one-day affair, "jus' to show Whitey what c'n happen if he don't straighten up an' start flyin' right."

At 10:30, Elizabeth got dressed and left with Sam for the East Laurelton Police Headquarters. Duke followed them in his Jaguar. In the office of Captain Harry Larch, in charge of Criminal Identification, Ralph Atkins, Lyle Emerson and Elizabeth were seated at a long table, each examining a book of mug shots of known burglary offenders. As each book was passed from one to the other and examined carefully, it was removed and replaced with another. Full face, left profile, right profile. Sam and Duke stood to one side, waiting silently, since no conversation was permitted in the room.

When she first entered the room, she was surprised to see Lyle and Ralph already engaged in the search task. She shook hands with Ralph and barely nodded to Lyle, conscious of the presence of her father and brother, and Captain Larch, a heavyset, phlegmatic man with a red, pock-marked face and pale blue eyes. There was another officer present, a pleasant young man who made himself useful by bringing coffee and later, sandwiches, as the hour moved past noon. Occasionally, Elizabeth glanced across the table at Lyle, to find his eyes on her, but controlled her desire to speak or smile at him.

At a little before two o'clock, a fourth book was given to Lyle Emerson and on page 11, he found what he was searching for. As prearranged, he raised one finger in Larch's direction. Larch came to the table and took a hard look at the picture, nodded and closed the book.

"All right, Miss Shackleford," he said, "will you go through this book and see if you can make an identification."

Elizabeth began inspecting each page carefully, aware that Lyle had identified at least one of the suspects. Slowly, she turned the pages, scrutinizing each set of photographs meticulously, unwilling to err by influence. Reaching page 11, she gasped suddenly. Larch was standing directly behind her and took the book at once, closed it and carried it to Atkins, who began his own examination. Under the captain's watchful eye, he passed over page 11, came back to it and said, "This is the one Mr. Emerson was grappling with on the floor when I reached the manual-training classroom. I'm sure of it. I got a clear look at him when he got up and ran out."

Larch called off the number on the mug shot and the officer-assistant went to a steel cabinet, searched through it and removed a similarly numbered file.

Tucker Rollins. Nickname(s) or Alias(es): Tuck, Rolly. His record extended back to his 13th year. He was 26 now and since his 21st year had been arrested and convicted of larceny, car theft, burglary, assault with a deadly weapon, two counts, mugging, two counts. Of his 26 years, he had spent 10 in reform school or prison.

The second man's picture was not in the files.

Outside the police building, Duke said, "Pa, how about lettin' me have Lizabeth for a little while. I didn' bring her no present from New York an' I like to buy her somethin' now."

"I don't need a present, Duke," Elizabeth protested.

"You got nothin' to say about it, sugar, an' every pretty girl needs presents. If you don't come along, you goin'a get

579

somethin' you got to exchange for somethin' you want. All right, Pa?"

Sam saw the look of expectancy light up in Elizabeth's eyes and said, "All right, son. You take good care of her." He got into his Ford and drove off.

In the Jaguar, Duke cruised slowly along in the rain. Pedestrian traffic was heavy and umbrella-ed, but seemed good-natured in the joy of a cool, albeit rainy day after the long hot spell; but curiously, there were few Negroes abroad for a Saturday. Both felt it, but neither remarked on this minor phenomenon.

"Where's the best shop in town, Lizabeth?" Duke asked.

"For what?"

"For a dress, a suit, shoes, raincoat, everything. The works. You goin'a get the best dressin' up you ever had in your whole life, Sis."

"Well, I usually shop at Millicent's on Grand Avenue—"

"Not over there. Here. What's the best shop over here?"

"Duke—"

"Where at?"

"I guess The Mall, but I've never bought anything there. Too expensive."

"Then that's for us. Just point the way."

Driving along rain-drenched Taylor Avenue in bumper-to-bumper traffic, something clicked in Duke's mind and he turned suddenly and said, "Hey! That Emerson fella—"

The mention of Lyle's name so suddenly took Elizabeth by surprise and it showed on her face as she looked up quickly. "What about him?"

"Who's he? What he doin', teachin' at the Center?"

"Just that, Duke. He teaches history at Laurelton High and an adult class in voter registration at the Center at night, the same as I do."

"I mean, how come? Just because he's one-legged?"

"No, Duke. He's just a very fine person who believes in many of the same things we do. That there's a need to educate the illiterates, teach them to read and write so they'll be able to communicate with others and exercise their right to vote."

"Another hundred years from now?" Duke scoffed.

"If necessary, for another thousand years. It needs to be done and it's got to start somewhere and sometime, even a hundred years too late."

"Yeah, well—" For the moment, he addressed himself to the car ahead, which had suddenly braked to a stop. "Damn traffic. Worse'n New York." The car ahead moved on and Duke followed. "That fella—"

"What fellow?"

"The Whitey. Emerson. I seen him eyein' you—"

"That's crazy, Duke. Lyle—Mr. Emerson is simply a kind, good man."

"How come you say Ralph Atkins get to you first an' Ralph say Emerson was wrasslin' with the man when he got there?"

"I—I don't know. It was dark until someone turned a light on. Everything was happening at once. Maybe I was confused."

Eyes on the traffic ahead, Duke said, "There somethin' between you an' that fella, Lizabeth?"

In an angry voice, Elizabeth replied, "If you're serious, Duke, I wish you'd turn back and take me home."

"That the way they learn you to answer a question in that fancy college, sugar, not to answer it at all?"

"Duke—"

"I seen the way he lookin' at you, Lizabeth, an' I know a look when I see it."

"Stop it, Duke. You're imagining things that aren't so."

"I seen it in his face an' I seen it in yours. There *is* somethin', ain't there? I c'n see it there now."

Heatedly, she replied, "I don't know what you think you saw, or what you think you see now, but whatever it is, Bubba, my life is my own and nobody else's business. Not even yours, even if you did pay my way through U.S.C."

"Now you hold on, Sis. I ain't askin' for you to pay me back for nothin'. I'm just askin' you if there's somethin' between you an' this ofay, an' you can't answer me a straight 'Yes' or 'No.' I guess that's enough answer for me."

"I won't answer because you haven't any right to ask or question me."

"An' I guess you answered me, all right."

"Duke—"

His face hardened, lips drawn in a single tight line. "Like you say, it ain't none of my business what my sister does. I guess if I slep' with my share of white women, a white man's got the right to sleep with my sister, hey? Is that what you mean by integration?"

She turned away from him angrily, her face flushed. The car pulled up to a red light and stopped. After a second's hesitation, Elizabeth reached for the door latch. Duke grabbed her arm and pulled her back toward him. "Don't you go jumpin' out on me, Sis," he said. "You do an' I'll look your white boy friend up an' beat the livin' shit outa him. You don't want me to do that, do you? An' what'll Pa

581

say if you don't come home with them presents I tol' him I
was goin'a buy you?"

3

On Friday night, when Tish told Corey that Kenneth would
not be home for dinner, he had telephoned Brookhill, but
Leona told him Drew had gone for a drive and didn't know
when she would be back. Paula called while he was eating
his solitary dinner and when he returned her call, he was
first amused then annoyed by her pique at his refusal to remain after the others had left the party on the Saturday
night before. More than anything else, he resented the pos-
sessiveness in her attitude.

"What about Polk, Paula?" he asked pointedly.

"What *about* Polk?" she parried.

"I've got a feeling he's interested—"

"And you're too much the gentleman to step in?"

"Perhaps not. Maybe too much of a friend."

Paula's laugh was high-pitched. "Corey, don't be so naïve,
for heaven's sake! All the time we were steadying at the
University, Polk was trying his best to cut in on you."

"Paula, that was another world. Life is too short to work
at making enemies. No matter what, I can't cut in on Polk."

"Or do you prefer Hilary Fields?"

"Thanks for the suggestion—" There was a *click!* as
Paula hung up. Deliberately, he dialed Hilary's number and
found her in. "I've tried to call you twice this week," he
said, "but you're probably the busiest woman in town."

She laughed happily. "Advertising is a hard taskmaster.
We've been putting an important presentation together,
trying to steal a big account from a competitor, and that
takes a lot of doing."

"I'd like to hear more about it."

"I doubt that very much. Anyway, it's all top secret and
very sneaky. All I can tell you is that we wrapped it up late
this afternoon."

"Then more about you. Are you free?"

"Well, I had intended spending the evening doing all the
girl-things I haven't had time for this week. Hair, nails and
other vital necessities."

"But you could be talked out of it until tomorrow?"

"Well—yes. No work tomorrow."

"Eight-thirty?"

"Eight-thirty will be fine."

"See you then."

Shortly after 8:30, he was there, carrying a bottle of pre-chilled champagne. Hilary was wearing comfortable hostess pajamas, flowing bottoms with a sheath topper that fell to below-hip length, a fetching costume. She offered her mouth for a kiss. "For the Greek bearing gifts. How nice."

"And another gift I couldn't bring inside with me. It has just begun to rain."

"Really? How nice and cozy." She went to the curtains and drew them, revealing sliding glass doors that opened onto a small balcony. She opened the doors just as a flash of lightning raced across the sky simultaneously with a grinding rumble of thunder and a heavy sheet of rain which almost blotted out the view of the city lights. She drew back and closed the doors. "Bless the Lord for small favors. I'd love to take off my clothes and dance in it."

"Why don't we?" he proposed.

"I've done it in the country, but not in view of an entire city." She opened the doors again experimentally. "Help me pull these chairs back." They moved the porch furniture back as far as the glass wall would permit and went back inside to prepare an ice bucket for the champagne. Hilary got out a bottle of brandy, some bitters and sugar cubes.

"Hey! What—?"

"French 75s. Champagne, brandy and a sugar cube soaked with bitters," Hilary said. "Surprising how much more effective champagne becomes. Game?"

"Lead on, MacDuff. Let's play it your way."

They snuggled together on the sofa, drank French 75s, kissed and fondled each other teasingly, neither with any doubt that their evening would culminate in bed. Without tension, the time passed in a pleasant euphoria of anticipation. Hilary slipped off the lower half of her pajamas and the sleeveless tunic blouse barely covered her hips. They made love in a burst of passion and returned to the living room sofa for more of the champagne and brandy.

Hilary talked briefly of her husband, Greg, who had fallen victim to ambition in New York; of their decision to come to Laurelton to make a fresh start, only to learn that Greg's total absorption in his work was too overwhelming for the change of locale and scenery to overcome.

"It must have been a terrible shock, breaking up, I mean," Corey said.

"The finality of it, yes, but once he'd left, it wasn't too bad. I think I'd conditioned myself for it."

Having started on the subject, it was as though she couldn't stop now. "We grew up together, had known each other since our first school days—" Corey thought of him-

583

self and Drew—"and through high school. Maybe that was it, that we'd known each other too well and too long. Just after college, we began sleeping together. Greg was ambitious even about that. Aggressive and almost arrogant. I didn't recognize that at first because it was great with Greg, then he got even more ambitious and started playing around with a vice-president's wife, then started on the president's daughter. When her mother found out, she quietly arranged for his transfer here."

"How did you find *that* out, for God's sake?"

"From an anonymous letter from the vice-president's wife. I got it about the same time the president's wife got one just like it. I compared the handwriting with a written note inviting us to their place on Long Island the summer before. I never told Greg."

"How could you not tell him?"

"Because I didn't give a damn any more and was planning to divorce him. Then came the transfer and he begged for another chance and I suppose because I didn't give a damn, I agreed. But he couldn't stick it out here and needed to get back to New York where the action was. And the president's daughter, I assume."

"When did you meet the Willards, Perry and Joyce?"

"Perry was Greg's department head. Joyce was very friendly and when Greg left, Joyce talked Arnold Fuller into giving me a trial at Fuller and Conwell. I'd worked for an ad agency in New York before Greg and I were married, so it all came out very well. Now about you."

"What about me?"

"Well—you and Paula. I hear you were quite a torrid twosome before you went into the army."

"It was long before that, just a college romance. Nothing serious or permanent."

Hilary laughed then. "That's not the way I heard it. I think Joyce pushed us together to prevent the old ashes from igniting."

"And instead, ignited a new conflagration."

"Well—Corey—"

"What?"

"We're not in college now."

"What does that mean?"

"Just this. I know about you and the rich Warren girl I've never seen. I don't intend to remain here and I don't want anything or anyone to try to keep me here. I'm only waiting to regain my sense of balance, and when I do, I'm going back to New York."

He felt a sense of relief surge over him. "You have my promise not to interfere," he said.

Hilary looked up quickly, smiling. "You, sir, are a louse. You might have put up a tiny ounce of resistance. Just for that, I'm going to make you leave—right after breakfast."

In the morning, it was still raining. At nine o'clock the phone awakened them and Corey nudged a sleepy Hilary into action. She answered the phone, grimacing under a slight hangover. It was Oren Easterwood, her copy chief, with a query about the presentation. "You'll find the photostats in the upper left-hand drawer of my desk, Oren. No, I'm sorry I can't come in this morning. I'm in bed with a slight cold. I'm sure I'll be all right by Monday morning." When she hung up, she slipped into Corey's arms with, "Hello, Slight Cold."

He was home by 10:30 and Kenneth had not come down yet. At 11, when he did appear, he asked no questions and Corey volunteered nothing about his night out. Corey sipped coffee while Kenneth ate a hearty meal. When Kenneth went up to dress, Corey went to the study to scan the morning paper.

His eyes leaped first to the picture of Lyle Emerson. He read the item with great interest, then dialed Lyle's number, but got no answer. Picturing the scene, Lyle and Elizabeth, he remembered them together, that first night he had seen Lyle; the very attractive, light-skinned girl who sat between them, refusing to allow Lyle to drop her closer than a full block from her house. And he remembered tall, fair, blonde Jill Tinsley with sudden anger.

Corey finished reading the paper, went upstairs and shaved, then dressed casually. The rain was still coming down heavily when the rest of his civilian clothes arrived from Weinstock's, and that took an hour to examine, try on and hang in his closet. Kenneth looked in on him to say he was driving to Atlanta on business and would return on Monday morning. Corey had planned to discuss the Shadow Hills project more thoroughly, but Kenneth's departure voided that. His mind still on Lyle, he dialed his number, but there was still no answer. He telephoned Brookhill and learned that Drew was taking a nap. He toyed with the thought of calling Polk, but for some reason, perhaps the triangular involvement with Paula, dropped the idea. Drowsily, he went up to his room to take a nap. Before he fell asleep, he tried once more to reach Lyle and failed. He promised to try again when he woke up, perhaps spend the evening with Lyle. He might even, he thought, discuss the Shadow Hills project with Lyle, offer to bring him into it in

585

some executive capacity that wouldn't require too much physical movement. He fell asleep thinking of Hilary Fields.

4

When she got out of the car in front of the Shackleford house, Elizabeth said, "I'm not going to thank you for these, Duke," indicating the two dress boxes she carried.

"I'n askin' you no thanks. All's I ask was if you carryin' on with that ofay."

"The answer to that is that I'm not 'carryin' on' with anybody, white or Negro, and if I were, I wouldn't tell you. I'm over twenty-one and not accountable to you, Duke, no more than you are accountable to the rest of the family for your behavior. If we're going to be friends, for God's sake consider me intelligent enough to live my own life as I see fit."

"Yeah. Well—"

"Are you coming in?"

"No. It just start up another wrangle. I'll be by some other time."

He drove away and Elizabeth ran up the walk, head down to keep the rain off her face. She didn't see Larry Powell until she stood at the door, wiping her shoes on the cocoa-brown mat, fumbling for her door key.

"It's open," Larry said, coming forward to take the packages from her.

"Larry. You startled me—"

"Let me see your face."

"It's nothing that won't disappear within a few days."

"Did you identify either of them at the police station?"

"How did you know about that?"

"Your mother told me."

"Is Pa home yet?"

"No. He stopped off to do the grocery shopping for your mother. This rain—"

"Come in, Larry, won't you? I'm sure Mom has some coffee on."

"I'd like to, but I'm due at work. A rainy Saturday always fills the place up."

"Larry, why won't you let Pa get you a job at Warren's, or let me talk to the principal about a teaching job?"

"Elizabeth, I can't. I wish I could tell you why, but I guess I've got to do this for myself, on my own."

"I don't understand why, but it's a shame to let your edu-

586

cation go to waste in a dirty poolroom, with people who hang around doing nothing."

"Hey, hey! That's extremist talk against your own people," Larry said with an exaggerated laugh. "Whose side are you on, anyway?"

She opened the door and went inside. "You sure you won't come in for some coffee?"

"I wish I could, Elizabeth. Best I can do is ask for a raincheck."

"All right, you've got it."

"See you. Take care of that pretty face, you hear?"

At 4:30, Corey dialed Lyle Emerson's number again. This time, Lyle answered, his voice thickened by what Corey assumed was liquor.

"We identified one of the men," Lyle told him. "The police have an alert out for him and they're sure they'll get the second guy if they pick up the first,"

"How about me coming by and we'll have dinner together in some quiet place?" Corey asked.

"I'd like that, Corey, but the truth is, this rainy weather is giving my leg hell—"

"Then I'll pick up a couple of steaks and come by anyway. We'll have an indoor picnic, if you've got guts enough to gamble on my cooking."

"Sure. Come on over. I'd like that. About seven."

When Corey hung up he went to the kitchen to ask Tish if there were two large steaks in the freezer which could start defrosting. As he reached the kitchen, the phone rang. Tish answered, held the receiver out toward him. "For you, Mist' Corey. Miss Warren."

"I'm sorry Sue-Ann didn't wake me when you called earlier, Corey," Drew said apologetically. "I woke up only a few minutes ago."

"I was only checking up on you, Drew. How do you feel?"

"Better, but this place is so gloomy with all this rain, welcome as it is. Are you busy this evening?"

At once, he regretted having made the dinner date with Lyle. "I'm sorry, Drew. I'd just finished talking with Lyle Emerson and we made a date for dinner."

"I saw the item in the paper this morning. Is he all right?"

"He's fine. What about tomorrow?"

"I'm free. How about lunch?"

"If it's late enough."

"Come out any time and we'll make it a—" She laughed

587

and it cheered Corey to hear its familiar ring—"If breakfast and lunch is 'brunch' what would lunch and dinner be?"

"I don't know—how about 'dunch,' or 'lunner'?"

"Dunch," Drew agreed. "We'll start it any time you get here."

"I'll ring you first."

"Don't bother. Just come out."

On that Saturday morning, Lyle Emerson had awakened in pain. The incident at the Center the night before, combined with the dampness in the air, sent excruciating twinges up into his stump and through his body. After driving Elizabeth home, he had taken two pain capsules, with little relief. He took two more and added a nembutal capsule, but the pain hardly lessened. Then he turned to the bourbon and drank nearly half a bottle before he fell into a numbed, fuzzy sleep. And dreamed of Elizabeth. In his apartment. In his robe. In his arms.

This dismal morning, the pain was back, his stump a solid ache, and the thought of fitting it into the foam-rubber-cushioned socket of his prosthesis palled on him, as though it were lined with heavy-duty sandpaper. He used his crutches to go to the kitchen, where he put the coffee on a low flame, then took a liberal drink of bourbon before going to the bathroom. After shaving, he brought the *Herald* in from the hallway, went back to the kitchen to start fixing bacon and eggs, poured out some bottled orange juice. With crutches, every action was more laborious, but less painful.

He poured more bourbon into the orange juice and drank it while turning the bacon in the pan, beating three eggs in a bowl, adding milk, salt and pepper. He buttered the second pan, placed six strips of bacon on a sheet of paper toweling, covered it with another sheet to drain. Eggs in the pan, he dropped two slices of bread in the toaster.

At the table, he read the story of the attempted robbery at the Center, examined his picture, the youthful one taken a million years ago, the broad, open smile somewhat out of character now. He noted the coupling of his name with Elizabeth's, the "hero" tag with reference to himself. Elsewhere, the news from Viet Nam was brief, the Viet Cong casualties, as usual, reported to be "heavy," with U.S. and Vietnamese dead and wounded "light." He muttered "Bullshit!" beneath his breath.

The switchboard telephoned that a police officer was asking to see him and he met Officer John West at the door.

588

West asked if it would be convenient for Lyle to come down to headquarters on a photo-identification mission. Lyle agreed and went back to the kitchen for another cup of coffee and the paper. Drought broken . . . demonstration at the Arcadia Theater broken up by rain . . . a teen-aged girl brought into Memorial Hospital in a psychedelic coma . . . rain causes numerous auto crashes . . . man electrocuted when electric heater falls into bathtub . . . .

He put the paper aside, washed the dishes and sat in his leather reading chair to rest his throbbing stump. And thought of Elizabeth again, on the floor struggling to get free of the man who held her, heard her penetrating scream again . . . his arms around her in this very room, wondering if—if—Lord, how he had yearned for her at that moment, to bed her down . . . in his mind an erotic vision as she undressed, coupled with him, accepting him willingly, even eagerly. . . .

Then his eyes fell on the obscene stump and he cursed himself for his thoughts, having fallen prey to the fault of many white men who, as boys, had been taught by older boys that all Negro women were whores who learned their art at the age of six, from brothers and fathers, and who looked forward to the day when they could screw white boys and men.

This and other myths; that all Negroes were cowards, thieves, rapists; were filthy, diseased, depraved, immoral; were lazy and shiftless with one ambition: to get on the county welfare rolls, County Bounty; lived in adultery and incest, hungered for white girls and women; were "hung" like animals because they *were* animals, by instinct and fact, inherited from their animal ancestors in Africa.

He recalled that his first participation in the sex act, at the age of 15, had been a "gang" affair when he and two of his classmates each paid a 16-year-old colored girl a quarter each for a brief, spiritless sexual exercise that had left him disgusted, worried and disappointed, yet had established a certain status for him among his friends. The girl had been the daughter of a day worker in the home of one of the two other boys and later, when the daughter came to work in the Emerson home as a once-a-week laundress, he had been unable to face her knowing, amused stare.

In time, he had found willing white girls and, once again, after a fraternity stag party in Athens, had taken a Negro stripper in the back seat of a friend's car. Then he had met Jill Tinsley, forgoing all others. Jill was *it*, the one, the only. He had never been unfaithful to her, not even while in training, nor in Viet Nam. After he lost his leg, and Jill, the thought of exposing himself to a woman, any woman, made him cringe. And yet the want, the desire was there, as strong as ever before, perhaps even stronger because he had put it out of his reach, reviling himself as a cripple: an obscenity.

Elizabeth. Sweet, golden-hued, lovely, kind; stamped with the ugly classification, Nigger.

He shook himself out of the lethargy of self-pity and took great care with his dress, knowing that Elizabeth and Ralph Atkins would be at the headquarters building. And this thought of seeing her again, perhaps, seemed to lessen the physical ache he felt.

He returned to his apartment from the police task at 2:30, changed from street clothes into something more casual, pinning the right pant leg to keep it from dangling uselessly, returning to crutches to relieve the pressure of the artificial leg. He brought a fresh bottle of bourbon and a glass from the kitchen to his reading chair, turned on the radio and listened to the news of the bread and milk strike, the labor slowdown elsewhere. He fell into a light sleep . . .

The phone rang and woke him. It rang a second time, then a third. It seemed to come from afar and he realized it was the bedroom telephone, a private line that bypassed the downstairs switchboard. It continued to ring until he reached it. "Hello," he said into the receiver.

There was no reply. "Hello. This is Lyle Emerson—"

Still no answer. The line was open, but he heard no voice. He said, "Hello," for a third time and heard a *click!* then the dial tone. Lyle hung up and lay down on the bed, his eyes closed, seeing Elizabeth again, this time at the table at police headquarters, the swelling gone, the purplish bruise covered cosmetically. The face of her anxious father. And that of her brother, Duke, cold with unyielding animosity.

Ten minutes later, the phone rang again. He picked up the receiver and said, "Hello." This time it was Corey Armour and he was tempted to ask Corey if he had called a few minutes ago and decided against it. He agreed to have dinner with Corey here in his apartment and hung up, lying back again to try to recapture his earlier thoughts.

In a public phone booth only two blocks away from Emerson's apartment house, Duke Shackleford hung up the receiver, went out to his car and started it. He checked the street signs against the one given in the telephone directory, found the correct one and saw the thin line of neon that identified his goal. Tower Apartments. He drove around to the rear and parked the Jaguar near the back entrance. Inside, he walked along the hallway to the front lobby, grateful there was no one in sight but the lone girl behind the counter, sitting at the switchboard reading a paperback novel. She was colored. "Help you?" she asked.

"Yeah. What number is Mist' Emerson's apartment?"

"Eight-oh-two. Who's calling, so I can announce you?"

"No need to, Sis. I'm just bringin' somethin' he forgot at the school las' night."

"Oh. You from the Center?"

"Yeah. I just telephoned him a little while ago. He's expectin' me."

"Okay. Elevator's to the left in the corridor. Eight-oh-two."

"Thanks. I'll find it."

On the eighth floor, Duke found 802 and rang the bell. He rang it four times before he heard the thump of steps coming toward him. Then the door opened and he saw Lyle Emerson's face forming a questioning frown. The door opened wider and Duke saw the crutches under Lyle's armpits and stared at the trouser leg pinned up just below the hip.

"You're—Elizabeth's brother, aren't you?" Lyle said. "I saw you at police headquarters with your father—"

"Yeah, that's right. C'n I come in f'just a minute?"

"Of course. Is Elizabeth all right?"

"She's all right."

Duke closed the door behind him and followed Lyle into the living room. Lyle turned and nodded toward the sofa. "Sit down. Duke, isn't it?"

Hat in hand, Duke remained standing. "What I got to say, it take only a minute. You sit down, rest yourself." Lyle eased himself into his leather chair and leaned the crutches against it.

"What can I do for you, Duke?" he asked.

"I'll tell you, white man." Lyle stiffened at the last two venom-infected words. "Like you said, I'm Elizabeth's brother. I want you to know just one thing. We don't want her to have no white friends—"

"Just a minute—"

"Don' argue with me, white man. I'm tellin' you just one more time an' no more. I ever find out you hangin' aroun' my sister, I'm goin'a look you up an' break you in little pieces. I don' want to hurt no cripple, else I'd do it right now, so you gettin' off easy, with just a warnin'. Keep away from Elizabeth, you understan' me?"

Lyle stared up at Duke Shackleford, tasting defeat, the stinging tears of futile anger in his eyes. Duke towered over him, lithe, strong, whole; and he knew he was no match for the incensed fighter. "Duke," he said, "there isn't anything, nor has there been anything, between Elizabeth and me in the way you mean it. We both teach at the Center—"

Duke waved the explanation aside without any change of expression. "Don' make no diff'rence what you say, Emerson. You stay clear of my sister, else I'll come after you. Ain't no place you c'n hide from me, man, an' I got friends who'll be glad to keep an eye on you. That's it, so you be goddam careful." Duke turned then, went quickly to the door. He paused for a moment and looked back, about to speak, then changed his mind and went out.

Lyle's first thought was for Elizabeth. Rather than use the house phone on the table beside him, he went to the bedroom to use the direct outside line and dialed the Shackleford number, hoping Elizabeth would answer, and was relieved when he heard her soft "Hello."

"Elizabeth—"

"Yes. Who is it, please?"

"Lyle. Are you all right?"

The strange tone of his voice alarmed her. "Yes, of course. Why?"

"I—this thing hasn't caused you any difficulty, has it? At home, I mean."

"Difficulty? No. Some concern, of course, but no difficulty. Why? What is it? Why are you asking?"

"I—ah—nothing—"

"Tell me," Elizabeth insisted. "I know there must be a reason. You sound—"

"Elizabeth, I just had a caller. Your brother—"

"What!"

Lyle took note that she hadn't mentioned his name, or Duke's, obviously because some member of her family was within hearing. While he paused, he heard her voice, now in an incisive whisper. "What happened? Tell me—"

"Nothing happened. Don't be alarmed."

"Then what did he do, accuse you—us—threaten you?"

"Something of the sort. I don't want to—all I wanted was to be sure you were all right."

"Yes. Yes, I am." A pause, then, "I want to know more about it but I can't talk any more. Can I call you later, perhaps meet you somewhere?"

"Later. Call me between nine and nine-thirty."

"Between 9:00 and 9:30." She hung up. Lyle at once dialed Corey's number.

592

"Corey, can I have a raincheck on our dinner? My leg is bothering hell out of me. I've just taken a sedative and want to turn in early."

Corey sounded genuinely regretful. "Sure, Lyle. I hope it feels better by morning."

At a few minutes past nine o'clock, the bedroom telephone rang and Lyle was already there, waiting. It was Elizabeth, calling from a pay phone in the lobby of the Goldfield Theater in West Laurelton. She planned to take a bus across the bridge and would get off at Latham Drive and Carteret Street in a quiet residential area. Lyle said he would go there at once and park just behind the bus stop.

The bus reached Latham and Carteret at 9:30. Elizabeth, wearing a dark blue raincoat with a hood that covered most of her face, got off, came to his car at once and got in. Lyle had started the motor when he saw her get off the bus and now pulled away quickly.

"Where can we go?" she asked.

"My apartment?"

"No, please. It may not be safe."

"Then—we'll keep driving. Out toward Riverton."

The Riverton highway was only four blocks away, the traffic exceptionally light in the steady rain. When they were finally on it, Elizabeth said, "Tell me about Duke. What did he say?"

"It wasn't very pleasant. He assumed that there was *something,* he called it, between us, and warned me to stay away from you. I tried to explain that it was all a coincidence, both of us teaching at the Center, but he wasn't in any mood to listen."

"Lyle, are you worried?"

"Only for you."

"He can be dangerous."

"That doesn't bother me."

"He could hurt you. Badly."

"He could do that to you as well. Easier—"

"He wouldn't hurt me, Lyle."

"Don't be too sure of that."

"It's you I'm worried about."

"Or what would happen to him?"

"Partly. Mostly, it's you—"

"Because of—" With his right hand, he touched his thigh.

"No, Lyle, not because of that. Duke is a professional fighter, made his living with his fists. He could even—"

"Then he probably knows that the law considers his hands to be deadly weapons and that an attack on another person is a felony assault."

593

"What if he didn't think about that in time?"

"Elizabeth, please don't worry about me. I'm only concerned about what he might do to you."

She laughed then, nervously. "That's funny. Here we are, not concerned for ourselves, only for each other."

For a few moments, he said nothing. "Lyle?"

"What?"

"What are you thinking?"

"You may not like it."

"Tell me. Please."

"I was thinking that in a way, perhaps Duke is right."

"About what?"

"That there is something between us, something we can't deny no matter how much we try."

Elizabeth did not reply. "Is there?" Lyle asked.

"I don't know," she said slowly. "Maybe. Maybe there is."

"I've felt it stronger than ever since last night."

"It can't be, Lyle. It can't. It's just too—crazy," she protested.

"Why can't it be? We're the same two human beings we were last night, whether you'll admit it or not. Why not? Color can't determine—"

"Don't, Lyle."

"Elizabeth, can you be honest?"

"I—think so."

"You're unwilling to admit that there's something between us. I know there is. Otherwise, we wouldn't be here together now, like this, concerned for each other's safety. You wouldn't have come to my apartment last night. You can't possibly deny there is 'something' between us, can you?"

"All right, suppose I do admit it. What does *something* mean? What does it amount to?"

"As much as we'll allow it to mean or amount to."

"I can't—couldn't—"

"Then what is it with you, pity?"

"Pity? Oh, no, Lyle. I've told you. It hasn't anything to do with your leg. You're a lot more sensitive about it than I am, naturally. I don't even think of it. I swear that whatever it is, it isn't pity."

"Can you accept the word 'love,' or are you afraid?"

"Don't say it, Lyle. You know nothing can come of it."

"Yes. If we steel ourselves against it, deny its existence, fight it, we might even manage to keep it from happening."

"Please, please, you're looking at it from your own point of view only."

"The white man who is trying to become a Negro?"

"I'm sorry I said that to you. It wasn't fair."

"But you believe it, don't you?"

Again she fell silent. Up ahead, Lyle saw a yellow light flashing, indicating a crossroad. Route 112. He braked the car gently and made a right turn into it.

"Where are we going?" Elizabeth asked.

"Nowhere. I want to find some place to turn around so I can take you back to town."

"Are you that angry with me?"

"No, not angry, Elizabeth."

"Then disappointed."

"No—perhaps—"

He saw a side road coming up, turned into it and stopped. Before he could shift into reverse, Elizabeth said, "Go ahead. See if there's a place where we can stop and talk."

Half a mile down the narrow road, Lyle turned off onto a piece of flat, grassy ground that was partially protected by a small grove of trees. He braked the car to a stop and turned the lights off, lowered his window a few inches to clear the trapped air from the car. The smell of wet pines carried him back to his boyhood, carefree days and long-ago summer rains when he thought of little more than finding some means to idle the hours away; swimming, fishing, boating, prowling the woods, reading, eating, the movies, a girl. Now he had a girl. More girl than any he had ever known, Jill included. No rebound this. The real thing, with a terrible urgency to hold her, possess her, forever.

He turned and she was facing him, hardly more than a shadow, moving into his arms. He felt her arm on his shoulder, her hand around his neck, touching his cheek, drawing him closer. Then her lips were impressed upon his, soft, warm and gentle, and he kissed her firmly, then her cheek, throat, her lips again. She drew back after a few moments and said, "Lyle—"

"What?"

"If you want to—"

"Not this way, Elizabeth. Not to be kind. You don't owe me anything."

"I'm not paying a debt, Lyle. I'm here and I'm willing."

"That's not the way it should be. Willing. It sounds like a sacrifice of some kind."

Puzzled. "I don't understand. I don't know what you want—"

"Can you say 'I love you'?"

"Would you want me to say it if I didn't honestly feel it?"

"Then that's the answer."

"That's the answer if you want to accept it as an answer."

Lyle didn't say anything and Elizabeth drew back a few inches. "Now I feel ashamed," she said.

"Don't be. You've nothing to be ashamed about. A kiss—"

"It was more than a kiss."

"But not for love."

"Lyle, I don't *know*. I wanted to, but I—maybe I don't know love the way you do."

She began to cry and he took her into his arms. "Don't, Elizabeth. There's nothing to cry over. Maybe I don't know what it is, either, but I can't cheapen it, or us, by trying to convince you if you don't really feel it."

"Lyle—I'm so embarrassed—"

"Don't be. You're honest and that's probably best for both of us until you know for sure. Let's get you back to town now."

"What time is it?"

He turned the dashlight on. "Five minutes past ten."

"The Goldfield show doesn't break until after eleven-thirty. That's where I'm supposed to be."

"Elizabeth—"

"What?"

"Say it and mean it. I love you. Say it. If you can't, let's get out of here. I'll take you back—"

She said it quickly. "I love you, Lyle. It's hopeless, but I love you."

For a moment, he stared at her, in the direction of her face, unable to distinguish her features in the darkness, sensing them, touching her, moving from behind the wheel toward her, embracing her hungrily, drawing her closer to him, caressing and kissing her. Unmindful of the ache in his stump and upper leg, one hand on her thigh, touching her breast. Then the moments of silent, almost furtive, adjustment to each other, the fear of exposing the leather harness to her touch, the edges of the obscenity of the artificial leg. He squirmed, tortured by the unseen *thing*.

"Let me help you, Lyle."

He lay back and allowed her to accommodate herself to his position. Suddenly, with electrifying awareness, she was there, over him, blending them into one being, and he forgot everything else on earth but Elizabeth, her warmth, inside and out, the passion and drive of her body against his own, her lips on his, her gentle utterances, giving, receiving, quickening, driving. And then dissolving into his arms, weeping, feeling the tears on her cheeks, lingering.

"Oh, Lyle, Lyle—"

"Darling—"

"I feel—"

Apprehensively, "What, darling?"

"Exhausted. Wonderful."

He fondled her breasts, kissing them. "You are wonderful," he said. "I love you, Elizabeth."

"I'm cold now." She raised herself from him and squirmed into her panties, then pulled her dress down and drew the raincoat around herself, readjusted herself on his lap.

"Lyle—"

"Let's don't talk for a while."

"I've got to say this. We've done it, but it's still hopeless, isn't it?"

"Not if we don't want it to be. There are other places. We'll get out of here, get married. There are states where the law will allow us to marry and live."

"Lyle, it's a dream, a crazy dream."

"Not if you're willing."

"We'll think about it."

"Don't put it to one side. Let's talk about it now."

"Right now? This very minute?"

"This very minute, I'd like to—"

"That's what I was thinking." She kissed him and it was beginning all over again.

"What time is it now?"

The dashboard light came on. "Eleven."

"If we leave now I can make it to the Goldfield in time."

"I'll drive you there."

"No. I can get the bus where you picked me up."

He started the car, eased it back into the narrow road, then into Route 112 and south toward Laurelton. Near the bus stop, he parked. "Elizabeth, you're not going to let Duke frighten you, are you?"

"He won't scare me away from the Center, if that's what you mean."

"We'll work something out."

"I don't know. Back there it seemed possible. Here—"

"If we don't, what happened back there will become cheap. Nothing. A white man who took an unfair advantage of a colored girl."

"I know it wasn't that, Lyle."

597

"I love you, Elizabeth. Remember that. Keep on remembering it."

She was saved from answering by the approach of a pair of bright headlights from the east. "My bus," she said. He leaned toward her. She kissed him quickly, got out of the car and hurried to the bus stop, her hood covering her head and face. He waited, saw her get on, drop her fare in the box and look in his direction. Then she was gone.

CHAPTER IV

1

By Sunday morning the intensity of the rain that had begun falling on Friday night had lessened, but continued in heavy gusts of drizzle before the cold wind that had driven it down from Canada. An icy tinge in the air awakened Laurelton to the need to check its furnaces, fireplaces, wood- and kerosene-burning stoves, neglected chimneys and clogged rainspouts. Mothers and daughters burrowed into closets, wardrobes and trunks to dig out the family's heavier clothing and prepared their lighter garments for winter storage.

At the Nigerian Motel, Dr. Rhama and Brother Leonard entertained Duke Shackleford and eight of Duke's followers at breakfast. Luke Tolbert, Odie Bilson, Jake Runnels, Dave Sharkey, Booker Dance, Eli Buller, Mace Bodie and Jim Cuddy. When the meal was finished, all retired to Dr. Rhama's cottage where Luke Tolbert and Booker Dance reported in detail on the driver walkouts at Ainslee Farm Dairy and Cloverland Bakeries.

"Don' look like it doin' much good," Luke said disappointedly. "When the milk didn' show up at the stores, they send their own trucks an' cars over to pick it up. We try to stop 'em, but they jus' run right on through us. Then the cops come an' makin' us get to one side an' let everybody through. Home deliveries the same. People come to the dairy to load up an' cuss us out."

Booker's experience was similar. "All's we got now is a bunch of drivers with no jobs to go to tomorrow mornin'. Colored people come by to buy their baked goods, they no better'n the whites, cuss us out for makin' trouble for 'em. Mist' Manley tellin' us we all fired, goin'a have a whole new white crew come Monday mornin'. Las' night when they shut down, platform boss tellin' us they sold more bread, cake, buns an' doughnuts than they ever sold on a reg'lar Sat'dy. We out there cold an' wet, wasn't one driver didn' want to ask for his job back and promise not to strike no more. Platform boss say, Nothin' doin'. You strike, you stay struck."

Duke, standing at the window looking out at the rain, turned around and said, "Like I been sayin', you can't get nowheres thataway. You got to do somethin' to hit 'em in the face to wake 'em up. A few busted windows, a couple little strikes, they don't ruffle nobody much. What we got to do, we got to wake everybody up, white man, black man, bring 'em face to face with one another, let 'em see who they enemy is."

Dr. Rhama was nodding, smiling. "You're right, Brother Duke," he said, "but we've got to lead up to it, let it come by a natural progression of actions and awaken the whole community to the fact that the sleeping black man is waking up and sharpening his claws. I agree that the broken windows, the Arcadia demonstration, the two strikes are only tokens, but the white man now realizes that the long, hot summer doesn't end when the outside temperatures drop, that he faces a long winter of continued disruption from his Negro brothers. What we're doing is putting him on notice that there's more to come. Brother Leonard?"

Brother Leonard was opening one of a dozen large cartons, from which he removed a handful of black cardboard fezzes, cheaper models of those he and Dr. Rhama wore. He handed one to each man present, then held one up by its black tassel for all to see.

"This is our symbol," Brother Leonard said. "Without a single spoken word, it tells any man who sees it that it represents Black Power. Wherever we have gone, these caps, worn by black men and women and children, on the streets, in schools, speak out louder than words. They say the one thing the white man fears more than anything else. They say, 'We are unified and in unity there is strength. Black strength. Black Power.' In these cartons there are enough fezzes to put on the head of every Negro boy, girl, man and woman in West and South Laurelton. Your first job will be to distribute them and encourage the people to wear them. Don't hold them in your hands, gentlemen, put them on your heads where they belong."

Duke and the others put the fezzes on.

"Look around you now and see if you don't get the message," Brother Leonard said.

The men looked around at each other and slowly, their faces lighted up in self-conscious grins. Jim Cuddy said, "I be damned!"

Dr. Rhama's face broke into a smile. "You see? They give you the same feeling of unity a uniform gives a policeman or a soldier. Wear it, see it worn by others, and you *belong* to something, together. You're not alone any longer, but part of an organization, fighting for the same things."

Duke said, "What about the schools, people on the job? White people won't let 'em wear these things."

"Maybe not," Brother Leonard said, "but by the time they decide, the fezzes will have been seen. The children in schools will be ordered to take them off. So will the workers in white stores and plants. But nobody can stop them from wearing them *to* school, *to* work, *after* school and *after* work, can they? Hand them out. Make it a disgrace *not* to wear a black fez on the streets. Let the white police, the white authority see them. Let them be reminded every day and every night that the black man is unified, waiting to strike at him."

Dr. Rhama took over now. "The white man has lived with that fear ever since the beginning of the slavery system he imposed on the black man. On his plantations, where the slaves outnumbered the white owners and overseers, he rode his lands, ate his meals, entertained his friends, and slept behind locked doors in fear of an uprising. Trouble was, only a few slaves knew this and those who knew it couldn't convince the others. There was no unity then, there is no total unity today.

"Some day, there will be. Here, in Central and South America, in Africa, Asia, India, around the world, all men of color will unite, and when they do, they will learn that they outnumber the white men. They will rise up then and crush him, make him the slave of the majority. Then the black man will emerge and take his rightful place in the world.

"This fez—" he held his own up high for all to see—"is the talisman, the amulet, the symbol of our superiority. By itself, it is a piece of black cardboard with a black tassel, which costs only a few cents. Worn by hundreds of millions of nonwhites, it represents an army of destruction to White Supremacy.

"The white man has hidden behind white hoods and robes. We don't need that. We don't need to burn crosses. All we need is for the black man to wear this symbol on his head proudly, where everybody can see it and look into his determined eyes."

"So we wear the fez," Duke said. "What comes next?"

Dr. Rhama smiled wisely, his fingers tented piously on his stomach. "We wear the fez," he replied. "Later, there will be an incident, and it will be an important one."

"You mean a riot?" Duke asked.

"A riot that will wake everybody up, white *and* black."

"So we burn an' smash up a few stores an' buildings. Question is, what comes of it?"

Dr. Rhama stood up and crossed the room to face Duke directly. The smile evaporated and his eyes glittered. "All right, Duke, I'll tell you what comes next. Once Whitey is aware of us, and what we can do to him, we make our demands. *Full desegregation! White jobs for equal pay NOW! Fifty black cops on the force, all working among the black community! Thirty black firemen! Better black schools! Black teachers! Doctors! Lawyers! Judges! City councilmen! County supervisors! Black tax money to build homes, factories and stores for black people!* What we want here, and everywhere, is *black in its correct percentages! Black towns! Black cities! And some day, a whole Black State! For blacks, with blacks, by blacks!* Does that answer your question?"

Duke was taken aback by the fierce sincerity of Dr. Rhama, pounding his fist as he emphasized each point. "Does it?" he asked again.

"It does."

Dr. Rhama smiled again. "Then let's do it one step at a time, but do it well. First, the fez. We'll make it a moral offense for any black man, woman or child *not* to wear it, proudly, like a crown. The symbol of black unity—"

2

The rain that had dampened the spirits of most churchgoers that morning did little to discourage the normal patronage at Webster's, where Laurelton came to pick up the Sunday editions of the Atlanta *Journal-Constitution* and other out-of-town papers which had been shipped in by plane, train, bus and truck. This was a Sunday morning ritual; the New York, Philadelphia, Baltimore, Washington, Richmond and New Orleans papers, a cup of coffee, even breakfast, at Blanchard's Cafeteria, pleasant small talk with friends, neighbors and business acquaintances.

Others, nonregulars, who sniffed at the chilly air with nostalgia for their duck blinds and the woods, drifted into Blanchard's from Willard's Hardware laden with boxes of shotgun shells and rifle cartridges, cans of oil, bottles of solvent, packages of cleaning patches, and newly purchased hunting licenses.

The talk eventually shifted to the inconvenience created by the milk and bread strike which had been duly reported in the morning *Herald,* and comments leaped from table to table. When Adam Cameron came in, dressed as most were in plaid shirt, peaked hunting cap, twill trousers, jacket and short boots, almost everyone had a question for him. He moved along the service counter, loaded orange juice, eggs, bacon, a roll and coffee on his tray and took his place at a large round table.

"How about it, Ad? What's with this damn' silly strike?" Sime Price asked.

"Nothing to it, Sime. Ainslee and Cloverland will be back on regular home and store deliveries in the morning with new crews."

"What the hell's going on?" Howard Wyatt demanded. "They pullin' that old boycott crap on us like they did a few years ago?"

"I don't know, Howie," Ad replied. "We couldn't seem to run it down anywhere. One thing for sure, Amos Hart isn't behind it. Probably just an unorganized wildcat thing."

"Unorganized, my ass," Jim Stedman retorted angrily. "My brother tells me there's a rumor this Dr. Rhama and his Black Fezzes are in town." Stedman's brother, Arnie, was a sergeant at the 12th Precinct in Angeltown. "There's talk going around over there that he's going to pull all the switches and put on a show here like he did down in Atlanta."

"What about it, Ad?" Ed Altshuler asked.

"We know he's in town, Ed, but I haven't seen him or talked with anyone who has. Pete LaSalle tells me that Dr. Rhama and one of his aides, a Brother Leonard, came to town the other day. That's all I know."

"And we had two strikes pulled yesterday."

"I wouldn't tie those in with him. Rhama goes in for bigger, better organized action. You'll know more about him if, suddenly, you see a lot of Negroes walking around wearing those black fezzes he hands out free, his trademark."

"I've seen some of 'em already, over on the other side of the bridge," someone added.

"Tell you," Stedman said, "the first one I see, I knock off—"

"That's exactly what Rhama wants you to do, Jim," Adam said, "give him all the reason he needs to work both sides up against each other."

"Well, goddam it, Ad, you think we ought to let him walk in and stir the people up that way?"

"Jim, if you want to know what and how I think, all you have to do is read the editorial page of the *Herald*."

Ben Coster leaned over from the next table. "Sure, all

you'll find out is, the *Herald* wants us to let 'em move in next to us and give 'em instant good manners, culture, cleanliness and brains. Also, we ought to give 'em our jobs."

"Now that's pretty damned silly, Ben, and you know it," Ad replied, "or else you're reading some other paper."

"Well, you and your daddy are always standing up for 'em."

"Only when they're right, never when they're wrong."

"Who's to say?"

"It's a matter of decency and judgment."

"Well, if it's mine against yours, that makes us even, don't it? Except that I haven't got a newspaper to make my opinions known."

"The *Herald* will publish any letter you will sign and send us, Ben," Adam said with a smile. "Just keep it down under five thousand words and edit out the cuss words."

A small group had drawn chairs around the table, interested in the exchange. From among the standees, Frank Everts said, "The whole damned thing is like cancer. It all began in the army, back in Korea, puttin' niggers in the same barracks and messhalls with white men. You-all seen what happened when they come home again, wantin' our jobs, workin' alongside of white folks, their kids goin' to our white schools, ridin' anywhere on buses. Now they want to move into our neighborhoods—"

"Oh, knock it off, Frank," Ad said. "What they want is decent treatment, decent schools, decent jobs and decent housing. If they had that, it wouldn't make any difference what part of town they lived in, and I'm not so sure they'd want you or any of us for neighbors."

"Where else they goin'a get it except take it away from us?" Randy Hammersmith asked, his voice indignant.

"Randy, I don't want to start World War III here in Blanchard's. I think that any reasonable man knows what the problems are and when we begin recognizing them, we'll start ironing them out."

"This strike yesterday, was that reasonable?" Frank Everts asked. "Ainslee and Cloverland used to have all-white drivers a few years ago. Then somebody pressured them to put a couple of niggers on. First thing you know, it was all nigger."

"Frank, that's only one side of the story. What happened was the white drivers refused to stay on and walked off the job. Ainslee and Cloverland had to replace them with Negroes. Even at that, the Negroes were drawing twelve dollars a week less than the white drivers for the same job,

604

same hours. *That* is yesterday's strike issue. What would you have done?"

"I'm not a nigger, Ad, don't ask me what a nigger would do, for Christ's sake," Everts replied hotly.

Someone laughed and Everts turned around to face him. "What the hell are you laughing about, Jody? Didn't I see you in the crowd tryin' to bust up the school integration thing?"

Jody Clark said, "Difference between us, Frank, I learned a hell of a lot since then. People said, 'Let 'em in white schools, they'll take 'em over.' We let 'em in, but they didn't. Back in slave times, people said, 'Free the niggers, they'll take us over.' They set 'em free, but the South never got taken over or died. Now they're sayin' 'Treat 'em like equals, they'll take us over.' Hell, I say, if they do, it'll be because we deserve it."

Don Staley eyed Jody Clark coldly. "What'll you think will happen to your job if I tell Bob Goodrich what you just said here?"

"Go ahead and tell him, Don. If Bob Goodrich fires me for saying what I think, I don't want to work for him. But I think I know Bob a little better'n you do. When I said I learned a lot since that school integration ruckus, I did most of my learnin' from Bob, so screw you, friend."

Adam Cameron sipped the last of his coffee. He stood up and said, "Gentlemen, peace." And went out.

3

Reverend Amos Hart's congregation numbered less than 100 that morning, about 80 who were middle- and old-aged, with a sprinkling of small children, those of their sons and daughters. There were very few in the African Zion Baptist Church between the ages of 14 and 30. And this was duly noted by Amos Hart. The church normally seated 400, with movable benches for another 250 if the occasion demanded, and although the rain kept many away, Hart knew that even if the day had been bright, cool and clear, not more than another 50 or 75 would have come.

On his way to the pulpit, he stopped to talk to Sam and Lutie Shackleford. "I heard about your Elizabeth, Sister Lutie, Brother Sam. I hope her injury was slight."

"Yes, Reverend," Lutie replied, "but the marks still show some, so—"

"I understand. I'd hoped to see your son Duke."

Sam muttered, "Don't count on him, Reverend. He got other plans for reachin' God."

"Well, deacon, we'll keep trying. If Duke finds a better way than ours, I wish you'd have him come around and tell me what it is."

"Seems like the more we try, the more we lose," Sam replied.

Hart clamped Shackleford's shoulder and smiled. "Faith, deacon. It has moved mountains. If we have enough faith, we may even move a few hearts."

"Amen," Sam and Lutie said together.

When the service was over Amos Hart looked up over the edge of the lectern. Only two elderly couples had entered the church since he had begun the service. He shuffled a few notes in his hands, put them aside and began the sermon. His audience squirmed into more comfortable positions, restless with expectancy, knowing he would touch on the vandalism and strike incidents, wondering how deeply he would go into the subjects. As usual, Hart smiled and began in a light vein; and as usual, it was expected that he would warm up to his intended message, filling the near-empty hall with his rich, booming voice.

"I welcome you brave Baptists who have courageously defied the elements to come and listen to the word of God. In weather like this, I know there are no members of this congregation idling on golf courses, dallying over fishing poles or enjoying the sunshine and fresh air at picnics or in the woods, and since it has never been my practice to belabor the faithful for the absence of their lagging brethren, I thank and bless those present for their attendance."

He paused for a moment while his audience settled down for what would come next; waiting, casting benign eyes over each other's faces.

"I hear murmurs of discontent," Hart continued, "and the rumblings of unrest among us. I have seen with my own eyes the wanton, senseless destruction of the property of our white neighbors across the bridge, and the retaliation visited upon us by white youths seeking vengeance. And I ask you: what profit has black gained from white; or white from black, in an exchange of vandalism that might have caused death as well? Who has gained the most, lost the most, by what has happened during the past week?

"We have known this state of affairs before, and it is as though we are watching actors replaying their parts, but the actors this time are youngsters who are acting in hatred, in lust. In that other time a few years ago, we marched, demonstrated and sat in to gain a rightful place in society, the white man's society, if you please. We were beaten, spat upon, cursed. We were vilified and jailed, but we won some of our battles with honor. We won a place for our children in white schools, the right to the seat of our choice in buses, the right to eat in some restaurants we could not enter before except as janitors or dishwashers. In our City Hall and County Building, no longer are all the employees white. On our police department rolls are a representative number of our sons. The fire department has not yet allowed one of us to join its ranks, but resistance is weakening under pressure.

"That, brothers and sisters, is Progress. It is not enough, but it is Progress we have not seen in over a full century."

Hart paused to sip some water. "There are those who say we are moving too slowly, and perhaps they are right. If we are making haste slowly, it is because white eyes and white minds react slowly to the right of ALL men to be equal. And yet, there was a time when we had the Power. Did you know that, brothers and sisters? Let me tell you about a bit of history few of you know.

"Once in this Southland of ours, we tasted and knew Power. Black Power. Yes. It was after the War Between the States, and Negroes were seated in State Legislatures throughout the whole South, with the legal right to enact laws, with the police powers to enforce them. The courts of the land and the military backed us, encouraged us, and we were the majority voice.

"Did you know that, my brothers and sisters? Did your parents or grandparents ever tell you of those days of Negro power and glory in the white man's land?"

There was silence and more shifting of bodies. "Oh, yes," Hart went on, "it is true, believe me. *We had the Power!* We held in our hands the power the white man held before we were freed! The power he holds today! The power our young people are shouting for today. *Black Power!*

"Yes. We had it and we threw it away. Lost it because we had no leaders or educators to teach us, guide us to use it wisely. Lost it because we were too ignorant, illiterate, ill-prepared to know what to do with it.

"And so, we ran wild with our power, searching for ways to capitalize on it for personal gain. We confiscated the white man's lands and houses, taxed him into poverty, seeking revenge. An eye for an eye, the Bible tells us, but we wanted two eyes for one. We mixed hate into our power, revenge into our new strength. We abused it. And all we proved was that we were no better, no wiser, no more charitable than the men we knew to be evil, unwise, and uncharitable. We took our vengeance happily, yes, and there was black joy in the land with our black power.

"But we know, don't we, that he who takes his own revenge will himself come to know the vengeance of another. And we did. We lost that power and have been trying to win it back for a hundred years, and I pray that when we win it this time, however little, however great, we will have the wisdom to keep it and build upon it.

"I know as well as you that what we have gained today *is not enough,* that we are far from sharing equality with the white man, that we must have more. But we have got to get it by making the people who withhold it from us see the wisdom and reasonableness of our right to have it.

"During the past week, we have seen again that senseless violence is not the answer. Attack and counterattack is ignorance, and promotes wars neither side wins. Yet, it was our side that started a self-destroying war. Our sons, brothers and sisters. I can't name them for you, but they were Negro boys who vandalized white property. And I ask you: If this is a sample of how we hope to win our rights, an example of what is called Black Power, can we expect to win more, or will we lose what we have already gained? If it is, hear my voice and remember that the Negro lost his power a hundred years ago because he got too much too soon and wasn't prepared to understand its wonderful uses.

"Like our absentees, I know I am belaboring the wrong people. Those vandals, those demonstrators, are not in this House of God to hear my voice. In fact, I see none of those of that age here this morning. You are their parents and grandparents, and I ask you: Where are your children, those who need God and God's guidance most? Sleeping away the hours they lost last night in poolrooms and bars and beer taverns and pleasure palaces? Where are their bright, intelligent faces this morning, these stalwart young men and women who want the power and equality they believe belongs to them?

"Brothers, sisters, we need them to hear the words they need most to hear. A short while back, three of our sons, all under seventeen years of age, were trapped by police in the act of robbing a merchant. They couldn't deny the act, so they yelled, 'Police brutality!' hoping the false charge would create sympathy for them. Dr. Betts, who sits among you, and I saw the three boys that same morning, examined them and found no evidence to back up their claims. So, in addition to becoming robbers at the tender ages of fourteen, sixteen and seventeen, they have become conscious, practiced liars. And my question is: Where were you when they

608

needed you most? Can you justly blame the church, the schools, the police for the behavior of your children?

"These children talk of Black Power, of a force to 'take over' and I say that if they take over by force, they will meet the same kind of force, with violence and death and the loss of the compassionate who know our plight and want to help us.

"Schools! Education! Training! Jobs! Understanding! Those needs come first and they are close at hand. The need for Negro doctors, nurses, lawyers, writers, scientists, businessmen and political leaders to guide them toward their futures! Today! Now!"

They were shaken and Amos Hart knew it, knew that he could not press harder without losing them. He gave them a moment to let his words sink in, then, with kindliness in his voice, he said, "And now, please rise for the benediction—"

4

Drew came down to breakfast for the first time since Anderson's funeral. It was 10:15 and Theodore was still at the table with the Sunday *Herald* and an after-breakfast cup of coffee. He stood when she entered and said, "Good morning, Drew."

"Good morning, Father," she responded. "It's nice to see some rain for a change, isn't it?"

"I'm sure everyone has been looking forward to it."

She sat down, aware that neither was unable to continue with small talk. The last conversation they had had together was the lengthiest either had known and in the serious vein of the future of the Company; anything less would now seem vapid. Sue-Ann came in with a large glass of orange juice bedded in crushed ice and waited for Drew to order her breakfast. "Nothing else, Sue-Ann," Drew said. "I'll have some coffee and toast with this."

Sue-Ann went out. Theodore poured a cup of coffee for Drew and passed it to her, then folded the paper and stood up. "I'll be in your grandfather's study when you've finished, Drew. May I see you for a few minutes?"

"Of course."

For some reason, his use of the expression "your grandfather's study" reechoed in her mind and she saw it as a reflection of Theodore's lack of attachment for, or sense of belonging to, anything that had been left behind by Anderson: Brookhill, the Company, even Laurelton. It saddened her to think that he would be able to leave everything Gran had built and loved so much and never look back in regret.

And what about me? she thought. Bruce and I were born in this house, grew up here. Gran, Grandmother Cleo and Bruce are still here, and how can I ever leave them? No matter what has happened or will happen, I'm still as much a part of it as it is of me.

Of one thing she was certain: Theodore had come to a decision and she would learn what it was within a very short time.

She scanned the front page headlines with little interest, nibbled at her toast and drank the hot black coffee. Leona bustled in to see if she could change Drew's mind about breakfast, but Drew insisted she had had enough, remembered to tell her that Corey would be coming by later for a late lunch or early dinner, or a combination of both, and was rewarded with a smile of approval.

When she was finished, she went directly to Gran's study where she found Theodore at the scarred old desk that had been Anderson's first, a scattering of papers before him, Gran's safe open. To one side stood a long-forgotten silver jewel chest that had once belonged to Cleo, and it evoked memories of the distant past, knowing what it contained.

Theodore looked up when she entered the room. "Ah, Drew. Sit down, please. Here." She sat in the worn leather chair nearest the desk and Theodore pointed to the chest. "I've been going over some personal papers and records in your grandfather's safe, Drew. I ran across your grandmother's—"

"I remember it," Drew said.

"It belongs to you. She left it to you in her will, you know."

"Yes. I'd forgotten about it. I asked Gran to put it away for me and haven't thought of it since."

"It already belongs to you, so it won't be mentioned in your grandfather's will. A few days before he died, he reminded me of it and asked me to be sure you got it."

"Thank you. I think I'll take it now." She went to the desk and stood for a moment, running her fingers over the raised silver figures and flowers. It was locked and Theodore handed her a small envelope with her name scrawled across its face in Gran's bold, angular handwriting. "Have you decided about the Company, Father?" she asked.

Theodore swiveled around in the chair and faced her directly. "That is what I wanted to discuss with you. I had a lengthy talk with Kenneth Armour on Thursday. I think there may be some difficulty."

"In what way?"

"It seems the Intercon people are very determined about wanting to either buy in with enough to give them control, or if we are agreeable, buy us out completely."

"You wouldn't have to do either, would you, unless you wanted to? I mean, they can't force you to sell if you don't want to, can they?"

"There's some possibility they can, Drew. If Intercon can accumulate enough of the outstanding stock to give them more than fifty per cent, they can simply vote that stock to elect their own president and board of directors and run the Company as they see fit. If they can't do that, they might go directly to the stockholders with a cash tender offer, or force us into a proxy fight. Ken Armour made it very clear to me they stand a reasonably good chance to win. A proxy fight would not only be costly to both sides, and very unpleasant, but they are thoroughly experienced and unscrupulous in that sort of thing."

"I don't understand."

"It's rather complicated. Intercon is prepared to publicly level charges of gross mismanagement, citing the fact that the Company has refused to pay an increased dividend despite having accumulated a considerable amount of cash reserves. Also, abuse of Company funds, an unwillingness to modernize our facilities, expand into other fields as many other related companies have been doing. In short, they would hit on our lack of progressiveness. By making these charges and backing them up, they can pick up enough proxies from dissatisfied stockholders to demand sufficient places on the board of directors, name their own president and take over control."

"What right have they to bring such charges against us? This has always been a family-managed company from the very start—"

"Drew, you must understand that the Company is responsible to its stockholders for its conduct, operation, profits and dividends, the prime reason why they buy our stock. Even if Intercon fails to get enough proxies to assume control, the charges and implications will stand and could possibly affect the price of the stock. Even our sales, to some extent."

"Can't we fight them? Buy up proxies the same way they can?"

"I suggested that, but Armour warned me that Intercon may already be well on their way to controlling a majority of the outstanding stock. In which case, any fight we put up would be futile."

"But until you *know* that, there's still a chance, isn't there?"

"A very small one."

"Then what you are suggesting is that we give in to Intercon without even putting up a fight."

"There's an alternative, Drew. If we negotiate amicably there will be no open fight. Certainly, we could come out handsomely as far as the financial—"

"That's not really the point, is it?" Drew said sharply.

"I don't think I understand you."

"You don't want the Company, do you? You'd like to get rid of it, the responsibilities, convert everything to easy cash and be free of it, wouldn't you?"

"Drew—"

"Father, don't play games with me at this stage of my life. I'm not a child. If you decided to put up a fight, you could beat Intercon or anyone else who tried to take the Company away from us. I would put up everything I've got in my own name to help you. The Warren Company is ours, yours and mine, and all you can think of is some easy way to dispose of it so you will be free to run off somewhere again. For God's sake, doesn't the work Gran put into it mean anything to you? Can't you see—?"

Her words broke off abruptly, unable to continue, tears filling her eyes and threatening to spill over.

Theodore sat watching her silently for a moment, his fists clenched tightly. "Father—please—" she added brokenly.

"Does it mean so much to you, Drew?" he asked finally.

"Yes. Yes. It means—everything—to live for—"

"I didn't know you felt so strongly."

"N-not for myself. For—for the memory of Gran, for Bruce, for Grandmother Cleo. They meant for it to be what everybody lives for, to leave some permanent mark behind, a worthwhile memory—"

Theodore pulled himself up from the chair and came to the edge of the desk closest to Drew. He took her hands into his own and said, "Drew, I honestly didn't know—realize—"

"There's so little we know about each other, isn't there, Father, now that there are only two of us left?"

Theodore sighed deeply and sadly. "Drew, do you think—"

She looked up through tear-dimmed eyes. "There must be some way to fight this kind of piracy, isn't there?"

"Perhaps. There's the question of time, but I'm sure we could get expert help. Ken Armour has been inclined to go along with Intercon's offer, but I think I—my attitude—has been largely to blame for that. We could talk to Duncan

612

Collins in New York, bring in a firm of attorneys capable in these matters."

"Then I say, *do it!*" Drew felt a sudden lift in Theodore's willingness to even consider the impending battle. "Father, do it, please. I'd rather go down fighting than simply give up and let them walk in and take over your Company." She placed a deliberate emphasis on those last two words and saw a bright reaction in his eyes. "Grandfather would have fought them. I'm sure Uncle Chase would, too."

"Yes," Theodore said. "I'm sure Chase would be more at home than I in a proxy fight. It's more his way of doing business."

"Then you will call Mr. Collins?"

"Yes. Perhaps I'll arrange to go to New York to see him in person."

Drew was smiling. "I'm sure something will come of it, Father. I know it would make Gran happy if he knew that the Company will remain in family hands. He would be very proud of you."

Theodore smiled grimly in return. "Drew, I—we'll do our best."

"Thank you, Father. I'm sure you will."

When she left the study, Theodore felt all the old doubts again. Chase. Anderson. Cleo. Louise. Bruce. Each, in his way, represented a failure of his own, and he wondered if, at this stage of life, it was all worth the effort. They were all gone now, beyond recall. Only Chase remained. And Drew. He thought of Anderson, whom he had never, somehow, seemed to be able to understand. Or reach. And Cleo, to whom he had once been so close, and the searing torment of the three years he had spent away from her, tramping all over the country because of Anderson's insistence that he follow in Chase's footsteps.

He sat back in the large leather chair and stared across the room, seeing faces that were not there, hearing voices—

"For heaven's sake, Theodore, where have you been, you're so filthy?"

"Playing with Matt and Cora down at the water trough, Mama. We were washing Hungry, their pig."

"Oh, Theodore! I've asked you time and again not to play with those children."

"They're fun, Mama."

"Well, from now on I want you to keep out of the field hands' quarters."

"Then who'll I play with?"

613

"Can't you play with your brother Chase?"

"Chase hates me."

"Chase does not hate you. He's your brother."

"He won't let me play with him. He calls me a little snot-nose. And he's always reading books."

"That's because it's sometimes more fun to read than run out in the fields getting your clothes muddy and torn."

"Mama, I'm too little to read."

"Chase?"

"What do you want?"

"Play with me?"

"Go away, snotnose. Can't you see I'm busy?"

"Chase?"

"What?"

"Why won't you play with me?"

"Because."

"Because why?"

"Because you're a baby and I don't play with babies."

"You're not so big yourself."

"I'm nine years older than you. I don't play with dirty niggers the way you do, and I don't wet my bed. I've got my own pony and saddle—"

"I'm going to tell Papa you said a bad word."

"What word?"

"Nigger."

"You do and I'll whip you. Now go out and play with your nigger friends."

"Theodore—"

"Yes, ma'am."

"Your brother is going off to college this morning. Go say good-bye to him."

"I don't want to."

"Theodore!"

"I don't care, Mama. He doesn't like me and I don't like him and I'm glad he's going. I hope he stays there forever."

"Theodore, Theodore, what are we going to do with you? This is the second letter we've had from the dean about your drinking."

Silence.

"Theodore, if your father were home—"

"I know, Mother. He'd raise holy hell."

"Theodore, please don't swear."

"I'm sorry, Mother."

"Please, darling, can't you be more like Chase? You don't

614

know what you're doing to your life, to those who love you."

"Mother, it's my life. The only reason you're concerned is because Chase is in New York, doing exactly what Father wants him to do. I'm not Chase and I don't want to be like him. He's a war hero and he's in the business. All right. Father doesn't need two of us. He's satisfied with Chase. So are you. Why can't you let me alone?"

"Theodore—"
"Yes, sir."
"For the last time, you got to cut out this damfool drinking and cutting up before it goes too far."
"How far is too far, Father?"
"Don't get smart-alecky with me, boy. Too far is when a young, spoiled brat needs a whiskey bottle to give him the courage to face up to life. You listen to me. Chase or no Chase, you're going to come into the Company some day because you and he are going to own it when I'm gone."
"I don't want to own anything with Chase."
"That'll change when you're out of college, but you can't use a bottle for a crutch. Drinking, gambling, running wild with a lot of tarts and whores. I'm telling you, straighten yourself out or you'll die a drunkard's death in disgrace."
"Like your father did?"
"You dirty little—"

Listening at a sitting room door, overhearing:

"Anderson what are we going to do?"
"Uh—I don't rightly know, Cleo. I can't break through his crazy reasoning. He's a coward and a weakling, can't face up to the simple problems of everyday living."
"Maybe a doctor—"
"Doctor! Hell, I've talked to half a dozen doctors, the best. I even told 'em about my own father. Some just shake their heads and the others talk about heredity or environment, or some other damfool thing. Repressed personality, psycho-something, schizo-something—"
"Do you think he's another Christian Warren, Anderson?"
"God only knows that, Cleo. All we can do is keep trying and hoping. We've tried to give him the best."
"If we'd only remained close to him, both of us, the way you were with Chase."
"Ah, Cleo, who could tell? I was busy running around to get the Company started, put it on its feet—"

615

"It's not your fault, Anderson. Mine, if anybody's. I didn't see it happening. I was sick for so long—"

"Don't be faulting yourself, Cleo honey. He'll be out of college next week, and I'm taking him up to New York, turn him over to Duncan Collins—"

"What about his plans to spend the summer in Europe? Do you think you should force him—"

"The sooner the better. I'm getting tired of giving in to him."

The phone rang, waking him from his reverie. He looked at his watch and saw it was nearly two o'clock. He waited for a few minutes, then picked up the receiver and heard the dial tone and dialed Kenneth Armour's number. Tish answered and told him that Kenneth was in Atlanta and was expected back sometime later that evening. Theodore asked Tish to have Kenneth call the moment he returned, that the matter was very important.

5

Corey arrived shortly after two o'clock. There had been a lull in the rain, falling gently now, but an ominous blanket of dark clouds hung low over the city. Now, the newscasters talked of the rising river and the possibility of some flooding if no break came during the next forty-eight hours.

Drew met him at the door and Sue-Ann took his hat and raincoat. On their way to the smaller sitting room, they met Theodore coming from the study and Corey exchanged a few brief words for a few moments before Theodore left the house.

"Hungry?" Drew asked when they were seated in her small sitting room.

"Not at all. I didn't have breakfast until sometime past noon."

"Then we'll wait. Drink?"

"It's much too early for me, even on a gloomy day like this."

"I'm enjoying it. There's something tranquil about a drowsy day, as though the world's energy were slowing down to take a short rest."

"I'm sure the police would agree with you. I know they must be happy with the end of this heat spell."

It seemed to Corey that their words were forced, clumsily trying to make conversation to bridge the gap that had widened during the past three years, yearning for the casual

616

ease that had once existed between them before Bruce's death. And yet, unlike their more recent meeting, she was making more of an effort.

"Have you heard any more about your project?" Drew asked suddenly, providing him with a subject that could bring some meaning to the conversation.

"Yes. I had a meeting with Wayne and Johnny on Thursday. They had some rough preliminary plans and we discussed it in general terms. They are very definitely interested and are going ahead with the next steps, engineering, topographical studies, surveys—"

He elaborated on the design concept of the planned community development, the homes, services, with the lake as its centerpiece. "Corey, I want to be the first to put in my bid for a lakefront lot," Drew said finally. "As soon as you have a plan, I'd like to choose it, then bring in an architect to design it exactly the way I want it, with a private beach, boat house and dock, tennis courts, stable—it will be such fun to plan something entirely new, for me, with my own ideas! How long before—?"

The sudden heightening in her voice broke the torpid atmosphere, infected Corey with its enthusiasm. "Hold on, Drew. This thing isn't even on the drawing boards yet. All I've seen is a rough pencil sketch, the bare skeleton that has to have the flesh put on before it can be dressed up. Even if everything goes off like clockwork, we couldn't possibly be ready to turn the first shovelful of earth before next summer. There's the big factor to settle first, financing—"

"How much will it take?"

"Just guesswork, the figure runs to between fifteen and twenty million before the first home will be built. There's the dam, piping the water in from the Cottonwood, streets, roads, subdivisions, sewers and other utilities and services—"

"Will it be open to private investors?"

"We haven't gone into that deeply, but there's that possibility."

"Corey, I'd like to be an investor, put up some money or buy stock in it. I think it's a wonderful idea!"

"And I think you should get some good, practical advice before you start flinging money around, particularly into something you know so little about."

Unabashed, smiling, "Well, you're an attorney, aren't you? Suppose I were a client asking for advice?"

"Then I would have to advise you that there is the matter of a conflict of interests added to my own lack of practi-

617

cal experience, and send you to somebody more qualified than I to give you the advice and protection you need."

"Conflict of interests?"

"Yes. Advising a client to invest in a project in which I stand to make a profit, possibly at your expense."

"I'm not what you could call a pauper, Corey. I can afford the risk."

"I'm sure you can, but I don't like to see you substitute hunches, sentiment or feminine intuition for hard, practical dollar-sense, Drew."

"Can't you see? That's exactly what I would be relying on you for."

Corey smiled helplessly. "It's still in the gamble stage, Drew."

"Gran always said that the right time to get into a good thing was at the ground level while others were wasting time making up their minds. If you and Cousin Wayne are willing to gamble, why shouldn't I?"

"Then I'd suggest you talk it over with Wayne before you make your decision. It's possible he and Johnny may want to swing the entire deal through their bank without outside help."

"Then why can't I put up my money through you?"

"I couldn't do that, Drew. I couldn't be responsible—"

"I'm not asking for guarantees, Corey."

"And I wouldn't want to risk your capital."

"I can afford it. You'd do it if—" She broke off suddenly.

"If what?" Corey asked.

"Nothing."

"Say it, Drew."

She turned away from him. "I don't know what I was going to say," she said evasively.

"What made you change your mind so suddenly?"

"Don't, please don't, Corey—"

"Drew, tell me. It had to do with you and me, didn't it? There's an answer I want and I think you were on the verge just then. You can't keep it bottled up forever."

He saw the agony in her eyes before she looked away again. "Corey, it won't do either of us any good—"

He waited but there was nothing more for a few moments. Drew got up and went to the door and pushed a wall-buzzer. A few moments later Sue-Anne appeared. "Yes, ma'am?"

"Bring us—" She turned to Corey. "What would you like to drink, Corey?"

"Bourbon on ice."

"Bring a bottle of bourbon, some brandy and some ice, Sue-Ann."

"Yes, ma'am." Sue-Ann glided out of the room.

"Drew, does it do any good?"

"It helps sometimes."

"When did it start, the drinking, I mean?"

She smiled sadly. "Ages ago."

"After Bruce died?"

"Y-yes—"

"Drew, unless you let it come out, it will kill you. Talk about it, can't you?"

"I talk about it. Nights. When I'm alone—"

"It's not the same. That's brooding, living with it—"

"Corey, please. It's my problem."

"It's *our* problem."

"No. Not any more."

"Drew—" he began, but Sue-Ann was back with the tray of brandy, bourbon and ice. She placed the tray on a table and Drew said, "Thank you, Sue-Ann. We'll help ourselves." She poured bourbon over several ice cubes and the brandy without ice for herself. She drank the brandy quickly, before Corey had more than tasted his drink, then poured another for herself and went to the sofa.

"Drew," Corey said, "you're heading for trouble and I want to help. I feel that I'm partly to blame for whatever it is, that in some way, I failed you."

"No, not you. If anything, I failed myself."

"Then for what we once meant to each other, won't you tell me?"

"I can't. It's—painful. I don't want to hurt you, too."

"But you are hurting me, deeply."

"I'm sorry—"

"Drew, why are you warning me off with all this nonsense about being a different person than the Drew Warren I knew, the girl who once said she loved me?"

"You're only making it more difficult for both of us."

"Are you saying all this for my benefit, to keep from hurting me?"

"I—all right, yes."

She had finished her second drink and went to the table to pour another, drinking it there as if unwilling to return to him.

"Who was he, Drew?" She heard Corey say it and for a startled moment, she couldn't answer. "Who was he?" Corey said again.

"Who was who?"

"The man you can't talk about."

"Corey—" She walked to the window, drink in her hand, and looked across the rainswept tennis courts and swimming pool, to the empty stables and the woods in the background. Then she realized that Corey was standing beside her. "Light a cigarette for me, please?"

He lighted one and handed it to her, knowing now that he had hit on a likely answer, feeling embarrassed to ask or know more. "I'm sorry, Drew," he said. "It isn't any of my business. I'll go now."

"No. You asked the question—"

"Forget it."

"But you won't, will you, now that you know?"

"I don't know anything. It was a shot in the dark, a guess."

"It hit a mark. Shall I tell you about it—him?"

"Only if you want to."

"I don't really know if I do—or if I can tell it so you will understand."

"I promise I'll try."

"Then— Corey, understand that I'm not blaming anyone but myself for what happened. It was all me, in my mind. If you can believe that a temporary—mental aberration—can result in a physical act, a meaningless physical act—" She stubbed her cigarette out and walked back to the sofa and sat down, staring at the last half inch of brandy in her glass, then downed it quickly and put the glass down on the end table. Corey sat down beside her. "Tell me," he said.

She took a deep breath and began again. "It's not a very pretty story."

"Tell me," he repeated. "I want to know."

Drew looked away and said in a low voice, "You know what happened when Bruce died. I was completely out of control, totally disoriented, as though I were living in a state of panic. Emotionally empty and abandoned. All I could feel was anger. And hate. Hate for a girl I'd never even seen. Diana Cross. It was stupid to blame her for Bruce's death when I should have realized it was the other way around.

"I blamed my grandfather and grandmother for things that happened long before I was born. I blamed my father and mother for what happened after I was born. I blamed you—I don't know why—maybe for not having been a closer friend to Bruce. And myself. I honestly felt that if I had been more of a sister to Bruce, more *than* a sister, given him what he wanted from Diana Cross, he would have lived. I know that shocks you, that I was crazy to think that. I can't explain it, only what I felt then.

"After you left to go back to law school, there was only Gran and myself. Father had gone off somewhere, I don't even know where, to get away from it all. Just Gran and me, each of us reproaching himself, both drenched in self-pity and guilt. I felt so alone, as though the whole world had turned its back on me. I couldn't stand it, watching Gran, Gran watching me.

"I went to Dr. Ballard and told him some of what I felt. I suggested going abroad and he agreed it might help to get away. He gave me the name of a doctor in Zurich, a psychiatrist. I went to see the man. He was a kind and gentle old man who really tried to help me, reassure me.

"But I couldn't go on with it, stripping my mind naked before a stranger, having my deepest emotions exposed and labeled with names as though they were packaged—things —items of merchandise with strange names. All it did for me was give me newer doubts and stronger feelings of introversion. The whole thing was a total failure. The more I tried to talk about myself, the less I understood about any of us. All I could think of was that I was alone, taut and tense, trying to push a mountain aside in order to see, feel and breathe like other people. Spending an hour or two at a time in a doctor's office seemed so useless and unrewarding because of the long, lonely hours in between. It lasted only a month.

"I left Zurich without telling the doctor. I remember sending you cards from along the way, going from one place to another, meeting people, moving on, meeting others and suddenly moving again. That became the important thing to do, to keep going, moving. I wrote my mother and went to Rome, hoping she would see me, but when I got there, she was off somewhere with her husband.

"I went back to Paris; it was wintertime and very cold and inhospitable. I was trying to decide where to go next, to some warmer climate. Then I ran into some people I'd met in Montreux. They were planning a yachting cruise to the Mediterranean and the Greek Islands and invited me to come along. The owner of the yacht was an older man, not particularly attractive, but somewhat sad. He had lost his wife less than a year before and hadn't gotten over it. She was a lot younger than he, my own age, his second wife. There was something there, between us, some kind of a sympathetic bond of understanding—or loss—without either of us having discussed it in depth.

"There was the excitement of getting ready for the trip, shopping, more people arriving, and finally we sailed, sixteen passengers, everyone happy to be leaving the Continent behind in a bitterly cold snowstorm.

"We were ashore in Crete one night for dinner at the home of the owner's brother. Even though he had planned the dinner party, both he and I were the only two who seemed out of it. We walked out on it and strolled back to the yacht. He told me about his wife and I told him about Bruce and my own deep sense of loss and guilt. He was very understanding. His own sense of guilt was as deep and strong as my own because his wife had always depended on him so much and he had laughed away her fears when she first developed a lump in her breast.

"Later, when she became more alarmed, he consented to take her to a doctor. She was hospitalized, a biopsy performed, and they told her the breast would have to be removed. That night, she leaped from the hospital window, a suicide.

"He tried to convince me I was wrong in my feelings for Bruce, but I wouldn't allow myself to be convinced. I think I grew hysterical. He took me back to my cabin on the yacht. I don't know how it happened that night, Corey, but —well, it did. When I awoke the next morning, he was gone. I couldn't understand it then, no more than I can explain it now.

"I could tell you that it began and ended there, but I won't lie to you. We stayed on Crete for a week, but the incident didn't recur there. We remained apart until after the cruise was resumed. In Piraeus, I decided to leave the yacht and went to Athens, where I checked into the Gran Bretagne. The next night at dinner, he was there. He had left the party, too, and had been searching for me.

"We stayed in Athens for almost ten days, then flew back to Paris together. He took me to his home, a chateau in the country, and asked me to marry him; and suddenly, I realized that he was searching for a substitute for his wife, just as I had been looking for a substitute for Bruce. I came out of my trance and insisted he drive me into Paris. The next morning I flew to New York.

"It was a difficult period, the worst of all, in New York. I thought I was going out of my mind, unable to think coherently, unable to eat or sleep. That was when the drinking started, then the addiction to sleeping pills.

"There—in New York—was another man, the doctor I went to, who gave me the sleeping pills and later, a stronger drug. That lasted for two or three months until I realized that I had to get out or turn to suicide. One morning, I packed and flew home. I went back to Dr. Ballard for help.

I told him the whole story and begged him to keep it from Gran. Dr. Ballard put me in the hospital for several weeks. He got me over the drug problem, but the drinking part is taking a longer time.

"When I returned to Brookhill, I couldn't remember their faces or anything about them—the man in Paris, the doctor in New York, only what had happened, something I had done that couldn't become undone. If anything, it made me realize that I couldn't have changed what had happened to Bruce. What I'd believed was an abnormal incestuous love, or need, for Bruce, was gone.

"There it is. You wanted me to tell you."

She stopped then and Corey saw the tears that had welled up in her eyes. "Drew—" he began, reaching a hand toward her.

"Corey, please don't do or say anything out of kindness. I don't want that. I don't deserve it. I couldn't stand it." She sat with her hands clasped in her lap, head bowed, and he knew the tears were flowing now. He reached for the handkerchief in his breast pocket and handed it to her. Through small sobs, she said, "When I realized the enormity—of what I had done—it isn't a pretty picture, is it, Corey?"

"Drew—"

She shook her head from side to side, the handkerchief held to her eyes, her words choked. "Don't try to make it easier for me, Corey. Now you can understand why I'm not the same person you knew before."

"Drew, listen. This isn't out of pity or some imagined nobility. Please believe me. You've committed no crime against me or the world. What happened couldn't be helped. You were sick. It's over now. It couldn't happen again in a hundred years. A part of it is my fault. That night we learned about Bruce, I had intended telling you I was in love with you and wanted you to wait until I was out of law school—"

"If you had—"

"I wish now that I had, but I decided at the last moment to wait. I've regretted it ever since. By the time we got to Brookhill and learned about Bruce, it was too late. The question is, what happens now?"

"I don't know, Corey. I've told you what happened, but I can't explain why I let it happen. I'm in no position to ask for anything."

"Drew, stop torturing yourself with this thing that is in the past. Give yourself a chance to forget it."

"And if I do, I mean if that were possible, can I pick up where I was three years ago, as though it hadn't happened?"

"Give yourself a chance to find out."

She smiled wanly. "I've talked more in the last half hour than I have in weeks, months. And I haven't given you the lunch or dinner I promised. Would you forgive me if we made it another time? I'm so tired. I don't think I can make sense."

"Of course, Drew. I'll run along for now and call you tomorrow."

6

It was a little past three when Kenneth Armour returned home and found the two messages to call Theodore Warren. He had gone into the study to make the call when the phone rang and it was Theodore, calling for the third time.

"Ken, I've got to see you at once," he said.

"Can't it wait until morning, Theodore? I've just got back from Atlanta."

"I don't think it can wait another hour, Ken. It's terribly important."

Kenneth hesitated for a moment. "Ken, please. I need your advice."

"Very well, Theodore. Would you like me to come out to Brookhill?"

"No. If it is convenient, I'll come over to your house."

"Very well. I've got something to tell you, too."

Theodore Warren spoke the words with combined shock and awe. "Chase? My brother Chase?"

Kenneth nodded. "Your brother Chase," he replied, then repeated, "Chase." Theodore's melancholy eyes widened with disbelief and his mouth went slack as his hands began to tremble.

"How long have you known this, Ken?"

"Since Friday, when I walked into that motel suite to meet Tom Shelby. I had no idea Chase was any part of this thing, Intercon. When he came in on us, I realized for the first time that Dillingham and Shelby were merely his front men, his corporation stooges."

"My God. After all these years——"

"Yes."

"Ken, I don't know what to say, except to thank you for your loyalty."

"I hardly deserve that, Theodore," Kenneth said frankly. "I was prepared to throw in with Intercon until I learned of Chase's part in it."

624

"I blame myself for that," Theodore said. "I had intimated often enough that I was willing to go along. I would have, except for Chase. Also, I've had a long talk with Drew that changed my mind irrevocably. The thing now is, how can we hope to fight him?"

"I can see only one chance. The twenty per cent held by your Warren cousins, unless Chase already has that locked up. I think it might be worthwhile to take a quick trip to Baltimore and Richmond and have a talk with Austin and Ralph Warren."

Theodore was shaking his head in doubt. "I don't think Chase would have made his move until he had gotten their proxies, Ken. The only members I've met in the last thirty years are those who came to my father's funeral and I don't think we exchanged more than a few words."

"Still, they came, so there's some sense of family attachment."

Theodore said wryly, "I might remind you that Chase came, too, and he is no less related to them than I am."

"Nevertheless, it's a chance we can't afford to overlook."

"What about Duncan Collins?"

"I'm sure we can count on his loyalty. We'll need him to help us with a public counteroffer if it becomes necessary. I suggest we call Collins now and fly up to meet him. We could stop off in Baltimore and Richmond on the way back."

"All right, Ken, let's do that first. You make the arrangements while I talk with Collins."

Duncan Collins had just returned from taking their cocker spaniel for a walk around the block when Diane met him at the door. She took Rompy's leash and said, "Call Theodore Warren at Brookhill. He's waiting there for your call-back."

"Eh? On Sunday?"

"Sunday, and I'd say it's very important. I could sense it in his voice. He was calling from Ken Armour's house, but was on his way back to Brookhill." Diane took Duncan's hat. "Better use the private line in your den. I'm expecting a call from Mother. We're having dinner there tonight, remember?"

Duncan groaned a small protest. "Don't commit us too definitely until I've finished with my call. You may have to make it alone."

"Then hurry and find out."

When Diane's mother phoned half an hour later, and Duncan had not yet emerged from his den, she canceled the dinner engagement and sent Martha to tell the cook to ready a pair of steaks for the broiler on short notice. Another twenty minutes passed before Duncan reappeared, his face grim and puzzled.

"Darling—"

"I've already canceled out. Annie has two steaks ready for the broiler. Get cleaned up—" She read his appreciation in his first two words.

"Ah, Diane—"

"Problems?"

He nodded. "Big problems. I need your ear."

"Let me tell cook to go ahead." She rang for Martha and gave her the message, followed Duncan to his bathroom where he washed his hands and talked. "That unmitigated sonofabitch—"

"Which of our dear friends are you memorializing, darling?" Diane asked.

Duncan smiled as though it were painful. "Chase Warren."

"Chase? What is our modern-day robber baron up to now?"

"He's up to snatching the bread and butter from out of our mouths, the filthy blackguard. Listen—"

He told Diane of his conversation with Theodore, then with Kenneth Armour; of Chase's treachery, the years Chase had maintained his friendship with Duncan, which had given him a certain amount of freedom in the Warren offices.

"What could he gain there, Duncan?"

"For one thing—do you remember that incident, oh, five-six months ago, I think, when we received a new stockholders' list from Laurelton, that when Miss Chapman went to put it in the special locked compartment of the vault, the 1966 copy was missing?"

"I remember something about it."

"And a few days later, just as mysteriously as it had disappeared, it reappeared again?"

"Yes—"

"Well, at the time, Jim Letterman told her he had taken the list to double-check it against the envelopes that had been run off for the dividend notices. I didn't attach any importance to it and thought Letterman was being a little too cautious because the address plates were run off from a verified list taken directly from the list itself. I gave orders that in the future, the list was never to be removed from Miss Chapman's office unless I personally issued the order on my own memo form and personally signed it."

626

"And?"

"Since that time, I've issued no such memo. I just called Miss Chapman at her home, who called Mrs. Wharton in Accounting. Mrs. Wharton told her she had accepted an initialed memo from Jim Letterman about a month ago and let him take the latest list. It was gone for two days, long enough for someone to photocopy every new change. Names, addresses, amount of stock, dates of purchase, transfers, everything. That memo from me was a forgery. The week after the list was returned, Jim Letterman quit his job. I'm sure I can guess who he's working for now."

"Chase?"

"Of that, from what I've just heard, I'm sure."

"Oh, Duncan!"

"Yes, oh, Duncan." He had scarcely touched his steak and now pushed the plate to one side and lit a cigarette. "I don't know how I'm going to do it, but if there's a way to trip that dirty scoundrel, I'll find it. Theodore and Ken Armour are coming up tomorrow."

"Do they know about the lists?"

"Not yet, but I'll tell them the moment they arrive. I wish I could deliver Letterman's head to them. And Chase's."

"Duncan—"

"What?"

"May I offer a suggestion for what it may be worth?"

"Ordinarily, darling, I'd say no, but in this case I'd be willing to listen to almost anything from anybody if I thought it would help."

"Victoria Warren," Diane said.

"Victoria Warren what?"

"I see I'm going to have to break a confidence."

"Love, what you're doing is confusing me with your riddles. What confidence? Whose confidence?"

"Victoria Warren's, you thickheaded Scots-Irishman."

"Will you please, for God's sake, make some sense, woman?"

"Let's go back to your den where we can't be overheard."

Duncan listened and learned and told himself that if he lived to be a thousand years old, he would never understand how any woman could tell another of the hatred she had for a man with whom she continued to share a roof. He listened and wondered how Diane could possess that rare quality of trust that would draw to her other women who needed a sympathetic, understanding ear. And he wondered, finally, what great and good thing he had done in his life to

627

deserve the love of a woman such as the one he had married.

He was still thinking these thoughts as he stared at the back of Diane's head and heard her one-sided telephone conversation with Victoria Warren, hopeless as he was certain it would be, then saw her hang up the receiver and turn to face him with a quick, open smile.

"Victoria will call me back later," she said, "after she has had a talk with her mother."

"Andrea Vanderkuyl? What the devil does Andrea have to do with this—what we are talking about?"

"Don't ask too many questions and take any favor you can get graciously," Diane retorted. "And if you underestimate the strength of Andrea Vanderkuyl, you could be making a bigger mistake than when you married the daughter of a pure Irishman."

"Ah, love, I may be a stupid man in many other respects, but I'll never stop blessing the day I overlooked my Scots-Irish ancestry."

"And you're beginning to sound more Irish than Scotch."

"And if I didn't need you so desperately in this moment of great trial, I'd paddle your lovely behind until it was the color of your cheeks."

"Go, mon, an' dream yer dreams of glory that come only to aging, balding men."

At 8:30, the call came. Not from Victoria for Diane, but from Andrea Vanderkuyl for Duncan. He listened, nodded, said, "Yes," several times and hung up.

"What?" Diane asked.

"A summons from the Empress of Vanderkuyl. I don't know what it will bring, but I can't afford to overlook even the smallest bet. Also, whether it pays off or comes to naught, I owe you anything your darling Irish heart desires."

"A trip to Europe next spring?"

"Even to that barren, benighted land that sent your starving ancestors here to bring forth a wife for me." Duncan kissed Diane warmly. "Don't wait up for me. From her voice, I think I may be in for a long session."

7

Momentarily, a feeling of strange relief engulfed Drew. It was the first time since it had happened that she had been able to unburden herself of its weight, ironically, inexplicably, compulsively to the one person she had told herself many times must never know. Nor was it less puzzling that Corey had accepted her open confession so calmly, with an almost clinical understanding; yet she was aware there must be a period of considered evaluation of her act. And then—

Her eyes misted with self-pity as she went slowly to her room, conscious of her desire for a drink, yet determined not to succumb. She lit a cigarette and paced nervously back and forth, then undressed and took a shower to rid herself of the state of drowsy lethargy that was beginning to overcome her. Toweling herself dry, she examined her face and figure carefully and was for the moment satisfied that the mental ravages of the past three years seemed not to have affected the outward attractiveness of the woman who, in turn, soberly examined her from the mirrored walls of her dressing room.

It had been a long time since she had felt the need and desire for exercise and she again determined to restock the Brookhill stables and kennels. Why? she asked herself. For what purpose? What friends?

And suddenly the desire was gone.

Introspectively, she had never, until Bruce's death, considered that she had been lonely; not until her third week of talks with the psychiatrist in Zurich, when it became apparent that since early childhood she had chosen to substitute Bruce for the mother and father who had deserted them, the grandfather who was too frequently away on business, the grandmother who spent much of her time in bed, ill. Bruce had become the substitute figure around whom her dreams were formed: brother, friend, lover, husband.

Bruce's friends had become her friends and although the differences in their ages made it provokingly difficult to keep up, eventually time erased the age gap and they were always together until Bruce went off to college.

There had never been a shortage of boys, but most, excepting Corey Armour, seemed shy, perhaps intimidated by the open display of Warren wealth. At 17, none had a car as expensive, sporty or powerful as Bruce's or Drew's. None could compete with Brookhill's stables, tennis courts or pool, the skeet-shooting range. At parties she was aware of excessive politeness and care not to offend; and Drew realized even then that there was no single girl of her acquaintance with whom she was intimate enough to share girlish confidences or secrets. Lacking such an exchange, she became inordinately bored with meaningless, inane chatter and, among the boys, conversations that were overly suggestive for their years. Or hers.

629

Long before she realized it, she had singled out Corey as her favorite among Bruce's friends. Perhaps because they had known each other since early childhood, he talked with her as he would with Bruce, dismissing the small difference in their ages. Corey had, as with Bruce, sharpened her tennis game and taught her to breathe properly and improve her swimming speed and stroke. Often, she would enter into mature discussions between Corey and Bruce and in no way did either suggest she was too young or immature to participate. From the time she was 14, she had played girlish dream games about Corey, but it wasn't until after the Loon Lake incident with Lucas Warren that she had begun serious romantic thoughts that culminated in her unabashed declaration of love to him the following New Year's Eve. She hadn't taken his rejection seriously, interpreting the uncertainty of his mild rebuff as a form of brotherly protection for a sister.

Of those who had played important roles in her life, only two were left now: Theodore, still an unknown quantity, and Corey, whom she had once abandoned and now wanted very much.

And in the background, the Company which had touched them all; even Corey, through his father. And for that reason, the Company had suddenly taken on a fresh, new meaning. She was a part of it as much as it was a part of her, had been a part of Anderson, Cleo and Bruce. If the Company were to be lost to Intercon, there would be nothing left to hold her dreams together.

She lighted another cigarette and tried to remember some of her former schoolmates and found that aside from several family names, Willard, Corbin, Constable, Thurgood, their first names were difficult to properly tie up with faces. Her college years had been spent abroad in an effort to compel Corey to think of her as a woman instead of a child. How, she wondered, can one person be so completely surrounded and yet be so alone?

She stubbed out her cigarette, dressed in a skirt and sweater and went downstairs, just as Theodore returned home. Shad closed the door, took Theodore's hat, topcoat and briefcase as Theodore, his back to Drew, was saying, "Put my briefcase in the study, Shad. I'll be leaving for New York in the morning and I'll want you to drive me to the airport around five-thirty—" He turned then and saw Drew as she reached the bottom step.

"Hello, Father."

"Drew. You—you're looking very well."

630

"Thank you. I heard you tell Shad you're going to New York."

"Yes. I went to have a talk with Ken Armour and we called Duncan Collins. Collins is arranging a meeting with someone. Ken and I will take the Company plane to Atlanta and catch the early plane to New York."

"Have you had dinner?"

"No."

"I'll tell Leona—"

"Don't bother now, Drew."

"It's no bother." She went toward the kitchen while Theodore took the opposite direction to the study. Drew returned and found him there a few minutes later, looking through some of the papers he had removed from his briefcase.

"A half hour, Father."

"Thank you, Drew. Will you sit down, please. I've had a rather disturbing piece of news from Ken Armour. I think you should know about it."

She sat in the chair nearest the desk, anxiety showing on her face. "What is it?"

Theodore almost had to force himself to speak. "Don't hold out too much hope, Drew," he said finally. "Ken is not too encouraging about the situation, but we'll give it a try. On our way back, we'll stop in Baltimore and Richmond and have a talk with our cousins there."

"Is that what disturbs you?" Drew asked.

"It's a part of it, but not all." He took a deep breath and said, "Intercon. The corporation that is eager to buy the Company—"

"Yes?"

"Intercon is owned by my brother. Your Uncle Chase Warren."

"Uncle Chase? Why, Father? I've always heard he was never really interested in the Company. Gran said so many times—"

"It all goes back a long way, Drew. It seems that Chase wasn't interested because your grandfather kept the control in his own hands, and Chase couldn't stand that. We know now that he has been picking up Warren stock, in Intercon's name and through private individuals wherever possible. We believe he holds about twenty-two per cent and suspect he may have the twenty per cent held by our Warren cousins tied up. If he has, and makes a tender offer to pick up another nine per cent—"

"What if—what if he does?"

"Then control will be in Chase's hands and we will be

forced out. The physical properties will remain, of course, but the Company will be directed by Chase from New York with new officers and board of directors."

Drew stood up and walked to the window. Lights from the house were reflected in the pool, its waters whipped by the brisk wind, leaves falling on its surface like a flotilla of small, storm-tossed ships. Suddenly, Brookhill seemed to have aged into decay, as near death as the Company.

If the Company is lost, she thought, I won't continue to live here. Father won't want it, either. This house where Bruce and I were born will die and become a ghost. There will be nothing left but the mausoleum.

She remembered Laurellen's conversation on the day of Gran's funeral, the intimation that Uncle Chase was "up to something," and knew that Ken Armour's suspicions were most likely correct, that somehow the Maryland and Virginia twenty per cent of the Warren stock must already be in Chase's hands.

"Drew," she heard Theodore's voice saying, "if we lose, will it mean so much to you?"

She turned back to him with a wintry smile. "No, Father," she lied, "it won't matter. Not at all."

"And Brookhill?"

"We can talk about that later. When it is over."

"Yes. Well—it has been a long day. I'll wash up for dinner now. And Drew—"

"Yes, Father?"

"We won't give up easily. I promise I'll do my very best."

8

After leaving Brookhill, Corey drove aimlessly in the rain, reliving Drew's confession that had shaken him, in spite of the calm with which he had accepted it, trying not to show how much it was affecting him. Without knowing why he had chosen to turn north, he found himself approaching Riverton and pulled in at a roadside truck stop for coffee. The restaurant was small, dim, shabby, overly warm and badly ventilated, boisterous with the hearty conversation between half a dozen long distance haulers and the man and young girl behind the counter, who exchanged strong opinions on the war in Viet Nam, Washington, Moscow, state's rights, and civil rights.

Which brought up the subject of the recent activity in Laurelton and stringent, vigorous suggestions to curb what might become a show of open, outright rebellion. The

owner, a small, wizened, volatile man in his sixties broke
off in the middle of a sentence to slide a thick mug of coffee
across the counter to Corey and ask, "Somethin' else, son?"

"No, thank you," Corey replied and was at once ignored
by the man who addressed himself to his audience-at-large.

"—take them goddam niggers an' string 'em up by the
balls 'til we run out of lampposts an' trees. I don' know
what the hell's happened to people in these parts any more,
I purely don't. Back when I was just a tyke, nobody'd ever
take a pinch of their goddam uppity talk—"

"More coffee, Pop," one of the drivers said. Without
stopping, Pop reached for the coffee pot and sloshed the
black liquid into and over the rim of the mug. "Tell you,
we got at least fifty men up here ready to go down there,
they break loose, an' give 'em their comeuppance—"

"Pop," the girl called through the opening into the
kitchen, "two beef stews gettin' cold a-waitin'."

Corey dropped a quarter on the counter and left his
half-filled mug of coffee. He turned the Thunderbird toward
Laurelton, suddenly aware that what he had regarded as a
community problem was no longer a local matter. He
thought again of the more pressing inquiry into his own
feelings about Drew, remembered his promise to Anderson
Warren, *"I'll be there if she needs me."* Brave words to a
dying man who had sought reassurance, wondering if he
had assumed an enforced obligation.

She hadn't allowed him to commit himself, giving him
this opportunity for second thoughts and cool reappraisal
before coming to a decision; and he had taken the easy way
out. Now he questioned whether he would, had he remained, have declared his understanding and love with honesty and without false compassion.

Certainly she hadn't gone into affairs with two chance
strangers, men whom she could not remember, with im-
probity or lewdness; and yet it was difficult to understand
how it could happen. Who, he asked himself now, am I to
judge or condemn? How much different would it be if she
had married the men and later divorced them?

He thought of his own sexual dalliances during his high
school days, at Loon Lake, his college and recently renewed
affair with Paula, brief romances with others at home and
abroad, the spark of lust ignited by Hilary Fields, these with
a greater sense of awareness than Drew's momentary fall
from logic. Logic. In daily human conduct, logic was probably life's greatest question mark. And chastity? Only that
which one illogically expects from, and assigns to, others.
Morality? What about my own morality?

The drive home was deliberately slow and by the time he turned into the driveway on Old Colony Lane, Corey had almost convinced himself that the separation could be bridged as though it had never occurred. Kenneth's car was in the garage and Corey found himself thinking that the lack of close communication here at home was another gap that needed closing. He entered the house through the rear door and came upon Tish and Jemmy listening to the six o'clock news program on the kitchen radio.

"Lord, Mist' Corey, you been out in that ugly weather all day? Mist' Kenneth done et. I'll fix you—" Tish began.

"I'm not hungry, Tish. I had something earlier. Where is Dad?"

"He havin' his coffee in the study," Jemmy replied.

"Don't bother. I'll have some with him." Corey dropped his raincoat and hat on a chair in the entrance hallway and went to the study. Kenneth was at his desk, looking over a Warren Company annual statement. He glanced up with a brief smile. "Hello, Corey. I hoped it was your car I heard driving in. Coffee?"

"Yes, thanks." At that moment Jemmy knocked and came in with a cup and saucer on a small tray, poured the coffee for Corey and went out.

"Blustery day," Kenneth said.

"It's still nasty out and that fireplace is a cozy sight. It must have been an unpleasant trip back from Atlanta."

"Yes." Kenneth smiled and added, "But it was something that had been put off too long and had to be done." He stood up and walked to the fireplace and shifted the logs about. "Had a devil of a time getting this thing started, but it's fine now." He turned back to the desk and asked, "Haven't heard anything more from Wayne, have you?"

"No. I don't think it has reached that stage yet."

Kenneth sipped more coffee then put his cup down. "Corey, there may be a change, a rather important one, in my plans," he said.

"Nothing adverse, I hope."

"That depends largely on how one sees it. Something has come up to make me change my mind about the Intercon offer. In fact, I've already rejected it."

"That's rather sudden, isn't it, Dad?"

"Yes, and rather unexpected, the way it happened. It means that I will remain in Laurelton, but not with the Company." When Corey raised his eyebrows in silent question, "I think I owe you an explanation. This recent development, I mean."

Kenneth then took Corey back in time to his first contact

634

with Tom Shelby, the subsequent meetings and discussions with Kirk Dillingham and finally, the surprising introduction of Chase Warren into the picture. "It is my offhand opinion," he concluded, "that Chase probably controls enough stock and proxies to take the Company over at the annual meeting in January. Since I have refused to go along with him, my association with the Company will come to an end."

"There won't be any opposition to the takeover?"

"If I'm correct in my assumption, Corey, a fight would be meaningless."

"For God's sake, can he just walk in and— What about Theodore Warren?"

"He left here less than an hour ago. He knows about Chase now and wants to fight. In fact, we've both talked with Duncan Collins in New York and are leaving early in the morning to meet with him. Collins feels the way I do, that knowing Chase, he wouldn't have come out into the open unless he was certain of his strength."

"Does that mean he controls the stock held by the Warrens in Maryland and Virginia?"

"Very likely, since those two blocks represent twenty per cent and are the key to control, although according to the stockholder list, there are still some fifteen per cent outstanding. I think Chase is already prepared to pick up the nine or ten per cent he needs in order to give him the necessary fifty-one per cent—"

Corey's mind went back to Loon Lake, trying to remember the Warrens who would be within his own age range. Lucas and Laurellen, Brad and Charlotte, dimly remembered; Clyde, the ascetic law student; Chris, a shadowy memory; wondering if they might have some voice in the disposition of the stock.

"—that Chase has no doubt romanced the Maryland and Virginia branches of the family into turning their proxies over to him. After all, he is as closely related to them as Theodore, who has scarcely made any effort to keep in touch."

"He's really a bastard, isn't he? Chase, I mean."

"Well, let's say he's a very practical bastard at the least. I'm sure you are as aware as I that Chase and Theodore have been estranged for many years, probably as far back as the day Theodore was born. Chase always had grandiose ideas and used anyone he could to promote his own ambitions. He could have had the Company all to himself, with Anderson's blessings and without any opposition from Theodore, but he was hungry to own, to possess, to prove

635

he was a bigger man than his father before him. Now, unless he takes over control of the Company and pushes it ahead, he'll never be able to prove his point."

"I wish there were some way to trip him—" Corey began.

"So do I, but I doubt if Chase can be stopped. His track record is too strong. Taking over the Company will be his crowning achievement, it's that important to him."

"Then Drew doesn't know about this yet."

"Not unless Theodore has told her since he left here. I'm sure she knows about Intercon's original offer. I would guess Drew is the reason why Theodore changed his mind about accepting." Kenneth sighed and added, "At least, Chase can't hurt Theodore or Drew financially.

"That's hardly the point, is it?"

"No," Kenneth said softly, "it really isn't."

"What about your plans, Dad?"

Kenneth smiled wearily. "For the present, to see what I can do to keep the Company from falling into Chase's hands. When that issue has been resolved, one way or the other, I'll begin to work on plans for the future. If we win, well—"

Corey broke in quickly. "Dad, I'm sorry if I've been less than understanding about Shana. I'm certain you would have married her long ago if it hadn't been for me."

"Until now, Corey, I don't think I could have expected more."

"I want you to know that I wish you both every happiness in the world and certainly there are no objections on my part."

"That pleases me more than I can tell you, son. It makes a big difference to me and I know it will to Shana. Which brings us to another matter. This house. Would you consider selling it to me?"

"I've never really thought of it as belonging to me. Would you and Shana accept it as a wedding gift from me?" When Kenneth hesitated, "Please, Dad. I'd never think of trying to maintain it by myself. Tish and Jemmy would probably go with you, so why not keep the whole thing intact? I can take an apartment in town and if the Shadow Hills project works out, it would be more convenient for me—"

Kenneth said simply, "Thank you, Corey. You know we'd want you to stay on here, with us."

"We can discuss that later." He stood up. "Well—we've covered a lot of ground tonight, haven't we? If you don't mind, I think I'll go up to my room and try to digest it.

Good night, Dad. If I don't see you in the morning, I hope you have a good, successful trip to New York."

"Good night, son," Kenneth replied, feeling a new sense of pride.

"And if Chase does win," Corey added from the doorway, "I'll need a knowledgeable partner in the Shadow Hills project."

9

In order to attract as many Negro ministers—and their congregations—as possible, Amos Hart had received permission from the Center to use its auditorium for his meeting on Sunday night. The hour had been set for 8 o'clock, but by 7:30 the seats and benches in the long, narrow, former cotton warehouse, now used for amateur plays and musical recitals, were filling up. Only two other Negro ministers showed up. The black-topped parking lot had filled up quickly. Both sides of the roadway were choked with cars and the overflow were parking at odd angles in the surrounding open, soggy field. The two Negro officers sent to control traffic radioed in for help and two more were detailed from the 12th Precinct to lend assistance.

Inside, the overhead lights were on and from a heavy crossbeam, a bank of spots and floodlights illuminated the center of the stage where a lectern and eight chairs stood. New arrivals added to the confusion of conversation, calling greetings as they peeled off raincoats and hats and moved to their seats.

Promptly at 8 o'clock, Reverend Amos Hart came out of the wings and approached the lectern to some scattered applause from the noisy crowd. Behind him came Dr. Royal Betts, Amylee Todd, Milo Roose, Henry Clark and Walter Lynch, representing the Negro half of the Laurelton Civil Rights Committee, then two of the seven other Negro ministers from West and South Laurelton, Harry Lang and Charles Duckworth. The six men and Mrs. Todd seated themselves onstage as Amos Hart tested the microphone and raised it to accommodate his height.

Looking out over the sea of faces, Hart was pleased to see a good sprinkling of younger people, some in their early teens and twenties, faces he hadn't seen over a long period of time, some never before. It was a gratifying turnout for a meeting called on such short notice, and for a rainy night. Emily Hart sat at the piano playing hymnal music that

637

could hardly be heard above the shuffling feet and raised voices as people continued to arrive.

Hart tapped the microphone, blew into it again and waited. Walter Lynch came to the lectern and struck the gavel against a block of wood, saying, "Take your seats, please, ladies and gentlemen. Please find your seats quickly —please—"

The conversational hum decreased and the audience grew silent. Bowing his head, Hart's next words were intoned into the microphone. "Rise, brothers and sisters.

"We are gathered here in the sight and presence of the Almighty to seek His inspiration, wisdom and guidance, to help us forge a common bond of understanding among our people.

"Almighty God, visit Thy radiance and blessing upon this meeting tonight that we may know and understand Thy goodness and mercy. Place Thy hand upon us that we may see reason and know eternal love toward all men and dwell in everlasting brotherhood. Let our thoughts, deeds, works, and lives lead us into the path of justice and righteousness. This Thy humble servant prays for all men of good faith everywhere in this troubled world. And let us say, Amen."

To the asked for "Amen" were added, "Yes, Lord," "It's the truth Lord," "Be with us, Lord." Hart waited for the murmur to diminish, observing that the back of the auditorium was now filled with standees.

"I have asked you to come to this meeting, brothers and sisters, because I feel there is a dangerous mood abroad, an infection that is spreading among our people, one that may bring harm to all of us if it is not curbed now. I speak to all ages present and ask you to consider that the actions of a few misguided people may cause us to lose that which we have fought and bled for in recent years. You know that I am talking about the recent uncalled for vandalism which took place in East Laurelton and the retaliation suffered in West Laurelton as a result."

The audience stirred restlessly and the murmuring rose. "There are among us," Hart continued, "the scoffers who have come under duress, or for entertainment. What you will hear from me tonight will be Truth; and I know it is not always pleasant or entertaining to hear Truth. I am not going to tell you that all is well, that we are all well-fed, well-housed, well-clothed, well-paid, and that there are no needy poor, sick, hungry, tired and weary.

"I know as well as many, and better than most, that there have been, and still are, injustices and inequalities; and that man's patience grows thin and brittle. But no matter how

From the rear came shouts of encouragement. Others rose to their feet crying for order. For a few moments, as ushers tried to quiet the protagonists and antagonists, it seemed that the meeting would be over. Hart waited patiently until the uproar wore itself out slowly. Then he spoke into the microphone again.

"Who profits by hate? Who profits by riot, fire, looting and destruction? It's the same hate that starts wars between nations and no one, not even the victor, has ever won a war. He only inherits the misery it leaves behind to breed another war. I am called an Uncle Tom, a handkerchief head, because I preach for peace and love. What have you followers of Black Power violence gained except the loss of dignity and friends not of your own color? Whose homes have been burned out and how many of your own color have been burned out of their jobs by this violence? I don't speak against my people, but right is right and wrong is wrong and there's little to gain by setting your own house on fire, bringing down the law on your heads in anger, destroying the gains, however few, we've made, gains on which we should be building a future!"

Hart's thundering voice came to a pause amid total silence and then another voice came from the audience. "Reverend Hart!"

"Yes, sir?"

A thin, slightly built man walked down the aisle from among the standees in the rear. As he came forward, he placed a black fez on his head and the audience murmur rose as fingers pointed toward him, then shouts of "Dr. Rhama! Dr. Rhama!" rose. Behind him, as though guarding him, walked Brother Leonard, also wearing a fez. Dr. Rhama stopped as he reached the edge of the stage. "May I join you, Reverend Hart?" he asked.

"Please do, Dr. Rhama," Hart invited.

Dr. Rhama went to the stairs and mounted the stage. Brother Leonard followed and stood behind the row of chairs in back of the lectern. "Thank you, Reverend Hart," Dr. Rhama said. "I would like to address your audience, if I may."

"This is an unusual request, Dr. Rhama," Hart said, his mouth close to the microphone. "Do you offer the same courtesy to listeners at your meetings?"

"I have been known to do so, Reverend," Dr. Rhama replied, "but if you are unwilling for some reason—"

From the audience came shouts of "Let him talk!" "He got a right to speak!" and similar calls of approval. Hart glanced at his supporters on the stage, but drew no comfort from their puzzled, pained expressions. "Very well, Dr. Rhama," Hart said and indicated the microphone, stepping to one side, but not out of the spotlights.

Dr. Rhama smiled as he faced the expectant audience. "The good Reverend has told you that nothing good has come from violence, that nobody wins a war. I say he is misguided and the proof is that we have survived. We have lived through the white man's war on us for over three centuries of slavery, at first legal, now illegal, but always immoral. We have been at war in order to survive and our casualties, known and unknown, can't be totaled.

"Good people, I am not a man of religion, but you and Reverend Hart know that more people have been killed in religious wars and crusades than all other wars put together, proving only that religion may benefit a man's soul in the hereafter, but it does not offer survival. I say we have survived, but survival is not enough."

At the back of the room, others had crowded inside. The air had become humid and stagnant. Many were using handkerchiefs to mop their faces, waving hands to stir the fetid air. Even on the stage, Hart and the others were sweating profusely. The calmest man, despite his necktie and buttoned jacket, was Dr. Rhama. The pause he took now was aimed at his expectant, receptive audience, a deliberate move to keep them on edge.

"The good Reverend talks about living with our white brothers and I'll believe that when our white brother comes to live among his black brothers so we can see how much love he will share when he lives in wooden shacks, too hot in summer, too cold in winter, dirt streets, dirt floors, with rats and roaches and outhouses. He talks of keeping our children under restraint until they are educated and learn to hold jobs, but how much can a child learn in an inferior, third-rate school, taught by antiquated methods, when his mind is on his empty belly or a rat bite on his leg or arm or face?

"Love, brothers and sisters, is not a one-sided thing. It takes two to love, to make a marriage, to live together. And while we're being told how to live in peace with Mr. White Man, who is telling him, his wife, sons and daughters how to live in peace with us?"

The applause from the audience was loud and Dr. Rhama was cheered from the back rows and standees; and now, more black fezzes appeared on the heads of the younger element.

As Reverend Hart moved toward the microphone, Dr. Rhama said, "Just this, Reverend," then into the microphone, "the trouble is, our own people are working with Mr. White Man against us, people who have no hunger wrinkles in their bellies." One sweep of his thin hand included Hart and his supporters on the stage. "People who live in clean houses, Negro merchants and businessmen who have made it from their Negro brethren's sweat, like the white exploiters of the black race. They wear no second-hand clothes, drive no secondhand cars, use no secondhand furniture, dishes, pots and pans like the rest of their second-hand brothers. To them, everything is new, beautiful and right, but it is just as evil to be right for the wrong reasons as it is to be wrong for the right reasons.

"One last thing. Reverend Hart is right when he tells you we must have pride. Yes, we must have pride, but not so much pride that we don't fight for what is rightfully ours, what the law has said is ours. Equal justice, equal rights. Equality. And now, not tomorrow. Today! Now!"

Without another glance at Hart, Dr. Rhama strode from the stage, Brother Leonard at his heels. He went swiftly up the aisle amid a tumult of applause and stamping feet and whistling, touching hands that sought to touch him. When he reached the rear of the auditorium, he continued into the outer lobby, now followed by a stream of shouting young men and women. Among them was Duke Shackleford and his followers, who had generated and stimulated the applause. In the lobby, Brother Leonard, Jim Cuddy and Jake Runnels were distributing tasseled cardboard fezzes into eager hands.

Inside the auditorium, the exodus had left an uncertain audience, highly vocal in both agreement and disavowal, and Amos Hart seemed adrift for the moment. He held a brief consultation with Roose and Lynch, then with the two ministers, joined by Amylee Todd. From the third row, Sam Shackleford rose and went to the stage and spoke with Hart, who pointed to the steps. While Sam mounted the stage, Hart rapped his gavel for attention and asked for quiet. At this point, almost half his audience had defected.

"Brothers and sisters," Hart announced, "you have heard me speak and Dr. Rhama answer in rebuttal. I would like now for you to hear from our brother, Sam Shackleford, a member of the African Zion Congregation, who is well-known to all of you. Please give him your attention. Deacon—"

Shackleford waited until quiet was restored, clutching self-consciously at the lapels of his heavy black suit. "I ain't no speaker like the good Reverend here," he said, "and I ain't got any big educated words to th'ow at you. I'm an

643

ordinary man been workin' for more'n forty years. I learned to read an' write a little as a boy but my Lizabeth, she help me along when she was a little girl goin' to school. Now, she's a college-educated teacher, teachin' your chil'ren in a bigger, better school than I ever saw in my time.

"Most of you know me. I work for the Warren Company an' I'm a foreman, got sixty men workin' under me. I got what used to be a white man's job an' I'm gettin' a white man's pay. My men drawin' down white pay, too. That's progress, I tell you."

The seated audience listened to Shackleford as they would to a man they respected, but from the rear of the auditorium came a flood of booing and catcalls that disturbed and unnerved him. He looked around to find Amos Hart standing behind him.

"Go on, brother," Hart encouraged.

"They don' want to listen, Reverend."

"Stand where you are. It will pass."

The noise died down as Hart predicted. Sam Shackleford braced himself and began again.

"Me, my wife an' my daughter, we live in Angeltown all our lives. I'm gettin' on to be sixty-five, born when this century was only a few years old. Anybody in this room can't see no changes for the good, it's because he ain't old enough to remember what it was like. Lemme tell you." Shackleford wiped his forehead with a large white handkerchief.

"I seen times when no Nigra owned his own piece of land, a horse, a plow, tools, his own house or shack. I seen Nigras burned, hung, beat to death, and shot, just for *thinkin'* what I hear goin' aroun' these days.

"We got school an' bus integration by peaceful demonstration, only sometimes it was less peaceful than others. We got beat up, spit on, went to jail, but we kept comin' back 'til we got what we was askin' for. We got other things, too, by talkin' things out, with the law on our side. And that was progress, too.

"Why? Because we found out the white folks didn' want trouble no more'n we did. Like the Reverend said, nobody wins a war. They can rebuild what we can burn or smash, but over here, we lose ten-twenty years in time."

Someone shouted, "Sit down, old man, you said enough," but it was a lone voice in the crowd.

"Maybe," Sam said sadly, "but I got this to say, too, friend. I seen times when a man finish his workin' year with less'n a dollar in his pocket, all because he couldn't read, add, subtract or multiply. Come to think of it, that's the one thing he could do best, multiply." There was scattered laughter and hooting. "Except he was only multiplyin' the number of mouths he had to feed.

"We was poor, yes, mighty poor, but we had love from our parents an' that love was strong, strong enough to keep us together. We worked an' we had pride in our families an' we moved along. Slowfully, but we moved.

"Them days are long behind us. We got more money now, we got cars, we don't ride the back of the bus, and our chil'ren go to school with white chil'ren. We can eat an' buy in some places we never could before. Maybe it seems like it don't move fast enough to the younger folks, but long's it moves ahead, we gainin' a lot.

"The Reverend is right when he say that education an' trainin' is the answer. Maybe not for my generation, but for the young ones an' their young ones. That's where it's goin'a tell. Today, you c'n see thirty-forty nice, shiny-bright colored boys an' girls workin' at the City Hall, another twenty-thirty for the County, all in offices with desks an' typewriters. That's a real start. It's *their* chil'ren goin'a see it work, make it work.

"Maybe it's too late for us old an' middle-year folks, but our mamas an' papas, wherever they are, they lookin' down at us thinkin', 'Well, thank the good Lord my chil'ren got it better'n we had it.' Just like your chil'ren'll have it better'n you, an' theirs better'n them. The colored problem ain't new. It's as old as time, since they brought the first slaves in. It's comin' late, Lord, yes, but it's better now'n it ever was an' it be a lot better if you give it a chance to work, an' work with it to help it along. All's I'm sayin' is, you don't help it by ruckusin' in the streets, smashin', burnin'. That's all I got to say."

The room exploded with applause as Shackleford leaped down and rejoined Lutie, but it was not loud enough to drown out the scattered boos and catcalls that came from the back of the room. More of the audience got up and moved toward the back of the hall and Hart knew he had lost them. Dr. Rhama's strong words had captured and held them even after he had gone.

Hart came to the lectern to offer a prayer of benediction and the meeting was over.

645

Apart from the residue of overcast, Monday was a typical fall day. The rain had stopped sometime after midnight and the air was crisp and cool with a weak sun trying to break through the clouds. This October Monday also marked the official birth of the Black Fez movement throughout Laurelton.

Negro children on both sides of the bridge proudly wore the tasseled caps. Young Negro men reported to their jobs with the symbol perched on their heads at rakish angles. Before very long, the full meaning of the Black Fez had made itself known and the reaction was almost universal. Principals of all Negro elementary and secondary schools sent word to teachers forbidding the wearing of the Black Fez in school buildings or playgrounds. In integrated schools, self-appointed monitors prevented the fez-wearers from entering the school grounds. Fights broke out and police were called to maintain order, but the fez-wearers were required to go to their classes bareheaded, leaving their newly adopted headgear in their lockers.

White employers ordered their workers to get rid of the new headpieces or get off the job. In several instances, Negroes walked off the job in protest. Delivery boys and truck drivers wore their fezzes openly and the pickets at Ainslee's and Cloverland wore them defiantly and marched more erectly.

After school, numerous fights broke out and spread when white students delightedly organized a "fez hunt," snatching the headpieces from Negro students. Gangs formed and roamed the streets searching for offending fez-wearers. Rocks were thrown, windows broken, cars and trucks attacked. Police switchboards lit up and patrol cars scurried about, breaking up street fights, trying their best to disperse the militant youths of both races. Two Negro boys were beaten sufficiently to require medical care and a white boy and girl were taken to Laurelton Memorial Hospital with stab wounds and cuts.

At the induction center, seven fez-wearing Negroes refused induction, asserting they were members of the Black Fez Movement and were, therefore, conscientious objectors. They were escorted to the Federal Building by marshals where they were held for arraignment. Within an hour, a hundred Negro men, women and youths had gathered in front of the Federal Building to demonstrate, all wearing black fezzes and carrying posters protesting the arrests.

By nightfall, many off-duty officers had been called in and peace was partially restored, but in South and West Laurelton, possession of a black fez became paramount to every young Negro. Without the tasseled headpiece, he seemed to lack a sense of belonging. Negro business establishments, well supplied by Duke Shackleford's followers, handed out the fezzes free of charge. Children whose fezzes had been confiscated by their parents had little trouble finding replacements.

Older Negroes, who saw danger in flaunting the flimsy symbol of black unity, were taunted by younger Negroes as they shopped and walked along the streets.

At the Warren Company, Sam Shackleford warned his warehouse crew at the end of the working day: "You wear that thing to work tomorrow, you won't find no job waitin' for you."

"How come, Sam?"

" 'Cause you can't work an' demonstrate at the same time. On this job, you do what you get paid to do an' nothin' else."

Dave Sharkey said, "Okay, then, I quit."

"That's your right, Dave. Anybody else want to quit?"

No one else spoke up, but Sam felt the resentment and tension in his force of 61 men, now reduced by one. "I'll tell you now, all of you. You don't need no piece of black cardboard an' black strings to tell the world you're black, no more'n you need somebody you never knowed before to tell you how to fight the white man an' get killed to get what you got comin' to you by the law. You got your jobs without a black hat an' without this Dr. Rhama, but if you want to lose your jobs because of him, I can get five men for every job here. Before you jump, go home an' sleep on it, see if it worth givin' up your jobs just to wear a black hat."

On Velie Street and Grand Avenue later that night, the black fez was the predominant piece of headgear on both male and female heads. At the 2-2-2 Club every head displayed the fez; customers, bartenders, waitresses, musicians, even the chorus line. It seemed that most Negroes appearing in public would have as soon appeared naked as without a black fez.

In the private meeting room at the 2-2-2 Club, Luke Tolbert and Booker Dance reported on the strike at Ainslee and Cloverland. White drivers had replaced all Negroes on the delivery trucks, and at higher hourly pay rates. Despite pickets in front of stores and supermarkets on both sides of the bridge, whites and Negroes alike were buying Ainslee and Cloverland products. In a dozen cases, pickets at white-owned stores had been jeered at, insulted, their fezzes knocked from their heads. Dave Sharkey told of Sam Shackleford's ultimatum and that he alone, of 61 employees, had resisted and quit his job.

Among the 15 present at the meeting called for by Duke Shackleford, Dr. Rhama and Brother Leonard sat behind a small table, the others on folding chairs in a semicircle.

"Then you can all see," Dr. Rhama said, "the need for black unity, not only here, but throughout the country, all over the world. Our greatest immediate problem is not from the white man without, but from our own people within.

"Laurelton has always been a special case because the Negro here has had a little more than his brethren in other cities. There are more jobs for him here, so he is satisfied, even though he will never rise into a position of real authority or equality. He has been permitted to ride in the front of the bus and believes that this is full equality. He is allowed to eat in a few white restaurants, which the whites now shun. He may shop in a few white stores, but must wait and be humble until all white customers have been served. He is allowed to register, but is afraid to vote for fear of white retaliation; and when he does, he votes the white ticket permissively in appreciation for being allowed to vote.

"Why? Because he has no pride in himself, his race, his fellow-Negroes. And this is what we—you—must change."

"How we goin'a change somebody who don't want to be changed?" Jack Runnels asked.

"How? First, by giving him pride in himself. Second, by demonstrating the value of strength and unity. Strength *in* unity. Already, you have seen what has happened among our young people by the simple act of wearing the black fez openly. They have thrown fear into the white man. Let me tell you, and you tell everyone who will listen to you, that this is what we must all do, *throw fear into the white man.*

"Listen, my black brothers, and learn something about your own heritage, the Negroes who were once kings in Africa. In ancient times, in the period from 1700 to 1550 B.C., African Negroes invaded Egypt and held the most important positions in government. In 741 B.C. Negroes initiated a campaign of conquest and held Egypt in subjugation for a hundred years. The Negro kingdom of Melle flourished from the thirteenth to fifteenth century and included most of what became French West Africa. We were kings in Songhay in the eighth century.

"In those times, slavery was a tradition everywhere, in Europe as well as Africa, but in 1460 hundreds of Africans were taken to Portugal as slaves and by the seventeenth century slave trade became a profitable European enterprise. Why? Because the African tribes were not unified. We have been in the Americas since about 1500, as slaves under the white man's heel.

"Yet, in the Boston Massacre, Negroes died fighting white men for the freedom of other white men. Remember that a Negro, Crispus Attucks, was one who died there. Five thousand Negroes fought the British for American freedom, but not their own. In 1775, Peter Salem, a Negro, was among those who died in battle. In 1812, in 1846, in 1861, in 1898, in 1918, in 1941, in 1950, Negroes have fought and died for the white man's freedom, but not their own. Today, fifty thousand Negroes are in Viet Nam, fighting other men of color for a country in which he is held in contempt by the men he is fighting for.

"Ask yourself: how many black men have died to protect freedom for the white man, then returned to slavery conditions? Can you guess how many Negro women have nursed and raised white children? Tell yourself and others that given equal opportunity, the black man is equal, often superior, to the white man. Frederick Douglass, Josiah Henson, Sojourner Truth. Henri Christophe, Jean Jacques Dessalines. Phyllis Wheatley. Harriet Tubman. Booker T. Washington, William E. DuBois. Langston Hughes. And many more. Writers, scholars, poets, inventors, scientists, warriors. Who knows how many more could have climbed the heights if we had been given the equal rights and opportunities from the time the Constitution was written?

"We have been discussed and analyzed almost to death, but we have survived. We're still here and we're going to stay here and fight for what is ours—full equality. The white man may not approve, he may not like us, he may

649

not even want us, but I will tell you, and you must tell others, *he can no longer ignore us!*"

Dr. Rhama's speech had ignited his listeners and they rose as one to applaud and cheer him long and loudly. He listened for a full minute before he raised his pink palm for quiet. When they were seated, he began speaking again, more softly.

"We have had our martyrs down through the centuries unto today." He waited, then the one name exploded from his lips. "Medgar Evers!" A pause, then, "He represents every Negro who has been lynched by the white man, the millions who have been brutalized and died for their black brothers, for you, for me.

"Never forget that we are related to every black man on this earth, on every continent, wherever he may be. We are related to those who liberated their people from the French rule in Haiti, from the British and French and Dutch in Africa. We are brothers to every West Indian black man who seeks to escape white rule. And we know by the color of their skins who are brothers are, something the white man will never know among his own.

"Let me tell you again: we are the friend of every black man on earth and the enemy of every white man on earth. *He is the enemy! The universal enemy!* That is the message for you to carry to your friends, your parents, to every pair of black ears that will listen to you. There is no brotherhood of white and black, only white against black, black against white. Every Negro who *knows*, knows we can't work together because we are not allowed to live together. If we must continue to live, we've got to be prepared to die, not for white freedom this time, but for our own!

"I say to you: arm yourselves any way you can. I say to you: defend your own on the streets!

"Among the Indian tribes, none could be called a man until he had killed an enemy. Among African tribes, it was the same. I say to you now: It is no different today than it was then."

There was no cheering when the meeting came to its end moments later, but each man left the room in sober reflection, his black fez settled a little firmer in place on his head.

3

At the Center on this Wednesday night, as on the preceding Monday night, all classes were more heavily attended than on any night since the new fall term had begun in September

ber. A good number of absentees returned to resume their studies and there were nearly 30 new applicants for the two Voter Registration classes, placing new burdens upon Elizabeth Shackleford and Lyle Emerson. The sudden surge of activity toward these classes came perhaps as a result of Amos Hart's Sunday night plea for political action; but no matter as long as interest heightened.

Dave Hill's workshop, the largest classroom on the second floor, was comprised mainly of younger men, nine of whom were veterans of Viet Nam, all eagerly pursuing a course in the assembly of electronic components. Hill, a Pennsylvania Negro, a graduate of Lehigh and M.I.T., had been brought to Laurelton by the Taylor Electronics Corporation and was encouraged to make use of the Center's facilities to build and train prospects as an integral part of the Taylor recruitment program, necessitated by the growing demand for skilled workers.

On this night, Dave Hill was very displeased by the sight of at least two dozen of his class of 42 who appeared wearing the tasseled black fezzes. He waited patiently for the class to settle down in their places at their work benches before outlining a complex wiring problem to be tackled as the project of the evening. A hum of conversation at the back of the room persisted. Dave Hill turned back to the class from the blackboard and rapped his pointer against the edge of his desk.

"If the class will come to order, please," he began, but his plea went unheeded. "Will the gentlemen at the rear of the class please remove your hats so that we may begin with tonight's problem, one that will require your close attention—"

He waited, but the dozen or so offenders ignored the request, although the volume of their conversation lessened a little.

"I gave you an order and I expect it to be obeyed. Before we continue, please remove your headgear in class," Hill said more firmly. There was no reaction to the request, only silent, sullen defiance.

Support for Dave Hill came from an unexpected source when Cliff Loomis urged, "Come on, you guys, take off the dunce caps and let's get down to work. You're only holding the rest of us up."

"Uncle Tom Loomis," one of the fezz-wearers called out in derision.

"And Uncle Tom Hill," another voice taunted.

Dave Hill tried to suppress his angry annoyance. "All right, gentlemen, let's have it out right now," Hill announced. "I will repeat what I told you at the start of this

651

class last month. Since I organized this class two years ago, thirty-seven students have qualified for apprentice jobs at Taylor Electronics. Of those thirty-seven, thirty-five are working at regular assembly, finishing, inspection and trouble-shooting jobs, some as unit heads, all drawing equal pay. Several of those not yet qualified, Mr. Loomis among them, are here for important refresher work.

"I do not get paid for the three evenings each week I give to teaching at this Center. I work a full week at my regular job at T.E. and teach this course in order to supply a needed demand and at the same time help my fellow Negroes to advance themselves in positions not normally available to them. For this opportunity given you, I must demand two things: your devoted attention and respect for the rules of the Center.

"Let me make one thing clear. I do not care about your politics, but I cannot permit you to bring them into this classroom and interfere with the rights of others to learn, perform their experiments and study in peace. The hats you are wearing are a political symbol and I must ask you to remove them under the rule that prohibits the wearing of any hats, regardless of significance, in a classroom—"

"This ain't no hat," Olin Childs retorted. "It's a Black Fez. Where's yours, blood brother?" Approval came from Olin's supporters in raised voices and applause at the rear of the room.

"Whatever you choose to call it," Hill replied, "it is a hat and I want you to remove it. Furthermore, we will have no name-calling in this classroom." He sat on the edge of his desk and indicated the wall clock with his pointer. "At the end of sixty seconds, if those hats are not removed, you people will be asked to leave the room. If you refuse, the entire class will be dismissed and on Friday night the offenders will be refused admission to the class unless each individual makes a public apology to the other members of the class. Sixty seconds."

At the end of the allotted time, no one had made a move beyond some vocal resentment toward the offenders. Hill remained impassively aloof. He stood up and began to address the class when Robbie Baldwin, the apparent leader of the group of Army veterans, approached the platform.

"Mr. Hill?"

"What is it, Robbie?"

"Mr. Hill, I been talkin' to some of the boys who are here to learn something. We decided to ask you if you'd leave us alone for about ten minutes so we can solve this problem—"

652

Hill smiled bleakly. "I'm sorry, Robbie, but nothing doing. There's about six thousand dollars' worth of equipment in this room that was donated on my recommendation by Taylor Electronics. I don't want to see it destroyed in a stupid, useless fight that won't prove a damned thing."

Robbie sighed with defeat. "Okay," he said and returned to the veterans hovering around his bench. Hill said, "Time is up, gentlemen. Either remove your hats or leave the classroom."

The dissident students made no move except to fold their arms across their chests to emphasize their defiance. "Make us," Olin Childs challenged.

"Very well," Hill said briefly. "Class is dismissed. Please file out quietly and don't disturb the students in other classes on your way out." He turned his back to his desk and began replacing textbooks in his briefcase.

Robbie Baldwin leaped up on his bench. "Goddam it, wait a minute, you guys! I come here every school night to learn a decent trade to help me get a better job than carrying a hod full of bricks and cement all day long. Mr. Hill, he's giving us his time free to teach us. If you black beret heroes want to quit, that's fine, but you've got no right closing this class down on the rest of us who want to make something out of ourselves. Far's you're concerned, how the hell you ever going to do it unless you learn something, hey?"

"What good it do us to learn, man, do we hafta go up against Mist' Charley when we get through?" Charley Anderson shouted.

"Boy, why don't you take a good look around you and see what's going on? Everybody who went through this class is working for T.E. for the same pay your Mist' Charley's getting. He ain't as much your enemy as you are to yourself. You talk about getting equal rights from him, how about you taking our right to learn away from us? Man, you just simple-minded, throwing away a chance to learn, get a job, do something important for a change—"

"So we c'n get sent to Viet Nam an' kill somebody ain't never done nothin' to us?"

"Look, smartass, what the hell do you know about Viet Nam? I was there and I came back with a lot more'n I went there with. You want to talk about Viet Nam, let's go outside and talk, but it's got nothing to do with this class. Now get that stupid dunce cap off your head and—"

"Don't tell me what to do, nigger!" Olin Childs shouted, rushing toward Robbie Baldwin.

"Nigger? Goddamn you, boy, I soldiered with a hell of a

653

lot of white men who never called me nigger. I was made sergeant by a white captain who didn't look to see what color I was. Let's you and me go outside and you call me that just once more, hey?"

"I'm your man," Childs accepted.

Amid partisan urgings, Childs and Baldwin led the rest of the class out and down the rear steps to an open outside area within the building lights. Dave Hill went quickly down the front stairs to the administration office and reached for the phone on Daisy Church's desk. "What's the police station number?" he asked.

"4444. What's wrong, Mr. Hill? I heard the noise—"

Hill dialed the number without replying. Two other instructors had left their classes unattended and edged into the office to hear his request for a patrol car and receive assurances that it would be sent at once. "Just keep your classes from joining the fight," Hill pleaded. "Anything else will only aggravate matters." He turned and went to the rear of the building and outside, where the two adversaries were circling each other in preparation for the battle. The rest of the disrupted class, the music rehearsal group and basketball team were joined in the circle around them.

To Hill's satisfaction, Olin Childs was proving one thing: for all his additional height and weight advantage, he was no match for Army-toughened Robbie Baldwin. Childs was bleeding at the mouth from the first blow, one eye badly puffed, finding difficulty with his breathing. Baldwin stood off, charitably waiting for Childs to make the offensive moves, stepping inside Olin's ineffective flailing arms. Robbie pushed him off twice, pleading, "Man, why don't you give up?" But Childs continued his futile efforts, spurred on by his fez-topped supporters.

Car No. 27 arrived with two Negro officers who stepped in and separated the belligerents, bringing the fight to an abrupt end. On pleas by Dave Hill and Ralph Atkins, who had been given the word by Daisy Church, the officers agreed to drop the matter. Childs and his followers left the grounds in sullen retreat. Robbie Baldwin went to Dave Hill and asked, "Can the rest of us go back to class, Mr. Hill?"

"Sure, Robbie," Hill grinned. "Follow me."

When the 9:30 dismissal bell rang, Dave Hill was surrounded in the snack room for his firsthand account of the incident. The black fezzes had appeared in other classrooms that evening, he learned, but had, on request, been removed before classes were started.

Lyle Emerson waited for Elizabeth, who had joined the

circle around Dave Hill, then came to him when he was seated with a mug of coffee. "It makes me nervous," Elizabeth said.

"Dave handled it fine, Elizabeth. I don't think there's anything to worry about," Lyle replied.

"Don't you, Lyle? We almost had the same situation at day school today. They're being worked up by this Dr. Rhama—"

"Elizabeth, don't agitate yourself over it. I'm sure reason will prevail."

"Reason, Lyle, or force?"

"It won't come to that, I'm sure."

"I wish I could feel as sure as you do. Those damned fezzes are all over town."

"Drink your coffee." As she sipped at her mug, "Do you have a lift tonight?"

"I—ah—I'll get one—"

"Why bother? I'll drive you."

"Lyle, it's too risky. Things are getting worse over here. I'd rather not."

"I'll go out now. Follow me in five minutes. I'm on the far side of the parking lot."

"Lyle—I—"

He stood up. "Five minutes," he said and limped away.

Duke Shackleford reached the Center at 9:20, driving Eli Buller's 1957 Buick, a fair exchange for the Jaguar, considering his purpose. He parked outside the Center's grounds on Division Street, but within sight of its driveway, then slid down behind the wheel and waited. At 9:45, he saw the Dodge come out of the driveway and turn right. Duke let it reach the corner before he started the Buick and followed. In the next block, he allowed a station wagon to drop in between himself and the Dodge, but the station wagon continued straight on as the Dodge turned into Reed. Duke followed the Dodge as it crossed Churchill, then ran a red light to cross behind them. He trailed the Dodge cautiously until it turned into Crescent and headed toward Riverside. Duke assumed that Emerson was merely driving to kill time, reasoning that as long as the car kept moving, nothing could happen between Elizabeth and her white boy friend except conversation.

In the Dodge, Elizabeth said, "I can't run out on my responsibilities, Lyle. It's not fair of you to ask me to do that."

"Elizabeth, you've got a responsibility to yourself, too."

655

"And what about you, your dedication to elevating the Negro—"

"We could do that in Los Angeles, too, couldn't we?"

"Oh, Lyle, you knock down every argument I can raise to prove you're wrong about us."

"If you love me, Elizabeth, I'm not wrong."

"And I've told you, I don't *know*. I'm not honestly *sure*."

"I think we've already proved that, but you're allowing other issues to cloud your mind. Shut them out, darling, please. Try to see us apart from duty and responsibility to Laurelton. We'll take that up in Los Angeles, doing what we want to do together."

"Lyle, I can't think now. I'm upset by what happened tonight. Those fools in their black fezzes, disrupting an entire school because of a demagogue who trades on hatred."

"It will pass, I tell you. I know it will."

"Take me home now, Lyle? Please."

"All right." He wheeled the car into a turn at the corner of Grand and caught a glimpse of headlights in his rearview mirror. He turned into Exeter.

"Where are we going?" Elizabeth asked.

"Taking you home by a roundabout route," Lyle said with a lightness he did not feel. The car behind had followed. He slowed down on Exeter, reached the corner as the yellow light came on, then shot across the street, barely avoiding a pickup truck on his right, hearing the curse flung at him by its driver. But the pursuing car had been trapped at the red light and blocked by cross traffic.

Lyle turned into a strange street, a left, a right, a straight stretch for eight blocks on a dark street with no lights behind him.

"Was someone following us?" Elizabeth asked.

"I think not. I'm sure of it now."

"Lyle, we can't keep this up, having to look over our shoulders every minute we're together, afraid to breathe, or live—"

"We can if it's worth it, and it's worth it to me, Elizabeth. And to you, or you wouldn't be here with me."

She said nothing until he dropped her at the corner nearest her house. "Good night, Lyle," she said then.

Lyle drew her to him and kissed her. She responded less eagerly than before, then pulled away, opened the door and got out quickly. He waited until he saw her go up the steps, then turned up Wallace and by the time he reached her house, she had disappeared inside.

Lyle thought of the expression "star-crossed" and knew now that it applied to the situation that existed between himself and Elizabeth; then, as he cut back into Grand Avenue, the most direct approach to the bridge, he wondered about the car that had been following them earlier, and how long it had been tailing them before he noticed it; probably since they had left the Center. He had little doubt that the driver had been her brother, Duke. Or had it been merely a coincidence escalated into suspicion by his own—and Elizabeth's—fears?

He couldn't entirely dismiss the matter, but he put it aside for the moment and thought of Elizabeth and the problems he was creating for her within her family, possibly her community. He knew the other instructors at the Center had begun to notice. It had become obvious because he sought out no one but her after classes. The others were polite and coolly standoffish, regarding him perhaps, as Elizabeth had told him, as the white man who was trying to cover his sense of guilt by crawling into a black skin.

In the time since he had returned, Lyle had turned away from his former friends. They had been kind and warm, but he saw the pity for his loss of limb, pity for his loss of Jill Tinsley, pity in the offer of the school board to return him to his teaching job even before he had requested reinstatement. And he had had more than his share of pity. He had been tempted to reject the school board offer; in fact, had made it difficult by requesting assignment to an all-Negro school in Angeltown, which had been denied; but teaching was what he had done best in civilian life and without the job to cling to, his life would have become meaningless.

His days had been full, but the nights were long and sleepless; and then, the idea of offering his services to teach night classes at the Center came to him. He had been accepted because he had a certain skill that was needed, but like the other white instructors who were on the teaching staff then, he felt excluded from the Negro instructors. Even when the four white instructors, for one reason or another, resigned from the Center, Lyle had stubbornly refused to give in to what he secretly termed reverse intolerance and remained. Or was it because Elizabeth had understood his need and given him warmth instead of cool politeness, encouragement instead of subtle indifference?

The dilemma of rejection; by Jill because he was a cripple; by Elizabeth because he was white.

He was caught by a red light at Grand and Mercer and turned right when the light turned green. This was the action section of the Avenue by night. The scene. Swingers and cats. Taverns, restaurants and honky-tonk amusement places that rocked and rolled in store-fronted establishments whose neon did little to disguise shabbiness. Like Velie Street, Grand was noisy with human and vehicular traffic as Angeltown moved about restlessly in search of distraction from the cares of the day, following the pied pipers whose lures were a new beat, a hip combo, a new adventure.

A mini-skirted figure, wearing a tasseled fez, suddenly dashed across the street in midblock, a grinning youth in hot pursuit, and Lyle jammed his brakes on to avoid hitting the pursuer. There was a loud squeal of brakes behind him as Lyle brought the Dodge to an abrupt halt only inches from the boy. The car behind him, a 1955 Buick, rammed into him, front bumper locked with Lyle's rear bumper. The fez-topped youth who had escaped injury came around to the driver's side, saw a white man behind the wheel and substituted a snarl for the grin of apology.

"What th' hell's th' matter with you, white man? You don't own no streets over here," he shouted, attracting the attention of passersby. A small knot of men and women gathered as the driver of the Buick got out to check for damage. Lyle opened the door and slid out on his left leg, using both hands to swing his right leg around. Traffic began to stack up in both directions and the air was filled with the added noise of impatient hands on horns.

The driver of the Buick was an elderly Negro, who approached him smilingly. "Sorry, Mister," he said to Lyle. "You stopped so fast I didn't have time——"

"It's all right, sir," Lyle replied. "There's no damage. Just our bumpers locked. We'll need some help to separate them."

From the outer rim of the gathered curious came the questions: "What's up?" "What happen?"

Someone called back, "Ol Mist' Charley here hot-roddin' his jalopy."

"Hit somebody?"

"I think so. A boy——"

Angry mutterings from the outside circle. Lyle looked around him in surprise, into a sea of hostile faces and black fezzes. "No one was hurt——" he began.

"Says you——"

"He lyin'. Boy was hit."

658

The Buick driver said loudly, "Look. Nobody was hit an' it wasn't this man's fault. The boy ran across the street in front of him, chasin' after a girl. You help us get untangled, we be out of here in a minute."

"Well, if it ain't Uncle Tom, suckin' up to Mist' Charley," came a derisive cry.

"Goddam it, you people crazy? If he wasn't white, wouldn't nobody even stop to look," the driver spat angrily. "If anybody got hurt, where is he, huh?"

Two men came forward and stepped on Lyle's bumper, tugging at the Buick's front bumper. Freed, the second car moved backward a few inches. Lyle said, "Thank you," to the men. To the driver, "If you want my name and license—"

"No need," the driver replied. "Couldn't tell the new scratches from the old ones."

Lyle moved back toward the door. A hand shot out and grabbed his left arm. "Hol' on, Whitey. What about the boy you hit?"

"I didn't hit anyone," Lyle began, when he saw the first friendly face in the crowd, a Negro officer who had pushed through to the inner circle.

"All right, folks," the officer chanted ritually, "let's break it up now and get the traffic moving."

"He hit a boy," came a shout, repeated by others.

The officer said, "All right, where's the boy? Let's see him."

There was a rumbling among the crowd, but no boy came forward. Smiling affably, the officer said, "Get along now. You-all blocking traffic. This is between these two men and nobody else."

"White man's nigger!" came the virulent taunt.

The officer's jaws tightened, struggling to maintain his smile and composure. He turned to Lyle and the other driver. He listened to both, saw there was no damage, recorded their names and license numbers in his book, this more for the benefit of the onlookers, then motioned them both back into their cars. But the dissatisfied crowd had pushed forward, blocking the front left door of Lyle's car.

The officer toyed with his whistle. "Get back now," he ordered. "I've got a partner less than a block from here. I blow this whistle, he'll call in for police assistance. You people know what will happen then, don't you? Nobody's been hurt and no damage was done. Now let's get out of the way and start the traffic moving."

For a moment the situation was tense, then from somewhere inside the crowd, a voice called out, "Let him alone. He's the crippled teacher from the Center. He's okay."

The crowd began to inch back. Lyle got into his car and started the motor, flushing with embarrassment and anger at the identification. Slowly, a path cleared in front of him and he moved eastward on Grand, feeling the wetness of his shirt against his body. As he eased forward, he heard catcalls hurled at him by several fez-topped faces, felt their fists beating against the sides of his car.

The incident only emphasized Elizabeth's fears, the fear he had felt only moments ago; and hatred as implacable as that he had seen in the faces of enemy Viet Cong prisoners. As he came onto the bridge, he saw a patrol car parked to one side. On the east end, another patrol car, both probably checking for any sudden increase of traffic in either direction. Ticklish as driving in Saigon, through checkpoints, not knowing when the bomb or grenade would explode.

He drove through Laurelton's quiet commercial center quickly, turned off a block before the Mall and drove to the rear of his apartment building. It was nearing 11 o'clock when he pulled in between two cars nearest the rear entrance door. He got out, locked the car and started toward the door. The voice, low and sharp, hissed, *"Hey!"*

He turned and looked back. In the narrow aisle between his car and the one on his left he saw the dark figure moving toward him. No crowd this time, no officer. Only himself and the swift-moving figure. They were no more than 30 feet apart. Only 20 yards from the rear door of the building, but Lyle knew he could never make it to safety in time. He braced himself against a fender and said, "Who is—?"

Then he saw the fist as it flashed upward, came directly at his jaw, felt the second blow in his abdomen, another chopping downward to his head as he doubled over in pain. He came up, turned toward his assailant, grabbed for the right hand that was aimed toward his jaw, ducked and held it for a second, but it tore loose from his grasp and caught him along the jaw. His mouth was bleeding and the pain in his midsection ran down into the nerve ends of his stump. He buckled, but the man caught him, held him by the lapels of his coat with his left hand and pummeled him with his right.

One of his eyes was almost closed by a blow and he could no longer see, except for some sharp splinters of light that were unnatural; then he felt himself falling. The ground came up and struck him and for a moment he heard only his own gasping breath and the angry, short breaths of his assailant. Then he felt the harsh stamp of a shoe crunch down on the upper part of his prosthetic, heard the voice grind out, "You ofay sonofabitch, I warned you." And then a merciful blackness.

When he came to, a woman was kneeling beside him doing something to his face with a handkerchief. For a moment he thought he had been blinded, heard her saying, "Please. Don't move. My husband is getting someone to help you. Lie still, please."

He lay back on the asphalt paving, reached an aching arm upward and touched the swollen eye, then pushed the sticky lid of his left eye up and caught the dim glimpse of the kneeling woman. "Wha—"

"We were visiting friends," she said. "We came out a few minutes ago and found you lying here beside our car. Are you all right?"

"I don't—know," Lyle said. His head ached and his ribs felt as though they had been beaten with steel rods. He twisted and felt the pain grinding into his stump.

"Was it a holdup? My God, I was afraid to wait here with you. Don't move, please. There may be something broken. My husband said to keep you still until—" She was kneeling, speaking to him, but her head was raised, looking around anxiously. There was the sound of a door slamming and she said with relief, "Here they come."

One man carried a chair. The other got into his car and backed it away to give them more room. Then both men lifted him carefully and placed him into the chair, carried him toward the building. The woman ran ahead to open the door. Inside, the night desk man waited, holding the door to the service elevator open. "It's Mr. Emerson," he said. "I've got a passkey. Doctor's on his way. Poor guy—"

Undressing him became complicated by the harness arrangement, but the woman worked efficiently and he felt himself between the cool sheets of his own bed, naked and covered to his neck with a blanket. He barely heard the night clerk tell the two men that this was the lieutenant who had been shot down in Viet Nam. The woman found a bottle of bourbon on the sideboard, poured a few inches into a glass and held it for him as he drank it quickly. Then she found a bottle of alcohol in the bathroom and bathed his face with a damp washcloth.

"Pills—" he whispered, pointing to the night table. The woman picked up one of several small boxes of pills and capsules. He nodded at one marked *For pain—one every four hours,* and gave him two to swallow. He was asleep

—or unconscious—by the time the doctor arrived, and when he awoke again he was in a room in the Laurelton Memorial Hospital, his ribs taped, a bandage covering part of his head and slanted down over his left eye.

The nurse held a glass tube to his mouth while he sipped water gratefully, then gave him an injection that sent him back into the safety of darkness.

5

At midmorning, Lyle was awake again. The nurse, young and attractive for a change, smiled and said, "Welcome back, Mr. Emerson. Ready for some food?"

"Where—?"

"Are you?" she finished for him. "In a private room at Memorial. I'm Jane Corbett, your private nurse. You were brought in late last night and there's an officer waiting to ask you some questions, but the doctor will see you first."

"How bad is it? My eye—"

"The doctor will be here in a few minutes, Mr. Emerson. He'll tell you all about it. I'll order a soft-boiled egg and toast for you and if you feel like it, you can have a big steak by dinnertime. All right?"

"Get the doctor for me, will you, nurse? And one favor, please. Let's not be so goddamned cheerful about it."

"You sound like you're almost fully recovered," Miss Corbett said, still smiling. "Back in a few minutes. Don't try to get out of bed, you hear?"

She returned with a white-coated serious young man who introduced himself as Dr. Bass, the resident on duty. Bass checked his left eye carefully and seemed satisfied, evidenced by his first smile. "You'll be fine, Mr. Emerson. I was worried about that eye more than anything else, but the swelling is subsiding nicely. No broken bones, no concussion, luckily, and we're giving you something to relieve the pain and soreness. You should be up and around within a day or two."

"Thank you, Doctor."

"Can you remember what happened? I'm assuming it was a holdup."

"I can't recall much. It happened so suddenly, from behind."

"Well—I suppose it's all right to let the police see you for a few minutes. I'll tell them to keep it as brief as possible and I'll drop in on you later this afternoon."

"Thanks, Doctor. By the way, this room and the private nurse—"

"The night clerk at your apartment house found a book of telephone numbers and called the first person on the list. A Corey Armour. He ordered the room and nurse and guaranteed everything. I'm to call him as soon as you're up to seeing anyone. Shall I?"

"Yes, please."

"Later, then. You can have anything you want to eat, so feel free."

The nurse returned with a tray of soft-boiled eggs, toast and a pot of coffee. "Ready for company?"

"That depends."

"The police. Two detectives."

"All right. Send them in."

Detectives Rossiter and Jansen came in and began the routine questioning. Lyle plotted the evening preceding the attack. "I left the Center a few minutes after nine-thirty and drove around a little while before I came home—"

Rossiter said, "What about the run-in you had on Grand Avenue at—" he consulted a small notebook—"10:20. We have an officer's report—"

"Oh, that. It wasn't anything. Just a tangle of bumpers—"

"A considerable crowd gathered, didn't it, Mr. Emerson? Some harsh names called, pushing around?"

"I tell you it was nothing. No damage. It lasted less than five minutes."

Jansen asked, "Did you notice anyone following you when you left the scene of the accident?"

"No-o. I'm sure I'd have noticed if someone had followed me for that distance, across the bridge and all."

"Did you get a glimpse of the man or men who attacked you?"

"No. I'm sure it was one man. He came from behind and struck before I could turn fully around. There was too little light to see him clearly."

"Did he say anything that might give us a clue to either his identity or why he attacked you? Demand your money or other valuables?"

"No. Not a word."

"Puzzling," said Rossiter. "A man attacks you, but leaves your watch and wallet with sixty-seven dollars intact. There was no one around to stop him from robbing you, yet he didn't. Do you have any personal enemies, Mr. Emerson?"

"None I know of."

"Anyone from high school or the Center who might have

663

some kind of a grudge to work off? Someone who failed a test, argued with—"

"I can assure you on that subject and answer with a positive no."

"The man *was* a Nigra, wasn't he?"

After a brief hesitation, "Yes. But I didn't recognize him. It took place between two cars and the light was bad."

"Can you give us any kind of a description? Approximate height, weight, build, anything at all?"

"I'm sorry. I was at a disadvantage. He may have been my own height, weight and build. Five feet eleven inches, about one hundred and seventy pounds. I don't think I can give you anything more than that."

"Well, let's look for something else. Could it have been either of the men you identified at Headquarters in the Center burglary matter?"

"No. I think I can be fairly positive about that. If it had, I think I would have been robbed. But I don't really know. I'm tired—"

"All right, Mr. Emerson, we'll let that hold us for the time being. If you can remember anything else, no matter how slight or unimportant you may think it is, give us a ring, will you? I'll leave a card on your table here." Jansen took a card from his wallet. Rossiter added his card to it and placed both on the table within Lyle's reach. "Good luck," Rossiter said and both men left.

Miss Corbett returned to remove his tray, take his temperature and give him a pill to swallow. The telephone rang and she answered, held her hand over the mouthpiece as she asked, "Do you want to talk to a Miss Page, the assignments secretary at the Recreational-Vocation Center?"

There was no Miss Page at the Center and Lyle knew it was Elizabeth. He said, "Yes. They'll have to get someone to fill in for me while I'm out." He took the receiver and said, "Hello."

"Lyle, can you talk?"

"I'm fine, Miss Page, but I won't be able to take any classes for a day or two," he replied.

"Oh, Lyle, I'm so sorry. I know it's my fault. I know it. I wish I could come to see you—"

"How did you hear about it, Miss Page?"

"It's in the morning paper. Haven't you seen it?"

"No."

"It said you were attacked by a suspected prowler when you returned home last night from your class at the Center. It was him, wasn't it, Lyle?"

664

"I—ah—yes, thank you, Miss Page. I'll return as soon as I'm discharged. Yes. Good-bye."

"Good-bye, darling. I'm so sorry—"

Corey arrived at 4:30. The room was brighter with flowers from Lyle's high school class, the Center, Ad Cameron, and a large basket of fruit from Corey. The nurse adjusted the bed into a sitting position and went out, admonishing Lyle not to move around too much. Corey dropped a carton of Warren Imperials on the table and remained standing.

"What the hell was it all about, Lyle?"

"You read it in the paper, Corey. One of those things. I came home, parked my car, and probably disturbed some prowler. Just an accident in timing. A few minutes either way and it would never have happened."

"That's what the paper said. I talked with Ad. He told me it was a rough guess on the part of the police until they could talk with you about it. You didn't get a look at the guy?"

"No. Only a glimpse in the dark. Before I could turn around fully, I was down between two cars. He came at me from behind."

"Too damned bad. Negro, wasn't he?"

"Yes. Makes any identification all the harder. Probably a car thief, mugger, nothing as important as a gunman—"

"Ad tells me the police checked and found nothing had been taken."

"That's right. He was probably scared off."

"Or was it something else, Lyle?"

"What are you suggesting?"

"Well, I keep thinking—"

"What?"

"Skip it. I'm getting out of line."

"You suspect it has something to do with Elizabeth, don't you?"

"I said skip it."

A moment of silence passed between them, then Lyle said, "Okay, chum. I gave Elizabeth a lift home from the Center. Somebody was following us, but I managed to hang him up at a red light and lost him there. After I dropped her, I headed for home, but got into a minor traffic tangle with another car on Grand Avenue. The police have a report on that. When I got home, he was waiting there for me. The rest of it happened the way I told the police."

"Except that you know who it was."

"Yes. Her brother. Duke Shackleford. I didn't see him

665

too clearly, but I recognized his voice and something he said to me."

"Which you didn't report to the police."

"How the hell can I without dragging her into it?"

"Lyle, you're playing out of your league. He could kill you next time."

"I'll worry about that later. Just keep what I've told you to yourself."

"Lyle—"

"It's my problem, Corey. Don't get involved."

"Ad told me the other day that with things popping the way they are, you'd be smart as hell to stay away from the Center and out of Angeltown until the situation cools off. This could be a good excuse to drop out for a while. The whole town is edgy and headed for an eyeball confrontation—"

"That's ridiculous, Corey. People have a way of magnifying insects into roaring, clawing beasts. It's only another phase that will work itself out. This Black Fez thing will blow over and they'll forget about it."

"I wish you could convince Ad and some of the others I've heard recently. Frankly, it disturbs me, too."

"Let's forget it for the moment. What are you doing to keep yourself occupied?"

"That's something else again. Lyle, do you remember the air base the Seabees put down in that jungle country in the Tuyen Duc province?"

"Hell, I ought to. I operated out of there when it was first opened. Why?"

Corey told Lyle about his conversation with Hall Peterson and his plans for developing the Shadow Hills property into a permanent home and resort community. Lyle's response was at once enthusiastic. "Jesus, Corey, what a hell of a great idea. Do you think Taylor will spring for it?"

"So far, he and John Curran are interested enough to conduct a thorough survey. The reason I'm breaking this to you, Lyle, is that I'd like you to think about coming in on the deal, take over and run the school system we'll need up there. Between two thousand and twenty-five hundred families will require elementary and high schools—"

"Hold it, old son. You're coming on too fast for me."

"I know it's a brand-new thing, Lyle, but why not give it some thought? No rush. There's plenty of time before we make any kind of move. If we make it at all."

"Corey, I'm a teacher. What you need is an administrative type, somebody who knows the cost of operations, books, teacher personnel recruitment and salaries. Somebody who can coordinate school programs, buy furniture, toilet paper, wastepaper baskets, set up lunch programs, organize a P.T.A., that sort of thing."

"Well," Corey smiled, "why not you? It will get you out of the teacher level and into the higher plateaus of education. Think about it, man."

"I am. It sounds great at the start, but— Let me ask you this: what about Negroes, will they be a part of the community?"

"That hasn't come up yet, but I suppose it will as plans develop. There will be jobs for them to fill and we can't expect them to commute from Laurelton or Riverton. People will want maids, gardeners—"

It suddenly struck Lyle that this was folly. No new community would include homes for Negroes. They would be welcomed as day workers, laborers, delivery boys, janitors. They would have to build a separate community of shacks somewhere nearby, a ghetto slum from which to emerge every morning and retreat to every night. Like bedbugs or roaches or rats. And what about the Center, Elizabeth?

"Corey, it's too big to take in so quickly—"

"Think about it, Lyle. I don't expect an off-the-top-of-the-head answer. There's plenty of time and there'll be other problems to think about and work out."

"Let's let it rest a while, shall we?" Lyle said.

"Sure. We'll talk about it another time. What about some reading matter? Anything special you'd like to have?"

"Not right now, thanks. I've got this bunged-up eye and the makings of a splitting headache."

"All right, chum. I'll take off now and let you get some rest. See you tomorrow. Ad said he'd drop in on you later."

"Thanks, Corey. I appreciate everything."

"My pleasure, Lieutenant."

6

Most of them were of school age, but there were at least 20 adult men and women among them as they paraded into Taylor Square and began marching in double ranks before the Federal Building, each wearing a tasseled black fez. By noon, there were about 80 in the group. Earlier, five more Negro youths had reported to the Induction Center, but refused to take the step forward as a condition of their willingness to accept service in the Army. They were hastily arraigned and placed in detention cells pending further action.

Newspaper and television photographers had recorded the scene and walked beside the marchers, interviewing them. By midafternoon, city, county and federal employees watched from windows of the buildings that lined three sides of the square and people who had business to conduct passed the demonstrators with self-conscious glances. So far, there had been no major disturbances.

In response to several complaints that the Negroes were blocking entrances to the Federal Building and thus interfering with the civil rights of others, Inspector LaSalle had ordered several prowl cars with both white and Negro officers into the square to assist federal marshals and several sheriff's deputies in keeping the demonstrators moving and corridors open before the entrances.

The trouble began as soon as schools were dismissed for the day. The ranks of the demonstrators swelled to over 200 and more city police were sent for to keep order. Hastily painted signs were passed out to the marchers, demanding the release of the Negro conscientious objectors. The signs also demanded that ten whites be inducted for each Negro as a fair and equal proportion.

At four o'clock, a countermarch was begun by about 60 white youths and men also carrying posters and placards, but these were at once provocative and offensive, using acronyms which caught the eyes of the onlookers, to the delight of some and the embarrassment of others. These read:

Slobs,	Foul-
Hogs,	Ups,
Idiots,	Colored
Traitors,	Kowards,
Go Home!	*Beat it!*

The first four letters of each sign were larger and heavier than the others and were painted in bright red, producing deliberate obscenities to add to insult. The Negroes bore their humiliation for a few minutes before laughter from the countermarchers and passersby provoked an attempt to capture the odiously phrased signs. The clash brought more police, deputy sheriffs and marshals into the fray and city, county and federal government came to a virtual standstill as employees watched the action in the square.

There were 43 arrests. Four Negroes and one white man required medical attention. The offensive signs were confiscated and the remaining marchers and countermarchers continued to parade, kept apart by vigilant enforcement officers.

Peter LaSalle sat in his car at the north end of the square and watched the demonstration, wondering if, when the trouble came, it would begin here. Of one thing he was certain: when it did come, it would be explosive and fast. A shouted curse, even a virulent look, could set it off. He had sat in on two strategy meetings and attended conferences with County Sheriff Will Apperson during the day, while Lee Durkin had been in touch with the Governor's office to discuss the possible use of the State Highway Patrol and the National Guard in case of emergency. Both Durkin and the Governor were reluctant to use troopers, but both agreed on the steps to be taken if a general riot broke out. Every fire department in Cairn County had been alerted and most of the equipment that could be spared was placed on standby, to be rushed into Laurelton on call from Fire Chief Gary Hobbs. Recalling the Watts riots in Los Angeles in August of 1965, and the rooftop snipers who had shot at firemen, it was agreed to assign two heavily armed sheriff's deputies or city policemen to each fire vehicle called out.

Durkin, certain that any outbreak would come in Angeltown, decided to strengthen Captain Price's 12th Precinct with as many reserves as possible, assigning skeleton units of regulars, with police trainees for support in the Laurelton area, and roadblocks on the east and west approaches to the bridge. The single police boat, *Ranger,* would take on the almost impossible job of patrolling the Cottonwood to prevent crossings from one side to the other by small craft. At the first sign of trouble, sheriffs of adjoining counties would set up checkpoints along the main roads into East Laurelton to search all vehicles for weapons.

LaSalle listened to the communicator's voice issuing orders, receiving call-ins. Except for the earlier incident in the square, there had been no major disturbances elsewhere. Out on Green Haven Avenue and Pall Mall Road, pickets marched in front of Ainslee Farm Dairy and Cloverland Bakery, but there had been no clashes. Several retail outlets in Angeltown had been struck, but milk and bread were basic necessities and shoppers ignored the pickets, although they asked the store clerks to put the milk containers and bread into paper bags to avoid incidents with the pickets.

It was six o'clock. LaSalle started back to Headquarters.

669

CHAPTER VI

1

Corey found Adam Cameron in Lyle's room when he called at the hospital later that night. Lyle was on his feet exercising his leg and arm muscles and but for some minor facial bruises and a small patch over one eye, showed great improvement over the day before. "If the doctor is satisfied with my eye in the morning, he'll take the patch off and I can check out of here by early afternoon," Lyle told Corey.

"Great, but why rush it? Why not take an extra day or two of luxury living?"

"Exactly what I suggested," Ad said.

Lyle laughed lightly. "Look, will you guys stop worrying about me? I'll guarantee that nobody will slip up behind me again. It was pure accident or coincidence, nothing more. Nobody's out to get me or anything like that."

Corey caught the quick glance Lyle threw him and nodded imperceptibly, aware that Ad knew no more of the story than Lyle had told the police.

"Damned strange," Ad commented. "I don't get it. Hell, all the guy had to do was slip his hand into your jacket pocket and—"

Lyle shrugged. "Who knows how these things happen, Ad? He may have started going for my wallet when he heard that couple and ran. Anyway, it's all over now and I'll be out of here sometime tomorrow at the latest."

"I've been bringing Lyle up to date on the situation in town," Ad said to Corey.

"Just what is it, Ad?" Corey asked.

"Not good. This Black Fez thing is stirring up some of our better known hotheads. We've had hundreds of calls at the paper, threats from the usual white-sheet boys to move into Angeltown and clean it out of the Communist-led Negroes unless the police put a stop to the Black Power movement. The radio and television stations have been getting pretty much the same thing. Over at the City Hall and County Building there must be half a dozen meetings going on, trying to find some way to pour oil over troubled waters. The police have worked out a strategy plan with the

670

Sheriff's Department and Durkin has his finger on the panic button, ready to call in the Highway Patrol and National Guard. This morning less than half the Negro kids were in school, a stay-out to voice their protest against the arrest of those conscientious objectors. It doesn't look promising. One match to the fuse and we've got a real ten-alarm explosion on our hands."

"God, I hope not," Lyle said.

"When and if it comes," Ad continued, "I'd hate like hell to be caught over there in Angeltown."

"What about police protection for the white merchants over there," Lyle asked.

"Lyle, boy, use your imagination. Those white merchants will be the prime targets. There aren't enough police to give individual protection to every white-owned or operated store. All merchants, black and white, realize that when hell breaks loose and the looting begins, color won't mean one goddamned thing. They'll all get caught up in the ruckus."

"What about the Center? They won't hurt that, will they?"

"You're being naïve. When a mob gets itself worked up, anything in its way becomes a bull's-eye. Fire hasn't any way to take sides. It just spreads."

"What about this Dr. Rhama?"

"He could damned well be the match that lights the fuse, and the worst part of it is, the police have nothing on him, no way to stop him. Freedom of speech—"

2

It looked like any other panel delivery truck except that it was sparkling new and carried no identification. It was black, glistening with touches of chrome, and drew little more than casual attention from passersby and loiterers when it parked at the corner of Velie and Harrison, one block west of Banjo's Place. The fez-topped driver and his two front-seat companions got out, went to the rear and opened both doors. Inside, a fourth man began handing out several cone-shaped objects which the other three carried up an aluminum ladder and began attaching to a post built into the center of the truck roof—four loudspeakers, facing the cardinal points of the compass.

This activity drew the attention of the loiterers, then the passersby, who gathered at the curb to watch the operation. When the silver-hued speakers were in place, the man inside the panel truck clamped a set of earphones on and began blowing into a microphone for a power test. The O.K. signal was relayed to him from one of the men listening on the vehicle's roof. Another of the foursome removed a large carton from the truck and opened it to reveal stacks of black cardboard fezzes. He held one up and called out, "You brothers and sisters who don't have one, step up and get one. They're free, Dr. Rhama's compliments. Don't be bashful, just come up and take one. Wear it wherever you go. Come on, brother, you there with your friends—"

At once, eager hands pressed in to receive the tasseled fezzes: men, women, boys and girls. On the wooden steps next to the Capital Laundromat, two elderly men and a woman who was holding an infant, sat watching stoically. The man dispensing the fezzes, crossed the pavement and held out three of the black caps.

"How about it, brothers, sister, you with us?" he asked with a wide, disarming smile.

"The one I got on, it's good enough for me," one man replied, touching the brim of his worn brown hat.

"Looks kinda foolish to me," the second man said.

The woman stared blankly without speaking.

"Tell you, black folks," the fez dispenser said, "you're going to look a little foolish being the only ones not wearing the black fez of brotherhood. Time's coming soon when you're going to have to show you're with us or against us—"

The first man interrupted impatiently. "You just lookin' for trouble, man. All's you doin', you's stirrin' up somethin' bad for all of us. You gettin' our chil'ren all riled up, but when the white man come shootin' an' bustin' heads, where you goin'a be? With us, or a hun'red mile from here in your fancy truck?"

"All right, Uncle Tom, you-all just sit there, just the way you've been sitting there all your life, doing nothing to help yourself or your people." Still smiling, but cold-eyed, the disciple of Dr. Rhama turned back to the curb to help his companions distribute more of the fezzes to eager youngsters, some of whom wore several that were telescoped on top of each other.

Within a few moments, another car drew up behind the sound truck. Four fez-topped men got out, Brother Leonard and Dr. Rhama among them. The four wore ankle-length black robes that were embroidered with half moons and stars, a clenched fist, a burst of flame with a sword rising from it. Nodding, smiling to the gathered crowd of about 30 men and women, Dr. Rhama walked to the sound truck and took a microphone from the technician inside. He walked around and mounted a small, three-step platform that had been set up on the pavement and began speaking. As soon as he did, others crossed the street to join the assembly, now increased to about a hundred.

"Brothers, sisters, I bid you welcome. I am Dr. Rhama and these are my loyal brethren who have followed me to many cities where I have conducted my Crusade for Black Brotherhood."

The response was immediate, with calls of "Yeah, brother!" "Amen!" "Say it, brother, say it!"

"You have heard me on radio, seen me on television, read my words in the press. In many cities and towns, I have been arrested, beaten and harassed for speaking those words. Arrested, beaten and spat upon out of fear, the fear of the white man who knows that he must keep black men and women apart and disunited in order to keep them in perpetual slavery.

"They have said, 'Wait.' They have said it since slavery was abolished. Wait. And we have waited for over a hundred years only to find that we are still in bondage to the white master.

"We have waited through one hundred years of suffering, and they still say, 'Wait.' One hundred years of lynchings, abominations and terror, and they still say, 'Tomorrow.' One hundred years of man's inhumanity to man, of degradation to his spirit and soul, and they still say, 'Have patience.' One hundred years of educational and economic starvation, and they still say, 'You are not our intellectual equal.' One hundred years of humiliation and bestial intolerances, and they still say, 'You can't have it overnight.' "

Dr. Rhama paused and slowly looked over his growing audience, recognizing the signs he had seen often before, knowing he had captured and was holding them. He relaxed now, waiting until the murmurs of "Amen" diminished.

"And for one hundred years, we have waited for his promises to come true. Well, brothers and sisters, the blame doesn't fall on Mr. White Man's shoulders alone. No. Some of it is ours, yes, our fault, the fault of the black man because for one hundred years, we—you, us, together—have sat back and agreed with what Mr. White Man has said. We accepted his lies and did nothing but what he told us to do, Wait. We waited and watched our children and grandchildren beaten, ground down while they waited, giving in, accepting slavery in shame, living in fear of death, with death itself.

"You have taken Whitey's promises and given up your heritage and your manhood with it, believing that it was freedom. You have accepted his meaningless laws and what have you gotten in return?"

In Car No. 4, Officers Ben Hammond and Paul Green turned into Harrison Street from Grand Avenue and headed south toward Velie. The morning, despite the school stay-out in Angeltown, had been relatively quiet, hardly more then a schoolless Saturday. All squad cars had been warned to keep a close watch on the white-owned shops in the 26-by-12-block commercial area that ran north from Velie to Grand and west from the bridge to Exeter. As they turned into Harrison now, Paul Green stirred, then came alert. "Ben—"

"What?"

"Up ahead, some kind of a crowd. Looks like Velie."

Hammond pulled to his left to clear the truck ahead of them which was obscuring his vision. "Yeah," he said. He maneuvered No. 4 behind the large truck again and reached for the microphone. "Central Communications, this is No. 4. Come in. Over."

The response was immediate. "Cent-Com. Come in, No. 4. Over."

"Crowd formed at Velie and Harrison. Can't make it out from where we are, but it looks like a big one. We're three blocks north on Harrison, just south of Grand, heading toward it to investigate. Over."

"Cent-Com standing by, No. 4. Over and out."

This was the new routine. In any case where you approach a gathered crowd, notify Cent-Com. Keep one man in the car to maintain communication and call in a Code 9 (Request for Assistance) at the first sign of trouble.

"You stay with the car, Paul," Hammond said as they drew within a block of Velie. "I'd better handle this one."

"You think maybe it would be better if I—"

"No—o. I'll give it a go. You stick close to the mike."

At Velie, the truck in front of Car No. 4 braked and sounded its horn. The crowd had spilled over into the intersection, partially blocking vehicular traffic. Slowly, the crowd gave way. The truck passed through the intersection and the black-and-white police car stood exposed in the open. At once, the atmosphere became charged with hostility. Hammond stopped the car a few feet beyond the far edge of the crowd and brought it to a halt at the curb. Green slid across the seat and got behind the wheel, the microphone in his right hand, held partly concealed beneath the dashboard.

From the periphery of the human ring that surrounded

674

the sound truck, Dr. Rhama's voice blared his message and Ben Hammond listened to the inflammatory, incisive words.

"—so the law tells us we are free and equal and I ask you: What does free and equal mean to you as a Negro? Let me tell you. It means that you are free and equal only to another Negro, but not to the white man, rich, poor, ignorant or illiterate; not to the white man who wrote those words, spoke those words, passed those laws. But those words and laws were in effect when Emmett Till, Medgar Evers, Jimmie Lee Jackson and James Chaney were murdered out of the white man's fears."

Dr. Rhama paused and, in pausing, saw Ben Hammond on the edge of the crowd, beginning to press slowly, gently through to the inner circle. "I see a minion of the law," Dr. Rhama said, "the white man's law, in our midst, and I welcome him. Come up, Officer, and refute, if you can, anything I have said here to my people. Please. Make room, brothers, sisters, for the majesty of the White Law."

The crowd turned toward Hammond, far less cool than he appeared to be, and a narrow aisle was opened for his passage, pressing against him, and then they were face to face, Dr. Rhama looking down upon the white officer from his raised platform.

"I'm not here to answer your questions or to debate with you," Hammond said in a controlled, polite voice, "only to ask a question. Do you have a city permit to conduct a public rally in West Laurelton, Dr. Rhama?"

Dr. Rhama smirked and replied through his microphone. "This officer has just demanded to know if I have a permit to speak to my people. My answer to him is, no. I have no permit, nor do I need a permit to address my brothers and sisters in peaceful assembly as guaranteed by the Constitution of the United States. Does that answer your question, Officer?"

"It's an answer," Hammond replied, "but there's a city ordinance against blocking traffic. Your people are blocking this pavement, the north side of Velie Street, the east side of Harrison Street, and part of the intersection. I'll have to ask you to break this rally up and take it to some place where you won't interfere with the right of others to free passage."

"Where would you suggest we go?" Rhama asked.

In Car No. 4, Paul Green tried to ignore the small band of youths who had encircled the vehicle, peering through the opened front windows; grinning, taunting faces that mocked him as he sat behind the wheel. Moments later, a boy of 15 mounted the front bumper and began to bounce

675

up and down upon it, swaying the car. Then came a counter-bumping and rocking from the rear, and Green knew he would have to control the situation before it got out of hand; and yet, there was the firm order: One man stays close to the mike at all times. He drew the mike closer to his mouth, depressed the "Talk" button. "Cent-Com—"

"Here—"

"No. 4. You'd better send us some assistance. No sirens or lights, but quick, just for show. Over."

"Check. On the way. Over and out."

The press of bodies against the car was so great now, he could scarcely open the left door. He slid back on the seat, put his foot against the door and pushed. When it gave, he pushed it open with both hands, got out and stood beside it. "All right, kids, hands off the car and off those bumpers. Move back." With the baton in his left hand, he warded off an open hand that clutched at it from behind another boy. "Move!"

"Get back," someone shouted, "or that white nigger'll mow us down with his machine gun. Brat-tat-tat-tat-tat! Big man with a gun! Do like he tellin' you. He eats li'l kids like us for his breakfus'."

"All right, wise guy, knock it off and move back," Green ordered. "I know you, Joey-Lee Mason—"

"Shuh, you know me. I know you, too. Knowed you when you live down the street from us, you stuck-up nigger."

The circle became a sea of white teeth set in dozens of grinning, laughing faces. "Listen. If you kids don't want any trouble, get off this car. In a minute there'll be four more cars here and—"

"They comin'!" came a shout from the rear.

The crowd of youths on the curbside of the car acted spontaneously and in concert, although no order was given. About a dozen of them bent over, grabbed the bottom edge of the car and heaved mightily. A few men drifted over from the main crowd and lent their strength to the action. In seconds, the car was tipped over on its side, those on the wheel-side narrowly escaping injury as it rocked and tottered back and forth. Gasoline erupted from the tank and began to spread over the paved street. Green had leaped aside and with baton raised, ran to the curbside, but the offenders were already scattered. He saw Hammond's face among the haze of black faces that blocked his progress, then turned toward the rear of the car, now lying on its left side. He heard someone cry out, "Hurry up with that thing, man!" and saw a boy of about 16 in the clear, striking a

676

match, holding it for a moment, then dropping it into the pool of gasoline. It caught, raced toward the tank and the crowd dissolved.

Green stood still, watching the flames with fascinated horror as they crept up and engulfed the rear end of No. 4. He felt himself grabbed and dragged away from the car and tried to tear himself free, angrily clutching his baton in one hand, reaching for his service pistol with the other.

"Paul! For Christ's sake, don't be a goddam fool!"

It was Hammond who brought him back to sanity. As Cars No. 12, 16 and 22 arrived and an emergency call for a fire truck was placed, the crowd began scattering into nearby stores, doorways and houses across the street, and the first cries of "Scorch it, man, scorch it!" were heard.

Police Sergeant Boley Carter, the senior officer present, quickly assessed the situation and ordered everyone back fom the burning vehicle. Two officers were shooting jets from their fire extinguishers on the flames with little results. Hammond quickly gave Carter his version; then Green, his eyes tear-filled with anger and frustration, gave his own. Carter looked around him in mild dismay and saw the open defiance and restrained glee in the faces that surrounded them, with no reasonable way to dispel it. During the excitement, Dr. Rhama's sound truck and car had disappeared.

Two fire trucks arrived and put the blaze out with foam and chemicals, began hosing the excess gasoline away while traffic was rerouted east and west on Velie under the eyes of almost 500 Negroes. Carter called in for a tow truck and the eight officers maintained a close watch until the wrecked No. 4 was righted, hooked up and removed. Then Hammond and Green returned to the 12th Precinct in No. 22 where they would write their separate reports.

The crowd lingered until the burned police car was hauled away and, on orders from Captain Price, Sergeant Carter ordered his men out of the area until the people dispersed; then to resume normal patrols. An hour later, vehicular and pedestrian traffic had resumed. By dusk it was as though the incident had not occurred.

3

Enforced freedom, when everyone he knew was at work, gave Corey more time than he knew how to cope with. With Hugh Brock and Sam Driscoll married, Lin Dorsey living in New York and Les Delevan in Richmond, there were Ad Cameron, a busy newspaper executive, Perry Willard, an engineer on the Taylor Industries staff, and Polk Holderby, remaining from his college days. He knew that Perry had been assigned to the Shadow Hills project and so avoided him lest he be accused of seeking advance information.

He had lunched with Hugh and Sam and turned down their invitations to dinner. Joyce Willard phoned to ask him to dinner, "and why don't your bring Hilary? She thinks you're something special." He had put Joyce off "until I get squared away," sensing in her the incipient qualities of a matchmaker. He had called Polk twice, but Polk had returned neither call and he knew that his return, at a time when Polk had renewed a serious interest in Paula, was at least one reason for the apparent coolness on Polk's part.

Three days had passed since he had seen or talked with Drew and he wondered if he could tempt her to leave Brookhill to have dinner with him. He dialed the number and spoke with Leona, who told him Drew "just got back two hours ago." He wondered idly about it, then heard her voice, pitched a little higher than he had heard it recently.

"Corey? Hi!"

"Drew, you sound—"

"Out of breath. I've been in Atlanta shopping. It's been so long, it was a real adventure. I flew down with my father and yours on Monday morning and got back just a few minutes ago."

"You sound so excited—"

"It was exciting, the new styles, everything. I even went to a movie last night. I spent a fortune—"

"Good. You're a patriotic citizen, spreading all that money around to improve the economy. Are you exhausted or would you consider having dinner with me?"

She hesitated, then asked, "How about here?"

"That's exactly what I did not have in mind. I want to start getting acquainted with some of the old places. Fisher's Landing, the Marina Club—"

"Oh, Corey, it's so—so public."

"That's why I suggested it. Let's make it the Marina. The food is good, the view of the river is pleasant and I'm sure there's still music and dancing." Before she could object, "I'll pick you up at seven. That gives you three full hours to do everything you need to do to get ready. Wear something you bought in Atlanta. I'll make the reservation for eight o'clock."

"Corey—" He ignored the mild protest in her voice.

"Seven o'clock or I'll drag you out, ready or not, even if

678

your hair is still in curlers." He hung up without waiting to hear her reply just as Tish came in to ask if he was having dinner at home. "My, my," she said approvingly, "Army sure done you a lot of good. Never heard you givin' orders to nobody like that before."

"Maybe it's because you and your mother didn't bring me up right, Tish."

Tish giggled. "I never had no say with you. Sounds good to hear somebody snappin' words aroun' this house." Corey knew she was referring to Kenneth and Caddy; that if his father had shown a firmer hand with his mother, things might have turned out differently between them. It was useless to try to explain to Tish that when that certain magic had evaporated between them, the rules of the game were changed, that firmness built belligerence instead of respect. He finished his drink and went upstairs to nap for a while.

On the dot of seven, he arrived at Brookhill and found Drew ready and waiting in the downstairs sitting room. Her hair, he noticed at once, had been cut and restyled into windblown nonchalance, her dark eyes made more luminous with delicately shaded accents, and the shallow depressions beneath her cheekbones made her face seem narrower, her lips fuller. The dress she wore was black, a most favorable color for Drew, with touches of white piping at the throat and across two false pockets. From its narrow standup collar to her knees, it embraced her as though it had been sculpted onto her body, emphasizing her breasts and hips, slenderizing her waist. The jacket matched the color and texture of the dress and was fully lined in coral. She wore a single strand of pearls at her throat, which matched the single pearl in each ear lobe. When she came toward him, there was a fluid grace in her long, smooth legs that provoked a feeling of sensuality in him, and he smiled to cover his awareness of the fact.

"Beautiful!" he exclaimed softly.

"You really like it?"

"How could I not like it?"

"It's been so long since I've felt like shopping, I wasn't quite sure."

"I'm so sure that I don't know if I want to share you with the world, but our reservation is for eight, so let's get out and give the natives a treat."

They drove slowly past the old Taylor plantation, Laurel, into River Road and toward the bridge where two police cars and four officers scanned each car that crossed from either side. Corey pulled up at a signal light and one of the officers leaned into the open window on Drew's side, then touched the rim of his cap with a finger in salute.

"Evening, Miss Warren. You folks headed for Angeltown?"

"No," Corey replied, "the Marina Club."

"Okay. When you cross, take the shore road, please, and avoid the central section of town on your way back."

"More trouble, Officer?"

"None since earlier today, but things are kind of shaky. No use getting caught up in anything that might break out. The Club is in safe territory, though."

"Thank you—"

The green light came on and Corey swung the Thunderbird onto the bridge. Traffic at this hour was light. On the west side were two more police cars and four officers performing the same duty. As they came off the bridge, Corey turned left into the road that bordered the Cottonwood and took them directly into the Marina Club's well-lighted parking area. At the water's edge was a maze of finger piers lined with small craft and cabin cruisers, some darkened, others alight and readying for an evening on the river, music filling the air, men in denims and rope-soled shoes carrying food, drinks and ice aboard. Two work barges, in tandem, slid past with running lights flashing, heading south with their cargoes like trailer trucks on a highway, sounding their horns in warning to all small craft in the yacht club area.

They were early and the dining room was filled, with a dozen or more people waiting to be seated. Corey let the maitre d' know they were there and the smiling captain, wearing a yachting cap, suggested the bar.

"Drew?"

"I think not. I'd rather look out over the water."

They stepped out of the side door onto a broad veranda and sat in rocking chairs, watching small cruisers maneuver in and out of their berths, larger yachts anchored out beyond the piers. Music from the dining room flowed onto the veranda through a loudspeaker arrangement. Corey lighted two cigarettes and handed one to Drew. "I didn't remember how pleasant this could be," Drew said. "Thank you for insisting, Corey."

"There's so much you've been shutting out of your life, Drew. If you'll let me, I'd like to help you remember other things."

"Like?"

"Things we once enjoyed together. Tennis, swimming, riding. I'd like some day to go back to Loon Lake—"

680

"Loon Lake," Drew said. "It doesn't even belong to us any more. We gave it to Lucas and Laurellen for a wedding present. But I'm sure I could borrow it—perhaps—some day—" she added.

"Drew—"

"What, Corey?"

"Last Sunday. I don't want anything you told me to come between us. I'd like to pick up from the night we came back from that wedding in Atlanta, before we reached Brookhill, when I wanted to tell you I loved you and wanted you to wait."

She turned her head away and said, "Corey, how can we go back so far? So much has happened since to change everything."

"Not everything, Drew. Some things, yes. For one thing, you've finally accepted the loss of Bruce. The other thing could only have happened to a sick person and I'm sure you're over that. One thing it didn't change is my feelings for you. I love you. I want you to marry me."

Drew took a full fifteen seconds before she said, "Are you sure, Corey?"

"I've never been more sure of anything in my life."

"I wish I knew what makes you—and others—so sure of yourselves."

"I'm just as curious about why you're so uncertain of yourself."

"I don't know. I can't explain it, except that now I don't think I've ever really been sure of anything in my life. Gran and Bruce had it, but it seems to have skipped over my father and me."

"Maybe it has to do with accepting life as it is, coping with the everyday problems of living in a world that rejects weakness."

"Coping with life," Drew said. "What a horrid expression. It's as though we're born into hostility and have to overcome it from birth. That's a rather sorry outlook, isn't it?"

"Not necessarily, Drew, and not all life is hostile. You were happy enough growing up, weren't you? Was there anything you were ever denied?"

Again she hesitated, then said slowly, "Yes. My mother, I guess. I barely knew her. I suppose that is why I needed Bruce so much, why his loss affected me so deeply."

"Drew, there are things that are denied all of us. We live through the good and the bad, but we can't go back to recapture the past, however much we may miss it, long for it. If we could, I sometimes doubt if we would want it. Life is lived by moving forward into the future, not back to a re-membered past."

Drew laughed lightly. "When did you turn philosopher, Corey?"

"If that is philosophy, I suppose it happened while I was in Viet Nam; that among other things. The uselessness of wars that have never solved anything, the need to get through one day safely because there's a tomorrow that might be better. Hope is what keeps us going, looking ahead, Drew. Regression is for Monday morning quarter-backs."

He heard his name announced over the loudspeaker system. "Mr. Armour's table is ready. Mr. Armour, please."

Corey stood up, taking Drew's hand. They were standing closely together, shadows in the dark. "Drew?" he said.

"Philosophizing can't repair what I've done, Corey," she said. "I can't forget it. It would always be there between us."

"Remembering can also help overcome a mistake, but it needn't cripple either of us."

"Can you be so sure?"

"Why not give it a chance? That is, if you still love me. As I recall, you were pretty sure of that a long time ago."

"I wish I could be as sure of myself now as I was then. Corey, don't take that as a negative answer. Just give me a little time to adjust to the idea. It's like—something—like it was happening for the first time."

He kissed her then and felt some warmth in her response. "All right, Drew, take the time you want. I'll wait." The loudspeaker called his name again and they went inside.

Police were still guarding the west and east ends of the bridge when Drew and Corey returned sometime after 11 o'clock. Laurelton was quiet as they drove through it on their way to Brookhill. They had touched on many subjects which affected them singly, but not together. They had discussed the Company and Chase Warren's injection into the picture, Theodore and Kenneth's trip to New York, the Shadow Hills project and the chances of Wayne and John-ny's participation in it; and the possibility, if they rejected it, of proposing the project to an outside organization.

"Suppose they do turn it down, Corey, what then?"

"I'd guess I would let it ride for a while. Maybe give up the idea and open a law office."

"Suppose you could arrange other financing?"

"Other financing," he said. "You are talking about your-self?"

"Why not? Perhaps with Dad."

"I might consider that if I could find out where Hall Peterson is, get the organization he was with when they built the same sort of thing in Michigan—"

"Corey, let's!"

He laughed then. "Well, we could kick it around a little. We've talked a lot of other nonsense tonight, why not this? So many topics, and not a single answer."

"Nice nonsense," Drew replied. "I can't tell you how much it has meant to me. Getting out like this—like old times. For a while, I'd forgotten a lot—"

"Because it's no longer important, Drew. That's what really counts. Today and tomorrow. We'll work it out. Together." He paused to light a cigarette. "I think that I should forewarn you now, there's a fairly large-sized skeleton rattling around in the Armour closet."

"A real one?"

"Very real. Dad and Shana Pierce."

Drew laughed. "Oh, that. I've known about it for a long time. Bruce told me about it when he first went to work for the Company that summer."

"Well, I'll be goddamned!" Corey exploded.

"Don't be so shocked. I guess we all have skeletons we try to hide."

Corey thought of Paula and Hilary. "Yes. All of us," he said and let the subject die.

4

When they met for lunch at Victoria's request, which held a hint of urgency, since this was an off-day for their usual meetings, Walter Cunningham was further surprised that Victoria, usually tardy, was already seated at their table in the out-of-the-way French restaurant that had long been their private rendezvous. As he entered the dining room, he responded briefly to Jean Pierre's greeting. "Madame is already seated, m'sieu. The usual?"

"Yes, please." Jean Pierre signaled the barman for two martinis and showed Walter to the table. He brushed Victoria's cheek with his lips, sat beside her on the leather bench and leaned back to examine her more closely.

"I've ordered martinis, but I don't think you really need one in your present state," he said with an indulgent smile.

"I don't really want one," said Victoria.

"Nonsense. Your face is flushed, either from the wind or

—" He ended the sentence with a dangling question mark in his voice.

"News," Victoria said happily.

"Good, I take it."

"Very good. The best." She laughed and said, "On second thought, I do want a drink."

"Now I'm sure you *don't* need one. I've never seen you so quietly excited in broad daylight." The waiter placed the martinis on the service plates before them and Walter ordered two more before touching the rim of his glass to Victoria's. "To your very good health, darling."

"And my news." Victoria sipped her drink and put the glass down. "Walt, it may very well upset your equilibrium."

"The way it has upset yours? Suppose you stop chattering like a school girl and tell me."

"I actually feel like one."

"All right, tell it in your own way and in your own time. I've canceled my appointments for the rest of the afternoon."

"Oh, Walt. I'm sorry. Forgive me?"

"There wasn't a single thing that won't keep. Get on with it."

For a few moments she was an artist who had completed a painting she couldn't bring herself to part with, knowing that as soon as someone else even saw it, it would be no longer hers. She simply sat still and stared at Walter's face. He was, she knew, 54, and there was a whitening tinge that edged the gray at his temples, but most of his hair was still black. His eyes, humorous and tender, were bright, not old, yet not youthful, but there was the same quality of kindness she had first seen in him when what she needed most of all in her life was kindness, tenderness and the love they had discovered in each other.

And there was the danger that over the years, he had become set in his ways and would not welcome any changes now, when it could easily disrupt his well-ordered life.

"Walt, within a short time, I'll be a free woman."

His head jerked upward in surprise. "What—"

"I said—"

"I heard what you said. What's happened?"

"Chase has finally tripped over his own ambitions."

His patience came to an end. "Will you for pity's sake stop talking in riddles and make sense?"

Again Victoria laughed happily. "Walt, Walt. Thank heaven I've lived to see the day when I can upset your dignified aplomb."

684

"Vicky, I'm warning you—"

"All right, darling, listen—"

Excitement, Walter thought, brought added beauty to her; the same beauty he had seen in her that first time in Palm Beach; the second time when he returned from Asian waters early in 1946. How miraculous that it could be recaptured now, 21 years later, by two people reaching their middle-50's, even though neither thought of himself as being middle-aged. In the passing years, both had marveled over this and Walter decided that perhaps it was because they had been separated by circumstances that kept them eager with expectation of their next meeting.

Victoria had arranged numerous occasions when Walter could observe Victor; shopping, lunching, attending a matinee with her, spending an afternoon in Central Park, during long summer weekends at Ogonquit where he could see them together, enjoy his resemblance to his son. Now, with Victor grown into handsome young manhood—

Victoria's voice came to an abrupt end. "Are you sure you were listening to me, Walt?"

"Of course I'm sure. How your fantastic mother has been compiling years of investigative reports on Chase without you knowing a damned thing about it. Some superspy agency—"

"And you don't think that strange, or—"

"From the little I remember of Andrea and from what you've told me over the years, I think her behavior is perfectly normal, exactly what I would have expected. Go on, please."

"Well— Then, last Sunday night, I got a telephone call from Diane Collins—"

"Who is Diane Collins?"

"We were at Miss Hotchkiss's together before I went abroad to school. She was Diane Foster, a fifth or sixth cousin, several times removed. We've met a number of times since, class reunions, luncheons, shopping—"

"Collins. Tobacco. Would that be Duncan Collins, the tobacco man?"

"Yes, and will you stop interrupting, please? I don't want to forget anything."

"Go on, dear."

"I'd told Diane how it was with Chase and me long before I met you. We gossiped for a while, then Diane came out with it. Something that involved Chase and his family's company, the Warren Tobacco Company. Chase's kind of shenanigans. I told her I didn't know anything about it, but that perhaps Mother, who gets some sort of an annual report of—"

"Andrea again."

"Hush. Anyway, I phoned Mother and asked if she would talk to Diane. Mother agreed and I phoned Diane. Then Mother phoned Duncan and he went to see her. Next morning, Mother had me to a late breakfast. You remember I called and had to beg off?"

"Yes."

"That's when I found out that Mother has had Chase under close observation by a firm that specializes in industrial and financial investigations, and another that goes deeper into more personal things."

"In short, a private detective agency. Good old Andrea."

"You could say it with more emphasis. She deserves it. *Good old Andrea.* Like that."

"Are you getting a bit loaded, darling?"

"No, I am not getting a bit loaded. Good old Andrea discovered that Chase had helped himself to a liberal amount of Vanderkuyl money in order to set up his very own financial empire. A thing called Intercon."

"Intercon? Chase Warren owns Intercon?"

"Yes. Built with money that didn't belong to him. Vanderkuyl money. Mother's, Vanessa's and mine."

Walter chuckled. "Good old Andrea, and this time with proper respect and emphasis," he said. "Then what?"

"Well, if you thought I was excited, you should have seen Mother while she was telling me about it. She's known it almost from the start and has been waiting. Chase began with a company he started in Mexico during the war and has been adding companies to it, hiding behind the Intercon name."

"And done very well. I've been tempted several times to pick up some of the Intercon stock."

"Wouldn't that have been ironical," Victoria said.

"And profitable. I wonder why on earth he did it?" Walter said. "He had everything any man could possibly want or need—"

"You don't understand a man like Chase, Walt. When we were first married, he walked out on the Warren Tobacco Company in a snit because his father wouldn't give him the authority to do as he pleased with it. I've told you what happened when my father died and Chase threatened to leave me unless Mother, Vanessa and Leander, and I gave him complete control over the estate—"

"If only he had—"

686

"If only I'd known you then," Victoria said, "he could have gone with my blessings. But Andrea, and I suppose I, too, had firmer ideas about the sanctity of marriage then. It wasn't pleasant to think of being pointed out as the woman Chase Warren divorced despite her fortune."

"Ah, the pity of it."

"It seems that with his father dead, Chase is trying to take the Company away from his brother, Theodore, and Theodore's daughter. If he does, it will probably affect Duncan Collins as well—"

"And so, Andrea has finally decided to lower the well-known boom on her son-in-law."

"Yes. With injunctions, court orders, a lawsuit charging fraud, grand larceny—"

"Wait a minute. Are you telling me that Chase never re-paid the initial—uh—loan he used to start his first com-pany?"

"Of course I'm telling you that, which is where he slipped up in the first place. When Mother's investigators learned about his trips to Mexico and had them looked into more thoroughly, they reported their findings to Mother and she asked her accountants to look into the matter. They found a hodgepodge of tricky stock transfers and other things I can't remember or even understand. Mother never pressed the issue and Chase probably thought he was so far in the clear, he decided there was no use wasting his ill-gotten gains by repaying the estate. Or out of sheer overconfidence or carelessness. But one thing is certain: he never paid a cent of the money back."

"And Andrea let him go ahead and get so high up that the fall be all the harder."

"There are other things, too. Personal. A record of Chase's infidelities—"

Walter squirmed. "And, I presume, ours?"

The waiter brought two more martinis. Victoria sipped, then said, "Darling Walt, Mother has known about us since Palm Beach. Oh, don't be shocked—"

"Extraordinary," Walt said. "A woman who objected to your divorcing Chase, but condones an extramarital affair between her daughter and a stranger."

"But such a darling, handsome stranger."

"Thank you, darling. Am I to assume, then, that Andrea knows I am Victor's father?"

"Of course. She noticed the resemblance even before I did. In fact, that was when she told me she knew about us. You were away in the Pacific then—"

687

"Then I can also assume that where Chase Warren is concerned, our sins can be equated with good and his with evil."

Victoria stared at him blankly. "I've never looked at us as being sinful," she said, "or evil."

"Nor have I, despite the fact that we could hardly expect others to see it that way. Excepting Andrea, of course."

"Walt, you—you're not unhappy about this, are you?"

"That Andrea is about to brutally execute your husband, perhaps yes. That it will free you to marry me, no."

Victoria sighed a deep breath of relief. "We can't have it both ways, can we?"

"That depends on several things. One, how deeply Andrea's need for vengeance runs. Two, the publicity and how it will affect you, your sons, our son. Three, I am in a rather respectable seat as president of Com-Tex—"

"Oh, Walt! I hadn't thought—"

"Unless—"

"Unless what?"

"Unless we can discuss the whole thing reasonably with Andrea and compromise the matter in some way that will bring Chase around to allowing you to get a quiet Sun Valley, Florida or Nevada divorce. He would necessarily wield some bargaining influence—"

"You mean get away with some of it."

"Not everything. Hardly that. His skin and a good bit of money his Intercon has made. Think it over while we have lunch. I hate to upset even a part of Andrea's plans, but total revenge on Chase might have an adverse effect on all of us."

"Suddenly," Victoria said soberly, "I feel conspicuous."

"See someone you know?" Walter asked, looking around.

"Someone I don't even recognize. Myself."

Walter laughed without mirth. "Vicky, darling, we're not children and this isn't a child's game. If we were twenty-one years younger, as we were when we first met, I would probably feel as electrified at the proposal as you were half an hour ago. I love you as deeply now as I did then. More, even, if that is possible, but the war cured me of most of my destructive tendencies. Once, I could hunt deer, ducks, quail, pheasant, even squirrels and rabbits, but today, I wince at the thought of killing or harming any living, breathing thing. Say I've mellowed and can't stand brutality to humans or animals."

"Walt, I feel so ashamed."

"Don't. Instead, let's go and have a talk with Andrea and tell her how we feel about the whole thing. And us."

"After lunch?"

"After lunch."

5

Andrea Vankerkuyl had enjoyed a light dinner and now dozed in her favorite chair, dreaming of the years before Chase Warren had come into their collective world. It had been a good marriage and life with Marshall, one in which she had played a prominent part, although she realized she had not been much more than a sounding board for her husband's ideas. Yet, she could not complain. They were sound ideas and he had done well, very well, for a man who had inherited his money.

She had given Marshall two daughters and not once had he showed his disappointment that they were not sons who could follow in his footsteps. Even when Victoria had wanted to go abroad for her secondary schooling, she had had Vanessa; and when Vanessa eloped, Victoria was ready to come home. They had enjoyed wealth and good living and had been happy—until Chase had swept Victoria off her feet. Marshall had been enthusiastic about Chase's capabilities, but Andrea had seen him through a woman's eyes and although she had consented, remained wary. And then Chase's ambitions had begun to chip away at the foundation of their happiness.

She thought of Victoria and Walter as she had seen them this afternoon. She had known about Walter and Victoria even in Palm Beach and could not bring herself to spoil the temporary happiness they had found in each other. Ordinarily, she would never have permitted the affair to begin, but she saw in it a measure of revenge on Chase, whom she despised; a hatred she actually enjoyed.

She had given tacit consent to the continuation of the affair when the war ended and Walter came back to New York; consent by silence. It had heartened her when Victoria came to her one night and told her that Walter was back and would remain in New York; but by then, Andrea had known every time she looked at young Victor's face, that Walter was his father; and she could do nothing, say nothing to prevent Victoria's reunion with Victor's father. And again, she had remained silent when Victoria told her and left the room without waiting for an answer. She had not asked for permission, Andrea knew, but was merely telling

689

her what course she had adopted. Andrea had wanted then to suggest divorce to Victoria, but could not bring herself to bring the subject up. All she could hope for was that Victoria and Walter would be careful.

Until today, she had not seen Walter Cunningham since those first days in Palm Beach; still a youngish man, strong, virile, almost handsome. She had listened first to Victoria, then Walter, both pleading for a sane approach to the problem so than none would suffer greatly. It was much to ask of Andrea, who had quietly planned for Chase's ultimate destruction as a general plans war upon his enemy; and yet, she could not deny that her personal vengeance was secondary to the happiness of her daughter and the man she had loved for so long; the father of her second son.

She sighed deeply and rang for Morris. When the butler entered the room, she indicated the section of walnut paneling and stood beside him when he moved it to one side to disclose the wall safe. Morris waited silently while Andrea went to her desk, adjusted her glasses, unlocked the center drawer, removed a flat box from which she extracted a small leather booklet. Turning the pages, she found the one she wanted and began to read the combination to him, a useless ritual since Morris knew the combination from the memory of years. When the doors were opened, Andrea said, "Thank you, Morris. I am expecting Mr. Collins and two other gentlemen at eight o'clock. When they arrive, please notify me, then show them here."

"Yes, madam," Morris replied, and left.

Andrea pored through the safe and removed two files. Back at her desk, she examined the first file, labeled: Atlas Research Associates, from which she removed a single sheet of paper dated October 1st, headed:

File A. V./20-67 CONFIDENTIAL
For: Mrs. Andrea Vanderkuyl
Subject: Intercontinental Corporation of America (INTERCON)
Re: Continuing report of September 1, 1967.

1. It has been ascertained through a reliable source that Intercon is preparing a campaign to acquire outstanding Warren Tobacco Company stock by public solicitation (via tender offer). Letters and brochures to known stockholders have been printed, addressed, and are ready for mailing on the as yet undisclosed date, which will no doubt coincide with a contemplated advertising campaign in financial papers and newspaper

publicity releases previously reported under discussion (see report of September 1, 1967, File A. V./19-67).

ATLAS RESEARCH ASSOCIATES, INC.
Frank Brownlee, Director

Andrea closed the file and with a slow smile began reading a report from the second folder. It was dated October 16th, 1967.

CONFIDENTIAL, INC.

Memorandum for: Mrs. Andrea Vanderkuyl
From: Norton Harsh

1. Acting on information contained in ARA, Inc. report A.V./20-67, dated October 1, 1967, subject Chase Warren returned to New York from his recent visit to Fairview, Ga., with Mr. Thomas Shelby. We are reliably informed that Mr. Kenneth Armour, vice-president and chief of legal staff of Warren Tobacco Co., Laurelton, Ga., has rejected participation in Intercon takeover plan on learning of Chase Warren's involvement as previously undisclosed chief executive of Intercon.

2. Upon return to this city, Chase Warren, in a meeting with Mr. Kirk Dillingham and Shelby, ordered release of mail campaign to reach Warren stockholders on Friday, October 27, with advertisements to break in financial papers on Sunday, October 29, this in order to take advantage of a full weekend of financial inactivity.

3. There has been no change in Intercon's financial status.

4. Followup report: Auto-Mex continues operations as previously reported. No changes.

5. Verification of new interest reported by ARA in Report of August 1, 1967. Intercon has now acquired a total of 83,000 shares of West Coast Film Productions, Inc. producers of film documentaries for television, continuing purchases in blocks of 100 to 500 shares. Added to recent stock acquisitions in Bayliss Bros. Film Corp., it would appear that Intercon's next major move, after Warren Company, will be in film making and distribution.

6. Add to previous reports on subject Chase Warren's social conduct. Mrs. Joan Condon, recently divorced in Mexico by Robert John Condon, of Dallas, Texas, his third wife. Photo of Joan Condon enclosed, taken with subject in Palm Springs. Age 28, brown hair, hazel eyes, five feet three inches, former bit-

player under name of Joan Barton, married three times. Address: Compton Hall, Sutton Place, on lease to subject. Further particulars will be forthcoming as they occur.

7. No change in reports on subjects Mrs. Chase Warren and Mr. Walter Cunningham. Subjects continue to meet twice each week for lunch and at male subject's apartment on occasions when subject Chase Warren is absent from the city.

End report.

CONFIDENTIAL, INC.
Norton Harsh, General Manager

Andrea closed the second file with a sense of satisfaction. Morris knocked on the door and entered. "The three gentlemen have arrived, madam," he announced.

"Show them in at once, Morris."

"Yes, madam."

Duncan Collins entered first, Kenneth Armour and Theodore Warren behind him. Collins held Andrea's thin, blue-veined hand as he greeted her and introduced his colleagues. "Thank you for calling us so soon, Mrs. Vanderkuyl. Mr. Armour and Mr. Warren are naturally anxious to meet you after our conversation last Sunday night."

"And I," Andrea replied as she looked imperiously from Kenneth to Theodore, "am pleased to meet Mr. Armour and Mr. Warren. Please be seated, gentlemen. Would you care for some brandy?" When they refused, she said, "Nothing more, Morris. See that we are not disturbed. I shall ring when I want you." The old retainer went out and closed the door.

"I feel," Andrea continued, "as though I have known Mr. Warren and Mr. Armour for a long time." Her lips drew back slightly in a wintry smile. "I shall not explain that remark except to say that I know of you and, after my discussion with Mr. Collins last Sunday night, am aware of the situation which concerns all of you."

"If I may speak for all of us," Kenneth said, "I don't believe Mr. Warren or I can add greatly to what Mr. Collins has already told you, Mrs. Vanderkuyl, except that should your son-in-law manage a successful campaign to take control of the Warren Tobacco Company for Intercon—"

Andrea raised one of her parchment-skinned hands and cut Kenneth off at that point. "Mr. Armour, Mr. Collins may have indicated to you that for years I have not been in full sympathy with my son-in-law. For reasons I do not

692

wish to disclose at this time, I have no desire to expand that statement. However, I am not without certain resources which I believe may be helpful to you, Mr. Warren and Mr. Collins.

"I have asked my attorneys and accountants to meet with me tomorrow afternoon to discuss the details of a plan I have in mind. If they are in agreement with me, I shall be in touch with Mr. Collins. At this moment, you may take comfort, however minimal, that whatever I am able to do will be of little cheer to Mr. Chase Warren."

Kenneth Armour exchanged swift glances with Duncan Collins, who was nodding his head in satisfaction with what they had heard. To Andrea, Kenneth said, "I am sure I speak for the three of us when I say we are deeply indebted and grateful to you, Mrs. Vanderkuyl."

Again, the thin-lipped smile that gave a hint of cruelty to whatever it was Andrea had in mind. The silence in the room hung for a moment as she stared at each of the men who faced her. There seemed to be nothing more to discuss and she said finally, "If there is nothing more, gentlemen, I will ask you to excuse me and say good night. I have had a long and tiring day."

She rang for Morris as Collins, Kenneth and Theodore rose to their feet, thanked her and left. In Collins' car, Duncan said, "Don't for one minute underestimate that little old lady. She's a hater if I ever saw one and I'd almost rather be in anybody's shoes than Chase's."

693

At 7:30 on Thursday morning, the Emergency Plan briefing session conducted by Inspector Peter LaSalle in the Police Training School gymnasium came to an end. The 146 men represented the off-duty men of the Police Department (65), County Sheriff's Department (54), and Police Trainee Class (27). In addition, there were State Highway Patrol Lieutenant Henry Parker, Fire Chief Gary Hobbs, and County Sheriff Will Apperson.

Squad leaders distributed mimeographed copies of orders complete with area charts of each squad's emergency duty station, which had appeared on the three blackboards during the two-hour session, these to be studied and memorized. "Remember," Inspector LaSalle cautioned the group, "the emergency alarm will be given through our Civil Defense warning system. For our purpose, the signal will be one long blast of ten seconds, followed by three short blasts, then repeated. Off-duty men will assemble according to the written orders now being handed out to you. You will report as quickly as possible to your squad leaders at the designated points. They will assign you and your partner to a specific area for foot or car patrol. Once assigned, you will remain within that area and leave it only on direct order of your squad leader or a superior officer who will be wearing a green band on his left arm.

"On dismissal, police regulars will change into uniform and report for their eight o'clock tour of duty. Trainees will remain here to continue their classes. Members of the Sheriff's Department will report back to their normal duties. Dismissed."

The class broke and filed out. Sheriff Apperson, Lieutenant Parker and Fire Chief Hobbs remained with LaSalle for a last-minute discussion. A uniformed officer of the training staff brought in a pot of coffee, containers of milk, sugar and paper cups, which the men present accepted gratefully. Sheriff Apperson removed the dead cigar he had been chewing and sipped at the strong, black coffee. Lieutenant Parker

694

took one sip, put his cup down and said, "I've got to get back and report to the captain. I'd like to add one comment, Inspector. I think the single most effective control would be a strict curfew—"

"We have it in mind, Lieutenant," LaSalle said, "but we will put it in effect only if it appears likely that we will be forced to bring in the National Guard. Otherwise, we don't have enough personnel to enforce it. We've got clearance from the Governor and have an open line to General Drummond at Camp Fitch, who has been alerted. If the emergency arises, Chief Durkin will make the request to Mayor Cameron, who will notify General Drummond directly. Within three hours, we will have a minimum of eight hundred Guardsmen here to back us up."

Parker nodded. "Very well then, Inspector. I'll check all of this through with Captain Hughes." He nodded to the Sheriff and Chief Hobbs and left.

"As I understand it, Pete," Hobbs said to LaSalle, "we'll have two of Will's deputies, fully armed, riding on every piece of equipment answering a call. Is that correct?"

"That's correct, Chief," LaSalle replied. "The Sheriff's dispatcher will assign the fire truck guards according to the list you will furnish him by no later than noon today. At the emergency signal, the deputies assigned to your department will report to designated fire stations to ride shotgun. If attacked, they will defend and radio the nearest command post for additional deputies or police officers being held in reserve."

"All right. Will, your man will have the list of stations by noontime." Hobbs then left and LaSalle was alone with Sheriff Will Apperson.

"Will?"

Apperson pushed his near-white felt hat back on his head and grinned at LaSalle. "If you don't mind me saying so, Pete, I still think you people are chickenshit. You let me turn my boys loose over in Nigger Heaven and I'll guarantee you there won't be any ruckusin' goin' over there."

"With your dogs and cattle prods, Will?"

"You're goddam well right. I don't see no sense in babyin' them people the way you been doin' for years now. You-all got it in your heads that they're somethin' special, just because they got a few outside niggers preachin' about their black power. Take a good look at it an' you'll see it's us who's got the power an' too scared to use it because of newspaper opinion. If I was runnin' this show—"

Wearily, LaSalle said, "That's all been settled, Will. Lee

695

Durkin is in full command and you're backing him up with his deputies."

"Like I was sayin', if I was runnin' this show, first thing I'd do, I'd get hold of that sonofabitchin' Dr. Rhama an' shove a cattle prod up his black ass 'til it come shootin' sparks out of his mouth. Then I'd march my boys, yeah, with their dogs an' riot guns, down Grand Avenue and up Velie Street, then through every neighborhood around an' let 'em all know who the hell is boss in this town. I'd shoot the first nigger who put a foot on the bridge to cross over into Laurelton and string him up on a light pole, and shoot any nigger I caught on the street after sundown and until sunrise.

"Thing I hate is havin' to call out the National Guard in a situation we could handle right here in our own family, between us. Kinda gives the whole county a bad name. People get to feel they can't depend on their police and Sheriff's Department—"

LaSalle grinned now. "What you mean, Will, is that when election time comes around, a lot of Cairn County voters are going to remember, and one of your opponents will be sure to remind them, that Will Apperson wasn't out there in front with his dogs and cattle prods, isn't it?"

"Well, Pete, we'll see. We'll just by God see."

"Any other questions, Will?"

"Nope." Apperson stood up, yawned, then crumpled his paper cup and threw it into the wastepaper basket. "You tell Lee hello for me, you hear." He pulled his wide-brimmed hat down over his deeply sunburnt forehead and went out.

Lee Durkin had had three hours of sleep on a cot in his office. When LaSalle reported back to him, Durkin was on the private line to Captain Price's 12th Precinct in West Laurelton. He was unshaven, tie askew, clothes rumpled, holding a mug of hot coffee in his right hand. "Thanks, Jim," he said into the receiver. "Keep on top of it and keep me posted." He hung up and swung around to face LaSalle with a wry grin. "You look like death warmed over, Pete. You get any sleep at all?"

"I looked in on Nora for a couple of hours last night, then showered and shaved and made the briefing at 5:30. I'm that far ahead of you, anyway."

Durkin rubbed his wiry stubble. "I'll get around to it in a little while. How's Nora?"

"Going into her ninth month and the only complaint so

far, thank God, is that her child will be fatherless. She sends you her love."

"Tell her I'll make it up to you and her as soon as I can. I'm too embarrassed to face up to her, else I'd drop by."

"Also, there's a standing invitation for you to come to dinner any time you get a few spare moments."

Durkin yawned, covered it with a huge hand. "If only I could." He reached into his desk drawer and brought out an electric razor, threw the loose end of the cord to LaSalle. "Plug that in for me, will you, Pete?" LaSalle plugged the cord into a wall receptacle. "Anything new from Captain Price?" he asked.

"Not since about four o'clock. Somebody fired four shots from an alley off Division Street and hit one of Jim's prowl cars. Officer Dan Shaw got a thigh wound when he got out to investigate. Not serious, but he'll be out of action for a while. The general situation is still nervous over there. Jim was giving me a rundown on gun sales." Durkin broke off long enough to shave the corners of his mouth. "He got Berman's Sports Shop to take every rifle and shotgun off display, the same thing in the three pawnshops. Dacey, the colored secondhand and loan shop, claims he's out of stock, but there's a rumor he's doing a hell of a big back door business. That checks out with what Larry Powell phoned in last night. Anything more on his report of kids collecting bottles for possible use as Molotov cocktails?"

"Nothing, and just about impossible to run down. Or do anything about it if we did find a lot of kids collecting bottles to take back to the stores for a cash rebate. What worries me just as much is the gun sale over on this side. Willard's Hardware, Warneke's Gun Shop, Lindstrom's Sporting Goods and Loman's Loan Company have been doing a land office business in handguns, rifles, shotguns and hunting licenses. Anything else from Powell?"

"No more than he's given us before. There's still an undercurrent of restlessness that's hard to define or point up. The older people are scared of what the younger ones are going to do and the younger people seem to be waiting around for something to set them off. What they call The Word. Touchy as hell. It's anybody's guess as to what, when or where it will happen, but all the signs are there."

Durkin shut off the razor. "That's what our Emergency Plan is all about, isn't it, Pete?"

At 8:30 a series of meetings began in the office of Wayne Taylor. The first was with Police Chief Lee Durkin and lasted an hour. At 9:30, Reverend Amos Hart, Walter

697

Lynch and Dr. Royal Betts arrived and remained for three-quarters of an hour. At 10:15 Edgar Roche of the Mercantile Club, Ben Kelton of the Restaurant Men's Association and Baylor Claypool, president of the Hotelmen's Association, arrived and stayed until 11:30. There followed a brief telephone discussion between Wayne and Shana Pierce, who informed him that Kenneth Armour and Theodore Warren were out of the city on business.

The luncheon hour was reserved for Mayor Tom Cameron, who arrived just as the table in the private dining room next to Wayne's office was being set. John Curran joined them for a drink, then left them together. To ease Cameron's obvious apprehension, Wayne poured a second drink, which the mayor accepted gratefully. With the tense situation in the city and local elections eight months away, Cameron was totally sensitive to the political implications of this meeting.

"Tom," Wayne said in opening the discussion, "you know that since the deaths of my Grandfather Jonas and my father, I have deliberately avoided taking an active part in local politics, apart from some financial support to the candidates of my personal choice, of which you have been one. When you were campaigning last time, I supported your platform of progress—"

"I've done my best, Wayne. I can point to a dozen or more improvements and changes over Max Hungerford's term."

"I've read the statistics, Tom, but what I'm concerned about is the people. During the past three years, the City Council has voted the largest budgets in Laurelton's history, but there has been no sign of physical improvement over in West and South Laurelton. Now we're faced with a major rebellion that has been smoldering for years. Street and housing improvements are nonexistent, sanitation and sewers are still lacking, street lighting is bad, there hasn't been a new playground or library, and people are still complaining about the bus service—"

"Wayne, eighty per cent of the funds for those budgets comes from East Laurelton and it's only fair that the money be spent where it comes from."

"That's one hell of a moot question, Tom, since the major industries who supply a large portion of that tax money are located in West and South Laurelton, even if their owners and executives live in East Laurelton. Regardless of that, what is fair is to spend money where it is most needed and not where it comes from. I know that's not the

698

way to win votes over on this side, but there are plenty of potential votes across the bridge, too."

"Promises won't help the situation today or tomorrow, Wayne."

"No. I'll agree that the time for promises is over. The people have been overburdened with promises and, if I may coin a word, underwhelmed by the lack of performance. For several days, I've been holding meetings with various people and groups——"

"I know." Cameron's words were rimmed with mild criticism.

"——in order to come to some reasonable understanding of what we, who *can* do something about the situation, *should* do as quickly as possible. Not after next June's primary, but now. At once."

The ultimatum was clear. The name Taylor, the image and fortune of Jonas Taylor, Cameron knew, was still powerful. Any man supported actively by Wayne Taylor would become Laurelton's next mayor.

"What do you have in mind, Wayne?"

"A number of things. I don't know how the present situation will be resolved, but hopefully, it will pass. When it does, we're going to see that it never happens again, God and reasonable men willing." Wayne began to outline a program from a sheet of paper upon which he had written a lengthy list of notations. Cameron listened, but his appetite for the meal that was being served had lessened considerably.

2

At 9:30 that morning, Corey was dressing when Jemmy came up to tell him that Adam Cameron was on the phone; also, that Drew Warren had phoned while he was in the shower and asked that he call her back. He took Adam's call in the dining room where Jemmy had plugged the phone in, and talked with Adam while having his orange juice and coffee.

"How are you fixed for lunch, Corey?" Adam asked at once.

"Free and clear if you can tear yourself away from your typewriter. Is this social, or something special?"

"Both, I think, but I don't want to discuss it over the phone. Dad keeps popping in and out of my office."

"What time?"

"Twelve-thirty? Stop by and we'll grab a sandwich at Spurling's down the street."

"Twelve-thirty. You can't give me a hint, can you?"

"Well—something to do with a friend of ours."

"Which friend?"

"Lyle Emerson."

"I'll be there, Ad."

"Check. I'll look for you."

Corey dialed the Brookhill number. "Drew? Good morning. Sleep well?"

"Better than I have in months. I called for two reasons. First, to thank you again for last night. It was lovely, Corey, and I enjoyed it so much. Second, Dad called from Mr. Collins' office in New York this morning. I also spoke with your dad. He asked me to tell you that everything is going smoothly and that he and Father are going to Baltimore and Richmond. If all goes well, they should be home sometime on Saturday."

"That sounds encouraging, Drew. At least, there's still some hope. About last night, how about a repeat?"

"Any time you like."

"Let me call you later. I'm going into town to have lunch with Ad Cameron."

"*Ciao.*"

Over toast and a second cup of coffee, he scanned the headlines of the *Herald* and read the detailed story of the police car that had been burned the day before. Later, there had been several arrests when two women were picked up for shoplifting in a supermarket and a group of belligerent watchers attempted to rescue the prisoners from the police. Another item described an act of vandalism in a white high school in East Laurelton during the night. Desks had been broken into and rifled, blackboards defaced with obscenities, offices littered with torn records, two typewriters were smashed, the cafeteria left in a shambles and every faucet in the rest rooms had been turned on. Damage was estimated at $7,500. Still later, a cruising police car had been fired upon, one officer wounded.

The editorial page took note of these incidents and deplored the lack of parental guidance and authority over children who were bent on destructive courses by permissiveness that exceeded the bounds of reason, giving little comfort to those who "feel that teen-agers must find a means of expressing themselves as individuals in purely aggressive terms."

"These actions," the editorial went on, "are not those of 'individuals' but the combined efforts of hoodlums who gang up to express contempt for their parents and constituted authority, whether it be in the home, school, church or police. It is not unreasonable to assume that if this contemptuous behavior is not curbed from within the home, laws must eventually be passed to place the financial responsibility of the culprits upon their parents until they reach an age when they can be tried as adults and, if found guilty, jailed for their transgressions."

Brad Cameron, owner and publisher of the *Herald,* was in Adam's office when Corey arrived. He greeted Corey warmly, asked after Kenneth, then left them alone.

"Problems?" Corey asked.

Ad grinned ruefully. "My editorial this morning. We've already had over two dozen calls from irate subscribers and advertisers, threatening to cancel subscriptions and advertising for advocating, quote, Communistic laws, unquote, and why the hell don't *we* find something for their kids to do after school. *We,* not they. Christ, the more I see of some parents, the more I find myself leaning toward enforced birth control. Or sterilization. Let's get out of here."

They walked the two blocks to Spurling's and found a place at a table already occupied by two television men. The talk all around them was focused on the civil rights problem, vandalism, the threatened Negro action encouraged by Dr. Rhama, and probable retaliation by the white community.

"We took a count yesterday on gun sales over here and you can't find a rifle, shotgun or revolver anywhere for love or money," Seth Apley confided. "Sergeant Dickerson over in the 12th Precinct tells me it's the same over in West Laurelton. Jim Price has been warning white merchants to keep their eyes open, their cash in their pockets, and their eyes on the back door at the first sign of trouble. Boy, this is getting damned spooky."

"You really think it's that close, Seth?" Adam asked.

"You'd better by God believe it, man. If I get a call to make that scene, I'm not moving in without police protection."

Andy Dallas munched on his sandwich through this exchange, then said, "Tell you something, and you can quote me. Any sonofabitch lays a hand on my camera or touches one of my sound crew, he's going to get to pick a load of buckshot out of his hide, if he's still alive. That last thing down in Atlanta, I had about two thousand dollars' worth of equipment smashed. This time, I'm going to do some smashing first."

701

"How about you, Ad?" Apley asked.

"I'll have about six men covering, three teams of two, but we're not going to search them for weapons before they move in. Anything more on the National Guard thing?"

"Last I heard, Cameron was in touch with the Governor," Dallas said.

"I can give you something later than that," Ad said, "direct from the Camp Fitch P.R.O. They're on standby with eight hundred men. If Durkin hits the panic button, they'll be here within three hours."

"Three hours? Can't they move quicker than that?"

"Orders. They don't move a man or truck until they get the word to the C.O., General Drummond."

"A hell of a lot of wood and real estate can burn in three hours," Apley observed.

"Long as it burns over there, it's okay with me," Dallas added. "Tell you, they make a move to cross that bridge, they're going to run into a lot of bullets that've been sold this last week or two. You ready, Seth?"

Apley rose, waved a hand and left with Dallas. "This has all the familiar earmarks of a Viet Nam briefing," Corey said.

"Let's hope it won't come off. It will be a rough sonofabitch if it does." A perspiring waitress took their order and hurried away. "One thing going for it is that Amos Hart and some of his people are working hard to keep the fire banked, but this bastard Rhama keeps adding fuel. What may happen—"

"Let's get back to Lyle Emerson, Ad. I'm concerned about him."

"All right. You're probably closer to him than anyone else in town, having known him in Viet Nam. I've been trying to get a message across to him, but he's so goddamned withdrawn since he returned. This obsession with helping the Negro cause—"

"Let's say it's dedication rather than obsession."

"Whatever the hell it is, he's asking for trouble."

"In what way?"

"For one thing, I'd like to find some way to warn him to stay away from a certain piece of yellow tail he's been shagging at the Center—"

"Hold on, Ad—"

"Let me finish, Corey. This isn't just idle gossip or rumor. I'd warn him because that spade brother of hers happens to be a professional boxer. Also, I'm not buying any of that business about his having been beaten up by a so-called prowler who didn't bother to rob him when his wallet was within easy reach, just as his wrist watch wasn't taken. One plus one still equals two, except in this case, when it adds up to three."

Corey said, "Where are you collecting your garbage these days, Ad?"

"From the usual reliable and well-informed sources. I make it a policy never to reveal a source, but in your case, I'll make an exception this one time. For instance, the mother of one of our pressroom gang is a student in Lyle's Voters' Registration class at the Center. Say what you want about Negroes, they're damned quick to take in a white-colored situation, this one in particular. They've been seen talking together, driving away from the Center in his car after hours. That kind of thing gets talked about among their own. This boy who told me about it is a bright-eyed kid, a sort of protégé of mine, so it comes straight from the horse's mouth."

The sandwiches and coffee arrived, saving Corey from immediate comment, and he knew it was useless to refute Adam's information. When the waitress was gone, Ad said, "I can't find a way to reach Lyle. I'd probably get the back of his hand for trying to butt in, but if I were a close friend, I'd hint that he isn't being very b-r-i-g-h-t about this cockeyed, integrated romance of his."

Corey remained silent, nibbling at his sandwich. Ad dropped the subject then and took on a new one. "I hear you broke the female hermit out of her cave last night."

"Another of your usual reliable and well-informed sources?" Corey asked.

"Well, you'll admit the Marina Club dining room isn't exactly a secret hideaway, won't you?"

"So?"

"So that almost makes it a news item. Drew Warren, one of Georgia's most attractive heiresses, takes off for Europe, remains away for over a year without a word, not a single line of publicity from the usually news-hungry European press. No show at the better known resorts, spas, gambling casinos, no romantic fortune hunters following her. She returns as quietly as she left, checks into Memorial Hospital, then holes up at Brookhill like a recluse, comes out suddenly when former boy friend Corey Armour returns from Viet Nam. Any comment for the press, sir?"

"Knock it off, Ad. You know how close she was to Bruce. She left town shortly after the funeral—"

"And after you went back to Athens."

"—after his funeral, to get away from everything that reminded her of him. She returned when Anderson Warren's
703

health began to fail. She identifies me with a more happy period of her life. Don't try to embroider that into more than what it is."

"Okay, I'll take your word for it, even though she wouldn't see a reporter or talk to me on the phone when she got back, and buddy, I tried a dozen times or more. So what else is new?"

"Not a thing, Ad. Why the hell don't you stay with birth and death statistics, accidents, fires, the city and county budgets and what progress our axe-handle Governor has been making in the civil rights department?"

Ad grinned mischievously. "We've got all of that covered. One of my jobs is to dig up new leads—"

"Even if you have to dig inside someone's coffin?"

"—like, whatever became of Theodore Warren's brother, Chase Warren? And how does he figure in Anderson's will? And will he come back to the Warren Tobacco Company? And if he does, what happens to Theodore, the long distance runner? And Drew—"

"You've really become a nosy bastard, haven't you?"

"All in a day's work, Corey. You can't run a newspaper by overlooking possibilities."

"Now I'm wondering just why you got me down here, to tell me about Lyle or dig up something on the Warrens?"

"Whatever you believe, Corey, I'm serious about Lyle. If anything breaks in Angeltown and he's caught over there, he won't have much of a chance, particularly with that gal's brother out gunning for him. That's as straight as I can give it to you."

3

From the *Herald*, Corey drove to Memorial Hospital, only to learn that Lyle Emerson had been discharged at noon. Instead of telephoning, Corey drove directly to Lyle's apartment house. Lyle opened the door and Corey saw the links of chain stretched across the opening. The door closed, the chain was removed, and Corey went in. Lyle slipped the chain back into place. He was on crutches, a robe concealing the stump of his leg, the swelling over his eye reduced to near normal, showing little physical evidence of the attack.

"Sit down, Corey, let me finish this phone call," Lyle said, returning to the chair beside the telephone. On the table next to the chair was a half-filled bottle of bourbon, a glass, a partially stripped .38 automatic, clip, box of cartridges, a small ramrod, a can of oil and some cleaning patches.

Into the phone, Lyle was saying, "—of course. No, I'm fine and I'll take the class as usual tonight, Miss Church. Please call him and tell him it won't be necessary to substitute—yes, that's correct. Thank you, I'll be there at 7:30." He hung up and indicated the bottle. "Drink, Corey?"

"No, thanks, Lyle." He pointed to the stripped-down .38. "You planning on reenlisting?"

Lyle laughed and picked up the barrel of the automatic and began fitting it into the frame. "This? Hell, no. I'm just taking out a small insurance policy."

"That's not being very wise, is it?"

"Just following the Boy Scout creed. Be prepared."

"You could do better than that by not showing up, couldn't you?"

Lyle snapped the loaded clip into the handle and flipped the safety catch on. "I do what I have to do, Corey," he said in a voice that had suddenly hardened. "No sonofabitch is going to tell me what I can do and what I can't do. Period."

"Lyle—"

"Corey, I'm big enough to take care of my own problems. I've got a job to do that means a lot to me. I'm accepted because I contribute to a needy cause. Everybody needs—needs—"

He broke off suddenly, reached for the bottle and poured a drink. Corey said, "I'm not knocking it, Lyle. I'm glad you've found something so useful and self-satisfying. All I'm asking is that you wait until this trouble blows over. It could settle down in a few days."

"Goddam it, Corey, whatever anybody else may think, I'm still a *man*—"

"You don't have to prove that to me."

"Maybe I've got to prove it to myself, but make no mistake about it. I'm going to the Center tonight and every school night, to my job at Laurelton High every school day. Period."

"Period. Now that we've settled that, how about having dinner with me tonight? My father is out of town and I'm on the loose. I'll call Tish and have her set another place. We'll eat early enough to get you to the Center by 7:30."

The invitation, made that way, was difficult to refuse. Lyle said, "Okay. Six?"

"Six will be fine. You know the way?"

"Old Colony Lane, isn't it?"

At 6 P.M. in the social hall of the African Zion Baptist Church, a hastily prepared supper was being served to 34 Negroes who were between the ages of 21 and 28. Of the 34, 12 were employed in permanent jobs, 9 in temporary jobs and 13 were unemployed. Sixteen were married, 6 divorced or separated and 12 were single. Seven of the employed and 9 unemployed were attending night classes at the Center. The one thing they had in common was that all were veterans of the Viet Nam conflict. Their army ranks had varied from PFC to First Sergeant Davis Lipscomb, a tall, robust, intelligent man who was an electrician at the Water and Power Company and operated a television and radio repair business from his home at night and weekends.

The 34 were all that could be contacted on such short notice among West and South Laurelton's veterans who were willing to attend the "square meeting" on Amos Hart's invitation, despite the efforts of Hart, Walter Lynch, Dr. Royal Betts and Henry Clark; but, Hart thought as the meal progressed, it was a good start. Emily Hart had pressed seven women into service to prepare the fried chicken supper, which was served hot from the social hall kitchen. Milo Roose, not present, had supplied the beer, two cans for each man. Dr. Betts was absent by reason of a heavy schedule at his clinic.

The discussion began during the dessert and coffee when Hart asked, "Do any of you know the meaning of the Latin expression *quid pro quo?*"

"Means something received in return for something given," Davis Lipscomb replied quickly.

"Very good, Mr. Lipscomb," Hart said. "You've had a good supper and I hope you enjoyed it. I know you expect me to ask for something in return. *Quid pro quo.* But I won't ask for much, only that you listen to an old man whom your generation calls a square. And I won't hold you to anything, so that at any time any of you feels like it, you are free to get up and walk out. I won't try to hold you back.

"I'll say this much, however; if you believe that what I have to say is important to the future of our community, and the future of every one of us, I will ask more of you. I make no promises. You will listen and accept or walk out and forget it. I'm gambling you will stay and accept, but the choice is your own."

The 34 men stirred, squirmed, looked at each other self-consciously, then settled back in their chairs to listen.

"Good," Hart said with a beaming smile. "That took exactly fifty-five seconds and nobody walked out. Light up your cigarettes if you want to."

Several of the men laughed, a few grinned, but mostly they regarded Hart seriously. Hart said, "By actual count, eight of you came here wearing a black fez. I don't know how many more of you put your fezzes aside before you came in. It makes no difference at the moment because I want to talk about another kind of hat. In Viet Nam, some of you wore green berets. I know the rest of you wore battle helmets with no less pride. Why? Because you were proud men doing a necessary and patriotic job that made all men respect and admire you, there and back here.

"You left many of your black brothers there, some in hospitals, some who will never return. There are upwards of fifty thousand Negroes there now, most of whom will come back one day. And more will go and return, decorated with honors, robed in pride, just as you have.

"To what? To what will they return?

"That question, you soldiers, is one you may help answer here tonight. Yes, you may well speak for all your brethren in uniform who are absent."

"Reverend," Robbie Baldwin spoke up, "I don't mean to step out of line, but like you said, we're all vets and we're used to getting things told without the fancy buildup. Some of us are married, some due for classes at the Center."

"All right, son. This isn't a Sunday sermon, so we'll skip the soup and get to the meat."

There was a slight break while the men poured the last of their beer and others lighted cigarettes. Hart resumed quickly. "I have looked carefully at my own generation and yours and I see the distrust that lies between us. And yet, it is your generation which must carry the burden, just as mine once carried it. We have made some progress, more than our fathers' generation did, but it is not enough. Your generation will accomplish more, perhaps, and still, it will not be enough. But the burden is yours whether you want to assume it or not, to make it succeed or fail. We had certain advantages over our fathers, just as you have certain advantages we never had."

"Like what?" Joe Beeman asked loudly.

"You have been trained in teamwork, to be leaders, to accept responsibility for other men's lives. That you are alive today proves that. You have educational benefits, subsidized by the government. You have lived and fought be-

707

side white men on an equal basis, eaten, bathed and slept beside them. You know it can work because you have seen it work, that it can be made to work; that it worked because you showed you were equal to any man in courage, intelligence and a willingness to share danger together.

"Your brothers who are still in Viet Nam will return and ask, 'What have you been doing while we were over there fighting on?' and what will you tell them?

"You can tell them you have made a start in which they can join, follow, and improve. You can tell them you are changing the image of the Negro here just as you did over there. You can show him progress in your work, education, industry and home life; that you are working with the generation growing up behind you to better their lives and futures. That you have not joined the street nomads and wastrels who only 'hang around' waiting for a job to find them, or for a money handout. That you have earned your way and enjoy the respect of your fellow man, regardless of color, as a man.

"There are thirty-four of you present, thirty-four of over a hundred local veterans here tonight, but even thirty-four men of determination can change the direction of all our lives, the course of the earth itself."

Hands began to fly upward, but Hart wigwagged them into silence. "Let me finish first, please.

"You men have been exposed to the dangers of combat, led others into it. I don't have to tell you that what is going on in our streets at this moment is a danger greater than that in Viet Nam because it is one-sided. This time, the civilians won't be Vietnamese men, women and children. They will be yours.

"Let me tell you, or do I have to, about other riots in other cities and towns. You've heard and read about them. All I can ask you is: What good did the rioting, looting and burning do? Who gained? Who lost? Who got beaten up, jailed, and burned out? Who suffered most for the few who smashed and stole and set fire to stores, even when white-owned, but where Negroes were employed and are jobless now?"

Davis Lipscomb said, "Reverend, we been taking it as long as we can remember. You asking us to lay down and keep on doing nothing? Is that what our training and leadership amounts to, more of the same?"

"No!" Hart thundered the word at him. "No, that is *not* what I'm asking of you. What I'm asking is that you show our Negro community that you young men are men of responsibility. I'm asking that you help to control our young people and others, prevent this stupid wholesale rioting and not allow us to lose what we have gained so far, what my generation was beaten and jailed for. School and bus integration, open vote registration, equal pay for equal jobs in city, county and some industrial jobs.

"What we gained, I will admit, is not everything we want, what we deserve and have earned, but how much more will we win by riot and the torch? As citizens, we have the law on our side. As outlaws, we have nothing. It's asking a lot of you men, but we've got no other way to go. We have among us a group of outsiders who call themselves the Black Fez, black nationalists. Dr. Rhama's people have gone from city to city, stirring Negro communities into revolt and riot against constituted authority—"

"The white man's authority, Reverend," Claude Morris said.

"All right, Claude, the white man's authority, if you will, but it is legal authority, voted by the majority. But some day enough black people will learn the value of their votes and share in that authority as councilmen, assemblymen, senators, and reach even higher.

"Dr. Rhama preaches black nationalism, black internationalism. Of what nation or nations can we become a part and not be aliens, foreigners? What Dr. Rhama is preaching is black violent revolution and that idea is as useless as it is senseless. We can't allow purposeless destruction of lives, property and our advancement, nor permit black militants to push us back instead of forward. To destroy others is to destroy ourselves and eliminate any chance of forward progress."

Robbie Baldwin's hand shot up. "Reverend, what can just a handful of us do against so many? You go out and count all the black people who are wearing black fezzes. There's thousands against us."

"You're right, Robert, but remember that many are wearing those fezzes because no one has given them anything else to show them they are not alone. Still, there are many who have refused to wear them, decent people who know in their hearts that violence breeds violence and nothing more. Henry?"

Henry Clark had risen and Hart gave over to him. Clark was tall and thin, almost ascetic in appearance with deep hollows beneath high cheekbones that emphasized his flat nose and heavy lips. "Maybe you think I'm against Dr. Rhama because, as a businessman, I am self-supporting and stand to lose more by opposing him. Let me tell you that the men he calls 'handkerchief heads' and Uncle Toms

709

have been on the city's Civil Rights Committee with Reverend Hart since it began here. Just being on it with Mayor Cameron and other white leaders is progress. Since 1954, all of us have seen changes few other cities have seen. We have tried to encourage black participation in these affairs, but even those who were eligible to vote in the last election didn't exercise their right to vote. That is one of the curses on the black man, his apathy, his lack of respect for himself, his disbelief in the black man who runs for office. Those who went to the polls voted for white councilmen from black districts. This is another point on which we have worked alone and without support from our own community, in which our people have indicated by their apathy that they are satisfied with white rule. And this is an attitude we must all work together to change. The big question is, will you help us to bring this about?"

Davis Lipscomb, the ex-first sergeant, rose. He was the eldest of the young veterans present and had held the highest rank among them. He stood an even six feet tall, broad-shouldered, deep-chested, and spoke with a commanding voice as he addressed himself to Hart and Clark.

"What you gentlemen have been telling us makes a lot of sense, but what I think, when I've heard it all is, What's the use? We're not in the army where we had the chance to show what we are, what we can do. What kind of chance have we got here? The army gave us equality in rank, food, quarters, pay. Even when we slept in foxholes and ditches, we complained together and shared what we had. And still, not all white men were the same, just like all Negroes were not the same. Both sides had hate in 'em and battle action was only a temporary truce between 'em.

"What we learned was, we had a chance to fight for equality and we had to work damned hard to win it. But we did it. Point is, they gave us the *chance* to prove we could do it. Maybe that's what we need here, the *chance* to prove we can do it and hold down a job like everybody else and not look to welfare to keep alive. Here, there's nothing to fight for because the cards are stacked. Who says that if we go your way instead of Dr. Rhama's we'll get our chance to be equal to the white man?"

"A good question, Davis," Hart responded promptly, "and I'll give you an answer. You know that nobody has been more fair to our people than Mr. Wayne Taylor, and his father before him, Ames Taylor. This morning, Walter Lynch, Dr. Betts and I met with Mr. Taylor in his office and I can tell you that when this messy situation facing us is cooled off, things are going to happen that will surprise you. It may be that Laurelton will show the way for the rest of the country in civil rights because he is determined that this will never happen again in our city. There will be changes—"

"More promises, Reverend?" Arthur Goodwin asked. "We've heard 'em all by now, haven't we?"

"I can tell you this: Mr. Taylor asked me specifically *not* to make any specific promises when I told him what I had in mind, but to ask you to take it on faith that a change is coming. He has also met with other civic leaders, Chief Durkin and the mayor, and has their assurances that these will not be token changes, but the real thing.

"To get to the point of *this* meeting, what we are asking is that you show your leadership to everybody, white and black, by taking to the streets, if it becomes necessary, and help the police maintain law and order, prevent rioting from spreading, control looting, and show our people that not all of us are fez-headed or fez-minded. Dr. Rhama can shout, 'Hell, no! We won't go!' but you've already been there. You know how to do this kind of a job. You've been trained for it. The question is: Will you do it?"

"How?" Anson Warner, an ex-staff sergeant asked. "We go out and start clobberin' our own people around?"

"No," Hart replied. "I met with Chief Durkin and Inspector LaSalle and Captain Price at the 12th Precinct this afternoon. Captain Price will furnish helmets to every man who indicates a willingness to cooperate with the police, to persuade hotheaded youths to keep out of their way and not create riot conditions. You will have no weapons, no authority to make arrests, only your qualities of leadership to use on would-be lawbreakers who attempt to prevent police or firemen who try to do their jobs.

"You may even be able to restrain some police from using their clubs on our people who have been caught up in a crush of onlookers. You may help officers keep traffic moving so that fire trucks can get to where they are needed. You won't be asked to fight your own people, only to help control them. We don't know how many other ways there are to be helpful, but we feel your own resourcefulness will find those ways. There isn't very much time left, men. If you are with us, I urge you to go among your friends, veterans or not, and begin enlisting them on your side. This is one of the most important contributions you can make and we urge you, plead with you, to accept the challenge. You may use this social hall as your headquarters and I will personally clear you and any of your veteran friends who weren't able to get here this evening with Captain Price."

711

When Corey reached home, he telephoned Drew and explained the situation in part and accepted her invitation to dine at Brookhill the following night. Lyle appeared promptly at six. Jemmy served them drinks and they dined on steak, pan-fried potatoes, peas, corn and a huge tossed salad. Coffee and apple pie.

They talked of Viet Nam, of Corey's plan for Shadow Hills, and Corey noticed an increasing interest on Lyle's part, thinking. It may work out yet.

At seven, Lyle left for the Center and Corey was not unaware of the slight bulge the flat .38 made in Lyle's hip pocket. He waited until the Dodge was out of sight, then went to his own car and drove into town and parked on the lot behind the *Herald* Building. Ad was in his office, on the phone, signaling with his free hand for Corey to take a seat. When he concluded his conversation, "What's up, soldier?"

"That's what I dropped by to find out."

"Could be a long night. I'm going to take a ride across the bridge to snoop around. I could use some company. Interested?"

"Very much, if I won't be in your way."

"Hell, you've lived closer to this kind of thing than I have. Let's go." He dialed his inside operator and told her she could reach him by mobile phone. In Adam's Lincoln, they headed for Angeltown.

"There's talk going around of a white vigilante group forming up to, quote, protect white lives and property, unquote. Outside the city limits on a farm somewhere. Rumor also has it that they have Will Apperson's blessing and approval."

The car turned into Taylor Avenue and headed west. "Take a look at the shops." Corey noticed that lights burned in most of them. "Owners and some of their help are in there, loaded for bear. At the first threat of any black invasion, or a gasoline bomb, World War III is going to break loose right here. I'll bet a dollar to a pumpkin seed that eight out of ten stores in the commercial area are being guarded the same way."

"What's the solution, Ad?"

"If I knew that, I could settle the war in Viet Nam, the unrest in the Middle East and become a one-man United Nations. One thing I'm sure of is that there's as little unity among the Negroes as there is between white and black.

Force and threat will solve nothing. Black nationalism can't win over white supremacy and vice versa because they're both as wrong and phony as a three-dollar bill. Until both sides decide to accept the simple truth and find some way to sit down and compromise, but sincerely, the best we can hope for is what we're getting now, a Mexican standoff. The 'have-nots' want what's due them, the 'haves' refuse to turn loose with what they've got, and the reasonable people on both sides are caught in a trap between them."

"What about the federal government?"

Adam snorted. "The government are a lot of unrealistic men who think human problems can be solved with strong statements made in loud ringing voices, little deeds and big money. Figure up how much money has been spent and what it has accomplished. Add to that the cost of all property that has been destroyed, the lives lost. The government spends and greedy politicians at state, county and city levels argue about who will administer the funds in order to control the greatest number of votes in the next election. What sifts down to the needy is peanuts and propaganda. Poverty programs, Great Societies, Head Starts, Youth Economic projects, nothing has really worked as it was intended. What they need is a Peace Corps type of operation with jobs, education and decent housing as their goals. Also, an effort to knock out profitable slum landlordism."

"What about the Center?"

"Corey," Adam said, "if Katie Willard's Recreational-Vocational Center could be multiplied, spread into thousands of communities throughout the world and supported by civic, industrial, business and religious leaders, we'd solve most of the world's poverty problems. If they were organized honestly as training, recreational and educational institutions in every industrial and agricultural area, we'd have the answer to school dropouts, open rebellion, vandalism, even war. Oops! The gendarmes."

At the east end of the bridge, the six lanes had been blocked down to two, one in each direction, with officers permitting cars to proceed only after cursory examination of the occupants. To one side, several cars with Negro passengers, heading eastward into Laurelton, were halted while officers questioned occupants as to destination and purpose. Some were being turned back. Adam dropped his sun visor to exhibit his official PRESS identification and was waved on.

The west end of the bridge was similarly guarded and traffic moved slowly, bumper-to-bumper, across the Cottonwood River. The night was warm and there were numerous boats on the river, and Corey wondered what measures were being taken to examine these.

"They've got roadblocks set up on the Riverton and Fairview roads leading into Laurelton," Adam continued when they came off the bridge into West Laurelton. "Sheriff Apperson's boys. I hope they won't have to be brought into this. Durkin is fine, even though he's got a lot of hardnoses on the force, but Apperson is strictly for blood and thunder. Also, he's up for reelection next June and the publicity would help him a lot. Thank God Durkin ruled out those goddamned vicious dogs and cattle prods."

They passed several police cars, all moving slowly through the congested traffic on Grand Avenue, Velie and Division Streets and the many cross streets that comprised the central section. Most of the stores were dark, excepting for supermarkets, drugstores, service stations, the Goldfield Theater, bars, restaurants, poolrooms and neon-lighted, tinselly night clubs. Knots of young people were gathered on every well-lighted corner, talking, shuffling feet to the music that spewed out of the taverns and night clubs. Most noticeable was the number of black fezzes being worn by men, women, boys and girls. They were everywhere. Symbol of unity. Symbol of power. Symbol of hatred for the common enemy, the white man.

And other symbols; crudely painted signs on store windows: NEGRO-OWNED; BLOOD BROTHER; DON'T BURN A BROTHER; COOL IT, MAN, I'M ONE OF YOU.

Adam stopped beside a car and talked for a moment with a *Herald* reporter and photographer who were parked on an unlighted side street. Waiting expectantly. The reporter indicated with a shrug that nothing of reportable importance was happening, but the current was there waiting only to be turned on.

They drove north on 22nd Street to Division and turned right on Division. As they came toward the Center, Adam slowed down. They saw the lights of the two-storied administration building, several one-storied buildings and the converted barn that was the gymnasium. "Looks quiet enough," Adam said.

"I hope it can stay that way," Corey replied.

"Well, let's take one more turn around and get back, shall we?" He headed south toward the central area again. The police radio, its volume turned low, began sputtering. Adam reached for the phone and called in to the *Herald* desk.

Ivy had bathed, applied makeup and was slipping into her dress when Duke awoke. "What time is it?" he asked.

"Half-past seven."

"Hey! Didn't I tell you to wake me half-past seven?"

"You awake, ain't you?"

Duke's eyes opened wider. He yawned, laughed and said, "Yeah. I am, ain't I?"

"You hungry?"

"Jesus, no. Just a little boguey."

"I got three left 'til I get some more from Connie tomorrow night. You want me to turn you on?"

"Yeah. I'm gettin' itchy."

Ivy went to her dresser and pulled the top drawer out, inserted her hand and withdrew a small cellophane envelope which had been scotch-taped to the underside of the top slab of mahogany. From the false bottom of a wicker laundry hamper, she took a small leather hypodermic kit, then went to the kitchen where she dissolved the heroin in a small amount of heated water, drew the fluid into the barrel. Duke had taken one of Ivy's stockings and tightened it into a tourniquet around his upper left arm. When she returned from the kitchen, he was ready. She injected the fluid into a bulging vein, withdrew the needle, rinsed the hypodermic and replaced it in the hamper. Duke lay back on the bed, eyes closed, while Ivy finished dressing and applied a coat of polish to her nails. When they were dry, she gave her lips a final touch of lipstick.

"How you fixed, Duke?"

"Ah-h—just fine, baby." He sat up, eyes brightened with a freshened sense of awareness. "That done it."

"You got any left at your place?"

"Some. Why?"

"The way you shootin' it, you goin'a need a connection all your own. You got it big, ain't you?"

Duke laughed with new confidence. "Don't you worry, baby, I'll get it. All I need."

"Okay, if you say so. You comin' by the Club?"

"Later. Got to go by an' see The Man first."

"You gettin' on pretty thick with Banjo, ain't you?"

Duke stood up and began dressing. "Well, right now I need him. In a little while, it'll be different."

"How different?"

"You wait an' see. I told you once before, I'm cuttin' me

715

a piece of his cake. It works out, I'll come out with a bigger piece'n he ever had."

Skeptically, "An' I told you before, you better watch out, Duke."

"I'm watchin' out, baby. For me. For you, too."

"Duke, honey, I'm warnin' you. Banjo ain't nobody to be foolin' around with. I know at least half a dozen men thought they could outsmart Banjo who ain't around no more."

"Sure. Like Benny Tupper." Duke laughed again as he pulled up his tie. "I'm around, Ivy, an' I'm goin'a be around a long time, but I'm goin' first class like I always travel."

Ivy began to reply, then realized the effort was useless. "Okay," she said resignedly. "Make sure the door is locked when you leave, huh?"

Duke finished dressing, let himself out of the house, tried the front door to make sure it was locked, then walked south to the end of the block where his Jaguar was parked. He got in and drove to Banjo's Place for the scheduled 8:00 o'clock meeting.

7

For the first time since he had become The Man among Angeltown's vice fraternity, Banjo Nichols was worried. The back room of his pool parlor that was now his office and the scene of an occasional high-stakes poker game and meeting place for his "business" associates, had once been the only horse parlor in town, operated by one Bookie Bill Baker, whom Lee Durkin banished when Baker tried to parlay the one into a multiple operation in South and West Laurelton. The tightening process began after Cuban Joe Androz moved his gambling and night club to New Orleans. Coley Walsh and Con Coverly were driven out when they tried to expand their illicit whiskey operation. Eddie Jackson retired and moved to Atlanta. The gambling partnership of Bailey Gordon and Deacon Fish ended when Gordon died of cancer. Chocolate Charlotte and Miss Angie were still operating their houses under Ben-Joe Nichols' umbrella of police protection.

With Baker's departure, Ben-Joe had fallen heir to the poolroom. He at once moved the bookmaking operation to another location and put Charlie Beckwith in charge. Similarly, he took over the Walsh-Coverly whiskey setup and the Jackson, Gordon and Fish gambling enterprises. As long as the operations were quiet and contained, Captain Price was inclined to look the other way, but as time passed, Ben-Joe gave in to threats from the New Orleans and Atlanta narcotics syndicate to send their own men into the area. Ben-Joe thought this over and brought in his brother-in-law, Connie Clark, a night club and gambling house operator from Phenix City, Alabama, when the federal and state clamped down on that city of vice, and furnished the money to open the 2-2-2 Club to base the narcotics outlet.

Within three weeks of its birth, the 12th Precinct vice squad had run down the source of marijuana that had begun to flourish. By the time four small-time pushers had been picked up, the 2-2-2 Club had been tabbed and a plainclothes vice squad man made a call on Connie at his home at four o'clock one morning. Connie listened and said, "I'll let you know something inside of forty-eight hours."

"You'll let me know something by ten o'clock tonight, mister," the vice cop replied, "or you'll be in jail and out of business. Also, you try going over my head and you'll be cold, stone dead."

Connie did not use his telephone, suspecting it may have been tapped. He waited until he was sure he was not being followed, then drove to Ben-Joe's house in Riverside. Ben-Joe was willing, even eager to write the entire adventure off as a loss, but Connie pointed out that if he did, the syndicate would move in, accept the police protection offer and continue the lucrative operation without Ben-Joe. Or Connie Clark.

"You know what that means, Ben-Joe?" Connie asked. "I seen it happen before. They move in, they take over. First thing you know, all's you goin'a be runnin' is a two-bit poolroom. You play with the cops, they'll keep the syndicate out."

"I never had no police trouble before, Connie. I don't want none now. They don't mind a little gamblin', a few whorehouses, some moonshinin', 'cause people goin'a find some way to do it anyhow, but this dope business—"

"Take it or leave it, Ben-Joe, but it got to be one way or the other. All or nothin'. We got us a Club—"

"*I* got a Club, Connie," Ben-Joe snapped quickly.

"Okay, *you* got a Club. Thing is, what you got to keep it doin' is jumpin', else it no different than any other Club. You nervous about gettin' knocked over, this is what you need, protection. Man, you got to realize you been gettin' away lucky for a long time. I never been in nothin' where I didn't have to pay somebody off, a hell of a sight more'n this boy is askin'."

"Well," Ben-Joe said uncertainly, "I don't know. I just don't know."

"You got 'til ten o'clock tonight to make your mind up. You shake this deal off, I'm pullin' out."

"The Club ain't big enough for you?"

"It's big enough for me, but I been up against syndicates before, Ben-Joe. Time they take their cut to send back to Cleveland, Detroit, Miami, Chicago an' a few other places, all's you doin' is workin' for coffee an' doughnuts." Connie paused and added significantly, "Ain't nowhere near enough to keep a nice house like this goin'."

Ben-Joe reflected silently for a few moments. "How's a thing like this work, Connie?"

"What thing?"

"The police payoff."

"Nothin' to it, much. You talk to the man and make a deal. He comes aroun' like a landlord, once a week, to pick up the money. He spread it where it needs spreadin'. Once in a while, they tip you off ahead of time they got to knock off one or two of your people, one of your joints. You finger somebody who don't know too much, couple-a pushers, maybe a gamblin' joint you clean out first, a couple-a whores. That keeps 'em out of the Club an' you stay in business."

"I don't like it, Connie."

"Man, you ain't got no choice. You don't play ball, somebody else moves in, takes over the same deal and first thing you know, you out. That's all she wrote."

"You go along home now. I'll call you by nine o'clock tonight."

At nine that night, Ben-Joe made the call and at ten o'clock Connie talked with the vice squad man. At one o'clock, Ben-Joe and the plainclothes man sat in a car near Willow Grove and the deal was made. In the four years that followed, narcotics had become the single largest and most profitable source of Ben-Joe's revenue, but the costs had increased proportionately. The syndicate prices had gone up and protection became more costly. How the payoff money was distributed locally had remained a mystery to Ben-Joe and Connie, but Nichols knew that the top men, Price, La-Salle and Durkin were not sharing in the money. Also, there were the chiselers; beat men who dropped in on their own at the poolroom or the Club for a handout, hinting of some deeper knowledge, accepting a few dollars that went into their own pockets. Not much, but a constant irritation. And this, perhaps, was why Banjo was lenient with men like Jim Cuddy, Jake Runnels and Eli Buller who were on his personal payroll and were dipping into the money they collected from the various operators. Again, not much, but enough to annoy Banjo, knowing they would be hard to replace; and knew too much to be fired outright.

What worried him now was that he was not too sure he had not committed an error of judgment in the matter of Dr. Rhama. At first, the idea had appealed to him very strongly. Angered by the repeated increases in the protection bite he was paying, the thought of creating problems for the police seemed to be a logical outlet for the revenge he sought. He went to Atlanta and located Brother Leonard, a known follower of Dr. Rhama. Two days later, Dr. Rhama flew into Atlanta, listened to Ben-Joe Nichols, asked many questions, then decided that Laurelton was an ideal focal point for a major demonstration project. Ben-Joe agreed to the $5,000 "expense" cost and returned home. If, after the demonstration was under way, Ben-Joe could emerge as the peacemaker, many of his problems, he reasoned, would be solved. He could then bargain with the police higher-ups for favors, get the do-gooders like Hart, Lynch, Betts and others off his back.

Until now, the Black Fez Movement seemed a reasonable solution, something the people wanted. Action. Now, the whole business was no longer in his own hands, but in Dr. Rhama's; burning police cars and growing threats of total violence were more than Ben-Joe had bargained for. Only last night he had protested to Dr. Rhama, whose cold eyes were answer enough.

"I'm not a Messiah, Brother Nichols," Rhama replied. "I talk to people, but I don't control their actions. I speak the truth to them, but what action they see fit to take in order to control the white devils' evil is in their own hands. Destruction is one way of manifesting their dissatisfaction, their need to throw off the yoke of slavery, the only one to which the white authority will pay attention. Once it starts, no one but the people themselves can control it. It rolls on and on—"

"I didn't ask to get our town burned, or people shot. All's I asked for was demonstrations—"

"And you're getting what you asked for. The degree is in the hands of the people, not mine. Remember, brother, I didn't come to you. You came to me."

"All right, I'm askin' you to leave it where it is, just go on back to Atlanta and forget it."

"I have taken your money and given my word, brother. When my work is done, I will leave, not before."

And there wasn't a damned thing, Ben-Joe reflected now,

719

that he could do about it. The people had accepted Dr. Rhama as their saviour. They listened, accepted, and were reaching toward him.

He heard the signal rap on the back door. When it was repeated, he got up heavily and unlocked the door to admit Duke Shackleford, then shot the two bolts back into place. "Anybody see you?" Ben-Joe asked.

"Nobody out there to see."

"Sit down." The two men faced each other across the green-covered poker table, Ben-Joe's thick fingers busy with the inevitable deck of cards, shuffling, cutting, shuffling, cutting. "When you see Dr. Rhama and Brother Leonard last?" he asked finally.

"Last night around eleven o'clock. Right after they seen you."

"Rhama say anything about me?"

Duke smiled with a trace of venality. "Some. Said you wantin' to call the whole thing off."

Eyes on the cards, Ben-Joe nodded. "This whole thing, it was a mistake, Duke."

"You gettin' what you asked for, what you paid for, ain't you?"

"I didn't ask for what this thing is comin' to."

"Little late for that, ain't it? The people, they ready to go, start swingin'."

"Listen, Duke—"

"What's the matter, Ben-Joe, you startin' to show piss in your blood?"

"Look, boy, I don't need no smart talk from you." The fingers stopped shuffling and ice crept into Ben-Joe's voice. The ugly scar on his face had gone from pink to purple and his eyes became two bright pinpoints of light beneath their reptilian hoods.

"You can't back off now, is all I'm sayin'," Duke replied.

"An' I don't need no goddam advice from a junkhead. Look, boy, I know what goes with you. An' I know what goes with you an' Ivy. Onliest thing's save you from gettin' bombed out with a shot of battery acid instead of H so far is me. I told you before, this is my town and if you want to stay alive in it, you better get it straight in your mind who The Man is. Banjo Nichols. Me."

Across the table, Duke stared back at Banjo with a light, cruel smile on his lips and no trace of fear. "Banjo," he said coolly, "you ain't got the class it takes to be The Man. If you did, you'da run Rhama an' his stooge all the way back to Atlanta barefooted. He put you down an' you're bleedin' to death because you ain't got the guts to let him turn the people on. Well, he's goin'a do it anyhow, whether you like it or not. An' when they finished, you're goin'a be finished, too. You're small time, trying to act biggety, but you ain't got what it takes. You tried to put me down because I wanted to start up a numbers thing an' cut you in, but all's you was, was afraid, an 'a man who's afraid, he's got no class. In a little while, you an' Connie, you goin'a be through, Banjo, an' I'm goin'a be The Man."

"You junkie bastard! You a dead man—"

Duke showed little reaction to Ben-Joe's outburst. He reached across the table and picked up the deck of cards, riffled them once, then threw them in Ben-Joe's distorted face. "Watch yourself, man. You got high blood pressure. You could crap out any minute, you let yourself get excited that way."

Duke got up and walked to the door that led into the poolroom, shot the bolts and walked out, smiling and waving to the pool players as he made his way to the food counter. He passed Larry Powell and patted him on the back with a patronizing, "How you doin', Larry?" then ordered a beer from Noah Smith and leaned against the counter while he drank it. He saw Hinky Liggett's chair come upright away from the wall. Hinky got up and went into the back room, closing the door after him. Duke finished the beer, paid for it, called out, "See you-all," and went out. He walked north to his car and began driving toward the Nigerian Motel.

After an hour with Dr. Rhama and Brother Leonard, Duke telephoned the 2-2-2 Club and asked for Odie Bilson. After a few moments, Odie came to the phone. "Odie, listen an' get this straight the first time. I want you to get hold of Dave Sharkey, Mace Bodie, Luke Tolbert, Booker Dance and get hold of Larry Powell, too. Nobody else, just the six of you. Meet me at my place a little after midnight. Yeah, the Nigerian. Keep it to yourself an' tell the others the same."

"How about Jim Cuddy—?"

"Forget Jim Cuddy, Jake Runnels and Eli Buller. Just you an' the other five. You got that?"

"I got it. Ivy been askin' for you, Duke. Connie, too."

"You don't know where I am, Odie. Get the boys an' be here after midnight. Okay?"

"Okay, Duke. We be there."

It was shortly past two in the morning when Larry Powell called in from a pay phone outside a closed service station. Inspector LaSalle was spending the night at headquarters, poring over a large city map upon which he and Lee Durkin had earlier marked the emergency disposition of all available manpower. He responded to the Two-Five quickly. "What's up, Larry?"

"A lot. A hell of a lot, Inspector. Around 8:45, Duke and Banjo had a meeting in the back room. I don't know what happened between them, but Banjo left early, about ten o'clock, looking like he'd been poisoned. Or shook up. About 11:30, Odie Bilson got word to me that Duke wanted me to be present at a meeting at the Nigerian. I got there a little after midnight. Duke, Bodie, Sharkey, Tolbert, Dance—"

LaSalle was listening intently, making rapid notes, then began asking questions. "How many gasoline bombs?"

"I don't know. All he said was, there'd be enough to go around."

"Any details, Larry? Time, places?"

"Nothing definite. He talked in general terms, but I've got a hunch that Dr. Rhama will be the sparkplug. Duke will give them the what and where sometime tomorrow. Trouble is, I won't be with them then. He wants me to be at the poolroom until he sends me word, then I'm to meet him at some designated place and work with him on this side."

"This side?"

"Yes. He's sending the rest of them over to East Laurelton with some of the bombs to create a diversion, try to pull the police away from Angeltown or at least to keep any reserves from coming in. Question is, what do you want me to do?"

"Don't show, Larry. When you get the word, ignore it. When this hell breaks loose, nobody on the force will know you, and you could get cut down. You understand?"

"Yes, sir, but what do I do when it starts happening?"

"If it breaks out into a general riot, try to get through to Captain Price at the 12th. By phone or in person. I'll clear you with him and ask him to work something out for you. I'm sorry I can't give you any more, but chances are I'll be out in the field where you can't reach me."

"Yes, sir. Anything else?"

"I've got some of the names. What about Buller, Cuddy and Runnels?"

"They weren't at this meeting. They're Banjo's boys, on his payroll, which gives me the idea there's been a split between Banjo and Duke."

"Could be. All right, Larry, go along with it as long as you can, but you are not to get involved in any outside street action. And if you get any information before anything breaks out, and can get to a phone, call it in to me. If we can, we'll put a tail on Shackleford and the rest of his boys when they cross the bridge."

"Yes, sir, but you'll have to watch it closely. I think Duke has a plan up his sleeve for delivering the stuff to East Laurelton."

"All right. We'll see what we can do from this end."

"Okay, sir. Good night."

9

On Friday morning, the ranks of the demonstrators in front of the Federal Building had again swelled and now more than 200 people were marching with signs, singing songs of freedom and liberation. Sheriff's deputies from the County Building were sent to help the handful of federal marshals keep the demonstrators moving, opening passageways to permit employees and those with legitimate business to enter the building. Around the U-shaped plaza, a squad of city policemen, eight in number, sat on their motorcycles, ready to respond to Sergeant Roland Moss, who was in charge of the detail.

There were frequent verbal brushes with whites who, in passing through the lines, cursed at the Negroes and who, in turn, were roundly cursed by the marchers, secure in the strength of growing numbers; but the exchange between Negro employees on their way to their jobs, and the demonstrators, was even more bitter and virulent. From the upper floors of the City Hall, Federal Building, Courthouse and County Building, faces stared down upon the marchers with eyes that were angry, puzzled or hurt.

By noon, when the civic buildings began emptying out for the lunch hour, the demonstrators were loudly chanting their demands that the Negro conscientious objectors be released. Shoppers and employees from nearby stores and office buildings joined the onlookers until the grass lawns and walkways were packed solid with the curious and expectant, taxing the lawmen to keep pavements and streets clear for vehicular traffic. Television, radio and newspaper reporters and photographers shot pictures and talked with the marchers and white passersby, asking for opinions and predictions. There were several isolated exchanges of blows and one major fight when four white youths barged through the lines repeatedly, knocking down two sign-bearing men and two women. Deputies and police rushed in and led the four youths away while white onlookers shouted for "equal rights" for the objectors.

An outraged white man kicked over one of the empty police motorcycles and was hustled off to jail. In the doorway of the City Hall, an alert police officer grabbed another white man, relieved him of a .45 caliber automatic that was bulging in his right hip pocket and arrested him. The officer was booed by white onlookers, but no one attempted to interfere.

A pickup truck arrived with sandwiches, coffee and water for the demonstrators. Sheriff's deputies refused permission for the truck to park at the curb, which was marked FOR OFFICIAL VEHICLES ONLY. The marchers surrounded the truck and four deputies and it appeared that a major clash was imminent, but Inspector LaSalle arrived at that opportune moment and ordered the disappointed deputies away and permitted the food and drinks to be distributed to the hungry demonstrators. When the truck finally left, carrying the debris of sandwich wrappers and paper cups with it, LaSalle left the scene and went directly to police headquarters.

In the Riot Control Center, the precinct captains and lieutenants, chief of detectives and operational department heads of Communications, Transportation and Training had been briefed by Chief Durkin and handed mimeographed procedure orders for the Emergency Plan to be passed along to the men under their commands. On a separate larger sheet was a map of the city, a reproduction of the one that occupied an entire wall in the assembly hall which would become the Emergency Communications Room when the Plan was put into effect. The map identified each police precinct with a red square, each fire station with a blue circle, the boundaries of each ward indicated by heavy green lines. Durkin was alone in the room, studying the map, when LaSalle entered.

"Anything new, Pete?"

"Status quo, Lee, but far from normal. I've just finished the check with Personnel. Except for eleven on the sick list, we've got a full roster on duty or standing by for the whole weekend."

"What about the utility installations?"

"Water and Power, the telephone exchange buildings and major industrial plants will be under private double guard. I've deputized six private power boats for river patrol with a sheriff's deputy assigned to each boat. Apperson's men will guard the two hospitals and lights will be kept on throughout the night at all schools and schoolyards, with two deputies on the roof of each building, using walkie-talkies. How did the briefing go?"

"Good. There were some changes suggested, so let's run over it once more." Using narrow strips of black tape that were held in place by pushpins, Durkin had boxed off the central commercial section of West Laurelton, twenty-six blocks running east and west, twelve blocks north and south. The area contained 85% of the taverns, night clubs, restaurants, poolrooms, stores, schools, churches and used-car lots. On its periphery were the 13th, 17th, 19th and 21st police precincts, four fire substations, these apart from the 12th Precinct Headquarters and the West Laurelton Fire Battalion Headquarters.

Indicating the 26-by-12 block area, Durkin said, "No matter where it starts, this will be the vulnerable area. We've got to contain the trouble inside these lines and not let it go beyond. The minute anything breaks out, we've got to close in and keep closing this area down to its minimum, using every man available. If it's a choice between looters and fire, we've got to ignore the looters, get the fire equipment through and protect the firemen while they work. I don't want any punches pulled with snipers and I don't give a goddam how many are killed, but I'll burn the ass off any man who shoots an unarmed civilian. We've got plenty of tear gas for them.

"We also agreed that all plainclothes, vice squad and special duty officers will get into uniform when the emergency alarm goes off and that no unmarked police cars will be used, this in order to avoid identification problems. Trainees will not be sent into the riot area unless we're backed up against a wall. The Negro trainees have been assigned to Jim Price to work with the booking officers at the 12th. I want you working over there with Jim, and out of the 12th. If this turns out to be the real thing, I'll turn Emergency Communications over to Captain Archer and pick you up at the 12th or in the field. By four o'clock, every man will have his orders. Helmets, shotguns and tear gas in every car and no car left unattended. We'll keep the motorcycles on this side of the bridge. If it's a situation that can't be handled, officers in cars will put in an emergency Code 3 and pull back or use tear gas until help arrives. We've got our finger on the Civil Defense Warning System, all set to go, and I want you to be the man who orders it turned on."

"Okay, Lee. I'll get over to the 12th now and make a few dry runs to size up the situation."

Durkin nodded. "For Christ's sake, Pete, take care. I don't want to have to face Nora with any bad news."

"I'll do my best to spare you that embarrassment, Lee. Good luck."

An ominous note crept into early afternoon newscasts. Forewarned by their legmen at police headquarters and the 12th Precinct, television and radio announcers hardly needed to warn the city of impending danger. It was only necessary to report on the precautions being taken by the police to avert disaster. Switchboards at the City Hall, police headquarters, the *Herald* office, television and radio stations began to light up as irate citizens demanded that "something be done" to ward off the threat.

Parents created traffic jams in the vicinity of every school when they went directly to classrooms to take their children home. At the end of the school day, groups of teen-agers swarmed through the downtown streets in cars or on foot, eager for some part, however small, in what was to come. There was an air of near-hilarity among the hundreds of boys and girls searching for "where the action is." At the east end of the bridge, sheriff's deputies turned back the steady stream of student-laden cars attempting to cross over into West Laurelton and blocking every traffic lane in protest until the officers began issuing traffic violation tickets and threatened to call for tow trucks.

The scene was hardly different on the west side of the bridge. Negro students took to cars and the streets, brandishing baseball bats, tire chains and sand-filled bottles and beer cans. These, too, were turned back from the bridge and paraded along West Laurelton's main thoroughfares in a gleeful holiday mood, hurling insults at those whose heads were not covered with a black fez.

Police cars kept in constant motion, windows closed and doors locked, drivers and partners hoping there would be no need to stop to make an arrest; thus, minor traffic violations, common drunks, loitering, and small street fights were virtually ignored, along with calls from supermarket and variety store operators complaining of open, defiant shoplifting. Only when necessary were arrests made, usually with a second police car as backup support; runs were made swiftly and without the use of red lights or sirens. Fire battalion chiefs toured their districts in their red cars, alert for possible arsonists, plagued by false alarms.

In the vicinity of the white-owned supermarkets, drug, furniture, clothing and appliance stores, and the single block that contained three pawnshops, police cars were in more frequent evidence, but this did not prevent loiterers from shouting obscenities and pointing to the stores to indicate that they were marked for destruction. When passage was momentarily blocked by heavy traffic, Negro youths swaggered over, shouted incoherently, and banged fists on the sides and trunks of the police cars.

The smaller of the white-owned stores had closed early and owners escaped roughing-up or injuries by using alley exits to reach their cars. On the other hand, the police had warned all white store-owners that an early closing could precipitate window-smashing and looting that might not come off at all if the public mood changed. Those owners, in turn, demanded police protection, but Captain Price and Inspector LaSalle were agreed that to station an officer, even two, in each market or store might very well inflame customers as well as passersby and escalate hostility into overt action.

After a light lunch, Drew Warren returned to her room to listen to the radio broadcasts which were giving on-the-scene running accounts of the activity on both sides of the bridge, direct interviews, official and public opinions, eye-witnessed arrests. At 1:30 she turned the radio off and tried to nap, but the lingering thought of an outbreak of violence stirred her into restlessness. She got up, walked out onto the veranda, returned for a cigarette, but her pack was empty. She went to a dresser to get a fresh one and saw the silver jewel chest in the drawer.

Drew recalled the times when Grandmother Cleo used the chest to amuse her with its glittering hoard of pins, necklaces, rings, brooches and watches which, except for very special occasions, she never wore. Each represented a birthday, anniversary, Christmas, or a trip Gran had taken without her. The box was large and heavy and engraved with numerous small figures in a garden, a castle in the background, the work of an Italian silversmith who had lived in the 18th century, itself a priceless art object.

She found the key and carried the chest to her bed, unlocked it. In the velvet-lined top tray, each piece in its own place, were more than a dozen gold, silver and enameled pins and brooches, some simple and unadorned, others set

727

with diamonds, rubies, emeralds and pearls. In the bottom compartment, protected in chamois sacks or leather-lined boxes, were the necklaces, bracelets, rings, a four-strand pearl-and-diamond choker, gem-studded watches and, never worn, a diamond tiara which Grandmother Cleo would place on Drew's head and call her "Princess." She lifted each piece carefully and arranged them all on the counterpane, a child playing store, trapped by the twinkling lights; an adventurous young maiden discovering a rich pirate treasure.

And at the bottom of the chest, she saw the envelope, certainly a more recent addition than the rest of its contents. Her name was scrawled across it in Gran's loose, bold hand: *Drew;* and beneath it, the word: *Personal,* underlined twice.

She opened it slowly and removed the three sheets of Anderson Warren's seldom-used personal stationery, the top sheet dated on the day before he had taken his life.

Dear, beloved Drew:

For several moments she could only stare at those three words that slanted shakily upward, his last message to anyone on earth, coming now as though from his crypt. Then she began reading the body of the letter.

When I finish this, I will ask your father to bring your Grandmother's jewel case from the safe in my study. I will lock this inside it and remind your father it was left to you by your Grandmother and that he is to give it to you sometime after my funeral.

Drew, darling, forgive me for what I am about to do. We both know the end is near and I prefer to die in dignity. I ask you not to mourn for me. I will be in peace with your grandmother, Bruce, and our son, Clyde, who died in his second week on earth.

I have never tried to interfere with or influence your life because there were too many years and generations between us for common understanding. Nor can I counsel you with any great degree of wisdom now. I know how deeply Bruce's death affected you and yet I could do nothing to ease your sorrow, but Drew, I can say now what I could not say then. He is gone and you can't keep him with you except in fond memory. Let him go. If you can't let him die, he won't let you live.

My death will no doubt create problems for you. I don't know how much help your father will be to you, but I hope he will feel a sense of freedom that will free

728

him from the past, that he will take up the responsibili-
ties I have laid down. If you are in need of help or
advice beyond his capacity to give it, I offer you the
names of two men in whom I have the greatest faith
—your cousin, Wayne Taylor, and my friend of many
years, Duncan Collins.

To these names, I would add one more, someone of
your own generation, Corey Armour. I have seen him
grow from boy to man and I like what I see. He has a
good background and I hope you have the same high
regard for him I know you once had.

No mourning, Drew. A few quiet tears, yes, but no
more. I am now with those who, except for you, I have
loved most during my many years on earth.

Be happy, darling Drew. Make a life with a husband
you love, children to cherish, care for, and be loved
by. Nothing else can be more rewarding or important.

Your loving grandfather,

ANDERSON WARREN

She read the last sheet through misted eyes, tried to re-
read it, but the words were too blurred to see. Still holding
the letter in her hand, she lay back and fell into a peaceful
sleep.

At 4:00 P.M., apprehension had driven most of the normally heavy Friday afternoon shopping crowd out of the
East Laurelton commercial area. A number of smaller
shops and stores had closed, and some office workers released. Business was brisk at Lindstrom's Sporting Goods,
Warneke's Gun Shop, Willard's Hardware and Loman's
Loan Company, mostly in ammunition for hunting rifles,
shotguns. In a number of stores, owners announced their intention to remain throughout the night, armed against any
invasion of looters, no matter the source or color.

Despite the efforts of news broadcasters to maintain a
note of moderation in their on-the-hour programs, restraint
somehow managed to overemphasize a feeling of impending doom. The most popular afternoon programs
were "Telephone Open Line" and "Speak Your Piece,"
which invited public participation between caller and announcer and which, today, were jammed by riot-conscious
listeners with suggestions, advice, angry demands, invective,
criticism and pure outrage. The early afternoon edition of
the *Herald* featured riot pictures from Buffalo and Cincin-
nati, captioned in earthy tones, "Cool it, baby. The next

729

house that burns may be your own." Editorially, it asked everyone to think carefully and be guided by the wisdom of preservation over misguided destruction; that plans were under way to eliminate many of the ills of the past; that any outbreak of violence could delay or even put an end to any such progress; and finally, that while might was not necessarily right, laws must be rigorously enforced and order preserved at any cost.

Corey, after listening to the news reports, had called Drew shortly after noon, but Leona told him that Drew had had a sleepless night and was taking a nap. He hung up with an uneasy feeling, wondering if she had resorted to her former reliance on alcohol. Eventually, he knew, he must face the fact of her instability. At the Marina, she had been fine, the Drew he remembered from his pre-Viet Nam days, but she had had Corey to lean on. Alone, what happened to her self-assurance? And what could he hope to do to help her if she couldn't accept his help?

The one o'clock news was a repetition of the noon and eleven o'clock news. The demonstration at the civic center. Several arrests. Whites harassing the Negro marchers. In Angeltown, eighteen arrests for drunkenness, brawling, obstructing officers in the performance of their duties. Motorcycle police were beginning to appear wearing steel helmets, jeered at as they maneuvered through the streets, eyes flicking from side to side with anxiety. In South Laurelton, a number of Negroes had walked off their jobs with the announced intention to go up to West Laurelton to "hang around and see the doin's."

Private security guards, the announcer went on, had been called in by the Taylor and Warren plants, the Telephone Company, and Water & Power installations. Two radio station helicopters had been borrowed by Sheriff Apperson to patrol power lines and towers. Three houses in West Laurelton had been raided and caches of arms taken, their owners, all members of the rising Black Fez movement, placed under arrest.

Corey switched off the radio and telephoned Ad Cameron at the *Herald*.

"Hiya soldier!" Ad greeted. "You calling from your foxhole? How come you're not with some vigilante group planning to stop a Nat Turner invasion?"

"Is it that bad, Ad?"

"Knock on any door and ask. All sorts of rumors flying around. They just had a bomb scare phoned in at the Emporium. Had to clear out a couple hundred customers while the police looked for the bomb. Probably a phony, but they

730

can't take any chances. A good gimmick to keep the police tied up and out of the way. The fire department has already answered thirty false alarms since early this morning. Hold it, my other phone."

Corey could hear Ad barking out crisp instructions, then he was back on the line. "A Ku Klux Klan scare. A car filled with white-hooded guys just tossed some gasoline bombs into a vacant lot on Tracton Street in Angeltown, started a grass fire, but there are a lot of wooden shacks all around it."

"You planning on going over, Ad?"

"About six-thirty or seven. You want another escorted tour?"

"I'd feel safer in a press car."

"You might be better off in a police car with riot guns and tear gas, but you're welcome to come along. How about five-thirty? We'll grab something to eat and shove off." Corey could hear the other phone ringing again. "Got to go now, Corey. Five-thirty?"

"Five-thirty."

Leona Waters came into Drew Warren's room, stood over her sleeping form for a moment, then turned to leave. Drew woke then, blinked her eyes and said, "Leona?"

"It's just me, honey. I only looked in to see if you awake."

"What time is it?"

"Past four o'clock." She indicated the jewelry. "You been playin' store with your grandma's things?"

"Oh. Yes."

"I better put them away." Leona began picking up the pieces of jewelry.

"Lord, I feel as though I've been asleep for days."

"I guess you needed it. Can I bring you something?"

"No—yes. Would you send Sue-Ann up with some coffee?"

"Sue-Ann went home to be with her mother. They pretty worried over there."

"Has there been any more news?"

"Radio says some people arrested. One fire over in Angel-town some Ku Kluxers started. Burned down two houses before they got it put out."

"Ku Klux Klan, Leona? That's crazy."

"That's what the man said. Five men wearin' white hoods and robes. Throwed some gasoline bombs and started it. Time the firemen got there, two houses was burned to the ground."

731

"Good Lord! They've gone out of their minds."

"Sure have. I'll bring you the coffee. Anything else?"

"I'd better not or I won't be able to touch my dinner."

"I'll—oh, I forgot. Mr. Corey called. He said not to wake you."

"Thank you, Leona." As Leona went out, Drew reached for the phone and dialed the Armour number. "Corey? Hi. I'm glad I caught you."

"Hello, Drew. Have a nice nap?"

"Nap? It was almost a full night's sleep. I feel so refreshed. I couldn't fall asleep at all last night."

"You're not worrying about this stupid riot business, are you?"

"Not worried, but I am concerned. About other things, too."

"The Company?"

"Not particularly. Some of the things we talked about. Or didn't."

"Worried, or concerned?"

"Neither. Would you like to come out for dinner?"

"I'd love to, Drew, but I've already made a date for dinner."

"Someone I know?"

"Jealous?"

"If you're serious, yes. If you're not, no."

"It's with Ad Cameron. I'm going to drive over to West Laurelton with him afterward."

"Corey, please don't get mixed up in anything—"

"We'll be safe enough in a press car, Drew."

"But why?"

"Why? I suppose because I want to see it for myself, remember it. One of these days I may be able to help do something about it."

"Corey, it's not your problem—"

"Of course it is, Drew. Yours, too. And everyone else's in Laurelton, in the whole country."

There was a brief, hushed pause, then Drew said, "I'm sorry. I wasn't thinking clearly. Of course it is. But I hate to think of you being in it."

"It won't be that strange to me, Drew."

"This isn't Viet Nam."

"We're not that far away from it. Besides, I'm concerned about Lyle Emerson. If anything happens at the Center, he'll be in trouble."

"Corey?"

"What?"

"Will you come out when you get back?"

732

"Yes, if we're not too long——"

"Come out any time, no matter how late it is."

"The Center closes at nine-thirty. I'll make sure Lyle is safe, then drive out."

"I'll be here," she said softly.

Leona came in with the coffee, placed the tray on the night table and handed the cup and saucer to Drew. As she took it, she looked up into Leona's eyes and Leona said, "Lord, child, what you cryin' about? Here, drink this——"

"It's nothing bad, Leona. These are happy tears."

"Mr. Corey?"

"Yes."

"That's good. I'm glad. It's going to be all right, honey. I knowed that since you were children."

Drew leaned her head against Leona and took comfort from the woman who had raised her from birth, and knew that Leona was crying for her happiness. Leona said, "About time somebody in this house had somethin' good happen."

"Oh, Leona, Leona, what ever happened to a family that had so much to live for? Lord——"

"Shush, honey. Don't take your sorrows out on the Lord. My people been askin' the same question for hundreds of years. What has to happen, it happens, and it don't make much difference who it happens to, or where. He taken our son, Cord, just like He taken your brother. What for? Maybe because He need 'em for somethin' He got in mind. Like a sickness, or people's color, you got to learn to live with things. Sometimes you get to thinkin' you can't, but you lives through it the best way you can. Now comes your turn to be happy. Maybe it bring some happiness to your daddy, to Shad an' me, too." Leona sat down, one arm around Drew, forcing the cup upward to her lips. "Drink your coffee, baby. From now on, we goin'a have us a happy house, children to raise, horses, dogs, everything, the way it used to be. My, won't your daddy and Mr. Kenneth be somethin' to see when you tell 'em. My, my——"

At ten minutes to seven, Elizabeth came into the kitchen, dressed for school, and began helping Lutie distribute the supper dishes among the various cabinets over the sink. "You don't need to help me, honey," Lutie said. "You'll get your nice new dress all messed up."

"I've got time, Mama. Papa isn't ready yet and I can reach higher than you can."

"Honey, I wish you wasn't goin' out tonight."

733

"Mama, don't start that up again. I had enough trouble with Papa at dinner—"

"Well, you heard what he say about the way people carryin' on."

"They wouldn't hurt anybody at the Center."

"Somebody hurted you over there las' Friday night, didn't they?"

"That was different, an accident. It didn't have anything to do with this business, this riot talk. It couldn't happen again in a whole lifetime, Mama."

"Your Pa an' me, we seen it happen a lot of times in our lifetime. Baby, don't go out, please?"

"Mama, I've got people depending on me to be there. If I stay away, why shouldn't they? Besides, it's too late to find a substitute for tonight."

Sam Shackleford came in, shrugging into his jacket. "You ready, honey?"

"In a minute, Pa, as soon as I put these away—" The phone rang. "It's probably for me," Elizabeth said, and went to the front hallway to answer it. "Hello."

"Lizabeth?" It was Duke and the sound of his voice raised some slight anger in her which she tried to hide.

"Yes."

"Elizabeth, you fixin' to go to that school tonight?"

"Why?"

"Because if you are, I'm tellin' you not to."

"Why not?"

"I'm just tellin' you. Don't go out tonight."

"Thank you," Elizabeth replied, trying to control her voice, "but I'm going anyway. Papa is waiting for me now, so if that's all—"

"Look, girl, I'm tellin' you for your own good—"

"Was it for my own good you did what you did on Monday night?"

"Like what?"

"Like attacking a defenseless man on a parking lot?"

For a moment, all she heard was Duke's heavy breathing, then, "Okay, Lizabeth. I told you what I'd do if you kep' on seein' him. Like I'm tellin' you now, stay away from—"

"I'm going. Right now."

"He goin'a be there, too?"

"What I do, what he does, is none of your damned business, Duke." She hung up and returned to the kitchen.

"Who was it?" Lutie asked.

"Daisy Church at the Center," Elizabeth lied glibly. "She reminded me about four new students who registered yester-

734

day and today. I'll have to interview them before classes begin to see how I can fit them in. Ready, Pa?"

From the public phone in the empty office at the Nigerian Motel, Duke walked slowly back to his cottage. *Goddam stubborn bitch! Worst thing coulda happened, sendin' her off to college, come back so goddam uppity, she don't know what's good for her. Big ideas, messin' aroun' with a no-good cripple, an ofay, big-mouthin' me. No sense at all in her head for all the education she got. An' that fink, Powell. Send him word to meet me here when he go out for his supper, an' he don't show up. That ex-cop bastard. I'll take care of him before the night is over. Get him, Big Mouth Banjo together.*

He entered the cottage. Ivy lay stretched out on the sofa wearing a lacy red bra and pair of pants to match, fingers clasped behind her head. "Who bit you?" she asked.

"Bit me? Nobody—"

"Then why couldn't you use the phone here, 'stead of the one in the office?"

"Don't bug me, Ivy. I got things on my mind."

"I know that. Why don't you tell me what happened between you and Banjo?"

"I told you, nothin' happened."

"Then why did Connie tell me to drop you before he drops me?"

"He's jealous, that's all. Get dressed. Time to go."

"I don't like it, Duke. I don't want to get mixed up in this thing. Cops all over the place—"

"I told you, Ivy. You won't get mixed up in nothin'. Nobody's goin'a stop one girl in a car. You know what to tell them cops at the bridge. They pass you through, then all's you got to do is drive Dave's car to where I told you. They be waitin' for you. They unload the stuff from the trunk, then you turn aroun' an' come back, leave the car on the lot at the Club an' go on to work. That's all there is to it."

"Suppose the cops get nosy and look in the trunk? I'm lookin' at five years up in Mayfield."

"I keep tellin' you. You tell 'em what I told you to tell 'em an' nobody's goin'a look in no trunk. Just speak up."

"Duke—"

"Look, Ivy, after tonight, you won't have to worry about Banjo, Connie, nobody. I'll be The Man an' from then on, it's you an' me. You want to buy in or cut out?"

"Well—"

"Say it now. In or out?"

"In," Ivy said.

"All right. Get dressed an' let's get goin'."

Traffic at the Grand Avenue entrance to the bridge was slowed down to a crawl. Buses carrying day-workers from East Laurelton back to West Laurelton were waved through in the extreme right lane, but all trucks, buses and passenger cars headed east were stopped for examination. Cars whose passengers could give no valid reason for crossing from one side to the other were turned back with stern warnings.

The lights were on when Ivy, driving Dave Sharkey's car, reached the roadblock behind an out-of-state trailer truck. Two sheriff's deputies and two city police officers checked the truck expertly and waved it through. A Negro officer walked back to the next car in line and touched a finger to the brim of his white helmet, then flashed a light inside the car. Satisfied that only the girl was in it, he said politely, "Where are you going in East Laurelton, miss?"

Ivy turned on a smile and replied, "Same place I go every night this time. To pick my mother up, bring her home. She day-works for Mrs. Kirk Russell, 1014 Patterson Street."

A sheriff's deputy approached, flashed his light into the car from the other side. "Okay?" he asked.

The Negro officer nodded. "Okay."

"Move it, lady," the deputy said and waved her through.

The car behind was a black convertible that had seen better days. As it moved up in line, the officer threw a beam of light inside, saw that the man was white and passed him through without comment, then waved to the city bus, carrying a dozen Negro youths and several white men, motioning the driver to one side. At once he forgot the pretty girl and prepared to board the bus to check its passengers out.

There was no inspection on the other side of the bridge. Ivy made a sharp right turn a block beyond and took South River Road, which followed the east bank of the river. Three and two-tenths miles by the car's odometer, she slowed down, saw the red bandana tied to a branch of an oleander bush on the right side of the road. Thirty yards ahead was the narrow entrance into a dirt road and another 60 or 70 yards brought her out into a clearing with a view of the river. There was a small building on the river bank, from which a pier extended into the river. A faded sign on the shack read: BAIT—TACKLE, BOATS RENTED. Beneath that sign was another which read: FOR SALE OR LEASE. PHONE LAURELTON 6212. OWNER.

Ivy turned the headlights off and at once a figure emerged from the shack and came toward her. "Ivy?"

736

"Who—?"

"It's me, Odie. Gimme the keys."

Ivy handed the car keys to Odie Bilson. He whistled softly and three other figures came from the shack. They went directly to the back of the car and removed several small cartons which they carried to other cars that were parked a short distance away among the trees. Odie handed the keys back to Ivy and said, "So long, sugar. Goin'a be a hot time in the ol' town tonight." He picked up the fourth carton and followed the others. Ivy started the car and headed back toward the bridge.

The black convertible had followed Ivy across the bridge, made the same right turn into South River Road. There was no other traffic and the man in the convertible turned his headlights off and used the tail lights on Dave Sharkey's car as a guide. He slowed down when Ivy hit her brakes, but when she disappeared farther on, the man was unable to find the narrow, tree-lined entrance into the dirt road. At a point where he believed he had last seen the tail lights, he pulled off the road, parked among the trees and waited.

Twenty minutes later, he heard a car grinding out of a side road. He got out of his car and waited, saw the same car he had been following as it stopped, then made a left turn and speeded back toward the bridge. He returned to his car, reached for the telephone receiver that was concealed beneath the dashboard.

"12th Precinct, Sergeant Ledbetter."

"Sergeant Webb, badge 631. Inspector LaSalle."

"Hold on."

A few moments later, LaSalle came on. "Webb? Where are you?"

Webb gave him his exact location and added. "I know the place now. An old bait and boat rental deal, vacant for over a year. There's a shack and a pier in there. The girl went in and came out twenty minutes later. She's on her way back, alone. I'd guess there was somebody there to take the stuff and will wait 'til after dark when it's safe to come out. Any orders, sir?"

"Wait where you are, Webb. I'll send somebody over to help you."

"Yes, sir." Webb replaced the receiver and relaxed against the seat. And at that moment the night splintered into a million jagged flashes of light.

"You get him, Luke?" Mace Bodie asked.

"Got 'im good. Let's get out of here fast."

"You go 'head. I'll see if he's got a gun on him."

737

"Never mind, I'll do it." Quickly, Luke Tolbert frisked the unconscious sergeant, relieved him of his .38 service revolver and $22 that were in his wallet. He ran back to where the cars were parked and a few minutes later, four nondescript cars, driven by Luke Tolbert, Mace Bodie, Odie Bilson and Booker Dance, were on their way into East Laurelton, each car carrying three Molotov cocktails.

10

At exactly 8:00 P.M., Dr. Rhama's sound truck arrived at the corner of Velie and Porter Streets, its panels now decorated with signs boldly urging: *Join the Black Fez Movement to Freedom!* From the interior, two men leaped out and arranged the speaking platform on the pavement, then brought out two cartons from which they began dispensing the already familiar black fezzes into eager young hands. Dr. Rhama and Brother Leonard arrived a few moments later, bedecked in full-length black robes, and immediately a crowd of loiterers, shoppers and passersby began congregating. Taking the microphone from one of his assistants, Dr. Rhama mounted the platform and began addressing his eager audience.

Pearson's Supermarket, Dubner's Drug Store and Blue Front Discount Sales, all white-owned, all open for Friday night business, occupied three of the corners at the intersection. On the fourth stood a three-storied office building tenanted by several lawyers, Dr. Royal Betts, a dentist, an insurance firm and an optometrist, all Negro. Within seconds, the gathering crowd around the sound truck had filled the pavement and begun flowing over into the streets, interfering with passing traffic and blocking exists of two crowded parking lots.

Homer Pease, the Negro manager of Blue Front, reported the unusual, but not unexpected, activity to Roy Haley, the white owner, who was checking invoices against bills of lading in the glass-fronted office at the rear. Haley went to the front door to see it for himself, then went back to his office and called the 12th Precinct.

"Thank you. We'll have someone there in a minute," he was told. All thought of resuming the clerical work fled from his mind. He returned to the front of the store to watch and listen to Dr. Rhama's inflammatory words.

"—but don't let me put the thought into your heads that they hate us. Oh, no. NO! Our good, gentle, Christian white brothers and sisters don't hate us. They *love* us! They love

738

us in our place—living in roach- and rat-infested slums and ghettos, shining their shoes, sweeping their floors, collecting their garbage, digging ditches and graves, chopping cotton, cleaning white houses, raising white children, cooking and serving white food, driving white cars and trucks, doing everything that is beneath white dignity. Yes, and serving time, hanging from trees, floating face down in muddy creeks and in swamps—"

The air resounded with loud, "Amens," "That's God's own Truth!" "You sayin' it, brother!" and other expressions of approval.

Two blocks south on Porter, Officer Paul Green and a rookie police trainee Billy-Lee Hawkins, on orders to investigate the gathering crowd with caution, pulled Car No. 17 into the curb, but left the motor running. Both were Negroes and Hawkins was visibly nervous, fingering his baton and darting quick glances at Green.

"Looks bad, don't it?" Hawkins said.

"Not as bad as it can get," Green replied. He sat behind the wheel watching the stream of slow-moving traffic, hearing the raucous horn-tooting of exasperated motorists trying to fight through the intersection.

"We got to break it up?" Hawkins asked.

Green snorted. "Might as well try to break up a steel wall. Could be a lot less troublesome, too. No, Billy-Lee, what we do, according to the orders, we call in and report." And so saying, he picked up the hand mike and reported the situation and his location.

"Hold it where you are," the police communicator replied. "We are sending assistance. Do not attempt single action. Over."

"Check," Green replied. "Over and out." To Hawkins, "That's how you do it, sonny. By orders."

At the corner less than a block away, four loudspeakers were blaring out Dr. Rhama's message above the noise of the traffic. "Now, for the benefit of any police spies in this crowd, and I know you are here among us, I'm not telling anybody to go out and kill the first white man, woman or child you see, nor burn his property or loot his stores to take what rightfully belongs to you, to all of you. No! What I'm telling you over and over again is that all black people, no matter where they are, are true blood brothers. They have got to band together as one and show a solid black front to the white man in every village, town and city, the man who is our natural enemy! Then—then, brothers and sisters, we will be ready to fight and do what we must do to survive as human beings, to remove his foot from our

739

necks, put in our own judges and juries who will give us black justice and black rights because we have the force of black power. They will fight back, yes, but we will have an army of our own, a sea of proud black faces, and we'll be ready to do battle. Yes, some of us may die, *will* die, but they will die, too. Many more of them because we will be fighting for decent, human rights!

"You, you, you—" pointing—"and you, can do all of this, and more, if you understand the importance and force of Black Unity! The black fez you are wearing at this moment is more than a covering for your head. It is the symbol of that Black Unity, the Black Power all over the country. I repeat—"

At that moment a rock flew through the air and crashed into one of the windows of Pearson's Supermarket. The huge sheet of glass, liberally sprinkled with advertised "specials," crumpled and fell in large shattered pieces, scattering the huddle of listeners who were standing there. Shards of glass, like spears and arrows, flew toward the fleeing men and women, inflicting serious and minor cuts. Angered, a number of men and youths turned back, seeking weapons with which to revenge the outrage. A boy of 15 seized a shopping cart, and with the help of another youth, hurled it through another window. The crowd applauded with shouts of laughter and curses, enthusiastically endorsing the action. Others, thus encouraged, followed suit and within moments not one of the 12 windows bordering both streets was whole. At once, men, women and children stormed into the store and began looting, filling shopping bags and carts and arms with any goods their hands touched; canned goods, cigarettes, candy, baked goods, fresh and smoked meats, fruit and vegetables.

The Negro manager and clerks were driven into the back room, identified as "the enemy" by their green smocks. Some removed their green garments and joined the looters. Cashiers began stuffing money into their pockets, strewing bills and coins on the floor amid hysterical screams of innocent shoppers and howls of glee from the looters. The sound of breaking glass, shrieking voices and the sight of crowd movement reached Car No. 17 and Billy-Lee Hawkins began sweating profusely. "Jesus. Looks like it's started. All hell's breakin' loose up there. What do we do now?"

Green was leaning over the seat back. He came up with two helmets, two riot guns and six tear gas cartridges. "What we do, Billy-Lee, we put these on, keep the riot guns on our laps, stick the tear gas bombs in our belts and wait for that assistance. And while we wait, we hope they don't set anything on fire or find any ofays in them stores, on the streets or in cars." Green had the hand mike up to his mouth. "Car No. 17 to Cent-Com. Come in, emergency."

"Cent-Com. Over."

"It's started. Velie and Porter. Window-smashing, looting. No fires yet. Over."

"Check. We've got it already. Help is on the way. Over."

"It better get here fast, man. Over and out."

Pearson's had more than its share of the crowd and the overflow turned on Blue Front and Dubner's Drug Store. Blue Front's stock of portable radios and television sets and appliances were being carried, wheeled or thrown out into the street. Roy Haley and his assistant quickly locked the office door, then ran out through the back door and got into Haley's car, but a group of eight or ten youths attacked it with 2-by-4s and hand tools, smashing glass and denting metal. Haley got the car started and plowed through the youths, hitting two, brushing the others off.

Sirens wailed from east on Velie and south on Porter. Car No. 17's lights and siren came on, but the line of traffic blocked them in and no one seemed to care in the slightest. Already, giggling, shrieking looters were running past them, carrying, pulling and dragging stolen merchandise. As Hawkins started to get out of the car, Green said sharply, "Let 'em go. You just spittin' in the wind, tryin' to stop a few kids."

In Pearson's, shelves had been stripped and merchandise had been transferred into pockets, shirts, baskets and shopping carts. In one corner, a frenzied young woman began emptying gallon jugs of kerosene on a stack of cut wood which had been tied up in bundles. A man and two boys went to her aid, scattering the kerosene on emptied shelves, hurling filled jugs against the walls. Then the screaming woman lighted a match and threw it on the woodpile, just as one of the watching boys yelled, "Go, Mama, go! Scorch it, baby, scorch it!"

From the doorway leading into the back storage area, the Negro manager's enraged voice shouted, "You goddam crazy bastards, you burnin' us out of forty-three jobs!"

No one seemed to hear or care.

Now, Dubner's and Blue Front were burning and although the sirens and flashing red lights came closer, passage through the traffic and street debris was slow. Cars No. 2, 22, 6 and 7 helped clear the way, drawing more crowds from their houses and apartments into the streets. When the cars were momentarily blocked, fez-topped youths threw rocks, bottles, bricks, garbage can lids and the cans themselves at the officers, black and white. At two corners, tear gas was used to break mob formations and eventually, after pushing several cars up onto pavements, cleared a path for the fire equipment. By the time the firemen reached Velie and Porter and had run their tangle of hoses out, their principal purpose had become to keep the fire from spreading to nearby houses rather than the futile attempt to save the Pearson, Dubner or Blue Front buildings, all three now beyond saving.

At the 12th Precinct, Inspector LaSalle and Captain Price monitored the mounting calls that were flooding in over the loudspeaker, issued crisp orders, drew manpower from as yet unaffected areas to where they were needed. At 8:17, LaSalle reported a condition of general riot to Chief Durkin, who put the Emergency Plan into effect. Within ten seconds, Civil Defense sirens sounded on both sides of the bridge and all officers and sheriff's deputies on standby alert began reporting to their assigned stations. Sheriff Apperson, waiting in his office in the County Building, buckled on his pistol belt, selected a riot gun from a rack and went out into the civic center plaza.

Deputies had earlier replaced city police in the plaza where about 200 Negro demonstrators still marched before the entrance to the Federal Building. Apperson waited for five impatient minutes until he saw a half dozen large County Roads Commission trucks pull into the plaza. Six deputies, armed with riot guns, dismounted from the last truck as the marchers came to a stop and watched the arrival of the armed white men.

An aide handed Apperson a bullhorn. Into it, he announced, "This is Sheriff Apperson. You people are being taken into custody for your own protection. You ain't under arrest unless you resist. Get into them trucks and go along quietly."

Into the plaza came a group of white men, each armed with a rifle, pistol or shotgun, a white handkerchief tied around his upper left arm.

"These men are my sworn deputies and won't hurt nobody who don't offer resistance. Move fast, else you won't get no second chance, you hear—"

At 8:30, Lee Durkin picked up the direct line phone to Mayor Tom Cameron's office and said, "Okay, Tom. It's here. I hate to do it, but we'd better order the Guard in."

"Christ, Lee, are you sure? This is going to make us look bad as hell everywhere."

"If we don't, Tom, we'll look a hell of a lot worse by morning. We agreed—"

"All right."

"I'm going across the bridge. You can contact me through the 12th Precinct if—"

"Wait for me, Lee. I'm going with you."

"Tom, it could get a lot worse before it gets any better."

"I'm going anyway. Wait for me."

"All right. Get over here right away."

"As soon as I put this call through."

A sergeant burst into Durkin's office without knocking, and reported the action of Sheriff Apperson in the plaza.

Durkin's face reddened with anger. "Where's the sonofa-bitch taking 'em?"

"I don't know, but I'd guess he's hauling them out to the County Fair Grounds. One of the deputies told me they put up a bobwire stockade out there this afternoon."

"That double-crossing bastard. Well, there's nothing I can do about it right now. We'll see about it in the morning. Let's go. The Mayor's meeting us downstairs. Get a helmet for him and see if you can rustle up one of those old bul-let-proof vests—"

At 8:45, a dark gray 1959 Plymouth headed east on Reed Street, one block south and parallel to Taylor Avenue. Behind the wheel, Luke Tolbert, less confident than when he, Mace Bodie, Booker Dance and Odie Bilson were together in the fishing shack, looked from side to side, searching out a likely target for one of the Molotov cocktails which stood upright in the small carton on the seat beside him.

Traffic on Reed Street, of secondary importance, was light, the stores on both sides dark. Luke was, according to the plan outlined by Duke Shackleford, to set off the first fire somewhere east of Semmes Drive. This would draw the 6th Fire Battalion away from Taylor and Wilton. The second bomb would be set off by Odie Bilson on Warren Avenue, which paralleled Taylor on the north, and would occupy the 4th Fire Battalion. Then, Mace Bodie would make his "hit" in the Mall while Booker Dance took on the Ta-Ran Shopping Center at Avalon and Barrett. From that point on, all remaining gasoline bombs would be used on various targets on Taylor Avenue, with the Arcadia Theater singled out as No. 1 on the list.

A prowl car passed the Plymouth and Luke's hands grew moist on the wheel, but the two officers didn't even look at him. He continued eastward and saw his target, Constable's Furniture Mart, a two-storied building of white brick, green-and-white-striped awnings, with dim lights in each furniture-filled display window. There were several cars parked on both sides of the street, but no moving vehicles in sight. Luke circled the block once and came around to the front again, parked at the curb. He left the motor running, turned off his lights, got out with a wick-tongued bottle under his arm, leaving the door open. He lit a match, touched it to the wick and raised his arm to throw it.

"Drop it, you nigger bastard!"

Luke gasped and looked up. Over the rim of the rooftop he saw the shapes of two heads and pairs of shoulders. And the glint of shotgun barrels aimed directly at him. The wick was flaming brighter, illuminating him into a target. To drop the bottle meant he would die in flames. To throw it would seal his fate from the muzzles of two shotguns. With a curse, he drew his arm back further and both shotguns roared. The charge tore into his body and hurled him back into the Plymouth, the flaming bottle still in his hands; and as he lay dying across the seat a part of his burning sleeve touched the wicks of the two remaining Molotov cocktails.

On Warren Avenue, Odie Bilson moved along the line of moderate traffic, a windbreaker on the seat beside him covering his cargo of three Molotov cocktails. He stopped for a red light at Fremont and another at Exeter, then went through three green lights. As he approached the Phillips Place intersection, the light flashed yellow, then turned red. Odie braked the old Chevy hard. It squealed, shuddered, pulled to the right and glanced off the fender of a '66 Oldsmobile. The outraged white driver sounded his horn in a series of angry blasts, but a frightened Odie turned the wheel left and shot across Phillips Place on the red light.

A patrol car going south on Phillips saw the Chevy run the light and turned east on Warren, red light twirling, siren blasting, to give chase. Four blocks later, Officer Willis Johns pulled ahead, turned sharply to the right and ran Odie into the curb, his motor dead on impact. Johns' partner, Trainee Doug Dressen, leaped out and, with revolver in hand, approached the Chevy. He looked inside and called out to Johns, "Jesus! He either fainted or died of fright."

Odie had, in fact, fainted. When the two officers pulled him out of the car, Doug Dressen lifted the windbreaker and found the three gasoline bombs.

In West Laurelton, four more stores were hit by fire bombs: a supermarket, a clothing store and two secondhand shops, all white-owned, but the fires, unable to differentiate between black and white, began eating into black-owned stores and surrounding houses. Now, innocent Negroes became incensed and began attacking young window-smashers and looters, but the elders were outnumbered by the destruction-bent fez-wearers.

At the scene of the burnings, firemen were being attacked from rooftops where a group of Negroes had collected an arsenal of bricks and sand-filled cans and bottles. Deputies riding guard on the fire equipment fired tear gas shells, but the gas drifted away and was generally ineffective. Then from one rooftop, shots were fired at the deputies. A fireman and a deputy were hit by rifle bullets. Other deputies replied with riot guns and the rooftops were hurriedly cleared. Before an ambulance could get though, the fireman was dead. Two men, one 19, the other about 26, lay dead on the roof of a nearby house.

Roving bands, their appetites whetted by the fires and looting, began operating away from Velie and Porter Streets, which were getting most of the police attention. When one group broke into a closed liquor store, another band discovered them and a fight over the spoils broke out. Shops on either side of the liquor store were broken into and that which could not be eaten, drunk or carried away was thrown into the streets; nor did it matter in the least that these were Negro-owned stores.

At 12th Precinct, 122 youths, men and women were in cells intended to hold no more than 50 and newly arriving prisoners were herded into a parking lot which had been cleared for that purpose and enclosed by a chain link fence. Armed guards, posted outside the fence, were cursed and spat upon by the prisoners from inside and similarly harassed by crowds gathered across the street. As each new batch arrived, they were dumped into the compound until they could be properly charged and booked, many with torn clothes and showing signs of effective baton work.

The emergency rooms and hallways of the ancient West Laurelton General Hospital overflowed with victims of splintered glass, knife, bullet and brick wounds. A small, weary corps of nurses, aides, and totally unskilled helpers patched, painted and sewed cuts and other minor wounds while Dr. Betts and two assistants operated on the more critical cases, bitterly profaning the air with maledictions at the needlessness and stupidity of it all. Despite the desperate need, only two white doctors, two residents and one intern had been sent from East Laurelton. Private physicians could not be reached and Laurelton Memorial could not, in the emergency, spare more of its staff. By 9:15 there were 3 known dead, 92 injured, moderate to critical, and 167 arrests.

There were no pool shooters in Banjo's Place, all having deserted the hangout to take to the streets to witness the excitement and furor, the total breakdown of law and order. Only Hinky Liggett, who sat in the chair beside the door to the back room, somnolent as usual, the sawed-off poolcue within easy reach. Noah Smith, with no one to serve, nervously slicing cold meats and making sandwiches behind the counter; Larry Powell standing in the front doorway looking over the butterfly doors at the crowds of people moving along Velie Street in the direction of the "action." Nothing on these four corners had been touched yet, and he wondered how soon the anger and swiftly moving virus would reach them.

Children as young as six and seven ran wild down the pavements, upsetting garbage cans, stopping to pick up a stone or brick to throw in any direction, at any vehicle, without reason. If there was innocence among them, Larry thought, it was overshadowed by the infectious evil of the general mood, their determination to do as others were doing; invade, destroy, crush, burn, without realizing that what they were destroying was their own, themselves.

Old Noah Smith moved over from the counter to stand beside Larry. "You believe it?" he asked incredulously.

"I see it," Larry replied, "but it'll take some time before I believe it." He thought then of his own ineffectiveness, standing here in the empty poolroom, without definite orders from Inspector LaSalle. Useless and helpless. Then he thought of Elizabeth at the Center and prayed that this hell wouldn't reach as far north as Division Street. He stepped outside and looked up at the sky north and east of him and saw with relief that it was still black, untinged by fire as was the sky to the west. He walked back inside to where Hinky sat like a fat Buddha. Hinky looked up and said, "You want somethin', boy?"

"Yes. Is Banjo inside?"

"You didn' see him go out, did you?"

"No, but there's a back door and he could leave without me seeing him."

"Well—" Hinky spat into the cuspidor near his chair— "he inside but he busy. Go on back to your work."

"There's no work. I'm leaving. I want him to know."

"You leave, he'll know it soon enough, boy, an' your ass'll be fired out of here."

"Tell him I had to go. I've got to see if the things in my room are safe."

"I told you, you leave, you fired."

Larry turned and went back to the front door. To Noah, he said, "I'm going to check my room. I've got some things I can't afford to lose."

Noah nodded without reply, his watery eyes on the passing parade outside. Larry walked eastward against the fluid crowd. At Elgin, he turned south and three blocks away began running until he came to a service station with an outside phone booth. People were still emptying out of their houses, moving like lemmings toward Velie Street, calling to each other, infected by the excitement. Larry dialed the Headquarters number and snapped, "Inspector LaSalle. This is a Two-Five, emergency."

"Everything is a goddam emergency tonight. The Inspector is working out of the 12th. Hold on and I'll connect you." Larry held for almost a full minute before LaSalle came on.

"Powell, Inspector. I can't take any more of this—"

"Where are you, Larry? How far from the 12th?"

"About seven or eight blocks."

"Come on in. I'm with Captain Price. Ask for me."

"Yes, sir!" Larry hung up and began running again. And running, he thought once more of Elizabeth and that perhaps he should be running in the opposite direction, toward the Center.

As the first bulletins flashed over the air, former First Sergeant Davis Lipscomb left his radio and walked a block toward Robbie Baldwin's house, but Robbie was already outside, coming to meet him. Two blocks east, they met Artie Goodwin and Claude Morris in front of Joe Beeman's house, and a moment later, Anse Warner joined them there. As they walked in a group toward the 12th Precinct, avoiding the main thoroughfares, they picked up others of the group that had met at the African Zion the evening before. When they reached the 12th, they were 26 in number. In the supply room, a property clerk handed each a bronze-colored helmet which had a decal of the police emblem on the front, now partially defaced in a hurried effort to remove it. And with the helmets, a warning from a thickset sergeant.

"Just you remember, you ain't the law. You can't make no arrests and you can't carry clubs, knives or saps. All you can do is try to keep people from breaking, entering and looting—"

"We know, Sergeant," Lipscomb replied. "We've been told."

747

"Okay, go ahead, but I still think you guys are nuts."

Outside, Lipscomb divided his men into groups of nine, nine and eight, taking the smaller group for himself. "All right, let's move out. No goofing off and where we go, we work with the cops. Let's show our people and theirs what we learned over there."

In Captain Price's office, Peter LaSalle and Lee Durkin eavesdropped on Mayor Cameron's telephone conversation with Amos Hart, trying to persuade the minister to join him in front of the television cameras in an appeal to the Negro community to take no part in the rioting.

"Mr. Mayor," Hart replied, "I can see no point—"

"Reverend, if you consider yourself a leader in your community, with an interest in preserving law and order, saving lives and property of your own people—"

"Mr. Mayor," Hart retorted impatiently, "the people you are trying to reach are not at home watching television sets. They're out in the streets stealing them, and that's where I'm heading right now. Good night, sir."

Cameron hung up, thinking over Hart's words. He went to the press room then and announced to the gathered newsmen that he intended taking to the streets, "where the action is, gentlemen, and where I belong. Among the people." His aide then ordered a portable public address system to be placed in the Mayor's car and a short while later, Cameron left at the head of a parade of press cars.

The Mall, in the easternmost section of East Laurelton, was relatively quiet. Normally open for business until nine o'clock on Friday nights, the 32 shop-owners had agreed during the afternoon to remain closed after 5:30 because the threat of violence could easily make them a choice target by Negroes seeking revenge. Above at least a dozen stores, such as Paula's Casuals, were apartments occupied by several owners or leased out for private living quarters.

Mace Bodie had parked the borrowed Ford on one of the lots reserved for Mall shoppers. The only other cars there belonged to the nearby apartment dwellers. Inside his windbreaker, Bodie carried two quart-sized bottles of gasoline, their wicks exposed. He waited nervously, clinging to the dark shadows under the extended awnings. The lights in the center of the parkway and in some of the apartments above the stores were on but the Mall was empty of foot traffic. And while he waited for the sky to turn red in the direction of Reed Street or East Warren Avenue, he chose the two largest stores in the Mall as his targets, both two stories high and without living quarters above them.

And waiting, he grew impatient and nervous and cursed Luke and Odie for their delay. He wanted to smoke one of the reefers he had in his pocket, but knew he couldn't, or shouldn't, strike a light until he was ready to touch it to the wicks of his Molotov cocktails. He waited in the shadows, shifting from one foot to the other, praying that this far east of the bridge there would be no night watchmen. And then, patience exhausted, the need to act overcame him. To hell with Luke, to hell with Odie. Here goes.

He withdrew the first bottle, held it firmly in his left hand and took a lighter from his windbreaker pocket with his right. He snapped the lid open, thumb on the sparking wheel and got set to make his move. Connaught's would be his first target, beautiful with two large show windows filled with decorator wallpaper, draperies and paints. Anderson's directly opposite Connaught's, was his second choice, its windows filled with burnable furniture. After the first strike, he need only turn, light the second wick, throw it and get out fast.

Man, what a sight that goddam paint store was going to make!

From the south end of the Mall, he ran along the east pavement, unseen beneath the store canopies and awnings that stretched outward to cover half the pavement. Opposite Connaught's, he dashed across the grassy parkway in the center, struck the light and held it for a second before he touched it to the wick.

Polk Holderby lay flat on his back staring up at the off-white ceiling, painting pictures on its stark blankness, one arm cocked behind his head. The pillow lay on the floor beside the bed, but he didn't want to move from his present position and waken Paula, who was fast asleep, sprawled face-down on the bed beside him after a satisfactory climax. Face down, nude, one arm flung across him, her hand cupping his upper thigh.

Except for one thought, Polk was in a state of euphoric happiness. Since Paula had returned to Laurelton from New York, divorced from Bob Bennett, it had all been so simple; so easy, in fact, that he often wondered if she hadn't a nymphomaniacal touch in her. He was more than reasonably certain that during their college years together in Athens, Corey had frequently tapped this wellspring of sexual delight, although he could get neither Corey nor Paula to admit it. With conceit, or vanity, Polk liked to think that if he hadn't been able to make it with Paula after her breakup with Corey, neither had Corey; but having seen them together too often, this self-serving thought had been shaken.

When she returned from New York an exciting sophisticate, Polk, a seasoned campaigner after two years in Washington, was ready, willing and able; particularly with Corey away in Viet Nam. Paula was hardly established in her new apartment and shop, with considerable help from Polk, when he decided that enough time had elapsed and made his move; and was completely bowled over when Paula laughed and said, "Polk, you're about as subtle as an explosion. Here, help me out of this."

He had, he confessed to himself, known no one like Paula. She gave willingly, even enthusiastically, with the single-minded thought of earthy physical satisfaction. There were no subtleties, no devices, no demands, no complaints. The act, at which she was sublimely expert, was the thing, and a most satisfactory, satisfying thing it was.

She turned now and her arm moved upward and across his abdomen, stirring him with desire. He lifted his head and looked down over his own length and Paula's outstretched body, always a stimulating sight, the small hillocks and curves, legs outstretched provocatively. He twisted so that her arm fell between his naked thighs and he crossed his ankles to increase the delightful, yet gentle, pressure on her warm arm. She stirred again, turned her face toward him, pressed her lips against his left side. He felt her tongue touch his flesh, then her teeth in a small, nuzzling bite. He tightened his grip on her arm with his thighs. "Hey, sleepyhead," he whispered.

"Hm-m-m—?"

"You asleep?"

"Mm-hm-m—" She opened her eyes for a moment, then closed them. "What are you doing?"

"Waiting for you to come alive."

"Wait—" Her eyes closed again. She moved closer into the curve of his arm. The hand lying between his legs moved upward caressing him. Polk sighed happily and relaxed.

Jesus, was there ever another woman like Paula? he mused.

Usually it was Polk who called Paula. If he caught her in the right mood, the invitation came quickly. At other times, he dropped in at the shop at closing time, waited through the flurry of getting the last customers out, the salesgirls, fitter and porter, locking up. Sometimes, they had dinner at Marco's, the Marina Club, or took a drive to some distant, out-of-the-way restaurant to give Paula a chance to unwind. Occasionally, after locking up, they made love in her back room office on the chaise, sometimes in the apartment upstairs, then threw a meal together from whatever might be found in the refrigerator.

Tonight, Paula had called Polk. "I'm worried," she said.

"What about?"

"This damned civil rights trouble. I don't want my pretty shop burned out."

"You're covered by insurance, aren't you?"

"Of course I am, but I still don't want to be burned out, insurance or no insurance. What are you doing?"

"I'm planning on taking a run over to Angeltown with a few of the boys."

"You're not one of those vigilantes, are you, for God's sake?"

"I'm just another guy who's determined not to let a lot of animals burn this town to the ground. If that's being a vigilante, I'm a vigilante."

"What about the roadblocks on the bridge?"

"There aren't any roadblocks if you cross over by boat, say somewhere down around Fisher's Landing."

"Polk, please don't. You're just asking for trouble."

"You're damned right I am. I'd like to get my sights on some of those animals—"

"Why don't you come over and wait for them to come to you? In that case whatever you do would be purely defensive, wouldn't it?"

"Well, it's not the same thing."

"But it could be a lot nicer."

"I can't deny that."

"Well, how about it? And bring a bucket of water in case of fire."

"I— Okay. And I'll do better than that. I'll stop by Marco's and have them fix up a couple of gourmet dinners. We'll wine and dine like kings—"

"Like Nero, before Rome burned?"

"Oh, come on now—"

"Polk, I'm really worried. I mean it."

"All right. I'll bring something else along."

He brought the food, wine and a shotgun with a box of shells—"even though nothing's going to happen in this part of town. There's a roadblock at the bridge and you can bet they won't let any plunder-bound niggers through."

"Is that why you brought the shotgun?"

"Purely psychological. It's my security, like a kid's blanket."

751

Somehow, the shotgun was a comfort to Paula, too. They ate, washed dishes, and just as naturally as breathing, she had pulled off her clothes and said, "If they're going to do it, it won't be until well after dark." So they had made love and were temporarily spent.

Some months ago, while in the act, Polk had asked, "Was it this way with Bob?"

"Why," Paula replied, "do men have to know how it was with someone else? Why can't they be satisfied with doing it, enjoying it, and letting sleeping dogs lie?"

"Why? Because—well, it's so damned good with you."

"Then what else is important?"

What else was important, he said to himself. Well, what the hell else *was* important? Bob Bennett didn't bother him; but then, he hadn't known Bob, had never seen him, so he couldn't imagine him and Paula in bed together. But he could clearly visualize her in bed with Corey Armour. Nights and weekends in Athens, Atlanta, elsewhere. This body, these arms, legs, this mouth, this waterfall of soft hair, Corey poised over her, inside her. And Paula, the night of her party, trying to maneuver Corey into staying behind—

She stirred again, removed her hand and turned over, her back to him, one leg touching his own. He moved toward her, running his hand down her spine. "Uh-uh," she said. "I'm going to take a shower."

"Let's take one together," Polk suggested.

She turned toward him, her hair tangled like jungle growth around and over her face, one hand on his chest to prevent him from moving in and over her. "You're a sex fiend, aren't you?"

He laughed. "That's funny as hell. When I want it, I'm a sex fiend. When you want it, all the rules change."

Paula drew one finger down the center of his forehead, nose, lips and chin. "You know," she said, "you've come a long way since college. Washington was good for you."

"The way New York was for you?"

"It helped." She giggled and he reached for her, kissed her. "Don't get too nosy, huh, Polk?"

He said, "I wish to Christ you'd get serious for once."

"About what?"

"About us."

"How much more serious can we get than this?"

"I'm not talking just about *this*. I'm talking about getting married. Us. You and me."

She drew back and stared into his eyes. "Do you mean that?"

"Keep looking at me. Listen, woman, I've been crazy about you ever since Athens. For a while, after you dropped Corey, I thought I had it made, then I got the idea you were only trying to make him jealous—"

"Polk—"

"I'm not asking for any explanations about Corey—"

"I'm not making any. Not about him or anyone else."

"Look, I don't need any. All I know, feel, is that you and I are more alike than we're different. If we ever make it legal, we'll probably fight like cats and dogs, but one thing is for sure, we know it won't be dull."

"Well— Polk, what about—?"

"What about nothing. There's you, there's me, and nobody else. If you can see it that way, we can make it. How about it?"

"How about love, which you haven't mentioned?"

Exasperatedly, "What the hell else can I be talking about while we're lying here naked, teasing each other into a state of rape?"

"Don't raise your voice to me like that, Polk."

"Then don't talk like a sixteen-year-old hipster. You're twenty-seven and I'm twenty-eight and why don't we start acting like it?"

"You know, suddenly I don't know what to say."

"Then why don't you take sixty seconds to consider it while we're—"

But she drew away again and laughed. "Polk, you've suddenly become an interesting proposition. I never thought—"

"Proposal is the word, not proposition."

"That's what makes it so sudden."

"Well, how about it?"

"What?"

"Marry me."

She sighed. "Well, why not? Yes—" She slipped into his arms. He kissed her, felt her opening herself to him, the heat of desire enveloping them simultaneously.

When he awoke next, she was gone. He sat up, listened for some sound of her and heard the soft hissing of the shower. He lay back, eyes closed, but could not regain his earlier euphoria. Then suddenly, he sat up again, remembering. She had said she would marry him.

He was wide awake now. He found his cigarettes and lighter, lit one and drew deeply on it, watching the red tip bite into the paper. He stood up, pulled on shorts and trousers only and went into the living room and poured a drink, sitting on a stool at the bar. Thinking of what marriage to

753

Paula would be like. They would probably live here. He would take trips with her, buying trips to Atlanta, New York. His job? To hell with Archer & Moseley. He'd quit, invest their money in stocks, be his own client and customer's man. Help Paula. Maybe open another shop. A chain. Spread out to Fairview, Riverton, Augusta, Macon, even Atlanta. Hell, why not? Not for a while. Get some organization and merchandising data somewhere, the University, study this business—

"How about one for me?" It was Paula, bright, fresh, a short robe, partially open, a towel around her neck. He grinned, poured a drink for her and gave her a cigarette.

"What's doing outside?"

"Still as a mouse in a corncrib."

Cigarette and drink in hand, she went to one of the windows facing down into the Mall parkway. Lights on, not a soul in sight. Eerie, spooky silence.

"Polk—"

"What?"

"Polk, I see something—"

"Is it bigger than a breadbox?" he jibed.

"Polk, please." There was a quality of fear in her voice that made him go to her, instinctively picking up the shotgun on his way.

"What? Where?" he asked.

She pointed. "A little to my left, there—*coming out from under that awning—look—!*"

Before he could bring the lighter flame and wick together, Mace Bodie heard a window thrown up hastily somewhere behind him, then a man's voice shouting, "Hey! Hey! Put that down or I'll blast hell out of you!"

But Bodie's hand movements were committed. Flame touched the soft, gasoline-soaked wick. It caught at once, flaring up, and now the need was to get rid of it. He cocked his arm back, heard the voice call out again, "Hey, you—" As his arm moved forward in a throwing arc, he felt the force of a truck strike from behind, a roaring in his brain as though he had been hit by lightning and enveloped by thunder. He started to fall and felt another shock which spun him almost completely around. He felt himself floating for a moment, then fell headlong on the wide paved stretch between the parkway and his target.

The flaming bottle hit the door and shattered the glass. Inside, the burning gasoline reached the carpeting and touched the edge of the curtains that hung on either side of the door. Some of the gasoline, like a burning fuse, dripped on the pavement and began running downhill to where Bodie's inert body lay, and finally reached the pool of gasoline that formed under him when the second bottle, which he had been carrying inside his windbreaker, broke when he fell upon it.

From the apartments above the stores, people came running, shouting to attract the attention of others. None made the slightest effort to reach or save the burning man as they concentrated their fire extinguishers on Connaught's to keep the flames from spreading.

At the Ta-Ran Shopping Center, which occupied an entire block, the Avalon Supermarket and ave–You Drug Store were doing the bulk of the business. Most of the other neighboring shops were still open—book store, candy shop, several women's wear shops, shoe stores, beauty shop, hardware, variety and other stores. The huge parking area was well lighted and cars were driving through its marked lanes searching for vacancies between the white lines.

Booker Dance followed the line of traffic into one of the entrances on Barrett, rather than the more conspicuous Avalon Boulevard. There was ample parking at the far end of the lot, but most of the shoppers habitually searched for a space closer to the shops they intended to patronize. Booker pulled out of the line and headed toward the far end and turned to back into a space, choosing one between two other cars in order to blend the 1958 Volkswagen into anonymity. He turned off his lights, ran the windows up, locked the doors from the inside and slumped down behind the wheel as far as he could, then bent his upper body across the seat, hidden from outside view. The shopping center would close at 9:30. The parking lot would be emptied by no later than ten. He lay on the seat in discomfort, planning how he would tackle the Avalon Supermarket first, ave-You second, flee the area and find a likely target for his third and last gasoline bomb.

Booker lay there thinking of what lay ahead when Negro black power had been won. With somebody like Duke Shackleford in the saddle, what more could he ask for? That cat was fat, man, fat where it counted most. Ol' Duke, he knew up from down, an ace boon coon to tie up to. This was gin time, the payoff. By tomorrow or the next day, they'd have it made. On top, man. Plenty of bread, a hot lookin' ragtop, a stone fox. Livin', man, livin'. Show 'em whitey squares how to hip it. Show 'em they can't put us down, the Charley goons, the whole goddam lot of ofays an'

burrhead Toms. Warm up my bed, sugar, here come
Booker D. Show 'em—

From the outer edges of the 26-by-12 block area designated as critical on Lee Durkin's "war map," the police
began moving in toward the affected area in a containment
effort. The task, at this point, presented few problems because it seemed as though everyone but the very old and
very young had been attracted to the center of the conflagration, easily marked by reddened skies. Block after block,
keeping contact by walkie-talkie, car and motorcycle radios,
the police passed a clutter of shacks and houses where
frightened old people were congregated on doorsteps and
sat staring, wondering, praying, mute as the armed police
marched up the street cautioning, "Take it easy, folks. Just
stay where you are and take it easy."

At 25th and Velie, where the commercial began mingling
with the residential, they came upon a group of small
stores, grocery, shoe repair, sceondhand clothing and furniture, shoes, variety, appliances, hardware and liquor, all
dark, but protected from two groups of loot-bent youngsters
by owners who were armed with 2-by-4s, axe handles and
lengths of iron pipe, one with a double-barreled shotgun.
The windows of some of the stores had been broken by
rocks thrown from a distance, but the youths, like coyotes
waiting for the strength of their prey to ebb, stood off, circled, dodged in and out, watching for an opportunity to
strike.

When the store-owners called out for help, the patrol officer in charge paused for a moment to order the youths
away, but they stood off and faced the handful of police defiantly, grinning evilly, taunting them with filthy obscenities,
divining that these men had more important fish to fry.
Jerry Parris, a Negro officer, stepped forward. "Sergeant,"
he volunteered, "you leave me here, I think I can handle
this."

The sergeant weighed the request briefly. "These people'll
have to do for themselves for the time being," he replied.
"We're needed more where we're going. All right, move
up." The two bikemen took the lead, two prowl cars behind
them, and the unit moved slowly eastward, its eight footmen
flanking the vehicles. When they reached 22nd Street, four
blocks west of Porter, they came upon a car with two men
in it, parked at the curb. White men. Sergeant Russell
flashed a light inside and said, "For Christ's sake, what the
hell are you two goddam fools doing here, waiting for your
own execution?"

"Press, Sergeant. *Herald*," Ad Cameron replied.

"Press or no press, you're asking for it, parked here like that. You'd better move to hell out of here." He flashed the light on Corey Armour. "You press, too, mister?"

Ad said, "One of my reporters—"

"Well, we've got orders to cooperate with the press, but I've also got to prevent killing. You'd better pull out of here, Mr. Press."

"All right, which way? Everything is pretty well blocked off up ahead."

"Go west to Blankenship, north to Division and east on Division. It's still clear up there if you get going right now."

"All right, Officer, thank you." Ad started the motor, turned back in the direction from which the patrol had come. The sergeant remembered then and used his walkie-talkie to call in to the command post at the Cherry Hill Elementary School. "If any of those Nigra vets are looking for business," he requested, "send a few over to 25th and Velie. Four men can handle it."

At Orange and Linden, barely within the 26-by-12-block area to the south, Robbie Baldwin and his eight-man squad came on another marauding band of between 15 and 20 youths, four girls among them, who had broken into a small food store. More than half were still inside drinking canned beer, their pockets and shirt fronts bulging with looted goods. The owner and his wife, a middle-aged couple named Rosenstock, were on the floor, the man unconscious, his head bleeding, the woman seated beside him in terror, wiping the blood from his head with the hem of her undergarment, weeping in the midst of the terror around them.

Looters, already laden, stood outside holding off several older men and women who lived close by. As the helmeted veterans approached, several men and women ran ahead toward them.,"You better get them kids outa there and see what happen to them two white people. They—"

The eight vets moved in swiftly and the outside guards ran. Robbie led the way inside the wrecked store. The last man in closed the door.

Inside, the trapped boys and two girls faced the veterans, laughing amid the shambles and havoc of cartons, cans, bottles, overturned counters and ripped wall shelves. Meat, milk, butter and eggs were scattered and piled in the center of the floor. The vets stared in disbelief at the sight. One man expressed the hopelessness of it all when he said, "Sweet Jesus, they're animals."

757

It seemed so. Eight boys and two girls, caught up with the need to demolish and destroy with senseless lust, devoid of reason or purpose except revolt against the world they had been born into, schooled and tutored by the hatred of their elders in a society which had rejected them. There seemed to be no point in trying to talk to the defiant youngsters. Robbie and Sam Lincoln picked the old man up. Except for a few bruises and torn dress, the woman seemed able to move under her own power. Several of the older Negroes came into the store, horrified by the spectacle.

"Anybody around here got a car?" Robbie asked. "This man needs a doctor."

There were no cars. A woman said, "Poor Mist' Rosenstock. He a good Jew-man, always he'p us out when we broke. They got no reason doin' this to him."

Another woman was comforting the silently weeping Mrs. Rosenstock, kneeling with her over Dave Rosenstock's unconscious form. "Where do they live?" Robbie asked.

"Too far to carry him," one of the men replied.

"Take him to my place," a woman offered. "It's just across the street. We look after him 'til we c'n get a doctor."

"Okay." Two men carried Dave Rosenstock across the street.

"What about these hellions?" another man asked.

"They're going to start cleaning this place up as best they can," Robbie said in a voice directed at the looters. "They're going to start in right now with the shelves and counters, put everything back that wasn't busted." He glared into the ring of young defiant faces. "And if they don't get moving right here and now, we're going to start beating the living hell out of every one of 'em. *Move!*"

They moved.

The police were moving in from Division north, Linden south, Frazier east and 22nd Street west; and the 26-by-12-block area shrank down to 18 by 6, ringed with loosely scattered police. So far, the 12 fires that raged were within those blocks in six different locations. Additional fire equipment had been sent across the bridge from East Laurelton. Riverton, Fairview and Tenboro had sent token replacements, this with some reluctance to strip themselves in case their own Negro communities became incited to similar violence by the radio newscasts coming out of Laurelton.

Within the fire-struck area, it was impossible to attempt to bring order out of the existing chaos. Streets were blocked by cars that had been parked at curbs before the fires erupted, now trapped by fire equipment and tangled hoses that made passage impossible. Every effort was being concentrated on the ramshackle houses and apartments above the stores, to which the fires had spread, and others nearby. Tenants who had fled earlier were returning to gather in the streets with their few pitiful possessions, carrying children and pets in their arms, pleading with the harassed firemen to save their homes, or what was left of them.

As young looters ran past, gleefully clutching clothing, radios, foodstuffs and liquor bottles in their arms, the anger of the dispossessed turned upon them, attacking with fury, slapping, cursing, clawing, berating, using bare hands, fists, bottles, rocks, any weapons they could get—and these, in the rubble of broken glass and ripped boards and loose bricks, were plentiful. The few police and sheriff's deputies refused to interfere, their eyes sweeping nearby rooftops for snipers.

It was a holiday of terror for the young. Taverns, poolrooms, eating places and the Goldfield Theater were empty except for their worried owners. On the streets, hordes of fez-topped youths and young adults scampered, shouting, laughing and hooting as though participating in one last, wild game. And on every corner, there were the sober-faced watchers, smoldering, yearning to lash out in any direction against armed police, deputies, firemen, or their own.

In the thick of the action at Velie and Porter, where it had first begun, Inspector LaSalle, a bullhorn in his hands, repeated an order for everyone to get out of the area. Three of the four corners had already been destroyed but the battle for containment of the fires continued. Forty or more cars, trapped on parking lots, had been damaged and all but destroyed, and other, smaller stores were also burning. Four blocks away, a small mob had attacked two firemen and a deputy, snatched two fire axes and chopped three hose lines before they were repelled by tear gas and a blast from a riot gun that had killed one boy and wounded four others. An ambulance, on its way to pick up the injured, was overturned and set afire; two other wounded picked up en route died in it.

At Velie and Exeter, a city bus was similarly attacked and burned. The white driver had been beaten severely, but half a dozen Negro passengers saved the lives of four white riders by fighting off the raiders. The whites were sheltered in the nearby homes of Negroes.

It was a fantastic nightmare to whites and Negroes alike, the urge to destroy so great that it made little difference who was hurt, which property was sacked. Along with white-owned stores, others, clearly marked BLOOD BROTHER, NEGRO-OWNED and WE DON'T SELL TO WHITEY, had been invaded, looted, and wrecked. Latecomers to the scene, in envy of loot-laden vandals, formed gangs of their own to seek out unprotected stores in other areas. Here, owners lay in wait, determined to fight off the invaders.

Larry Powell reached the 12th Precinct shortly before nine o'clock. The streets surrounding it were jammed with cars, the fenced-in portion of the parking lot crowded with prisoners, the inside of the station overflowing with white residents and Negroes, either demanding protection or trying to find missing sons and daughters, some volunteering their services to the police.

Larry had considerable difficulty pushing his way through to the desk where Lieutenant Perrin had taken over from Sergeant Ruark. A group of helmeted officers assigned from Laurelton Headquarters began emerging from a small assembly room where they had been receiving last-minute briefing from Captain Price, and Larry recognized at least three men who had been in his training class, now veterans with two years of service on the force. One of these eyed him with curiosity and pointed him out to another, but there was no time for any exchange between them.

He heard a patient voice saying, "Let 'em through, folks, let 'em through. You people are holding them up—" Larry turned and saw a burly sergeant who was trying to open an aisle for the officers.

"What do you want, boy?"

Larry wheeled and faced a hard-visaged officer who was pressing through the crowd to reach the desk. "I want to see Captain Price."

"Captain's busy and so is everybody else. Why don't you go along so we can do what we need to do?" The officer turned aside, but Larry grabbed his arm and the officer swiveled back, angry now. "Goddam it, boy—"

"Officer, this is official, a Two-Five. Please, I've got to see Captain Price."

"Oh— Over there. Through that door and to your right."

"Thanks." Then, pointing to the uniformed sergeant near the door. "Can you tell me who that sergeant is?"

"Which one? We're up to our ass in sergeants all of a sudden."

"That one, near the doorway."

"Carter. Boley Carter. Vice squad, but in uniform for the

760

duration, like ever'body else." The officer plunged through an opening and was gone. Larry made it to the green door, opened it and found a helmeted, riot-gun-armed Negro officer on guard in the hallway, barring his way. He recognized Ed Purvis, who had been in his training class.

"What are you doing here, Powell?" Purvis asked with little friendliness in his voice or manner.

"Hello, Ed. I'm here to see Captain Price."

"He's busy. Go back outside and see the desk lieutenant."

"Ed—"

"Don't argue with me, Powell, I've got my orders. Captain's got his hands full with more important matters. Go see—"

"I'm seeing Captain Price on orders from Inspector LaSalle, goddam it, and I haven't got time to fool around. Let me through."

Purvis didn't move except to raise the short barrel of his riot gun in Larry's direction. "All right, Ed, I'm a Two-Five. Okay?"

"Two-Five? You?"

"Yes, me. The classroom foul-up." He brushed past Purvis and went down the hallway and knocked on the door which had the words *Station Commander* lettered in white on it. A uniformed officer opened the door and Larry saw Captain Price standing before a large map, moving pushpins about. Price turned then and said, "What the hell—"

"Sir," Larry said, "my name is Powell. Larry Powell."

"Oh. Inspector LaSalle cleared you through. Come in. What happened?"

"I'm blown, I guess. I wasn't doing anything but watching everything going up around me. I called in to Inspector LaSalle and he told me to come in. Is the Inspector around?"

"No, he was called out into the field."

"Captain, what can I do to help?"

"I don't know that there's anything you can do here. I can't put you into uniform or arm you. We're doing what we can and we're just about doing better than holding our own. There's nothing you can do around here."

Larry looked at the map and saw that a group of the pins were within several blocks of Division and Hartman, which would place the Center within striking range. "Any trouble at the center yet, sir?" he asked.

"Not yet. They called in earlier and we advised them to dismiss classes and shut up shop. I don't know if they did, but we've had no calls from them since."

"If you can't use me, will it be all right if I see what I can do at the Center?"

"As far as I'm concerned, it's all right. I don't think I can reach Inspector LaSalle, so—"

"Thank you, Captain." He got to the door, turned and said, "Captain?"

Price, facing the wall, listening to the radio reports on the loudspeaker, said, "What is it?"

"Sir, there's a Sergeant Carter on duty here at the 12th—"

"Boley Carter," Price acknowledged. "What about him?"

"Sir, a little while back, I told Inspector LaSalle about seeing a man in the back room of Banjo's Place, taking a payoff."

"He mentioned it to me and I've had Internal Security checking on it, but we haven't come up with anything. Are you suggesting that Carter is the man?"

"Yes, sir. He was in civilian clothes when I saw him, but I'll swear it was Sergeant Carter."

For a few moments Price said nothing, his head turned back to the map, one hand on a pushpin, not hearing the radio chatter. Then, "You're sure about that, Powell?"

"Yes, sir. I'm sure." Price jabbed the pin into the map angrily. "I saw him under the light for just a few seconds, no more than two or three, before he got up and moved to a dark corner," Larry continued. "I don't think I could be wrong about that profile and build. He was the man and he was counting the money in the envelope when I came in. When he got up he put the envelope in his inside coat pocket."

"An eighteen-year man," Price said as much to himself as to Larry.

"I hate to be the one to put the finger on him, Captain."

"It's got to be done, Powell. All right, I'll begin running a check on him, how he lives, bank accounts, safety deposit boxes, everything. I don't guess I have to warn you to keep this to yourself, except for Inspector LaSalle. I'll pass it along to him myself and we'll set up a new investigation squad to work on it."

"Yes, sir."

"You can go now." Price addressed himself to the map and his pushpins and Larry went out. He pushed through the milling crowd in the front room and reached the doorway. Carter was nowhere in sight. The skies to the north and west were still red. He got through the huddle of people and headed north and east toward the Center and once he was clear of the crowd, began running again.

In the office of the Center, Daisy Church heard the first riot news on her transistor radio shortly before 8:30 when the NBC network symphony concert was interrupted by the local station to broadcast the constant stream of bulletins that were flowing in from the scene in West Laurelton. Quickly, she dialed her home and was assured that her family was out of the danger area. She then went upstairs to notify Ralph Atkins. Atkins left the class in charge of a student-monitor and returned to the office with Daisy. He listened to the rapid-fire news flashes for a few moments. Mrs. Clemmons, in charge of the snack room, came in, her face registering alarm. She had been listening to the broadcast on her radio in the kitchen while preparing the after-class food and coffee for the instructors. Her staff of two volunteer helpers had already left for home.

Atkins dialed the 12th Precinct and after several attempts to get through, finally reached a Sergeant Holcomb, who said, "I can't tell you any more than you're getting on your radio."

"What do you think we ought to do, Sergeant. We've got a lot of people here."

"Well, I don't rightly know. Maybe you ought to close down."

"If we do, it means sending a couple hundred more people into the danger area. Are we close to any of the rioting?"

"So far, no. You've got a point about not closing down. Suppose I try to reach the Captain and we'll call you back after I talk to him about it."

"All right, Sergeant. Ask for Miss Church."

Charlie Eaton, one of the first-floor class instructors, was taking a smoking break and stopped at the office just as Atkins was hanging up. He heard the continuing flashes on the radio and exclaimed, "What the hell!"

Atkins said, "Well, you can't say we weren't expecting it Charlie, you take this floor. I'll take the upper floor. Take it easy and ask every instructor to meet us in the snack room as quickly as possible. Make sure you're not overheard. Daisy, you phone the gymnasium and auto repair class and tell the instructors to leave monitors in charge and meet us here. Don't tell them what it's about. They'll probably see it when they come outside and look at the sky."

Twenty minutes later, Atkins had informed the 18 gathered instructors of the situation and turned the kitchen radio up so they could hear the bulletins for themselves. "I'm waiting right now for a call from the 12th Precinct to advise us what to do—"

763

At that moment, Daisy Church came in from the office and reported that Sergeant Holcomb had called advising the Center to close down. Atkins mentioned the possibility that this could add to the problem of releasing the students and asked for an opinion. It was suggested a vote be taken, which resulted in a 16-to-2 vote in favor of dismissal, since the school was due to close in little more than half an hour anyway, and for each instructor to advise his students to avoid the central area in reaching their homes. By 9:10, the students and all but half a dozen instructors were gone.

In the downstairs hallway, Elizabeth waited at the pay telephone, third in line, visibly concerned. Atkins, Eaton, and the others who remained were lined up at the free phone in the office. In the front doorway, Lyle Emerson stood watching the red glow in the sky to the south and west, occasionally glancing over his shoulder to see if Elizabeth was closer to the phone. A moment later, Ralph Atkins joined him.

"What do you think Ralph?" Lyle asked.

"I'm thinking about Harlem, Chicago, Watts, Birmingham and Rochester. And I'm thinking of what a goddam shame it is to have it happen here, what tomorrow and next week, next month, will look like. And I'm also thinking you'd better get out of here as fast as you can. If this thing moves toward us, white is going to be the most unpopular color I can think of."

"If you try to stop them, Ralph, black won't be much more popular than white, will it?"

"Take a look at that sky, man, and tell me if you think I've got any intention of trying to stop anybody. Lord Jesus, what a pity. If they hit the Center, they'll only be driving another nail into their own coffins." He shook his head from side to side. "I wonder what our fearless leaders across the bridge are thinking now? How much they've saved by neglecting the thousands of people over here."

Lyle had no answers. He hadn't believed this would—could—happen, and now it was here. He looked over his shoulder toward the telephone again and saw that Elizabeth was next in line. "I mean it, Lyle," Atkins persisted. "You'd better get out of here while the getting is safe. Get across the bridge into white country. Keep to the side streets and if you see a group of prowlers—"

"I'll stay for a little while, Ralph."

Atkins shrugged. "It's your choice, but if you don't mind my saying so, you're out of your mind." Then, to Lyle's further confusion, "If you're worried about Elizabeth, I'll

764

look out for her. She'll be a hell of a lot safer with me than with you."

Lyle shot a quick look at Atkins' face, but there was nothing there he could interpret except a sincere desire to be helpful; nothing to indicate feeling one way or the other as far as anything else was concerned. So Ralph Atkins knew. Duke Shackleford knew. Corey Armour knew. How many others? he wondered. He turned again and saw Elizabeth take Wally Harding's place at the telephone, dialing now. He walked to her and simply stood beside her, listening.

"No, Mama, I'm all right. There's no trouble here. Cross my heart, Mama. Please don't worry." She listened for a moment, then, "If Papa calls again, tell him what I told you. I know he can't reach me. Everybody here has been using the telephone and others are waiting. No, I don't want him to leave the plant to come and get me. I've got transportation home when I want it. Yes, Mama, I'll come home when it's safe. Of course, there's Mr. Atkins and Mr. Harding and Mr. Eaton and two or three others who will give me a lift. I've got to hang up now, someone else is waiting to use the phone. Please don't worry."

She hung up, her face showing anxiety. Atkins had gone back to the office. Lyle and Elizabeth walked to the front door to look up at the sky. "Elizabeth, let's get out of here. I don't like what I see," Lyle said.

"I can't," Elizabeth said, shaking her head.

"Why not"

"It's crazy, Lyle. All that has to happen is for somebody —anybody—to stop us. What do you think would happen to you, to both of us?"

"We can go east to River Road, then south to Grand and the bridge and cross over into East Laurelton."

"We can't, Lyle. We'd have to pass the roadblocks. If those white officers see us together, it will be just as bad. Maybe worse. Please, Lyle, don't insist. I've caused you enough trouble already. This time, I can't predict what might happen. Why don't you get out now, while it's still safe for you?"

But Lyle refused to be swayed.

"I have just received the latest casualty count from the 12th Precinct in West Laurelton," the announcer reported to the city's radio listeners. "As of 9:25 there have been 166 arrests for looting, interference with officers in the performance of their duties, resisting arrest, refusing to move out of danger areas and destroying property. Three

765

Negroes, as yet unidentified, killed by gunfire, two others dead by means not described, two dead in fires, seventy-six injured and being cared for at the West Laurelton General Hospital. A shortage of plasma is being filled by Laurelton Memorial Hospital and a spokesman has reported that their blood bank is now dangerously low. There is a need for blood donors in West Laurelton. The need for doctors and nurses persists. Known white dead are James Garrison, 322 Myrtle Avenue, a fireman killed by a sniper; Fred Scott, 1266 Borden Street, a sheriff's deputy, killed by a sniper. Six white officers have been injured. White civilians, fifteen known to be hurt sufficiently to warrant hospitalization. We have been informed that many more may be injured, but these have not been reported to the authorities. Sniping at firemen from rooftops continues sporadically, despite efforts of guards to protect them.

"I have just been handed a bulletin. Two Negroes, operating separately in attempts to fire-bomb stores in East Laurelton, have been thwarted in the attempts. In the first, the Negro was killed when struck by shotgun fire and his bomb was set off when it dropped at his feet. In the second attempt, the Molotov cocktails were found in a car stopped by police for a traffic violation and the driver taken into custody. There has been no further word from the National Guard at Camp Fitch, which was alerted by Mayor Cameron earlier. Last report was that the unit was en route, due to arrive here sometime around midnight. Listeners are again cautioned to remain away from the central areas of East and West Laurelton. There is grave danger, repeat, grave danger.

"And another bulletin—from the 18th Precinct in South Laurelton. That station was attacked about ten minutes ago by a group of young Negroes who threw a gasoline bomb into the main entrance from a moving car. Another bomb crashed on the steps. Return fire by police is believed to have hit the car as it sped off. One officer injured by flying debris, one burned severely, one hit by a pistol shot. All three are being treated at the station. The fire is under control and twenty-two prisoners are being transferred to another jail.

"In West Laurelton, there is still much—"

Duke Shackleford was listening to the report, disturbed by the news that two—which two, he did not know—of his men had been nailed down before they could carry out their assignments. Two down, two to go. The rest of the news cheered him. Show those ofay bastards what they're up against. Not just here, but everywhere else. Long hot summer is so much shit for the birds. We'll show 'em October and December won't be no different than July or August.

He was two blocks north of Banjo's Place, his car parked on Preston, the first in line on the block, in position to get out quickly. All the action was south of him and before it could get this far, he would have accomplished what he had come to do. He had used one of his six gasoline bombs effectively and now it was time to put another to good use. He got out of the car and looked toward the flickering neon sign over the poolroom two blocks south. On the street, several Negroes were walking and running toward Velie Street to where the action was. The scene. The houses between where he was and Velie were dark, but he knew that there were terrified people behind those windows.

He took one of the bottles from the carton on the floor behind him and cradled it under his left arm. It was wrapped in a piece of cloth, the wick extended, waiting to be lit. He walked down Preston to Velie and stood on the opposite corner facing the poolroom. The doors were closed, but the lights were on inside. He crossed the street and tried the door and found it open. He stuck his head inside. Only Hinky Liggett was there, in his chair, leaning against the wall in his usual position. Duke was disappointed that Larry Powell was nowhere in sight. He entered and walked toward Hinky, who looked up and tilted his chair forward so that all four legs rested on the floor.

"What you doin' here?" Hinky asked.

"I got somethin' for Banjo. He inside?"

"He inside. Whyn't you go 'roun' the back like you suppose to?"

"It's blocked. People all over the place."

Hinky stood up and rapped the cuestick against the door. Duke was walking toward him and had reached the center of the room when the door to the back room opened and Banjo was standing in the doorway. He stared at Duke in complete surprise. "What the—?"

Duke had placed a cigarette between his lips and held a lighter up to it, but suddenly he touched the flame to the exposed wick of the covered bottle he was carrying, drew his arm back and threw it. "Somethin' for both of you," he called, then turned and ran toward the front door. Banjo put up his hands to deflect the flaming object, but it struck his chest. Hinky turned and made a grab for it as it fell to the floor, crashed and broke, exploding flaming gasoline on both of them.

Outside, the press of people surged past, paying little attention. Duke turned north and began to run toward his car. He got into it, started the motor, pulled out north toward Division Street, where he turned right, heading eastward. One more to go, Duke thought with satisfaction. Make sure Elizabeth ain't there, then—

On Grand Avenue and Ascot, Ad Cameron and Corey Armour drove over the street litter in a block where there had been no fire. This was the unwanted debris of several looted stores, rubble that hadn't been worth taking; odd shoes and garments, cans of paint, a smashed cash register, a keg of nails spilled over, fixtures that had been battered and torn apart, store furniture. Ad was on his car phone calling information in to a rewrite man, describing what he saw as they drove along. At the conclusion, the rewrite man said, "Hold it. Your father wants to talk to you."

Brad Cameron's gruff voice came on. "Adam?"

"Yes, sir?"

"Can you come in? I need your help here, coordinating the news that's coming in. We'll probably be running our presses all night, and we're shorthanded."

"All right, sir, As soon as I can get through." He replaced the phone beneath the dashboard. To Corey, "Had enough?"

"More than enough."

"Let's cut out."

"What time is it?"

Ad switched the dash light on. "Nine seventeen."

"Can we swing past the Center?"

"It's on the way."

"Let's take a look and see if Lyle's car is still there."

"Okay, but even if it is, that stubborn bastard won't budge an inch." Ad raised the volume level of the radio and heard his Uncle Tom Cameron's voice come on. The Mayor was in West Laurelton, it announced, broadcasting simultaneously to the people on the streets.

"—and I urge every citizen within hearing of my voice to leave this area of destruction at once and go to your homes. Please get off the streets and out of the way of the police and firemen who are doing their utmost to save lives and property. Your lives and property. If this insanity continues, the destruction can only spread to your homes. This damage is the work of irresponsible hoodlums and not our decent citizens who have worked hard for years to buy homes and possessions they cannot afford to lose.

"Please leave the area at once. There are snipers firing at police and firemen and you may be struck down. In the

768

darkness of night, accidents will occur and you may become innocent victims instead of spectators. Hospital facilities are already overcrowded. The death toll is rising. I urge all parents to exercise control over their children and keep them out of harm's way."

There was a pause, a rumbling of static, then Mayor Cameron's voice came on again. "To everyone listening, hear this. If these instructions are not obeyed by ten o'clock, I shall declare a citywide curfew commencing at ten o'clock until six A.M. This means that anyone not authorized to be on the streets between those hours will be placed under immediate arrest regardless of age. We do not want to do this, but it will become necessary in order to—"

Ad turned the volume lower. "Well," he said, "that ought to separate the men from the boys. I hope to hell it works."

"How does it end, Ad?" Corey asked.

"Who the hell knows? I sure as hell don't. This is the result of a lot of talk and damned little of doing. One spark was all it needed to set the blaze going. Putting it out is another matter."

"Let's get to the Center," Corey said.

Lee Durkin, who had been born and raised on a small farm in Angeltown and remained a familiar and popular figure in West and South Laurelton, was in the area of Velie and Porter Streets where the outbreak had begun. He was questioning several witnesses who were present when Dr. Rhama had begun making his speech. Less than a hundred yards away, firemen were still battling blazes that had spread from Pearson's, the Blue Front and Dubner's Drug Store to adjacent stores and houses. On the Pearson parking lot, a tangle of twenty or more cars, unable to escape because of blocked traffic, had suffered destruction from fire damage.

"—an' then, Mist' Durkin," Elias Birch was relating, "this damfool fella, I seen him on the far side of the crowd, he th'owed somethin', looked like a rock, maybe a brick, an' it hit the window, bust it to smithereens. After that, ever'thing started happenin', ever'thing, ever'body gone crazy—"

"What did Dr. Rhama and his people do then, Lias?" Durkin asked.

"I don' know. I was watchin' the doin's in Pearson's. Crazy, just plumb crazy."

"I was on the pavement listenin' to him," Sarah Potts chimed in. "When the glass broke, most of the people ran across the street to Pearson's. The doctor, he an' his people

769

they shut up shop fast. Put ever'thing back in the truck an' car an' got away from here."

"Lias, did you see the man who threw the rock, his face? Do you know who he was?" Durkin asked.

"Nossir. Don' think I ever seen him before."

"Think you'd know him if you saw him again?"

"I think so. Yessir, I think I would. He started the whole thing, smashin' the window. Burn me an' Sally right outen our house, all these people—" Lias' eyes were brimming with tears of anger. "Burned out. Didn' save a thing, we had to get out so fast. Lost ever'thing we own."

"Anybody else see him?" Durkin asked. Heads were shaking negatively. Durkin looked among the groups and saw a youth of about 17 who neither confirmed nor denied. "What's your name, son?" Durkin asked.

The boy remained mute. Beside him, his father said, "Speak up when the chief talk to you, boy. Tell him your name."

"Duddy."

"You got a las' name," the father prodded. "Tell him."

"It's all right, Sime," Durkin said to the man. To the boy, "Were you there, Duddy?"

The boy nodded. "Did you see the man?"

"I—uh—seen him."

"You know him?"

The boy did not answer. His father, Simon Decker, gripped Duddy's shoulder. "Answer the chief, boy."

The boy winced under the pressure on his shoulder. "Pa —don't—"

"Then speak up, else you'll get a lot worse."

"I know him. I seen him aroun' the 2-2-2."

"What's his name?" Durkin asked quietly.

"Buddy Duke. The fighter."

"You mean Duke Shackleford?"

Duddy nodded and Simon tightened his grip to remind the boy to speak up. "Yessir. Duke Shackleford."

"Thank you, Duddy, Sime, Lias. I'll talk to you later." He went to the curb where Lloyd Cooper sat behind the wheel of his car. Les Williams, a tough ex-Marine, and Tony Shattuck, a nine-year veteran and Bronze Star winner in Korea, were on the back seat. Only one of the three officers was white.

"Let's go," Durkin said. "Up Grand, east to the bridge, then west again on Velie. Shattuck, Cooper, Williams, keep your eyes out for Duke Shackleford. Owns a maroon Jaguar. Medium colored, about five-nine or -ten, about 160 pounds. He's been hanging around the 2-2-2 and Banjo's

Place, but he's probably not there now." Durkin reached for the radio mike, changed the frequency for car-to-car communication and picked up Inspector LaSalle. "Pete, where are you?"

"At the Marquette Elementary command post on South Mercer. All's quiet for the moment."

"Take a run out to the Nigerian and see if you can find Dr. Rhama and any of his crew. Pick them up for questioning. I'm calling in a pickup order on Duke Shackleford. I've got witnesses who saw him throw the first rock into Pearson's. Over."

"On my way, Lee. Over and out."

At the Nigerian, the cottage occupied by Dr. Rhama and Brother Leonard was dark. Likewise, the one rented by Duke Shackleford. Roy Herbert came back from the office with Vern Webb, the manager, who unlocked the doors to admit the officers. Dr. Rhama's cottage showed every indication of a hurried departure. No clothes, a toothbrush and tube of paste left in the bathroom, mimeographed copies of Dr. Rhama's speeches, other printed literature, wall posters showing Rhama's stony portrait, with fez, a quantity of other black fezzes of cheaper make strewn around the living room and bedroom.

"I told the man," Webb repeated, "they checked out in a hurry, over half an hour ago—"

The two men who had inspected Shackleford's cottage returned with several small packets wrapped in brown paper, and a leather box. "H," John Farmer announced. "I'd guess about three ounces, and the works. Found it taped to the bottom of the toilet tank."

"Mark it for identification, John."

Roy Herbert had been sifting through the accumulation of papers and brought a sheet of typed matter with two illustrations on it to LaSalle. "Anything to this, Inspector?"

The sheet described in detail the procedure for manufacturing a gasoline bomb, complete with illustrations and instructions for use. "It's something, Roy. Enough to tie him into a criminal charge. Mark it and bring it along with the other material."

In his car, LaSalle called the information back to Lee Durkin, who called Captain Price and ordered an APB broadcast to pick up Dr. Rhama, Brother Leonard and four John Does known to be with them, driving a 1967 Ford panel truck equipped with broadcasting equipment, dark green with wood-grained trim, license number—

"—hear this. If these instructions are not obeyed by ten o'clock, I shall declare a citywide curfew between the hours of ten and six A.M. This means that anyone not authorized to be on the streets between those hours will be placed under immediate arrest—"

Duke checked the time. 9:35. Six blocks to go. Time to spare. He braked for the stop sign at Division, entered it and turned right. There were only four cars moving, three coming toward him and one a good distance behind him, its headlights faintly visible in his tinted rear-view mirror. Another two blocks and the only car in view was the one behind him. He came to the Center and turned left into the driveway. With the exception of the ground floor of the two-storied building, the others were dark, the outdoor lights of the parking lot turned off. Duke assumed that the lights in the hallway were for the convenience of the night watchman. As he pulled into the paved parking area, his lights swept over the two cars there. A Plymouth sedan and a Dodge. Ofay Emerson's Dodge. To whom did the Plymouth belong? The night watchman? Probably. Duke switched the lights of the Jaguar off and waited to see if his arrival had been noticed.

In the office, Ralph Atkins, Daisy Church, Elizabeth Shackleford and Lyle Emerson listened to the radio and sipped coffee from paper cups. Atkins was munching a sandwich and Elizabeth had gone to the coffee percolator to refill her cup. Next to the table, the window blind had been drawn, but she saw the beam of light as it struck the inch of space between the blind and the window. She moved the blind another inch and peeked through it just as the lights were turned off. Lyle, watching her, said, "Something out there, Elizabeth?"

"A car just pulled into the parking lot."

"Probably a prowl car, checking," Atkins said.

"They parked and turned their lights off," Elizabeth added.

"I'll let them in." Atkins went out of the office and toward the front doorway. He returned a few minutes later, puzzled. "Nobody," he reported. "Not a soul."

"It was a car," Elizabeth said firmly. "I saw it as it came in and turned its lights off." She went to the window and pulled the blind back. Lyle hobbled over to her and said, "Wait a minute, Elizabeth. Whoever it is will be able to see you better than you can see him. Or them. Daisy, turn the room lights off, please."

Daisy was closest to the wall switch. She pressed a button and the overhead and desk lights went off, plunging the room into darkness. Lyle raised the blind and the four of them stared out across the lawn toward the parking lot.

Atkins said, "Can't see a thing—"

"Where are the parking lot lights?" Lyle asked.

"In the hall, just outside the office. I'll get it." He went to the doorway and a moment later the parking lot lights came on.

"My Dodge, Ralph's Plymouth. And—" Lyle's voice faded. Atkins said, "Looks like a foreign job. Hey, that's a Jaguar. Anybody know anybody who owns a Jag?"

Daisy said, "Uh-uh." Lyle and Elizabeth said nothing.

"A Jag," Atkins repeated. "Now that's a real hunk of iron." He heard some movement in the room and pulled the blind down. Daisy crossed the room and switched the lights on again, to discover that she and Atkins were alone.

"Hey," Ralph said, "where did they get to?"

"Out in the hall, I guess," Daisy replied. "Ralph, I'm worried. I'd like to go home."

"Okay. I guess it's safe now. We can circle around the trouble. Nothing more we can do here."

But Elizabeth and Lyle were not in the hallway. Daisy called their names, but got no reply. She started toward the snack room and Atkins said, "Let's go, Daisy. They probably left something in one of the classrooms." Atkins opened the front door and they went out. As he closed the door, the spring lock snapped into place. From where he stood in the dark beside the building, Duke flattened against the wood siding, heard Daisy Church say, "—but who was in the car?"

And Atkins' reply, "I don't know. Maybe somebody lives close by, parking off the street to keep it safe from vandals."

In the darkened snack room, Lyle said, "They've gone—"

"Lyle, he's here. Somewhere. It's his car."

"Yes, but you'll be all right. He won't find you."

"It's not me I'm worried about as much as I am about you."

"Elizabeth, please don't worry about me. I promise you I can handle this. What I want you to do is walk out through the front door. Here are the keys to my car. Get in and drive home."

"And leave you here, alone with him? Lyle, he's dangerous. He warned me not to come here tonight."

"When?"

"He telephoned just before I left the house tonight."

"Did he say why he didn't want you to be here?"

"No. Just— Oh, Lord!"

773

"What is it?"

"He asked me if you'd be here. I told him it wasn't any of his business and hung up. I just remembered."

"Elizabeth, get out of here, please. Here, take these keys." He pushed them toward her hand in the darkness and Elizabeth clutched at his hand, but did not take the keys from him. "No, Lyle. If I'm here, maybe I can talk to him—promise him—"

"Promise him what?"

"Not to see you again, ever. That's what he wants. I'll drop out for a while if you won't—"

Lyle put his arms around her. "You can't do that, Elizabeth."

"I can if it will stop him from— Oh, Lyle, Lyle, what have we got ourselves into?"

He kissed her, felt the tears on her face with his lips, then her lips on his own. "It doesn't change anything," Elizabeth said. "He's still out there somewhere."

"Take the keys, for God's sake," Lyle urged again.

"No. I won't take the keys and I won't leave you here alone with him out there."

"Goddam it, Elizabeth— All right, then, let's get out of here."

"Where?"

"I'll turn the hall and parking lot lights off. You go upstairs to your classroom. I'll phone the police from the office."

"You go upstairs and let me phone."

"No. As far as he knows, you're not here. Wait." Lyle opened the door, peered out, then moved to the wall switches outside the office and cut the hall and parking lot lights off. The building was in total darkness.

Outside, crouching in the shadow of the building, Duke Shackleford watched as Daisy Church and Ralph Atkins crossed to where the two cars stood almost side by side. He saw Atkins hold the door open for Daisy, then walk around to the driver's side, get in, start the car, switch on its headlights and drive out of the school grounds. After a moment, Duke cradled the bottle of gasoline in one arm and grinned to himself. "That leaves you all by yourself, you sonofabitchin' cripple," he said. "You in there an' you goin'a burn in there."

He went up the steps and tried the door. It was locked. He walked around to the east side of the building toward the back, feeling his way carefully, one hand against the wooden siding, stepping cautiously over the ground stubble. At the rear, he tried the door and found that it was locked, too. He returned to the east side where the building was separated from a chain link fence by a ten-foot width of more stubble. Moving closer to the fence, he walked along until he reached the halfway mark, then stopped, and looked up and stared at a second-floor window. He leaned against the fence, gauging the distance carefully.

In the downstairs office, Lyle dialed the "O" and asked the operator for the nearest police precinct. "Is this an emergency, sir?" the operator asked.

"Yes, Operator, very much so." He waited, then heard a quick, gruff, "Ninthprecinctsergeantlewis. Helpyou?"

"Yes, Sergeant. This is the Recreational-Vocational Center—"

"What'stheproblem?"

"There's a prowler—"

"Prowler? *Prowler?* Man, we can't spare no time for prowlers. We got a full-sized, wide-open riot on our hands. Lock all the doors and windows. If—"

Lyle realized it was a waste of time and hung up. He went out, feeling his way along the wall until he reached the stairway, then mounted the steps slowly. In the upper hallway, he heard Elizabeth's voice. "Lyle?" she called softly.

"Here, Elizabeth. Where are you?"

"Outside my classroom." He continued feeling his way until he felt her outstretched hand drawing him into the darkened room. "Did you get the police?" she asked.

"Yes."

"Are they sending someone?"

"As soon as they can locate a car," he lied.

"Let's sit down and keep quiet. I've locked the door. Don't make any noise."

He sat in the chair beside her and put an arm around her.

When Ad reached the Center, the building was dark. He hesitated at the driveway entrance and said, "Too late. Looks like everybody's gone."

"Yes," Corey replied not without some relief at the thought that Lyle had left and was either home or on his way there.

"At least," Ad said, "that's one worry off your mind. Let's head for the barn. We'll be up all night at the paper with this."

"Do you think the curfew will work?"

"Hell, no. Not enough police to enforce it, and a little over two hours before the National Guard can get here."

He reached for the car phone. "I'll check in with the office and tell 'em I'm on my way."

Even the few minutes of waiting became intolerable. Elizabeth was as taut as a tightly drawn bow, trembling with the strain. Lyle's arm around her offered little comfort or reassurance. Somewhere below, at the front, rear or sides of the building, was Duke, searching for Lyle, and she knew now that a confrontation between them, despite her presence, could end only in tragedy. She told herself she should have left with Ralph and Daisy, that if Duke had seen her leaving, he might have—but she knew in her heart that it would not have mattered. Duke was bent on revenge and must have it. She stirred and said in a whisper, "Oh, Lord—"

Lyle stood up and hobbled across the room to one of the four windows, starting out into the darkness, his eyes barely able to distinguish the trees and shrubbery from the black backdrop of night.

"Can you see anything?" Elizabeth asked in a low voice.

"No. Nothing," he replied without turning. "Black as the inside of a tar barrel. Elizabeth—"

"What?"

"You can still leave. You're not helping matters by staying here. Take my car keys and get out. If you run into Duke, tell him I left earlier with someone else and left my keys in the office."

"It's too late, Lyle. He'd see through that and come for you."

Silently, helplessly, Lyle agreed.

Well, let him come, Lyle thought. I hate to do it in front of her, but if he walks into this room—

Lyle's hand moved back to his right hip pocket where the .38 automatic rested. He felt its grip and replaced both hands on the windowsill, staring outward and downward, trying to accustom his eyes to the darkness.

Below, Duke made his decision. It didn't make much difference which window as long as his throw was accurate. The old building would go up like wood shavings. And when it started to burn, Mr. Emerson would either burn with it or come a-running. And then—

Duke removed the book of matches from his jacket pocket, pulled one out and closed the book carefully. He struck the match, touched it to the wick, reached his arm back to throw the bottle. It arced upward—

From the window above, the matchlight caught Lyle's eye. He looked to his left and saw it touch something and flare up, the arc as it was drawn back, knowing what it was he was seeing. Instinctively, his hand drew back to his hip pocket and withdrew the .38. The movement caused Elizabeth to look in his direction and with the faint gray light entering the window, saw the shadow of the automatic in his hand.

"Lyle!"

He was aiming the automatic downward as she came out of her chair and ran toward him, but before she could reach him, he had fired twice in rapid succession, then twice more.

"Lyle! For God's sake, don't!"

As she reached him and grabbed for his arm, she heard more breaking glass, the sound coming from the classroom to the right of them.

"He threw a Molotov cocktail," Lyle said. "The next room. We've got to get out of here!"

"Duke! Was it Duke?"

"I don't know. I guess so. I saw him light the wick and throw it. We've got to get out."

Below, Duke had watched in that split second of triumph as the bottle arc-ed upward, smashed through the pane of glass and dropped inside the classroom. In that instant, he saw flames erupt, emitting a sheet of glaring light from the window. And in that same plit second, he felt the force as the first bullet hit his ankle and even before he could fall, the second struck his left knee. And falling, he heard the next two bullets whistle over his head.

When he tried to stand, his leg gave way under him and he fell again. He grabbed for the ankle with one hand, his knee with the other, felt the warm blood and the same intense pain he had felt when his knuckles were broken. Sweat broke out over him as he hopped up on his right foot, fell again, then began crawling painfully, desperately, toward his car.

Outside the Center, Ad Cameron had been in the act of hanging up his receiver when a sheet of bright red light flashed up on the far side of the administration building and caused him to retract his hand. "Mike!" he shouted into the receiver. "You still on?"

"Yo, Ad. What's up?"

"Get this! The Center has just been hit. A gasoline bomb, I think. Call it in to Fire Control Center, then get a photographer here. I'll cover the story. Out."

Corey was already out of the car, but he leaned in again. "Where's your gun, Ad?"

"Glove compartment." He leaped out on the driver's side and began running toward the front entrance of the building. Corey got the .38 Police Special out of the glove compartment, shoved it into his waist belt and ran across the street after Ad. Inside the grounds, Corey called, "This way," and cut across the parking lot where, in the light of the flames that were rising from the right side of the wooden structure, he saw Lyle's car and the one close to it.

"That's Lyle's Dodge, Ad!" Corey shouted as they ran toward the front entrance.

"Somebody's there with him," Ad called back. "Who the hell owns a Jag?"

Corey didn't answer. He ran up the steps and tried the doors. They were locked. He pulled the .38 out, grasped it by the barrel and broke the glass, then inserted one hand, felt for the lock, found it and unlocked the door. He pushed both doors open and stumbled back, choking on the smoke that rushed out. Ad grabbed his jacket and pulled him back.

"Get out, you damned fool! You'll be overcome by smoke!"

Upstairs, the sudden smashing of glass and the roar that followed it caused Elizabeth to jump suddenly, her hands still gripping Lyle's arms. "My God! What was—?"

The windows lighted up red, coming in waves, like a sea rolling up on a shore. "Fire. Dave Hill's classroom. We've—"

"Lyle!"

"—got to get out of here, fast. This building will go up like a piece of Kleenex—"

He hopped on his left leg, dragging his right, reached the door and unsnapped the spring lock. From the hallway, a mass of smoke poured into the room. He slammed the door shut, leaned against it for a moment, then pushed himself away. He groped for the light switch, pressed the buttons, but no lights came on.

"Lyle—where—?"

"Here, Elizabeth! The window! Get to the window!" He hobbled, limped and stumbled, knocking chairs over. Elizabeth had reached a window and he saw her form outlined against the red-tinted panes, struggling to raise the lower portion. Lyle reached her, tried the window. It was locked. He reached up and unlocked it, threw the window open and looked out and saw the flames roaring out of Dave Hill's classroom, next to them. Above the roar of flames, he heard

778

Elizabeth gasping, clutching the windowsill, standing next to him. He looked out and down, approximating the distance to the ground.

"Listen, Elizabeth." He saw the numb, desperate glaze in her eyes, the fright spread across her face. He caught her by the arms and it was as though she was without bone or muscle. "Elizabeth! Listen to me!" Her head rolled loosely from side to side. He slapped her face and she seemed to come awake momentarily. "Listen to what I'm saying!" She nodded.

"I want you to get up on this sill, facing me, with your arms around my neck. When I say 'Go!' I'll help push you out, then grab your wrists. I'll lower you as far as I can, then drop you to the ground. It's not too far. When you hit the ground, run or crawl away from the building. I'll drop down behind you and we'll—"

He saw her eyes go blank again, felt her going limp in his arms, on the verge of fainting. He put an arm around her and held her up. "Elizabeth! For Christ's sake, listen to me—"

It was useless. She couldn't see or hear him. If there were something—anything—a rope—but he knew there was none in the classroom. He shouted, "Help!" at the top of his voice, again and again, until smoke began to pour in through the window as the air grew hotter, almost suffocating him.

Outside and below, Corey said, "Ad, did you hear—?"

Ad said, "Around the side, someone—"

They ran toward the burning side of the building and saw the flames shooting outward and upward from the window, reaching for the roof.

"Jesus!" Ad exclaimed. "Anybody caught in that—"

"*Lyle's in there—*" Corey shouted, and running, heard the cry again. "Help!" He looked up and saw a dim figure at the near window, partially engulfed by smoke. "*Lyle! Lyle! Here! Here!*"

Lyle bent down as low as he could over the sill. "G-got a—"

"Lyle! Jump! There are two of us here. Hang from the sill and drop down! We'll catch you!"

"C-can't. Girl here. Passed out. Ladder—"

"Where?"

"Tool shed. Behind this one—"

"I'll try to find it, Corey," Ad said and ran toward the back of the building.

779

"H-hurry—" Lyle's voice croaked. "Fire eating the wall—"

"Lyle! Try to bring her to. If you can't, lift her and drop her down to us. We'll catch her, or break her fall. Then you—"

Lyle had disappeared inside the room again. Corey stood there helplessly, looking upward, listening. He heard the faint wail of sirens in the distance and wondered if he were only imagining it.

In the classroom, Elizabeth was slumped down on the floor at the base of the window. Lyle bent over her, rubbed her wrists, patted her face, then slapped harder as he pleaded with her to come out of it. "Elizabeth! Listen to me! It's your life! For God's sake, look up. It's me, Lyle. I love you, Elizabeth, I love you. Don't die like this—"

She stirred, coughed and moaned. "Elizabeth, wake up! There's help down there! Listen, I can get you out. Try to stand up. Please!"

Hands under her arms, he wrestled her up, but her knees sagged. He dropped his arms around her waist and drew her tightly against him, dragged and tugged her back to the window. More smoke billowed in and Elizabeth broke into a paroxysm of coughing. Lyle bent her downward, out of the smoke, her waist across the sill, arms extended downward. He leaned down beside her, his eyes watering, heard Corey's voice, but could see nothing. He looked back into the room as a flash of light erupted and saw that the north wall was burning furiously, leaping toward the chair and desk on the raised platform, licking at paint, varnish. The American flag in its wooden stand in the corner exploded into a brief burst of red-orange.

Lyle screamed, "The ladder!"

Corey shouted, "Ad! Here! Quick!"

Ad came running back. "The goddam shed was locked. I broke the door in. There's no ladder there." He stood beside Corey panting, peering upward. "What—?"

"It's the girl. She's out." Hands cupped to mouth, Corey shouted, "Lyle! Ad is here with me. No ladder. Drop her and we'll catch her. Lyle! DROP HER!"

Lyle heard, but could not answer. He put his arms around Elizabeth's waist, lifted and turned her back toward him. He bent and caught her behind the knees, drew her upward until her feet cleared the sill, sat her upon it, facing outward. He steadied her against his chest and slid his arms upward and followed her arms until his hands gripped her wrists tightly. Leaning against her now, he pushed forward until her buttocks slipped off the sill. As she dropped, he braced himself. The shock of her dead weight almost pulled him out of the window after her, but he held on grimly. Then he heard Corey's voice faintly, as though it were coming from a million miles across a jungle, "Drop—drop—"

He let go then and the sudden freedom of the weight forced him upward and backward. He staggered and his body twisted around. He felt a wave of pain shoot down into the stump of his leg as his weight drove it deeper into the socket. He lurched, turned and fell and his chin struck the edge of the chair in which Elizabeth had been sitting earlier. And as he hit the floor, it seemed that this was something that had happened before, this feeling of falling, flames erupting and exploding around him, the crackle or shots—darkness.

Below, Corey and Ad stood beneath the window, Ad against the wall, bracing himself, Corey facing him with about three feet between them, both shouting, "Drop her! Let her go!" Looking upward through the smoke, they saw her feet extending down from the sill, hanging in space, and extended their arms to make the catch, waiting for the shock of first contact. And then, suddenly, she came hurtling downward in a rush. Her feet slipped through Corey's arms and both he and Ad grabbed for her body, enveloped her as the three of them fell to the ground in a single heap.

Corey leaped up and began shouting, "Lyle! Lyle!" but there was no answer, no figure at the window, only the heavy rolls of red-tinted smoke billowing out. Ad was dragging Elizabeth over the stubble by her arms, heard someone say, "Let me help you. I'll take her." It was a young, strong Negro who lifted her and carried her away to safety. There were others now, neighbors who had been attracted by the flames, men and women who stood back and stared at the fire-eaten building. Some followed the man who was carrying the unconscious Elizabeth.

Ad started back to where Corey stood waiting helplessly. Someone grabbed his arm and said, "Don't go back there, mister—" Ad pulled out of the man's grip and said, "Let go. There's a man up there—"

"Oh, my God!" a woman cried.

Flames were shooting upward through the roof when the first piece of fire equipment arrived. A battalion chief's car swung into the parking lot followed by two heavier pieces, including a ladder truck. Hoses were run out, ladders raised and helmeted firemen broke into the lower floor while others negotiated the forward section of the roof. Four armed sheriff's deputies herded the gathering crowds back.

Ad ran to the battalion chief, who pushed him aside with a curt, "Out of the way, friend—"

"There's a man in there, goddam it!" Ad shouted back.

"Where?"

Ad ran back with the chief following. Corey stood back from the building watching the flames leaping outward and upward, with sparks falling all around him. Ad pointed to the burning room and the chief said, "In *there?*" Ad nodded. The chief stared at the window, then at Corey and Ad. "Jesus!" he breathed, then ran back to issue an order to a hose-bearing unit.

A deputy, dodging falling sparks and debris, ran down the right side of the building to where Corey and Ad stood helplessly. "You'll have to move back out of here. For Christ's sake, you want this thing to collapse on you?" When they ignored him, he shouted angrily, "Come on, goddam it, move!"

They turned and walked back slowly, mourning silently. Ad said, "I've got to get to my car and call this in, Corey."

"Sure. Go ahead, Ad. I'll wait here."

When he reached his car, Duke knew he was in a critical situation. He had propelled himself through weeds and across grass and the macadam parking lot on hands and one knee, dragging his wounded left leg behind him, feeling each jolt of excruciating pain driving upward into his upper thigh and groin; but the need to get away was of prime importance. He pulled himself up by the handles of the Jaguar, opened the door and got inside, using his hands to lift his throbbing leg as he slid across the seat. The pain in his kneecap was almost more than he could bear as he gripped it, trying to stem the flow of blood. Below the kneecap, his leg was numb. He found a handkerchief and tried to tie it above his kneecap, but this was more pain than he could stand. He mopped at his knee with the handkerchief, but the blood continued to ooze out.

Becoming aware of the need to get away from here, he reached into his pocket for his car keys, then saw two figures racing toward him across the parking lot.

Quickly, he threw his upper body down and across the front seat, but soon heard their footsteps pass him, running toward the blazing building. He raised himself and watched the men mount the steps, then run to the right and down the side of the structure where the flames were erupting, lighting the area around it. There was the reek of gasoline in his car, coming from the rear compartment where the gas-

782

oline bombs had stood; leakage, no doubt, through the wicks that had hung outside the bottles.

For a moment he was trapped with fascination as flames and smoke billowed up and he thought with satisfaction, "That's one ofay sonofabitch goin'a get paid off. Burn, you bastard, like you been burnin' niggers for years." And watching, he wondered what was left of Banjo's Place. Of ape-faced Banjo. And his gorilla, Hinky.

Gotta get out of here, get to a doc. Jesus. First, my hand, now my knee an' ankle. Wish to Christ I had a shot with me. Wonder if I can get to Peach Alley, find Ivy. No, hell, no. She'll be out on the street, makin' the scene. Better get to my room, get a shot an' worry about the doc later. Got to go see Connie, too, make a deal, but I'll be The Man, take over. Connie, he'll play ball without Banjo aroun'.

Someone else, a man and a woman, were coming across the parking lot and Duke shook himself out of his momentary reverie. He again reached into his trousers pocket for his keys, thinking, So long, you ofay corpse. I like to see Lizabeth's face when she hears about you.

He guided his hand into his left trousers pocket cautiously, shrinking from the pain the movement caused. The keys weren't there. Sweat broke out on his face and he could feel it running down the crease between his well-developed pectoral muscles, not only from the heat, but from fear. He felt again and his fingers touched a pack of cigarettes, a book of matches, the key to his motel cottage attached to an oval of leather. He tried his right pocket and felt a wad of bills, some coins, a small penknife. He leaned forward and jammed his hands into his jacket pockets knowing the keys were not there. He always put them in his left trousers pocket when he got out of the car, a habit of years.

Jesus, Duke prayed. I got to get out of here. I can't walk. He saw the Dodge. The ofay's Dodge. Standing there only a few feet away. An irony, to escape in his victim's car. He slid across the seat again, wincing with pain, opened the door and got out on his right foot, then hopped across the short open space to the Dodge. He tried the door on the driver's side. Locked. He was tempted to hop around to the other side, but reason dictated that a man who locked one door would certainly lock the other. And the effort would cost too much. He could feel the grinding of bone splinters in his kneecap, the wetness of his trouser leg. Where could he have dropped his keys? Wherever it was, he was in no shape to go crawling around looking for them. He thought of trying to creep toward the hedges, burrow into them, use his shirt to bandage his knee and ankle, stem the flow of the blood; beyond the burning building to the old gymnasium where he had learned to box as a youngster, the playground beyond it—plenty of places to hide there, if he could make it. But the car, leaving the car here would place him at the scene, with the stench of gasoline inside— Oh, Christ! Christ Almighty!

Others were coming into the grounds now, running toward the right side of the burning building, shouting, calling to one another. He leaned against the Dodge, trying to decide what to do, and the simple act of holding his left foot off the ground sent knives stabbing into it, telling him, You can't make it, boy. You can't make it.

Then he opened the rear door of the Jaguar and climbed in. He lay across the back seat and eased his left leg inside, then began to pull his shirt from under his jacket, ripping it to make bandages; waiting dejectedly, wearily, and in physical agony, for what must inevitably come.

The fire was contained and the crowd had thinned out. Only a handful remained despite warnings from the deputies that they would be subject to arrest for violation of the curfew law now in effect. They drifted to one side, but remained in a knot, watching as the battalion chief ordered the ladder truck back to the station for further orders, the other pieces to remain until no longer needed. Then the ambulance came and removed the blanket-wrapped figure the firemen had brought down from the upper floor.

Corey looked aside when the ambulance driver and his helper carried the stretcher past him and placed it in the vehicle. Neither man was a doctor or intern. The charred corpse was beyond medical help. He wondered what had become of the girl. Elizabeth. Elizabeth Shackleford. And assumed someone had driven her home.

A police car pulled in and two helmeted figures, begrimed and sweat-stained, got out and began asking questions. The taller of the two walked over to the knot of remaining onlookers and spoke with them, warning them of the curfew restrictions. The group broke up then and drifted out of the Center grounds toward their homes.

The white officer asked Corey for his name and address and why he was here. Reluctantly, he responded.

"You know the deceased?"

"I knew him."

"What was his name, address, anything else you can tell me."

"He was—First Lieutenant Lyle Emerson, U.S. Air Force—"

"The guy who was shot down in Viet Nam?"

Corey glared at the officer and walked away. The officer said, "Look, friend, don't take it out on me."

Adam Cameron came over to the officer then. He identified himself with his press card. "I'll tell you what you want to know, Officer."

"Thanks. What's the matter with him?" he asked, indicating Corey with the tip of his pencil.

"They were buddies over in Viet Nam. Lyle Emerson, occupation, history teacher at Laurelton High, also taught classes here at the Center. Lives at—"

The Negro officer walked over to the Dodge and flashed his light inside, then tried the door. Locked. Corey was leaning against the front fender, smoking a cigarette. "Your car, mister?" the officer asked.

"No. It belongs—belonged to the deceased. Lyle Emerson."

"Friend of yours?"

"Yes."

"I'm sorry." He glanced at the Jaguar. "Do you know who that one belongs to?"

"No."

"Never seen one like it before." He started walking around toward it as Corey said absently, "It's a Jaguar."

"Jag." The officer stopped and reached for the notebook in his shirt pocket. "Jaguar. We got a pickup out for—" He was at the back of it, out of range of Corey's hearing, checking the plate number. New York— "Hey, Walker!" he called out to the white officer. "This is that New York Jaguar we got on the hot list a while ago."

Walker broke off his conversation with Ad and joined the Negro officer at the rear of the Jaguar, then walked around to the side and flashed his light inside, startled by the sight of the man lying on the rear seat. He shifted the flashlight to his left hand, opened the door and put his right hand on his service revolver. "Who are you, boy? What's your name?"

"Buddy Duke."

"You're Duke Shackleford, owner of this car?"

Painfully, but not without some pride, "That's me."

"All right, come out of there, slow-like. Put your hands out in front of you."

"I can't, man. I got a shot-up knee an' ankle."

Then the Negro officer was beside Walker, Ad Cameron behind him. Walker said, "Cuff his hands, Sonny. Watch out, he's a fighter." He shot a beam of light down on

785

Duke's knee and ankle and saw the blood-soaked trousers, the trail of blood on the carpet.

Sonny said, "He can't do anything, the shape he's in." He walked around and got into the car from the other side and frisked Duke. "He's clean."

Walker's head was inside the car, sniffing the air. To Duke, "You been haulin' gasoline in here, boy?"

"Screw you, ofay," Duke replied.

"Looks like you screwed yourself plenty, big shot." To Sonny, "Keep an eye on him while I call for another ambulance and a tow truck. We may have the guy who set this thing off." He went to the police car with Ad Cameron trailing him.

"Boy," Sonny said to Duke, "you only making it tough on yourself, shooting off your mouth like that."

Duke looked up at Sonny with disdain. "An' I don' need no advice from no white nigger, either."

"If I was you, boy, I'd start thinking about who I was going to get it from, because one thing you sure as hell need is some good advice."

Duke looked away angrily. I need me a lawyer, a good lawyer. Maybe Sam—

Ad Cameron went to his car to call his paper, learned that there had been no photographers in contact with the desk. Ad told the desk man to keep trying, and began relaying the story to a rewrite man. Walker came back to the Jaguar. "All right, Sonny, let's get him out of there and into the car. No ambulances available. Impound truck will be here in a couple of minutes." Sonny put his arms around Duke and raised him off the seat while Walker lifted him by the calves of his legs. They rested him on the floor of the car for a moment and Walker said to Sonny, who was still inside, "Reach over and get those keys while you're there, Sonny."

Duke's head snapped up. "What keys?"

"The keys in the ignition lock," Walker replied. "What keys you think I mean?"

Sonny reached across the back seat and removed the keys and when he pulled back, Duke saw them dangling from his hand; the keys he had forgotten, in his hurry, to remove; unable to remember one time since he owned the car, that he had forgotten to take the keys with him when getting out of it. His shoulders began to shake convulsively, sobbing, "Ah, man, man—ah, Jesus—"

The car pulled up in front of the Wallace Street house and Lutie Shackleford came running down the steps as Larry

Powell helped Elizabeth out, still unsteady on her feet, weeping into a handkerchief. Larry thanked the driver, who waved a hand and drove off quickly, hoping to avoid arrest for violating the curfew order. Lutie was sobbing, "Baby, baby, oh, Lord, Lord—" and between them, they got Elizabeth up the steps and into her room and on the bed. She turned over on her face, burrowed into the pillow and wept bitterly. Larry said, "I've got to go now, Mrs. Shackleford, but I'll come back tomorrow some time. She isn't hurt, but it was a real shaky thing."

"Thank you, son. You run along. I'll undress her an' get her to sleep. She'll be all right—"

"Where is Mr. Shackleford?"

"He's at the plant. They brung the whole day shift in tonight just to make sure. We'll be all right."

"Yes, ma'am." Larry went out and started north, hoping to find a prowl car.

They came back across the bridge and went directly to the *Herald* where Corey had left his car. Radio reports indicated that the situation was being slowly contained. In the hour during which the curfew had been in effect, most of the streets on both sides of the bridge were empty, but in West Laurelton small roving groups were still on the prowl and several snipers at work.

Police Chief Durkin had been lavish in his praise of what he called Reverend Amos Hart's Veterans' Brigade, which had contributed much to the police effort to prevent more widespread destruction and looting. The latest figures showed over 300 arrests, excluding the demonstrators held by Sheriff Apperson; 250 injured; 16 known dead, six by gunshot, ten by fire and other causes, including Lyle Emerson, Ben-Joe Nichols, James P. Balter, a sheriff's deputy, Albert Deming, a merchant, George P. Harris, a fireman.

"Come in for a drink, Corey?" Ad asked.

"No, thanks, Ad. I've had it, and you've got a full night ahead of you. On second thought, I'd like to make a call."

"Come on."

In an empty cubicle, Corey dialed the Brookhill number. On the second ring, Drew answered. "Corey! I've been so worried. I've been watching it on television and listening to the radio."

"Did you hear about Lyle Emerson?"

"Yes. I'm so terribly sorry, Corey."

"Well—it's all behind him now."

"Where are you, Corey?"

"At the *Herald*, ready to leave."

787

"Come by, Corey."

"It's close to midnight, Drew."

"I'm wide awake and I'm sure you won't be able to sleep. It might be better for you to talk it out. And I've got something to say."

"All right, I'll call Tish first. I know she'll be worried, too. Then I'll drive out."

"Corey—"

"What?"

"Please hurry."

It was 11:40 when prowl car No. 37, Officers Eckhart and Petry, took another swing through the Ta-Ran parking lot at Avalon and Barrett before taking their midnight coffee break. The stores were dark except for night security lights. In the parking area, only 10 per cent of the lights were on as a normal precautionary measure. Both men were concentrating on the radio chatter that had been constant and exciting most of the night. Eckhart, who was 44 years old and the father of four, considered that he was damned well out of it. All it took was one hothead in a moment of anger and Ellen Eckhart would become a widow with four hungry mouths to feed on a small police pension.

Not so George Petry, who was an energetic 22, single, powerfully built, lived at home and had little on his mind except a redheaded waitress named Carrie Lambert and a souped-up hot rod to support.

"Sounds like it's about over," Petry said with some regret.

"Yeah," Bill Eckhart replied hopefully. "Boys doing a good job. Time the Guard gets here, won't be any use for 'em."

"Well, maybe it'll break loose again tomorrow."

"Could be. These damned things don't end in one day's action."

"Sure—" Petry saw the Volkswagen sitting all alone against the far wall. "Bill, was that VW there last time we came through?"

"I didn't notice. Let's have a look." Eckhart wheeled the car over and parked it broadside to the front of the VW and waited, his motor running. Petry got out, baton in one hand, flashlight in the other. He held the light up to the window on the driver's side and pushed the door lever forward. Locked. He saw the figure of the sleeping Negro lying across the seat. Petry rapped the end of his baton against the window and saw the Negro's eyes blink, stare up into the bright light and turn away. He pushed himself upward as Petry called out to him. "Open up, boy."

Booker Dance could not see the man behind the beam of light, but recognized the familiar voice of authority. At that moment, he had forgotten the three bottles of gasoline that were standing in the cardboard carton on the floor behind the seat. He rolled the window down about three inches and said, "Put that thing out, man. You blindin' me."

Petry turned the light to one side, but kept it on. "All right, boy, open up and come on out."

"What for? I'n doin' nothin'. I got tired an' took me a little sleep, is all."

"I said come on out," Petry replied more firmly. "Or do you want me to bust this window and haul you out?"

"Man, go 'way, f'Chrissakes. What'm I doin' wrong?"

"That's what I'm going to find out. Let's move it, boy."

Booker reached for the handle and came fully awake, now remembering the cargo he was carrying. "Look, mister," he said, "lemme alone. I didn' do nothin', I ain't doin' nothin'. All's I want to do is go home."

Petry shot the beam toward Eckhart, rotating it to attract his attention. Eckhart got out of the prowl car and joined his young partner. "What's up?"

"This burrhead won't get out of his car."

Eckhart leaned close to the window and said, "You got just five seconds to open up or have your window broken. If we have to smash it, we take you in for resisting arrest. One —two—"

Booker had no choice. They were both on the same side of the car. He could open the other door and run, but they had guns.

"—three—four—" Petry had the baton raised.

"I'm comin'." Booker opened the door and got out.

"Face against the car, hands over the top, legs spread—"

Resignedly, "I know. I been there before."

"I'll bet by God you have," Petry said and began frisking him. Eckhart leaned through the open door, flashed his light over the front compartment, aimed the beam at the back, then along the floor. He reached into the carton and lifted one of the bottles, which had been wrapped in rags to prevent breakage while driving. There was little need to sniff at its penetrating odor.

"Cuff him, George. Quick."

Booker started to turn, but Petry called out, "Hold it!" and jammed the end of his baton into Booker's spine, driving him against the car, whimpering with pain. Or the utter fruitlessness of his life. "Hands together behind your back," Petry ordered.

With mounting dejection, Booker removed his hands

789

from the top of the car. As he dropped them to his side, he turned and lashed out at Petry, catching him flush on the jaw and throwing him off balance. Petry fell and Booker took off, making for the police car. Caught by surprise, Eckhart had the bottle in one hand, his flashlight in the other, but George Petry had rolled over, drawn his service revolver. Eckhart leaped backward, out of the line of fire. Petry sighted in on Booker's back and fired. Booker staggered and fell against the side of the police car and hung there. Petry got off another shot that plowed a furrow up the seat of Booker's trousers.

"Hold it, George, that's enough!" Eckhart shouted, and ran toward Booker as he was sliding down to the ground.

"Oh, you lousy—ofay—mother—all I done—I fell asleep." Those were Booker Dance's last conscious words.

At 11:30 P.M., Durkin and LaSalle concluded a curbside conference in front of the Walter Lynch Building at Velie and Porter, scorched but otherwise unharmed. Where Pearson's, the Blue Front and Dubner's Drug Store had stood, nothing remained but the outer shells, burned mountains of rubble, with roof timbers lying or hanging at idiotic angles. Smoke and occasional sparks flew out of the tangle as firemen continued to play streams of water over the unrecognizable rubbish. All around them were piles of household possessions which had been hurriedly carried from nearby houses, and despite the curfew order, sad and weeping owners and their young guarded their meager goods: bedding, television sets, radios, furniture, dishes, clothing.

Occasionally, a man or woman came up to the two officers to ask, "What do we *do*? Where can we *go*? We didn't have no part in this, Mister Durkin." And Durkin would reply, "You get through tonight somehow. In the morning, if we've got things under control, we'll see what we can do. It gets too cold out here, go over to the African Baptist Church. Reverend Hart's opened it up for everybody who got burned out. Got food there, coffee, mattresses to sleep on."

"What *are* we going to do, Lee?" LaSalle asked.

Durkin snorted. "All the planning we did, we didn't give anything like this a thought. Last count I had from Hobbs, a total of a hundred and ten houses burned out. Could affect three-four hundred people. Thirty-two commercial buildings. You got a late casualty check, Pete?"

"Latest I had about twenty minutes ago, over three hundred arrests, sixteen known dead, about two hundred injured. No estimate on money value of the damage. That

790

doesn't include the people Will Apperson hauled off to the County Fair Grounds."

"Apperson." The name ground out between Durkin's teeth. "Pete, you keep an eye out here. It's—" checking his watch—"eleven thirty-two. The Guard is due at the Fair Grounds at midnight. I think I'll go over and have a little talk with Will."

Durkin went to his car where Lloyd Cooper and Les Williams lounged on the front seat and Sergeant Tony Shattuck stood waiting on the curb.

"Lloyd, Les," Shattuck warned. Both men sat up and adjusted their helmets. Shattuck opened the rear door for Durkin and got in behind him. "Where to, sir?" Cooper asked.

"Fair Grounds. As fast as you can make it without lights or siren."

They were there by 11:50 and Durkin found Apperson seated in a chair on the porch of the Fair Administration Building which faced a chain link fence enclosure, now topped with barbed wire, behind which there were close to 200 milling, angry, shouting Negroes, most of them in their teens. Outside the enclosure, armed deputies and snarling sentry dogs were patrolling. On Durkin's arrival, the shouting increased and Durkin, after a brief look toward them, went up the steps of the Administration Building. Apperson grinned, turned the volume of his transistorized short-wave radio down, but did not stand up. He called to a deputy, "Sam, get the chief a chair out here."

Durkin said, "All right, Will, turn 'em loose. Get your trucks in here and take 'em back to town."

"You're in the county now, Lee. We're out of your jurisdiction," Apperson replied, still grinning.

"You know goddam well you made an illegal wholesale arrest that won't stand up for a minute, Will."

"That ain't for you to decide, Lee. You want 'em out find yourself a judge to issue a writ."

"I'll do better than that. Turn 'em loose or I'll call in every newspaper, radio and television man—"

"They been tryin' to get in all night, Lee. Didn't you see 'em down at the gate?"

"I saw 'em, and I'll use 'em. I'll go back down there and make a statement you'll never live down."

"Best vote-getting job anybody could do for me, Lee. I'd purely appreciate it."

"Will, I promise you that by tomorrow you may be a hero to the hardnosed Ku Kluxers and white supremacy boys, but you won't get a cent's worth of support anywhere else. Not from Taylor, Warren, not a solitary Negro, and I'll personally campaign against you."

Apperson stood up and hitched his belt a notch tighter around his belly. "You're talkin' mighty big, mister."

"I'm through talking, Will. Let those people out and truck 'em back to town or I'll make your name a curse word in the whole county and all over the state. I'll have witnesses to back me up and I'll go you one better than that. I'll run one of my people against you and beat you next June. You got five minutes to make up your mind."

Durkin turned and went back to his car. Apperson went inside the building. Three minutes later, the County Roads trucks began wheeling up to the wire enclosure. The gates were opened and the shouting, singing Negroes climbed aboard for the ride back to town. Apperson did not reappear and Durkin watched until the last of the trucks pulled away.

"Where to, Chief?" Lloyd Cooper asked.

"Wait right here. The Guard is due any minute," Durkin replied. "Smoke up if you boys like."

A few minutes past midnight, Colonel Wesley Slater and his National Guard troops arrived from Camp Fitch. The gates were opened and the jeep-led trucks rolled into the Fair Grounds, debarked and moved into the buildings set aside for the troops as newsmen, photographers, radio and television men crowded around. Tom Cameron arrived and went into immediate conference with Slater, Durkin and Apperson. After a 15-minute appraisal of the situation, during which the Mayor and Sheriff firmly insisted that the Guard unit be sent into West Laurelton at once, Slater heard Durkin's equally insistent opposition: that to do so would incite the extremist fringe, temporarily dormant, to come out of hiding and gamble on their ally, darkness, to help inflict death on the inexperienced reservists who, by their very numbers, would become easy targets.

Slater stated that his orders were to cooperate with the law enforcement authority, but use his own judgment to prevent bloodshed and do nothing to aggravate the situation. He finally sided with Durkin. Apperson appealed the decision, but Durkin was adamant and insisted that with the curfew in effect, the situation was reasonably under control and unless violence erupted when the curfew would end at six A.M., he did not want the Guard to make an appearance on the streets of Laurelton. Cameron gave in, then Apperson. Slater gave the order for his Guardsmen to turn in and get as much sleep as they could.

Durkin returned to his headquarters and found Inspector

LaSalle waiting for him with the news that Duke Shackleford had been booked on charges of suspicion of narcotics possession and use, two counts of arson, one count of first degree murder (Ben-Joe Nichols) and one count of voluntary manslaughter (Lyle Emerson). Shackleford's wounds had been treated and he was asleep in a cell in the basement.

"Statement?" Durkin asked.

"Nothing that can be repeated or printed. He wants a lawyer."

"What have we got on him?"

"Omar Liggett, alias Hinky, one of Nichols' men who was witness to the bombing of Banjo's Place. He's still alive at General, and under close guard. He made a statement, accusing Shackleford. Dr. Betts is hopeful that Liggett may make it, but there's some doubt. Duke was found at the scene of the Center fire, his car stained with gasoline—"

"That's not too much to go on, Pete. Liggett's statement, though—"

"Maybe not, Lee, but in another eight or ten hours, that monkey he's got on his back is going to start crying to be fed."

"Yeah. Well, we'll see."

"Powell fingered Boley Carter as the man Banjo Nichols was paying off. That confirms some suspicions Jim Price has had. I'm going to throw a suspension and charges at Carter tomorrow. Jim thinks that will start Carter talking. Lee?"

"What?"

"Would I be out of line if I made a policy suggestion?"

"You'd be out of line if you didn't. What's on your mind?"

"This riot. It's very possible that it might be a blessing in disguise, one we could make good use of—"

"What?"

"I mean it, Lee. The best time to start a meaningful movement is when you've got no other way to go except up. If we can get the reasonable people on both sides together while this thing is fresh in mind, it's logical to assume they might reach some obvious conclusions. If they can, Cameron, the City Council and County Commissioners will have the pressure on them to get some real action started toward some progress instead of a lot of talk. With the press, Taylor, Warren, Hart, Betts and other responsible citizens working together—"

Durkin listened and thought, There's always a beginning and never an end. Wayne is no Jonas Taylor and Theodore is sure as hell no Anderson Warren, but even Pete knows that no matter what or how little, you've got to keep trying. They won't do it willingly, that's for sure, but if we keep pushing hard enough, maybe they'll make some kind of a start, and that's about all we can hope for.

He said, "Pete, it sounds good. It's been a long time since we had a Taylor active in politics. Maybe he's ready for it. I'll talk to Wayne as soon as I can find him. And if I can, I'll try to get Johnny Curran's feet wet, too. He's an old Angeltowner like me. That Armour boy, like as not, will marry the Warren girl. He's a vet and he's lost a buddy tonight. That could help, too. Not just the money, but— Ah, what the hell. We'll try it because it's the only thing we've got left to try. You talk to Nora tonight?"

"I not only talked to her, I saw her about an hour ago for about ten minutes."

"Saw her? Where?"

"Laurelton Memorial. A seven-pound three-ounce girl."

"Girl? Wouldn't you know it? Knocks my police recruitment program all to hell."

The direct line to the 12th Precinct flashed and Durkin answered, listened, then said, "Thanks, Jim. I'll be here if you want me. LaSalle will be sleeping at Laurelton Memorial tonight if you want him, but don't call him unless it's an absolute emergency." He hung up and grinned at LaSalle. "Ninety per cent quiet and the other ten per cent folding. All fires out or under control. A few snipers got away, but if we can hold it there, we can get rid of the Guard and Apperson's men. We've got Hart's Veteran Brigade working on our side, and that's something we'll have to encourage.

"Pete, got to hell out of here and over to Memorial. I don't want to see you for another twenty-four hours unless I call you personally. And give Nora a kiss for me, and Nora, Junior a pat on the behind from her godfather."

On his way out, LaSalle turned at the door and said, "I'll kiss Nora for you, but you'll have to pat Miss LaSalle's behind for yourself. And only until she's three."

CHAPTER VIII

1

On Saturday morning the city began to emerge and take stock of its wounds and the damage. In West Laurelton, it began at six o'clock when the curfew ended. They came out of their houses quietly, looking about them cautiously, first at the overhead blanket of smoke, then up and down the streets to make sure there were no armed police to order them back inside. Beyond the affected area, there were few signs of the havoc they had seen the night before along Grand Avenue and Velie Street, the horror in the faces of friends and neighbors as they watched the fez-wearers racing through alleys and side streets to avoid police, seeking to burn, loot and destroy. They came for another reason: to search for sons and daughters who had not returned home after the curfew had gone into effect.

And converged on the prime area of devastation, as if drawn by a magnet, to view the debris and ashes of ruined buildings, fire-gutted houses, and those untouched except for smashed windows. The streets were a litter of tangled fire hoses, scorched brick, blackened lumber, and incredible heaps of glass, paper, cartons and boxes; odds and ends of looted merchandise that had been dropped or discarded as too heavy, useless or valueless; chairs, sofas, bureaus, china-ware, smashed television sets, major appliances, men's and women's wearing apparel, odd shoes, broken cash registers, scales; items of hardware and tools, fresh and canned food-stuffs, beer and whiskey bottles; a crushed guitar, a set of drums with heads slashed open, dress store mannikins, cheap jewelry items and all manner of interesting junk to be picked up, pored over, carried off or discarded.

Inside a roped-off area, a single brick wall collapsed and became part of the rubble that lay strewn at its feet and across the pavement, all that remained of Woody's Tavern and the four apartments above it, sending clouds of dust and smoke upward in rolling billows. Firemen were still pouring streams of water into small mountains of smolder-ing timbers and helmeted, red-eyed police wearily called out

795

warnings to the people to keep out of the roped-off areas. Young and old, the curious walked along the middle of the streets, gaping in awe and sorrow at the destruction of once-familiar structures.

Even the young, many who had taken an active part in the action the night before, seemed subdued in daylight. On some corners, fez-topped young men and women looked on with a certain defiant pride and arrogance as baton-carrying police moved silently, warily past, ignoring them. Generally, the face of Angeltown was one of peaceful innocence, but few doubted that by nightfall it could all happen again.

Among the viewers were some who pointed to the devastation and placed the blame firmly upon Mist' Whitey and Mist' Charley, charged the police with brutality, and a plot by white authority to starve the Negroes out by destroying their homes and food sources, burning them out of their businesses in order to force them out of the state, or back into slavery. In an atmosphere of such confusion, many were ready to accept the accusations as reasonable.

"Keep moving! Keep moving!"

They moved along among strange, nightmarish sights.

"Look, Mama, Miz Hadley's house—" A hushed silence, then, "I see it, honey. I see it." "My God, Gabe, that's Henry Hall's grocery store!" "Yeah. Ain't much left of it now." And seeing, would remember these further injustices and iniquities of white against black.

They saw some of their own, black men in police uniforms; others who wore ordinary clothes and police helmets; walking the streets in pairs, urging children to stay out of the wrecked buildings, now attractive for exploration, places to find endless treasures. Men carried shelving from wrecked buildings to board up their own smashed windows and doors. A boy of ten discovered a trumpet buried among a pile of sodden garments and began blowing into its mouthpiece, emitting raucous noises. In front of several establishments which had been untouched, owners and their families stood guard to prevent further looting. From somewhere came the sound of music, a record-player blared out, *Nobody knows the trouble I've seen—*

They moved past the shells of Pearson's, Dubner's and Blue Front, the scorched, but otherwise unharmed Lynch Building, past row after row of empty, fire-scorched stores and taverns, the wrecked lobby of the Goldfield Theater, past Banjo's Place, its inside gutted, its huge neon sign a tangle of wires and molten glass. And wherever fire had struck, piles of furniture, bedding and other family posses-

796

sions heaped in the center of the street where owners had piled it and now stood guard against pilferers.

There were Whiteys among the parade of the curious, some store-owners and merchants who had been the first to taste black anger, mournfully surveying the wreckage; believing now that despite years of coexistence, the theory that blacks and whites could live and work together amicably was impossible. The insured had some small hope, the uninsured none at all; for the latter, it was all gone, the work of years wiped away in a few hours of fury and terror.

Other whites who lived on the west side of the bridge came out of curiosity, parked their cars outside the restricted area and walked among, but not with, the Negroes, in solemn awe at the havoc wrought in blind anger born of frustration, despair and a need for revenge.

The only moving vehicles were those belonging to the police and fire departments. Bus service had been partially resumed, but had been routed outside the affected area. Few day workers would report for work in East Laurelton's white homes today, and not many more store or shop workers would show up on their jobs across the bridge. It was a day to see, talk, wonder about tomorrow, and what would come of the debacle; a day to find food stores that were still doing business, to commiserate with the homeless, count the dead and injured.

At the West Laurelton General Hospital, those with minor wounds and injuries were discharged to make room for more serious cases that continued to come in. The accident room, hallways and waiting rooms overflowed with patients not yet attended, with two operating rooms busy since 8:30 the night before. To Dr. Royal Betts, it was a World War II and Korean field hospital all over again.

The 12th Precinct was the scene of the greatest turmoil, its cells filled to above normal capacity, the overflow clamoring in the guarded parking compound, the streets surrounding it tangled with cars and milling crowds seeking missing sons and daughters, wives and husbands, crying, cursing with rage. Inside, beleaguered officers and civilian clerks labored over mountains of paperwork to process those in custody and new arrivals, harassed by angry parents, relatives, attorneys and bail bondsmen. Bail for those accused of burglary and looting had been set at $2,500, for which a fee of 10%, plus the cost of $50 for a writ, was necessary. Few could come up with the required $300. The city attorney sought to deny bail on any felony charge in order to keep known offenders off the streets. Courts were open and every available judge had been pressed into service.

797

Every person entering the 12th Precinct was searched for weapons and this created storms of angry protest, "treatin' us like criminals just because we come to look for our people, try to get 'em out." The searchers found no weapons, nor had they expected to find any, but the order stood. There were others who accepted the indignity, understanding that under the circumstances, the police could hardly do less and must do what they had been ordered to do.

There were floods of complaints that officers had deliberately fired into Negro-owned business houses outside the riot area, only because windows had been soaped with the words, BLOOD, BLOOD BROTHER, or NEGRO-OWNED. Irate parents brought children in with bruises and bandaged cuts, charging that these had been inflicted by police.

Reports of the cumulative damage to property, coming from newspaper, television, radio and police sources, varied and were approximate or inaccurate guesses, but the consensus was that the total would run well over one million, perhaps as much as two million dollars. There was a report that Mayor Cameron had called the Governor and asked that Laurelton be declared a disaster area. Meanwhile, the National Guard remained on the alert at the Fair Grounds against the eventuality of a further outbreak on Saturday night, a promising possibility as the temperature rose into the 70s and the day became heavily humid. Nor did it help matters when the demonstrators who had been out of the "action" were released from the Fair Grounds by Apperson, and returned to West Laurelton in a mood for vengeance.

A citywide ban was placed on the sale of all liquor and beer, and all bars and taverns were ordered to remain closed until Monday. Police radios crackled out messages of scattered resistance and disturbances. "Two men on roof of store at 23rd and Mercer, suspected of having arms. Approach with caution. . . . Looting reported at 242 Prince Street. . . . Report two men on Division Street in gray Ford sedan, heading south toward Riverside, suspected of looting. . . . Group of white youths armed with bike chains loitering in the vicinity of Division and Washington Deadline. . . ."

In East Laurelton, most of the commercial establishments were open for Saturday business, but there were few cars in the shopping area. Police cruised the downtown streets, trying not to take notice of the groups of men who had gathered on corners and parking lots close to the east end of the bridge, undoubtedly armed and waiting for something, any incident, to send them into action. There was not one Negro abroad in "white country." Almost every large

798

store had hired extra help to guard against sudden attack. Nor was it surprising that most people remained close to their homes, not too far away from a rifle or shotgun.

2

Sam Shackleford sensed something wrong the moment he entered the house at six o'clock after spending the entire night at the Warren plant in charge of guarding the warehouse and garage areas against invasion by vandals. Lutie was in the kitchen, head down on folded arms on the table, fully clothed and asleep. He put one hand on her shoulder lightly. "Lutie," he said softly.

She came awake with a start and her arm almost swept a coffee-stained mug from the table. "Sam? Oh, Sam. You all right?"

"I'm all right. We had a couple little run-ins. They th'owed a few fire bombs over the fence from cars, but didn' do no harm. We put 'em out fast."

Lutie stood up wearily. "I'll put a light under the coffee, get you somethin' to eat."

"I'll do it. You rest yourself." He went to the stove and put a match to the burner beneath the coffeepot, then returned to the table. "Ain't you been to bed at all?"

"I got some sleep. A little—"

"Lizabeth sleepin'?"

"She's sleepin'."

He caught the strange, quiet note in Lutie's voice, a subdued alarm, and studied her face for a moment. "What happen, Lutie?"

"Drink your coffee first. Lemme fix you some—"

He put out a hand and clasped it around her wrist and held her in the chair. "Lutie, what happen? Is Lizabeth all right?"

"She'll be all right, Sam. It's Duke." Her voice cracked as she mentioned the name.

"Duke? All right, Lutie, tell me."

She began telling him, weeping as she talked of Elizabeth's close brush with death; that after bringing her home in a hysterical state, Larry Powell had gone out somewhere and returned with some sleeping pills for her. He had come back sometime after 4:30 to break the news about Duke to her.

Sam heard Lutie out in stoic silence and when she finished, he got up and went to Elizabeth's room where she slept heavily under sedation. He knelt beside the bed and kissed her. "I wish you could sleep through this whole thing, baby," he whispered tenderly. "Lord help all of us."

When he came out of her room, he could hear Lutie moving around in the kitchen, preparing his breakfast. He went to the bathroom and washed up, then began to put on his white shirt, necktie and black Sunday suit. In the kitchen, Lutie was frying bacon. She looked up puzzled when he came in. "Sam, you eat somethin' an' go to sleep. You been up all night."

"I got things to do, Lutie."

"What c'n you do half-past six in the mornin'?"

"I c'n go to the jail an' see what I can do for Duke, what he needs. Then I c'n go see who I c'n find to help us. I don' know who or what good it do, but we got to try."

"We got to try," Lutie repeated blankly.

"How come," Sam asked, "Larry Powell know all about Duke? Was he workin' in Banjo's Place when it happen?"

"No. He find out at the police station later, after he leave here. When he came back again, he told me he been a policeman all the time, doin' detective work. Gettin' kicked out of school, that was part of it." Hopefully, "Sam, maybe Larry c'n help—"

"I'll try, Lutie. Everything I can. Maybe Mist' Armour—"

"They'll send him to Parkton, won't they?"

"Guess so."

"They kill your brother Matt up there."

"I know. Lutie, listen. If Duke kill Banjo an' that other man dies, if he had somethin' to do with that white man gettin' burned in the Center, you know he got to pay for it. We get him some help, maybe he get off with a prison sentence. He's strong. Maybe he come out alive some day. What he almost did to Lizabeth, well—maybe we c'n forgive him that, too, some day."

Lutie was weeping openly. "Our Duke. He try so hard when he only a boy. Workin' at Clark's, his newspaper route— I 'member the time your leg was broke—"

"I know, Lutie. I know. It was another time an' he was another boy then. Somethin' happen, I don't rightly know what, or whose fault it was. I'll go see what I can do now. You look after the baby."

"Baby," Lutie sobbed. "Lord, Lord, I wish they'd stayed babies. I wish—"

Larry Powell returned a little after nine o'clock. Elizabeth was fast asleep, Lutie's eyes still glazed with fear, apprehension and lack of sleep.

"I came by to see if you needed anything," he said.

"There are a few stores still open and one of the supermarkets is getting a lot of new stock brought in."

"I don't know, Larry. I need some things—I can't think. I don't know where Sam is, uptown somewhere seein' what he can do to help Duke. He'll be wantin' to talk to you."

"I'll be around. Let me make a list and get you the things you need. It'll take some time getting through the crowds. I'm not working today or tomorrow."

In the kitchen, Lutie sat down and began to recite automatically the few items she knew were in short supply while Larry listed them in a small notebook. When she stopped, he looked up and said, "Don't worry about Elizabeth, Mrs. Shackleford. She'll be all right. It will take a little while, but she'll come through fine."

"It's Duke, Larry. He's in bad trouble."

"I know. Maybe a good lawyer will be able to help some. Maybe."

"Oh, Lord, Lord," she prayed. "Look down on my poor boy an' do somethin', somethin'—"

3

In Laurelton, the emergency meeting called for nine o'clock by Mayor Tom Cameron was attended by all invited. In the City Council chambers were gathered the members of that body, five County Commissioners, members of the Laurelton Civil Rights Committee, with the exceptions of Police Chief Durkin and Dr. Royal Betts. At their usual desks sat the Council members, with chairs brought in from a conference room to seat the County Commissioners. Facing them were Wayne Taylor, Reverend Wyatt Miller, John Curran and former Mayor Max Hungerford, representing the white members of the Civil Rights Committee, and Reverend Amos Hart, Henry Clark, and Walter Lynch, representing the Negro community.

Mayor Cameron entered and the buzz of conversation ended. Before seating himself, he announced, "I've just spoken to the Governor and assured him that the rioting and fires have been brought under control, but that we will keep the Guard unit at the Fair Grounds in the event something else sets it off again. Gentlemen, I will make a statement of assessment before the general discussion begins."

Barred from the council chambers, the corps of newsmen and members of the electronic media, their ranks swelled by representatives of AP, UPI, CBS, NBC, ABC, the news weeklies and independents from within and outside the state, waited impatiently in the too-small press room and hallways. Soon, many of the photographers and television crews were dispatched with a handful of reporters to gather interviews and background material not yet covered.

At 10:30 A.M. the Warren Company plane arrived from Atlanta with Theodore Warren and Kenneth Armour. Aware of the violence by press and radio reports, Armour ordered the pilot to circle the scene of activity, but with other planes and helicopters brought in by the more enterprising news media, the larger Warren plane was forced to fly at a level too high for its passengers to get more than a glimpse through the smoke and overcast. They landed in South Laurelton and were driven to their homes in Company cars.

Corey was asleep when Jemmy came up to tell him that Kenneth was on his way home from the airport in South Laurelton. At eleven, he was dressed and on his way downstairs when Kenneth arrived.

"Hello, Dad," Corey greeted with extended hand. "Glad to see you back safe. Have your breakfast yet?"

"Very early, and I'm famished. Join me?"

"I haven't had mine yet. Jemmy woke me a little while ago."

Tish bustled in to welcome Kenneth back while Jemmy took his briefcase, hat and topcoat. In the dining room, Tish poured coffee and announced that breakfast would be on the table in exactly one minute. The newspaper lay on the table beside Kenneth's place and after a brief glance at the eight-column headline and single photograph that filled the upper half of the front page, asked, "Was it as bad as the reports we've been getting by radio and in the Atlanta papers? We passed by the plant. There was no damage there, but the smoke was hanging over everything."

"It was bad enough. Like having a nightmare while awake. I can't begin to describe what it was like over there."

"You were in it?"

"Only a small part of it. I went over with Ad Cameron. Dad, Lyle Emerson was killed last night, trapped in the fire at the Center."

"Oh, Lord! I'm terribly sorry, Corey. I know how hard that must have hit you." A moment of silence passed. "Did you say the Center? How in God's name could they burn down something that has done so much for them?"

"It's absolutely crazy, of course. It was just one building, fortunately, administration and some classrooms. The two-storied one. Everything else is safe. The damnedest thing, all of it, the last I'd expect to see here in this country. Fires raging out of control, people simply running wild, screaming, laughing, cursing, looting. I've seen mobs before, in Viet Nam, but this was hysterical insanity, kids only eight and nine years old hauling liquor, food, useless junk, anything that wasn't nailed down. Teen-agers running amok, some older people trying to control them. Dad?"

"What?"

"Shackleford. I remember a Shackleford who worked in one of the Warren plants."

"You must mean Sam Shackleford, a warehouse and shipping foreman. He's been with the Company for years. A good man." Apprehensively, "What about him?"

"It was his son. Duke. Buddy Duke, the fighter—"

"I didn't know he had a son. A daughter, I think. What about the son?"

"He was the one who set the fire at the Center that killed Lyle."

"Are you sure, Corey?"

"The police are. He was caught at the scene. The details are in the paper. They've booked him on two counts of arson, one on suspicion of murder, one on attempted murder, and in Lyle's case, voluntary manslaughter." He told Kenneth what he had read in the earlier edition of the *Herald,* of what had happened at Banjo's Place, what he personally knew of the Center fire and Duke's capture, except for Lyle's involvement with Elizabeth Shackleford and that they had been together at the time.

Kenneth said, "Corey, I know how you must feel about Lyle Emerson, but I'll have to do everything I can to give Sam Shackleford what help he needs, get him an attorney to represent his son if he asks it."

"I—" Corey broke off abruptly.

"Corey, he's entitled to everything the law allows. That's the kind of law my father and his father practiced, the kind I would want to practice and would expect you to practice."

"I understand, Dad."

"I won't offer my own services, of course. I've been out of that sort of thing for too long, but by tradition and policy, the Company will help in any way it can. It was one of Anderson Warren's firmest—"

"I said I understand, Dad. What happened in New York?"

Jemmy poured more coffee and began removing dishes. "The best I can say about New York is that we're very hopeful. We've got some help from a rather unexpected
803

source, but I'm not at liberty to reveal what it is. Privileged, a sort of gentleman's agreement, although the gentleman in this case happens to be a very unusual lady. We may know something more definite in a week or ten days."

"And the Baltimore and Richmond stops?"

Kenneth pursed his lips into a half smile. "An unknown quantity. There was a lot of hedging without anything definite, so we must assume that Chase has been doing a good bit of homework with his cousins."

"I'll be pulling for you."

"Thanks. I don't suppose anything has happened with your Shadow Hills project."

"No. Too many more important things are afoot at the moment. There's an emergency combined City Council-County Commission-Civil Rights meeting going on at the City Hall right now. Everybody's busy locking stables now that the horses are out."

"I don't know what the implications are, Corey, but we've all got to become seriously involved in this problem. Not only the rebuilding, but the causes that must be eliminated. We can't continue to live with a gun at each other's heads. Theodore and I were discussing that subject on the way up from Atlanta. I'm particularly upset about the Center."

"So am I and lots of others. Ad intends to start a rebuilding campaign aimed at the general public, with a lot of heavy pressure on the mayor, council and commissioners. Last night after I got back, I went out to Brookhill to see Drew. Most of what we talked about was what we, as individuals, could do to help eliminate the causes. She's very determined to become involved."

"Good for her. She could become very influential."

"Even politically dangerous, to hear her ideas. I think Anderson Warren would have been proud if he could have heard her last night. Drew is ready to ask some embarrassing questions of what she calls 'our fearless leaders,' which include the church, business and industry."

"For instance?"

"Well, why should our elected officials be housed in multimillion-dollar civic buildings with every possible convenience and luxury when they refuse, or are unable to come up with, solutions to the housing problems of the people who pay to keep them in office. One solution is to move them out into warehouse buildings and make them work there until they come up with some practical answers. And other answers like why must minority groups pay more for lower grade meats, foods and other basic goods? Also, the

804

phantom charges that are written into most credit contracts that keep them perpetually broke. And many more injustices that are separate from the financial. We were discussing the potential voting power of the Negro population in Cairn County alone and statistically, at least, there's enough latent power to make every public official sit up and take notice, or be voted out of quite a number of offices if these people begin voting in blocs."

"Statistically, perhaps," Kenneth said, "but what about actual practice?"

"Not yet, of course, but if last night's anger can be channeled in that direction, even the white community can be awakened to the need for readjustments, or be prepared to see a realignment in the political structure. It's only reasonable to realize that it will come in time."

"You're beginning to make sounds like a politician," Kenneth said.

"It's a tempting thought."

"Very interesting. We've never had an Armour who was active in politics. It might be something to think about."

"I haven't given it that much serious thought yet. And Dad?"

"What?"

"There's one more thing. Drew and me. It's official now. All we have to agree on is the date."

Kenneth's head jerked upward with a broad smile. "Congratulations, son. I'm very happy for both of you."

"Thank you." Corey stood up. "Would you mind if I run out on you, Dad? I've got an errand to take care of."

Corey parked his Thunderbird at the curb and went up the walk to the porch. He rang the bell and waited for a few moments and was about to ring a second time when the door opened and he saw her for the first time in years, although he had spoken to her on the phone the day before he arrived from Washington.

Shana Pierce stepped back a pace in surprise. "Hello, Corey," she said in a low, soft voice.

"May I come in, Shana?"

"Of course. I'm sorry. I wasn't expecting—anyone." She opened the door to admit him. "Don't look around too closely," she said, making conversation. "My maid hasn't been in since the trouble started. Horrible, isn't it? I was glued to my television set most of yesterday and last night. Would you like some coffee?"

"If you'll have some with me."

"I overslept and have just finished breakfast, but I'll take a second cup. Please sit down, Corey."

She went to the back of the house, not entirely at ease. Corey sat in a chair in the living room, very definitely a man's chair; deep, maroon leather, matching ottoman, beside a leather-topped octagonal-shaped table; and Corey wondered how many times over how many years Kenneth's body had rested in this chair he now occupied. Shana was as handsome as he remembered her from years back, still youthful and shapely, belying her years. Instinctively, he tried to compare her to his memory of Caddy, but failed because he could not imagine them together.

Shana was wearing a pair of white slacks, an article of clothing Caddy had never succumbed to. Over the slacks, she wore a loose matching tunic with a modest V-neck and short sleeves. Where it ended just below her waistline, the tunic was edged in a gold metallic band which was duplicated at the V and edges of the sleeves. Her bare feet were thrust into a pair of open white sandals with thin, golden straps. She returned with two cups of coffee on a tray, placed it on the octagonal table and sat in a club chair that almost faced him. "Well, Corey," she said, "if one is permitted to use coffee to make a toast, here is to your return and happiness."

"Thank you, Shana," Corey replied. "And to yours."

She smiled and said, "I haven't been anywhere."

"I meant your happiness."

The smile faded only a little. "I wish I could believe you mean that."

"I do, Shana, sincerely. If you've been wondering why I called on you this morning, you know now."

"Corey——" she began, then, "Does your father know about this, your coming to see me?"

"No. He got home about three-quarters of an hour ago. This is something I've been building up to for several days. Last night I was determined not to put it off any longer."

Shana was looking down into her coffee cup and she held it up between her hands now, her eyes suspiciously moist. "Why, Corey?" she asked. "Why now?"

"Because I understand a lot of things better than I did before I left here. Dad, you, myself. And because I know that everyone has a right to happiness if he has the capacity for it. Unfortunately, there are some who never had that capacity, who never will have it. I loved my mother and I was always closer to her than I was to Dad. Perhaps, in some way, it was arranged that way. I don't know. What I realize now is that for some reason, my mother had never been a

806

happy girl and couldn't become a happy woman. Whatever it was, I can't begrudge my father the happiness you've given him.

"He told me you and he were planning to marry and I suspect I am the reason it hasn't happened sooner. For that, I'm sorry. What I came here to say is that I hope you will feel free to do so whenever you wish, and that we'll be good friends."

Shana put her cup down and stood up quickly. "Corey— I—I—" She turned and left the room, but returned after a few moments, more composed. "Thank you, Corey," she said. "If you'll pardon the choice of words, I think you're a hell of a man and I wish you were my own son, I'm that proud of you."

Now Corey stood up, flushed with embarrassment. "I've told Dad I'd like you to have the house as a wedding gift from me. I meant it, and hope you will accept. I can't think of a nicer place for me to visit from time to time."

"And what about you, Corey? Where would you live?"

He grinned. "I've got plans of my own."

"You're not thinking of leaving Laurelton, are you?"

"No. You'll hear about it soon, but the house isn't included in my plans. Besides, I don't know how Dad could get along without Tish and Jemmy."

If Kenneth had ever mentioned or hinted anything about the house to Shana, she showed no sign or indication of it. She said, "Thank you, Corey. I don't think I need tell you how much I love and admire Kenneth—"

"As much, I'm sure, as I suspect he loves and admires you."

"And thank you for that. Corey, would it be proper for me to kiss my stepson-to-be?"

"I'm sure it would be perfectly legal, proper, and for me, enjoyable." She embraced and kissed him. "Thank you, Shana," he said with a smile. "I think my father is a very lucky man."

The telephone rang. "If that's Dad, this never happened. Promise?"

"Promise." She went to the telephone and answered. "Good morning, darling. When did you get back?" She nodded to Corey. He waved a hand in response, picked up his hat and let himself out.

The emergency meeting began with Mayor Cameron's opening speech, followed by County Commission Chairman Miles Crump, then Bryce Henderson, president of the City Council. Other members of the commission and council took turns expressing their views, opinions and concerns; and by noon, not a single suggestion had been put forth which was not keyed to the need for massive federal and state funds. City and county officials glibly absolved themselves and laid the blame at the doorstep of "these impatient people who want instant prosperity handed to them at the expense of citizens who have worked long and industriously to achieve a certain way of life."

Frequently, the members of the Civil Rights Committee exchanged bored, patient looks as the elected officials used their time to whip ancient and overworked phrases and issues into life. When Councilman Elbert Andrews concluded his remarks, Mayor Cameron rapped unnecessarily for order and said, "Mr. Taylor?"

Wayne rose to his feet, spread a few sheets of notes in front of him. "Gentlemen," he began, "this is an historic occasion, the first time these three bodies have met in joint session to discuss the problems that beset us all; the cause and ways to prevent violent outbreaks that have occurred elsewhere and which we are now experiencing in our own community.

"We have smugly told ourselves, 'It can't or won't happen here,' and now we realize full well that it can happen here, and has. Even before we can begin to estimate the cost in dead, injured and inconvenienced, apart from the overall destruction and damage to property, I am sure we realize that more of the same may easily recur. This morning, we have listened to our County and City leadership and as I stand here addressing you, nothing has been suggested that, in my opinion, will alleviate or mitigate the probability that what has already happened will not happen again."

Heads leaned together and a low, angry buzz came from the semicircle of public officials. Cameron looked on either side of him and rapped his gavel for order as Wayne Taylor waited calmly for quiet.

"I have listened," he continued, "and am dismayed when I realize that all that has been said this morning leads to but one conclusion, a distinct desire to return to the same conditions that existed prior to the violence, but with greater police powers, unless federal and state agencies assume the financial burdens and responsibilities to better those conditions.

"Gentlemen, I say to you that this is not leadership. It is an abdication of the purposes and powers for which you were elected. I say that what has happened last night must not be allowed to happen again, and I do not mean that it must be prevented by police action alone, but by an honest effort of responsible officials and citizens to eliminate the causes which drive people to burn, smash, loot and kill in order to achieve some sense of identification and equality.

"We have heard you place the blame for this situation on outside extremists, hoodlums, the discontented, the seekers of more free welfare handouts, and so on. To some extent, this is undoubtedly correct. But if the blame for the basic cause must be placed, it must in all honesty be shared by all of us, white and black alike. On government at every level, on the business and industrial community, on the practice of unions which bar Negroes from apprenticeships and membership, on churches which are guilty by silence, on our civic and educational institutions by their willing acceptance of the status quo, and yes, upon the average citizen who walks the streets and looks aside from the problem, which is no less an act of bigotry.

"We have heard it said, repeated, and emphatically stated that the Negroes in our community are good people who have been temporarily led astray by outside extremists, but it is my firm conviction that good people cannot be enticed to commit irrational, evil acts, particularly upon themselves and against each other, unless there are justifiable causes. Good people did not create the havoc of last night, gentlemen. These were the deeds and actions of a desperate people, though only a small percentage of the Negro community.

"Since dawn this morning, the Civil Rights Committee members present have been in meeting to work out a program of requirements which I am sure will come as no surprise to any of you. You have seen and heard them before. However, we feel impelled to call them to your attention once more for immediate remedial action—"

Mayor, councilmen and commissioners stirred restlessly in their chairs. They were seeing Wayne Taylor, but hearing the voice of his grandfather, Jonas, a voice that carried forcibly an underlying threat: *Get down to business or I will use the Taylor name and fortune to defeat you at the polls, replace you with men of my own choice.*

"I feel it hardly necessary," Wayne continued, "to remind

you that federal, state and local projects to increase job training, job opportunities, housing and other benefits have failed because of official bureaucratic delays, fumbling and inertia, this not without political implications. The principal problem, as we are well aware, is a lack of jobs, jobs with equal pay for black and white. The equal opportunities program offered by Taylor Industries and Warren Tobacco Company are cases in point, an indication that the Negro community can undertake responsibility if it is given them, accompanied by equal pay. To the age-old question, Can we live and work together? the answer is an unqualified, Yes. We not only can, we have. And we must. It remains only to encourage this program of progress and peaceful coexistence with a spirit of willing cooperation.

"First, jobs. Until now, the Katie Willard R-V Center has been supported privately. We recommend that the city take an active, cooperative role in its teacher and training services. Taylor Industries, and, I am informed, Warren Tobacco, expect to enter into expansion programs which will enable us to absorb many qualified Negroes of all working ages and pay those trainees while receiving instruction. Others must be persuaded to do likewise, particularly in government and business.

"Second, housing. We recommend that the city and county rigidly enforce every health, sanitation and fire-hazard ordinance on the books and compel every landlord to bring their East, West and South Laurelton properties up to established standards or face legal action, even condemnation proceedings. Then, systematically, and with the use of available federal and state funds, replace our ancient slums with decent, low-cost housing.

"Third, the city will begin at once a full-scale campaign of street repair, sewer installation, proper lighting, better bus service and garbage collection to match the services in East Laurelton, employing people from the affected areas on a permanent basis and in supervisory jobs wherever they are capable of handling them."

"Wayne," Cameron interjected in protest, "the budget—"

"Mr. Mayor, the Council must face its problems just as the citizenry must face theirs. We have operated too long under a system of deliberate neglect. Progress and change are inevitable and the start must be made now. I might remind you gentlemen that my Grandfather Jonas Taylor fought unionism all his life, but my father and Anderson Warren brought the first unions into Laurelton and we have learned to live together. I intend, gentlemen, to propose to our unions that Negroes be admitted—"

810

"You're asking for a holy war, Mr. Taylor," Commission Chairman Crump growled.

"So be it, Mr. Crump, but the change must come, and with the support of our elected officials." Wayne paused to sip from a glass of water. "On our part, and with support of the industrial and business community, we will undertake the rebuilding of the R-V Center, improve it with a swimming pool, enlarged recreational facilities, outdoor and indoor, for all ages. Athletic activities will be sponsored by Chief Durkin's Police Athletic League which has been permitted to lapse because its funds were cut off. We intend to ask that juvenile delinquents found guilty of a first or second offense be paroled to the R-V Center for vocational training. School dropouts will be given that opportunity as well in order to retain them within the community. We shall solicit the support of every church, of every denomination, in all of Laurelton.

"For the immediate present, we must restore order, clean up what we can and begin rebuilding the destruction created—"

When he finished, there was total silence in the chamber. Finally Cameron said, "Reverend Hart?"

Hart rose and said, "Gentlemen, I think Mr. Taylor has clearly expressed the feelings of this entire Committee. It remains only to make the start. I am sure that if these suggestions are approved, I can make proper appeals to the Negro community to cooperate and rid themselves of any thoughts of further disorder. Mr. Taylor and the other members have agreed to appear on television and radio and bring your message of hope to them. I know that this is what they are anxiously waiting to hear, that they are not alone—" He paused and added, "But gentlemen, I hope you realize that mere talk or token gestures will not eliminate the causes. Failure will bring a resumption of what has happened here, just as it has elsewhere. Cities will burn and men of both races will needlessly die in the streets, the innocent among the guilty, and when that happens, be sure to examine your consciences carefully before you point your fingers—"

5

When Larry Powell returned to the Shackleford home it was after two o'clock and he was laden down with four sacks filled with more groceries than Lutie had asked for.

"Food's going to be hard to get for the next day or two," he said almost in apology. "I brought along some extras."

Sam was home and Elizabeth was awake, but remained in her room. "Thank you, son," Sam said. "I didn't even think about what we needed here at home. I got to see Chief Durkin after he come out of a meeting. He get the Company lawyer on the phone for me, Mist' Armour. He say they goin'a get Duke a lawyer an' the Company pay for it. He say Duke maybe got a little chance, but don't hope too much, except they won't strap him in the chair."

"How is Elizabeth?" Larry asked.

"She's in her room," Lutie said.

"Awake?"

"She was last time I look in on her."

"I'd like to see her for a minute if it's all right."

"I'll see if she's dressed for company." Lutie returned a moment later. "You c'n come in, Larry."

Elizabeth was sitting up in bed, a robe over her nightgown, the blinds pulled down. "Elizabeth?"

"Hello, Larry."

"How are you feeling?"

"A little better. Thank you for last night, Larry, everything—"

"That's all right. You weren't hurt?"

"No. Larry?"

"What?"

"Did you tell my folks that I—was in that room—with Lyle Emerson?"

"I didn't know it myself."

"I was. I want you to know that. We were hiding from Duke. He was looking for Lyle, wanted to kill him."

"Why, Elizabeth?"

"He thought there was—something—suspected us of—" She broke off, grateful that Larry had said nothing, asked for no further explanation. "He didn't know I was there, but he knew Lyle was because Lyle's car was still on the parking lot."

"Why didn't you call out to him? He wouldn't have hurt you."

"Maybe it wouldn't have mattered if he knew we were together."

"Together?"

"Yes, but it wasn't the way Duke thought it was."

"I see."

"Larry, it wasn't. I don't know exactly what it was. Or why. Lyle was doing so much for us, our people, and no one would be his friend. All he wanted was for somebody

812

to say, 'We appreciate what you're doing to help us.' But nobody did."

"Except you."

"Except me."

"I'm glad you did. Maybe if more of us could show it isn't all hate, we can come out of this stupid war like reasonable human beings."

She was struck by her own guilt and hovered on the precipice of confession, to rid herself of the burden, then decided against it, that it would only harm others without reason. "What about you, Larry?" she asked. "Mama told me about Banjo's Place. Duke again—"

"It wasn't my real job, Elizabeth. I've been a police officer all the time. I was working at Banjo's to help uncover the narcotics racket he was operating and the payoff system he was using to reach certain people on the police vice squad. That's over now. The whole ring was picked up this morning. Connie Clark, your cousin Ivy, Jake Runnels, Jim Cuddy, Eli Buller and most of the other pushers."

"Larry, I'm sorry I—misjudged you."

"I'm sorry I couldn't tell you before."

"What now?"

"I'm being reassigned to the 12th Precinct on Monday. Human relations in West Laurelton and coaching some of the kid teams for the Police Athletic League. The R-V Center is going to become a big thing, Elizabeth. Paid staff, city, state and federal help. You could be in line for a top supervisory job. This is going to be the biggest breakthrough we've ever seen here, with the backing of white and Negro leaders. We'll become the civil rights showcase for the whole country before the year is out. What's more, we won't be alone."

6

During the ensuing days, the weather had cooled and the temper of Laurelton cooled with it. On the following Monday, traffic flowed normally across the bridge in both directions. Working relationships were restored but the atmosphere was what one newscaster termed "edgy". There were minor incidents, but these were settled quickly by bystanders alert to the possibility of escalation. Certainly, there was a sullen hostility in the air, but the former militance had been dissipated; as though, for the moment of truce, everyone had had enough.

On Saturday evening, Mayor Cameron and Commissioner Crump had joined the members of the Civil Rights Committee on a special television program, broadcast simultaneously on radio, which was hosted by a panel of news media representatives. Specific questions were answered in specific detail and without hedging. Wayne Taylor and Reverend Hart made closing statements expressing the Committee's hopes for the future and outlined plans in progress to correct certain conditions, pleading for cooperation from the white and black communities. This was received with a tongue-in-cheek "Well, we'll see" attitude.

On Monday morning, crews were hired to begin removing the debris from the streets and pavements, but the skeletons of gutted buildings and houses stood as a tragic reminder of man's indifference to the needs of other men and the senseless waste born of frustration. Food, clothing and medical supplies were trucked into West Laurelton and dispensed to waiting lines from vacant stores rented by the city for that purpose. The homeless found quarters with friends and neighbors, and the Center's large gymnasium was thrown open to the overflow, with the costs borne by the city through its special emergency fund. Not too surprisingly, many of those who had rampaged through the streets on Friday night were busy working on the cleanup squads.

The courts, wherever possible, dismissed charges against most of the 520 arrested, the majority of whom were young and seemingly penitent after a weekend in jail and in the presence of their parents. Those found guilty of felony charges were sent to Mayfield, adults to Parkton, some held for grand jury action. Almost every attorney on both sides of the bridge came forward to offer his services.

At his arraignment, Duke Shackleford pleaded not guilty on charges of fire-bombing Ben-Joe Nichols' poolroom, causing his death and critical injuries to one Omar Liggett, alias Hinky Liggett; of fire-bombing the R-V Center and causing the death of Lyle Emerson. He was represented by Martin Weinstock by arrangement with Kenneth Armour, and held without bail.

520 arrests. 278 known injured, 84 requiring further hospitalization. Of the 16 dead by gunshot, fire and other causes, 4 were white, 12 were Negro. 32 commercial establishments had been burned and looted, 110 homes destroyed, two schools and one police precinct partially burned. The toll attracted national attention to, as *Time* reported, "this progressive community which, throughout the troublesome years the South has experienced, had remained as a veritable model of racial harmony."

On Tuesday, Corey Armour formally claimed Lyle Emerson's body and made arrangements for his funeral on the following day at three o'clock. It was one of 16 funerals, but the only one attended by both the white and Negro communities; colleagues and students from Laurelton High School mourned with colleagues and students from the Center. Civic officials came and an honor guard was sent by two veterans' organizations. Flowers overflowed the gravesite and Corey wondered which of the black-garbed, veiled women on the edge of the crowd was Elizabeth Shackleford. When the service was over, Corey accepted the precisely folded flag which had covered Lyle's casket.

In his pocket, he carried the letter Lyle had addressed to *Mr. Corey Armour, my attorney,* which the police had found in Lyle's apartment and turned over to him. It was dated on Thursday, the day before the riot, and read:

Dear Corey:
    If anything happens to me, I hereby appoint you Executor of my estate, such as it is. Please convert everything I own, car, furniture, etc. into cash. There are also a savings and checking account at Laurelton National, a safety deposit box with my G.I. insurance and another policy. After deducting any necessary expenses, please divide the remainder equally between Mr. and Mrs. Waters and Elizabeth. See that they receive this quietly and without embarrassment. There is no one else.
    Good-bye, old buddy. Thanks, good luck and much happiness to you.

                                   Lyle
P.S. If there is a flag, please see that Mr. and Mrs. Waters get it.

And so, Lyle's last debt to the Waters family would be wiped out. Perhaps now he could sleep in peace.

7

During the ensuing week, an unnatural, eerie truce was in effect on both sides of the bridge.

For West and South Laurelton, it was a cleanup period. The city and private industry sent in trucks to clean up and remove the debris and rubble left in the aftermath of the riot, but the open framework of fire-gutted homes and business establishments stood as blackened monuments to the frustration and rage of the disfranchised. The courts had moved swiftly, leniently, and most of those arrested had been released. Those who had jobs returned to their work, but there was a notable, sullen wariness in the relationship between employers and employees. There was hardly any mention of the riot, but the silent threat was ever-present.

The riot had created a corps of homeless, joined by those whose jobs had vanished when their places of employment disappeared in flames. These men, women, boys and girls stood on corners or sat on steps sadly watching as the work force moved what remained of their possessions into trucks, to be carried off to the city dump.

City officials were in constant meetings with the industrial, commercial and civic leadership of the community to find funds and means to restore the damage and solve the unsolvable problem of preventing a similar outbreak in the future; high on the list was some way of providing meaningful job training, to create jobs, develop recreational centers, playground facilities and activity programs to keep the youth occupied, to organize a massive human relations program.

There was both willingness and reluctance. The willing were faced with angry charges that they were giving in to threats and blackmail, the reluctant with blindness to the realization that the old order of life could no longer exist and must conform to the newly emerging Society of Man —to live in harmony or in constant fear of revolution.

Meanwhile, homeless families found temporary refuge in the homes of friends, neighbors, and the churches which had opened their doors to the friendless. The federal government had sent in truckloads of surplus food and the Red Cross and Salvation Army supplied clothing and medical assistance. Money poured in from private contributors, federal loans were made available. Some construction had already begun in the affected areas, using Negro labor wherever possible.

At noon on the following Tuesday, which was the last day of October, Duncan Collins telephoned from New York. Theodore Warren was not in his office and the call was transferred to Kenneth Armour. "What's up, Dunc? Anything new or good?"

"I can't say exactly, but I'm hopeful. I received a call from Andrea Vanderkuyl's attorney about half an hour ago asking if I could reach Theodore and have him come up tomorrow."

"Sounds promising," Kenneth said.

"Could be, but I've no inkling, except that she wants to see him. The attorney didn't mention anyone else, but if you can make it, Ken, I'd suggest you come along. If anything develops, it might need your legalistic thinking."

"Fine, Dunc. I'll reach Theodore and pass the word along. We can fly down to Atlanta tonight and take the first jet out in the morning."

"Four o'clock at Andrea's house. I was told to caution Theodore to be prompt. You know the address—"

"Yes."

"Phone me your arrival time and I'll meet you at the airport. I hope you're not delayed by weather. We're having some rather heavy rain today. If you're early enough we might have time for lunch."

"We'll do our best to make it. Keep your fingers crossed."

"They've been that way since Andrea called me. See you tomorrow."

The last half of the trip had been flown in a heavy overcast and when they arrived at Kennedy Airport they were welcomed by Collins in a heavy downpour. The trip into Manhattan was slow and bleak and Theodore sat huddled inside his topcoat while Kenneth and Duncan Collins spoke of what might lie in front of them. "I've got a little more on it since yesterday," Collins told them en route. "It seems that twice each year, Andrea meets with Chase Warren's comptroller, who gives her a semiannual rundown on Chase's administration of the Vanderkuyl holdings. This time, Andrea has insisted that Chase make the presentation personally. It may very well be the showdown."

They reached their suite at the Sherry by 2:20, changed clothes while Collins ordered lunch. Promptly at 3:30 Kenneth and Theodore said good-bye to Collins and stepped into a chauffeured limousine to keep their appointment. Fifteen minutes later, they arrived at the Vanderkuyl house where Morris showed them into a small, comfortable second-floor sitting room. A few minutes later Andrea joined them there.

Tall and erect, she wore a high-necked gray gown with a black woolen shawl draped over her shoulders despite the warmth thrown off by burning logs in the fireplace. The two men rose as she approached and it was evident from her manner that she was not entirely happy about the event in which she was about to participate. Her hands were clenched together and blue veins stood out from the parchment-like skin as she greeted them.

"Thank you for coming to New York, Mr. Warren, Mr. Armour," she said. "You are early. The others will not be here until four o'clock. There will be Chase Warren and my attorney, Mr. Mattson, besides ourselves. I don't think it will take long, but I shall ask you to remain here until I send Morris to bring you downstairs to my study." She paused, then added, "If you should want a drink or anything else, ring for Morris. The pull-bell is there beside the fireplace. You will please excuse me now."

She went out. Theodore sank down into a comfortable sofa and lit a cigarette. "Whatever she has in mind," he said to Kenneth, "I don't think she will enjoy it any more than I will."

Promptly at four o'clock, Morris answered the bell and admitted Paul Mattson, Andrea's attorney. Before he could close the door, a limousine drew up at the curb and Chase Warren, carrying a slim black attaché case, emerged and came up the steps. As Morris took their coats and hats, Mattson, a dignified, youngish-looking man despite graying hair, smiled lightly and said, "Mr. Warren?"

Chase acknowledged with a stiff nod of his head.

"I'm Paul Mattson." He extended a hand which Chase touched briefly.

"I've heard of your firm, Mr. Mattson. You represent Mrs. Vanderkuyl, I take it."

"Yes. And indirectly, her daughter, Vanessa Willis of Chicago."

"And my wife."

"Yes."

"This way, please, gentlemen," Morris said. "Mrs. Vanderkuyl is in her study."

When they entered the room, Andrea was seated behind her Florentine desk on which stood a thin vase with a single rose in it. Other than that, the desk was bare. "Thank you for coming, Mr. Mattson, Chase," she said at once. "You've met?" When both men nodded, "Will you please be seated."

They sat in the two chairs which had been arranged to face her across the desk. Chase placed the attaché case on the floor beside him, crossed his legs, clasped his hands in his lap and looked directly at Andrea. To Chase, she said, "Mr. Mattson is here by my specific request. Your Mr. Whatever-is-his-name, your comptroller. He is not with you?"

"His presence isn't necessary," Chase replied. "I have all the necessary figures with me."

"Very well. Shall we get on with it?"

"May I ask why your attorney has been invited to be present?" Chase asked.

"Yes, of course," Andrea replied. "There are several matters I wish to discuss with you and I think Mr. Mattson will be better able than I to answer any questions you may wish to ask."

Chase threw another quick glance at Mattson, then opened his attaché case and brought out a single file folder, which he opened. From a long sheet, he read off a number of figures that dealt with income, expenditures, the sale of one piece of property in Rochester, another in Newark. There were no new acquisitions during the preceding six months. He recited other facts and figures for another twenty minutes, then placed the statement on the desk in front of Andrea, who made no move to pick it up. Chase sat back in his chair and waited, feeling the air of civil hostility that pervaded the room.

"Mr. Mattson?" Andrea said.

"Yes," Mattson replied. "If you will permit me." He turned to face Chase more directly and said, "Mr. Warren, there has been no mention in this, or in previous reports, of a company called—ah—" Mattson withdrew a sheet of paper from his inside jacket pocket, glanced at it, then looked back to Chase "—Auto-Mex, a corporation operating in, let me see, one, two, three cities in Mexico, in which I understand you are the principal stockholder."

Chase Warren's head jerked up and around to face Mattson. "Ah—" he began.

"A corporation," Mattson continued, "which I believe is one of a number of holdings of what was later to become the parent corporation, Intercon."

Chase's expression turned to granite. He squirmed uncomfortably in his chair, then turned from Mattson to stare at Andrea, in whose steely, glittering eyes he saw little hope or comfort.

"Well, Chase?" Andrea said.

"What has all this to do with the—with—" For once, caught completely off guard, Chase was fumbling for words. Andrea opened a drawer in her desk and removed two file folders which she placed on the desktop before her, then moved them toward Chase.

"It has everything to do with you, Chase," she said. "With you, with Victoria, with Vanessa, with me, with the Vanderkuyl estate. If you will glance through these files, I think you will better understand what we are talking about, with little need for further explanations from Mr. Mattson or myself."

Chase reached for the files, took them up and began scanning through them. Andrea and Mattson said nothing, but waited for some reaction from Chase. He had glanced through the first file, then started on the second. When he came to the 8-by-10 photograph of himself and Joan Condon, he held it up and examined it closely, then looked over its top edge and said to Andrea, "Do you have similar photographs of Victoria and Walter Cunningham?"

Andrea's chalk-white face became faintly tinged with pink. "Victoria and Mr. Cunningham are not under discussion at the moment," she said coldly.

"Then are we discussing a matter of privileged morality?" Chase needled.

Andrea's lips compressed tightly, but she did not reply. Chase dropped the photograph back into the folder, closed it and placed both folders on the desk. "I congratulate you, my dear mother-in-law. I hadn't suspected you'd been so well advised."

"Shall we get down to the business at hand?" Andrea said.

Paul Mattson took over then. "Mr. Warren, you've just seen a small part of the accumulation of evidence that has been gathered by Mrs. Vanderkuyl over a long period of time. If you should want copies in order to discuss the situation with your attorneys, they are available."

From Mattson's very tone, Chase knew it was useless. He sagged back into his chair as the knowledge of defeat overcame him. He had moved fast over the last twenty years; perhaps too fast, and too carelessly, never dreaming that the need for vengeance in Andrea had been so great. More than anything else, at the moment, he wanted a drink, but could not bring himself to ask for it. Mattson was leaning forward in his chair, waiting for some reply and Chase had none. What he had seen in the folders gave him a clear insight as to how well and strongly prepared Andrea was to exact her last ounce of punishment from him. He turned back toward Andrea, ignoring Mattson.

"What is your price?" he asked.

If this was to be her moment of supreme revenge, Andrea did not show it. She straightened up in her chair and said in a low, calm voice, "Your immediate disassociation from the Vanderkuyl estate after a thorough audit of its accounts. A quiet divorce which Victoria will file either in Mexico or Florida without opposition from you, and without any question of rights on your part as far as the children are concerned."

"And Intercon?"

"I have no interest in Intercon. It is yours—with one condition."

"What condition?"

"That in exchange for whatever legal claims the Vanderkuyl estate may have in Intercon, you will sign over all stock Intercon has acquired in the Warren Tobacco Company without reimbursement."

Chase's fists clenched tightly, his jaws showing knots of hard muscle. "And just what is your interest in Warren Tobacco?" he asked.

"Whatever it is, I will not allow it to become another toy of Chase Warren's. Those are my terms and they are firm. If you decide to fight me, Mr. Mattson is authorized to commence proceedings against you, Intercon, and each of its holdings as having been gained by your fraudulent manipulations with funds belonging to Victoria, Vanessa and me. I can assure you, Chase, that we will not go into this matter lightly. I have had numerous conferences with Mr. Mattson and his associates—"

"I'm sure you have. And am I to take it that Victoria and Vanessa are in complete agreement with you in this action?"

"I hardly think there is a need for me to answer that."

"No. I suppose not." Chase looked at Mattson again, then back to Andrea. "The children—" he began, when Andrea interrupted.

"Don't try to make an issue of Marshall and Victor, Chase. They are not infants, and have been told just enough to understand this unpleasant situation. I can assure you their sympathies lie with Victoria, so spare yourself the further humiliation of contesting that point. For the sake of all of us, *you and Mrs. Condon included*, I hope you will act wisely and swiftly to bring this to its conclusion."

When Chase did not respond, Andrea continued, "Mr. Mattson's office has prepared all the necessary documents to dispose of this matter simply and quietly. Victoria is prepared to leave within a day or two to apply for her divorce. All that remains is your signature, turning over the Warren stock to me in exchange for my agreement not to prosecute you for fraud and present evidence of your adulterous conduct in open court."

"I would like a few days to think it over," Chase said.

"I'm afraid I have been more generous than my inclinations have dictated. If it were not for Victoria and the children, I would not settle for less than throwing this into the courts to strip you of everything you own in your own name. The only thing that can bring this to a swift conclusion is your immediate acceptance of the terms I have outlined here today. I must insist on your answer before you leave this house for the last time."

Chase studied Andrea carefully. He had known her far too long not to know that she had lost none of her earlier determination. To be exposed in court, to public ridicule—how many men would chortle with glee, he wondered. How many would be made happy to see Chase Warren, always protected in his dealings by the strength and weight of the Vanderkuyl money and Intercon, humbled publicly; and watching Andrea's face, he knew she was thinking his own thoughts.

"All right, Andrea," he said finally, "you win." He turned to Mattson now. "I suppose you have something prepared for my signature."

Mattson was already holding a blue-bound document in his hand. "A preliminary agreement to the points Mrs. Vanderkuyl had already outlined. Also, that in exchange for abdicating her claims on Intercon, you will deliver your shares of Warren Tobacco stock within twenty-four hours."

Chase took the agreement and read its two pages slowly and carefully, then shrugged imperceptibly and reached into a pocket for his pen.

"This will require witnesses," Mattson said.

Andrea, acting on cue, rang for Morris who appeared immediately. "Will you show the two gentlemen to the study, Morris, please."

While they waited, Chase said, "What next, Mr. Mattson?"

"Tomorrow morning at ten o'clock, I will expect you in my office with the Warren stock. At that time, the formal documents will be ready for your signature."

Then Theodore and Kenneth Armour entered the room. Chase's reaction of shock was indelibly registered upon his face. He started to rise to his feet, then slumped back into his chair. Theodore's step faltered for a moment, but was bolstered by Kenneth, who walked firmly to the desk. He nodded and said simply, "Chase."

Chase did not reply. He held the gold pen in his right hand which now lay limply in his lap. Theodore had reached the desk and was standing beside Kenneth, staring grimly at his brother, but there were no words of greeting from either. Mattson stood up and moved the agreement closer to Chase, turned the first page back to expose the signature sheet. Without a further word, Chase shakily inscribed his name on the line indicated by Mattson's index finger. Mattson then handed the document to Theodore and reached into his pocket to extract a copy of the agreement, which he handed to Chase. Chase's movements were those of an automaton as he took it, placed it in the attaché case and left the house without a word to anyone.

When Kenneth had signed his name, Mattson picked up the document, folded it and returned it to his pocket. "I think that is all for the moment," he said, then shook hands with Andrea, Theodore and Kenneth and permitted Morris to show him out.

Andrea sat motionless at the desk, her hands clenched with tension, her mouth drawn. The revenge she had sought for years had brought her no more than a hollow victory, one she could not, at her age, enjoy. There were tears in her eyes as she looked up at Theodore Warren's first words to her. "Mrs. Vanderkuyl," he said, "I can't begin to tell you how very deeply we are indebted to you. I don't know exactly what compelled Chase to give up his stock—"

"No, Mr. Warren, you don't. The price has been great and I have paid it willingly, if unhappily." She sighed deeply. "Intercon's stock in Warren Tobacco will be delivered to my attorneys sometime tomorrow morning. As soon as they are in my hands, I will turn them over to Mr. Collins at the current market price. That may take a few days, the legal transfer—" Her voice broke then and a few moments later, she said, "I am very tired now. If there is nothing more—"

8

Wayne Taylor's secretary telephoned Corey on Thursday evening and asked him to a luncheon conference set for one o'clock the following day. He tried to interpret her voice into something meaningful, but failed; she could have just as well been ordering a dozen pencils or a fresh typewriter ribbon from the stationery stockroom.

When he arrived on the dot of one the next afternoon, the same secretary smiled and ushered him into Wayne's office, where Johnny Curran and the lunch arrived at that precise moment. They exchanged informal greetings and light conversation until the waiter had withdrawn. There was something in Wayne's quiet, sober manner that increased Corey's earlier sense of uneasiness, the premonition of impending doom, which was borne out when, without preliminaries, Wayne said, "Corey, I hope this won't come as a disappointment to you—"

Corey's army-trained mind had already leaped ahead, searching for alternatives; if Chase Warren gained control of the Company, Kenneth would be out; and if the Shadow Hills project was to be abandoned, perhaps Kenneth and he could reopen law offices as Armour & Armour, later seek outside financing and backing for the project.

He heard Wayne's voice bridge over his own thoughts. "—and we've put enough information and technical data together to give us a very clear picture. We've even sent men to look over the Michigan project and first reports are exceptionally favorable."

"Then—"

"However, with the present local situation, we intend to focus our full attention and resources on a low-cost housing program in West and South Laurelton, rebuild the commercial section, the Center and whatever else needs to be done before going outside our immediate area of operations."

"I understand," Corey replied, then a little more brightly, accepting the decision, "There are other circumstances, personal, that help lighten my disappointment to some extent—"

"Hold on, Corey," Johnny put in quickly. "We're not pulling out of the deal. What we're about to suggest is that you hold on to your option on the Halstead land for the full year—"

"You're not abandoning the project?"

"Not at all," Wayne said, "only delaying it until we can get some higher priority projects completed here, where the situation is more criticial. By the time we're ready for Shadow Hills, we'll have a larger, better-trained labor pool."

Corey's optimism was reignited, heightened by the thought that the intervening year would come as a blessing, give him time to adjust, prepare himself for whatever lay ahead. He toyed with his food, listening to Johnny expand his own ideas with technical expertise, breathing life into what had begun as costs and statistics, translating them into tons of steel, cubic yards of earth, miles of pipelines; into streets, roads, lighting, finance—

"Finance," Wayne said. "We've already been approached with an offer from two interested investors."

"Who?"

"For one, a large mid-Western insurance company. For the other, and with your permission, my cousin Drew would like to buy into the project," Wayne said with a smile.

Corey felt himself reddening. Wayne said, "You can't keep it a secret within the family, Corey. Congratulations from the Taylors and Currans." He extended a hand across the table and Corey shook it, then Johnny's. "Drew came by to see Julie yesterday," Wayne added, "and Julie kept her there until I got home. Johnny and Susan came by for a little celebration drink later. We're all so happy Drew is her old self again."

"Thank you. With this on top of everything else, do you mind if I take off now? I think I'd like to get used to the idea for a few minutes, then—well, I don't know exactly what. Maybe leap up in the air a few hundred yards—"

Outside, he stopped in at Stocker's Drug Store to use the phone booth to call Shana Pierce. "Any news from New York?" he asked.

"I'll let your father tell you himself. He got in less than half an hour ago."

"No, don't put him on. I'll drive over to see him."

He drove across the bridge into West Laurelton feeling an urgent need to talk with Kenneth, to tell him that no matter how the Warren matter turned out, he wanted to be a part of Kenneth's plans, make Kenneth a part of his own; whether in a law office together or involved in the Shadow Hills project. He tried to form the proposal into words that would make the offer seem casual and acceptable without making it appear to be an offer, more a need of his own. In the Warren administration building, which he hadn't visited in many years, so many physical changes had been made that he felt he was in strange territory. At the main reception desk on the first floor, he gave his name and was asked to wait while he was announced. A few moments later, Shana emerged from an elevator and escorted him to Kenneth's suite on the top floor.

"You're excited about something," Shana said on the way up. "You can't have heard so soon."

"Heard what?"

"I—I think I'd better let your father tell you." The elevator came to a stop and its doors slid open quietly. "This way." She turned left and he quickened his pace to catch up.

"I don't know what it is," Corey said, "but I've got some news for Dad, too."

She opened one of the pair of doors into her office, crossed to a duplicate pair of doors, knocked lightly and entered. Kenneth was at his desk, his back toward them, speaking into a telephone.

"Yes, yes, Dunc. It was all settled before we left. Sorry you weren't available, but we were in a hurry to get back. You'll have the stock within a few days. Wonderful? It's more than that. Thank you, and my love to Diane. I hope to see you very soon. Good-bye."

Kenneth hung up and swiveled around, surprise on his

face at the sight of Corey and Shana together. "Come in, come in, both of you," he said with a beaming smile.

"Good news, Dad?"

"The very best. It's all settled. There will be no tender offer, no proxy fight and control remains with Theodore and Drew. Chase Warren is out of the picture now and forevermore."

"That's wonderful, Dad."

"Much as I would like to continue this, I've got to see Theodore for a few minutes. Will you both excuse me? Don't leave, Corey, please. There's something I need to discuss with you. Shana will entertain you."

When they were alone, Shana said, "What was your good news, Corey?"

He laughed lightly, trying to hide his exuberance. "After Dad's news, mine is only an anticlimax. The Shadow Hills project is in, but it will be delayed for about a year. I was trying to frame some way of inviting Dad to come in with me, but now—"

"I wouldn't be too conclusive about anything, Corey."

"No?"

Shana smiled and said, "No. I think both of you still have a lot to learn about each other, from each other."

"I wouldn't doubt that. I hope there's time enough left."

"I think there will be now. Talk it over with him, Corey. Make the offer, no matter what."

"Yes— Would you mind, Shana? I'd like to call Drew."

"Not in the least. Use the white phone, it's a direct outside line." She turned and left the office, closing the door after her.

He spoke with Drew at length, detailing the meeting with Wayne and Johnny, somehow suspecting that she already knew what he was telling her. When he finished, he sat in Kenneth's chair and waited until his father returned, calmer, less ebullient than when he had left. He motioned Corey to remain at the desk while he sank into the visitor's chair. "Well," Kenneth said, "another crisis passed."

"And I suppose Theodore is a happy man now, with the Company in safe hands."

"In his own hands, Corey, his very own hands."

"What about you, Dad?"

"A personal crisis to face, Corey. Ever since Chase got into the picture, I've been thinking how it would be if I stepped out and opened my own law office—"

"What about the Company?"

"At first, I considered there would be no Company if Chase held all the cards in his hands—"

"But the point is, he didn't win."

"No, he didn't, and the picture is much clearer without him. I've already discussed this with Theodore, Corey, and made my decision. After the annual meeting in January, I intend to resign from the Company to open my own law offices. My first client will be the Warren Tobacco Company."

Corey leaned back in his chair and laughed. "What's so amusing about it, Corey?" Kenneth asked.

"The coincidence. For a few moments at lunch today, when there was some doubt about the future of the Shadow Hills project, I was thinking of doing the same thing."

"Then you approve?"

"Approve? I'd say it was absolutely great."

"If you mean that—"

"Of course I do. I can't think of anything more appropriate than a continuation of the Armour name in the practice of law here."

"With the exception of a gap of many years intervening."

"I don't think that would mean a thing. Who in Laurelton, in Cairn County, in the entire state, won't remember the name Armour except for the younger generation?"

"Armour," Kenneth mused. "Armour & Armour. It rolls nicely, doesn't it?"

Then Corey realized that Kenneth had somehow always had this in mind. Armour & Armour. Marcus and Lewis then, Kenneth and Corey now. "I'm flattered, of course, Dad. I can't contribute very much to an association—"

"Partnership, Corey. You will be contributing more than you realize. My father came into his father's practice fresh from law school, with no more or less to offer than you."

Corey grinned suddenly. "More, I think. The Shadow Hills project is in, but it will be a year before it gets started. That's what I came to tell you. Wayne and Johnny both want it."

"Congratulations, Corey. This *is* a day for good things to happen."

"And more, Dad. It's all set with Drew and me. A small wedding at Brookhill on Thanksgiving Day. Family and a few friends. You and Shana, the Taylors, Currans, a few of the northern Warrens."

"Ah, Corey—"

"What about you and Shana, Dad?"

Kenneth grinned sheepishly. "I'm afraid we're just a little ahead of you, Corey. If you will remember back a few weeks ago, the day Anderson died and you had to locate me in Atlanta—"

827

"I remember."

"On that Saturday, Shana and I were quietly married in a civil ceremony just outside Atlanta, in order to keep the notice out of the larger newspapers. We're planning our honeymoon for January following the annual meeting and my resignation."

The silence hung between their grinning faces for a moment before Corey said, "That's wonderful, Dad. I'm glad it happened. For both of you."

"Shana told me you went to see her the morning I got back from New York about a week later."

"She didn't tell me you were married—"

"I know. She wanted it to come from me."

"Well. Of course, the offer of the house still goes. Choose your own time. Right away, if it won't make either of you uncomfortable having me around until Thanksgiving."

"I'm sure— I'll discuss it with Shana. And again, our thanks."

Corey stood up. "Do you mind if I kiss the bride on my way out?"

"I'll come along and watch the effect. I'll need to get used to it."

They walked together across Brookhill, hand in hand, skirting the unused stables, the empty kennels, along the edge of woods where the vacant cabins of long-departed field workers stood in a neat row. Beyond were four cottages where only the families of the estate maintenance workers now lived, spirals of smoke rising from their chimneys on this crisp November Sunday afternoon. Drew stopped and turned to look back at the silhouette of the huge old house which straddled the highest rise on the grounds.

Corey took advantage of the moment to light a cigarette. "What are you thinking, Drew?"

She whirled around to face him, her face bright, eyes shining. "That's not a fair question to ask a girl less than a week before her wedding day." She smiled and took a puff from his cigarette, then thrust one arm through his and jammed her hands into the pockets of her suede jacket, turning him toward the house. "It's so ugly," she said. "While I was away, just thinking about it made me hate it, even the thought of ever coming back to it. And now, suddenly, I love it and want to keep it always. No matter what."

"It wasn't the house you hated," Corey said.

"No. I know that now." She sighed deeply. "Gran and Grandmother Cleo planned it to hold dozens of children and grandchildren, but it didn't work out that way. Maybe we can complete their dream."

Corey smiled and said, "Bet on our giving it a real try."

Drew looked up and kissed him impulsively. "I'm so glad you feel that way about it, the house, I mean. I never realized before how deeply my roots are buried here." She sighed again. "We'll make changes, I know, and we'll have the summer place at Shadow Hills, perhaps others. And we'll travel when we can, but Brookhill will always be our home to come back to."

"Yes, Drew. I want it that way, too."

"Corey, have I told you lately how happy I am to be alive?"

He kissed her and said, "We'll keep it that way from now on, darling. Shouldn't we be getting back to the house? Dad and Shana will be arriving soon for dinner."

"I'm looking forward to meeting Shana. Do you think she'll like me?"

"She'll love you."

"Then why are you laughing?"

"Because she asked me that very same question about you only yesterday."

In one of the cottages, a dog barked sharply. A door opened and a child ran out, the dog nipping at his heels. They watched for a few moments until dog and child disappeared into the woods, then started toward the house on the hill.

In Laurelton, the air was one of contentment that comes with the feel and knowledge of forward progress being made. Plants and mills hummed with activity and business was brisk. Tensions were lowered as the rubble of gutted buildings and houses disappeared and crews were busy framing new structures where the old had stood.

The most notable change of all was that most of the crews were Negro, working under Center-trained Negro foremen with the sanction of local trade unions, faced with the threat of competing with rival all-Negro unions which could possibly control the local labor market in every field.

Federal, state, county and city authorities had begun coordinating a housing and public works program which, when it would begin operations in the spring would bring the unemployment figure in line with, perhaps below, the national average and provide jobs for most eligible youths during summer school vacations. New construction at the Center had already begun and enrollments in its building trades and mechanics classes were being rapidly filled. News of the Shadow Hills project had been made public, offering further insurance of a continuance of jobs for the future.

Elsewhere, thoughts turned to preparation for the Thanksgiving and Christmas holidays. Men and boys took to the fields with their dogs and guns or hunkered in their blinds in the early morning chill, waiting for the ducks and geese to come winging down from Canada on their way south, searching for grain in the marshes and fields west of the Cottonwood River. And everyone felt, or hoped, that the new year soon to be born would be a better, happier, more peaceful one.

In West and South Laurelton, there was new hope. Church attendance increased, as always when the weather turned cool. From the pulpits came messages of encouragement, expressed in the simple words of Reverend Amos Hart.

"We have learned many valuable lessons in recent weeks, and at a great and terrible cost. We have learned the importance of Unity for Good as opposed to Unity for Evil; that there is strength in the former and weakness in the latter. We know that in Unity for Good there is the Power we seek to correct the ills of poverty and other destructive diseases of mankind. Therefore, Unity can give us the Power of Progress.

"But Unity does not come with words of anger and hate, nor from black fezzes or other symbols of frustration and destruction. To be accepted by modern society, we must join that society just as other minority groups joined it long ago. Its membership is open to all of us, just as the right to vote is ours by the laws of this land. It is for us to learn how to use that vote for progress.

"The way is open, brethren and sisters. All that remains is the need to open our eyes and minds and travel the road together."

"More turkey, Lee?" Nora LaSalle asked.

Durkin passed his plate to Peter LaSalle. "Only a sliver, and more of the dressing. The grandest I ever tasted."

"Like mother used to make?" Nora said with a sly smile.

"Lord love you, no. If the truth be known, my father was a better cook than my mother, God rest them both. He had a touch, Grady had, but no better than yours, Nora."

"I'll bet you're something of a cook, too, living alone," Nora said.

Peter looked up and caught Durkin's broad grin. "The first time I've seen her in months and she's at it again," Durkin said.

"Nora—" Peter warned.

"All I said was—"

"Never mind, both of you," Durkin said with good humor. "Comes a family holiday like Thanksgiving and an important wedding, all wives get the matchmaking itch."

"The utter conceit of men," Nora sniffed. "Tell us more about the wedding at Brookhill today, Lee."

"I wasn't a guest, so there's little enough to tell. I went along with the special squad to make sure the rubbernecks didn't block traffic the way they did when Old Anderson passed on. It was noon, a quiet home affair with no more than two dozen guests, half of them from out of town. Drew Warren, like all new brides, was beautiful. Corey Armour, like all new grooms, was handsome—"

"And what about new fathers?" Peter demanded.

"Hush, Peter, let it be," Nora said. "Go on, Lee."

"There's hardly more. The bride and groom drove away in their fairy tale Rolls Royce pumpkin coach and at the airport they flew off to some special paradise of their own. Ah, it was a sight, though, a beautiful sight. And that was the end."

"The beginning," Nora interjected with emphasis.

"An end and a beginning," Durkin amended. He raised his glass of wine and Nora and Peter followed suit. "Peace to them, and to all of us on this day of Thanksgiving."